great story

Avon Books is
proud to publish
the history-making bestseller

THE THORN BIRDS

Spanning three generations and an infinite range of human emotions, THE THORN BIRDS is the story of a singular family, the Clearys, who leave New Zealand to live on a vast Australian sheep station, where their triumphs and tragedies are interwoven with the wonder and terror of a land ravaged by cycles of drought, fire, and torrential flood. But most of all, it is the story of Meggie, who falls madly in love with a man she can never marry, and of Ralph, a truly beautiful man, whose ambition takes him from Outback parish priest to the inner circles of the Vatican—but whose love for Meggie Cleary will lead to a passion he cannot control.

The novel begins in 1915 and ends more than half a century later, when the only survivor of the third generation, Justine, a brilliant London actress, sets a course of life and love halfway around the world from her roots.

(Kindly turn page...)

"A GREAT, WONDERFUL, MOVING, ENGROSSING, IMPOSSIBLE-TO-PUT-DOWN BOOK." Boston Herald American

"THE STORY IS SUPERBLY TOLD. Miss McCullough deals with the vast canvas of characters with assurance. Never for one moment does the pace flag. Never for an instant does her control fail her. There are times when you are left gasping at her audacity....This is an unself-conscious blockbuster of a book. I read it with immense pleasure, enjoyed every page, and heartily recommend it as a thumping 'good read.'" London Times

"THE NOVEL EXPLODES with a powerful sensitivity for human emotions...love deepens and mounts into an exhilarating crescendo bursting with happiness as well as pain." Pittsburgh Press

"A FINE, LONG, ABSORBING BOOK with the best heart-throb since Rhett Butler." The Washington Post

"A SUPERB WORK OF FICTION BY A BORN STORYTELLER." King Features Syndicate

"THERE'S SOMETHING FOR EVERYONE IN THIS BOOK....JUST JUMP IN AND ENJOY IT."
United Press International

"A PUBLISHING PHENOMENON OF EPIC PROPORTIONS...sex, violence, forbidden love, dark secrets, innocence wronged, decadent wealth, courage, weakness, vengeance, hate, and all those other juicy human indulgences. The characters are dramatically drawn...the plot whisks along at a hectic pace; one yearns to know what is on the next page."
Philadelphia Bulletin

"VASTLY ENTERTAINING...It has that certain something that happens only when a natural storyteller is thoroughly enjoying telling her story. It ingratiates, it holds, it lives." The New Haven Register

"REFRESHING, ADDICTIVE, INFECTIOUS AND FAST... a rich Proustian potpourri of times, places and people...an old-fashioned rattling good tale." Time

"SHE WRITES AS IF TO IMPROVE ON LIFE...Enjoy, Colleen, enjoy. You give pleasure with THE THORN BIRDS." The New York Times Book Review

THE THORN BIRDS

COLLEEN McCULLOUGH

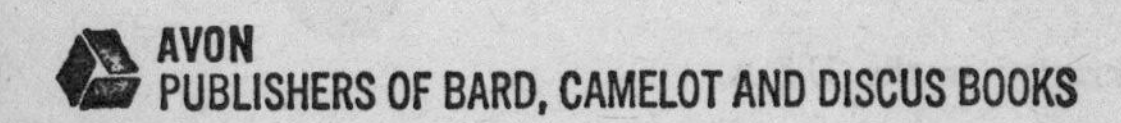

This is a work of fiction and any resemblance between the characters in this book and real persons is coincidental.

A portion of this work originally appeared in *Family Circle.*

Verses from "Clancy of the Overflow" by A. B. Paterson reprinted by permission of the copyright proprietor and Angus and Robertson Publishers.

Photograph of the author by Jim Kalett.

AVON BOOKS
A division of
The Hearst Corporation
959 Eighth Avenue
New York, New York 10019

Published by arrangement with
Harper & Row, Publishers, Inc.
Library of Congress Catalog Card Number: 76-26271
ISBN: 0-380-01817-9

First Avon Printing, June, 1978

for
“big sister”
Jean Easthope

CONTENTS

There is a legend about a bird which sings just once in its life, more sweetly than any other creature on the face of the earth. From the moment it leaves the nest it searches for a thorn tree, and does not rest until it has found one. Then, singing among the savage branches, it impales itself upon the longest, sharpest spine. And, dying, it rises above its own agony to outcarol the lark and the nightingale. One superlative song, existence the price. But the whole world stills to listen, and God in His heaven smiles. For the best is only bought at the cost of great pain. . . . Or so says the legend.

ONE

1915-1917 Meggie

I

On December 8th, 1915, Meggie Cleary had her fourth birthday. After the breakfast dishes were put away her mother silently thrust a brown paper parcel into her arms and ordered her outside. So Meggie squatted down behind the gorse bush next to the front gate and tugged impatiently. Her fingers were clumsy, the wrapping heavy; it smelled faintly of the Wahine general store, which told her that whatever lay inside the parcel had miraculously been *bought,* not homemade or donated.

Something fine and mistily gold began to poke through a corner; she attacked the paper faster, peeling it away in long, ragged strips.

"Agnes! Oh, Agnes!" she said lovingly, blinking at the doll lying there in a tattered nest.

A miracle indeed. Only once in her life had Meggie been into Wahine; all the way back in May, because she had been a very good girl. So perched in the buggy beside her mother, on her best behavior, she had been too excited to see or remember much. Except for Agnes, the beautiful doll sitting on the store counter, dressed in a crinoline of pink satin with cream lace frills all over it. Right then and there in her mind she had christened it Agnes, the only name she knew elegant enough for such a peerless creature. Yet over the ensuing months her yearning after Agnes contained nothing of hope; Meggie didn't own a doll and had no idea little girls and dolls belonged together. She played happily with the whistles and slingshots and battered soldiers her brothers discarded, got her hands dirty and her boots muddy.

It never occurred to her that Agnes was to play with. Stroking the bright pink folds of the dress, grander than any she had ever seen on a human woman, she picked Agnes up tenderly. The doll had jointed arms and legs which could be moved anywhere; even her neck and tiny, shapely waist were jointed. Her golden hair was exquisitely dressed in a high pompadour studded with pearls, her pale bosom peeped out of a foaming fichu of cream lace fastened with a pearl pin. The finely painted bone china face was beautiful, left unglazed to give the delicately tinted skin a natural matte texture. Astonishingly lifelike blue eyes shone between lashes of real hair, their irises streaked and circled with a darker blue; fascinated, Meggie discovered that when Agnes lay back far enough, her eyes closed. High on one faintly flushed cheek she had a black beauty mark, and her dusky mouth was parted slightly to show tiny white teeth. Meggie put the doll gently on her lap, crossed her feet under her comfortably, and sat just looking.

She was still sitting behind the gorse bush when Jack and Hughie came rustling through the grass where it was too close to the fence to feel a scythe. Her hair was the typical Cleary beacon, all the Cleary children save Frank being martyred by a thatch some shade of red; Jack nudged his brother and pointed gleefully. They separated, grinning at each other, and pretended they were troopers after a Maori renegade. Meggie would not have heard them anyway, so engrossed was she in Agnes, humming softly to herself.

"What's that you've got, Meggie?" Jack shouted, pouncing. "Show us!"

"Yes, show us!" Hughie giggled, outflanking her.

She clasped the doll against her chest and shook her head. "No, she's mine! I got her for my birthday!"

"Show us, go on! We just want to have a look."

Pride and joy won out. She held the doll so her brothers could see. "Look, isn't she beautiful? Her name is Agnes."

"Agnes? *Agnes?*" Jack gagged realistically. "What a soppy name! Why don't you call her Margaret or Betty?"

"Because she's Agnes!"

Hughie noticed the joint in the doll's wrist, and whistled. "Hey, Jack, look! It can move its hand!"

"Where? Let's see."

"No!" Meggie hugged the doll close again, tears forming. "No, you'll break her! Oh, Jack, don't take her away—you'll break her!"

"Pooh!" His dirty brown hands locked about her wrists, closing tightly. "Want a Chinese burn? And don't be such a crybaby, or I'll tell Bob." He squeezed her skin in opposite directions until it stretched whitely, as Hughie got hold of the doll's skirts and pulled. "Gimme, or I'll do it really hard!"

"No! Don't, Jack, please don't! You'll break her, I know you will! Oh, please leave her alone! Don't take her, please!" In spite of the cruel grip on her wrists she clung to the doll, sobbing and kicking.

"Got it" Hughie whooped, as the doll slid under Meggie's crossed forearms.

Jack and Hughie found her just as fascinating as Meggie had; off came the dress, the petticoats and long, frilly drawers. Agnes lay naked while the boys pushed and pulled at her, forcing one foot round the back of her head, making her look down her spine, every possible contortion they could think of. They took no notice of Meggie as she stood crying; it did not occur to her to seek help, for in the Cleary family those who could not fight their own battles got scant aid or sympathy, and that went for girls, too.

The doll's golden hair tumbled down, the pearls flew winking into the long grass and disappeared. A dusty boot came down thoughtlessly on the abandoned dress, smearing grease from the smithy across its satin. Meggie dropped to her knees, scrabbling frantically to collect the miniature clothes before more damage was done them, then she began picking among the grass blades where she thought the pearls might have fallen. Her tears were blinding her, the grief in her heart new, for until now she had never owned anything worth grieving for.

Frank threw the shoe hissing into cold water and straightened his back; it didn't ache these days, so perhaps he was used to smithying. Not before time, his father would have said, after six months at it. But Frank knew very well how long it was since his introduction to the forge and anvil; he had measured the time in hatred and resentment. Throwing the hammer into its box, he pushed the lank black hair off his brow with a trembling hand and dragged the old leather apron from around his neck. His shirt lay on a heap of straw in the corner; he plodded across to it and stood for a moment staring at the splintering barn wall as if it did not exist, his black eyes wide and fixed.

He was very small, not above five feet three inches, and thin still as striplings are, but the bare shoulders and arms had muscles already knotted from working with the hammer, and the pale, flawless skin gleamed with sweat. The darkness of his hair and eyes had a foreign tang, his full-lipped mouth and wide-bridged nose not the usual family shape, but there was Maori blood on his mother's side and in him it showed. He was nearly sixteen years old, where Bob was barely eleven, Jack ten, Hughie nine, Stuart five and little Meggie three. Then he remembered that today Meggie was four; it was December 8th. He put on his shirt and left the barn.

The house lay on top of a small hill about one hundred feet higher than the barn and stables. Like all New Zealand houses, it was wooden, rambling over many squares and of one story only, on the theory that if an earthquake struck, some of it might be left standing. Around it gorse grew everywhere, at the moment smothered in rich yellow flowers; the grass was green and luxuriant, like all New Zealand grass. Not even in the middle of winter, when the frost sometimes lay unmelted all day in the shade, did the grass turn brown, and the long, mild summer only tinted it an even richer green. The rains fell gently without bruising the tender sweetness of all growing things, there was no snow, and the sun had just enough strength to cherish, never enough to sap. New Zealand's scourges thundered up out of the bowels of the earth rather than descended from the skies. There was always a suffocated sense of waiting, an intangible shuddering and thumping that actually transmitted itself through the feet. For beneath the ground lay awesome power, power of such magnitude that thirty years before a whole towering mountain had disappeared; steam gushed howling out of cracks in the sides of innocent hills, volcanoes spumed smoke into the sky and the alpine streams ran warm. Huge lakes of mud boiled oilily, the seas lapped uncertainly at cliffs which might not be there to greet the next incoming tide, and in places the earth's crust was only nine hundred feet thick.

Yet it was a gentle, gracious land. Beyond the house stretched an undulating plain as green as the emerald in Fiona Cleary's engagement ring, dotted with thousands of creamy bundles close proximity revealed as sheep. Where the curving hills scalloped the edge of the light-blue sky Mount Egmont soared ten thousand feet, sloping into the clouds, its sides still white with snow, its symmetry so perfect that even those like Frank who saw it every day of their lives never ceased to marvel.

It was quite a pull from the barn to the house, but

Frank hurried because he knew he ought not to be going; his father's orders were explicit. Then as he rounded the corner of the house he saw the little group by the gorse bush.

Frank had driven his mother into Wahine to buy Meggie's doll, and he was still wondering what had prompted her to do it. She wasn't given to impractical birthday presents, there wasn't the money for them, and she had never given a toy to anyone before. They all got clothes; birthdays and Christmases replenished sparse wardrobes. But apparently Meggie had seen the doll on her one and only trip into town, and Fiona had not forgotten. When Frank questioned her, she muttered something about a girl needing a doll, and quickly changed the subject.

Jack and Hughie had the doll between them on the front path, manipulating its joints callously. All Frank could see of Meggie was her back, as she stood watching her brothers desecrate Agnes. Her neat white socks had slipped in crinkled folds around her little black boots, and the pink of her legs was visible for three or four inches below the hem of her brown velvet Sunday dress. Down her back cascaded a mane of carefully curled hair, sparkling in the sun; not red and not gold, but somewhere in between. The white taffeta bow which held the front curls back from her face hung draggled and limp; dust smeared her dress. She held the doll's clothes tightly in one hand, the other pushing vainly at Hughie.

"You bloody little bastards!"

Jack and Hughie scrambled to their feet and ran, the doll forgotten; when Frank swore it was politic to run.

"If I catch you flaming little twerps touching that doll again I'll brand your shitty little arses!" Frank yelled after them.

He bent down and took Meggie's shoulders between his hands, shaking her gently.

"Here, here there's no need to cry! Come on now,

they've gone and they'll never touch your dolly again, I promise. Give me a smile for your birthday, eh?"

Her face was swollen, her eyes running; she stared at Frank out of grey eyes so large and full of tragedy that he felt his throat tighten. Pulling a dirty rag from his breeches pocket, he rubbed it clumsily over her face, then pinched her nose between its folds.

"Blow!"

She did as she was told, hiccuping noisily as her tears dried. "Oh, Fruh-Fruh-Frank, they too-too-took Agnes away from me!" She sniffled. "Her huh-huh-hair all falled down and she loh-loh-lost all the pretty widdle puh-puh-pearls in it! They all falled in the gruh-gruh-grass and I can't *find* them!"

The tears welled up again, splashing on Frank's hand; he stared at his wet skin for a moment, then licked the drops off.

"Well, we'll have to find them, won't we? But you can't find anything while you're crying, you know, and what's all this baby talk? I haven't heard you say 'widdle' instead of 'little' for six months! Here, blow your nose again and then pick up poor . . . Agnes? If you don't put her clothes on, she'll get sunburned."

He made her sit on the edge of the path and gave her the doll gently, then he crawled about searching the grass until he gave a triumphant whoop and held up a pearl.

"There! First one! We'll find them all, you wait and see."

Meggie watched her oldest brother adoringly while he picked among the grass blades, holding up each pearl as he found it; then she remembered how delicate Agnes's skin must be, how easily it must burn, and bent her attention on clothing the doll. There did not seem any real injury. Her hair was tangled and loose, her arms and legs dirty where the boys had pushed and pulled at them, but everything still worked. A tortoise-shell comb nestled above each of Meggie's ears; she tugged at one until it came free, and began to comb Agnes's hair, which was genuine human hair, skillfully knotted onto a base of glue and gauze, and bleached until it was the color of gilded straw.

She was yanking inexpertly at a large knot when the dreadful thing happened. Off came the hair, all of it, dangling in a tousled clump from the teeth of the comb. Above Agnes's smooth broad brow there was nothing; no head, no bald skull. Just an awful, yawning hole. Shivering in terror, Meggie leaned forward to peer inside the doll's cranium. The inverted contours of cheeks and chin showed dimly, light glittered between the parted lips with their teeth a black, animal silhouette, and above all this were Agnes's eyes, two horrible clicking balls speared by a wire rod that cruelly pierced her head.

Meggie's scream was high and thin, unchildlike; she flung Agnes away and went on screaming, hands covering her face, shaking and shuddering. Then she felt Frank pull at her fingers and take her into his arms, pushing her face into the side of his neck. Wrapping her arms about him, she took comfort from him until his nearness calmed her enough to become aware of how nice he smelled, all horses and sweat and iron.

When she quietened, Frank made her tell him what was the matter; he picked up the doll and stared into its empty head in wonder, trying to remember if his infant universe had been so beset by strange terrors. But his unpleasant phantoms were of people and whispers and cold glances. Of his mother's face pinched and shrinking, her hand trembling as it held his, the set of her shoulders.

What had Meggie seen, to make her take on so? He fancied she would not have been nearly so upset if poor Agnes had only bled when she lost her hair. Bleeding was a fact; someone in the Cleary family bled copiously at least once a week.

"Her eyes, her eyes!" Meggie whispered, refusing to look at the doll.

"She's a bloody marvel, Meggie," he murmured, his face nuzzling into her hair. How fine it was, how rich and full of color!

It took him half an hour of cajoling to make her look at Agnes, and half an hour more elapsed before he could persuade her to peer into the scalped hole. He showed her how the eyes worked, how very carefully they had been aligned to fit snugly yet swing easily opened or closed.

"Come on now, it's time you went inside," he told her, swinging her up into his arms and tucking the doll between his chest and hers. "We'll get Mum to fix her up, eh? We'll wash and iron her clothes, and glue on her hair again. I'll make you some proper hairpins out of those pearls, too, so they can't fall out and you can do her hair in all sorts of ways."

Fiona Cleary was in the kitchen, peeling potatoes. She was a very handsome, very fair woman a little under medium height, but rather hard-faced and stern; she had an excellent figure with a tiny waist which had not thickened, in spite of the six babies she had carried beneath it. Her dress was grey calico, its skirts brushing the spotless floor, its front protected by an enormous starched white apron that looped around her neck and tied in the small of her spine with a crisp, perfect bow. From waking to sleeping she lived in the kitchen and back garden, her stout black boots beating a circular path from stove to laundry to vegetable patch to clotheslines and thence to the stove again.

She put her knife on the table and stared at Frank and Meggie, the corners of her beautiful mouth turning down.

"Meggie, I let you put on your Sunday-best dress this morning on one condition, that you didn't get it dirty. And look at you! What a little grub you are!"

"Mum, it wasn't her fault," Frank protested. "Jack and Hughie took her doll away to try and find out how the arms and legs worked. I promised we'd fix it up as good as new. We can, can't we?"

"Let me see." Fee held out her hand for the doll.

She was a silent woman, not given to spontaneous conversation. What she thought, no one ever knew, even her husband; she left the disciplining of the children to him, and did whatever he commanded without comment or complaint unless the circumstances were most unusual. Meggie had heard the boys whispering that she stood in as much awe of Daddy as they did, but if that was true she hid it under a veneer of impenetrable, slightly dour calm. She never laughed, nor did she ever lose her temper.

Finished her inspection, Fee laid Agnes on the dresser near the stove and looked at Meggie.

"I'll wash her clothes tomorrow morning, and do her hair again. Frank can glue the hair on after tea tonight, I suppose, and give her a bath."

The words were matter-of-fact rather than comforting. Meggie nodded, smiling uncertainly; sometimes she wanted so badly to hear her mother laugh, but her mother never did. She sensed that they shared a special something not common to Daddy and the boys, but there was no reaching beyond that rigid back, those never still feet. Mum would nod absently and flip her voluminous skirts expertly from stove to table as she continued working, working, working.

What none of the children save Frank could realize was that Fee was permanently, incurably tired. There was so much to be done, hardly any money to do it with, not enough time, and only one pair of hands. She longed for the day when Meggie would be old enough to help; already the child did simple tasks, but at barely four years of age it couldn't possibly lighten the load. Six children, and only one of them, the youngest at that, a girl. All her acquaintances were simultaneously sympathetic and envious, but that didn't get the work done. Her sewing basket had a mountain of socks in it still undarned, her knitting needles held yet another sock, and there was Hughie growing out of his sweaters and Jack not ready to hand his down.

Padraic Cleary was to home the week of Meggie's birthday, purely by chance. It was too early for the shearing season, and he had work locally, plowing and planting. By profession he was a shearer of sheep, a seasonal occupation which lasted from the middle of summer to the end of winter, after which came lambing. Usually he managed to find plenty of work to tide him over spring and the first month of summer; helping with lambing, plowing, or spelling a local dairy farmer from his endless twice-a-day milking. Where there was work he went, leaving his family in the big old house to fend for themselves; not as harsh an action as it seemed. Unless one was lucky enough to own land, that was what one had to do.

When he came in a little after sunset the lamps were lit, and shadows played flickering games around the high ceiling. The boys were clustered on the back veranda playing with a frog, except for Frank; Padraic knew where he was, because he could hear the steady clocking of an axe from the direction of the woodheap. He paused on the veranda only long enough to plant a kick on Jack's backside and clip Bob's ear.

"Go and help Frank with the wood, you lazy little scamps. And it had better be done before Mum has tea on the table, or there'll be skin and hair flying."

He nodded to Fiona, busy at the stove; he did not kiss or embrace her, for he regarded displays of affection between husband and wife as something suitable only for the bedroom. As he used the jack to haul off his mud-caked boots, Meggie came skipping with his slippers, and he grinned down at the little girl with the curious sense of wonder he always knew at sight of her. She was so pretty, such beautiful hair; he picked up a curl and pulled it out straight, then let it go, just to see it jiggle and bounce as it settled back into place. Picking the child up, he went to sit in the only comfortable chair the kitchen possessed, a Windsor chair with a cushion tied to its seat, drawn close to the fire. Sighing softly, he sat down in it and pulled out his pipe, carelessly tapping out the spent dottle of tobacco in its bowl onto the floor. Meggie cuddled down on his lap and wound her arms about his neck, her cool little face turned up to his as she played her nightly game of watching the light filter through his short stubble of golden beard.

"How are you, Fee?" Padraic Cleary asked his wife.

"All right, Paddy. Did you get the lower paddock done today?"

"Yes, all done. I can start on the upper first thing in the morning. Lord, but I'm tired!"

"I'll bet. Did MacPherson give you the crotchety old mare again?"

"Too right. You don't think he'd take the animal himself to let me have the roan, do you? My arms feel as if they've been pulled out of their sockets. I swear that mare has the hardest mouth in En Zed."

"Never mind. Old Robertson's horses are all good, and you'll be there soon enough."

"Can't be soon enough." He packed his pipe with coarse tobacco and pulled a taper from the big jar that stood near the stove. A quick flick inside the firebox door and it caught; he leaned back in his chair and sucked so deeply the pipe made bubbling noises. "How's it feel to be four, Meggie?" he asked his daughter.

"Pretty good, Daddy."

"Did Mum give you your present?"

"Oh, Daddy, how did you and Mum guess I wanted Agnes?"

"Agnes?" He looked swiftly toward Fee, smiling and quizzing her with his eyebrows. "Is that her name, Agnes?"

"Yes. She's beautiful, Daddy. I want to look at her all day."

"She's lucky to have anything to look at," Fee said grimly. "Jack and Hughie got hold of the doll before poor Meggie had a chance to see it properly."

"Well, boys will be boys. Is the damage bad?"

"Nothing that can't be mended. Frank caught them before it went too far."

"Frank? What was he doing down here? He was supposed to be at the forge all day. Hunter wants his gates."

"He was at the forge all day. He just came down for a tool of some sort," Fee answered quickly; Padraic was too hard on Frank.

"Oh, Daddy, Frank is the best brother! He saved my Agnes from being killed, and he's going to glue her hair on again for me after tea."

"That's good," her father said drowsily, leaning his head back in the chair and closing his eyes.

It was hot in front of the stove, but he didn't seem to notice; beads of sweat gathered on his forehead, glistening. He put his arms behind his head and fell into a doze.

It was from Padraic Cleary that his children got their various shades of thick, waving red hair, though none had inherited quite such an aggressively red head as his. He was a small man, all steel and springs in build, legs bowed from a lifetime among horses, arms elongated from years shearing sheep; his chest and arms were covered in a matted golden fuzz which would have been ugly had he been dark. His eyes were bright blue, crinkled up into a permanent squint like a sailor's from gazing into the far distance, and his face was a pleasant one, with a whimsical smiling quality about it that made other men like him at a glance. His nose was magnificent, a true Roman nose which must have puzzled his Irish confreres, but Ireland has ever been a shipwreck coast. He still spoke with the soft quick slur of the Galway Irish, pronouncing his final *t*'s as *th*'s, but almost twenty years in the Antipodes had forced a quaint overlay upon it, so that his *a*'s came out as *i*'s and the speed of his speech had run down a little, like an old clock in need of a good winding. A happy man, he had managed to weather his hard and drudging existence better than most, and though he was a rigid disciplinarian with a heavy swing to his boot, all but one of his children adored him. If there was not enough bread to go around, he went without; if it was a choice between new clothes for him or new clothes for one of his offspring, he went without. In its way, that was more reliable evidence of love than a million easy kisses. His temper was very fiery, and he had killed a man once. Luck had been with him; the man was English, and there was a ship in Dun Laoghaire harbor bound for New Zealand on the tide.

Fiona went to the back door and shouted, "Tea!"

The boys trailed in gradually, Frank bringing up the rear with an armload of wood, which he dumped in the big box beside the stove. Padraic put Meggie down and walked to the head of the non-company dining table at the far end of the kitchen, while the boys seated themselves around its sides and Meggie scrambled up on top of the wooden box her father put on the chair nearest to him.

Fee served the food directly onto dinner plates at her worktable, more quickly and efficiently than a waiter; she carried them two at a time to her family, Paddy first, then Frank, and so on down to Meggie, with herself last.

"Erckle! Stew!" said Stuart, pulling faces as he picked up his knife and fork. "Why did you have to name me after *stew?*"

"Eat it," his father growled.

The plates were big ones, and they were literally heaped with food: boiled potatoes, lamb stew and beans cut that day from the garden, ladled in huge portions.

In spite of the muted groans and sounds of disgust, everyone including Stu polished his plate clean with bread, and ate several slices more spread thickly with butter and native gooseberry jam. Fee sat down and bolted her meal, then got up at once to hurry to her worktable again, where into big soup plates she doled out great quantities of biscuit made with plenty of sugar and laced all through with jam. A river of steaming hot custard sauce was poured over each, and again she plodded to the dining table with the plates, two at a time. Finally she sat down with a sigh; this she could eat at her leisure.

"Oh, goodie! Jam roly-poly!" Meggie exclaimed, slopping her spoon up and down in the custard until the jam seeped through to make pink streaks in the yellow.

"Well, Meggie girl, it's your birthday, so Mum made your favorite pudding," her father said, smiling.

There were no complaints this time; no matter what the pudding was, it was consumed with gusto. The Clearys all had a sweet tooth.

No one carried a pound of superfluous flesh, in spite of the vast quantities of starchy food. They expended every ounce they ate in work or play. Vegetables and fruit were eaten because they were good for you, but it was the bread, potatoes, meat and hot floury puddings which staved off exhaustion.

After Fee had poured everyone a cup of tea from her giant pot, they stayed talking, drinking or reading for an hour or more, Paddy puffing on his pipe with his head in a library book, Fee continuously refilling cups, Bob immersed in another library book, while the younger children made plans for the morrow. School had dispersed for the long summer vacation; the boys were on the loose and eager to commence their allotted chores around the house and garden. Bob had to touch up the exterior paintwork where it was necessary, Jack and Hughie dealt with the woodheap, outbuildings and milking, Stuart tended the vegetables; play compared to the horrors of school. From time to time Paddy lifted his head from his book to add another job to the list, but Fee said nothing, and Frank sat slumped tiredly, sipping cup after cup of tea.

Finally Fee beckoned Meggie to sit on a high stool, and did up her hair in its nightly rags before packing her off to bed with Stu and Hughie; Jack and Bob begged to be excused and went outside to feed the dogs; Frank took Meggie's doll to the worktable and began to glue its hair on again. Stretching, Padraic closed his book and put his pipe into the huge iridescent paua shell which served him as an ashtray.

"Well, Mother, I'm off to bed."

"Good night, Paddy."

Fee cleared the dishes off the dining table and got a big galvanized iron tub down from its hook on the wall. She put it at the opposite end of the worktable from Frank, and lifting the massive cast-iron kettle off the stove, filled it with hot water. Cold water from an old kerosene tin served to cool the steaming bath; swishing soap confined in a wire basket through it, she began to wash and rinse the dishes, stacking them against a cup.

Frank worked on the doll without raising his head, but as the pile of plates grew he got up silently to fetch a towel and began to dry them. Moving between the worktable and the dresser, he worked with the ease of long familiarity. It was a furtive, fearful game he and his mother played, for the most stringent rule in Paddy's domain concerned the proper delegation of duties. The house was woman's work, and that was that. No male member of the family was to put his hand to a female task. But each night after Paddy went to bed Frank helped his mother, Fee aiding and abetting him by delaying her dishwashing until they heard the thump of Paddy's slippers hitting the floor. Once Paddy's slippers were off he never came back to the kitchen.

Fee looked at Frank gently. "I don't know what I'd

do without you, Frank. But you shouldn't. You'll be so tired in the morning."

"It's all right, Mum. Drying a few dishes won't kill me. Little enough to make life easier for you."

"It's my job, Frank. I don't mind."

"I just wish we'd get rich one of these days, so you could have a maid."

"That *is* wishful thinking!" She wiped her soapy red hands on the dishcloth and then pressed them into her sides, sighing. Her eyes as they rested on her son were vaguely worried, sensing his bitter discontent, more than the normal railing of a workingman against his lot. "Frank, don't get grand ideas. They only lead to trouble. We're working-class people, which means we don't get rich or have maids. Be content with what you are and what you have. When you say things like this you're insulting Daddy, and he doesn't deserve it. You know that. He doesn't drink, he doesn't gamble, and he works awfully hard for us. Not a penny he earns goes into his own pocket. It all comes to us."

The muscular shoulders hunched impatiently, the dark face became harsh and grim. "But why should wanting more out of life than drudgery be so bad? I don't see what's wrong with wishing you had a maid."

"It's wrong because it can't be! You know there's no money to keep you at school, and if you can't stay at school how are you ever going to be anything better than a manual worker? Your accent, your clothes and your hands show that you labor for a living. But it's no disgrace to have calluses on your hands. As Daddy says, when a man's hands are callused you know he's honest."

Frank shrugged and said no more. The dishes were all put away; Fee got out her sewing basket and sat down in Paddy's chair by the fire, while Frank went back to the doll.

"Poor little Meggie!" he said suddenly.

"Why?"

"Today, when those wretched chaps were pulling

her dolly about, she just stood there crying as if her whole world had fallen to bits." He looked down at the doll, which was wearing its hair again. "Agnes! Where on earth did she get a name like that?"

"She must have heard me talking about Agnes Fortescue-Smythe, I suppose."

"When I gave her the doll back she looked into its head and nearly died of fright. Something scared her about its eyes; I don't know what."

"Meggie's always seeing things that aren't there."

"It's a pity there isn't enough money to keep the little children at school. They're so clever."

"Oh, Frank! If wishes were horses beggars might ride," his mother said wearily. She passed her hand across her eyes, trembling a little, and stuck her darning needle deep into a ball of grey wool. "I can't do any more. I'm too tried to see straight."

"Go to bed, Mum. I'll blow out the lamps."

"As soon as I've stoked the fire."

"I'll do that." He got up from the table and put the dainty china doll carefully down behind a cake tin on the dresser, where it would be out of harm's way. He was not worried that the boys might attempt further rapine; they were more frightened of his vengeance than of their father's, for Frank had a vicious streak. When he was with his mother or his sister it never appeared, but the boys had all suffered from it.

Fee watched him, her heart aching; there was something wild and desperate about Frank, an aura of trouble. If only he and Paddy got on better together! But they could never see eye to eye, and argued constantly. Maybe he was too concerned for her, maybe he was a bit of a mother's boy. Her fault, if it was true. Yet it spoke of his loving heart, his goodness. He only wanted to make her life a little easier. And again she found herself yearning for the day when Meggie became old enough to take the burden of it from Frank's shoulders.

She picked up a small lamp from the table, then put it down again and walked across to where Frank was squatted before the stove, packing wood into the big firebox and fiddling with the damper. His white arm was roped with prominent veins, his finely made hands too stained ever to come clean. Her own hand went out timidly, and very lightly smoothed the straight black hair out of his eyes; it was as close as she could bring herself to a caress.

"Good night, Frank, and thank you."

The shadows wheeled and darted before the advancing light as Fee moved silently through the door leading into the front part of the house.

Frank and Bob shared the first bedroom; she pushed its door open noiselessly and held the lamp high, its light flooding the double bed in the corner. Bob was lying on his back with his mouth sagging open, quivering and twitching like a dog; she crossed to the bed and rolled him over onto his right side before he could pass into a full-fledged nightmare, then stayed looking down at him for a moment. How like Paddy he was!

Jack and Hughie were almost braided together in the next room. What dreadful scamps they were! Never out of mischief, but no malice in them. She tried vainly to separate them and restore some sort of order to their bedclothes, but the two curly red heads refused to be parted. Softly sighing, she gave up. How they managed to be refreshed after the kind of night they passed was beyond her, but they seemed to thrive on it.

The room where Meggie and Stuart slept was a dingy and cheerless place for two small children; painted a stuffy brown and floored in brown linoleum, no pictures on the walls. Just like the other bedrooms.

Stuart had turned himself upside down and was quite invisible except for his little nightshirted bottom sticking out of the covers where his head ought to have been; Fee found his head touching his knees, and as usual marveled that he had not suffocated. She slid her hand gingerly across the sheet and stiffened. Wet again! Well, it would have to wait until the morning, when no doubt the pillow would be wet, too. He always did that, reversed himself and then wet once more. Well, one bed-wetter among five boys wasn't bad.

Meggie was curled into a little heap, with her thumb in her mouth and her rag-decorated hair all around her. The only girl. Fee cast her no more than a passing glance before leaving; there was no mystery to Meggie, she was female. Fee knew what her lot would be, and did not envy her or pity her. The boys were different; they were miracles, males alchemized out of her female body. It was hard not having help around the house, but it was worth it. Among his peers, Paddy's sons were the greatest character reference he possessed. Let a man breed sons and he was a real man.

She closed the door to her own bedroom softly, and put the lamp down on a bureau. Her nimble fingers flew down the dozens of tiny buttons between the high collar and the hips of her dress, then peeled it away from her arms. She slipped the camisole off her arms also, and holding it very carefully against her chest, she wriggled into a long flannel nightgown. Only then, decently covered, did she divest herself of camisole, drawers and loosely laced stays. Down came the tightly knotted golden hair, all its pins put into a paua shell on the bureau. But even this, beautiful as it was, thick and shining and very straight, was not permitted freedom; Fee got her elbows up over her head and her hands behind her neck, and began to braid it swiftly. She turned then toward the bed, her breathing unconsciously suspended; but Paddy was asleep, so she heaved a gusty sigh of relief. Not that it wasn't nice when Paddy was in the mood, for he was a shy, tender, considerate lover. But until Meggie was two or three years older it would be very hard to have more babies.

2

When the Clearys went to church on Sundays, Meggie had to stay home with one of the older boys, longing for the day when she, too, would be old enough to go. Padraic Cleary held that small children had no place in any house save their own, and his rule held even for a house of worship. When Meggie commenced school and could be trusted to sit still, she could come to church. Not before. So every Sunday morning she stood by the gorse bush at the front gate, desolate, while the family piled into the old shandrydan and the brother delegated to mind her tried to pretend it was a great treat escaping Mass. The only Cleary who relished separation from the rest was Frank.

Paddy's religion was an intrinsic part of his life. When he had married Fee it had been with grudging Catholic approval, for Fee was a member of the Church of England; though she abandoned her faith for Paddy, she refused to adopt his in its stead. Difficult to say why, except that the Armstrongs were old pioneering stock of impeccable Church of England extraction, where Paddy was a penniless immigrant from the wrong side of the Pale. There had been Armstrongs in New Zealand long before the first "official" settlers arrived, and that was a passport to colonial aristocracy. From the

Armstrong point of view, Fee could only be said to have contracted a shocking *mésalliance*.

Roderick Armstrong had founded the New Zealand clan, in a very curious way.

It had begun with an event which was to have many unforeseen repercussions on eighteenth-century England: the American War of Independence. Until 1776 over a thousand British petty felons were shipped each year to Virginia and the Carolinas, sold into an indentured servitude no better than slavery. British justice of the time was grim and unflinching; murder, arson, the mysterious crime of "impersonating Egyptians" and larceny to the tune of more than a shilling were punished on the gallows. Petty crime meant transportation to the Americas for the term of the felon's natural life.

But when in 1776 the Americas were closed, England found herself with a rapidly increasing convict population and nowhere to put it. The prisons filled to overflowing, and the surplus was jammed into rotting hulks moored in the river estuaries. Something had to be done, so something was. With a great deal of reluctance because it meant the expenditure of a few thousand pounds, Captain Arthur Phillip was ordered to set sail for the Great South Land. The year was 1787. His fleet of eleven ships held over one thousand convicts, plus sailors, naval officers and a contingent of marines. No glorious odyssey in search of freedom, this. At the end of January 1788, eight months after setting sail from England, the fleet arrived in Botany Bay. His Mad Majesty George the Third had found a new dumping ground for his convicts, the colony of New South Wales.

In 1801, when he was just twenty years of age, Roderick Armstrong was sentenced to transportation for the term of his natural life. Later generations of Armstrongs insisted he came of Somerset gentlefolk who had lost their fortune following the American Revolution, and that his crime was nonexistent, but none of them had ever tried very hard to trace their illustrious ancestor's background. They just basked in his reflected glory and improvised somewhat.

Whatever his origins and status in English life, the young Roderick Armstrong was a tartar. All through the unspeakable eight months' voyage to New South Wales he proved a stubborn, difficult prisoner, further endearing himself to his ship's officers by refusing to die. When he arrived in Sydney in 1803 his behavior worsened, so he was shipped to Norfolk Island and the prison for intractables. Nothing improved his conduct. They starved him; they immured him in a cell so small he could neither sit, stand nor lie; they flogged him to jellied pulp; they chained him to a rock in the sea and let him half-drown. And he laughed at them, a skinny collection of bones in filthy canvas, not a tooth in his mouth or an inch of his skin unscarred, lit from within by a fire of bitterness and defiance nothing seemed to quench. At the beginning of each day he willed himself not to die, and at the end of each day he laughed in triumph to find himself still alive.

In 1810 he was sent to Van Diemen's Land, put in a chain gang and set to hew a road through the iron-hard sandstone country behind Hobart. At first opportunity he had used his pick to hack a hole in the chest of the trooper commanding the expedition; he and ten other convicts massacred five more troopers by shaving the flesh from their bones an inch at a time until they died screaming in agony. For they and their guards were beasts, elemental creatures whose emotions had atrophied to the subhuman. Roderick Armstrong could no more have gone off into his escape leaving his tormentors intact or quickly dead than he could have reconciled himself to being a convict.

With the rum and bread and jerky they took from the troopers, the eleven men fought their way through miles of freezing rain forest and came out at the whaling station of Hobart, where they stole a longboat and set off across the Tasman Sea without food, water or sails. When the longboat washed ashore on the wild west coast of New Zealand's South Island, Roderick Armstrong and two other men were still alive. He never spoke of that incredible journey, but it was whispered that the three had survived by killing and eating their weaker companions.

That was just nine years after he had been transported from England. He was yet a young man, but he looked sixty. By the time the first officially sanctioned settlers arrived in New Zealand in 1840, he had hewn lands for himself in the rich Canterbury district of the South Island, "married" a Maori woman and sired a brood of thirteen handsome half-Polynesian children. And by 1860 the Armstrongs were colonial aristocrats, sent their male offspring to exclusive schools back in England, and amply proved by their cunning and acquisitiveness that they were indeed true descendants of a remarkable, formidable man. Roderick's grandson James had fathered Fiona in 1880, the only daughter among a total of fifteen children.

If Fee missed the more austere Protestant rites of her childhood, she never said so. She tolerated Paddy's religious convictions and attended Mass with him, saw to it that her children worshipped an exclusively Catholic God. But because she had never converted, the little touches were missing, like grace before meals and prayers before bed, an everyday holiness.

Aside from that one trip into Wahine eighteen months before, Meggie had never been farther from home than the barn and smithy in the hollow. On the morning of her first day at school she was so excited she vomited her breakfast, and had to be bundled back into her bedroom to be washed and changed. Off came the lovely new costume of navy blue with a big white sailor collar, on went her horrid brown wincey which buttoned high around her little neck and always felt as if it were choking her.

"And for heaven's sake, Meggie, next time you feel sick, *tell* me! Don't just sit there until it's too late and I've got a mess to clean up as well as everything else! Now you're going to have to hurry, because if you're late for the bell Sister Agatha is sure to cane you. Behave yourself, and mind your brothers."

Bob, Jack, Hughie and Stu were hopping up and down by the front gate when Fee finally pushed Meggie out the door, her luncheon jam sandwiches in an old satchel.

"Come on, Meggie, we'll be late!" Bob shouted, moving off down the road.

Meggie followed the dwindling forms of her brothers at a run.

It was a little after seven o'clock in the morning, and the gentle sun had been up several hours; the dew had dried off the grass except where there was deep shade. The Wahine road was a wheel-rutted earthen track, two ribbons of dark red separated by a wide band of bright green grass. White calla lilies and orange nasturtiums flowered profusely in the high grass to either side, where the neat wooden fences of bordering properties warned against trespassing.

Bob always walked to school along the top of the right-hand fences, balancing his leather satchel on his head instead of wearing it haversack style. The left-hand fence belonged to Jack, which permitted the three younger Clearys domain of the road itself. At the top of the long, steep hill they had to climb from the smithy hollow to where the Robertson road joined the Wahine road, they paused for a moment, panting, the five bright heads haloed against a puffily clouded sky. This was the best part, going down the hill; they linked hands and galloped on the grassy verge until it vanished in a tangle of flowers, wishing they had the time to sneak under Mr. Chapman's fence and roll all the way down like boulders.

It was five miles from the Cleary house to Wahine,

and by the time Meggie saw telegraph poles in the distance her legs were trembling and her socks were falling down. Ears tuned for the assembly bell, Bob glanced at her impatiently as she toiled along, hitching at her drawers and giving an occasional gasp of distress. Her face under the mass of hair was pink and yet curiously pallid. Sighing, Bob passed his satchel to Jack and ran his hands down the sides of his knickers.

"Come on, Meggie, I'll piggyback you the rest of the way," he said gruffly, glaring at his brothers in case they had the mistaken idea that he was going soft.

Meggie scrambled onto his back, heaved herself up enough to lock her legs around his waist, and pillowed her head on his skinny shoulder blissfully. Now she could view Wahine in comfort.

There was not much to see. Little more than a big village, Wahine straggled down each side of a tar-centered road. The biggest building was the local hotel, of two stories, with an awning shading the footpath from the sun and posts supporting the awning all along the gutter. The general store was the next-biggest building, also boasting a sheltering awning, and two long wooden benches under its cluttered windows for passers-by to rest upon. There was a flagpole in front of the Masonic hall; from its top a tattered Union Jack fluttered faded in the stiff breeze. As yet the town possessed no garage, horseless carriages being limited to a very few, but there was a blacksmith's barn near the Masonic hall, with a stable behind it and a gasoline pump standing stiffly next to the horse trough. The only edifice in the entire settlement which really caught the eye was a peculiar bright-blue shop, very un-British; every other building was painted a sober brown. The public school and the Church of England stood side by side, just opposite the Sacred Heart Church and parish school.

As the Clearys hurried past the general store the Catholic bell sounded, followed by the heavier tolling of the big bell on a post in front of the public school. Bob broke into a trot, and they entered the gravel yard as some fifty children were lining up in front of a diminutive nun wielding a willowy stick taller than she was. Without having to be told, Bob steered his kin to one side away from the lines of children, and stood with his eyes fixed on the cane.

The Sacred Heart convent was two-storied, but because it stood well back from the road behind a fence, the fact was not easily apparent. The three nuns of the Order of the Sisters of Mercy who staffed it lived upstairs with a fourth nun, who acted as housekeeper and was never seen; downstairs were the three big rooms in which school was taught. A wide, shady veranda ran all the way around the rectangular building, where on rainy days the children were allowed to sit decorously during their play and lunch breaks, and where on sunny days no child was permitted to set foot. Several large fig trees shaded a part of the spacious grounds, and behind the school the land sloped away a little to a grassy circle euphemistically christened "the cricket pitch," from the chief activity that went on in that area.

Ignoring muffled sniggers from the lined-up children, Bob and his brothers stood perfectly still while the pupils marched inside to the sound of Sister Catherine plunking "Faith of Our Fathers" on the tinny school piano. Only when the last child had disappeared did Sister Agatha break her rigid pose; heavy serge skirts swishing the gravel aside imperiously, she strode to where the Clearys waited.

Meggie gaped at her, never having seen a nun before. The sight was truly extraordinary; three dabs of person, which were Sister Agatha's face and hands, the rest white starched wimple and bib glaring against layers of blackest black, with a massive rope of wooden rosary beads dangling from an iron ring that joined the ends of a wide leather belt around Sister Agatha's stout middle. Sister Agatha's skin was permanently red, from too much cleanliness and the pressure of the knifelike edges of the wimple framing the front center of her head into something too disembodied to be called a face; little hairs sprouted in tufts all over her chin, which the wimple ruthlessly squashed double. Her lips were quite invisible, compressed into a single line of concentration on the hard business of being the Bride of Christ in a colonial backwater with topsy-turvy seasons when she had taken her vows in the sweet softness of a Killarney abbey over fifty years before. Two small crimson marks were etched into the sides of her nose from the remorseless grip of her round, steel-framed spectacles, and behind them her eyes peered out suspiciously, pale-blue and bitter.

"Well, Robert Cleary, why are you late?" Sister Agatha barked in her dry, once Irish voice.

"I'm sorry, Sister," Bob replied woodenly, his blue-green eyes still riveted on the tip of the quivering cane as it waved back and forth.

"Why are you late?" she repeated.

"I'm sorry, Sister."

"This is the first morning of the new school year, Robert Cleary, and I would have thought that on this morning if not on others you might have made an effort to be on time."

Meggie shivered, but plucked up her courage. "Oh, please, Sister, it was my fault!" she squeaked.

The pale-blue eyes deviated from Bob and seemed to go through and through Meggie's very soul as she stood there gazing up in genuine innocence, not aware she was breaking the first rule of conduct in a deadly duel which went on between teachers and pupils *ad infinitum:* never volunteer information. Bob kicked her swiftly on the leg and Meggie looked at him sideways, bewildered.

"Why was it your fault?" the nun demanded in the coldest tones Meggie had ever heard.

"Well, I was sick all over the table and it went right

through to my drawers, so Mum had to wash me and change my dress, and I made us all late," Meggie explained artlessly.

Sister Agatha's features remained expressionless, but her mouth tightened like an overwound spring, and the tip of the cane lowered itself an inch or two. "Who is *this?"* she snapped to Bob, as if the object of her inquiry were a new and particularly obnoxious species of insect.

"Please, Sister, she's my sister Meghann."

"Then in future you will make her understand that there are certain subjects we do not ever mention, Robert, if we are true ladies and gentlemen. On no account do we ever, ever mention by name any item of our underclothing, as children from a decent household would automatically know. Hold out your hands, all of you."

"But, Sister, it was *my* fault!" Meggie wailed as she extended her hands palms up, for she had seen her brothers do it in pantomime at home a thousand times.

"Silence!" Sister Agatha hissed, turning on her. "It is a matter of complete indifference to me which one of you was responsible. You are all late, therefore you must all be punished. Six cuts." She pronounced the sentence with monotonous relish.

Terrified, Meggie watched Bob's steady hands, saw the long cane whistle down almost faster than her eyes could follow, and crack sharply against the center of his palms, where the flesh was soft and tender. A purple welt flared up immediately; the next cut came at the junction of fingers and palm, more sensitive still, and the final one across the tips of the fingers, where the brain has loaded the skin down with more sensation than anywhere else save the lips. Sister Agatha's aim was perfect. Three more cuts followed on Bob's other hand before she turned her attention to Jack, next in line. Bob's face was pale but he made no outcry or movement, nor did his brothers as their turns came; even quiet and tender Stu.

As they followed the upward rise of the cane above her own hands Meggie's eyes closed involuntarily, so she did not see the descent. But the pain was like a vast explosion, a scorching, searing invasion of her flesh right down to the bone; even as the ache spread tingling up her forearm the next cut came, and by the time it had reached her shoulder the final cut across her finger-tips was screaming along the same path, all the way through to her heart. She fastened her teeth in her lower lip and bit down on it, too ashamed and too proud to cry, too angry and indignant at the injustice of it to dare open her eyes and look at Sister Agatha; the lesson was sinking in, even if the crux of it was not what Sister Agatha intended to teach.

It was lunchtime before the last of the pain died out of her hands. Meggie had passed the morning in a haze of fright and bewilderment, not understanding anything that was said or done. Pushed into a double desk in the back row of the youngest children's classroom, she did not even notice who was sharing the desk until after a miserable lunch hour spent huddled behind Bob and Jack in a secluded corner of the playground. Only Bob's stern command persuaded her to eat Fee's gooseberry jam sandwiches.

When the bell rang for afternoon classes and Meggie found a place on line, her eyes finally began to clear enough to take in what was going on around her. The disgrace of the caning rankled as sharply as ever, but she held her head high and affected not to notice the nudges and whispers of the little girls near her.

Sister Agatha was standing in front with her cane; Sister Declan prowled up and down behind the lines; Sister Catherine seated herself at the piano just inside the youngest children's classroom door and began to play "Onward, Christian Soldiers" with a heavy emphasis on two-four time. It was, properly speaking, a Protestant hymn, but the war had rendered it interdenominational. The dear children marched to it just like wee soldiers, Sister Catherine thought proudly.

Of the three nuns, Sister Declan was a replica of Sister Agatha minus fifteen years of life, where Sister Catherine was still remotely human. She was only in her thirties, Irish of course, and the bloom of her ardor had not yet entirely faded; she still found joy in teaching, still saw Christ's imperishable Image in the little faces turned up to hers so adoringly. But she taught the oldest children, whom Sister Agatha deemed beaten enough to behave in spite of a young and soft supervisor. Sister Agatha herself took the youngest children to form minds and hearts out of infantile clay, leaving those in the middle grades to Sister Declan.

Safely hidden in the last row of desks, Meggie dared to glance sideways at the little girl sitting next to her. A gap-toothed grin met her frightened gaze, huge black eyes staring roundly out of a dark, slightly shiny face. She fascinated Meggie, used to fairness and freckles, for even Frank with his dark eyes and hair had a fair white skin; so Meggie ended in thinking her deskmate the most beautiful creature she had ever seen.

"What's your name?" the dark beauty muttered out of the side of her mouth, chewing on the end of her pencil and spitting the frayed bits into her empty inkwell hole.

"Meggie Cleary," she whispered back.

"You there!" came a dry, harsh voice from the front of the classroom.

Meggie jumped, looking around in bewilderment. There was a hollow clatter as twenty children all put their pencils down together, a muted rustling as precious sheets of paper were shuffled to one side so elbows could be surreptitiously placed on desks. With a heart that seemed to crumple down toward her boots, Meggie realized everyone was staring at her. Sister Agatha was coming down the aisle rapidly; Meggie's terror was so acute that had there only been somewhere to flee, she would have run for her life. But behind her was the partition shutting off the middle grade's room, on either side desks crowded her in, and in front was Sister Agatha. Her eyes nearly filled her pinched little face as she stared up at the nun in suffocated fear, her hands clenching and unclenching on the desktop.

"You spoke, Meghann Cleary."

"Yes, Sister."

"And what did you say?"

"My name, Sister."

"Your *name!*" Sister Agatha sneered, looking around at the other children as if they, too, surely must share her contempt. "Well, children, are we not honored? Another Cleary in our school, and she cannot wait to broadcast her name!" She turned back to Meggie. *"Stand up when I address you,* you ignorant little savage! And hold out your hands, please."

Meggie scrambled out of her seat, her long curls swinging across her face and bouncing away. Gripping her hands together, she wrung them desperately, but Sister Agatha did not move, only waited, waited, waited. . . . Then somehow Meggie managed to force her hands out, but as the cane descended she snatched them away, gasping in terror. Sister Agatha locked her fingers in the bunched hair on top of Meggie's head and hauled her closer, bringing her face up to within inches of those dreadful spectacles.

"Hold out your hands, Meghann Cleary." It was said courteously, coldly, implacably.

Meggie opened her mouth and vomited all over the front of Sister Agatha's habit. There was a horrified intake of breath from every child in the room as Sister Agatha stood with the disgusting sick dripping down her black pleats onto the floor, her face purple with rage and astonishment. Then down came the cane, anywhere it could land on Meggie's body as she flung up her arms to shield her face and cringed, still retching, into the corner. When Sister Agatha's arm was so tired it did not want to lift the cane, she pointed toward the door.

"Go home, you revolting little Philistine," she said, turned on her heel and went through into Sister Declan's classroom.

Meggie's frantic gaze found Stu; he nodded his head as if to tell her she must do as she was told, his soft blue-green eyes full of pity and understanding. Wiping her mouth with her handkerchief, she stumbled through the door and out into the playground. There were still two hours to go before school was dismissed; she plodded down the street without interest, knowing there was no chance the boys would catch up with her, and too frightened to find somewhere to wait for them. She had to go home on her own, confess to Mum on her own.

Fee nearly fell over her as she staggered out of the back door with a full basket of wet washing. Meggie was sitting on the top step of the back veranda, her head down, the ends of her bright curls sticky and the front of her dress stained. Putting down the crushing weight of the basket, Fee sighed, pushed a strand of wayward hair out of her eyes.

"Well, what happened?" she demanded tiredly.

"I was sick all over Sister Agatha."

"Oh, Lord!" Fee said, her hands on her hips.

"I got caned, too," Meggie whispered, the tears standing unshed in her eyes.

"A nice kettle of fish, I must say." Fee heaved her basket up, swaying until she got it balanced. "Well, Meggie, I don't know what to do with you. We'll have to wait and see what Daddy says." And she walked off across the backyard toward the flapping half-full clotheslines.

Rubbing her hands wearily around her face, Meggie stared after her mother for a moment, then got up and started down the path to the forge.

Frank had just finished shoeing Mr. Robertson's bay mare, and was backing it into a stall when Meggie appeared in the doorway. He turned and saw her, and memories of his own terrible misery at school came flooding back to him. She was so little, so baby-plump and innocent and sweet, but the light in the eyes had been brutally quenched and an expression lurked there which made him want to murder Sister Agatha. Murder her, really murder her, take the double chins and squeeze. . . . Down went his tools, off came his apron; he walked to her quickly.

"What's the matter, dear?" he asked, bending over until her face was level with his own. The smell of vomit rose from her like a miasma, but he crushed his impulse to turn away.

"Oh, Fruh-Fruh-Frank!" she wailed, her face twisting up and her tears undammed at last. She threw her arms around his neck and clung to him passionately, weeping in the curiously silent, painful way all the Cleary children did once they were out of infancy. It was horrible to watch, and not something soft words or kisses could heal.

When she was calm again he picked her up and carried her to a pile of sweet-smelling hay near Mr. Robertson's mare; they sat there together and let the horse lip at the edges of their straw bed, lost to the world. Meggie's head was cradled on Frank's smooth bare chest, tendrils of her hair flying around as the horse blew gusty breaths into the hay, snorting with pleasure.

"Why did she cane all of us, Frank?" Meggie asked. "I told her it was my fault."

Frank had got used to her smell and didn't mind it any more; he reached out a hand and absently stroked the mare's nose, pushing it away when it got too inquisitive.

"We're poor, Meggie, that's the main reason. The nuns always hate poor pupils. After you've been in Sister Ag's moldy old school a few days you'll see it's not only the Clearys she takes it out on, but the Marshalls and the MacDonalds as well. We're all poor.

Now, if we were rich and rode to school in a big carriage like the O'Briens, they'd be all over us like a rash. But we can't donate organs to the church, or gold vestments to the sacristy, or a new horse and buggy to the nuns. So we don't matter. They can do what they like to us.

"I remember one day Sister Ag was so mad at me that she kept screaming at me, 'Cry, for the love of heaven! Make a noise, Francis Cleary! If you'd give me the satisfaction of hearing you bellow, I wouldn't hit you so hard or so often!'

"That's another reason why she hates us; it's where we're better than the Marshalls and the MacDonalds. She can't make the Clearys cry. We're supposed to lick her boots. Well, I told the boys what I'd do to any Cleary who even whimpered when he was caned, and that goes for you, too, Meggie. No matter how hard she beats you, not a whimper. Did you cry today?"

"No, Frank," she yawned, her eyelids drooping and her thumb poking blindly across her face in search of her mouth. Frank put her down in the hay and went back to his work, humming and smiling.

Meggie was still asleep when Paddy walked in. His arms were filthy from mucking out Mr. Jarman's dairy, his wide-brimmed hat pulled low over his eyes. He took in Frank shaping an axle on the anvil, sparks swirling round his head, then his eyes passed to where his daughter was curled up in the hay, with Mr. Robertson's bay mare hanging her head down over the sleeping face.

"I thought this is where she'd be," Paddy said, dropping his riding crop and leading his old roan into the stable end of the barn.

Frank nodded briefly, looking up at his father with that darkling glance of doubt and uncertainty Paddy always found so irritating, then he returned to the white-hot axle, sweat making his bare sides glisten.

Unsaddling his roan, Paddy turned it into a stall,

filled the water compartment and then mixed bran and oats with a little water for its food. The animal rumbled affectionately at him when he emptied the fodder into its manger, and its eyes followed him as he walked to the big trough outside the forge, took off his shirt. He washed arms and face and torso, drenching his riding breeches and his hair. Toweling himself dry on an old sack, he looked at his son quizzically.

"Mum told me Meggie was sent home in disgrace. Do you know what exactly happened?"

Frank abandoned his axle as the heat in it died. "The poor little coot was sick all over Sister Agatha."

Wiping the grin off his face hastily, Paddy stared at the far wall for a moment to compose himself, then turned toward Meggie. "All excited about going to school, eh?"

"I don't know. She was sick before they left this morning, and it held them up long enough to be late for the bell. They all got sixers, but Meggie was terribly upset because she thought she ought to have been the only one punished. After lunch Sister Ag pounced on her again, and our Meggie spewed bread and jam all over Sister Ag's clean black habit."

"What happened then?"

"Sister Ag caned her good and proper, and sent her home in disgrace."

"Well, I'd say she's had punishment enough. I have a lot of respect for the nuns and I know it isn't our place to question what they do, but I wish they were a bit less eager with the cane. I know they have to beat the three R's into our thick Irish heads, but after all, it was wee Meggie's first day at school."

Frank was staring at his father, amazed. Not until this moment had Paddy ever communicated man-to-man with his oldest son. Shocked out of perpetual resentment, Frank realized that for all his proud boasting, Paddy loved Meggie more than he did his sons. He found himself almost liking his father, so he smiled without the mistrust.

"She's a bonzer little thing, isn't she?" he asked.

Paddy nodded absently, engrossed in watching her. The horse blew its lips in and out, flapping; Meggie stirred, rolled over and opened her eyes. When she saw her father standing beside Frank she sat bolt upright, fright paling her skin.

"Well, Meggie girl, you've had quite a day, haven't you?" Paddy went over and lifted her out of the hay, gasping as he caught a whiff of her. Then he shrugged his shoulders and held her against him hard.

"I got caned, Daddy," she confessed.

"Well, knowing Sister Agatha, it won't be the last time," he laughed, perching her on his shoulder. "We'd better see if Mum's got any hot water in the copper to give you a bath. You smell worse than Jarman's dairy."

Frank went to the doorway and watched the two fiery heads bobbing up the path, then turned to find the bay mare's gentle eyes fixed on him.

"Come on, you big old bitch. I'll ride you home," he told it, scooping up a halter.

Meggie's vomiting turned out to be a blessing is disguise. Sister Agatha still caned her regularly, but always from far enough away to escape the consequences, which lessened the strength of her arm and quite spoiled her aim.

The dark child who sat next to her was the youngest daughter of the Italian man who owned and operated Wahine's bright blue café. Her name was Teresa Annunzio, and she was just dull enough to escape Sister Agatha's attention without being so dull that it turned her into Sister Agatha's butt. When her teeth grew in she was quite strikingly beautiful, and Meggie adored her. During lesson breaks in the playground they walked with arms looped around each other's waists, which was the sign that you were "best friends" and not available for courting by anyone else. And they talked, talked, talked.

One lunchtime Teresa took her into the café to meet her mother and father and grown-up brothers and sisters. They were as charmed with her golden fire as Meggie was with their darkness, likening her to an angel when she turned her wide, beautifully flecked grey eyes upon them. From her mother she had inherited an indefinable air of breeding which everyone felt immediately; so did the Annunzio family. As eager as Teresa to woo her, they gave her big fat potato chips fried in sizzling cauldrons of lamb dripping, and a piece of boned fish which tasted delicious, dipped as it was in floury batter and fried in the smoking well of liquid fat along with the chips, only in a separate wire basket. Meggie had never eaten food so delicious, and wished she could lunch at the café more often. But this had been a treat, requiring special permission from her mother and the nuns.

Her conversation at home was all "Teresa says" and "Do you know what Teresa did?" until Paddy roared that he had heard more than enough about Teresa.

"I don't know that it's such a good idea to be too thick with Dagos," he muttered, sharing the British community's instinctive mistrust of any dark or Mediterranean people. "Dagos are dirty, Meggie girl, they don't wash too often," he explained lamely, wilting under the look of hurt reproach Meggie gave him.

Fiercely jealous, Frank agreed with him. So Meggie spoke less often of her friend when she was at home. But home disapproval couldn't interfere with the relationship, confined as it was by distance to school days and hours; Bob and the boys were only too pleased to see her utterly engrossed in Teresa. It left them to career madly around the playground just as if their sister did not exist.

The unintelligible things Sister Agatha was always writing on the blackboard gradually began to make sense, and Meggie learned that a "+" meant you counted all the numbers up to a total, where a "−" meant you took the numbers on the bottom away from the numbers on the top and wound up with less than you had in the first place. She was a bright child, and would have been an excellent if not brilliant student had she only been able to overcome her fear of Sister Agatha. But the minute those gimlet eyes turned her way and that dry old voice rapped a curt question at her, she stammered and stuttered and could not think. Arithmetic she found easy, but when called upon to demonstrate her skill verbally she could not remember how many two and two made. Reading was the entrance into a world so fascinating she couldn't get enough of it; but when Sister Agatha made her stand to read a passage out loud, she could hardly pronounce "cat," let alone "miaow." It seemed to her that she was forever quivering under Sister Agatha's sarcastic comments or flushing bright red because the rest of the class was laughing at her. For it was always her slate Sister Agatha held up to sneer at, always her laboriously written sheets of paper Sister Agatha used to demonstrate the ugliness of untidy work. Some of the richer children were lucky enough to possess erasers, but Meggie's only eraser was the tip of her finger, which she licked and rubbed over her nervous mistakes until the writing smudged and the paper came away in miniature sausages. It made holes and was strictly forbidden, but she was desperate enough to do anything to avoid Sister Agatha's strictures.

Until her advent Stuart had been the chief target of Sister Agatha's cane and venom. However, Meggie was a much better target, for Stuart's wistful tranquillity and almost saintlike aloofness were hard nuts to crack, even for Sister Agatha. On the other hand, Meggie trembled and went as red as a beet, for all she tried so manfully to adhere to the Cleary line of behavior as defined by Frank. Stuart pitied Meggie deeply and tried to make it easier for her by deliberately sidetracking the nun's anger onto his own head. She saw through his ploys immediately, angered afresh to see the Cleary clannishness as much in evidence with the girl as it had always been among the boys. Had anyone questioned her as to exactly why she had such a down on the Clearys, she would not have been able to answer. But for an old nun as embittered by the course her life had taken as Sister Agatha, a proud and touchy family like the Clearys was not easy to swallow.

Meggie's worst sin was being left-handed. When she gingerly picked up her slate pencil to embark on her first writing lesson, Sister Agatha descended on her like Caesar on the Gauls.

"Meghann Cleary, put that pencil down!" she thundered.

Thus began a battle royal. Meggie was incurably and hopelessly left-handed. When Sister Agatha forcibly bent the fingers of Meggie's right hand correctly around the pencil and poised it above the slate, Meggie sat there with her head reeling and no idea in the world how to make the afflicted limb do what Sister Agatha insisted it could. She became mentally deaf, dumb and blind; that useless appendage her right hand was no more linked to her thought processes than her toes. She dribbled a line clean off the edge of the slate because she could not make it bend; she dropped her pencil as if paralyzed; nothing Sister Agatha could do would make Meggie's right hand form an *A*. Then surreptitiously Meggie would transfer her pencil to her left hand, and with her arm curled awkwardly around three sides of the slate she would make a row of beautiful copperplate *A*'s.

Sister Agatha won the battle. On morning line-up she tied Meggie's left arm against her body with rope, and would not undo it until the dismissal bell rang at three in the afternoon. Even at lunchtime she had to eat, walk around and play games with her left side firmly immobilized. It took three months, but eventually she learned to write correctly according to the tenets of Sister Agatha, though the formation of her letters was never good. To make sure she would never revert back to using it, her left arm was kept tied to her body for a further two months; then Sister Agatha made the whole school assemble to say a rosary of thanks to Almighty God for His wisdom in making Meggie see the error of her ways. God's children were all right-handed; left-handed children were the spawn of the Devil, especially when redheaded.

In that first year of school Meggie lost her baby plumpness and became very thin, though she grew little in height. She began to bite her nails down to the quick, and had to endure Sister Agatha's making her walk around every desk in the school holding her hands out so all the children could see how ugly bitten nails were. And this when nearly half the children between five and fifteen bit their nails as badly as Meggie did.

Fee got out the bottle of bitter aloes and painted the tips of Meggie's fingers with the horrible stuff. Everyone in the family was enlisted to make sure she got no opportunity to wash the bitter aloes off, and when the other little girls at school noticed the telltale brown stains she was mortified. If she put her fingers in her mouth the taste was indescribable, foul and dark like sheep-dip; in desperation she spat on her handkerchief and rubbed herself raw until she got rid of the worst of it. Paddy took out his switch, a much gentler instrument than Sister Agatha's cane, and sent her skipping round the kitchen. He did not believe in beating his children on the hands, face or buttocks, only on the legs. Legs hurt as much as anywhere, he said, and could not be damaged. However, in spite of bitter aloes, ridicule, Sister Agatha and Paddy's switch, Meggie went on biting her nails.

Her friendship with Teresa Annunzio was the joy of her life, the only thing that made school endurable. She sat through lessons aching for playtime to come so she could sit with her arm around Teresa's waist and Teresa's arm around hers under the big fig tree, talking, talking. There were tales about Teresa's extraordinary alien family, about her numerous dolls, and about her genuine willow pattern tea set.

When Meggie saw the tea set, she was overcome. It had 108 pieces, tiny miniature cups and saucers and plates, a teapot and a sugar bowl and a milk jug and a cream jug, with wee knives and spoons and forks just the right size for dolls to use. Teresa had innumerable toys; besides being much younger than her nearest sister, she belonged to an Italian family, which meant she was passionately and openly loved, and indulged to the full extent of her father's monetary resources. Each child viewed the other with awe and envy, though Teresa never coveted Meggie's Calvinistic, stoic upbringing. Instead she pitied her. Not to be allowed to run to her mother with hugs and kisses? Poor Meggie!

As for Meggie, she was incapable of equating Teresa's beaming, portly little mother with her own slender unsmiling mother, so she never thought: I wish Mum hugged and kissed me. What she did think was: I wish Teresa's mum hugged and kissed me. Though images of hugs and kisses were far less in her mind than images of the willow pattern tea set. So delicate, so thin and wafery, so beautiful! Oh, if only she had a willow pattern tea set, and could give Agnes afternoon tea out of a deep blue-and-white cup in a deep blue-and-white saucer!

During Friday Benediction in the old church with its lovely, grotesque Maori carvings and Maori painted ceiling, Meggie knelt to pray for a willow pattern tea set of her very own. When Father Hayes held the monstrance aloft, the Host peered dimly through the glass window in the middle of its gem-encrusted rays and blessed the bowed heads of the congregation. All save Meggie, that is, for she didn't even see the Host; she was too busy trying to remember how many plates there were in Teresa's willow pattern tea set. And when the Maoris in the organ gallery broke into glorious song, Meggie's head was spinning in a daze of ultramarine blue far removed from Catholicism or Polynesia.

The school year was drawing to a close, December and her birthday just beginning to threaten full summer, when Meggie learned how dearly one could buy the desire of one's heart. She was sitting on a high stool near the stove while Fee did her hair as usual for school; it was an intricate business. Meggie's hair had a natural tendency to curl, which her mother considered to be a great piece of good luck. Girls with straight hair had a hard time of it when they grew up and tried to produce glorious wavy masses out of limp, thin strands. At night Meggie slept with her almost knee-length locks twisted painfully around bits of old white sheet torn into long strips, and each morning she had to clamber up on the stool while Fee undid the rags and brushed her curls in.

Fee used an old Mason Pearson hairbrush, taking one long, scraggly curl in her left hand and expertly brushing the hair around her index finger until the entire length of it was rolled into a shining thick sausage; then she carefully withdrew her finger from the center of the roll and shook it out into a long, enviably thick curl. This maneuver was repeated some twelve times, the front curls were then drawn together on Meggie's crown with a freshly ironed white taffeta bow, and she was ready for the day. All the other little girls wore braids to school, saving curls for special occasions, but on this one point Fee was adamant; Meggie should have curls all the time, no matter how hard it was to spare the minutes each morning. Had Fee realized it, her charity was misguided, for her daughter's hair was far and away the most beautiful in the entire school. To rub the fact in with daily curls earned Meggie much envy and loathing.

The process hurt, but Meggie was too used to it to notice, never remembering a time when it had not been done. Fee's muscular arm yanked the brush ruthlessly through knots and tangles until Meggie's eyes watered and she had to hang on to the stool with both hands to keep from falling off. It was the Monday of the last week at school, and her birthday was only two days away; she clung to the stool and dreamed about the willow pattern tea set, knowing it for a dream. There was one in the Wahine general store, and she knew enough of prices to realize that its cost put it far beyond her father's slender means.

Suddenly Fee made a sound, so peculiar it jerked Meggie out of her musing and made the menfolk still seated at the breakfast table turn their heads curiously.

"Holy Jesus Christ!" said Fee.

Paddy jumped to his feet, his face stupefied; he had never heard Fee take the name of the Lord in vain before. She was standing with one of Meggie's curls in her hand, the brush poised, her features twisted into an expression of horror and revulsion. Paddy and the boys crowded round; Meggie tried to see what was going on and earned a backhanded slap with the bristle side of the brush which made her eyes water.

"Look!" Fee whispered, holding the curl in a ray of sunlight so Paddy could see.

The hair was a mass of brilliant, glittering gold in the sun, and Paddy saw nothing at first. Then he became aware that a *creature* was marching down the back of Fee's hand. He took a curl for himself, and in among the leaping lights of it he discerned more creatures, going about their business busily. Little white things were stuck in clumps all along the separate strands, and the creatures were energetically producing more clumps of little white things. Meggie's hair was a hive of industry.

"She's got lice!" Paddy said.

Bob, Jack, Hughie and Stu had a look, and like their father removed themselves to a safe distance; only Frank and Fee remained gazing at Meggie's hair, mesmerized, while Meggie sat miserably hunched over, wondering what she had done. Paddy sat down in his Windsor chair heavily, staring into the fire and blinking hard.

"It's that bloody Dago girl!" he said at last, and turned to glare at Fee. "Bloody bastards, filthy lot of flaming pigs!"

"Paddy!" Fee gasped, scandalized.

"I'm sorry for swearing, Mum, but when I think of that blasted Dago giving her lice to Meggie, I could go into Wahine this minute and tear the whole filthy greasy café down!" he exploded, pounding his fist on his knee fiercely.

"Mum, what is it?" Meggie finally managed to say.

"Look, you dirty little grub!" her mother answered, thrusting her hand down in front of Meggie's eyes. "You have these things everywhere in your hair, from that Eyetie girl you're so thick with! Now what am I going to do with you?"

Meggie gaped at the tiny thing roaming blindly round Fee's bare skin in search of more hirsute territory, then she began to weep.

Without needing to be told, Frank got the copper going while Paddy paced up and down the kitchen roaring, his rage increasing every time he looked at Meggie. Finally he went to the row of hooks on the wall inside the back door, jammed his hat on his head and took the long horsewhip from its nail.

"I'm going into Wahine, Fee, and I'm going to tell that blasted Dago what he can do with his slimy fish and chips! Then I'm going to see Sister Agatha and tell her what I think of her, allowing lousy children in her school!"

"Paddy, be careful!" Fee pleaded. "What if it isn't

the Eyetie girl? Even if she has lice, it's possible she might have got them from someone else along with Meggie."

"Rot!" said Paddy scornfully. He pounded down the back steps, and a few minutes later they heard his roan's hoofs beating down the road. Fee sighed, looking at Frank hopelessly.

"Well, I suppose we'll be lucky if he doesn't land in jail. Frank, you'd better bring the boys inside. No school today."

One by one Fee went through her sons' hair minutely, then checked Frank's head and made him do the same for her. There was no evidence that anyone else had acquired poor Meggie's malady, but Fee did not intend to take chances. When the water in the huge laundry copper was boiling, Frank got the dish tub down from its hanging and filled it half with hot water and half with cold. Then he went out to the shed and fetched in an unopened five-gallon can of kerosene, took a bar of lye soap from the laundry and started work on Bob. Each head was briefly damped in the tub, several cups of raw kerosene poured over it, and the whole draggled, greasy mess lathered with soap. The kerosene and lye burned; the boys howled and rubbed their eyes raw, scratching at their reddened, tingling scalps and threatening ghastly vengeance on all Dagos.

Fee went to her sewing basket and took out her big shears. She came back to Meggie, who had not dared to move from the stool though an hour and more had elapsed, and stood with the shears in her hand, staring at the beautiful fall of hair. Then she began to cut it—snip! snip!—until all the long curls were huddled in glistening heaps on the floor and Meggie's white skin was beginning to show in irregular patches all over her head. Doubt in her eyes, she turned then to Frank.

"Ought I to shave it?" she asked, tight-lipped.

Frank put out his hand, revolted. "Oh, Mum, no!

Surely not! If she gets a good douse of kerosene it ought to be enough. Please don't shave it!"

So Meggie was marched to the worktable and held over the tub while they poured cup after cup of kerosene over her head and scrubbed the corrosive soap through what was left of her hair. When they were finally satisfied, she was almost blind from screwing up her eyes against the bite of the caustic, and little rows of blisters had risen all over her face and scalp. Frank swept the fallen curls into a sheet of paper and thrust it into the copper fire, then took the broom and stood it in a panful of kerosene. He and Fee both washed their hair, gasping as the lye seared their skins, then Frank got out a bucket and scrubbed the kitchen floor with sheep-dip.

When the kitchen was as sterile as a hospital they went through to the bedrooms, stripped every sheet and blanket from every bed, and spent the rest of the day boiling, wringing and pegging out the family linen. The mattresses and pillows were draped over the back fence and sprayed with kerosene, the parlor rugs were beaten within an inch of their lives. All the boys were put to helping, only Meggie exempted because she was in absolute disgrace. She crawled away behind the barn and cried. Her head throbbed with pain from the scrubbing, the burns and the blisters; and she was so bitterly ashamed that she would not even look at Frank when he came to find her, nor could he persuade her to come inside.

In the end he had to drag her into the house by brute force, kicking and fighting, and she had pushed herself into a corner when Paddy came back from Wahine in the late afternoon. He took one look at Meggie's shorn head and burst into tears, sitting rocking himself in the Windsor chair with his hands over his face, while the family stood shuffling their feet and wishing they were anywhere but where they were. Fee made a pot of tea and poured Paddy a cup as he began to recover.

"What happened in Wahine?" she asked. "You were gone an awful long time."

"I took the horsewhip to that blasted Dago and threw him into the horse trough, for one thing. Then I noticed MacLeod standing outside his shop watching, so I told him what had happened. MacLeod mustered some of the chaps at the pub and we threw the whole lot of those Dagos into the horse trough, women too, and tipped a few gallons of sheep-dip into it. Then I went down to the school and saw Sister Agatha, and I tell you, she was fit to be tied that she hadn't noticed anything. She hauled the Dago girl out of her desk to look in her hair, and sure enough, lice all over the place. So she sent the girl home and told her not to come back until her head was clean. I left her and Sister Declan and Sister Catherine looking through every head in the school, and there turned out to be a lot of lousy ones. Those three nuns were scratching themselves like mad when they thought no one was watching." He grinned at the memory, then he saw Meggie's head again and sobered. He stared at her grimly. "As for you, young lady, no more Dagos or anyone except your brothers. If they aren't good enough for you, too bad. Bob, I'm telling you that Meggie's to have nothing to do with anyone except you and the boys while she's at school, do you hear?"

Bob nodded. "Yes, Daddy."

The next morning Meggie was horrified to discover that she was expected to go to school as usual.

"No, no, I can't go!" she moaned, her hands clutching at her head. "Mum, Mum, I can't go to school like this, not with Sister Agatha!"

"Oh, yes, you can," her mother replied, ignoring Frank's imploring looks. "It'll teach you a lesson."

So off to school went Meggie, her feet dragging and her head done up in a brown bandanna. Sister Agatha ignored her entirely, but at playtime the other girls caught her and tore her scarf away to see what she looked like. Her face was only mildly disfigured, but her head when uncovered was a horrible sight, oozing and angry. The moment he saw what was going on Bob came over, and took his sister away into a secluded corner of the cricket pitch.

"Don't you take any notice of them, Meggie," he said roughly, tying the scarf around her head awkwardly and patting her stiff shoulders. "Spiteful little cats! I wish I'd thought to catch some of those things out of your head; I'm sure they'd keep. The minute everyone forgot, I'd sprinkle a few heads with a new lot."

The other Cleary boys gathered around, and they sat guarding Meggie until the bell rang.

Teresa Annunzio came to school briefly at lunchtime, her head shaven. She tried to attack Meggie, but the boys held her off easily. As she backed away she flung her right arm up in the air, its fist clenched, and slapped her left hand on its biceps in a fascinating, mysterious gesture no one understood, but which the boys avidly filed away for future use.

"I hate you!" Teresa screamed. "Me dad's got to move out of the district because of what your dad did to him!" She turned and ran from the playground, howling.

Meggie held her head up and kept her eyes dry. She was learning. It *didn't* matter what anyone else thought, it didn't, it didn't! The other girls avoided her, half because they were frightened of Bob and Jack, half because the word had got around their parents and they had been instructed to keep away; being thick with the Clearys usually meant trouble of some kind. So Meggie passed the last few days of school "in Coventry," as they called it, which meant she was totally ostracized. Even Sister Agatha respected the new policy, and took her rages out on Stuart instead.

As were all birthdays among the little ones if they

fell on a school day, Meggie's birthday celebration was delayed until Saturday, when she received the longed-for willow pattern tea set. It was arranged on a beautifully crafted ultramarine table and chairs made in Frank's nonexistent spare time, and Agnes was seated on one of the two tiny chairs wearing a new blue dress made in Fee's nonexistent spare time. Meggie stared dismally at the blue-and-white designs gamboling all around each small piece; at the fantastic trees with their funny puffy blossoms, at the ornate little pagoda, at the strangely stilled pair of birds and the minute figures eternally fleeing across the kinky bridge. It had lost every bit of its enchantment. But dimly she understood why the family had beggared itself to get her the thing they thought dearest to her heart. So she dutifully made tea for Agnes in the tiny square teapot and went through the ritual as if in ecstasy. And she continued doggedly to use it for years, never breaking or so much as chipping a single piece. No one ever dreamed that she loathed the willow pattern tea set, the blue table and chairs, and Agnes's blue dress.

Two days before that Christmas of 1917 Paddy brought home his weekly newspaper and a new stack of books from the library. However, the paper for once took precedence over the books. Its editors had conceived a novel idea based on the fancy American magazines which very occasionally found their way to New Zealand; the entire middle section was a feature on the war. There were blurred photographs of the Anzacs storming the pitiless cliffs at Gallipoli, long articles extolling the bravery of the Antipodean soldier, features on all the Australian and New Zealand winners of the Victoria Cross since its inception, and a magnificent full-page etching of an Australian light horse cavalryman mounted on his charger, saber at the ready and long silky feathers pluming from under the turned-up side of his slouch hat.

At first opportunity Frank seized the paper and read the feature hungrily, drinking in its jingoistic prose, his eyes glowing eerily.

"Daddy, I want to go!" he said as he laid the paper down reverently on the table.

Fee's head jerked around as she slopped stew all over the top of the stove, and Paddy stiffened in his Windsor chair, his book forgotten.

"You're too young, Frank," he said.

"No, I'm not! I'm seventeen, Daddy, I'm a man! Why should the Huns and Turks slaughter our men like pigs while I'm sitting here safe and sound? It's more than time a Cleary did his bit."

"You're under age, Frank, they won't take you."

"They will if you don't object," Frank countered quickly, his dark eyes fixed on Paddy's face.

"But I do object. You're the only one working at the moment and we need the money you bring in, you know that."

"But I'll be paid in the army!"

Paddy laughed. "The 'soldier's shilling' eh? Being a blacksmith in Wahine pays a lot better than being a soldier in Europe."

"But I'll be over there, maybe I'll get the chance to be something better than a blacksmith! It's my only way out, Daddy."

"Nonsense! Good God, boy, you don't know what you're saying. War is terrible. I come from a country that's been at war for a thousand years, so I know what I'm saying. Haven't you heard the Boer War chaps talking? You go into Wahine often enough, so next time listen. And anyway, it strikes me that the blasted English use Anzacs as fodder for the enemy guns, putting them into places where they don't want to waste their own precious troops. Look at the way that saber-rattling Churchill sent our men into something as useless as Gallipoli! Ten thousand killed out of fifty thousand! Twice as bad as decimation.

"Why should you go fighting old Mother England's wars for her? What has she ever done for you, except bleed her colonies white? If you went to England they'd look down their noses at you for being a colonial. En Zed isn't in any danger, nor is Australia. It might do old Mother England the world of good to be defeated; it's more than time someone paid her for what she's done to Ireland. I certainly wouldn't weep any tears if the Kaiser ended up marching down the Strand."

"But Daddy, I *want* to enlist!"

"You can want all you like, Frank, but you aren't going, so you may as well forget the whole idea. You're not big enough to be a soldier."

Frank's face flushed, his lips came together; his lack of stature was a very sore point with him. At school he had always been the smallest boy in his class, and fought twice as many battles as anyone else because of it. Of late a terrible doubt had begun to invade his being, for at seventeen he was exactly the same five feet three he had been at fourteen; perhaps he had stopped growing. Only he knew the agonies to which he subjected his body and his spirit, the stretching, the exercises, the fruitless hoping.

Smithying had given him a strength out of all proportion to his height, however; had Paddy consciously chosen a profession for someone of Frank's temperament, he could not have chosen better. A small structure of pure power, at seventeen he had never been defeated in a fight and was already famous throughout the Taranaki peninsula. All his anger, frustration and inferiority came into a fight with him, and they were more than the biggest, strongest local could contend with, allied as they were to a body in superb physical condition, an excellent brain, viciousness and indomitable will.

The bigger and tougher they were, the more Frank wanted to see them humbled in the dust. His peers trod a wide detour around him, for his aggressiveness was well known. Of late he had branched out of the ranks of youths in his search for challenges, and the local men still talked about the day he had beaten Jim Collins to a pulp, though Jim Collins was twenty-two years old, stood six feet four in his socks and could lift horses. With his left arm broken and his ribs cracked, Frank had fought on until Jim Collins was a slobbering mass of bloodied flesh at his feet, and he had to be forcibly restrained from kicking the senseless face in. As soon as the arm healed and the ribs came out of strapping, Frank went into town and lifted a horse, just to show that Jim wasn't the only one who could, and that it didn't depend on a man's size.

As the sire of this phenomenon, Paddy knew Frank's reputation very well and understood Frank's battle to gain respect, though it did not prevent his becoming angry when fighting interfered with the work in the forge. Being a small man himself, Paddy had had his share of fights to prove his courage, but in his part of Ireland he was not diminutive and by the time he arrived in New Zealand, where men were taller, he was a man grown. Thus his size was never the obsession with him it was with Frank.

Now he watched the boy carefully, trying to understand him and failing; this one had always been the farthest from his heart, no matter how he struggled against discriminating among his children. He knew it grieved Fee, that she worried over the unspoken antagonism between them, but even his love for Fee could not overcome his exasperation with Frank.

Frank's short, finely made hands were spread across the open paper defensively, his eyes riveted on Paddy's face in a curious mixture of pleading and a pride that was too stiff-necked to plead. How alien the face was! No Cleary or Armstrong in it, except perhaps a little look of Fee around the eyes, if Fee's eyes had been dark and could have snapped and flashed the way

Frank's did on slightest provocation. One thing the lad did not lack, and that was courage.

The subject ended abruptly with Paddy's remark about Frank's size; the family ate stewed rabbit in unusual silence, even Hughie and Jack treading carefully through a sticky, self-conscious conversation punctuated by much shrill giggling. Meggie refused to eat, fixing her gaze on Frank as if he were going to disappear from sight any moment. Frank picked at his food for a decent interval, and as soon as he could excused himself from the table. A minute later they heard the axe clunking dully from the woodheap; Frank was attacking the hardwood logs Paddy had brought home to store for the slow-burning fires of winter.

When everyone thought she was in bed, Meggie squeezed out of her bedroom window and sneaked down to the woodheap. It was a tremendously important area in the continuing life of the house; about a thousand square feet of ground padded and deadened by a thick layer of chips and bark, great high stacks of logs on one side waiting to be reduced in size, and on the other side mosaic-like walls of neatly prepared wood just the right size for the stove firebox. In the middle of the open space three tree stumps still rooted in the ground were used as blocks to chop different heights of wood.

Frank was not on a block; he was working on a massive eucalyptus log and undercutting it to get it small enough to place on the lowest, widest stump. Its two-foot-diameter bulk lay on the earth, each end immobilized by an iron spike, and Frank was standing on top of it, cutting it in two between his spread feet. The axe was moving so fast it whistled, and the handle made its own separate swishing sound as it slid up and down within his slippery palms. Up it flashed above his head, down it came in a dull silver blur, carving a wedge-shaped chunk out of the iron-hard wood as easily as if it had been a pine or a deciduous tree. Sundered pieces of wood were flying in all directions, the sweat was running in streams down Frank's bare chest and back, and he had wound his handkerchief about his brow to keep the sweat from blinding him. It was dangerous work, undercutting; one mistimed or badly directed hack, and he would be minus a foot. He had his leather wristbands on to soak up the sweat from his arms, but the delicate hands were ungloved, gripping the axe handle lightly and with exquisitely directed skill.

Meggie crouched down beside his discarded shirt and undervest to watch, awed. Three spare axes were lying nearby, for eucalyptus wood blunted the sharpest axe in no time at all. She grasped one by its handle and dragged it onto her knees, wishing she could chop wood like Frank. The axe was so heavy she could hardly lift it. Colonial axes had only one blade, honed to hair-splitting sharpness, for double-bladed axes were too light for eucalyptus. The back of the axe head was an inch thick and weighted, the handle passing through it, firmly anchored with small bits of extra wood. A loose axe head could come off in midswing, snap through the air as hard and fast as a cannonball and kill someone.

Frank was cutting almost instinctively in the fast-fading light; Meggie dodged the chips with the ease of long practice and waited patiently for him to spy her. The log was half severed, and he turned himself the opposite way, gasping; then he swung the axe up again, and began to cut the second side. It was a deep, narrow gap, to conserve wood and hasten the process; as he worked toward the center of the log the axe head disappeared entirely inside the cut, and the big wedges of wood flew out closer and closer to his body. He ignored them, chopping even faster. The log parted with stunning suddenness, and at the same moment he leaped lithely into the air, sensing that it was going almost before the axe took its last bite. As the wood collapsed inward, he landed off to one side, smiling; but it was not a happy smile.

He turned to pick up a new axe and saw his sister sitting patiently in her prim nightgown, all buttoned up and buttoned down. It was still strange to see her hair clustering in a mass of short ringlets instead of done up in its customary rags, but he decided the boyish style suited her, and wished it could remain so. Coming over to her, he squatted down with his axe held across his knees.

"How did you get out, you little twerp?"

"I climbed through the window after Stu was asleep."

"If you don't watch out, you'll turn into a tomboy."

"I don't mind. Playing with the boys is better than playing all by myself."

"I suppose it is." He sat down with his back against a log and wearily turned his head toward her. "What's the matter, Meggie?"

"Frank, you're not really going away, are you?" She put her hands with their mangled nails down on his thigh and stared up at him anxiously, her mouth open because her nose was stuffed full from fighting tears and she couldn't breathe through it very well.

"I might be, Meggie." He said it gently.

"Oh, Frank, you can't! Mum and I *need* you! Honestly, I don't know what we'd do without you!"

He grinned in spite of his pain, at her unconscious echoing of Fee's way of speaking.

"Meggie, sometimes things just don't happen the way you want them to. You ought to know that. We Clearys have been taught to work together for the good of all, never to think of ourselves first. But I don't agree with that; I think we ought to be able to think of ourselves first. I want to go away because I'm seventeen and it's time I made a life for myself. But Daddy says no, I'm needed at home for the good of the family as a whole. And because I'm not twenty-one, I've got to do as Daddy says."

Meggie nodded earnestly, trying to untangle the threads of Frank's explanation.

"Well, Meggie, I've thought long and hard about it. I'm going away, and that's that. I know you and Mum will miss me, but Bob's growing up fast, and Daddy and the boys won't miss me at all. It's only the money I bring in interests Daddy."

"Don't you like us anymore, Frank?"

He turned to snatch her into his arms, hugging and caressing her in tortured pleasure, most of it grief and pain and hunger. "Oh, Meggie! I love you and Mum more than all the others put together! God, why weren't you older, so I could talk to you? Or maybe it's better that you're so little, maybe it's better. . . ."

He let her go abruptly, struggling to master himself, rolling his head back and forth against the log, his throat and mouth working. Then he looked at her. "Meggie, when you're older you'll understand better."

"Please don't go away, Frank," she repeated.

He laughed, almost a sob. "Oh, Meggie! Didn't you hear any of it? Well, it doesn't really matter. The main thing is you're not to tell anyone you saw me tonight, hear? I don't want them thinking you're in on it."

"I did hear, Frank, I heard all of it," Meggie said. "I won't say a word to anybody, though, I promise. But oh, I do wish you didn't have to go away!"

She was too young to be able to tell him what was no more than an unreasoning something within her heart; who else was there, if Frank went? He was the only one who gave her overt affection, the only one who held her and hugged her. When she was smaller Daddy used to pick her up a lot, but ever since she started at school he had stopped letting her sit on his knee, wouldn't let her throw her arms around his neck, saying, "You're a big girl now, Meggie." And Mum was always so busy, so tired, so wrapped in the boys and the house. It was Frank who lay closest to her heart, Frank who loomed as the star in her limited heaven. He was the only one who seemed to enjoy sitting talking to her, and he explained things in a way she could understand.

Ever since the day Agnes had lost her hair there had been Frank, and in spite of her sore troubles nothing since had speared her quite to the core. Not canes or Sister Agatha or lice, because Frank was there to comfort and console.

But she got up and managed a smile. "If you have to go, Frank, then it's all right."

"Meggie, you ought to be in bed, and you'd better be back there before Mum checks. Scoot, quickly!"

The reminder drove all else from her head; she thrust her face down and fished for the trailing back of her gown, pulled it through between her legs and held it like a tail in reverse in front of her as she ran, bare feet spurning the splinters and sharp chips.

In the morning Frank was gone. When Fee came to pull Meggie from her bed she was grim and terse; Meggie hopped out like a scalded cat and dressed herself without even asking for help with all the little buttons.

In the kitchen the boys were sitting glumly around the table, and Paddy's chair was empty. So was Frank's. Meggie slid into her place and sat there, teeth chattering in fear. After breakfast Fee shooed them outside dourly, and behind the barn Bob broke the news to Meggie.

"Frank's run away," he breathed.

"Maybe he's just gone into Wahine," Meggie suggested.

"No, silly! He's gone to join the army. Oh, I wish I was big enough to go with him! The lucky coot!"

"Well, I wish he was still at home."

Bob shrugged. "You're only a girl, and that's what I'd expect a girl to say."

The normally incendiary remark was permitted to pass unchallenged; Meggie took herself inside to her mother to see what she could do.

"Where's Daddy?" she asked Fee after her mother had set her to ironing handkerchiefs.

"Gone in to Wahine."

"Will he bring Frank back with him?"

Fee snorted. "Trying to keep a secret in this family is impossible. No, he won't catch Frank in Wahine, he knows that. He's gone to send a telegram to the police and the army in Wanganui. They'll bring him back."

"Oh, Mum, I hope they find him! I don't want Frank to go away!"

Fee slapped the contents of the butter churn onto the table and attacked the watery yellow mound with two wooden pats. "None of us want Frank to go away. That's why Daddy's going to see he's brought back." Her mouth quivered for a moment; she whacked the butter harder. "Poor Frank! Poor, poor Frank!" she sighed, not to Meggie but to herself. "I don't know why the children must pay for our sins. My poor Frank, so out of things . . ." Then she noticed that Meggie had stopped ironing, and shut her lips, and said no more.

Three days later the police brought Frank back. He had put up a terrific struggle, the Wanganui sergeant on escort duty told Paddy.

"What a fighter you've got! When he saw the army lads were a wakeup he was off like a shot, down the steps and into the street with two soldiers after him. If he hadn't had the bad luck to run into a constable on patrol, I reckon he'd a got away, too. He put up a real wacko fight; took five of them to get the manacles on."

So saying, he removed Frank's heavy chains and pushed him roughly through the front gate; he stumbled against Paddy, and shrank away as if the contact stung.

The children were skulking by the side of the house twenty feet beyond the adults, watching and waiting. Bob, Jack and Hughie stood stiffly, hoping Frank would put up another fight; Stuart just looked on quietly, from out of his peaceful, sympathetic little soul; Meggie held her hands to her cheeks, pushing and kneading at them in an agony of fear that someone meant to hurt Frank.

He turned to look at his mother first, black eyes into grey in a dark and bitter communion which had never been spoken, nor ever was. Paddy's fierce blue gaze beat him down, contemptuous and scathing, as if this was what he had expected, and Frank's downcast lids acknowledged his right to be angry. From that day forward Paddy never spoke to his son beyond common civility. But it was the children Frank found hardest to face, ashamed and embarrassed, the bright bird brought home with the sky unplumbed, wings clipped, song drowned into silence.

Meggie waited until after Fee had done her nightly rounds, then she wriggled through the open window and made off across the backyard. She knew where Frank would be, up in the hay in the barn, safe from prying eyes and his father.

"Frank, Frank, where are you?" she said in a stage whisper as she shuffled into the stilly blackness of the barn, her toes exploring the unknown ground in front of her as sensitively as an animal.

"Over here, Meggie," came his tired voice, hardly Frank's voice at all, no life or passion to it.

She followed the sound to where he was stretched out in the hay, and snuggled down beside him with her arms as far around his chest as they would reach. "Oh, Frank, I'm so glad you're back," she said.

He groaned, slid down in the straw until he was lower than she, and put his head on her body. Meggie clutched at his thick straight hair, crooning. It was too dark to see her, and the invisible substance of her sympathy undid him. He began to weep, knotting his body into slow twisting rails of pain, his tears soaking her nightgown. Meggie did not weep. Something in her little soul was old enough and woman enough to feel the irresistible, stinging joy of being needed; she sat rocking his head back and forth, back and forth, until his grief expended itself in emptiness.

TWO

1921–1928 Ralph

3

The road to Drogheda brought back no memories of his youth, thought Father Ralph de Bricassart, eyes half shut against the glare as his new Daimler bounced along in the rutted wheel tracks that marched through the long silver grass. No lovely misty green Ireland, this. And Drogheda? No battlefield, no high seat of power. Or was that strictly true? Better disciplined these days but acute as ever, his sense of humor conjured in his mind an image of a Cromwellian Mary Carson dealing out her particular brand of imperial malevolence. Not such a highflown comparison, either; the lady surely wielded as much power and controlled as many individuals as any puissant war lord of elder days.

The last gate loomed up through a stand of box and stringybark; the car came to a throbbing halt. Clapping a disreputable grey broad-brimmed hat on his head to ward off the sun, Father Ralph got out, plodded to the steel bolt on the wooden strut, pulled it back and flung the gate open with weary impatience. There were twenty-seven gates between the presbytery in Gillanbone and Drogheda homestead, each one meaning he had to stop, get out of the car, open the gate, get into the car and drive it through, stop, get out, go back to close the gate, then get in the car again and proceed to the next one. Many and many a time he longed to dispense with at least half the ritual, scoot on down the track leaving the gates open like a series of astonished mouths behind him; but even the awesome aura of his calling would not prevent the owners of the gates from tarring and feathering him for it. He wished horses were as fast and efficient as cars, because one could open and close gates from the back of a horse without dismounting.

"Nothing is given without a disadvantage in it," he said, patting the dashboard of the new Daimler and starting off down the last mile of the grassy, treeless Home Paddock, the gate firmly bolted behind him.

Even to an Irishman used to castles and mansions, this Australian homestead was imposing. Drogheda was the oldest and the biggest property in the district, and had been endowed by its late doting owner with a fitting residence. Built of butter-yellow sandstone blocks hand-hewn in quarries five hundred miles eastward, the house had two stories and was constructed on austerely Georgian lines, with large, many-paned windows and a wide, iron-pillared veranda running all the way around its bottom story. Gracing the sides of every window were black wooden shutters, not merely ornamental but useful; in the heat of summer they were pulled closed to keep the interior cool.

Though it was autumn now and the spindling vine was green, in spring the wistaria which had been planted the day the house was finished fifty years before was a solid mass of lilac plumes, rioting all over the outer walls and the veranda roof. Several acres of meticulously scythed lawn surrounded the house, strewn with formal gardens even now full of color from roses, wall-flowers, dahlias and marigolds. A stand of magnificent ghost gums with pallid white trunks and drifting thin leaves hanging seventy feet above the ground shaded the house from the pitiless sun, their branches wreathed in brilliant magenta where bougainvillaea vines grew intertwined with them. Even those indispensable Outback monstrosities the water tanks were thickly clothed in hardy native vines, roses and wistaria, and thus managed to look more decorative than functional. Thanks to the late Michael Carson's passion for Drogheda homestead, he had been lavish in the matter of water tanks; rumor had it Drogheda could afford to keep its lawns green and its flower beds blooming though no rain fell in ten years.

As one approached down the Home Paddock the house and its ghost gums took the eye first, but then one was aware of many other yellow sandstone houses of one story behind it and to each side, interlocking with the main structure by means of roofed ramps smothered in creepers. A wide gravel driveway succeeded the wheel ruts of the track, curving to a circular parking area at one side of the big house, but also continuing beyond it and out of sight down to where the real business of Drogheda lay: the stockyards, the shearing shed, the barns. Privately Father Ralph preferred the giant pepper trees which shaded all these outbuildings and their attendant activities to the ghost gums of the main house. Pepper trees were dense with pale-green fronds and alive with the sound of bees, just the right lazy sort of foliage for an Outback station.

As Father Ralph parked his car and walked across the lawn, the maid waited on the front veranda, her freckled face wreathed in smiles.

"Good morning, Minnie," he said.

"Oh, Father, happy it is to see you this fine dear mornin'," she said in her strong brogue, one hand holding the door wide and the other outstretched to receive his battered, unclerical hat.

Inside the dim hall, with its marble tiles and great brass-railed staircase, he paused until Minnie gave him a nod before entering the drawing room.

Mary Carson was sitting in her wing chair by an

open window which extended fifteen feet from floor to ceiling, apparently indifferent to the cold air flooding in. Her shock of red hair was almost as bright as it had been in her youth; though the coarse freckled skin had picked up additional splotches from age, for a woman of sixty-five she had few wrinkles, rather a fine network of tiny diamond-shaped cushions like a quilted bedspread. The only clues to her intractable nature lay in the two deep fissures which ran one on either side of her Roman nose, to end pulling down the corners of her mouth, and in the stony look of the pale-blue eyes.

Father Ralph crossed the Aubusson carpet silently and kissed her hands; the gesture sat well on a man as tall and graceful as he was, especially since he wore a plain black soutane which gave him something of a courtly air. Her expressionless eyes suddenly coy and sparkling, Mary Carson almost simpered.

"Will you have tea, Father?" she asked.

"It depends on whether you wish to hear Mass," he said, sitting down in the chair facing hers and crossing his legs, the soutane riding up sufficiently to show that under it he wore breeches and knee-high boots, a concession to the locale of his parish. "I've brought you Communion, but if you'd like to hear Mass I can be ready to say it in a very few minutes. I don't mind continuing my fast a little longer."

"You're too good to me, Father," she said smugly, knowing perfectly well that he, along with everybody else, did homage not to her but to her money. "Please have tea," she went on. "I'm quite happy with Communion."

He kept his resentment from showing in his face; this parish had been excellent for his self-control. If once he was offered the chance to rise out of the obscurity his temper had landed him in, he would not again make the same mistake. And if he played his cards well, this old woman might be the answer to his prayers.

"I must confess, Father, that this past year has been very pleasant," she said. "You're a far more satisfactory shepherd than old Father Kelly was, God rot his soul." Her voice on the last phrase was suddenly harsh, vindictive.

His eyes lifted to her face, twinkling. "My dear Mrs. Carson! That's not a very Catholic sentiment."

"But the truth. He was a drunken old sot, and I'm quite sure God will rot his soul as much as the drink rotted his body." She leaned forward. "I know you fairly well by this time; I think I'm entitled to ask you a few questions, don't you? After all, you feel free to use Drogheda as your private playground—off learning how to be a stockman, polishing your riding, escaping from the vicissitudes of life in Gilly. All at my invitation, of course, but I do think I'm entitled to some answers, don't you?"

He didn't like to be reminded that he ought to feel grateful, but he had been waiting for the day when she would think she owned him enough to begin demanding things of him. "Indeed you are, Mrs. Carson. I can't thank you enough for permitting me the run of Drogheda, and for all your gifts—my horses, my car."

"How old are you?" she asked without further preamble.

"Twenty-eight," he replied.

"Younger than I thought. Even so, they don't send priests like you to places like Gilly. What did you do, to make them send someone like you out here into the back of beyond?"

"I insulted the bishop," he said calmly, smiling.

"You must have! But I can't think a priest of your peculiar talents can be happy in a place like Gillanbone."

"It is God's will."

"Stuff and nonsense! You're here because of human failings—your own and the bishop's. Only the Pope is infallible. You're utterly out of your natural element in

Gilly, we all know that, not that we're not grateful to have someone like you for a change, instead of the ordained remittance men they send us usually. But your natural element lies in some corridor of ecclesiastical power, not here among horses and sheep. You'd look magnificent in cardinal's red."

"No chance of that, I'm afraid. I fancy Gillanbone is not exactly the epicenter of the Archbishop Papal Legate's map. And it could be worse. I have you, and I have Drogheda."

She accepted the deliberately blatant flattery in the spirit in which it was intended, enjoying his beauty, his attentiveness, his barbed and subtle mind; truly he would make a magnificent cardinal. In all her life she could not remember seeing a better-looking man, nor one who used his beauty in quite the same way. He *had* to be aware of how he looked: the height and the perfect proportions of his body, the fine aristocratic features, the way every physical element had been put together with a degree of care about the appearance of the finished product God lavished on few of His creations. From the loose black curls of his head and the startling blue of his eyes to the small, slender hands and feet, he was perfect. Yes, he had to be conscious of what he was. And yet there was an aloofness about him, a way he had of making her feel he had never been enslaved by his beauty, nor ever would be. He would use it to get what he wanted without compunction if it would help, but not as though he was enamored of it; rather as if he deemed people beneath contempt for being influenced by it. And she would have given much to know what in his past life had made him so.

Curious, how many priests were handsome as Adonis, had the sexual magnetism of Don Juan. Did they espouse celibacy as a refuge from the consequences?

"Why do you put up with Gillanbone?" she asked. "Why not leave the priesthood rather than put up with it? You could be rich and powerful in any one of a number of fields with your talents, and you can't tell me the thought of power at least doesn't appeal to you."

His left eyebrow flew up. "My dear Mrs. Carson, you're a Catholic. You know my vows are sacred. Until my death I remain a priest. I cannot deny it."

She snorted with laughter. "Oh, come now! Do you really believe that if you renounced your vows they'd come after you with everything from bolts of lightning to bloodhounds and shotguns?"

"Of course not. Nor do I believe you're stupid enough to think fear of retribution is what keeps me within the priestly fold."

"Oho! Waspish, Father de Bricassart! Then what *does* keep you tied? What compels you to suffer the dust, the heat and the Gilly flies? For all you know, it might be a life sentence."

A shadow momentarily dimmed the blue eyes, but he smiled, pitying her. "You're a great comfort, aren't you?" His lips parted, he looked toward the ceiling and sighed. "I was brought up from my cradle to be a priest, but it's far more than that. How can I explain it to a woman? I am a vessel, Mrs. Carson, and at times I'm filled with God. If I were a better priest, there would be no periods of emptiness at all. And that filling, that oneness with God, isn't a function of place. Whether I'm in Gillanbone or a bishop's palace, it occurs. But to define it is difficult, because even to priests it's a great mystery. A divine possession, which other men can never know. That's it, perhaps. Abandon it? I couldn't."

"So it's a power, is it? Why should it be given to priests, then? What makes you think the mere smearing of chrism during an exhaustingly long ceremony is able to endow any man with it?"

He shook his head. "Look, it's years of life, even before getting to the point of ordination. The careful development of a state of mind which opens the vessel to God. It's *earned!* Every day it's earned. Which is the purpose of the vows, don't you see? That no earthly things come between the priest and his state of mind—not love of a woman, nor love of money, nor unwillingness to obey the dictates of other men. Poverty is nothing new to me; I don't come from a rich family. Chastity I accept without finding it difficult to maintain. And obedience? For me, it's the hardest of the three. But I obey, because if I hold myself more important than my function as a receptacle for God, I'm lost. I obey. And if necessary, I'm willing to endure Gillanbone as a life sentence."

"Then you're a fool," she said. "I, too, think that there are more important things than lovers, but being a receptacle for God isn't one of them. Odd. I never realized you believed in God so ardently. I thought you were perhaps a man who doubted."

"I do doubt. What thinking man doesn't? That's why at times I'm empty." He looked beyond her, at something she couldn't see. "Do you know, I think I'd give up every ambition, every desire in me, for the chance to be a perfect priest?"

"Perfection in anything," she said, "is unbearably dull. Myself, I prefer a touch of imperfection."

He laughed, looking at her in admiration tinged with envy. She was a remarkable woman.

Her widowhood was thirty-three years old and her only child, a son, had died in infancy. Because of her peculiar status in the Gillanbone community she had not availed herself of any of the overtures made to her by the more ambitious males of her acquaintance; as Michael Carson's widow she was indisputably a queen, but as someone's wife she passed control of all she had to that someone. Not Mary Carson's idea of living, to play second fiddle. So she had abjured the flesh, preferring to wield power; it was inconceivable that she should take a lover, for when it came to gossip Gillanbone was as receptive as a wire to an electrical current. To prove herself human and weak was not a part of her obsession.

But now she was old enough to be officially beyond the drives of the body. If the new young priest was assiduous in his duties to her and she rewarded him with little gifts like a car, it was not at all incongruous. A staunch pillar of the Church all her life, she had supported her parish and its spiritual leader in fitting fashion even when Father Kelly had hiccuped his way through the Mass. She was not alone in feeling charitably inclined toward Father Kelly's successor; Father Ralph de Bricassart was deservedly popular with every member of his flock, rich or poor. If his more remote parishioners could not get into Gilly to see him, he went to them, and until Mary Carson had given him his car he had gone on horseback. His patience and kindness had brought him liking from all and sincere love from some; Martin King of Bugela had expensively refurnished the presbytery, Dominic O'Rourke of Dibban-Dibban paid the salary of a good housekeeper.

So from the pedestal of her age and her position Mary Carson felt quite safe in enjoying Father Ralph; she liked matching her wits against a brain as intelligent as her own, she liked outguessing him because she was never sure she actually did outguess him.

"Getting back to what you were saying about Gilly not being the epicenter of the Archbishop Papal Legate's map," she said, settling deeply into her chair, "what do you think would shake the reverend gentleman sufficiently to make Gilly the pivot of his world?"

The priest smiled ruefully. "Impossible to say. A coup of some sort? The sudden saving of a thousand souls, a sudden capacity to heal the lame and the blind. . . . But the age of miracles is past."

"Oh, come now, I doubt that! It's just that He's altered His technique. These days He uses money."

"What a cynic you are! Maybe that's why I like you so much, Mrs. Carson."

"My name is Mary. Please call me Mary."

Minnie came in wheeling the tea trolley as Father de Bricassart said, "Thank you, Mary."

Over fresh bannocks and anchovies on toast, Mary Carson sighed. "Dear Father, I want you to pray especially hard for me this morning."

"Call me Ralph," he said, then went on mischievously, "I doubt it's possible for me to pray any harder for you than I normally do, but I'll try."

"Oh, you're a charmer! Or was that remark innuendo? I don't usually care for obviousness, but with you I'm never sure if the obviousness isn't actually a cloak for something deeper. Like a carrot before a donkey. Just what do you really think of me, Father de Bricassart? I'll never know, because you'll never be tactless enough to tell me, will you? Fascinating, fascinating . . . But you *must* pray for me. I'm old, and I've sinned much."

"Age creeps on us all, and I, too, have sinned."

A dry chuckle escaped her. "I'd give a lot to know how you've sinned! Indeed, indeed I would." She was silent for a moment, then changed the subject. "At this minute I'm minus a head stockman."

"Again?"

"Five in the past year. It's getting hard to find a decent man."

"Well, rumor hath it you're not exactly a generous or a considerate employer."

"Oh, impudent!" she gasped, laughing. "Who bought you a brand-new Daimler so you wouldn't have to ride?"

"Ah, but look how hard I pray for you!"

"If Michael had only had half your wit and character, I might have loved him," she said abruptly. Her face changed, became spiteful. "Do you think I'm without a relative in the world and must leave my money and my land to Mother Church, is that it?"

"I have no idea," he said tranquilly, pouring himself more tea.

"As a matter of fact, I have a brother with a large and thriving family of sons."

"How nice for you," he said demurely.

"When I married I was quite without worldly goods. I knew I'd never marry well in Ireland, where a woman has to have breeding and background to catch a rich husband. So I worked my fingers to the bone to save my passage money to a land where the rich men aren't so fussy. All I had when I got here were a face and a figure and a better brain than women are supposed to have, and they were adequate to catch Michael Carson, who was a rich fool. He doted on me until the day he died."

"And your brother?" he prompted, thinking she was going off at a tangent.

"My brother is eleven years younger than I am, which would make him fifty-four now. We're the only two still alive. I hardly know him; he was a small child when I left Galway. At present he lives in New Zealand, though if he emigrated to make his fortune he hasn't succeeded.

"But last night when the station hand brought me the news that Arthur Teviot had packed his traps and gone, I suddenly thought of Padraic. Here I am, not getting any younger, with no family around me. And it occurred to me that Paddy is an experienced man of the land, without the means to own land. Why not, I thought, write to him and ask him to bring himself and his sons here? When I die he'll inherit Drogheda and Michar Limited, as he's my only living relative closer than some unknown cousins back in Ireland."

She smiled. "It seems silly to wait, doesn't it? He might as well come now as later, get used to running sheep on the black soil plains, which I'm sure is quite different from sheep in New Zealand. Then when I'm gone he can step into my shoes without feeling the pinch." Head lowered, she watched Father Ralph closely.

"I wonder you didn't think of it earlier," he said.

"Oh, I did. But until recently I thought the last thing I wanted was a lot of vultures waiting anxiously for me to breathe my last. Only lately the day of my demise seems a lot closer than it used to, and I feel . . . oh, I don't know. As if it might be nice to be surrounded by people of my own flesh and blood."

"What's the matter, do you think you're ill?" he asked quickly, a real concern in his eyes.

She shrugged. "I'm perfectly all right. Yet there's something ominous about turning sixty-five. Suddenly old age is not a phenomenon which will occur; it has occurred."

"I see what you mean, and you're right. It will be very pleasant for you, hearing young voices in the house."

"Oh, they won't live here," she said. "They can live in the head stockman's house down by the creek, well away from me. I'm not fond of children or their voices."

"Isn't that a rather shabby way to treat your only brother, Mary? Even if your ages are so disparate?"

"He'll inherit—let him earn it," she said crudely.

Fiona Cleary was delivered of another boy six days before Meggie's ninth birthday, counting herself lucky nothing but a couple of miscarriages had happened in the interim. At nine Meggie was old enough to be a real help. Fee herself was forty years old, too old to bear children without a great deal of strength-sapping pain. The child, named Harold, was a delicate baby; for the first time anyone could ever remember, the doctor came regularly to the house.

And as troubles do, the Cleary troubles multiplied. The aftermath of the war was not a boom, but a rural depression. Work became increasingly harder to get.

Old Angus MacWhirter delivered a telegram to the house one day just as they were finishing tea, and Paddy tore it open with trembling hands; telegrams never held good news. The boys gathered round, all save Frank, who took his cup of tea and left the table. Fee's eyes followed him, then turned back as Paddy groaned.

"What is it?" she asked.

Paddy was staring at the piece of paper as if it held news of a death. "Archibald doesn't want us."

Bob pounded his fist on the table savagely; he had been so looking forward to going with his father as an apprentice shearer, and Archibald's was to have been his first pen. "Why should he do a dirty thing like this to us, Daddy? We were due to start there tomorrow."

"He doesn't say why, Bob. I suppose some scab contractor undercut me."

"Oh, Paddy!" Fee sighed.

Baby Hal began to cry from the big bassinet by the stove, but before Fee could move Meggie was up; Frank had come back inside the door and was standing, tea in hand, watching his father narrowly.

"Well, I suppose I'll have to go and see Archibald," Paddy said at last. "It's too late now to look for another shed to replace his, but I do think he owes me a better explanation than this. We'll just have to hope we can find work milking until Willoughby's shed starts in July."

Meggie pulled a square of white towel from the huge pile sitting by the stove warming and spread it carefully on the work table, then lifted the crying child out of the wicker crib. The Cleary hair glittered sparsely on his little skull as Meggie changed his diaper swiftly, and as efficiently as her mother could have done.

"Little Mother Meggie," Frank said, to tease her.

"I'm not!" she answered indignantly. "I'm just helping Mum."

"I know," he said gently. "You're a good girl, wee Meggie." He tugged at the white taffeta bow on the back of her head until it hung lopsided.

Up came the big grey eyes to his face adoringly; over

the nodding head of the baby she might have been his own age, or older. There was a pain in his chest, that this should have fallen upon her at an age when the only baby she ought to be caring for was Agnes, now relegated forgotten to the bedroom. If it wasn't for her and their mother, he would have been gone long since. He looked at his father sourly, the cause of the new life creating such chaos in the house. Served him right, getting done out of his shed.

Somehow the other boys and even Meggie had never intruded on his thoughts the way Hal did; but when Fee's waistline began to swell this time, he was old enough himself to be married and a father. Everyone except little Meggie had been uncomfortable about it, his mother especially. The furtive glances of the boys made her shrink like a rabbit; she could not meet Frank's eyes or quench the shame in her own. Nor should any woman go through that, Frank said to himself for the thousandth time, remembering the horrifying moans and cries which had come from her bedroom the night Hal was born; of age now, he hadn't been packed off elsewhere like the others. Served Daddy right, losing his shed. A decent man would have left her alone.

His mother's head in the new electric light was spun gold, the pure profile as she looked down the long table at Paddy unspeakably beautiful. How had someone as lovely and refined as she married an itinerant shearer from the bogs of Galway? Wasting herself and her Spode china, her damask table napery and her Persian rugs in the parlor that no one ever saw, because she didn't fit in with the wives of Paddy's peers. She made them too conscious of their vulgar loud voices, their bewilderment when faced with more than one fork.

Sometimes on a Sunday she would go into the lonely parlor, sit down at the spinet under the window and play, though her touch had long gone from want of time to practice and she could no longer manage any but the simplest pieces. He would sit beneath the window among the lilacs and the lilies, and close his eyes to listen. There was a sort of vision he had then, of his mother clad in a long bustled gown of palest pink shadow lace sitting at the spinet in a huge ivory room, great branches of candles all around her. It would make him long to weep, but he never wept anymore; not since that night in the barn after the police had brought him home.

Meggie had put Hal back in the bassinet, and gone to stand beside her mother. There was another one wasted. The same proud, sensitive profile; something of Fiona about her hands, her child's body. She would be very like her mother when she, too, was a woman. And who would marry her? Another oafish Irish shearer, or a clodhopping yokel from some Wahine dairy farm? She was worth more, but she was not born to more. There was no way out, that was what everyone said, and every year longer that he lived seemed to bear it out.

Suddenly conscious of his fixed regard, Fee and Meggie turned together, smiling at him with the peculiar tenderness women save for the most beloved men in their lives. Frank put his cup on the table and went out to feed the dogs, wishing he could weep, or commit murder. Anything which might banish the pain.

Three days after Paddy lost the Archibald shed, Mary Carson's letter came. He had opened it in the Wahine post office the moment he collected his mail, and came back to the house skipping like a child.

"We're going to Australia!" he yelled, waving the expensive vellum pages under his family's stunned noses.

There was silence, all eyes riveted on him. Fee's were shocked, so were Meggie's, but every male pair had lit with joy. Frank's blazed.

"But, Paddy, why should she think of you so suddenly after all these years?" Fee asked after she had read the letter. "Her money's not new to her, nor is her isolation. I never remember her offering to help us before."

"It seems she's frightened of dying alone," he said, as much to reassure himself as Fee. "You saw what she wrote: 'I am not young, and you and your boys are my heirs. I think we ought to see each other before I die, and it's time you learned how to run your inheritance. I have the intention of making you my head stockman—it will be excellent training, and those of your boys who are old enough to work may have employment as stockmen also. Drogheda will become a family concern, run by the family without help from outsiders.' "

"Does she say anything about sending us the money to get to Australia?" Fee asked.

Paddy's back stiffened. "I wouldn't dream of dunning her for that!" he snapped. "We can get to Australia without begging from her; I have enough put by."

"I think she ought to pay our way," Fee maintained stubbornly, and to everyone's shocked surprise; she did not often voice an opinion. "Why should you give up your life here and go off to work for her on the strength of a promise given in a letter? She's never lifted a finger to help us before, and I don't trust her. All I ever remember your saying about her was that she had the tightest clutch on a pound you'd ever seen. After all, Paddy, it's not as if you know her so very well; there was such a big gap between you in age, and she went to Australia before you were old enough to start school."

"I don't see how that alters things now, and if she is tight-fisted, all the more for us to inherit. No, Fee, we're going to Australia, and we'll pay our own way there."

Fee said no more. It was impossible to tell from her face whether she resented being so summarily dismissed.

"Hooray, we're going to Australia!" Bob shouted, grabbing at his father's shoulder. Jack, Hughie and Stu jigged up and down, and Frank was smiling, his eyes seeing nothing in the room but something far beyond it. Only Fee and Meggie wondered and feared, hoping painfully it would all come to nothing, for their lives could be no easier in Australia, just the same things under strange conditions.

"Where's Gillanbone?" Stuart asked.

Out came the old atlas; poor though the Clearys were, there were several shelves of books behind the kitchen dining table. The boys pored over yellowing pages until they found New South Wales. Used to small New Zealand distances, it didn't occur to them to consult the scale of miles in the bottom left-hand corner. They just naturally assumed New South Wales was the same size as the North Island of New Zealand. And there was Gillanbone, up toward the top left-hand corner; about the same distance from Sydney as Wanganui was from Auckland, it seemed, though the dots indicating towns were far fewer than on the North Island map.

"It's a very old atlas," Paddy said. "Australia is like America, growing in leaps and bounds. I'm sure there are a lot more towns these days."

They would have to go steerage on the ship, but it was only three days after all, not too bad. Not like the weeks and weeks between England and the Antipodes. All they could afford to take with them were clothes, china, cutlery, household linens, cooking utensils and those shelves of precious books; the furniture would have to be sold to cover the cost of shipping Fee's few bits and pieces in the parlor, her spinet and rugs and chairs.

"I won't hear of your leaving them behind," Paddy told Fee firmly.

"Are you sure we can afford it?"

"Positive. As to the other furniture, Mary says she's readying the head stockman's house and that it's got everything we're likely to be needing. I'm glad we don't have to live in the same house as Mary."

"So am I," said Fee.

Paddy went into Wanganui to book them an eight-berth steerage cabin on the *Wahine;* strange that the ship and their nearest town should have the same name. They were due to sail at the end of August, so by the beginning of that month everyone started realizing the big adventure was actually going to happen. The dogs had to be given away, the horses and the buggy sold, the furniture loaded onto old Angus MacWhirter's dray and taken into Wanganui for auction, Fee's few pieces crated along with the china and linen and books and kitchen goods.

Frank found his mother standing by the beautiful old spinet, stroking its faintly pink, streaky paneling and looking vaguely at the powdering of gold dust on her fingertips.

"Did you always have it, Mum?" he asked.

"Yes. What was actually mine they couldn't take from me when I married. The spinet, the Persian carpets, the Louis Quinze sofa and chairs, the Regency escritoire. Not much, but they were rightfully mine." The grey, wistful eyes stared past his shoulder at the oil painting on the wall behind him, dimmed with age a little, but still showing clearly the golden-haired woman in her pale-pink lace gown, crinolined with a hundred and seven flounces.

"Who was she?" he asked curiously, turning his head. "I've always wanted to know."

"A great lady."

"Well, she's got to be related to you; she looks like you a bit."

"Her? A relation of mine?" The eyes left their contemplation of the picture and rested on her son's face ironically. "Now, do I look as if I could ever have had a relative like her?"

"Yes."

"You've cobwebs in your brain; brush them out."

"I wish you'd tell me, Mum."

She sighed and shut the spinet, dusting the gold off her fingers. "There's nothing to tell, nothing at all. Come on, help me move these things into the middle of the room, so Daddy can pack them."

The voyage was a nightmare. Before the *Wahine* was out of Wellington harbor they were all seasick, and they continued to be seasick all the way across twelve hundred miles of gale-stirred, wintry seas. Paddy took the boys up on deck and kept them there in spite of the bitter wind and constant spray, only going below to see his women and baby when some kind soul volunteered to keep an eye on his four miserable, retching boys. Much though he yearned for fresh air, Frank had elected to remain below to guard the women. The cabin was tiny, stifling and reeked of oil, for it was below the water line and toward the bow, where the ship's motion was most violent.

Some hours out of Wellington Frank and Meggie became convinced their mother was going to die; the doctor, summoned from first class by a very worried steward, shook his head over her pessimistically.

"Just as well it's only a short voyage," he said, instructing his nurse to find milk for the baby.

Between bouts of retching Frank and Meggie managed to bottle-feed Hal, who didn't take to it kindly. Fee had stopped trying to vomit and had sunk into a kind of coma, from which they could not rouse her. The steward helped Frank put her in the top bunk, where the air was a little less stale, and holding a towel to his mouth to stem the watery bile he still brought up, Frank perched himself on the edge beside her, stroking the matted yellow hair back from her brow. Hour after hour he stuck to his post in spite of his own sickness; every time Paddy came in he was with his mother, stroking her hair, while Meggie huddled on a lower berth with Hal, a towel to her mouth.

Three hours out of Sydney the seas dropped to a

glassy calm and fog stole in furtively from the far Antarctic, wrapping itself about the old ship. Meggie, reviving a little, imagined it bellowed regularly in pain now the terrible buffeting was over. They inched through the gluey greyness as stealthily as a hunted thing until that deep, monotonous bawl sounded again from somewhere on the superstructure, a lost and lonely, indescribably sad noise. Then all around them the air was filled with mournful bellows as they slipped through ghostly smoking water into the harbor. Meggie never forgot the sound of foghorns, her first introduction to Australia.

Paddy carried Fee off the *Wahine* in his arms, Frank following with the baby, Meggie with a case, each of the boys stumbling wearily under some kind of burden. They had come into Pyrmont, a meaningless name, on a foggy winter morning at the end of August, 1921. An enormous line of taxis waited outside the iron shed on the wharf; Meggie gaped round-eyed, for she had never seen so many cars in one place at one time. Somehow Paddy packed them all into a single cab, its driver volunteering to take them to the People's Palace.

"That's the place for youse, mate," he told Paddy. "It's a hotel for the workingman run by the Sallies."

The streets were thronged with cars seeming to rush in all directions; there were very few horses. They stared raptly out of the taxi windows at the tall brick buildings, the narrow winding streets, the rapidity with which crowds of people seemed to merge and dissolve in some strange urban ritual. Wellington had awed them, but Sydney made Wellington look like a small country town.

While Fee rested in one of the myriad rooms of the warren the Salvation Army fondly called the People's Palace, Paddy went off to Central Railway Station to see when they could get a train for Gillanbone. Quite recovered, the boys clamored to go with him, for they had been told it was not very far, and that the way was all shops, including one which sold squill candy. Envying their youth, Paddy yielded, for he wasn't sure how strong his own legs were after three days of seasickness. Frank and Meggie stayed with Fee and the baby, longing to go, too, but more concerned that their mother be better. Indeed, she seemed to gain strength rapidly once off the ship, and had drunk a bowl of soup and nibbled a slice of toast brought to her by one of the workingman's bonneted angels.

"If we don't go tonight, Fee, it's a week until the next through train," Paddy said when he returned. "Do you think you could manage the journey tonight?"

Fee sat up, shivering. "I can manage."

"I think we ought to wait," Frank said hardily. "I don't think Mum's well enough to travel."

"What you don't seem to understand, Frank, is that if we miss tonight's train we have to wait a whole week, and I just don't have the price of a week's stay in Sydney in my pocket. This is a big country, and where we're going isn't served by a daily train. We could get as far as Dubbo on any one of three trains tomorrow, but then we'd have to wait for a local connection, and they told me we'd suffer a lot more traveling that way than if we make the effort to catch tonight's express."

"I'll manage, Paddy," Fee repeated. "I've got Frank and Meggie; I'll be all right." Her eyes were on Frank, pleading for his silence.

"Then I'll send Mary a telegram now, telling her to expect us tomorrow night."

Central Station was bigger than any building the Clearys had ever been inside, a vast glass cylinder which seemed simultaneously to echo and absorb the din of thousands of people waiting beside battered, strapped suitcases and fixedly watching a giant indicator board which men with long poles altered by hand. In the gathering evening darkness they found themselves a part of the throng, their eyes on the steel concertina gates of platform five; though shut, they bore a large hand-painted sign saying GILLANBONE MAIL. On platform one and platform two a terrific activity heralded the imminent departure of the Brisbane and Melbourne night expresses, passengers crowding through the barriers. Soon it was their turn, as the gates of platform five squashed themselves open and the people began eagerly to move.

Paddy found them an empty second-class compartment, put the older boys by the windows and Fee, Meggie and the baby by the sliding doors which led into the long corridor connecting compartments. Faces would peer in hopefully in sight of a spare seat, to vanish horrified at the sight of so many young children. Sometimes being a large family was an advantage.

The night was cold enough to warrant unstrapping of the big tartan traveling rugs all the suitcases bore on their outsides; though the carriage was not heated, steel boxes full of hot ashes lay along the floor radiating warmth, and no one had expected heating anyway because nothing in Australia or New Zealand was ever heated.

"How far is it, Daddy?" Meggie asked as the train drew out, clanking and rocking gently across an eternity of points.

"A long way further than it looked on our atlas, Meggie. Six hundred and ten miles. We'll be there late tomorrow afternoon."

The boys gasped, but forgot it at the blossoming of a fairyland of lights outside; everyone clustered at the windows and watched while the first miles flew by and still the houses did not diminish. The speed increased, the lights grew scattered and finally went out, replaced by a constant flurry of sparks streaming past in a howling wind. When Paddy took the boys outside so Fee could feed Hal, Meggie gazed after them longingly. These days it seemed she was not to be included as one of the boys, not since the baby had disrupted her life and chained her to the house as firmly as her mother was. Not that she really minded, she told herself loyally. He was such a dear little fellow, the chief delight of her life, and it was nice to have Mum treat her as another grown-up lady. What caused Mum to grow babies she had no idea, but the result was lovely. She gave Hal to Fee; the train stopped not long after, creaking and squealing, and seemed to stand hours panting for breath. She was dying to open the window and look out, but the compartment was growing very cold in spite of the hot ashes on the floor.

Paddy came in from the corridor with a steaming cup of tea for Fee, who put Hal back on the seat, glutted and sleepy.

"What is it?" she asked.

"A place called Valley Heights. We take on another engine here for the climb to Lithgow, the girl in the refreshment room said."

"How long have I got to drink this?"

"Fifteen minutes. Frank's getting you some sandwiches and I'll see the boys are fed. Our next refreshment stop is a placed called Blayney, much later in the night."

Meggie shared her mother's cup of hot, sugary tea, suddenly unbearably excited, and gobbled her sandwich when Frank brought it. He settled her on the long seat below baby Hal, tucked a rug firmly around her, and then did the same for Fee, stretched out full length on the seat opposite. Stuart and Hughie were bedded down on the floor between the seats, but Paddy told Fee that he was taking Bob, Frank and Jack several compartments down to talk to some shearers, and would spend the night there. It was much nicer than the ship, clicking along to the rhythmic huff-a-huff of the two engines, listening to the wind in the telegraph wires, the occasional flurry of furious huffs as steel wheels slipped on sloping steel rails, frantically sought traction; Meggie went to sleep.

In the morning they stared, awed and dismayed, at

a landscape so alien they had not dreamed anything like it existed on the same planet as New Zealand. The rolling hills were there certainly, but absolutely nothing else reminiscent of home. It was all brown and grey, even the trees! The winter wheat was already turned a fawnish silver by the glaring sun, miles upon miles of it rippling and bending in the wind, broken only by stands of thin, spindling, blue-leafed trees and dusty clumps of tired grey bushes. Fee's stoical eyes surveyed the scene without changing expression, but poor Meggie's were full of tears. It was horrible, fenceless and vast, without a trace of green.

From freezing night it turned to scorching day as the sun climbed toward its zenith and the train racketed on and on and on, stopping occasionally in some tiny town full of bicycles and horse-drawn vehicles; cars were scarce out here, it seemed. Paddy opened both the windows all the way in spite of the soot which swirled in and settled on everything; it was so hot they were gasping, their heavy New Zealand winter clothing sticking and itching. It did not seem possible that anywhere outside of hell could be so hot in winter.

Gillanbone came with the dying sun, a strange small collection of ramshackle wooden and corrugated iron buildings along either side of one dusty wide street, treeless and tired. The melting sun had licked a golden paste over everything, and gave the town a transient gilded dignity which faded even as they stood on the platform watching. It became once more a typical settlement on the very edge of the Back of Beyond, a last outpost in a steadily diminishing rainfall belt; not far away westward began two thousand miles of the Never-Never, the desert lands where it could not rain.

A resplendent black car was standing in the station yard, and striding unconcernedly toward them through the inches-deep dust came a priest. His long soutane made him seem a figure out of the past, as if he did not move on feet like ordinary men, but drifted dreamlike;

the dust rose and billowed around him, red in the last of the sunset.

"Hello, I'm Father de Bricassart," he said, holding out his hand to Paddy. "You have to be Mary's brother; you're the living image of her." He turned to Fee and lifted her limp hand to his lips, smiling in genuine astonishment; no one could spot a gentlewoman quicker than Father Ralph. "Why, you're beautiful!" he said, as if it were the most natural remark in the world for a priest to make, and then his eyes went onward to the boys, standing together in a huddle. They rested for a moment with puzzled bewilderment on Frank, who had charge of the baby, and ticked off each boy as they got smaller and smaller. Behind them, all by herself, Meggie stood gaping up at him with her mouth open, as if she were looking at God. Without seeming to notice how his fine serge robe wallowed in the dust, he stepped past the boys and squatted down to hold Meggie between his hands, and they were firm, gentle, kind. "Well! And who are you?" he asked her, smiling.

"Meggie," she said.

"Her name's Meghann." Frank scowled, hating this beautiful man, his stunning height.

"My favorite name, Meghann." He straightened, but held Meggie's hand in his. "It will be better for you to stay at the presbytery tonight," he said, leading Meggie toward the car. "I'll drive you out to Drogheda in the morning; it's too far after the train ride from Sydney."

Aside from the Hotel Imperial, the Catholic church, school, convent and presbytery were the only brick edifices in Gillanbone, even the big public school having to content itself with timber frame. Now that darkness had fallen, the air had grown incredibly chill; but in the presbytery lounge a huge log fire was blazing, and the smell of food came tantalizingly from somewhere beyond. The housekeeper, a wizened old Scotswoman with amazing energy, bustled about showing them their rooms, chattering all the while in a broad western Highlands accent.

Used to the touch-me-not reserve of the Wahine priests, the Clearys found it hard to cope with Father Ralph's easy, cheerful bonhomie. Only Paddy thawed, for he could remember the friendliness of the priests in his native Galway, their closeness to lesser beings. The rest ate their supper in careful silence and escaped upstairs as soon as they could, Paddy reluctantly following. To him, his religion was a warmth and a consolation; but to the rest of his family it was something rooted in fear, a do-it-or-thou-shalt-be-damned compulsion.

When they had gone, Father Ralph stretched out in his favorite chair, staring at the fire, smoking a cigarette and smiling. In his mind's eye he was passing the Clearys in review, as he had first seen them from the station yard. The man so like Mary, but bowed with hard work and very obviously not of her malicious disposition; his weary, beautiful wife, who looked as if she ought to have descended from a landaulet drawn by matched white horses; dark and surly Frank, with black eyes, *black* eyes; the sons, most of them like their father, but the youngest one, Stuart, very like his mother, he'd be a handsome man when he grew up; impossible to tell what the baby would become; and Meggie. The sweetest, the most adorable little girl he had ever seen; hair of a color which defied description, not red and not gold, a perfect fusion of both. And looking up at him with silver-grey eyes of such a lambent purity, like melted jewels. Shrugging, he threw the cigarette stub into the fire and got to his feet. He was getting fanciful in his old age; melted jewels, indeed! More likely his own eyes were coming down with the sandy blight.

In the morning he drove his overnight guests to Drogheda, so inured by now to the landscape that he derived great amusement from their comments. The last hill lay two hundred miles to the east; this was the land of the black soil plains, he explained. Just sweeping, lightly timbered grasslands as flat as a board. The day was as hot as the previous one, but the Daimler was a great deal more comfortable to travel in than the train had been. And they had started out early, fasting, Father Ralph's vestments and the Blessed Sacrament packed carefully in a black case.

"The sheep are dirty!" said Meggie dolefully, gazing at the many hundreds of rusty-red bundles with their questing noses down into the grass.

"Ah, I can see I ought to have chosen New Zealand," the priest said. "It must be like Ireland, then, and have nice cream sheep."

"Yes, it is like Ireland in many ways; it has the same beautiful green grass. But it's wilder, a lot less tamed," Paddy answered. He liked Father Ralph very much.

Just then a group of emus lurched to their feet and commenced to run, fleet as the wind, their ungainly legs a blur, their long necks stretched out. The children gasped and burst out laughing, enchanted at seeing giant birds which ran instead of flying.

"What a pleasure it is not to have to get out and open these wretched gates," Father Ralph said as the last one was shut behind them and Bob, who had done gate duty for him, scrambled back into the car.

After the shocks Australia had administered to them in bewildering rapidity, Drogheda homestead seemed like a touch of home, with its gracious Georgian façade and its budding wistaria vines, its thousands of rosebushes.

"Are we going to live *here?"* Meggie squeaked.

"Not exactly," the priest said quickly. "The house you're going to live in is about a mile further on, down by the creek."

Mary Carson was waiting to receive them in the vast drawing room and did not rise to greet her brother, but forced him to come to her as she sat in her wing chair.

"Well, Paddy," she said pleasantly enough, looking past him fixedly to where Father Ralph stood with Meggie in his arms, and her little arms locked tightly about his neck. Mary Carson got up ponderously, without greeting Fee or the children.

"Let us hear Mass immediately," she said. "I'm sure Father de Bricassart is anxious to be on his way."

"Not at all, my dear Mary." He laughed, blue eyes gleaming. "I shall say Mass, we'll all have a good hot breakfast at your table, and then I've promised Meggie I'll show her where she's going to live."

"Meggie," said Mary Carson.

"Yes, this is Meggie. Which rather begins the introductions at the tail, doesn't it? Let me begin at the head, Mary, please. This is Fiona."

Mary Carson nodded curtly, and paid scant attention as Father Ralph ran through the boys; she was too busy watching the priest and Meggie.

4

The head stockman's house stood on piles some thirty feet above a narrow gulch fringed with tall, straggling gum trees and many weeping willows. After the splendor of Drogheda homestead it was rather bare and utilitarian, but in its appurtenances it was not unlike the house they had left behind in New Zealand. Solid Victorian furniture filled the rooms to overflowing, smothered in fine red dust.

"You're lucky here, you have a bathroom," Father Ralph said as he brought them up the plank steps to the front veranda; it was quite a climb, for the piles upon which the house was poised were fifteen feet high. "In case the creek runs a banker," Father Ralph explained. "You're right on it here and I've heard it can rise sixty feet in a night."

They did indeed have a bathroom; an old tin bath and a chipped water heater stood in a walled-off alcove at the end of the back veranda. But, as the women found to their disgust, the lavatory was nothing more than a hole in the ground some two hundred yards away from the house, and it stank. After New Zealand, primitive.

"Whoever lived here wasn't very clean," Fee said as she ran her finger through the dust on the sideboard.

Father Ralph laughed. "You'll fight a losing battle

trying to get rid of that," he said. "This is the Outback, and there are three things you'll never defeat—the heat, the dust and the flies. No matter what you do, they'll aways be with you."

Fee looked at the priest. "You're very good to us, Father."

"And why not? You're the only relatives of my very good friend, Mary Carson."

She shrugged, unimpressed. "I'm not used to being on friendly terms with a priest. In New Zealand they kept themselves very much to themselves."

"You're not a Catholic, are you?"

"No, Paddy's the Catholic. Naturally the children have been reared as Catholics, every last one of them, if that's what's worrying you."

"It never occurred to me. Do *you* resent it?"

"I really don't care one way or the other."

"You didn't convert?"

"I'm not a hypocrite, Father de Bricassart. I had lost faith in my own church, and I had no wish to espouse a different, equally meaningless creed."

"I see." He watched Meggie as she stood on the front veranda, peering up the track toward Drogheda big house. "She's so pretty, your daughter. I have a fondness for titian hair, you know. Hers would have sent the artist running for his brushes. I've never seen exactly that color before. Is she your only daughter?"

"Yes. Boys run in both Paddy's family and my own; girls are unusual."

"Poor little thing," he said obscurely.

After the crates arrived from Sydney and the house took on a more familiar look with its books, china, ornaments and the parlor filled with Fee's furniture, things began to settle down. Paddy and the boys older than Stu were away most of the time with the two station hands Mary Carson had retained to teach them the many differences between sheep in northwest New South

Wales and sheep in New Zealand. Fee, Meggie and Stu discovered the differences between running a house in New Zealand and living in the head stockman's residence on Drogheda; there was a tacit understanding they would never disturb Mary Carson herself, but her housekeeper and her maids were just as eager to help the women as her station hands were to help the men.

Drogheda was, everyone learned, a world in itself, so cut off from civilization that after a while even Gillanbone became no more than a name with remote memories. Within the bounds of the great Home Paddock lay stables, a smithy, garages, innumerable sheds storing everything from feed to machinery, dog kennels and runs, a labyrinthine maze of stockyards, a mammoth shearing shed with the staggering number of twenty-six stands in it, and yet another jigsaw puzzle of yards behind it. There were fowl runs, pigpens, cow bails and a dairy, quarters for the twenty-six shearers, small shacks for the rouseabouts, two other, smaller, houses like their own for stockmen, a jackaroos' barracks, a slaughter yard, and woodheaps.

All this sat in just about the middle of a treeless circle whose diameter measured three miles: the Home Paddock. Only at the point where the head stockman's house lay did the conglomeration of buildings almost touch the forests beyond. However, there were many trees around the sheds, yards and animal runs, to provide welcome and necessary shade; mostly pepper trees, huge, hardy, dense and sleepily lovely. Beyond in the long grass of the Home Paddock, horses and milch cows grazed drowsily.

The deep gully beside the head stockman's house had a shallow, sluggish stream of muddy water at its bottom. No one credited Father Ralph's tale of its rising sixty feet overnight; it didn't seem possible. Water from this creek was pumped up by hand to service the bathroom and kitchen, and it took the women a long time to get used to washing themselves, the dishes and the clothes in greenish-brown water. Six massive corrugated-iron tanks perched on wooden derricklike towers caught rain from the roof and provided them with drinking water, but they learned they must use it very sparingly, that it was never to be used for washing. For there was no guarantee as to when the next rains might come to fill the tanks up.

The sheep and cattle drank artesian water, not tapped from an easily accessible water table, but true artesian water brought from over three thousand feet below the surface. It gushed at boiling point from a pipe at what was called the borehead, and ran through tiny channels fringed with poisonously green grass to every paddock on the property. These channels were the bore drains, and the heavily sulphurated, mineral-laden water they contained was not fit for human consumption.

At first the distances staggered them; Drogheda had two hundred and fifty thousand acres. Its longest boundary stretched for eighty miles. The homestead was forty miles and twenty-seven gates away from Gillanbone, the only settlement of any kind closer than a hundred and six miles. The narrow eastern boundary was formed by the Barwon River, which was what the locals called this northern course of the Darling River, a great muddy thousand-mile stream that finally joined the Murray River and surged out into the southern ocean fifteen hundred miles away in South Australia. Gillan Creek, which ran in the gully beside the head stockman's house, merged into the Barwon two miles beyond the Home Paddock.

Paddy and the boys loved it. Sometimes they spent days on end in the saddle, miles away from the homestead, camping at night under a sky so vast and filled with stars it seemed they were a part of God.

The grey-brown land swarmed with life. Kangaroos in flocks of thousands streamed leaping through the trees, taking fences in their stride, utterly lovely in their grace and freedom and numbers; emus built their nests in the middle of the grassy plain and stalked like giants about their territorial boundaries, taking fright at anything strange and running fleeter than horses away from their dark-green, football-sized eggs; termites built rusty towers like miniature skyscrapers; huge ants with a savage bite poured in rivers down mounded holes in the ground.

The bird life was so rich and varied there seemed no end to new kinds, and they lived not in ones and twos but in thousands upon thousands: tiny green-and-yellow parakeets Fee used to call lovebirds, but which the locals called budgerigars; scarlet-and-blue smallish parrots called rosellas; big pale-grey parrots with brilliant purplish-pink breasts, underwings and heads, called galahs; and the great pure white birds with cheeky yellow combs called sulphur-crested cockatoos. Exquisite tiny finches whirred and wheeled, so did sparrows and starlings, and the strong brown kingfishers called kookaburras laughed and chuckled gleefully or dived for snakes, their favorite food. They were well-nigh human, all these birds, and completely without fear, sitting in hundreds in the trees peering about with bright intelligent eyes, screaming, talking, laughing, imitating anything that produced a sound.

Fearsome lizards five or six feet long pounded over the ground and leaped lithely for high tree branches, as at home off the earth as on it; they were goannas. And there were many other lizards, smaller but some no less frightening, adorned with horny triceratopean ruffs about their necks, or with swollen, bright-blue tongues. Of snakes the variety was almost endless, and the Clearys learned that the biggest and most dangerous-looking were often the most benign, while a stumpy little creature a foot long might be a death adder; carpet snakes, copper snakes, tree snakes, red-bellied black snakes, brown snakes, lethal tiger snakes.

And insects! Grasshoppers, locusts, crickets, bees, flies of all sizes and sorts, cicadas, gnats, dragonflies, giant moths and so many butterflies! The spiders were dreadful, huge hairy things with a leg span of inches, or deceptively small and deadly black things lurking in the lavatory; some lived in vast wheeling webs slung between trees, some rocked inside dense gossamer cradles hooked among grass blades, others dived into little holes in the ground complete with lids which shut after them.

Predators were there, too: wild pigs frightened of nothing, savage and flesh-eating, black hairy things the size of fully grown cows; dingoes, the wild native dogs which slunk close to the ground and blended into the grass; crows in hundreds carking desolately from the blasted white skeletons of dead trees; hawks and eagles, hovering motionless on the air currents.

From some of these the sheep and cattle had to be protected, especially when they dropped their young. The kangaroos and rabbits ate the precious grass; the pigs and dingoes ate lambs, calves and sick animals; the crows pecked out eyes. The Clearys had to learn to shoot, then carried rifles as they rode, sometimes to put a suffering beast out of its misery, sometimes to fell a boar or a dingo.

This, thought the boys exultantly, was *life*. Not one of them yearned for New Zealand; when the flies clustered like syrup in the corners of their eyes, up their noses, in their mouths and ears, they learned the Australian trick and hung corks bobbing from the ends of strings all around the brims of their hats. To prevent crawlies from getting up inside the legs of their baggy trousers they tied strips of kangaroo hide called bowyangs below their knees, giggling at the silly-sounding name, but awed by the necessity. New Zealand was tame compared to this; this was *life*.

Tied to the house and its immediate environs, the women found life much less to their liking, for they had not the leisure or the excuse to ride, nor did they have the stimulation of varying activities. It was just harder to do what women always did: cook, clean, wash, iron, care for babies. They battled the heat, the dust, the flies, the many steps, the muddy water, the nearly perennial absence of men to carry and chop wood, pump water, kill fowls. The heat especially was hard to bear, and it was as yet only early spring; even so, the thermometer out on the shady veranda reached a hundred degrees every day. Inside the kitchen with the range going, it was a hundred and twenty degrees.

Their many layers of clothing were close-fitting and designed for New Zealand, where inside the house it was almost always cool. Mary Carson, exercising gently by walking down to see her sister-in-law, looked at Fee's high-necked, floor-length calico gown superciliously. She herself was clad in the new fashion, a cream silk dress coming only halfway down her calves, with loose elbow sleeves, no waist and a low décolletage.

"Really, Fiona, you're hopelessly old-fashioned," she said, glancing round the parlor with its fresh coat of cream paint, the Persian carpets and the spindly priceless furniture.

"I have no time to be anything else," Fee said, curtly for her when acting as hostess.

"You'll have more time now, with the men away so much and fewer meals to get. Raise your hems and stop wearing petticoats and stays, or you'll die when summer comes. It can get fifteen to twenty degrees hotter than this, you know." Her eyes dwelled on the portrait of the beautiful blond woman in her Empress Eugénie crinoline. "Who's that?" she asked, pointing.

"My grandmother."

"Oh, really? And the furniture, the carpets?"

"Mine, from my grandmother."

"Oh, really? My dear Fiona, you've come down in the world, haven't you?"

Fee never lost her temper, so she didn't now, but her thin lips got thinner. "I don't think so, Mary. I have a good man; you ought to know that."

"But penniless. What was your maiden name?"

"Armstrong."

"Oh, really? Not the Roderick Armstrong Armstrongs?"

"He's my oldest brother. His namesake was my great-grandfather."

Mary Carson rose, flapping her picture hat at the flies, which were not respecters of person. "Well, you're better born than the Clearys are, even if I do say so myself. Did you love Paddy enough to give all that up?"

"My reasons for what I do," said Fee levelly, "are my business, Mary, not yours. I do not discuss my husband, even with his sister."

The lines on either side of Mary Carson's nose got deeper, her eyes bulged slightly. "Hoity-toity!"

She did not come again, but Mrs. Smith, her housekeeper, came often, and repeated Mary Carson's advice about their clothes.

"Look," she said, "there's a sewing machine in my quarters which I never use. I'll have a couple of the rouseabouts carry it down. If I do need to use it, I'll come down here." Her eyes strayed to baby Hal, rolling on the floor gleefully. "I like to hear the sound of children, Mrs. Cleary."

Once every six weeks the mail came by horse-drawn dray from Gillanbone; this was the only contact with the outside world. Drogheda possessed a Ford truck, another specially constructed Ford truck with a water tank on its tray, a model-T Ford car and a Rolls-Royce limousine, but no one ever seemed to use them to go into Gilly save Mary Carson infrequently. Forty miles was as far as the moon.

Bluey Williams had the mail contract for the district and took six weeks to cover his territory. His flat-topped dray with its ten-foot wheels was drawn by a magnificent team of twelve draft horses, and was loaded with all the things the outlying stations ordered. As well as the Royal Mail, he carried groceries, gasoline in forty-four-gallon drums, kerosene in square five-gallon cans, hay, bags of corn, calico bags of sugar and flour, wooden chests of tea, bags of potatoes, farm machinery, mail-order toys and clothes from Anthony Hordern's in Sydney, plus anything else that had to be brought in from Gilly or Outside. Moving at the clipping rate of twenty miles a day, he was welcomed wherever he stopped, plied for news and weather far away, handed the scribbled scraps of paper carefully wrapped around money for goods he would purchase in Gilly, handed the laboriously written letters which went into the canvas sack marked "Royal GVR Mail."

West of Gilly there were only two stations on the route, Drogheda closer in, Bugela farther out; beyond Bugela lay the territory that got mail only once every six months. Bluey's dray swung in a great zigzagging arc through all the stations southwest, west and northwest, then returned to Gilly before setting out eastward, a smaller journey because Booroo town took over sixty miles east. Sometimes he brought people sitting beside him on his unsheltered leather seat, visitors or hopefuls looking for work; sometimes he took people away, visitors or discontented stockmen or maids or rouseabouts, very occasionally a governess. The squatters owned cars to transport themselves, but those who worked for the squatters depended upon Bluey for transport as well as goods and letters.

After the bolts of cloth Fee had ordered came on the mail, she sat down at the donated sewing machine and began to make loose dresses in light cotton for herself and Meggie, light trousers and overalls for the men, smocks for Hal, curtains for the windows. There was no doubt it was cooler minus layers of underwear and tightly fitting outerwear.

Life was lonely for Meggie, only Stuart at the house among the boys. Jack and Hughie were off with their father learning to be stockmen—jackaroos, the young apprentices were called. Stuart wasn't company the way Jack and Hughie used to be. He lived in a world all his own, a quiet little boy who preferred to sit for hours watching the behavior of a throng of ants than climb trees, whereas Meggie adored to climb trees and thought Australian gums were marvelous, of infinite variety and difficulty. Not that there was much time for tree-climbing, or ant-watching for that matter. Meggie and Stuart worked hard. They chopped and carried the wood, dug holes for refuse, tended the vegetable garden and looked after the fowls and pigs. They also learned how to kill snakes and spiders, though they never ceased to fear them.

The rainfall had been mediocrely good for several years; the creek was low but the tanks were about half full. The grass was still fairly good, but apparently nothing to its lush times.

"It will probably get worse," said Mary Carson grimly.

But they were to know flood before they encountered a full-fledged drought. Halfway through January the country caught the southern edge of the northwest monsoons. Captious in the extreme, the great winds blew to suit themselves. Sometimes only the far northern tips of the continent felt their drenching summer rains, sometimes they traveled far down the Outback and gave the unhappy urbanites of Sydney a wet summer. That January the clouds stormed dark across the sky, torn into sodden shreds by the wind, and it began to rain; not a gentle downpour but a steady, roaring deluge which went on and on.

They had been warned; Bluey Williams had turned up with his dray loaded high and twelve spare horses behind him, for he was moving fast to get through his rounds before the rains made further provisioning of the stations impossible.

"Monsoons are comin'," he said, rolling a cigarette and indicating piles of extra groceries with his whip.

"The Cooper an' the Barcoo an' the Diamantina are runnin' real bankers an' the Overflow is overflowin'. The whole Queenslan' Outback's two foot under water an' them poor buggers is tryin' to find a rise in the groun' to put the sheep on."

Suddenly there was a controlled panic; Paddy and the boys worked like madmen, moving the sheep out of the low-lying paddocks and as far away from the creek and the Barwon as they could. Father Ralph turned up, saddled his horse and set off with Frank and the best team of dogs for two uncleared paddocks alongside the Barwon, while Paddy and the two stockmen each took a boy in other directions.

Father Ralph was an excellent stockman himself. He rode a thoroughbred chestnut mare Mary Carson had given him, clad in faultlessly tailored buff jodhpurs, shiny tan knee boots, and a spotless white shirt with its sleeves rolled up his sinewy arms and its neck open to show his smooth brown chest. In baggy old grey twill trousers tied with bowyangs and a grey flannel undershirt, Frank felt like a poor relation. Which was what he was, he thought wryly, following the straight figure on the dainty mare through a stand of box and pine beyond the creek. He himself rode a hard-mouthed piebald stock horse, a mean-tempered beast with a will of its own and a ferocious hatred of other horses. The dogs were yelping and cavorting in excitement, fighting and snarling among themselves until parted with a flick from Father Ralph's viciously wielded stock whip. It seemed there was nothing the man couldn't do; he was familiar with the coded whistles setting the dogs to work, and plied his whip much better than Frank, still learning this exotic Australian art.

The big Queensland blue brute that led the dog pack took a slavish fancy to the priest and followed him without question, meaning Frank was very definitely the second-string man. Half of Frank didn't mind; he alone among Paddy's sons had not taken to life on

Drogheda. He had wanted nothing more than to quit New Zealand, but not to come to this. He hated the ceaseless patrolling of the paddocks, the hard ground to sleep on most nights, the savage dogs which could not be treated as pets and were shot if they failed to do their work.

But the ride into the gathering clouds had an element of adventure to it; even the bending, cracking trees seemed to dance with an outlandish joy. Father Ralph worked like a man in the grip of some obsession, sooling the dogs after unsuspecting bands of sheep, sending the silly woolly things leaping and bleating in fright until the low shapes streaking through the grass got them packed tight and running. Only having the dogs enabled a small handful of men to operate a property the size of Drogheda; bred to work sheep or cattle, they were amazingly intelligent and needed very little direction.

By nightfall Father Ralph and the dogs, with Frank trying to do his inadequate best behind them, had cleared all the sheep out of one paddock, normally several days' work. He unsaddled his mare near a clump of trees by the gate to the second paddock, talking optimistically of being able to get the stock out of it also before the rain started. The dogs were sprawled flat out in the grass, tongues lolling, the big Queensland blue fawning and cringing at Father Ralph's feet. Frank dug a repulsive collection of kangaroo meat out of his saddlebag and flung it to the dogs, which fell on it snapping and biting at each other jealously.

"Bloody awful brutes," he said. "They don't behave like dogs; they're just jackals."

"I think these are probably a lot closer to what God intended dogs should be," said Father Ralph mildly. "Alert, intelligent, aggressive and almost untamed. For myself, I prefer them to the house-pet species." He smiled. "The cats, too. Haven't you noticed them around the sheds? As wild and vicious as panthers; won't let a human being near them. But they hunt magnificently, and call no man master or provider."

He unearthed a cold piece of mutton and a packet of bread and butter from his saddlebag, carved a hunk from the mutton and handed the rest to Frank. Putting the bread and butter on a log between them, he sank his white teeth into the meat with evident enjoyment. Thirst was slaked from a canvas water bag, then cigarettes rolled.

A lone wilga tree stood nearby; Father Ralph indicated it with his cigarette.

"That's the spot to sleep," he said, unstrapping his blanket and picking up his saddle.

Frank followed him to the tree, commonly held the most beautiful in this part of Australia. Its leaves were dense and a pale lime green, its shape almost perfectly rounded. The foliage grew so close to the ground that sheep could reach it easily, the result being that every wilga bottom was mown as straight as a topiary hedge. If the rain began they would have more shelter under it than any other tree, for Australian trees were generally thinner of foliage than the trees of wetter lands.

"You're not happy, Frank, are you?" Father Ralph asked, lying down with a sigh and rolling another smoke.

From his position a couple of feet away Frank turned to look at him suspiciously. "What's happy?"

"At the moment, your father and brothers. But not you, not your mother, and not your sister. Don't you like Australia?"

"Not this bit of it. I want to go to Sydney. I might have a chance there to make something of myself."

"Sydney, eh? It's a den of iniquity." Father Ralph was smiling.

"I don't care! Out here I'm stuck the same way I was in New Zealand; I can't get away from him."

"Him?"

But Frank had not meant to say it, and would say no more. He lay looking up at the leaves.

"How old are you, Frank?"

"Twenty-two."

"Oh, yes! Have you ever been away from your people?"

"No."

"Have you even been to a dance, had a girlfriend?"

"No." Frank refused to give him his title.

"Then he'll not hold you much longer."

"He'll hold me until I die."

Father Ralph yawned, and composed himself for sleep. "Good night," he said.

In the morning the clouds were lower, but the rain held off all day and they got the second paddock cleared. A slight ridge ran clear across Drogheda from northeast to southwest; it was in these paddocks the stock were concentrated, where they had higher ground to seek if the water rose above the escarpments of the creek and the Barwon.

The rain began almost on nightfall, as Frank and the priest hurried at a fast trot toward the creek ford below the head stockman's house.

"No use worrying about blowing them now!" Father Ralph shouted. "Dig your heels in, lad, or you'll drown in the mud!"

They were soaked within seconds, and so was the hard-baked ground. The fine, nonporous soil became a sea of mud, miring the horses to their hocks and setting them floundering. While the grass persisted they managed to press on, but near the creek where the earth had been trodden to bareness they had to dismount. Once relieved of their burdens, the horses had no trouble, but Frank found it impossible to keep his balance. It was worse than a skating rink. On hands and knees they crawled to the top of the creek bank, and slid down it like projectiles. The stone roadway, which was normally covered by a foot of lazy water, was under four feet of racing foam; Frank heard the priest laugh. Urged on by shouts and slaps from sodden hats, the horses managed to scramble up the far bank without mishap, but Frank and Father Ralph could not. Every time they tried, they slid back again. The priest had just suggested they climb a willow when Paddy, alerted by the appearance of riderless horses, came with a rope and hauled them out.

Smiling and shaking his head, Father Ralph refused Paddy's offer of hospitality.

"I'm expected at the big house," he said.

Mary Carson heard him calling before any of her staff did, for he had chosen to walk around to the front of the house, thinking it would be easier to reach his room.

"You're not coming inside like that," she said, standing on the veranda.

"Then be a dear, get me several towels and my case."

Unembarrassed, she watched him peel off his shirt, boots and breeches, leaning against the half-open window into her drawing room as he toweled the worst of the mud off.

"You're the most beautiful man I've ever seen, Ralph de Bricassart," she said. "Why is it so many priests are beautiful? The Irishness? They're rather a handsome people, the Irish. Or is it that beautiful men find the priesthood a refuge from the consequences of their looks? I'll bet the girls in Gilly just eat their hearts out over you."

"I learned long ago not to take any notice of lovesick girls." He laughed. "Any priest under fifty is a target for some of them, and a priest under thirty-five is usually a target for all of them. But it's only the Protestant girls who openly try to seduce me."

"You never answer my questions outright, do you?" Straightening, she laid her palm on his chest and held it there. "You're a sybarite, Ralph, you lie in the sun. Are you as brown all over?"

Smiling, he leaned his head forward, then laughed into her hair, his hands unbuttoning the cotton drawers;

as they fell to the ground he kicked them away, standing like a Praxiteles statue while she toured all the way around him, taking her time and looking.

The last two days had exhilarated him, so did the sudden awareness that she was perhaps more vulnerable than he had imagined; but he knew her, and he felt quite safe in asking, "Do you want me to make love to you, Mary?"

She eyed his flaccid penis, snorting with laughter. "I wouldn't dream of putting you to so much trouble! Do you need women, Ralph?"

His head reared back scornfully. "No!"

"Men?"

"They're worse than women. No, I don't need them."

"How about yourself?"

"Least of all."

"Interesting." Pushing the window all the way up, she stepped through into the drawing room. "Ralph, Cardinal de Bricassart!" she mocked. But away from those discerning eyes of his she sagged back into her wing chair and clenched her fists, the gesture which rails against the inconsistencies of fate.

Naked, Father Ralph stepped off the veranda to stand on the barbered lawn with his arms raised above his head, eyes closed; he let the rain pour over him in warm, probing, spearing runnels, an exquisite sensation on bare skin. It was very dark. But he was still flaccid.

The creek broke its banks and the water crept higher up the piles of Paddy's house, farther out across the Home Paddock toward the homestead itself.

"It will go down tomorrow," said Mary Carson when Paddy went to report, worried.

As usual, she was right; over the next week the water ebbed and finally returned to its normal channels. The sun came out, the temperature zoomed to a hundred and fifteen in the shade, and the grass seemed to take wing for the sky, thigh-high and clean, bleached brilliant as gilt, hurting the eyes. Washed and dusted, the trees glittered, and the hordes of parrots came back from wherever they had gone while the rain fell to flash their rainbow bodies amid the timber, more loquacious than ever.

Father Ralph had returned to succor his neglected parishioners, serene in the knowledge his knuckles would not be rapped; under the pristine white shirt next to his heart resided a check for one thousand pounds. The bishop would be ecstatic.

The sheep were moved back to their normal pasture and the Clearys were forced to learn the Outback habit of siesta. They rose at five, got everything done before midday, then collapsed in twitching, sweating heaps until five in the afternoon. This applied both to the women at the house and the men in the paddocks. Chores which could not be done early were done after five, and the evening meal eaten after the sun had gone down at a table outside on the veranda. All the beds had been moved outside as well for the heat persisted through the night. It seemed as if the mercury had not gone below a century in weeks, day or night. Beef was a forgotten memory, only a sheep small enough to last without tainting until it was all eaten. Their palates longed for a change from the eternal round of baked mutton chops, mutton stew, shepherd's pie made of minced mutton, curried mutton, roast leg of mutton, boiled pickled mutton, mutton casserole.

But at the beginning of February life changed abruptly for Meggie and Stuart. They were sent to the convent in Gillanbone to board, for there was no school closer. Hal, said Paddy, could learn by correspondence from Blackfriars School in Sydney when he was old enough, but in the meantime, since Meggie and Stuart were used to teachers, Mary Carson had generously offered to pay for their board and tuition at the Holy Cross convent. Besides, Fee was too busy with Hal to supervise correspondence lessons as well. It had been tacitly understood from the beginning that Jack and Hughie would go no further with their educations; Drogheda needed them on the land, and the land was what they wanted.

Meggie and Stuart found it a strange, peaceful existence at Holy Cross after their life on Drogheda, but especially after the Sacred Heart in Wahine. Father Ralph had subtly indicated to the nuns that this pair of children were his protégés, their aunt the richest woman in New South Wales. So Meggie's shyness was transformed from a vice into a virtue, and Stuart's odd isolation, his habit of staring for hours into illimitable distances, earned him the epithet "saintly."

It was very peaceful indeed, for there were very few boarders; people of the district wealthy enough to send their offspring to boarding school invariably perferred Sydney. The convent smelled of polish and flowers, its dark high corridors awash with quietness and a tangible holiness. Voices were muted, life went on behind a black thin veil. No one caned them, no one shouted at them, and there was always Father Ralph.

He came to see them often, and had them to stay at the presbytery so regularly he decided to paint the bedroom Meggie used a delicate apple green, buy new curtains for the windows and a new quilt for the bed. Stuart continued to sleep in a room which had been cream and brown through two redecorations; it simply never occurred to Father Ralph to wonder if Stuart was happy. He was the afterthought who to avoid offense must also be invited.

Just why he was so fond of Meggie Father Ralph didn't know, nor for that matter did he spend much time wondering about it. It had begun with pity that day in the dusty station yard when he had noticed her lagging behind; set apart from the rest of her family by virtue of her sex, he had shrewdly guessed. As to why Frank also moved on an outer perimeter, this did not intrigue him at all, nor did he feel moved to pity Frank. There was something in Frank which killed tender emotions: a dark heart, a spirit lacking inner light. But Meggie? She had moved him unbearably, and he didn't really know why. There was the color of her hair, which pleased him; the color and form of her eyes, like her mother's and therefore beautiful, but so much sweeter, more expressive; and her character, which he saw as the perfect female character, passive yet enormously strong. No rebel, Meggie; on the contrary. All her life she would obey, move within the boundaries of her female fate.

Yet none of it added up to the full total. Perhaps, had he looked more deeply into himself, he might have seen that what he felt for her was the curious result of time, and place, and person. No one thought of her as important, which meant there was a space in her life into which he could fit himself and be sure of her love; she was a child, and therefore no danger to his way of life or his priestly reputation; she was beautiful, and he enjoyed beauty; and, least acknowledged of all, she filled an empty space in his life which his God could not, for she had warmth and a human solidity. Because he could not embarrass her family by giving her gifts, he gave her as much of his company as he could, and spent time and thought on redecorating her room at the presbytery; not so much to see her pleasure as to create a fitting setting for his jewel. No pinchbeck for Meggie.

At the beginning of May the shearers arrived on Drogheda. Mary Carson was extraordinarily aware of how everything on Drogheda was done, from deploying the sheep to cracking a stock whip; she summoned Paddy to the big house some days before the shearers came, and without moving from her wing chair she told him precisely what to do down to the last little detail. Used to New Zealand shearing, Paddy had been staggered by the size of the shed, its twenty-six stands; now, after the interview with his sister, facts and figures warred inside his head. Not only would Drogheda sheep be shorn on Drogheda, but Bugela and Dibban-Dibban and Beel-Beel sheep as well. It meant a grueling amount of work for every soul on the place, male and female. Communal shearing was the custom and the stations sharing Drogheda's shearing facilities would naturally pitch in to help, but the brunt of the incidental work inevitably fell on the shoulders of those on Drogheda.

The shearers would bring their own cook with them and buy their food from the station store, but those vast amounts of food had to be found; the ramshackle barracks with kitchen and primitive bathroom attached had to be scoured, cleaned and equipped with mattresses and blankets. Not all stations were as generous as Drogheda was to its shearers, but Drogheda prided itself on its hospitality, and its reputation as a "bloody good shed." For this was the one activity in which Mary Carson participated, so she didn't stint her purse. Not only was it one of the biggest sheds in New South Wales, but it required the very best men to be had, men of the Jackie Howe caliber; over three hundred thousand sheep would be shorn there before the shearers loaded their swags into the contractor's old Ford truck and disappeared down the track to their next shed.

Frank had not been home for two weeks. With old Beerbarrel Pete the stockman, a team of dogs, two stock horses and a light sulky attached to an unwilling nag to hold their modest needs, they had set out for the far western paddocks to bring the sheep in, working them closer and closer, culling and sorting. It was slow, tedious work, not to be compared with that wild muster before the floods. Each paddock had its own stockyards, in which some of the grading and marking would be done and the mobs held until it was their turn to come in. The shearing shed yards accommodated only ten thousand sheep at a time, so life wouldn't be easy while the shearers were there; it would be a constant flurry of exchanging mobs, unshorn for shorn.

When Frank stepped into his mother's kitchen she was standing beside the sink at a never-ending job, peeling potatoes.

"Mum, I'm home!" he said, joy in his voice.

As she swung around her belly showed, and his two weeks away lent his eyes added perception.

"Oh, God!" he said.

Her eyes lost their pleasure in seeing him, her face flooded with scarlet shame; she spread her hands over her ballooning apron as if they could hide what her clothes could not.

Frank was shaking. "The dirty old goat!"

"Frank, I can't let you say things like that. You're a man now, you ought to understand. This is no different from the way you came into the world yourself, and it deserves the same respect. It isn't dirty. When you insult Daddy, you insult me."

"He had no right! He should have left you alone!" Frank hissed, wiping a fleck of foam from the corner of his trembling mouth.

"It isn't dirty," she repeated wearily, and looked at him from her clear tired eyes as if she had suddenly decided to put shame behind her forever. "It's *not* dirty, Frank, and nor is the act which created it."

This time his face reddened. He could not continue to meet her gaze, so he turned and went through into the room he shared with Bob, Jack and Hughie. Its bare walls and little single beds mocked him, mocked him, the sterile and featureless look to it, the lack of a presence to warm it, a purpose to hallow it. And her face, her beautiful tired face with its prim halo of golden hair, all alight because of what she and that hairy old goat had done in the terrible heat of summer.

He could not get away from it, he could not get away from her, from the thoughts at the back of his mind, from the hungers natural to his age and manhood. Mostly he managed to push it all below consciousness, but when she flaunted tangible evidence of her lust before his eyes, threw her mysterious activity with that lecherous old beast in his very teeth. . . . How could he think of it, how could he consent to it, how could he bear it? He wanted to be able to think of her as totally holy, pure and untainted as the Blessed Mother, a being who was above such things though all her sisters throughout the world be guilty of it. To see her proving his concept of her wrong was the road to madness. It had become necessary to his sanity to imagine that she lay with that ugly old man in perfect chastity, to have a place to sleep, but that in the night they never turned toward each other, or touched. Oh, God!

A scraping clang made him look down, to find he had twisted the brass rail of the bed's foot into an S.

"Why aren't you Daddy?" he asked it.

"Frank," said his mother from the doorway.

He looked up, black eyes glittering and wet like rained-upon coal. "I'll end up killing him," he said.

"If you do that, you'll kill me," said Fee, coming to sit upon the bed.

"No, I'd free you!" he countered wildly, hopefully.

"Frank, I can never be free, and I don't want to be free. I wish I knew where your blindness comes from, but I don't. It isn't mine, nor is it your father's. I know you're not happy, but must you take it out on me, and on Daddy? Why do you insist upon making everything so hard? Why?" She looked down at her hands, looked up at him. "I don't want to say this, but I think I have to. It's time you found yourself a girl, Frank, got married and had a family of your own. There's room on Drogheda. I've never been worried about the other boys in that respect; they don't seem to have your nature at all. But you need a wife, Frank. If you had one, you wouldn't have time to think about me."

He had turned his back upon her, and wouldn't turn around. For perhaps five minutes she sat on the bed hoping he would say something, then she sighed, got up and left.

5

After the shearers had gone and the district had settled into the semi-inertia of winter came the annual Gillanbone Show and Picnic Races. It was the most important event in the social calendar, and went on for two days. Fee didn't feel well enough to go, so Paddy drove Mary Carson into town in her Rolls-Royce without his wife to support him or keep Mary's tongue in its silent position. He had noticed that for some mysterious reason Fee's very presence quelled his sister, put her at a disadvantage.

Everyone else was going. Under threat of death to behave themselves, the boys rode in with Beerbarrel Pete, Jim, Tom, Mrs. Smith and the maids in the truck, but Frank left early on his own in the model-T Ford. The adults of the party were all staying over for the second day's race meeting; for reasons known best to herself, Mary Carson declined Father Ralph's offer of accommodation at the presbytery, but urged Paddy to accept it for himself and Frank. Where the two stockmen and Tom, the garden rouseabout, stayed no one knew, but Mrs. Smith, Minnie and Cat had friends in Gilly who put them up.

It was ten in the morning when Paddy deposited his sister in the best room the Hotel Imperial had to offer;

he made his way down to the bar and found Frank standing at it, a schooner of beer in his hand.

"Let me buy the next one, old man," Paddy said genially to his son. "I've got to take Auntie Mary to the Picnic Races luncheon, and I need moral sustenance if I'm going to get through the ordeal without Mum."

Habit and awe are harder to overcome than people realize until they actually try to circumvent the conduct of years; Frank found he could not do what he longed to do, he could not throw the contents of his glass in his father's face, not in front of a bar crowd. So he downed what was left of his beer at a gulp, smiled a little sickly and said, "Sorry, Daddy, I've promised to meet some blokes down at the showground."

"Well, off you go, then. But here, take this and spend it on yourself. Have a good time, and if you get drunk don't let your mother find out."

Frank stared at the crisp blue five-pound note in his hand, longing to tear it into shreds and fling them in Paddy's face, but custom won again; he folded it, put it in his fob pocket and thanked his father. He couldn't get out of the bar quickly enough.

In his best blue suit, waistcoat buttoned, gold watch secured by a gold chain and a weight made from a nugget off the Lawrence goldfields, Paddy tugged at his celluloid collar and looked down the bar for a face he might recognize. He had not been into Gilly very often during the nine months since he arrived on Drogheda, but his position as Mary Carson's brother and heir apparent meant that he had been treated very hospitably whenever he had been in town, and that his face was well remembered. Several men beamed at him, voices offered to shout him a beer, and he was soon in the middle of a comfortable little crowd; Frank was forgotten.

Meggie's hair was braided these days, no nun being willing (in spite of Mary Carson's money) to attend to its curling, and it lay in two thick cables over her shoulders, tied with navy-blue ribbons. Clad in the sober navy-blue uniform of a Holy Cross student, she was escorted across the lawn from the convent to the presbytery by a nun and handed over to Father Ralph's housekeeper, who adored her.

"Och, it's the wee bairn's bonnie Hielan' hair," she explained to the priest once when he questioned her, amused; Annie wasn't given to liking little girls, and had deplored the presbytery's proximity to the school.

"Come now, Annie! Hair's inanimate; you can't like someone just because of the color of her hair," he said, to tease her.

"Ah, weel, she's a puir wee lassie—skeggy, ye ken."

He didn't ken at all, but he didn't ask her what "skeggy" meant, either, or pass any remarks about the fact that it rhymed with Meggie. Sometimes it was better not to know what Annie meant, or encourage her by paying much attention to what she said; she was, in her own parlance, fey, and if she pitied the child he didn't want to be told it was because of her future rather than her past.

Frank arrived, still trembling from his encounter with his father in the bar, and at a loose end.

"Come on, Meggie, I'll take you to the fair," he said, holding out his hand.

"Why don't I take you both?" Father Ralph asked, holding out his.

Sandwiched between the two men she worshipped, and hanging on to their hands for dear life, Meggie was in seventh heaven.

The Gillanbone showground lay on the banks of the Barwon River, next door to the racecourse. Though the floods were six months gone, the mud had not completely dried, and the eager feet of early comers had already pulped it to a mire. Beyond the stalls of sheep and cattle, pigs and goats, the prime and perfect livestock competing for prizes, lay tents full of handicrafts and cooking. They gazed at stock, cakes, crocheted shawls, knitted baby clothes, embroidered tablecloths, cats and dogs and canaries.

On the far side of all this was the riding ring, where young equestrians and equestriennes cantered their bob-tailed hacks before judges who looked, it seemed to a giggling Meggie, rather like horses themselves. Lady riders in magnificent serge habits perched sidesaddle on tall horses, their top hats swathed with tantalizing wisps of veiling. How anyone so precariously mounted and hatted could stay unruffled upon a horse at anything faster than an amble was beyond Meggie's imagination, until she saw one splendid creature take her prancing animal over a series of difficult jumps and finish as impeccable as before she started. Then the lady pricked her mount with an impatient spur and cantered across the soggy ground, reining to a halt in front of Meggie, Frank and Father Ralph to bar their progress. The leg in its polished black boot hooked round the saddle was unhooked, and the lady sat truly on the side of her saddle, her gloved hands extended imperiously.

"Father! Be so kind as to help me dismount!"

He reached up to put his hands around her waist, her hands on his shoulders, and swung her lightly down; the moment her heels touched the ground he released her, took her mount's reins in his hand and walked on, the lady beside him, matching his stride effortlessly.

"Will you win the Hunting, Miss Carmichael?" he asked in tones of utter indifference.

She pouted; she was young and very beautiful, and that curious impersonal quality of his piqued her. "I hope to win, but I can't be sure. Miss Hopeton and Mrs. Anthony King both compete. However, I shall win the Dressage, so if I don't win the Hunting I shan't repine."

She spoke with beautifully rounded vowels, and with the oddly stilted phraseology of a young lady so carefully reared and educated there was not a trace of warmth or idiom left to color her voice. As he spoke to her Father Ralph's own speech became more pear-shaped, and quite lost its beguiling hint of Irishness; as if she brought back to him a time when he, too, had been like this. Meggie frowned, puzzled and affected by their light but guarded words, not knowing what the change in Father Ralph was, only knowing there was a change, and not one to her liking. She let go Frank's hand, and indeed it had become difficult for them to continue walking abreast.

By the time they came to a wide puddle Frank had fallen behind them. Father Ralph's eyes danced as he surveyed the water, almost a shallow pond; he turned to the child whose hand he had kept in his firmly, and bent down to her with a special tenderness the lady could not mistake, for it had been entirely lacking in his civil exchanges with her.

"I wear no cloak, darling Meggie, so I can't be your Sir Walter Raleigh. I'm sure you'll excuse me, my dear Miss Carmichael"—the reins were passed to the lady—"but I can't permit my favorite girl to muddy her shoes, now can I?"

He picked Meggie up and tucked her easily against his hip, leaving Miss Carmichael to collect her heavy trailing skirts in one hand, the reins in her other, and splash her way across unaided. The sound of Frank's hoot of laugher just behind them didn't improve her temper; on the far side of the puddle she left them abruptly.

"I do believe she'd kill you if she could," Frank said as Father Ralph put Meggie down. He was fascinated by this encounter and by Father Ralph's deliberate cruelty. She had seemed to Frank so beautiful and so haughty that no man could gainsay her, even a priest, yet Father Ralph had wantonly set out to shatter her faith in herself, in that heady femininity she wielded like a weapon. As if the priest hated her and what she stood for, Frank thought, the world of women, an exquisite mystery he had never had the opportunity to plumb. Smarting from his mother's words, he had wanted Miss Carmichael to notice him, the oldest son of Mary Carson's heir, but she had not so much as deigned to admit he existed. All her attention had been focused on the priest, a being sexless and emasculated. Even if he was tall, dark and handsome.

"Don't worry, she'll be back for more of the same," said Father Ralph cynically. "She's rich, so next Sunday she'll very ostentatiously put a ten-pound note in the plate." He laughed at Frank's expression. "I'm not so much older than you, my son, but in spite of my calling I'm a very worldly fellow. Don't hold it against me; just put it down to experience."

They had left the riding ring behind and entered the amusement part of the grounds. To Meggie and Frank alike it was enchantment. Father Ralph had given Meggie five whole shillings, and Frank had his five pounds; to own the price of admission to all those enticing booths was wonderful. Crowds thronged the area, children running everywhere, gazing wide-eyed at the luridly and somewhat inexpertly painted legends fronting tattered tents: The Fattest Lady in the World; Princess Houri the Snake Dancer (See Her Fan the Flames of a Cobra's Rage!); The India Rubber Man; Goliath the World's Strongest Man; Thetis the Mermaid. At each they paid their pennies and watched raptly, not noticing Thetis's sadly tarnished scales or the toothless smile on the cobra.

At the far end, so big it required a whole side for itself, was a giant marquee with a high boardwalk along its front, a curtainlike frieze of painted figures stretching behind the entire length of the board bridge, menacing the crowd. A man with a megaphone in his hand was shouting to the gathering people.

"Here it is, gents, Jimmy Sharman's famous boxing troupe! Eight of the world's greatest prize fighters, and a purse to be won by any chap game to have a go!"

Women and girls were trickling out of the audience as fast as men and boys came from every direction to swell it, clustering thickly beneath the boardwalk. As solemnly as gladiators parading at the Circus Maximus, eight men filed onto the bridge and stood, bandaged hands on hips, legs apart, swaggering at the admiring oohs of the crowd. Meggie thought they were wearing underclothes, for they were clad in long black tights and vests with closely fitting grey trunks from waists to midthighs. On their chests, big white Roman capitals said JIMMY SHARMAN'S TROUPE. No two were the same size, some big, some small, some in between, but they were all of particularly fine physique. Chatting and laughing to each other in an offhand manner that suggested this was an everyday occurrence, they flexed their muscles and tried to pretend they weren't enjoying strutting.

"Come on, chaps, who'll take a glove?" the spruiker was braying. "Who wants to have a go? Take a glove, win a fiver!" he kept yelling between the booms of a bass drum.

"I will!" Frank shouted. "I will, I will!"

He shook off Father Ralph's restraining hand as those around them in the throng who could see Frank's diminutive size began to laugh and good-naturedly push him to the front.

But the spruiker was very serious as one of the troupe extended a friendly hand and pulled Frank up the ladder to stand at one side of the eight already on the bridge. "Don't laugh, gents. He's not very big but he is the first to volunteer! It isn't the size of the dog in the fight, you know, it's the size of the fight in the dog! Come on now, here's this little bloke game to try—what about some of you big blokes, eh? Put on a glove and win a fiver, go the distance with one of Jimmy Sharman's troupe!"

Gradually the ranks of the volunteers increased, the young men self-consciously clutching their hats and eyeing the professionals who stood, a band of elite beings, alongside them. Dying to stay and see what happened, Father Ralph reluctantly decided it was more than time he removed Meggie from the vicinity, so he picked her up and turned on his heel to leave. Meggie began to scream, and the farther away he got, the louder she screamed; people were beginning to look at them, and he was so well known it was very embarrassing, not to mention undignified.

"Now look, Meggie, I can't take you in there! Your father would flay me alive, and rightly!"

"I want to stay with Frank, I want to stay with Frank!" she howled at the top of her voice, kicking and trying to bite.

"Oh, *shit!*" said Father Ralph.

Yielding to the inevitable, he dug into his pocket for the required coins and approached the open flap of the marquee, one eye cocked for any of the Cleary boys; but they were nowhere to be seen, so he presumed they were safely trying their luck with the horseshoes or gorging themselves on meat pies and ice cream.

"You can't take her in there, Father!" the foreman said, shocked.

Father Ralph lifted his eyes heavenward. "If you'll only tell me how we can get her away from here without the entire Gilly police force arresting us for molesting a child, I'll gladly go! But her brother volunteered and she's not about to leave her brother without a fight that will make your chaps look like amateurs!"

The foreman shrugged. "Well, Father, I can't argue with you, can I? In you go, but keep her out of the way, for—ah—pity's sake. No, no, Father, put your money back in your pocket; Jimmy wouldn't like it."

The tent seemed full of men and boys, milling around a central ring; Father Ralph found a place at the back of the crowd against the canvas wall, hanging on to Meggie for dear life. The air was foggy from tobacco smoke and redolent with sawdust they had thrown down to absorb the mud. Frank, gloves already on his hands, was the first challenger of the day.

Though it was unusual, it was not unknown for a man out of the crowd to last the distance against one of the professional boxers. Admittedly they weren't the best in the world, but they did include some of the best in Australia. Put up against a flyweight because of his size, Frank knocked him out with the third punch he threw, and offered to fight someone else. By the time he was on his third professional the word had got around, and the tent was so jammed they could not fit another eager spectator inside.

He had hardly been touched by a glove, the few blows he had taken only provoking his ever-smoldering rage. He was wild-eyed, almost spitting in passion, each of his opponents wearing Paddy's face, the yells and cheers of the crowd throbbing in his head like a vast single voice chanting *Go! Go! Go!* Oh, how he had ached for the chance to fight, denied him since coming to Drogheda! For to fight was the only way he knew of ridding himself of anger and pain, and as he landed the felling punch he thought the great dull voice in his ears changed its song, to *Kill! Kill! Kill!*

Then they put him with one of the real champions, a lightweight under orders to keep Frank at a distance and find out if he could box as well as he could punch. Jimmy Sharman's eyes were shining. He was always on the lookout for champions, and these little country shows had yielded several. The lightweight did as he was told, hard-pressed in spite of his superior reach, while Frank, so possessed by his hunger to kill that dancing, elusive figure he saw nothing else, went after him. He learned with every clinch and flurry of blows, one of those strange people who even in the midst of titanic rage still can think. And he lasted the distance, in spite of the punishment those expert fists had meted out; his eye was swelling, his brow and lip cut. But he had won twenty pounds, and the respect of every man present.

Meggie wriggled from Father Ralph's slackened clasp and bolted from the tent before he could catch hold of her. When he found her outside she had been sick, and was trying to clean her splattered shoes with a tiny handkerchief. Silently he gave her his own, stroking her bright, sobbing head. The atmosphere inside had not agreed with his gorge either, and he wished the dignity of his calling permitted him the relief of releasing it in public.

"Do you want to wait for Frank, or would you rather we went now?"

"I'll wait for Frank," she whispered, leaning against his side, so grateful for his calmness and sympathy.

"I wonder why you tug so at my nonexistent heart?" he mused, deeming her too sick and miserable to listen but needing to voice his thoughts aloud, as do so many people who lead a solitary life. "You don't remind me of my mother and I never had a sister, and I wish I knew what it was about you and your wretched family. . . . Have you had a hard life, my little Meggie?"

Frank came out of the tent, a piece of sticking plaster over his eye, dabbing at his torn lip. For the first time since Father Ralph had met him, he looked happy; the way most men did after what one knew was a good night in bed with a woman, thought the priest.

"What's Meggie doing here?" he snarled, not quite down from the exaltation of the ring.

"Short of binding her hand and foot, not to mention gagging her, there was no way I could keep her out," said Father Ralph tartly, not pleased at having to justify himself, but not sure Frank wouldn't have a go at him, too. He wasn't in the least afraid of Frank, but he was afraid of creating a scene in public. "She was frightened for you, Frank; she wanted to be near enough to you to see for herself that you were all right. Don't be angry with her; she's upset enough already."

"Don't you dare let Daddy know you were within a mile of this place," Frank said to Meggie.

"Do you mind if we cut the rest of our tour short?" the priest asked. "I think we could all do with a rest and a cup of tea at the presbytery." He pinched the tip of Meggie's nose. "And you, young lady, could do with a good wash."

Paddy had had a tormenting day with his sister, at her beck and call in a way Fee never demanded, helping her pick her fastidious, cross-patch way through the Gilly mud in imported guipure lace shoes, smiling and chatting with the people she greeted royally, standing by her side as she presented the emerald bracelet to the winner of the principal race, the Gillanbone Trophy. Why they had to spend all the prize money on a woman's trinket instead of handing over a gold-plated cup and a nice bundle of cash was beyond him, for he did not understand the keenly amateur nature of the race meeting, the inference that the people who entered horses didn't need vulgar money, instead could carelessly toss the winnings to the little woman. Horry Hopeton, whose bay gelding King Edward had won the emerald bracelet, already possessed a ruby, a diamond and a sapphire bracelet from other years; he had a wife and five daughters and said he couldn't stop until he had won six bracelets.

Paddy's starched shirt and celluloid collar chafed, the blue suit was too hot, and the exotic Sydney seafood they had served with champagne at luncheon had not agreed with his mutton-inured digestion. And he had felt a fool, thought he looked a fool. Best though it was, his suit smacked of cheap tailoring and bucolic unfashionableness. They were not his kind of people, the bluff tweedy graziers, the lofty matrons, the toothy, horsy young women, the cream of what the *Bulletin* called "the squattocracy." For they were doing their best to forget the days in the last century when they had squatted on the land and taken vast tracts of it for their own, had it tacitly acknowledged as their own with federation and the arrival of home rule. They had become the most envied group of people on the continent, ran their own political party, sent their children to exclusive Sydney schools, hobnobbed with the visiting Prince of Wales. He, plain Paddy Cleary, was a workingman. He had absolutely nothing in common with these colonial aristocrats, who reminded him of his wife's family too much for comfort.

So when he came into the presbytery lounge to find Frank, Meggie and Father Ralph relaxed around the fire and looking as if they had spent a wonderful, carefree day, it irritated him. He had missed Fee's genteel support unbearably and he still disliked his sister as much as he had back in his early childhood in Ireland. Then he noticed the sticking plaster over Frank's eye, the swollen face; it was a heaven-sent excuse.

"And how do you think you're going to face your mother looking like that?" he yelled. "Not a day out of my sight and you're back at it again, picking fights with anyone who looks at you sideways!"

Startled, Father Ralph jumped to his feet with a soothing noise half-uttered; but Frank was quicker.

"I earned myself money with this!" he said very softly, pointing to the plaster. "Twenty pounds for a few minutes' work, better wages than Auntie Mary pays you and me combined in a month! I knocked out three good boxers and lasted the distance with a lightweight champion in Jimmy Sharman's tent this afternoon. And I earned myself twenty pounds. It may not fit in with your ideas of what I ought to do, but this afternoon I earned the respect of every man present!"

"A few tired, punch-drunk old has-beens at a country show, and you're full of it? Grow up, Frank! I know you can't grow any more in body, but you might make an effort for your mother's sake to grow in mind!"

The whiteness of Frank's face! Like bleached bones.

It was the most terrible insult a man could offer him, and this was his father; he couldn't strike back. His breathing started coming from the bottom of his chest with the effort of keeping his hands by his sides. "No has-beens, Daddy. You know who Jimmy Sharman is as well as I do. And Jimmy Sharman himself said I had a terrific future as a boxer; he wants to take me into his troupe and train me. *And* he wants to pay me! I may not grow any bigger, but I'm big enough to lick any man ever born—and that goes for you, too, you stinking old he-goat!"

The inference behind the epithet was not lost on Paddy; he went as white as his son. "Don't you dare call me that!"

"What else are you? You're disgusting, you're worse than a ram in rut! Couldn't you leave her alone, couldn't you keep your hands off her?"

"No, no, no!" Meggie screamed. Father Ralph's hands bit into her shoulders like claws and held her painfully against him. The tears poured down her face, she twisted to free herself frantically and vainly. "No, Daddy, no! Oh, Frank, please! Please, please!" she shrilled.

But the only one who heard her was Father Ralph. Frank and Paddy faced each other, the dislike and the fear, each for the other, admitted at last. The dam of mutual love for Fee was breached and the bitter rivalry for Fee acknowledged.

"I am her husband. It is by God's grace we are blessed with our children," said Paddy more calmly, fighting for control.

"You're no better than a shitty old dog after any bitch you can stick your thing into!"

"And you're no better than the shitty old dog who fathered you, whoever he was! Thank God I never had a hand in it!" shouted Paddy, and stopped. "Oh, dear Jesus!" His rage quit him like a howling wind, he sagged and shriveled and his hands plucked at his mouth as if to tear out the tongue which had uttered the unutterable. "I didn't mean it, I didn't mean it! *I didn't mean it!*"

The moment the words were out Father Ralph let go of Meggie and grabbed Frank. He had Frank's right arm twisted behind him, his own left arm around Frank's neck, throttling him. And he was strong, the grip paralyzing; Frank fought to be free of him, then suddenly his resistance flagged and he shook his head in submission. Meggie had fallen to the floor and knelt there, weeping, her eyes going from her brother to her father in helpless, beseeching agony. She didn't understand what had happened, but she knew it meant she couldn't keep them both.

"You meant it," Frank croaked. "I must always have known it! I must always have known it." He tried to turn his head to Father Ralph. "Let me go, Father. I won't touch him, so help me God I won't."

"So help you God? God rot your souls, both of you! If you've ruined the child I'll kill you!" the priest roared, the only one angry now. "Do you realize I had to keep her here to listen to this, for fear if I took her away you'd kill each other while I was gone? I ought to have let you do it, you miserable, self-centered cretins!"

"It's all right, I'm going," Frank said in a strange, empty voice. "I'm going to join Jimmy Sharman's troupe, and I won't be back."

"You've got to come back!" Paddy whispered. "What can I tell your mother? You mean more to her than the rest of us put together. She'll never forgive me!"

"Tell her I went to join Jimmy Sharman because I want to be someone. It's the truth."

"What I said—it wasn't true, Frank."

Frank's alien black eyes flashed scornfully, the eyes the priest had wondered at the first time he saw them; what were grey-eyed Fee and blue-eyed Paddy doing with a black-eyed son? Father Ralph knew his Mendelian laws, and didn't think even Fee's greyness made it possible.

Frank picked up his hat and coat. "Oh, it was true! I must always have known it. The memories of Mum playing her spinet in a room you could never have owned! The feeling you hadn't always been there, that you came after me. That she was mine first." He laughed soundlessly. "And to think all these years I've blamed *you* for dragging her down, when it was me. It was *me!*"

"It was no one, Frank, no one!" the priest cried, trying to pull him back. "It's a part of God's great unfathomable plan; think of it like that!"

Frank shook off the detaining hand and walked to the door with his light, deadly, tiptoed gait. He was born to be a boxer, thought Father Ralph in some detached corner of his brain, that cardinal's brain.

"God's great unfathomable plan!" mocked the young man's voice from the door. "You're no better than a parrot when you act the priest, Father de Bricassart! I say God help *you,* because you're the only one of us here who has no idea what he really is!"

Paddy was sitting in a chair, ashen, his shocked eyes on Meggie as she huddled on her knees by the fire, weeping and rocking herself back and forth. He got up to go to her, but Father Ralph pushed him roughly away.

"Leave her alone. You've done enough! There's whiskey in the sideboard; take some. I'm going to put the child to bed, but I'll be back to talk to you, so don't go. Do you hear me, man?"

"I'll be here, Father. Put her to bed."

Upstairs in the charming apple-green bedroom the priest unbuttoned the little girl's dress and chemise, made her sit on the edge of the bed so he could pull off her shoes and stockings. Her nightdress lay on the pillow where Annie had left it; he tugged it over her head and decently down before he removed her drawers. And all the while he talked to her about nothing, silly stories of buttons refusing to come undone, and shoes stubbornly staying tied, and ribbons that would not come off. It was impossible to tell if she heard him; with their unspoken tales of infant tragedies, of troubles and pains beyond her years, the eyes stared drearily past his shoulder.

"Now lie down, my darling girl, and try to go to sleep. I'll be back in a little while to see you, so don't worry, do you hear? We'll talk about it then."

"Is she all right?" asked Paddy as he came back into the lounge.

Father Ralph reached for the whiskey bottle standing on the sideboard, and poured a tumbler half full.

"I don't honestly know. God in heaven, Paddy, I wish I knew which is an Irishman's greater curse, the drink or the temper. What possessed you to *say* that? No, don't even bother answering! The temper. It's true, of course. I knew he wasn't yours the moment I first saw him."

"There's not much misses you, is there?"

"I suppose not. However, it doesn't take much more than very ordinary powers of observation to see when the various members of my parish are troubled, or in pain. And having seen, it is my duty to do what I can to help."

"You're very well liked in Gilly, Father."

"For which no doubt I may thank my face and my figure," said the priest bitterly, unable to make it sound as light as he had intended.

"Is *that* what you think? I can't agree, Father. We like you because you're a good pastor."

"Well, I seem to be thoroughly embroiled in your troubles, at any rate," said Father Ralph uncomfortably. "You'd best get it off your chest, man."

Paddy stared into the fire, which he had built up to the proportions of a furnace while the priest was putting Meggie to bed, in an excess of remorse and frantic to be doing something. The empty glass in his hand shook in a series of rapid jerks; Father Ralph got up for the whiskey bottle and replenished it. After a long draft Paddy sighed, wiping the forgotten tears from his face.

"I don't know who Frank's father is. It happened before I met Fee. Her people are practically New Zealand's first family socially, and her father had a big wheat-and-sheep property outside Ashburton in the South Island. Money was no object, and Fee was his only daughter. As I understand it, he'd planned her life for her—a trip to the old country, a debut at court, the right husband. She had never lifted a hand in the house, of course. They had maids and butlers and horses and big carriages; they lived like lords.

"I was the dairy hand, and sometimes I used to see Fee in the distance, walking with a little boy about eighteen months old. The next thing, old James Armstrong came to see me. His daughter, he said, had disgraced the family; she wasn't married and she had a child. It had been hushed up, of course, but when they tried to get her away her grandmother made such a fuss they had no choice but to keep her on the place, in spite of the awkwardness. Now the grandmother was dying, there was nothing to stop them getting rid of Fee and her child. I was a single man, James said; if I'd marry her and guarantee to take her out of the South Island, they'd pay our traveling expenses and an additional five hundred pounds.

"Well, Father, it was a fortune to me, and I was tired of the single life. But I was always so shy I was never any good with the girls. It seemed like a good idea to me, and I honestly didn't mind the child. The grandmother got wind of it and sent for me, even though she was very ill. She was a tartar in her day, I'll bet, but a real lady. She told me a bit about Fee, but she didn't say who the father was, and I didn't like to ask. Anyway, she made me promise to be good to Fee

—she knew they'd have Fee off the place the minute she was dead, so she had suggested to James that they find Fee a husband. I felt sorry for the poor old thing; she was terribly fond of Fee.

"Would you believe, Father, that the first time I was ever close enough to Fee to say hello to her was the day I married her?"

"Oh, I'd believe it," the priest said under his breath. He looked at the liquid in his glass, then drained it and reached for the bottle, filling both glasses. "So you married a lady far above you, Paddy."

"Yes. I was frightened to death of her at first. She was so beautiful in those days, Father, and so . . . out of it, if you know what I mean. As if she wasn't even there, as if it was all happening to someone else."

"She's still beautiful, Paddy," said Father Ralph gently. "I can see in Meggie what she must have been like before she began to age."

"It hasn't been an easy life for her, Father, but I don't know what else I could have done. At least with me she was safe, and not abused. It took me two years to get up the courage to be—well, a real husband to her. I had to teach her to cook, to sweep a floor, wash and iron clothes. She didn't know how.

"And never once in all the years we've been married, Father, has she ever complained, or laughed, or cried. It's only in the most private part of our life together that she ever displays any feeling, and even then she never speaks. I hope she will, yet I don't want her to, because I always have the idea if she did, it would be *his* name she'd say. Oh, I don't mean she doesn't like me, or our children. But I love her so much, and it just seems to me she hasn't got that sort of feeling left in her. Except for Frank. I've always known she loved Frank more than the rest of us put together. She must have loved his father. But I don't know a thing about the man, who he was, why she couldn't marry him."

Father Ralph looked down at his hands, blinking.

"Oh, Paddy, what hell it is to be alive! Thank God I haven't the courage to try more than the fringe of it."

Paddy got up, rather unsteadily. "Well, I've done it now, Father, haven't I? I've sent Frank away, and Fee will never forgive me."

"You can't tell her, Paddy. No, you mustn't tell her, ever. Just tell her Frank ran away with the boxers and leave it at that. She knows how restless Frank's been; she'll believe you."

"I couldn't do that, Father!" Paddy was aghast.

"You've got to, Paddy. Hasn't she known enough pain and misery? Don't heap more on her head." And to himself he thought: Who knows? Maybe she'll learn to give the love she has for Frank to you at last, to you and the little thing upstairs.

"You really think that, Father?"

"I do. What happened tonight must go no further."

"But what about Meggie? She heard it all."

"Don't worry about Meggie, I'll take care of her. I don't think she understood more of what went on than that you and Frank quarreled. I'll make her see that with Frank gone, to tell her mother of the quarrel would only be an additional grief. Besides, I have a feeling Meggie doesn't tell her mother much to begin with." He got up. "Go to bed, Paddy. You've got to seem normal and dance attendance on Mary tomorrow, remember?"

Meggie was not asleep; she was lying with eyes wide in the dim light of the little lamp beside her bed. The priest sat down beside her and noticed her hair still in its braids. Carefully he untied the navy ribbons and pulled gently until the hair lay in a rippling, molten sheet across the pillow.

"Frank has gone away, Meggie," he said.

"I know, Father."

"Do you know why, darling?"

"He had a fight with Daddy."

"What are you going to do?"

"I'm going to go with Frank. He needs me."

"You can't, my Meggie."

"Yes, I can. I was going to find him tonight, but my legs wouldn't hold me up, and I don't like the dark. But in the morning I'll look for him."

"No, Meggie, you mustn't. You see, Frank's got his own life to lead, and it's time he went away. I know you don't want him to go away, but he's been wanting to go for a long time. You mustn't be selfish; you've got to let him live his own life." The monotony of repetition, he thought, keep on drumming it in. "When we grow up it's natural and right for us to want a life away from the home we grew up in, and Frank is a grown man. He ought to have his own home now, his own wife and family. Do you see that, Meggie? The fight between your daddy and Frank was only a sign of Frank's wanting to go. It didn't happen because they don't like each other. It happened because that's the way a lot of young men leave home, it's a sort of excuse. The fight was just an excuse for Frank to do what he's been wanting to do for a long time, an excuse for Frank to leave. Do you understand that, my Meggie?"

Her eyes shifted to his face and rested there. They were so exhausted, so full of pain, so *old*. "I know," she said. "I know. Frank wanted to go away when I was a little girl, and he didn't go. Daddy brought him back and made him stay with us."

"But this time Daddy isn't going to bring him back, because Daddy can't make him stay now. Frank has gone for good, Meggie. He isn't coming back."

"Won't I ever see him again?"

"I don't know," he answered honestly. "I'd like to say of course you will, but no one can predict the future, Meggie, even priests." He drew a breath. "You mustn't tell Mum there was a fight, Meggie, do you hear me? It would upset her very much, and she isn't well."

"Because there's going to be another baby?"

"What do you know about that?"

"Mum likes growing babies; she's done it a lot. And she grows such nice babies, Father, even when she isn't well. I'm going to grow one like Hal myself, then I won't miss Frank so much, will I?"

"Parthenogenesis," he said. "Good luck, Meggie. Only what if you don't manage to grow one?"

"I've still got Hal," she said sleepily, nestling down. Then she said, "Father, will you go away, too? Will you?"

"One day, Meggie. But not soon, I think, so don't worry. I have a feeling I'm going to be stuck in Gilly for a long, long time," answered the priest, his eyes bitter.

6

There was no help for it, Meggie had to come home. Fee could not manage without her, and the moment he was left alone at the convent in Gilly, Stuart went on a hunger strike, so he too came back to Drogheda.

It was August, and bitterly cold. Just a year since they had arrived in Australia; but this was a colder winter than last. The rain was absent and the air was so crisp it hurt the lungs. Up on the tops of the Great Divide three hundred miles to the east, snow lay thicker than in many years, but no rain had fallen west of Burren Junction since the monsoonal drenching of the previous summer. People in Gilly were speaking of another drought: it was overdue, it must come, perhaps this would be it.

When Meggie saw her mother, she felt as if an awful weight settled upon her being; maybe a leaving-behind of childhood, a presentiment of what it was to be a woman. Outwardly there was no change, aside from the big belly; but inwardly Fee had slowed down like a tired old clock, running time down and down until it was forever stilled. The briskness Meggie had never known absent from her mother had gone. She picked her feet up and put them down again as if she was no longer sure of the right way to do it, a sort of spiritual fumbling got into her gait; and there was no joy in her for the coming baby, not even the rigidly controlled content she had shown over Hal.

That little red-haired fellow was toddling all over the house, constantly into everything, but Fee made no attempt to discipline him, or even supervise his activities. She plodded in her self-perpetuating circle of stove, worktable and sink as if nothing else existed. So Meggie had no choice; she simply filled the vacuum in the child's life and became his mother. It wasn't any sacrifice, for she loved him dearly and found him a helpless, willing target for all the love she was beginning to want to lavish on some human creature. He cried for her, he spoke her name before all others, he lifted his arms to her to be picked up; it was so satisfying it filled her with joy. In spite of the drudgery, the knitting and mending and sewing, the washing, the ironing, the hens, all the other jobs she had to do, Meggie found her life very pleasant.

No one ever mentioned Frank, but every six weeks Fee would lift her head when she heard the mail call, and for a while be animated. Then Mrs. Smith would bring in their share of whatever had come, and when it contained no letter from Frank the small burst of painful interest would die.

There were two new lives in the house. Fee was delivered of twins, two more tiny red-haired Cleary boys, christened James and Patrick. The dearest little fellows, with their father's sunny disposition and his sweetness of nature, they became common property immediately they were born, for beyond giving them milk Fee took no interest in them. Soon their names were shortened to Jims and Patsy; they were prime favorites with the women up at the big house, the two spinster maids and the widowed childless housekeeper, who were starved for the deliciousness of babies. It was made magically easy for Fee to forget them—they had three very eager mothers—and as time went on it became the accepted thing that they should spend most of their waking hours up at the big house. Meggie just didn't have time to take them under her wing as well as managing Hal, who was extremely possessive. Not for him the awkward, unpracticed blandishments of Mrs. Smith, Minnie and Cat. Meggie was the loving nucleus of Hal's world; he wanted no one but Meggie, he would have no one but Meggie.

Bluey Williams traded in his lovely draft horses and his massive dray for a truck and the mail came every four weeks instead of every six, but there was never a word from Frank. And gradually his memory slipped a little, as memories do, even those with so much love attached to them; as if there is an unconscious healing process within the mind which mends up in spite of our desperate determination never to forget. To Meggie, an aching fading of the way Frank had looked, a blurring of the beloved lineaments to some fuzzy, saintlike image no more related to the real Frank than a holy-picture Christ to what must have been the Man. And to Fee, from out of those silent depths in which she had stilled the evolution of her soul, a substitution.

It came about so unobtrusively that no one noticed. For Fee kept herself folded up with quietness, and a total undemonstrativeness; the substitution was an inner thing no one had time to see, except the new object of her love, who made no outward sign. It was a hidden, unspoken thing between them, something to buffer their loneliness.

Perhaps it was inevitable, for of all her children Stuart was the only one like her. At fourteen he was as big a mystery to his father and brothers as Frank had been, but unlike Frank he engendered no hostility, no irritation. He did as he was told without complaint, worked as hard as anyone and created absolutely no ripples in the pool of Cleary life. Though his hair was red he was the darkest of all the boys, more mahogany, and his eyes were as clear as pale water in the shade, as if they reached all the way back in time to the very beginning, and saw everything as it really was. He was also the only one of Paddy's sons who promised adult handsomeness, though privately Meggie thought her Hal would outshine him when it came his turn to grow up. No one ever knew what Stuart was thinking; like Fee, he spoke little and never aired an opinion. And he had a curious knack of being utterly still, as still within himself as he was in body, and to Meggie, closest to him in age, it seemed he could go somewhere no one else could ever follow. Father Ralph expressed it another way.

"That lad isn't human!" he had exclaimed the day he dumped a hunger-striking Stuart back at Drogheda after he was left at the convent minus Meggie. "Did he say he wanted to go home? Did he say he missed Meggie? No! He just stopped eating and patiently waited for the reason why to sink into our thick skulls. Not once did he open his mouth to complain, and when I marched up to him and yelled did he want to go home, he simply smiled at me and nodded!"

But as time went on it was tacitly assumed that Stuart would not go out into the paddocks to work with Paddy and the other boys, even though in age he might have. Stu would remain on guard at the house, chop the wood, take care of the vegetable garden, do the milking—the huge number of duties the women had no time for with three babies in the house. It was prudent to have a man about the place, albeit a half-grown one; it gave proof of other men close by. For there were visitors—the clump of strange boots up the plank steps to the back veranda, a strange voice saying:

"Hullo, Missus, got a bit of tucker for a man?"

The Outback had swarms of them, swagmen humping their blueys from station to station, down from Queensland and up from Victoria, men who had lost their luck or were chary of holding a regular job, preferring to tramp on foot thousands of miles in search of only they knew what. Mostly they were decent fellows, who appeared, ate a huge meal, packed a bit of donated tea and sugar and flour in the folds of their blueys, then disappeared down the track headed for Barcoola or Narrengang, battered old billycans bouncing, skinny dogs belly down behind them. Australian itinerants rarely rode; they walked.

Occasionally a bad man would come, on the lookout for women whose men were away; with a view to robbery, not rape. Thus Fee kept a shotgun standing loaded in a corner of the kitchen where the babies couldn't get to it, and made sure she was closer to it than her visitor until her expert eye assessed his character. After Stuart was officially allotted the house as his domain, Fee passed the shotgun to him gladly.

Not all the visitors were swaggies, though they were in the majority; there was the Watkins man in his old model-T, for instance. He carried everything from horse liniment to fragrant soap unlike the rock-hard stuff Fee made in the laundry copper from fat and caustic; he had lavender water and eau de cologne, powders and creams for sun-dried faces. There were certain things one never dreamed of buying from anyone but the Watkins man; like his ointment, better by far than any drugstore or prescription salve, capable of healing anything from a rent in the side of a work dog to an ulcer on a human shin. The women would crowd around in every kitchen he visited, waiting eagerly for him to pop open his big suitcase of wares.

And there were other salesmen, less regular patrollers of the back-blocks than the Watkins man but equally welcome, hawking everything from tailor-made cigarettes and fancy pipes to whole bolts of material, sometimes even luridly seductive underwear and lavishly beribboned stays. They were so starved, these women of the Outback, limited to maybe one or two trips a year into the nearest town, far from the brilliant shops of Sydney, far from fashions and feminine furbelows.

Life seemed mostly flies and dust. There had not been any rain in a long time, even a sprinkle to settle the dust and drown the flies; for the less rain, the more flies, the more dust.

Every ceiling was festooned with long, lazily spinning helixes of sticky flypaper, black with bodies within a day of being tacked up. Nothing could be left uncovered for a moment without becoming either an orgy or a graveyard for the flies, and tiny speckles of fly dirt dewed the furniture, the walls, the Gillanbone General Store calendar.

And oh, the dust! There was no getting away from it, that fine-grained brown powder which seeped into even tightly lidded containers, dulled freshly washed hair, made the skin gritty, lay in the folds of clothes and curtains, smeared a film across polished tables which resettled the moment it was whisked away. The floors were thick with it, from carelessly wiped boots and the hot dry wind drifting it through the open doors and windows; Fee was forced to roll up her Persian carpets in the parlor and have Stuart nail down linoleum she bought sight unseen from the store in Gilly.

The kitchen, which took most of the traffic from outside, was floored in teak planks bleached to the color of old bones by endless scrubbing with a wire brush and lye soap. Fee and Meggie would strew it with sawdust Stuart carefully collected from the woodheap, sprinkle the sawdust with precious particles of water and sweep the damp, pungent-fragrant mess away out of doors, down off the veranda onto the vegetable garden, there to decompose itself to humus.

But nothing kept the dust at bay for long, and after a while the creek dried up to a string of waterholes, so that there was no water to be pumped up from it to kitchen or bathroom. Stuart took the tank truck out to the borehead and brought it back full, emptied it into one of the spare rain tanks, and the women had to get used to a different kind of horrible water on dishes and clothes and bodies, worse than muddy creek water. The rank, sulphur-smelling minerally stuff had to be wiped off dishes scrupulously, and made the hair dull and coarse, like straw. What little rain water they had was used strictly for drinking and cooking.

Father Ralph watched Meggie tenderly. She was brushing Patsy's curly red head, Jims standing obediently but a little rockily waiting for his turn, both pairs of bright blue eyes turned up to her adoringly. Just like a tiny mother, she was. It had to be a thing born in them, he mused, that peculiar obsession women had for infants, else at her age she would have regarded it as a duty rather than pure pleasure, and been off to do something more alluring as fast as she could. Instead she was deliberately prolonging the process, crimping Patsy's hair between her fingers to shape waves out of its unruliness. For a while the priest was charmed with her activity, then he whacked the side of his dusty boot with his crop and stared moodily off the veranda toward the big house, hidden by its ghost gums and vines, the profusion of station buildings and pepper trees which lay between its isolation and this hub of station life, the head stockman's residence. What plot was she weaving, that old spider up there at the center of her vast web?

"Father, you're not watching!" Meggie accused him.

"I'm sorry, Meggie. I was thinking." He turned back to her as she finished with Jims; the three of them stood watching him expectantly until he bent and scooped the twins up, one on either hip. "Let's go and see your Auntie Mary, shall we?"

Meggie followed him up the track carrying his crop and leading the chestnut mare; he toted the infants with easy familiarity and seemed not to mind, though it was almost a mile from the creek to the big house. At the cookhouse he relinquished the twins to an ecstatic Mrs. Smith and passed on up the walkway to the main house with Meggie by his side.

Mary Carson was sitting in her wing chair. She hardly ever moved from it these days; there was not the necessity any more with Paddy so capable of overseeing things. As Father Ralph came in holding Meggie's hand, her malevolent gaze beat the child's down; Father Ralph felt the increase in Meggie's pulse rate and squeezed her wrist sympathetically. The little girl dropped her aunt a clumsy curtsy, murmuring an inaudible greeting.

"Go to the kitchen, girl, have your tea with Mrs. Smith," said Mary Carson curtly.

"Why don't you like her?" Father Ralph asked as he sank into the chair he had come to think of as his own.

"Because you do," she answered.

"Oh, come now!" For once she made him feel at a loss. "She's just a waif, Mary."

"That's not what you see in her, and you know it."

The fine blue eyes rested on her sardonically; he was more at ease. "Do you think I tamper with children? I am, after all, a priest!"

"You're a man first, Ralph de Bricassart! Being a priest makes you feel safe, that's all."

Startled, he laughed. Somehow he couldn't fence with her today; it was as if she had found the chink in his armor, crept inside with her spider's poison. And he was changing, growing older perhaps, becoming reconciled to obscurity in Gillanbone. The fires were dying; or was it that he burned now for other things?

"I am not a man," he said. "I am a priest. . . . It's the heat, maybe, the dust and the flies. . . . But I am not a man, Mary. I'm a priest."

"Oh, Ralph, how you've changed!" she mocked. "Can this be Cardinal de Bricassart I hear?"

"It isn't possible," he said, a passing unhappiness in his eyes. "I don't think I want it anymore."

She began to laugh, rocking back and forth in her

chair, watching him. "Don't you, Ralph? Don't you? Well, I'll let you stew a little while longer, but your day of reckoning is coming, never doubt it. Not yet, not for two or three years, perhaps, but it will come. I'll be like the Devil, and offer you— Enough said! But never doubt I'll make you writhe. You're the most fascinating man I've ever met. You throw your beauty in our teeth, contemptuous of our foolishness. But I'll pin you to the wall on your own weakness, I'll make you sell yourself like any painted whore. Do you doubt it?"

He leaned back, smiling. "I don't doubt you'll try. But I don't think you know me as well as you think you do."

"Do I not? Time will tell, Ralph, and only time. I'm old; I have nothing but time left to me."

"And what do you think I have?" he asked. "Time, Mary, nothing but time. Time, and dust, and flies."

The clouds heaped themselves in the sky, and Paddy began to hope for rain.

"Dry storms," said Mary Carson. "We won't get rain out of this. We won't get any rain for a long time."

If the Clearys thought they had seen the worst that Australia could offer in the way of climatic harshness, it was because they hadn't yet experienced the dry storms of drought-dogged plains. Bereft of soothing dampness, the dryness of the earth and the air rubbed each other raw and crackling, an irritating friction which built up and up and up until it could end only in a gargantuan dissipation of accumulated energy. The sky dropped and darkened so much Fee had to light the lamps indoors; out in the stockyards the horses shivered and jumped at the slightest noise; the hens sought their perches and sank their heads into apprehensive breasts; the dogs fought and snarled; the tame pigs which rooted among the rubbish of the station dump burrowed their snouts into the dust and peered out of it with bright, skittish eyes. Brooding forces pent in the heavens struck fear into the bones of all living things, as the vast deep clouds swallowed the sun whole and prepared to spew solar fire over the earth.

Thunder came marching from far away with increasing tread, tiny flickers on the horizon cast soaring billows into sharp relief, crests of startling whiteness foamed and curled over midnight-blue depths. Then, with a roaring wind that sucked up the dust and flung it stinging in eyes and ears and mouths, came the cataclysm. No longer did they try to imagine the biblical wrath of God; they lived through it. No man could have kept himself from jumping when the thunder cracked—it exploded with the noise and fury of a disintegrating world—but after a while the assembled household grew so inured to it they crept out onto the veranda and stared across the creek at the far paddocks. Great forks of lightning stood ribbed in veins of fire all around the sky, dozens of bolts each and every moment; naphtha flashes in chains streaked across the clouds, in and out the billows in a fantastic hide-and-seek. Blasted trees alone in the grass reeked and smoked, and they understood at last why these lonely paddock sentinels were dead.

An eerie, unearthly glow seeped into the air, air which was no longer invisible but on fire from within, fluorescing pink and lilac and sulphur yellow, and smelling of some hauntingly sweet, elusive perfume quite beyond recognition. The trees shimmered, the red Cleary hair was haloed in tongues of fire, the hairs of their arms stood out stiffly. And all afternoon it went on, only slowly fading into the east to release them from its awesome spell at sunset, and they were excited, on edge, unappeased. Not a drop of rain had fallen. But it was like dying and coming back to life again, to have survived the atmospheric tantrum unscathed; it was all they could talk about for a week.

"We'll get a lot more," said Mary Carson, bored.

They did get a lot more. The second dry winter came

in colder than they had thought it could get without snow; frost settled inches thick on the ground at night, and the dogs huddled shivering in their kennels, keeping warm by gorging on kangaroo meat and mounds of fat from the homestead's slaughtered cattle. At least the weather meant beef and pork to eat instead of the eternal mutton. In the house they built great roaring fires, and the men were forced to come home when they could, for at night in the paddocks they froze. But the shearers when they arrived were in a mood for rejoicing; they could get through faster and sweat less. At each man's stand in the great shed was a circle of flooring much lighter in color than the rest, the spot where fifty years of shearers had stood dripping their bleaching sweat into the wood of the board.

There was still grass from the flood long ago, but it was thinning ominously. Day after day the skies were overcast and the light dull, but it never rained. The wind howled sadly across the paddocks, spinning drifting brown sheets of dust before it like rain, tormenting the mind with images of water. So much like rain it looked, that raggedly blowing dust.

The children developed chilblains on their fingers, tried not to smile with cracked lips, had to peel their socks away from bleeding heels and shins. It was quite impossible to keep warm in the face of that bitter high wind, especially when the houses had been designed to catch every stray puff of air, not keep it out. Going to bed in icy bedrooms, getting up in icy bedrooms, waiting patiently for Mum to spare a little hot water from the great kettle on the hob so that washing was not a teeth-chattering, painful ordeal.

One day small Hal started to cough and wheeze, and rapidly grew worse. Fee mixed up a gluey hot poultice of charcoal and spread it on his laboring little chest, but it seemed to give him no relief. At first she was not unduly worried, but as the day drew on he began to deteriorate so quickly she no longer had any idea what to do, and Meggie sat by his side wringing her hands, praying a wordless stream of Our Fathers and Hail Marys. When Paddy came in at six the child's breathing was audible from the veranda, and his lips were blue.

Paddy set off at once for the big house and the telephone, but the doctor was forty miles away and out on another case. They ignited a pan of sulphur and held him over it in an attempt to make him cough up the membrane in his throat slowly choking him, but he could not manage to contract his rib cage enough to dislodge it. His color was growing a deeper blue, his respiration was convulsive. Meggie sat holding him and praying, her heart squeezed to a wedge of pain because the poor little fellow fought so for every breath. Of all the children, Hal was the dearest to her; she was his mother. Never before had she wished so desperately to be a grown-up mother, thinking that were she a woman like Fee, she would somehow have the power to heal him. Fee couldn't heal him because Fee wasn't his mother. Confused and terrified, she held the heaving little body close, trying to help Hal breathe.

It never occurred to her that he might die, even when Fee and Paddy sank to their knees by the bed and prayed, not knowing what else to do. At midnight Paddy pried Meggie's arms from around the still child, and laid him down tenderly against the stack of pillows.

Meggie's eyes flew open; she had half fallen to sleep, lulled because Hal had stopped struggling. "Oh, Daddy, he's better!" she said.

Paddy shook his head; he seemed shriveled and old, the lamp picking up frosty bits in his hair, frosty bits in his week-long beard. "No, Meggie, Hal's not better in the way you mean, but he's at peace. He's gone to God, he's out of his pain."

"Daddy means he's dead," said Fee tonelessly.

"Oh, Daddy, no! He can't be *dead!*"

But the small creature in the pillowed nest was dead.

Meggie knew it the moment she looked, though she had never seen death before. He looked like a doll, not a child. She got up and went out to the boys, sitting hunched in an uneasy vigil around the kitchen fire, with Mrs. Smith on a hard chair nearby keeping an eye on the tiny twins, whose cot had been moved into the kitchen for warmth.

"Hal just died," said Meggie.

Stuart looked up from a distant reverie. "It's better so," he said. "Think of the peace." He got to his feet as Fee came out of the hallway, and went to her without touching her. "Mum, you must be tired. Come and lie down; I'll light a fire for you in your room. Come on now, lie down."

Fee turned and followed him without a word. Bob got up and went out onto the veranda. The rest of the boys sat shuffling for a while and then joined him. Paddy hadn't appeared at all. Without a word Mrs. Smith took the perambulator from its corner of the veranda and carefully put the sleeping Jims and Patsy into it. She looked across at Meggie, tears running down her face.

"Meggie, I'm going back to the big house, and I'm taking Jims and Patsy with me. I'll be back in the morning, but it's best if the babies stay with Minnie and Cat and me for a while. Tell your mother."

Meggie sat down on a vacant chair and folded her hands in her lap. Oh, he was hers and he was dead! Little Hal, whom she had cared for and loved and mothered. The space in her mind he had occupied was not yet empty; she could still feel the warm weight of him against her chest. It was terrible to know the weight would never rest there again, where she had felt it for four long years. No, not a thing to cry over; tears were for Agnes, for wounds in the fragile sheath of self-esteem, and the childhood she had left behind forever. This was a burden she would have to carry until the end of her days, and continue in spite of it.

The will to survive is very strong in some, not so strong in others. In Meggie it was as refined and tensile as a steel hawser.

Just so did Father Ralph find her when he came in with the doctor. She pointed silently to the hallway but made no effort to follow them. And it was a long time before the priest could finally do what he had wanted to do since Mary Carson phoned the presbytery; go to Meggie, be with her, give the poor little female outsider something from himself for her very own. He doubted that anyone else fully appreciated what Hal meant to her.

But it was a long time. There were the last rites to be administered, in case the soul had not yet left the body; and Fee to see, Paddy to see, practical advice to give. The doctor had gone, dejected but long used to the tragedies his far-flung practice made inevitable. From what they said, little he could have done anyway, so far from his hospital and his trained nursing staff. These people took their chances, they faced their demons and hung on. His death certificate would say "Croup." It was a handy malady.

Eventually there was nothing left for Father Ralph to see to. Paddy had gone to Fee, Bob and the boys to the carpentry shed to make the little coffin. Stuart was on the floor in Fee's bedroom, his pure profile so like her own silhouetted against the night sky outside the window; from where she lay on her pillow with Paddy's hand in hers, Fee never left her contemplation of the dark shape huddled on the cold floor. It was five o'clock in the morning and the roosters were stirring drowsily, but it would be dark for a long time yet.

Purple stole around his neck because he had forgotten he was wearing it, Father Ralph bent to the kitchen fire and built it up from embers into a blaze, turned down the lamp on the table behind, and sat on a wooden bench opposite Meggie to watch her. She had grown, put on seven-league boots which threatened to leave him behind, outstripped; he felt his inadequacy then more keenly, watching her, than ever he had in a life filled with a gnawing, obsessive doubt of his courage. Only *what* was he afraid of? What did he think he couldn't face if it came? He could be strong for other people, he didn't fear other people; but within himself, expecting that nameless something to come sliding into consciousness when he least expected it, he knew fear. While Meggie, born eighteen years after him, was growing beyond him.

Not that she was a saint, or indeed anything more than most. Only that she never complained, that she had the gift—or was it the curse?—of acceptance. No matter what had gone or what might come, she confronted it and accepted it, stored it away to fuel the furnace of her being. What had taught her that? Could it be taught? Or was his idea of her a figment of his own fantasies? Did it really matter? Which was more important: what she truly was, or what he thought she was?

"Oh, Meggie," he said helplessly.

She turned her gaze to him and out of her pain gave him a smile of absolute, overflowing love, nothing in it held back, the taboos and inhibitions of womanhood not yet a part of her world. To be so loved shook him, consumed him, made him wish to the God Whose existence he sometimes doubted that he was anyone in the universe but Ralph de Bricassart. Was this it, the unknown thing? Oh, God, why did he love her so? But as usual no one answered him; and Meggie sat still smiling at him.

At dawn Fee got up to make breakfast, Stuart helping her, then Mrs. Smith came back with Minnie and Cat, and the four women stood together by the stove talking in hushed monotones, bound in some league of grief neither Meggie nor the priest understood. After the meal Meggie went to line the little wooden box the boys had made, planed smooth and varnished. Silently Fee had given her a white satin evening gown long since gone to the hue of ivory with age, and she fitted strips of it to the hard contours of the box interior. While Father Ralph put a toweling padding in it she ran the pieces of satin into shape on the sewing machine, then together they fixed the lining in place with thumbtacks. And after that Fee dressed her baby in his best velvet suit, combed his hair and laid him in the soft nest which smelled of her, but not of Meggie, who had been his mother. Paddy closed down the lid, weeping; this was the first child he had lost.

For years the reception room at Drogheda had been in use as a chapel; an altar had been built at one end, and was draped in golden raiment Mary Carson had paid the nuns of St. Mary d'Urso a thousand pounds to embroider. Mrs. Smith had decked the room and the altar with winter flowers from Drogheda's gardens, wallflowers and early stocks and late roses, masses of them like pink and rusty paintings magically finding the dimension of scent. In a laceless white alb and a black chasuble free of any ornamentation, Father Ralph said the Requiem Mass.

As with most of the great Outback stations, Drogheda buried its dead on its own land. The cemetery lay beyond the gardens by the willow-littered banks of the creek, bounded by a white-painted wrought-iron railing and green even in this dry time, for it was watered from the homestead tanks. Michael Carson and his baby son were entombed there in an imposing marble vault, a life-size angel on top of its pediment with sword drawn to guard their rest. But perhaps a dozen less pretentious plots ringed the mausoleum, marked only by plain white wooden crosses and white croquet hoops to define their neat boundaries, some of them bare even of a name: a shearer with no known relatives who had died in a barracks brawl; two or three swaggies whose last earthly calling place had been Drogheda; some sexless and totally anonymous bones found in one of the paddocks;

Michael Carson's Chinese cook, over whose remains stood a quaint scarlet umbrella, whose sad small bells seemed perpetually to chime out the name Hee Sing, Hee Sing, Hee Sing; a drover whose cross said only TANKSTAND CHARLIE HE WAS A GOOD BLOKE; and more besides, some of them women. But such simplicity was not for Hal, the owner's nephew; they stowed his home-made box on a shelf inside the vault and closed elaborate bronze doors upon it.

After a while everyone ceased to speak of Hal except in passing. Meggie's sorrow she kept exclusively to herself; her pain had the unreasoning desolation peculiar to children, magnified and mysterious, yet her very youth buried it beneath everyday events, and diminished its importance. The boys were little affected save Bob, who had been old enough to be fond of his tiny brother. Paddy grieved deeply, but no one knew whether Fee grieved. It seemed she grew further and further away from husband and children, from all feeling. Because of this, Paddy was so grateful to Stu for the way he minded his mother, the grave tenderness with which he treated her. Only Paddy knew how Fee had looked the day he came back from Gilly without Frank. There had not been a flicker of emotion in those soft grey eyes, not hardening nor accusation, hate or sorrow. As if she had simply been waiting for the blow to fall like a condemned dog for the killing bullet, knowing her fate and powerless to avoid it.

"I knew he wouldn't come back," she said.

"Maybe he will, Fee, if you write to him quickly," Paddy said.

She shook her head, but being Fee went into no explanations. Better that Frank made a new life for himself far from Drogheda and her. She knew her son well enough to be convinced that one word from her would bring him back, so she must not utter that word, ever. If the days were long and bitter with a sense of failure, she must bear it in silence. Paddy hadn't been the man of her choice, but a better man than Paddy never lived. She was one of those people whose feelings are so intense they become unbearable, unlivable, and her lesson had been a harsh one. For almost twenty-five years she had been crushing emotion out of existence, and she was convinced that in the end persistence would succeed.

Life went on in the rhythmic, endless cycle of the land; the following summer the rains came, not monsoonal but a by-product of them, filling the creek and the tanks, succoring the thirsting grass roots, sponging away the stealthy dust. Almost weeping in joy, the men went about the business of the patterned seasons, secure in the knowledge they would not have to hand-feed the sheep. The grass had lasted just long enough, eked out by scrub-cutting from the more juicy trees; but it was not so on all the Gilly stations. How many stock a station carried depended entirely on the grazier running it. For its great size Drogheda was understocked, which meant the grass lasted just that much longer.

Lambing and the hectic weeks that followed it were busiest of all in the sheep calendar. Every lamb born had to be caught; its tail was ringed, its ear marked, and if it was a male not required for breeding it was also castrated. Filthy, abominable work which soaked them to the skin with blood, for there was only one way to wade through thousands upon thousands of male lambs in the short time available. The testicles were popped out between the fingers and bitten off, spat on the ground. Circled by tin bands incapable of expanding, the tails of male and female lambs alike gradually lost their vital bloody supply, swelled, withered and dropped off.

These were the finest wool sheep in the world, raised on a scale unheard of in any other country, and with a paucity of manpower. Everything was geared to the perfect production of perfect wool. There was crutching; around the sheep's rear end the wool grew foul with excrement, fly-blown, black and lumped together in what were called dags. This area had to be kept shaven close, or crutched. It was a minor shearing job but one far less pleasing, stinking and fly-ridden, and it paid better rates. Then there was dipping: thousands upon thousands of bleating, leaping creatures were hounded and yanked through a maze of runs, in and out of the phenyl dips which rid them of ticks, pests and vermin. And drenching: the administration of medicine through huge syringes rammed down the throat, to rid the sheep of intestinal parasites.

For work with the sheep never, never ended; as one job finished it became time for another. They were mustered and graded, moved from one paddock to another, bred and unbred, shorn and crutched, dipped and drenched, slaughtered and shipped off to be sold. Drogheda carried about a thousand head of prime beef cattle as well as its sheep, but sheep were far more profitable, so in good times Drogheda carried about one sheep for every two acres of its land, or about 125,000 altogether. Being merinos, they were never sold for meat; at the end of a merino's wool-producing years it was shipped off to become skins, lanolin, tallow and glue, useful only to the tanneries and the knackeries.

Thus it was that gradually the classics of Bush literature took on meaning. Reading had become more important than ever to the Clearys, isolated from the world on Drogheda; their only contact with it was through the magic written word. But there was no lending library close, as there had been in Wahine, no weekly trip into town for mail and newspapers and a fresh stack of library books, as there had been in Wahine. Father Ralph filled the breach by plundering the Gillanbone library, his own and the convent's shelves, and found to his astonishment that before he was done he had organized a whole Bush circulating library via Bluey Williams and the mail truck. It was perpetually loaded with books—worn, thumbed volumes which traveled down the tracks between Drogheda and Bugela, Dibban-Dibban and Braich y Pwll, Cunnamutta and Each-Uisge, seized upon gratefully by minds starved for sustenance and escape. Treasured stories were always returned with great reluctance, but Father Ralph and the nuns kept a careful record of what books stayed longest where, then Father Ralph would order copies through the Gilly news agency and blandly charge them to Mary Carson as donations to the Holy Cross Bush Bibliophilic Society.

Those were the days when a book was lucky to contain a chaste kiss, when the senses were never titillated by erotic passages, so that the demarcation line between books meant for adults and those meant for older children was less strictly drawn, and there was no disgrace for a man of Paddy's age to love best the books his children also adored: *Dot and the Kangaroo,* the *Billabong* series about Jim and Norah and Wally, Mrs. Aeneas Gunn's immortal *We of the Never-Never.* In the kitchen at night they would take turns to read the poems of Banjo Paterson and C. J. Dennis out loud, thrilling to the ride of "The Man from Snowy River," or laughing with "The Sentimental Bloke" and his Doreen, or wiping away surreptitious tears shed for John O'Hara's "Laughing Mary."

I had written him a letter which I had, for want of better
Knowledge, sent to where I met him down the Lachlan years ago;
He was shearing when I knew him, so I sent the letter to him,
Just on spec, addressed as follows, "Clancy, of the Overflow."

And an answer came directed in a writing
unexpected
(And I think the same was written with a
thumb-nail dipped in tar);
'Twas his shearing mate who wrote it, and
verbatim I will quote it:
"Clancy's gone to Queensland droving, and we
don't know where he are."

In my wild erratic fancy visions come to me of
Clancy
Gone a-droving "down the Cooper" where the
Western drovers go;
As the stock are slowly stringing Clancy rides
behind them singing,
For the drover's life has pleasures that the
townsfolk never know.
And the bush has friends to meet him, and their
kindly voices greet him
In the murmur of the breezes and the river on
its bars,
And he sees the vision splendid of the sunlit plains
extended,
And at night the wondrous glory of the
everlasting stars.

"Clancy of the Overflow" was everyone's favorite, "the Banjo" their favorite poet. Hoppity-go-kick doggerel, perhaps, but the poems had never been intended for the eyes of sophisticated savants; they were for the people, of the people, and more Australians of that day could recite them off by heart than knew the standard schoolroom pieces by Tennyson and Wordsworth, for their brand of hoppity-go-kick doggerel was written with England as inspiration. Crowds of daffodils and fields of asphodel meant nothing to the Clearys, living in a climate where neither could exist.

The Clearys understood the bush poets better than

most, for the Overflow was their backyard, the traveling sheep a reality on the TSRs. There was an official Traveling Stock Route or TSR winding its way near the Barwon River, free crown land for the transference of living merchandise from one end of the eastern half of the continent to the other. In the old days drovers and their hungry, grass-ruining mobs of stock had not been welcome, and the bullockies a hated breed as they inched their mammoth teams of from twenty to eighty oxen through the middle of the squatters' best grazing. Now, with official stock routes for the drovers and the bullockies vanished into legend, things were more amicable between vagabonds and stay-puts.

The occasional drovers were welcomed as they rode in for a beer and a talk, a home-cooked meal. Sometimes they brought women with them, driving battered old sulkies with galled ex-stock horses between the shafts, pots and billies and bottles banging and clanking in a fringe all around. These were the most cheerful or the most morose women in the Outback, drifting from Kynuna to the Paroo, from Goondiwindi to Gundagai, from the Katherine to the Curry. Strange women; they never knew a roof over their heads or the feel of a kapok mattress beneath their iron-hard spines. No man had bested them; they were as tough and enduring as the country which flowed under their restless feet. Wild as the birds in the sun-drenched trees, their children skulked shyly behind the sulky wheels or scuttled for the protection of the woodheap while their parents yarned over cups of tea, swapped tall stories and books, promised to pass on vague messages to Hoopiron Collins or Brumby Waters, and told the fantastic tale of the Pommy jackaroo on Gnarlunga. And somehow you could be sure these rootless wanderers had dug a grave, buried a child or a wife, a husband or a mate, under some never-to-be-forgotten coolibah on a stretch of the TSR which only looked the same to those who didn't know how hearts could mark out as singular and special one tree in a wilderness of trees.

Meggie was ignorant even of the meaning of a phrase as hackneyed as "the facts of life," for circumstances had conspired to block every avenue whereby she might have learned. Her father drew a rigid line between the males of the family and the females; subjects like breeding or mating were never discussed in front of the women, nor did the men ever appear in front of the women unless fully clothed. The kind of books that might have given her a clue never appeared on Drogheda, and she had no friends of her own age to contribute to her education. Her life was absolutely harnessed to the needs of the house, and around the house there were no sexual activities at all. The Home Paddock creatures were almost literally sterile. Mary Carson didn't breed horses, she bought them from Martin King of Bugela, who did; unless one bred horses stallions were a nuisance, so Drogheda didn't have any stallions. It did have a bull, a wild and savage beast whose pen was strictly out of bounds, and Meggie was so frightened of it she never went anywhere near it. The dogs were kept kenneled and chained, their mating a scientific, supervised exercise conducted under Paddy's or Bob's eagle eye, therefore also out of bounds. Nor was there time to watch the pigs, which Meggie hated and resented having to feed. In truth, there wasn't time for Meggie to watch anyone beyond her two tiny brothers. And ignorance breeds ignorance; an unawakened body and mind sleep through events which awareness catalogues automatically.

Just before Meggie's fifteenth birthday, as the summer heat was building up toward its stupefying peak, she noticed brown, streaky stains on her drawers. After a day or two they went away, but six weeks later they came back, and her shame turned to terror. The first time she had thought them signs of a dirty bottom, thus her mortification, but in their second appearance they became unmistakably blood. She had no idea where the blood was coming from, but assumed it was her bottom. The slow hemorrhage was gone three days later, and did not recur for over two months; her furtive washing of the drawers had gone unnoticed, for she did most of the laundry anyway. The next attack brought pain, the first non-bilious rigors of her life. And the bleeding was worse, far worse. She stole some of the twins' discarded diapers and tried to bind herself under her drawers, terrified the blood would come through.

Death taking Hal had been like a tempestuous visit from something ghostly; but this strung-out cessation of her own being was terrifying. How could she possibly go to Fee or Paddy to break the news that she was dying from some disreputable, forbidden disease of the bottom? Only to Frank might she have poured out her torment, but Frank was so far away she didn't know where to find him. She had listened to the women talk over their cups of tea of tumors and cancers, gruesome lingering deaths their friends or mothers or sisters had endured, and it seemed to Meggie sure to be some kind of growth eating her insides away, chewing silently up toward her frightened heart. Oh, she didn't want to die!

Her ideas about the condition of death were vague; she wasn't even clear on what her status would be in that incomprehensible other world. Religion to Meggie was a set of laws rather than a spiritual experience, it couldn't help her at all. Words and phrases jostled piecemeal in her panicked consciousness, uttered by her parents, their friends, the nuns, priests in sermons, bad men in books threatening vengeance. There was no way she could come to terms with death; she lay night after night in a confused terror, trying to imagine if death was perpetual night, or an abyss of flames she had to jump over to reach the golden fields on the far side, or a sphere like the inside of a gigantic balloon full of soaring choirs and light attenuated through limitless stained-glass windows.

She grew very quiet, but in a manner quite different from Stuart's peaceful, dreamy isolation; hers was the petrified freezing of an animal caught in the serpent's basilisk stare. If she was spoken to suddenly she jumped, if the little ones cried for her she fussed over them in an agony of expiation for her neglect. And whenever she had a rare moment to herself she ran away, down to the cemetery and Hal, who was the only dead person she knew.

Everyone noticed the change in her, but accepted it as Meggie growing up without once asking themselves what growing up for Meggie entailed; she hid her distress too well. The old lessons had been well learned; her self-control was phenomenal and her pride formidable. No one must ever know what went on inside her, the façade must continue flawless to the end; from Fee to Frank to Stuart the examples were there, and she was of the same blood, it was a part of her nature and her heritage.

But as Father Ralph paid his frequent visits to Drogheda and the change in Meggie deepened from a pretty feminine metamorphosis to a quenching of all her vitality, his concern for her mushroomed into worry, and then into fear. A physical and spiritual wasting away was taking place beneath his very eyes; she was slipping away from them, and he couldn't bear to see her become another Fee. The small pointed face was all eyes staring at some dreadful prospect, the milky opaque skin which never tanned or freckled was growing more translucent. If the process went on, he thought, she would one day disappear into her own eyes like a snake swallowing its tail, until she drifted through the universe as an almost invisible shaft of glassy grey light, seen only from the corner of the vision where shadows lurk and black things crawl down a white wall.

Well, he would find out if he had to wring it from her forcibly. Mary Carson was at her most demanding these days, jealous of every moment he spent down at the head stockman's house; only the infinite patience of a subtle, devious man kept his rebellion against her possessiveness hidden from her. Even his alien preoccupation with Meggie couldn't always overcome his politic wisdom, the purring content he derived from watching his charm work on such a cantankerous, refractory subject as Mary Carson. While that long-dormant care for the welfare of a single other person champed and stamped up and down his mind, he acknowledged the existence of another entity dwelling side by side with it: the cat-cold cruelty of getting the better of, making a fool of a conceited, masterful woman. Oh, he'd always liked to do that! The old spider would never get the better of him.

Eventually he managed to shake free of Mary Carson and run Meggie to earth in the little graveyard under the shadow of the pallid, unwarlike avenging angel. She was staring up into its mawkishly placid face with shrinking fear written on her own, an exquisite contrast between the feeling and the unfeeling, he thought. But what was he *doing* here, chasing after her like a clucky old hen when it was really none of his business, when it ought to be her mother or her father to find out what was the matter? Only that they hadn't seen anything wrong, that she didn't matter to them the way she mattered to him. And that he was a priest, he must give comfort to the lonely or the despairing in spirit. He couldn't bear to see her unhappy, yet he shrank from the way he was tying himself to her by an accumulation of events. He was making a whole arsenal of happenings and memories out of her, and he was afraid. His love for her and his priestly instinct to offer himself in any required spiritual capacity warred with an obsessive horror of becoming utterly necessary to someone human, and of having someone human become utterly necessary to himself.

As she heard him walk across the grass she turned to confront him, folding her hands in her lap and looking down at her feet. He sat near her, arms locked around his knees, the soutane in folds no more graceful than the easy length of the body inhabiting it. No sense beating around the bush, he decided; if she could, she would evade him.

"What's the matter, Meggie?"

"Nothing, Father."

"I don't believe you."

"Please, Father, please! I *can't* tell you!"

"Oh, Meggie! Ye of little faith! You can tell me anything, anything under the sun. That's what I'm here for, that's why I'm a priest. I am Our Lord's chosen representative here on earth, I listen on His behalf, I even forgive on His behalf. And, wee Meggie, there is nothing in God's universe He and I cannot find it in our hearts to forgive. You must tell me what the matter is, my love, because if anyone can help you, *I* can. As long as I live I'll try to help you, watch over you. If you like, a sort of guardian angel, better by far than that chunk of marble above your head." He took a breath and leaned forward. "Meggie, if you love me, *tell* me!"

Her hands gripped one another. "Father, I'm dying! I've got cancer!"

First came a wild desire to laugh, a great surge of uproarious anticlimax; then he looked at the thin blue skin, the wasting of her little arms, and there came an awful longing to weep and cry, scream of its unfairness to the roof of heaven. No, Meggie wouldn't imagine this out of nothing; there had to be a valid reason.

"How do you know, dear heart?"

It took her a long time to say it, and when she did he had to bend his head right down to her lips in an unconscious parody of the confessional pose, hand shielding his face from her eyes, finely modeled ear presented for the sullying.

"It's six months, Father, since it started. I get the most awful pains in my tummy, but not like a bilious attack, and—oh, Father!—a lot of blood runs out of my bottom!"

His head reared back, something which had never happened inside the confessional; he stared down at her shamed bent head with so many emotions assaulting him that he could not marshal his wits. An absurd, delicious relief; an anger at Fee so great he wanted to kill her; awed admiration for such a little thing as her, to bear so much so well; and a ghastly, all-pervasive embarrassment.

He was as much a prisoner of the times as she was. The cheap girls in every town he had known from Dublin to Gillanbone would deliberately come into the confessional to whisper their fantasies to him as actual happenings, concerned with the only facet of him which interested them, his manhood, and not willing to admit it lay beyond their power to arouse it. They muttered of men violating every orifice, of illicit games with other girls, of lust and adultery, one or two of superior imagination even going so far as to detail sexual relations with a priest. And he would listen totally unmoved save for a sick contempt, for he had been through the rigors of the seminary and that particular lesson was an easy one for a man of his type. But the girls, never, never mentioned that secret activity which set them apart, demeaned them.

Try as he would, he could not prevent the scorching tide from diffusing up under his skin; Father Ralph de Bricassart sat with his face turned away behind his hand and writhed through the humiliation of his first blush.

But this wasn't helping his Meggie. When he was sure the color had subsided he got to his feet, picked her up and sat her on a flat-topped marble pedestal, where her face and his were level.

"Meggie, look at me. No, *look* at me!"

She raised hunted eyes and saw that he was smiling; an immeasurable contentment filled her soul at once. He would not smile so if she were dying; she knew very well how much she meant to him, for he had never concealed it.

"Meggie, you're not dying and you haven't got cancer. It isn't my place to tell you what's the matter, but I think I had better. Your mother should have told you years ago, prepared you, and why she didn't is beyond me."

He looked up at the inscrutable marble angel above him and gave a peculiar, half-strangled laugh. "Dear Jesus! The things Thou givest me to do!" Then, to the waiting Meggie: "In years to come, as you grow older and learn more about the ways of the world, you might be tempted to remember today with embarrassment, even shame. But don't remember today like that, Meggie. There's absolutely nothing shameful or embarrassing about it. In this, as in everything I do, I am simply the instrument of Our Lord. It is my only function on this earth; I must admit no other. You were very frightened, you needed help, and Our Lord has sent you that help in my person. Remember that alone, Meggie. I am Our Lord's priest, and I speak in His Name.

"You're only doing what all women do, Meggie. Once a month for several days you'll pass blood. It starts usually around twelve or thirteen years of age—how old are you, as much as that?"

"I'm fifteen, Father."

"Fifteen? *You?*" He shook his head, only half believing her. "Well, if you say you are, I'll have to take your word for it. In which case you're later than most girls. But it continues every month until you're about fifty, and in some women it's as regular as the phases of the moon, in others it's not so predictable. Some women have no pain with it, others suffer a lot of pain. No one knows why it's so different from one woman to another. But to pass blood every month is a sign that you're mature. Do you know what 'mature' means?"

"Of course, Father! I read! It means grown up."

"All right, that will do. While ever the bleeding persists, you're capable of having children. The bleeding is a part of the cycle of procreation. In the days before the Fall, it is said Eve didn't menstruate. The proper name for it is menstruation, to menstruate. But when Adam and Eve fell, God punished the woman more than He did the man, because it was really her fault they fell. She tempted the man. Do you remember the words in your Bible history? 'In sorrow thou shalt bring forth children.' What God meant was that for a woman everything having to do with children involves pain. Great joy, but also great pain. It is your lot, Meggie, and you must accept it."

She didn't know it, but just so would he have offered comfort and help to any of his parishioners, if with a less intense personal involvement; so very kindly, but never identifying himself with the trouble. And, perhaps not so oddly, thereby the comfort and help he offered was all the greater. As if he had gone beyond such small things, so they were bound to pass. It was not a conscious thing in him, either; no one who came to him for succor ever felt that he looked down on them, or blamed them for their weaknesses. Many priests left their people feeling guilty, worthless or bestial, but he never did. For he made them think that he, too, had his sorrows and his struggles; alien sorrows and incomprehensible struggles, perhaps, yet no less real. He neither knew nor could have been brought to understand that the larger part of his appeal and attraction lay not in his person, but in this aloof, almost godlike, very human something from his soul.

As far as Meggie was concerned, he talked to her the way Frank had talked to her: as if she were his equal.

But he was older, wiser and far better educated than Frank, a more satisfactory confidant. And how beautiful his voice was, with its faint Irishness and pear-shaped Britishness. It took all the fear and anguish away. Yet she was young, full of curiosity, eager now to know all there was to know, and not troubled by the perplexing philosophies of those who constantly question not the *who* of themselves but the *why*. He was her friend, the cherished idol of her heart, the new sun in her firmament.

"Why shouldn't you tell me, Father? Why did you say it ought to be Mum?"

"It's a subject women keep very much to themselves. To mention menstruation or one's period in front of men or boys just isn't done, Meggie. It's something strictly between women."

"Why?"

He shook his head, and laughed. "To be honest, I really don't know why. I even wish it weren't so. But you must take my word for it that it is so. *Never* mention it to a soul except your mother, and don't tell her you discussed it with me."

"All right, Father, I won't."

It was damnably difficult, this being a mother; so many practical considerations to remember! "Meggie, you must go home and tell your mother you've been passing blood, and ask her to show you how to fix yourself up."

"*Mum* does it, too?"

"All healthy women do. But when they're expecting a baby they stop until after the baby is born. That's how women tell they're expecting babies."

"Why do they stop when they're expecting babies?"

"I don't know, I really don't. Sorry, Meggie."

"Why does the blood come out of my bottom, Father?"

He glared up at the angel, which looked back at him serenely, not troubled by women's troubles. Things were getting too sticky for Father Ralph. Amazing that she persisted when she was usually so reticent! Yet realizing he had become the source of her knowledge about everything she couldn't find in books, he knew her too well to give her any hint of his embarrassment or discomfort. She would withdraw into herself and never ask him anything again.

So he answered patiently, "It doesn't come out of your bottom, Meggie. There is a hidden passageway in front of your bottom, which has to do with children."

"Oh! Where they get out, you mean," she said. "I always wondered how they got out."

He grinned, and lifted her down from her pedestal. "Now you know. Do you know what makes babies, Meggie?"

"Oh, yes," she said importantly, glad she knew at least something. "You grow them, Father."

"What causes them to start growing?"

"You wish them."

"Who told you that?"

"No one. I worked it out for myself," she said.

Father Ralph closed his eyes and told himself that he couldn't possibly be called a coward for leaving matters where they stood. He could pity her, but he couldn't help her any further. Enough was enough.

7

Mary Carson was going to be seventy-two years old, and she was planning the biggest party to be held on Drogheda in fifty years. Her birthday fell at the start of November, when it was hot but still bearable—at least for Gilly natives.

"Mark that, Mrs. Smith!" Minnie whispered. "Do ye mark that! November the t'urrd herself was born!"

"What are you on about now, Min?" the housekeeper asked. Minnie's Celtic mysteriousness got on her own good steady English nerves.

"Why, and to be sure it means herself is a Scorpio woman, does it not? A Scorpio woman, now!"

"I haven't got the slightest idea what you're talking about, Min!"

"The wurrst sign a woman can find herself born into, Mrs. Smith darlin'. Och, they're children of the Devil, so they are!" said Cat, round-eyed, blessing herself.

"Honestly, Minnie, you and Cat are the dizzy limit," said Mrs. Smith, not a whit impressed.

But excitement was running high, and would run higher. The old spider in her wing chair at the exact center of her web issued a never-ending stream of orders; this was to be done, that was to be done, such and such was to be taken out of storage, or put into storage. The two Irish maids ran polishing silver and washing the best Haviland china, turning the chapel back into a reception room and readying its adjacent dining rooms.

Hindered rather than helped by the little Cleary boys, Stuart and a team of rouseabouts mowed and scythed the lawn, weeded the flower beds, sprinkled damp sawdust on the verandas to clear dust from between the Spanish tiles, and dry chalk on the reception room floor to make it fit for dancing. Clarence O'Toole's band was coming all the way from Sydney, along with oysters and prawns, crabs and lobsters; several women from Gilly were being hired as temporary helpers. The whole district from Rudna Hunish to Inishmurray to Bugela to Narrengang was in a ferment.

As the marble hallways echoed to unaccustomed sounds of objects being moved and people shouting, Mary Carson shifted herself from her wing chair to her desk, drew a sheet of parchment forward, dipped her pen in the standish, and began to write. There was no hesitation, not so much as a pause to consider the positioning of a comma. For the last five years she had worked out every intricate phrase in her mind, until it was absolutely word perfect. It did not take her long to finish; there were two sheets of paper, the second one with a good quarter of it blank. But for a moment, the last sentence complete, she sat on in her chair. The roll-top desk stood alongside one of the big windows, so that by simply turning her head she could look out across the lawns. A laugh from outside made her do so, idly at first, then in stiffening rage. God *damn* him and his obsession!

Father Ralph had taught Meggie to ride; daughter of a country family, she had never sat astride a horse until the priest remedied the deficiency. For oddly enough, the daughters of poor country families did not often ride. Riding was a pastime for the rich young women of country and city alike. Oh, girls of Meggie's background could drive buggies and teams of heavy horses, even tractors and sometimes cars, but rarely did they ride. It cost too much to mount a daughter.

Father Ralph had brought elastic-sided ankle boots and twill jodhpurs from Gilly and plumped them down on the Cleary kitchen table noisily. Paddy had looked up from his after-dinner book, mildly surprised.

"Well, what have you got there, Father?" he asked.

"Riding clothes for Meggie."

"What?" bellowed Paddy's voice.

"What?" squeaked Meggie's.

"Riding clothes for Meggie. Honestly, Paddy, you're a first-class idiot! Heir to the biggest, richest station in New South Wales, and you've never let your only daughter sit a horse! How do you think she's going to take her place alongside Miss Carmichael, Miss Hopeton and Mrs. Anthony King, equestriennes all? Meggie's got to learn to ride, sidesaddle as well as astride, do you hear? I realize you're busy, so I'm going to teach Meggie myself, and you can like it or lump it. If it happens to interfere with her duties in the house, too bad. For a few hours each week Fee is just going to have to manage minus Meggie, and that's that."

One thing Paddy couldn't do was argue with a priest; Meggie learned to ride forthwith. For years she had longed for the chance, had once timidly ventured to ask her father might she, but he had forgotten the next moment and she never asked again, thinking that was Daddy's way of saying no. To learn under the aegis of Father Ralph cast her into a joy which she didn't show, for by this time her adoration of Father Ralph had turned into an ardent, very girlish crush. Knowing it was quite impossible, she permitted herself the luxury of dreaming about him, of wondering what it would be like to be held in his arms, receive his kiss. Further than that her dreams couldn't go, as she had no idea what came next, or even that anything came next. And if she knew it was wrong to dream so of a priest, there didn't seem to be any way she could discipline herself into not doing it. The best she could manage was to make absolutely sure he had no idea of the unruly turn her thoughts had taken.

As Mary Carson watched through the drawing room window, Father Ralph and Meggie walked down from the stables, which were on the far side of the big house from the head stockman's residence. The station men rode rawboned stock horses which had never seen the inside of a stable in all their lives, just shuffled around the yards when penned for duty, or frisked through the grass of the Home Paddock when being spelled. But there were stables on Drogheda, though only Father Ralph used them now. Mary Carson kept two thoroughbred hacks there for Father Ralph's exclusive use; no rawboned stock horses for him. When he had asked her if Meggie might use his mounts also, she could not very well object. The girl was her niece, and he was right. She ought to be able to ride decently.

With every bitter bone in her swollen old body Mary Carson had wished she had been able to refuse, or else ride with them. But she could neither refuse nor hoist herself on a horse anymore. And it galled her to see them now, strolling across the lawn together, the man in his breeches and knee boots and white shirt as graceful as a dancer, the girl in her jodhpurs slim and boyishly beautiful. They radiated an easy friendship; for the millionth time Mary Carson wondered why no one save she deplored their close, almost intimate relationship. Paddy thought it wonderful, Fee—log that she was!—said nothing, as usual, while the boys treated them as brother and sister. Was it because she loved Ralph de Bricassart herself that she saw what no one else saw? Or did she imagine it, was there really nothing save the friendship of a man in his middle thirties for a girl not yet all the way into womanhood? Piffle! No man in his middle thirties, even Ralph de Bricassart, could fail to see the unfolding rose. Even Ralph de Bricassart? Hah! Especially Ralph de Bricassart! Nothing ever missed that man.

Her hands were trembling; the pen sprinkled dark-blue drops across the bottom of the paper. The gnarled finger plucked another sheet from a pigeonhole, dipped the pen in the standish again, and rewrote the words as surely as the first time. Then she heaved herself to her feet and moved her bulk to the door.

"Minnie! Minnie!" she called.

"Lord help us, it's herself!" the maid said clearly from the reception room opposite. Her ageless freckled face came round the door. "And what might I be gettin' for ye, Mrs. Carson darlin'?" she asked, wondering why the old woman had not rung the bell for Mrs. Smith, as was her wont.

"Go and find the fencer and Tom. Send them here to me at once."

"Ought I not be reportin' to Mrs. Smith furrst?"

"No! Just do as you're told, girl!"

Tom, the garden rouseabout, was an old, wizened fellow who had been on the track with his bluey and his billy, and taken work for a while seventeen years ago; he had fallen in love with the Drogheda gardens and couldn't bear to leave them. The fencer, a drifter like all his breed, had been pulled from the endless task of stringing taut wire between posts in the paddocks to repair the homestead's white pickets for the party. Awed at the summons, they came within a few minutes and stood in work trousers, braces and flannel undershirts, hats screwed nervously in their hands.

"Can both of you write?" asked Mrs. Carson.

They nodded, swallowed.

"Good. I want you to watch me sign this piece of paper, then fix your own names and addresses just below my signature. Do you understand?"

They nodded.

"Make sure you sign the way you always do, and

print your permanent addresses clearly. I don't care if it's a post office general delivery or what, so long as you can be reached through it."

The two men watched her inscribe her name; it was the only time her writing was not compressed. Tom came forward, sputtered the pen across the paper painfully, then the fencer wrote "Chas. Hawkins" in large round letters, and a Sydney address. Mary Carson watched them closely; when they were done she gave each of them a dull red ten-pound note, and dismissed them with a harsh injunction to keep their mouths shut.

Meggie and the priest had long since disappeared. Mary Carson sat down at her desk heavily, drew another sheet of paper toward her, and began once more to write. This communication was not achieved with the ease and fluency of the last. Time and time again she stopped to think, then with lips drawn back in a humorless grin, she would continue. It seemed she had a lot to say, for her words were cramped, her lines very close together, and still she required a second sheet. At the end she read what she had put down, placed all the sheets together, folded them and slid them into an envelope, the back of which she sealed with red wax.

Only Paddy, Fee, Bob, Jack and Meggie were going to the party; Hughie and Stuart were deputed to mind the little ones, much to their secret relief. For once in her life Mary Carson had opened her wallet wide enough for the moths to fly out, for everyone had new clothes, the best Gilly could provide.

Paddy, Bob and Jack were immobilized behind starched shirt fronts, high collars and white bow ties, black tails, black trousers, white waistcoats. It was going to be a very formal affair, white tie and tails for the men, sweeping gowns for the women.

Fee's dress was of crepe in a peculiarly rich shade of blue-grey, and suited her, falling to the floor in soft folds, low of neckline but tightly sleeved to the wrists, lavishly beaded, much in the style of Queen Mary. Like that imperious lady, she had her hair done high in back-sweeping puffs, and the Gilly store had produced an imitation pearl choker and earrings which would fool all but a close inspection. A magnificent ostrich-feather fan dyed the same color as her gown completed the ensemble, not so ostentatious as it appeared at first glance; the weather was unusually hot, and at seven in the evening it was still well over a hundred degrees.

When Fee and Paddy emerged from their room, the boys gaped. In all their lives they had never seen their parents so regally handsome, so foreign. Paddy looked his sixty-one years, but in such a distinguished way he might have been a statesman; whereas Fee seemed suddenly ten years younger than her forty-eight, beautiful, vital, magically smiling. Jims and Patsy burst into shrieking tears, refusing to look at Mum and Daddy until they reverted to normal, and in the flurry of consternation dignity was forgotten; Mum and Daddy behaved as they always did, and soon the twins were beaming in admiration.

But it was at Meggie everyone stared the longest. Perhaps remembering her own girlhood, and angered that all the other young ladies invited had ordered their gowns from Sydney, the Gilly dressmaker had put her heart into Meggie's dress. It was sleeveless and had a low, draped neckline; Fee had been dubious, but Meggie had implored and the dressmaker assured her all the girls would be wearing the same sort of thing—did she want her daughter laughed at for being countrified and dowdy? So Fee had given in gracefully. Of crepe georgette, a heavy chiffon, the dress was only slightly fitted at the waist, but sashed around the hips with the same material. It was a dusky, pale pinkish grey, the color that in those days was called ashes of roses; between them the dressmaker and Meggie had embroidered the entire gown in tiny pink rosebuds. And Meggie had cut her hair in the closest way she could to the shingle creeping even through the ranks of Gilly girls. It curled far too much for fashion, of course, but it suited her better short than long.

Paddy opened his mouth to roar because she was not his little girl Meggie, but shut it again with the words unuttered; he had learned from that scene in the presbytery with Frank long ago. No, he couldn't keep her a little girl forever; she was a young woman and shy of the amazing transformation her mirror had shown her. Why make it harder for the poor little beggar?

He extended his hand to her, smiling tenderly. "Oh, Meggie, you're so lovely! Come on, I'm going to escort you myself, and Bob and Jack shall take your mother."

She was just a month short of seventeen, and for the first time in his life Paddy felt really old. But she was the treasure of his heart; nothing should spoil her first grown-up party.

They walked to the homestead slowly, far too early for the first guests; they were to dine with Mary Carson and be on hand to receive with her. No one wanted dirty shoes, but a mile through Drogheda dust meant a pause in the cookhouse to polish shoes, brush dust from trouser bottoms and trailing hems.

Father Ralph was in his soutane as usual; no male evening fashion could have suited him half so well as that severely cut robe with its slightly flaring lines, the innumerable little black cloth buttons up its front from hem to collar, the purple-edged monsignor's sash.

Mary Carson has chosen to wear white satin, white lace and white ostrich feathers. Fee stared at her stupidly, shocked out of her habitual indifference. It was so incongruously bridal, so grossly unsuitable—why on earth had she tricked herself out like a raddled old spinster playacting at being married? She had got very fat of late, which didn't improve matters.

But Paddy seemed to see nothing amiss; he strode

forward to take his sister's hands, beaming. What a dear fellow he was, thought Father Ralph as he watched the little scene, half amused, half detached.

"Well, Mary! How fine you look! Like a young girl!"

In truth she looked almost exactly like that famous photograph of Queen Victoria taken not long before she died. The two heavy lines were there on either side of the masterful nose, the mulish mouth was set indomitably, the slightly protruding and glacial eyes fixed without blinking on Meggie. Father Ralph's own beautiful eyes passed from niece to aunt, and back to niece again.

Mary Carson smiled at Paddy, and put her hand on his arm. "You may take me in to dinner, Padraic. Father de Bricassart will escort Fiona, and the boys must make do with Meghann between them." Over her shoulder she looked back at Meggie. "Do you dance tonight, Meghann?"

"She's too young, Mary, she's not yet seventeen," said Paddy quickly, remembering another parental shortcoming; none of his children had been taught to dance.

"What a pity," said Mary Carson.

It was a splendid, sumptuous, brilliant, glorious party; at least, they were the adjectives most bandied about. Royal O'Mara was there from Inishmurray, two hundred miles away; he came the farthest with his wife, sons and lone daughter, though not by much. Gilly people thought little of traveling two hundred miles to a cricket match, let alone a party. Duncan Gordon, from Each-Uisge; no one had ever persuaded him to explain why he had called his station so far from the ocean the Scots Gaelic for a sea horse. Martin King, his wife, his son Anthony and Mrs. Anthony; he was Gilly's senior squatter, since Mary Carson could not be so called, being a woman. Evan Pugh, from Braich y Pwll, which the district pronounced Brakeypull.

Dominic O'Rourke from Dibban-Dibban, Horry Hopeton from Beel-Beel; and dozens more.

They were almost to the last family present Catholic, and few sported Anglo-Saxon names; there was about an equal distribution of Irish, Scottish and Welsh. No, they could not hope for home rule in the old country, nor, if Catholic in Scotland or Wales, for much sympathy from the Protestant indigenes. But here in the thousands of square miles around Gillanbone they were lords to thumb their noses at British lords, masters of all they surveyed; Drogheda, the biggest property, was greater in area than several European principalities. Monegasque princelings, Liechtensteinian dukes, beware! Mary Carson was greater. So they whirled in waltzes to the sleek Sydney band and stood back indulgently to watch their children dance the Charleston, ate the lobster patties and the chilled raw oysters, drank the fifteen-year-old French champagne and the twelve-year-old single-malt Scotch. If the truth were known, they would rather have eaten roast leg of lamb or corned beef, and much preferred to drink cheap, very potent Bundaberg rum or Grafton bitter from the barrel. But it was nice to know the better things of life were theirs for the asking.

Yes, there were lean years, many of them. The wool checks were carefully hoarded in the good years to guard against the depredations of the bad, for no one could predict the rain. But it was a good period, had been for some time, and there was little to spend the money on in Gilly. Oh, once born to the black soil plains of the Great Northwest there was no place on earth like it. They made no nostalgic pilgrimages back to the old country; it had done nothing for them save discriminate against them for their religious convictions, where Australia was too Catholic a country to discriminate. And the Great Northwest was *home*.

Besides, Mary Carson was footing the bill tonight. She could well afford it. Rumor said she was able to buy and sell the King of England. She had money in steel, money in silver-lead-zinc, money in copper and gold, money in a hundred different things, mostly the sort of things that literally and metaphorically made money. Drogheda had long since ceased to be the main source of her income; it was no more than a profitable hobby.

Father Ralph didn't speak directly to Meggie during dinner, nor did he afterward; throughout the evening he studiously ignored her. Hurt, her eyes sought him wherever he was in the reception room. Aware of it, he ached to stop by her chair and explain to her that it would not do her reputation (or his) any good if he paid her more attention than he did, say, Miss Carmichael, Miss Gordon or Miss O'Mara. Like Meggie he didn't dance, and like Meggie there were many eyes on him; they were easily the two most beautiful people in the room.

Half of him hated her appearance tonight, the short hair, the lovely dress, the dainty ashes-of-roses silk slippers with their two-inch heels; she was growing taller, developing a very feminine figure. And half of him was busy being terrifically proud of the fact that she shone all the other young ladies down. Miss Carmichael had the patrician features, but lacked the special glory of that red-gold hair; Miss King had exquisite blond tresses, but lacked the lissome body; Miss Mackail was stunning of body, but in the face very like a horse eating an apple through a wire-netting fence. Yet his overall reaction was one of disappointment, and an anguished wish to turn back the calendar. He didn't want Meggie to grow up, he wanted the little girl he could treat as his treasured babe. On Paddy's face he glimpsed an expression which mirrored his own thoughts, and smiled faintly. What bliss it would be if just once in his life he could show his feelings! But habit, training and discretion were too ingrained.

As the evening wore on the dancing grew more and

more uninhibited, the liquor changed from champagne and whiskey to rum and beer, and proceedings settled down to something more like a woolshed ball. By two in the morning only a total absence of station hands and working girls could distinguish it from the usual entertainments of the Gilly district, which were strictly democratic.

Paddy and Fee were still in attendance, but promptly at midnight Bob and Jack left with Meggie. Neither Fee nor Paddy noticed; they were enjoying themselves. If their children couldn't dance, they could, and did; with each other mostly, seeming to the watching Father Ralph suddenly much more attuned to each other, perhaps because the times they had an opportunity to relax and enjoy each other were rare. He never remembered seeing them without at least one child somewhere around, and thought it must be hard on the parents of large families, never able to snatch moments alone save in the bedroom, where they might excusably have other things than conversation on their minds. Paddy was always cheerful and jolly, but Fee tonight almost literally shone, and when Paddy went to beg a duty dance of some squatter's wife, she didn't lack eager partners; there were many much younger women wilting on chairs around the room who were not so sought after.

However, Father Ralph's moments to observe the Cleary parents were limited. Feeling ten years younger once he saw Meggie leave the room, he became a great deal more animated and flabbergasted the Misses Hopeton, Mackail, Gordon and O'Mara by dancing—and extremely well—the Black Bottom with Miss Carmichael. But after that he gave every unattached girl in the room her turn, even poor homely Miss Pugh, and since by this time everyone was thoroughly relaxed and oozing goodwill, no one condemned the priest one bit. In fact, his zeal and kindness were much admired and commented upon. No one could say their daughter had not had an opportunity to dance with Father de Bricassart.

Of course, had it not been a private party he could not have made a move toward the dance floor, but it was so nice to see such a fine man really enjoy himself for once.

At three o'clock Mary Carson rose to her feet and yawned. "No, don't stop the festivities! If I'm tired—which I am—I can go to bed, which is what I'm going to do. But there's plenty of food and drink, the band has been engaged to play as long as someone wants to dance, and a little noise will only speed me into my dreams. Father, would you help me up the stairs, please?"

Once outside the reception room she did not turn to the majestic staircase, but guided the priest to her drawing room, leaning heavily on his arm. Its door had been locked; she waited while he used the key she handed him, then preceded him inside.

"It was a good party, Mary," he said.

"My last."

"Don't say that, my dear."

"Why not? I'm tired of living, Ralph, and I'm going to stop." Her hard eyes mocked. "Do you doubt me? For over seventy years I've done precisely what I wanted to do when I wanted to do it, so if Death thinks he's the one to choose the time of my going, he's very much mistaken. I'll die when *I* choose the time, and no suicide, either. It's our will to live keeps us kicking, Ralph; it isn't hard to stop if we really want to. I'm tired, and I want to stop. Very simple."

He was tired, too; not of living, exactly, but of the endless façade, the climate, the lack of friends with common interests, himself. The room was only faintly lit by a tall kerosene lamp of priceless ruby glass, and it cast transparent crimson shadows on Mary Carson's face, conjuring out of her intractable bones something more diabolical. His feet and back ached; it was a long time since he had danced so much, though he prided himself on keeping up with whatever was the latest fad. Thirty-five years of age, a country monsignor, and as a power in the Church? Finished before he had begun. Oh, the dreams of youth! And the carelessness of youth's tongue, the hotness of youth's temper. He had not been strong enough to meet the test. But he would never make that mistake again. Never, never . . .

He moved restlessly, sighed; what was the use? The chance would not come again. Time he faced that fact squarely, time he stopped hoping and dreaming.

"Do you remember my saying, Ralph, that I'd beat you, that I'd hoist you with your own petard?"

The dry old voice snapped him out of the reverie his weariness had induced. He looked across at Mary Carson and smiled.

"Dear Mary, I never forget anything you say. What I would have done without you these past seven years I don't know. Your wit, your malice, your perception . . ."

"If I'd been younger I'd have got you in a different way, Ralph. You'll never know how I've longed to throw thirty years of my life out the window. If the Devil had come to me and offered to buy my soul for the chance to be young again, I'd have sold it in a second, and not stupidly regretted the bargain like that old idiot Faust. But no Devil. I really can't bring myself to believe in God or the Devil, you know. I've never seen a scrap of evidence to the effect they exist. Have you?"

"No. But belief doesn't rest on proof of existence, Mary. It rests on faith, and faith is the touchstone of the Church. Without faith, there is nothing."

"A very ephemeral tenet."

"Perhaps. Faith's born in a man or a woman, I think. For me it's a constant struggle, I admit that, but I'll never give up."

"I would like to destroy you."

His blue eyes laughed, greyed in the light. "Oh, my dear Mary! I know *that.*"

"But do you know why?"

A terrifying tenderness crept against him, almost

inside him, except that he fought it fiercely. "I know why, Mary, and believe me, I'm sorry."

"Besides your mother, how many women have loved you?"

"Did my mother love me, I wonder? She ended in hating me, anyway. Most women do. My name ought to have been Hippolytos."

"Ohhhhhh! That tells me a lot!"

"As to other women, I think only Meggie . . . But she's a little girl. It's probably not an exaggeration to say hundreds of women have wanted me, but loved me? I doubt it very much."

"I have loved you," she said pathetically.

"No, you haven't. I'm the goad of your old age, that's all. When you look at me I remind you of what you cannot do, because of age."

"You're wrong. I have loved you. God, how much! Do you think my years automatically preclude it? Well, Father de Bricassart, let me tell you something. Inside this stupid body I'm still young—I still feel, I still want, I still dream, I still kick up my heels and chafe at restrictions like my body. Old age is the bitterest vengeance our vengeful God inflicts upon us. Why doesn't He age our minds as well?" She leaned back in her chair and closed her eyes, her teeth showing sourly. "I shall go to Hell, of course. But before I do, I hope I get the chance to tell God what a mean, spiteful, pitiful apology of a God He is!"

"You were a widow too long. God gave you freedom of choice, Mary. You could have remarried. If you chose not to remarry and in consequence you've been intolerably lonely, it's your own doing, not God's."

For a moment she said nothing, her hands gripping the chair arms hard; then she began to relax, and opened her eyes. They glittered in the lamplight redly, but not with tears; with something harder, more brilliant. He caught his breath, felt fear. She looked like a spider.

"Ralph, on my desk is an envelope. Would you bring it to me, please?"

Aching and afraid, he got up and went to her desk, lifted the letter, eyed it curiously. The face of it was blank, but the back had been properly sealed with red wax and her ram's head seal with the big *D*. He brought it to her and held it out, but she waved him to his seat without taking it.

"It's yours," she said, and giggled. "The instrument of your fate, Ralph, that's what it is. My last and most telling thrust in our long battle. What a pity I won't be here to see what happens. But I *know* what will happen, because I know you, I know you much better than you think I do. Insufferable conceit! Inside that envelope lies the fate of your life and your soul. I must lose you to Meggie, but I've made sure she doesn't get you, either."

"Why do you hate Meggie so?"

"I told you once before. Because you love her."

"*Not* in that way! She's the child I can never have, the rose of my life. Meggie is an idea, Mary, an idea!"

But the old woman sneered. "I don't want to talk about your precious Meggie! I shall never see you again, so I don't want to waste my time with you talking about her. The letter. I want you to swear on your vows as a priest that you don't open it until you've seen my dead body for yourself, but then that you open it immediately, before you bury me. Swear!"

"There's no need to swear, Mary. I'll do as you ask."

"Swear to me or I'll take it back!"

He shrugged. "All right, then. On my vows as a priest I swear it. Not to open the letter until I've seen you dead, and then to open it before you're buried."

"Good, good!"

"Mary, please don't worry. This is a fancy of yours, no more. In the morning you'll laugh at it."

"I won't see the morning. I'm going to die tonight; I'm not weak enough to wait on the pleasure of seeing you again. What an anticlimax! I'm going to bed now. Will you take me to the top of the stairs?"

He didn't believe her, but he could see it served no purpose to argue, and she was not in the mood to be jollied out of it. Only God decided when one would die, unless, of the free will He had given, one took one's own life. And she had said she wouldn't do that. So he helped her pant up the stairs and at the top took her hands in his, bent to kiss them.

She pulled them away. "No, not tonight. On my mouth, Ralph! Kiss my mouth as if we were lovers!"

By the brilliant light of the chandelier, lit for the party with four hundred wax candles, she saw the disgust in his face, the instinctive recoil; she wanted to die then, wanted to die so badly she could not wait.

"Mary, I'm a priest! *I can't!*"

She laughed shrilly, eerily. "Oh, Ralph, what a sham you are! Sham man, sham priest! And to think once you actually had the temerity to offer to make love to me! Were you so positive I'd refuse? How I wish I hadn't! I'd give my soul to see you wriggle out of it if we could have that night back again! *Sham, sham, sham!* That's all you are, Ralph! An impotent, useless sham! Impotent man and impotent priest! I don't think you could get it up and keep it up for the Blessed Virgin herself! Have you ever managed to get it up, Father de Bricassart? *Sham!*"

Outside it was not yet dawn, or the lightening before it. Darkness lay soft, thick and very hot over Drogheda. The revels were becoming extremely noisy; if the homestead had possessed next-door neighbors the police would have been called long since. Someone was vomiting copiously and revoltingly on the veranda, and under a wispy bottle brush two indistinct forms were locked together. Father Ralph avoided the vomiter and the lovers, treading silently across the springy new-mown lawn with such torment in his mind he did not know or care where he was going. Only that he wanted to be away from her, the awful old spider who was convinced she was spinning her death cocoon on this exquisite night. At such an early hour the heat was not exhausting; there was a faint, heavy stirring in the air, and a stealing of languorous perfumes from boronia and roses, the heavenly stillness only tropical and subtropical latitudes can ever know. Oh, God, to be alive, to be really alive! To embrace the night, and living, and be free!

He stopped on the far side of the lawn and stood looking up at the sky, an instinctive aerial searching for God. Yes, up there somewhere, between the winking points of light so pure and unearthly; what was it about the night sky? That the blue lid of day was lifted, a man permitted glimpses of eternity? Nothing save witnessing the strewn vista of the stars could convince a man that timelessness and God existed.

She's right, of course. A sham, a total sham. No priest, no man. Only someone who wishes he knew how to be either. No! *Not* either! Priest and man cannot coexist—to be a man is to be no priest. Why did I ever tangle my feet in her web? Her poison is strong, perhaps stronger than I guess. What's in the letter? How like Mary to bait me! How much does she know, how much does she simply guess? What is there to know, or guess? Only futility, and loneliness. Doubt, pain. Always pain. Yet you're wrong, Mary. I *can* get it up. It's just that I don't choose to, that I've spent years proving to myself it can be controlled, dominated, subjugated. For getting it up is the activity of a man, and I am a priest.

Someone was weeping in the cemetery. Meggie, of course. No one else would think of it. He picked up the skirts of his soutane and stepped over the wrought-iron railing, feeling it was inevitable that he had not yet done with Meggie on this night. If he confronted one of the women in his life, he must also deal with the other. His amused detachment was coming back; she could not disperse that for long, the old spider. The wicked old spider. God rot her, *God rot her!*

"Darling Meggie, don't cry," he said, sitting on the dew-wet grass beside her. "Here, I'll bet you don't have a decent handkerchief. Women never do. Take mine and dry your eyes like a good girl.'

She took it and did as she was told.

"You haven't even changed out of your finery. Have you been sitting here since midnight?"

"Yes."

"Do Bob and Jack know where you are?"

"I told them I was going to bed."

"What's the matter, Meggie?"

"You didn't speak to me tonight!"

"Ah! I thought that might be it. Come, Meggie, look at me!"

Away in the east was a pearly luster, a fleeing of total darkness, and the Drogheda roosters were shrieking an early welcome to the dawn. So he could see that not even protracted tears could dim the loveliness of her eyes.

"Meggie, you were by far the prettiest girl at the party, and it's well known that I come to Drogheda more often than I need. I am a priest and therefore I ought to be above suspicion—a bit like Caesar's wife—but I'm afraid people don't think so purely. As priests go I'm young, and not bad-looking." He paused to think how Mary Carson would have greeted that bit of understatement, and laughed soundlessly. "If I had paid you a skerrick of attention it would have been all over Gilly in record time. Every party line in the district would have been buzzing with it. Do you know what I mean?"

She shook her head; the cropped curls were growing brighter in the advancing light.

"Well, you're young to come to knowledge of the ways of the world, but you've got to learn, and it always seems to be my province to teach you, doesn't it? I mean people would be saying I was interested in you as a man, not as a priest."

"Father!"

"Dreadful, isn't it?" He smiled. "But that's what people would say, I assure you. You see, Meggie, you're not a little girl anymore, you're a young lady. But you haven't learned yet to hide your affection for me, so had I stopped to speak to you with all those people looking on, you'd have stared at me in a way which might have been misconstrued."

She was looking at him oddly, a sudden inscrutability shuttering her gaze, then abruptly she turned her head and presented him with her profile. "Yes, I see. I was silly not to have seen it."

"Now don't you think it's time you went home? No doubt everyone will sleep in, but if someone's awake at the usual time you'll be in the soup. And you can't say you've been with me, Meggie, even to your own family."

She got up and stood staring down at him. "I'm going, Father. But I wish they knew you better, then they'd never think such things of you. It isn't in you, is it?"

For some reason that hurt, hurt right down to his soul as Mary Carson's cruel taunts had not. "No, Meggie, you're right. It isn't in me." He sprang up, smiling wryly. "Would you think it strange if I said I wished it was?" He put a hand to his head. "No, I don't wish it was at all! Go home, Meggie, go home!"

Her face was sad. "Good night, Father."

He took her hands in his, bent and kissed them. "Good night, dearest Meggie."

He watched her walk across the graves, step over the railing; in the rosebud dress her retreating form was graceful, womanly and a little unreal. Ashes of roses. "How appropriate," he said to the angel.

Cars were roaring away from Drogheda as he strolled

back across the lawn; the party was finally over. Inside, the band was packing away its instruments, reeling with rum and exhaustion, and the tired maids and temporary helpers were trying to clear up. Father Ralph shook his head at Mrs. Smith.

"Send everyone to bed, my dear. It's a lot easier to deal with this sort of thing when you're fresh. I'll make sure Mrs. Carson isn't angry."

"Would you like something to eat, Father?"

"Good Lord, no! I'm going to bed."

In the late afternoon a hand touched his shoulder. He reached for it blindly without the energy to open his eyes, and tried to hold it against his cheek.

"Meggie," he mumbled.

"Father, Father! Oh, please will you wake up?"

At the tone of Mrs. Smith's voice his eyes came suddenly very awake. "What is it, Mrs. Smith?"

"It's Mrs. Carson, Father. She's dead."

His watch told him it was after six in the evening; dazed and reeling from the heavy torpor the day's terrible heat had induced in him, he struggled out of his pajamas and into his priest's clothes, threw a narrow purple stole around his neck and took the oil of extreme unction, the holy water, his big silver cross, his ebony rosary beads. It never occurred to him for a moment to wonder if Mrs. Smith was right; he knew the spider was dead. Had she taken something after all? Pray God if she had, it was neither obviously present in the room nor obvious to a doctor. What possible use it was to administer extreme unction he didn't know. But it had to be done. Let him refuse and there would be post-mortems, all sorts of complications. Yet it had nothing to do with his sudden suspicion of suicide; simply that to him laying sacred things on Mary Carson's body was obscene.

She was very dead, must have died within minutes of retiring, a good fifteen hours earlier. The windows were closed fast, and the room humid from the great flat pans of water she insisted be put in every inconspicuous corner to keep her skin youthful. There was a peculiar noise in the air; after a stupid moment of wondering he realized what he heard were flies, hordes of flies buzzing, insanely clamoring as they feasted on her, mated on her, laid their eggs on her.

"For God's sake, Mrs. Smith, open the windows!" he gasped, moving to the bedside, face pallid.

She had passed out of rigor mortis and was again limp, disgustingly so. The staring eyes were mottling, her thin lips black; and everywhere on her were the flies. He had to have Mrs. Smith keep shooing them away as he worked over her, muttering the ancient Latin exhortations. What a farce, and she accursed. The smell of her! Oh, God! Worse than any dead horse in the freshness of a paddock. He shrank from touching her in death as he had in life, especially those flyblown lips. She would be a mass of maggots within hours.

At last it was done. He straightened. "Go to Mr. Cleary at once, Mrs. Smith, and for God's sake tell him to get the boys working on a coffin right away. No time to have one sent out from Gilly; she's rotting away before our very eyes. Dear lord! I feel sick. I'm going to have a bath and I'll leave my clothes outside my door. Burn them. I'll never get the smell of her out of them."

Back in his room in riding breeches and shirt—for he had not packed two soutanes—he remembered the letter, and his promise. Seven o'clock had struck; he could hear a restrained chaos as maids and temporary helpers flew to clear the party mess away, transform the reception room back into a chapel, ready the house for tomorrow's funeral. No help for it, he would have to go into Gilly tonight to pick up another soutane and vestments for the Requiem Mass. Certain things he was never without when he left the presbytery for an outlying station, carefully strapped in compartments in the little black case, his sacraments for birth, death, benediction, worship, and the vestments suitable for Mass at whatever time of the year it was. But he was an Irishman, and to carry the black mourning accouterments of a Requiem was to tempt fate. Paddy's voice echoed in the distance, but he could not face Paddy at the moment; he knew Mrs. Smith would do what had to be done.

Sitting at his window looking out over the vista of Drogheda in the dying sun, the ghost gums golden, the mass of red and pink and white roses in the garden all empurpled, he took Mary Carson's letter from his case and held it between his hands. But she had insisted he read it before he buried her, and somewhere in his mind a little voice was whispering that he must read it *now,* not later tonight after he had seen Paddy and Meggie, but *now* before he had seen anyone save Mary Carson.

It contained four sheets of paper; he riffled them apart and saw immediately that the lower two were her will. The top two were addressed to him, in the form of a letter.

My dearest Ralph,

You will have seen that the second document in this envelope is my will. I already have a perfectly good will signed and sealed in Harry Gough's office in Gilly; the will enclosed herein is a much later one, and naturally nullifies the one Harry has.

As a matter of fact I made it only the other day, and had it witnessed by Tom and the fencer, since I understand it is not permissible to have any beneficiary witness one's will. It is quite legal, in spite of the fact Harry didn't draw it up for me. No court in the land will deny its validity, I assure you.

But why didn't I have Harry draw this testament

up if I wanted to alter the disposition of my effects? Very simple, my dear Ralph. I wanted absolutely no one to know of this will's existence apart from you, and me. This is the only copy, and you hold it. Not a soul knows that you do. A very important part of my plan.

Do you remember that piece of the Gospel where Satan took Our Lord Jesus Christ up onto a mountaintop, and tempted Him with the whole world? How pleasant it is to know I have a little of Satan's power, and am able to tempt the one I love (do you doubt Satan loved Christ? I do not) with the whole world. The contemplation of your dilemma has considerably enlivened my thoughts during the past few years, and the closer I get to dying, the more delightful my visions become.

After you've read the will, you'll understand what I mean. While I burn in Hell beyond the borders of this life I know now, you'll still be in that life, but burning in a hell with fiercer flames than any God could possibly manufacture. Oh, my Ralph, I've gauged you to a nicety! If I never knew how to do anything else, I've always known how to make the ones I love suffer. And you're far better game than my dear departed Michael ever was.

When I first knew you, you wanted Drogheda and my money, didn't you, Ralph? You saw it as a way to buy back your natural métier. But then came Meggie, and you put your original purpose in cultivating me out of your mind, didn't you? I became an excuse to visit Drogheda so you could be with Meggie. I wonder could you have switched allegiances so easily had you known how much I'm actually worth? *Do* you know, Ralph? I don't think you have an inkling. I suppose it isn't ladylike to mention the exact sum of one's assets in one's will, so I had better tell you here just to make sure you have all the necessary information at your fingertips when it comes to your making a decision. Give or take a few hundred thousands, my fortune amounts to some *thirteen million pounds.*

I'm getting down toward the foot of the second page, and I can't be bothered turning this into a thesis. Read my will, Ralph, and after you've read it, decide what you're going to do with it. Will you tender it to Harry Gough for probate, or will you burn it and never tell a soul it existed. That's the decision you've got to make. I ought to add that the will in Harry's office is the one I made the year after Paddy came, and leaves everything I have to him. Just so you know what hangs in the balance.

Ralph, I love you, so much I would have killed you for not wanting me, except that this is a far better form of reprisal. I'm not the noble kind; I love you but I want you to scream in agony. Because, you see, *I know* what your decision will be. I know it as surely as if I could be there, watching. You'll scream, Ralph, you'll know what agony is. So read on, my beautiful, ambitious priest! Read my will, and decide your fate.

It was not signed or initialed. He felt the sweat on his forehead, felt it running down the back of his neck from his hair. And he wanted to get up that very moment to burn both documents, never read what the second one contained. But she had gauged her quarry well, the gross old spider. Of course he would read on; he was too curious to resist. God! What had he ever done, to make her want to do this to him? Why did women make him suffer so? Why couldn't he have been born small, twisted, ugly? If he were so, he might have been happy.

The last two sheets were covered by the same precise, almost minute writing. As mean and grudging as her soul.

I, Mary Elizabeth Carson, being of sound mind and sound body, do hereby declare that this is my last will and testament, thereby rendering null and void any such testaments previously made by me.

Save only for the special bequests made below, all my worldly goods and moneys and properties I bequeath to the Holy Catholic Church of Rome, under the hereby stated conditions of bequest:

First, that the said Holy Catholic Church of Rome, to be called the Church hereafter, knows in what esteem and with what affection I hold her priest, Father Ralph de Bricassart. It is *solely* because of his kindness, spiritual guidance and unfailing support that I so dispose of my assets.

Secondly, that the bequest shall continue in the favor of the Church only so long as she appreciates the worth and ability of the said Father Ralph de Bricassart.

Thirdly, that the said Father Ralph de Bricassart be responsible for the administration and channeling of these my worldly goods, moneys and properties, as the chief authority in charge of my estate.

Fourthly, that upon the demise of the said Father Ralph de Bricassart, his own last will and testament shall be legally binding in the matter of the further administration of my estate. That is, the Church shall continue in full ownership, but Father Ralph de Bricassart shall be solely responsible for the naming of his successor in administration; he shall not be obliged to select a successor who is either an ecclesiastical or a lay member of the Church.

Fifthly, that the station Drogheda be never sold nor subdivided.

Sixthly, that my brother, Padraic Cleary, be retained as manager of the station Drogheda with the right to dwell in my house, and that he be paid a salary at the discretion of Father Ralph de Bricassart and no other.

Seventhly, that in the event of the death of my brother, the said Padraic Cleary, his widow and children be permitted to remain on the station Drogheda and that the position of manager shall pass consecutively to each of his sons, Robert, John, Hugh, Stuart, James and Patrick, but excluding Francis.

Eighthly, that upon the demise of Patrick or whichever son excluding Francis is the last son remaining, the same rights be permitted the said Padraic Cleary's grandchildren.

Special bequests:

To Padraic Cleary, the contents of my houses on the station Drogheda.

To Eunice Smith, my housekeeper, that she remain at a fair salary so long as she desires, and in addition that she be paid the sum of five thousand pounds forthwith, and that upon her retirement she be awarded an equitable pension.

To Minerva O'Brien and Catherine Donnelly, that they remain at fair salaries so long as they desire, and in addition that they be paid the sum of one thousand pounds each forthwith, and that upon their retirements they be awarded equitable pensions.

To Father Ralph de Bricassart the sum of ten thousand pounds to be paid annually so long as he shall live, for his own private and unquestioned use.

It was duly signed, dated and witnessed.

His room looked west. The sun was setting. The pall of dust which came with every summer filled the silent air, and the sun thrust its fingers through the fine-strung particles so that it seemed the whole world had turned to gold and purple. Streaky clouds rimmed in brilliant fire poked silver streamers across the great bloody ball which hung just above the trees of the far paddocks.

"Bravo!" he said. "I admit, Mary, you've beaten me. A master stroke. I was the fool, not you."

He could not see the pages in his hand through the tears, and moved them before they could be blotched. Thirteen million pounds. *Thirteen million pounds!* It was indeed what he had been angling for in the days before Meggie. And with her coming he had abandoned it, because he couldn't carry on such a campaign in cold blood to cheat her of her inheritance. But what if he had known how much the old spider was worth? What then? He had no idea it was a tenth so much. Thirteen million pounds!

For seven years Paddy and his family had lived in the head stockman's house and worked themselves ragged for Mary Carson. For what? The niggardly wages she paid? Never to Father Ralph's knowledge had Paddy complained of being shabbily treated, thinking no doubt that when his sister died he would be amply repaid for managing the property on ordinary stockman's pay, while his sons did stockman's work for rouseabout's wages. He had made do, and grown to love Drogheda as if it were his own, rightly assuming it would be.

"Bravo, Mary!" said Father Ralph again, these first tears since his boyhood dropping from his face onto the backs of his hands, but not onto the paper.

Thirteen million pounds, and the chance to be Cardinal de Bricassart yet. Against Paddy Cleary, his wife, his sons—and Meggie. How diabolically well she had read him! Had she stripped Paddy of everything, his way would have been clear: he could have taken the will down to the kitchen stove and thrust it inside the firebox without a qualm. But she had made sure Paddy wouldn't want, that after her death he would be more comfortable on Drogheda than during her life, and that

Drogheda could not quite be taken from him. Its profits and title, yes, but not the land itself. No, he wouldn't be the owner of that fabulous thirteen million pounds, but he would be well respected, comfortably provided for. Meggie wouldn't go hungry, or be thrown shoeless upon the world. Nor would she be Miss Cleary, either, able to stand on an equal footing with Miss Carmichael and that ilk. Quite respectable, socially admissible, but not top drawer. Never top drawer.

Thirteen million pounds. The chance to get out of Gillanbone and perpetual obscurity, the chance to take his place within the hierarchy of Church administration, the assured goodwill of his peers and superiors. And all while he was still young enough to make up the ground he had lost. Mary Carson had made Gillanbone the epicenter of the Archbishop Papal Legate's map with a vengeance; the tremors would reach as far as the Vatican. Rich though the Church was, thirteen million pounds was thirteen million pounds. Not to be sneezed at, even by the Church. And his was the sole hand which brought it into the fold, his hand acknowledged in blue ink in Mary Carson's own writing. He knew Paddy would never contest the will; so had Mary Carson, God rot her. Oh, certainly Paddy would be furious, would never want to see him again or speak to him again, but his chagrin wouldn't extend to litigation.

Was there a decision? Didn't he already know, hadn't he known the moment he read her will what he was going to do? The tears had dried. With his usual grace Father Ralph got to his feet, made sure his shirt was tucked in all the way round, and went to the door. He must get to Gilly, pick up a soutane and vestments. But first he wanted to see Mary Carson again.

In spite of the open windows the stench had become a reeking fug; no hint of a breeze stirred the limp curtains. With steady tread he crossed to the bed and stood looking down. The fly eggs were beginning to hatch maggots in all the wet parts of her face, ballooning gases puffed up her fat arms and hands to greenish blobs, her skin was breaking down. Oh, God. You disgusting old spider. You've won, but what a victory. The triumph of one disintegrating caricature of humanity over another. You can't defeat my Meggie, nor can you take from her what was never yours. I might burn in Hell alongside you, but I know the Hell they've got planned for you: to see my indifference to you persist as we rot away together through all eternity. . . .

Paddy was waiting for him in the hall downstairs, looking sick and bewildered.

"Oh, Father!" he said, coming forward. "Isn't this awful? What a shock! I never expected her to go out like this; she was so well last night! Dear God, what am I going to do?"

"Have you seen her?"

"Heaven help me, yes!"

"Then you know what has to be done. I've never seen a corpse decompose so fast. If you don't get her decently into some sort of container within the next few hours you'll have to pour her into a petrol drum. She'll have to be buried first thing in the morning. Don't waste time beautifying her coffin; cover it with roses from the garden or something. But get a move on, man! I'm going into Gilly for vestments."

"Get back as soon as you can, Father!" Paddy pleaded.

But Father Ralph was rather longer than a simple visit to the presbytery demanded. Before he turned his car in that direction he drove down one of Gillanbone's more prosperous side streets, to a fairly pretentious dwelling surrounded by a well-laid-out garden.

Harry Gough was just sitting down to his dinner, but came into the parlor when the maid told him who had called.

"Father, will you eat with us? Corned beef and cabbage with boiled potatoes and parsley sauce, and for once the beef's not too salty."

"No, Harry, I can't stay. I just came to tell you Mary Carson died this morning."

"Holy Jesus! I was there last night! She seemed so well, Father!"

"I know. She was perfectly well when I took her up the stairs about three, but she must have died almost the moment she retired. Mrs. Smith found her at six this evening. By then she'd been dead so long she was hideous; the room was shut up like an incubator all through the heat of the day. Dear Lord, I pray to forget the sight of her! Unspeakable, Harry, awful."

"She'll be buried tomorrow?"

"She'll have to be."

"What time is it? Ten? We must eat dinner as late as the Spaniards in this heat, but no need to worry, it's too late to start phoning people. Would you like me to do that for you, Father?"

"Thank you, it would be a great kindness. I only came into Gilly for vestments. I never expected to be saying a Requiem when I started out. I must get back to Drogheda as quickly as I can; they need me. The Mass will be at nine in the morning."

"Tell Paddy I'll bring her will with me, so I can deal with it straight after the funeral. You're a beneficiary, too, Father, so I'd appreciate your staying for the reading."

"I'm afraid we have a slight problem, Harry. Mary made another will, you see. Last night after she left the party she gave me a sealed envelope, and made me promise I'd open it the moment I saw her dead body for myself. When I did so I found it contained a fresh will."

"Mary made a new will? Without *me?"*

"It would appear so. I think it was something she had been mulling for a long time, but as to why she chose to be so secretive about it, I don't know."

"Do you have it with you now, Father?"

"Yes." The priest reached inside his shirt and handed over the sheets of paper, folded small.

The lawyer had no compunction about reading them on the spot. When he finished he looked up, and there was a great deal in his eyes Father Ralph would rather not have seen. Admiration, anger, a certain contempt.

"Well, Father, congratulations! You got the lot after all." He could say it, not being a Catholic.

"Believe me, Harry, it came as a bigger surprise to me than it does to you."

"This is the only copy?"

"As far as I know, yes."

"And she gave it to you as late as last night?"

"Yes."

"Then why didn't you destroy it, make sure poor old Paddy got what's rightfully his? The Church has no right to Mary Carson's possessions at all."

The priest's fine eyes were bland. "Ah, but that wouldn't have been fitting, Harry, would it now? It was Mary's property, to dispose of in any manner she wished."

"I shall advise Paddy to contest."

"I think you should."

And on that note they parted. By the time everyone arrived in the morning to see Mary Carson buried, the whole of Gillanbone and all points of the compass around it would know where the money was going. The die was cast, there could be no turning back.

It was four in the morning when Father Ralph got through the last gate and into the Home Paddock, for he hadn't hurried on the return drive. All through it he had willed his mind to blankness; he wouldn't let himself think. Not of Paddy or of Fee, or Meggie or that stinking gross thing they had (he devoutly hoped) poured into her coffin. Instead he opened his eyes and his mind to the night, to the ghostly silver of dead trees standing lonely in the gleaming grass, to the heart-of-darkness shadows cast by stands of timber, to the full moon riding the heavens like an airy bubble. Once he stopped the car and got out, walked to a wire fence and leaned on its tautness while he breathed in the gums and the bewitching aroma of wildflowers. The land was so beautiful, so pure, so indifferent to the fates of the creatures who presumed to rule it. They might put their hands to it, but in the long run it ruled them. Until they could direct the weather and summon up the rain, it had the upper hand.

He parked his car some distance behind the house and walked slowly toward it. Every window was full of light; faintly from the housekeeper's quarters he could hear the sound of Mrs. Smith leading the two Irish maids in a rosary. A shadow moved under the blackness of the wistaria vine; he stopped short, his hackles rising. She had got to him in more ways than one, the old spider. But it was only Meggie, patiently waiting for him to come back. She was in jodhpurs and boots, very much alive.

"You gave me a fright," he said abruptly.

"I'm sorry, Father, I didn't mean to. But I didn't want to be inside there with Daddy and the boys, and Mum is still down at our house with the babies. I suppose I ought to be praying with Mrs. Smith and Minnie and Cat, but I don't feel like praying for her. That's a sin, isn't it?"

He was in no mood to pander to the memory of Mary Carson. "I don't think it's a sin, Meggie, whereas hypocrisy is. I don't feel like praying for her, either. She wasn't . . . a very good person." His smile flashed. "So if you've sinned in saying it, so have I, and more seriously at that. I'm supposed to love everyone, a burden which isn't laid upon you."

"Are you all right, Father?"

"Yes, I'm all right." He looked up at the house, and sighed. "I don't want to be in there, that's all. I don't want to be where she is until it's light and the demons of the darkness are driven away. If I saddle the horses, will you ride with me until dawn?"

Her hand touched his black sleeve, fell. "I don't want to go inside, either."

"Wait a minute while I put my soutane in the car."

"I'll go on to the stables."

For the first time she was trying to meet him on his ground, adult ground; he could sense the difference in her as surely as he could smell the roses in Mary Carson's beautiful gardens. Roses. Ashes of roses. Roses, roses, everywhere. Petals in the grass. Roses of summer, red and white and yellow. Perfume of roses, heavy and sweet in the night. Pink roses, bleached by the moon to ashes. Ashes of roses, ashes of roses. My Meggie, I have forsaken you. But can't you see, you've become a threat? Therefore have I crushed you beneath the heel of my ambition; you have no more substance to me than a bruised rose in the grass. The smell of roses. The smell of Mary Carson. Roses and ashes, ashes of roses.

"Ashes of roses," he said, mounting. "Let's get as far from the smell of roses as the moon. Tomorrow the house will be full of them."

He kicked the chestnut mare and cantered ahead of Meggie down the track to the creek, longing to weep; for until he smelled the future adornments of Mary Carson's coffin it had not actually impinged on his thinking brain as an imminent fact. He would be going away very soon. Too many thoughts, too many emotions, all of them ungovernable. They wouldn't leave him in Gilly a day after learning the terms of that incredible will; they would recall him to Sydney immediately. *Immediately!* He fled from his pain, never having known such pain, but it kept pace with him effortlessly. It wasn't something in a vague sometime; it was going to happen immediately. And he could almost see Paddy's face, the revulsion, the turning away. After this he wouldn't be welcome on Drogheda, and he would never see Meggie again.

The disciplining began then, hammered by hoofs and in a sensation of flying. It was better so, better so, better so. Galloping on and on. Yes, it would surely hurt less then, tucked safely in some cell in a bishop's palace, hurt less and less, until finally even the ache faded from consciousness. It had to be better so. Better than staying in Gilly to watch her change into a creature he didn't want, then have to marry her one day to some unknown man. Out of sight, out of mind.

Then what was he doing with her now, riding through the stand of box and coolibah on the far side of the creek? He couldn't seem to think why, he only felt the pain. Not the pain of betrayal; there wasn't room for that. Only for the pain of leaving her.

"Father, Father! I can't keep up with you! Slow down, Father, please!"

It was the call to duty, and reality. Like a man in slow motion he wrenched the mare around, sat it until it had danced out its excitement. And waited for Meggie to catch him up. That was the trouble. Meggie was catching him up.

Close by them was the roar of the borehead, a great steaming pool smelling of sulphur, with a pipe like a ship's ventilator jetting boiling water into its depths. All around the perimeter of the little elevated lake like spokes from a wheel's hub, the bore drains dribbled off across the plain whiskered in incongruously emerald grass. The banks of the pool were slimy grey mud, and the freshwater crayfish called yabbies lived in the mud.

Father Ralph started to laugh. "It smells like Hell, Meggie, doesn't it? Sulphur and brimstone, right here on her own property, in her own backyard. She ought to recognize the smell when she gets there decked in roses, oughtn't she? Oh, Meggie . . ."

The horses were trained to stand on a dangling rein; there were no fences nearby, and no trees closer than half a mile away. But there was a log on the side of the pool farthest from the borehead itself, where the water was cooler. It was the seat provided for winter bathers as they dried their feet and legs.

Father Ralph sat down and Meggie sat some way from him, turned side on to watch him.

"What's the matter, Father?"

It sounded peculiar, his oft-asked question from her lips, to him. He smiled. "I've sold you, my Meggie, sold you for thirteen million pieces of silver."

"*Sold* me?"

"A figure of speech. It doesn't matter. Come, sit closer to me. There may not be the chance for us to talk together again."

"While we're in mourning for Auntie, you mean?" She wriggled up the log and sat next to him. "What difference will being in mourning make?"

"I don't mean that, Meggie."

"You mean because I'm growing up, and people might gossip about us?"

"Not exactly. I mean I'm going away."

There it was: the meeting of trouble head on, the acceptance of another load. No outcry, no weeping, no storm of protest. Just a tiny shrinking, as if the burden sat askew, would not distribute itself so she could bear it properly. And a caught breath, not quite like a sigh.

"When?"

"A matter of days."

"Oh, Father! It will be harder than Frank."

"And for me harder than anything in my life. I have no consolation. You at least have your family."

"You have your God."

"Well said, Meggie! You *are* growing up!"

But, tenacious female, her mind had returned to the question she had ridden three miles without a chance to ask. He was leaving, it would be so hard to do without him, but the question had its own importance.

"Father, in the stables you said 'ashes of roses.' Did you mean the color of my dress?"

"In a way, perhaps. But I think really I meant something else."

"What?"

"Nothing you'd understand, my Meggie. The dying of an idea which had no right to be born, let alone nurtured."

"There is nothing which has no right to be born, even an idea."

He turned his head to watch her. "You know what I'm talking about, don't you?"

"I think so."

"Not everything born is good, Meggie."

"No. But if it was born at all, it was meant to be."

"You argue like a Jesuit. How old are you?"

"I'll be seventeen in a month, Father."

"And you've toiled all seventeen years of it. Well, hard work ages us ahead of our years. What do you think about, Meggie, when you've the time to think?"

"Oh, about Jims and Patsy and the rest of the boys, about Daddy and Mum, about Hal and Auntie Mary. Sometimes about growing babies. I'd like that very much. And riding, the sheep. All the things the men talk about. The weather, the rain, the vegetable garden, the hens, what I'm going to do tomorrow."

"Do you dream of having a husband?"

"No, except I suppose I'll have to have one if I want to grow babies. It isn't nice for a baby to have no father."

In spite of his pain he smiled; she was such a quaint mixture of ignorance and morality. Then he swung sideways, took her chin in his hand and stared down at her. How to do it, what had to be done?

"Meggie, I realized something not long ago which I ought to have seen sooner. You weren't being quite truthful when you told me what you thought about, were you?"

"I . . ." she said, and fell silent.

"You didn't say you thought about me, did you? If there was no guilt in it, you would have mentioned my name alongside your father's. I think perhaps it's a good thing I'm going away, don't you? You're a little old to be having schoolgirl crushes, but you're not a very old almost-seventeen, are you? I like your lack of worldly wisdom, but I know how painful schoolgirl crushes can be; I've suffered enough of them."

She seemed about to speak, but in the end her lids fell over tear-bright eyes, she shook her head free.

"Look, Meggie, it's simply a phase, a marker on the road to being a woman. When you've become that woman, you'll meet the man destined to be your husband and you'll be far too busy getting on with your life to think of me, except as an old friend who helped you through some of the terrible spasms of growing up. What you mustn't do is get into the habit of dreaming about me in any sort of romantic fashion. I can never regard you the way a husband will. I don't think of you in that light at all, Meggie, do you understand me? When I say I love you, I don't mean I love you as a man. I am a priest, not a man. So don't fill your head with dreams of me. I'm going away, and I doubt very much that I'll have time to come back, even on a visit."

Her shoulders were bent as if the load was very heavy, but she lifted her head to look directly into his face.

"I won't fill my head with dreams of you, don't worry. I know you're a priest."

"I'm not convinced I chose my vocation wrongly. It fills a need in me no human being ever could, even you."

"I know. I can see it when you say Mass. You have a power. I suppose you must feel like Our Lord."

"I can feel every suspended breath in the church, Meggie! As each day goes on I die, and in each morning saying Mass I am reborn. But is it because I'm

God's chosen priest, or because I hear those awed breaths, know the power I have over every soul present?"

"Does it matter? It just is."

"It would probably never matter to you, but it does to me. I doubt, I doubt."

She switched the subject to what mattered to her. "I don't know how I shall get on without you, Father. First Frank, now you. Somehow with Hal it's different; I know he's dead and can never come back. But you and Frank are alive! I'll aways be wondering how you are, what you're doing, if you're all right, if there's anything I could do to help you. I'll even have to wonder if you're still alive, won't I?"

"I'll be feeling the same, Meggie, and I'm sure that Frank does, too."

"No. Frank's forgotten us. . . . You will, too."

"I could never forget you, Meggie, not as long as I live. And for my punishment I'm going to live a long, long time." He got up and pulled her to her feet, put his arms about her loosely and affectionately. "I think this is goodbye, Meggie. We can't be alone again."

"If you hadn't been a priest, Father, would you have married me?"

The title jarred. "Don't call me that all the time! My name is Ralph." Which didn't answer her question.

Though he held her, he did not have any intention of kissing her. The face raised to his was nearly invisible, for the moon had set and it was very dark. He could feel her small, pointed breasts low down on his chest; a curious sensation, disturbing. Even more so was the fact that as naturally as if she came into a man's arms every day of her life, her arms had gone up around his neck, and linked tightly.

He had never kissed anyone as a lover, did not want to now; nor, he thought, did Meggie. A warm salute on the cheek, a quick hug, as she would demand of her father were he to go away. She was sensitive and proud;

he must have hurt her deeply when he held up her precious dreams to dispassionate inspection. Undoubtedly she was as eager to be done with the farewell as he was. Would it comfort her to know his pain was far worse than hers? As he bent his head to come at her cheek she raised herself on tiptoe, and more by luck than good management touched his lips with her own. He jerked back as if he tasted the spider's poison, then he tipped his head forward before he could lose her, tried to say something against the sweet shut mouth, and in trying to answer she parted it. Her body seemed to lose all its bones, become fluid, a warm melting darkness; one of his arms was clamped round her waist, the other across her back with its hand on her skull, in her hair, holding her face up to his as if frightened she would go from him in that very moment, before he could grasp and catalogue this unbelievable presence who was Meggie. Meggie, and not Meggie, too alien to be familiar, for his Meggie wasn't a woman, didn't feel like a woman, could never be a woman to him. Just as he couldn't be a man to her.

The thought overcame his drowning senses; he wrenched her arms from about his neck, thrust her away and tried to see her face in the darkness. But her head was down, she wouldn't look at him.

"It's time we were going, Meggie," he said.

Without a word she turned to her horse, mounted and waited for him; usually it was he who waited for her.

Father Ralph had been right. At this time of year Drogheda was awash with roses, so the house was smothered in them. By eight that morning hardly one bloom was left in the garden. The first of the mourners began to arrive not long after the final rose was plundered from its bush; a light breakfast of coffee and freshly baked, buttered rolls was laid out in the small dining room. After Mary Carson was deposited in the vault a more substantial repast would be served in the big dining room, to fortify the departing mourners on their long ways home. The word had got around; no need to doubt the efficiency of the Gilly grapevine, which was the party line. While lips shaped conventional phrases, eyes and the minds behind them speculated, deduced, smiled slyly.

"I hear we're going to lose you, Father," said Miss Carmichael nastily.

He had never looked so remote, so devoid of human feeling as he did that morning in his laceless alb and dull black chasuble with silver cross. It was as if he attended only in body, while his spirit moved far away. But he looked down at Miss Carmichael absently, seemed to recollect himself, and smiled with genuine mirth.

"God moves in strange ways, Miss Carmichael," he said, and went to speak to someone else.

What was on his mind no one could have guessed; it was the coming confrontation with Paddy over the will, and his dread of seeing Paddy's rage, his *need* of Paddy's rage and contempt.

Before he began the Requiem Mass he turned to face his congregation; the room was jammed, and reeked so of roses that open windows could not dissipate their heavy perfume.

"I do not intend to make a long eulogy," he said in his clear, almost Oxford diction with its faint Irish underlay. "Mary Carson was known to you all. A pillar of the community, a pillar of the Church she loved more than any living being."

At that point there were those who swore his eyes mocked, but others who maintained just as stoutly that they were dulled with a real and abiding grief.

"A pillar of the Church she loved more than any living being," he repeated more clearly still; he was not one to turn away, either. "In her last hour she was alone, yet she was not alone. For in the hour of our death Our Lord Jesus Christ is with us, within us, bearing the burden of our agony. Not the greatest nor the humblest living being dies alone, and death is sweet. We are gathered here to pray for her immortal soul, that she whom we loved in life shall enjoy her just and eternal reward. Let us pray."

The makeshift coffin was so covered in roses it could not be seen, and it rested upon a small wheeled cart the boys had cannibalized from various pieces of farm equipment. Even so, with the windows gaping open and the overpowering scent of roses, they could smell her. The doctor had been talking, too.

"When I reached Drogheda she was so rotten that I just couldn't hold my stomach," he said on the party line to Martin King. "I've never felt so sorry for anyone in all my life as I did then for Paddy Cleary, not only because he's been done out of Drogheda but because he had to shove that awful seething heap in a coffin."

"Then I'm not volunteering for the office of pallbearer," Martin said, so faintly because of all the receivers down that the doctor had to make him repeat the statement three times before he understood it.

Hence the cart; no one was willing to shoulder the remains of Mary Carson across the lawn to the vault. And no one was sorry when the vault doors were closed on her and breathing could become normal at last.

While the mourners clustered in the big dining room eating, or trying to look as if they were eating, Harry Gough conducted Paddy, his family, Father Ralph, Mrs. Smith and the two maids to the drawing room. None of the mourners had any intention of going home yet, hence the pretense at eating; they wanted to be on hand to see what Paddy looked like when he came out after the reading of the will. To do him and his family justice, they hadn't comported themselves during the funeral as if conscious of their elevated status. As goodhearted as ever, Paddy had wept for his sister, and Fee looked exactly as she always did, as if she didn't care what happened to her.

"Paddy, I want you to contest," Harry Gough said after he had read the amazing document through in a hard, indignant voice.

"The wicked old bitch!" said Mrs. Smith; though she liked the priest, she was fonder by far of the Clearys. They had brought babies and children into her life.

But Paddy shook his head. "No, Harry! I couldn't do that. The property was hers, wasn't it? She was quite entitled to do what she liked with it. If she wanted the Church to have it, she wanted the Church to have it. I don't deny it's a bit of a disappointment, but I'm just an ordinary sort of chap, so perhaps it's for the best. I don't think I'd like the responsibility of owning a property the size of Drogheda."

"You don't understand, Paddy!" the lawyer said in a slow, distinct voice, as if he were explaining to a child. "It isn't just Drogheda I'm talking about. Drogheda was the least part of what your sister had to leave, believe me. She's a major shareholder in a hundred gilt-edged companies, she owns steel factories and gold mines, she's Michar Limited, with a ten-story office building all to herself in Sydney. She was worth more than anyone in the whole of Australia! Funny, she made me contact the Sydney directors of Michar Limited not four weeks ago, to find out the exact extent of her assets. When she died she was worth something over thirteen million pounds."

"Thirteen million pounds!" Paddy said it as one says the distance from the earth to the sun, something totally incomprehensible. "That settles it, Harry. I don't want the responsibility of that kind of money."

"It's no responsibility, Paddy! Don't you understand yet? Money like that looks after itself! You'd have nothing to do with cultivating or harvesting it; there are hundreds of people employed simply to take care of it for you. Contest the will, Paddy, *please!* I'll get you the best KCs in the country and I'll fight it for you all the way to the Privy Council if necessary."

Suddenly realizing that his family were as concerned as himself, Paddy turned to Bob and Jack, sitting together bewildered on a Florentine marble bench. "Boys, what do you say? Do you want to go after Auntie Mary's thirteen million quid? If you do I'll contest, not otherwise."

"But we can live on Drogheda anyway, isn't that what the will says?" Bob asked.

Harry answered. "No one can turn you off Drogheda so long as even one of your father's grandchildren lives."

"We're going to live here in the big house, have Mrs. Smith and the girls to look after us, and earn a decent wage," said Paddy as if he could hardly believe his good fortune rather than his bad.

"Then what more do we want, Jack?" Bob asked his brother. "Don't you agree?"

"It suits me," said Jack.

Father Ralph moved restlessly. He had not stopped to shed his Requiem vestments, nor had he taken a chair; like a dark and beautiful sorcerer he stood half in the shadows at the back of the room, isolated, his hands hidden beneath the black chasuble, his face still, and at the back of the distant blue eyes a horrified, stunned resentment. There was not even going to be the longed-for chastisement of rage or contempt; Paddy was going to hand it all to him on a golden plate of goodwill, and *thank* him for relieving the Clearys of a burden.

"What about Fee and Meggie?" the priest asked Paddy harshly. "Do you not think enough of your women to consult them, too?"

"Fee?" asked Paddy anxiously.

"Whatever you decide, Paddy. I don't care."

"Meggie?"

"I don't want her thirteen million pieces of silver," Meggie said, her eyes fixed on Father Ralph.

Paddy turned to the lawyer. "Then that's it, Harry. We don't want to contest the will. Let the Church have Mary's money, and welcome."

Harry struck his hands together. "God damn it, I hate to see you cheated!"

"I thank my stars for Mary," said Paddy gently. "If it wasn't for her I'd still be trying to scrape a living in New Zealand."

As they came out of the drawing room Paddy stopped Father Ralph and held out his hand, in full view of the fascinated mourners clustering in the dining room doorway.

"Father, please don't think there are any hard feelings on our side. Mary was never swayed by another human being in all her life, priest or brother or husband. You take it from me, she did what she wanted to do. You were mighty good to her, and you've been mighty good to us. We'll never forget it."

The guilt. *The burden.* Almost Father Ralph did not move to take that gnarled stained hand, but the cardinal's brain won; he gripped it feverishly and smiled, agonized.

"Thank you, Paddy. You may rest assured I'll see you never want for a thing."

Within the week he was gone, not having appeared on Drogheda again. He spent the few days packing his scant belongings, and touring every station in the district where there were Catholic families; save Drogheda.

Father Watkin Thomas, late of Wales, arrived to assume the duties of parish priest to the Gillanbone district, while Father Ralph de Bricassart became private secretary to Archbishop Cluny Dark. But his work load was light; he had two undersecretaries. For the most part he was occupied in discovering just what and how much Mary Carson had owned, and in gathering the reins of government together on behalf of the Church.

THREE

1929-1932 Paddy

8

The new year came in with Angus MacQueen's annual Hogmanay party on Rudna Hunish, and still the move to the big house had not been accomplished. It wasn't something done overnight, between packing over seven years' accumulation of everyday artifacts, and Fee's declaration that the big house drawing room at least be finished first. No one was in the slightest hurry, though everyone was looking forward to it. In some respects the big house would prove no different: it lacked electricity and the flies populated it just as thickly. But in summer it was about twenty degrees cooler than outside, from the thickness of its stone walls and the ghost gums shading its roof. Also, the bathhouse was a true luxury, having hot water all winter from pipes which ran up the back of the vast fuel stove in the cookhouse next door, and every drop in its pipes was rain water. Though baths and showers had to be taken in this large structure with its ten separate cubicles, the big house and all the smaller houses were liberally endowed with indoor water-closet toilets, an unheard-of degree of opulence envious Gilly residents had been caught calling sybaritism. Aside from the Hotel Imperial, two pubs, the Catholic presbytery and the convent, the Gillanbone district survived on outhouses. Except Drogheda homestead, thanks to its enormous number of tanks and roofs to catch rain water. The rules were strict: no undue flushing, and plenty of sheep-dip disinfectant. But after holes in the ground, it was heaven.

Father Ralph had sent Paddy a check for five thousand pounds at the beginning of the preceding December, to be going on with, his letter said; Paddy handed it to Fee with a dazed exclamation.

"I doubt I've managed to earn this much in all my working days," he said.

"What shall I do with it?" Fee asked, staring at it and then looking up at him, eyes blazing. "Money, Paddy! Money at last, do you realize it? Oh, I don't care about Auntie Mary's thirteen million pounds—there's nothing real about so much. But *this* is real! What shall I do with it?"

"Spend it," said Paddy simply. "A few new clothes for the children and yourself? And maybe there are things you'd like to buy for the big house? I can't think of anything else we need."

"Nor can I, isn't it silly?" Up got Fee from the breakfast table, beckoning Meggie imperiously. "Come on, girl, we're walking up to the big house to look at it."

Though at that time three weeks had elapsed since the frantic week following Mary Carson's death, none of the Clearys had been near the big house. But now Fee's visit more than made up for their previous reluctance. From one room to another she marched with Meggie, Mrs. Smith, Minnie and Cat in attendance, more animated than a bewildered Meggie had ever known her. She muttered to herself continually; this was dreadful, that was an absolute horror, was Mary color-blind, did she have no taste at all?

In the drawing room Fee paused longest, eyeing it expertly. Only the reception room exceeded it in size, for it was forty feet long and thirty wide, and had a fifteen-foot ceiling. It was a curious mixture of the best and the worst in its decoration, painted a uniform cream which had yellowed and did nothing to emphasize the magnificent moldings on the ceiling or the carved paneling on the walls. The enormous floor-to-ceiling windows that marched uninterruptedly for forty feet along the veranda side were heavily curtained in brown velvet, casting a deep gloom over the dingy brown chairs, two stunning malachite benches and two equally beautiful benches in Florentine marble, and a massive fireplace of cream marble veined in deep pink. On the polished teak floor three Aubusson carpets had been squared with geometrical precision, and a Waterford chandelier six feet long touched the ceiling, its chain bunched round it.

"You are to be commended, Mrs. Smith," Fee pronounced. "It's positively awful, but spotlessly clean. I shall give you something worth caring for. Those priceless benches without anything to set them off—it's a shame! Since the day I saw this room, I've longed to make it into something every person who walks into it will admire, and yet comfortable enough to make every person who walks into it want to remain."

Mary Carson's desk was a Victorian hideousness; Fee walked to it and the phone which stood upon it, flicking its gloomy wood contemptuously. "My escritoire will do beautifully here," she said. "I'm going to start with this room, and when it's finished I'll move up from the creek, not before. Then at least we'll have one place where we can congregate without being depressed." She sat down and plucked the receiver off its hook.

While her daughter and her servants stood in a small bewildered huddle, she proceeded to set Harry Gough in motion. Mark Foys would send fabric samples on the night mail; Nock & Kirbys would send paint samples; Grace Brothers would send wallpaper samples; these and other Sydney stores would send catalogues specially compiled for her, describing their lines of furnishings. Laughter in his voice, Harry guaranteed to produce a competent upholsterer and a team of painters capable of doing the meticulous work Fee demanded. Good for Mrs. Cleary! She was going to sweep Mary Carson right out of the house.

The phoning finished, everyone was directed to rip down the brown velvet curtains at once. Out they went onto the rubbish heap in an orgy of wastefulness Fee supervised personally, even putting the torch to them herself.

"We don't need them," she said, "and I'm not going to inflict them on the Gillanbone poor."

"Yes, Mum," said Meggie, paralyzed.

"We're not going to have any curtains," said Fee, not at all disturbed over a flagrant breach of the decorating customs of the time. "The veranda's far too deep to let the sun come in directly, so why do we need curtains? I want this room to be *seen.*"

The materials arrived, so did the painters and the upholsterer; Meggie and Cat were sent up ladders to wash and polish the top windows while Mrs. Smith and Minnie coped with the bottom ones and Fee strode around watching everything with an eagle eye.

By the second week in January it was all done, and somehow of course the news leaked out on the party lines. Mrs. Cleary had made the Drogheda drawing room into a palace, and wouldn't it be only the civil thing for Mrs. Hopeton to accompany Mrs. King and Mrs. O'Rourke on a welcome-to-the-big-house visit?

No one argued that the result of Fee's efforts was absolute beauty. The cream Aubusson carpets with their faded bunches of pink and red roses and green leaves had been strewn rather haphazardly around the mirror-finished floor. Fresh cream paint covered the walls and the ceiling, every molding and carving painstakingly picked out in gilt, but the huge oval-shaped flat spaces in the paneling had been papered with faded black silk bearing the same bunches of roses as the three carpets, like stilted Japanese paintings in cream and gilt surrounds. The Waterford chandelier had been lowered until its bottom pendant chimed a bare six and a half feet from the floor, every prism of its thousands polished to a flashing rainbow, and its great brass chain tethered to the wall instead of being bunched up. On spindly cream-and-gilt tables Waterford lamps stood next to Waterford ashtrays and Waterford vases stuffed with cream and pink roses; all the big comfortable chairs had been re-covered in cream watered silk and placed in small cozy groupings with large ottomans drawn up to each one invitingly; in one sunny corner stood the exquisite old spinet with an enormous vase of cream and pink roses on it. Above the fireplace hung the portrait of Fee's grandmother in her pale pink crinoline, and facing her at the other end of the room was an even larger portrait of a youngish, red-haired Mary Carson, face like the youngish Queen Victoria, in a stiff black gown fashionably bustled.

"All right," said Fee, "now we can move up from the creek. I'll do the other rooms at my leisure. Oh, isn't it lovely to have money and a decent home to spend it on?"

About three days before they moved, so early in the morning the sun had not yet risen, the roosters in the fowl yard were cock-a-doodling joyously.

"Miserable wretches," said Fee, wrapping old newspapers around her china. "I don't know what they think they've done to crow about. Not an egg in the place for breakfast, and all the men at home until we finish moving. Meggie, you'll have to go down to the chook yard for me; I'm busy." She scanned a yellowed sheet of the *Sydney Morning Herald*, snorting over an advertisement for wasp-waisted stays. "I don't know why Paddy insists we get all the newspapers; no one ever has time to read them. They just pile up too fast to burn in the stove. Look at this! It's older than our tenancy of the house. Well, at least they're handy for packing."

It was nice to see her mother so cheerful, Meggie thought as she sped down the back steps and across the dusty yard. Though everyone was naturally looking forward to living in the big house, Mum seemed to hunger for it as if she could remember what living in a big house was like. How clever she was, what perfect taste she had! Things no one had ever realized before, because there had been neither time nor money to bring them out. Meggie hugged herself with excitement; Daddy had sent in to the Gilly jeweler and used some of the five thousand pounds to buy Mum a real pearl choker and real pearl earrings, only these had little diamonds in them as well. He was going to give them to her at their first dinner in the big house. Now that she had seen her mother's face freed of its habitual dourness, she could hardly wait for the expression it would wear when she received her pearls. From Bob to the twins, the children were agog for that moment, because Daddy had shown them the big flat leather case, opened it to reveal the milky opalescent beads on their black velvet bed. Their mother's blossoming happiness had affected them deeply; it was like seeing the start of a good drenching rain. Until now they had never quite understood how unhappy she must have been all the years they had known her.

The chook yard was huge, and held four roosters and upward of forty hens. At night they inhabited a tumble-down shed, its rigorously swept floor lined around the edges with straw-filled orange crates for laying, and its rear crossed by perches of various heights. But during the day the chooks strutted clucking around a large, wire-netted run. When Meggie opened the run gate and squeezed inside, the birds clustered about her greedily, thinking they would be fed, but since Meggie fed them in the evenings she laughed at their silly antics and stepped through them into the shed.

"Honestly, what a hopeless lot of chookies you are!"

she lectured them severely as she poked in the nests. "Forty of you, and only fifteen eggs! Not enough for breakfast, let alone a cake. Well, I'm warning you here and now—if you don't do something about it soon, the chopping block for the lot of you, and that applies to the lords of the coop as well as wives, so don't spread your tails and ruffle up your necks as if I'm not including you, gentlemen!"

With the eggs held carefully in her apron, Meggie ran back to the kitchen, singing.

Fee was sitting in Paddy's chair staring at a sheet of *Smith's Weekly,* her face white, her lips moving. Inside Meggie could hear the men moving about, and the sounds of six-year-old Jims and Patsy laughing in their cot; they were never allowed up until after the men had gone.

"What's the matter, Mum?" Meggie asked.

Fee didn't answer, only sat staring in front of her with beads of sweat along her upper lip, eyes stilled to a desperately rational pain, as if within herself she was marshaling every resource she possessed not to scream.

"Daddy, Daddy!" Meggie called sharply, frightened.

The tone of her voice brought him out still fastening his flannel undershirt, with Bob, Jack, Hughie and Stu behind him. Meggie pointed wordlessly at her mother.

Paddy's heart seemed to block his throat. He bent over Fee, his hand picking up one limp wrist. "What is it, dear?" he asked in tones more tender than any of his children had ever heard him use; yet somehow they knew they were the tones he used with her when they were not around to hear.

She seemed to recognize that special voice enough to emerge from her shocked trance, and the big grey eyes looked up into his face, so kind and worn, no longer young.

"Here," she said, pointing at a small item of news toward the bottom of the page.

Stuart had gone to stand behind his mother, his hand lightly on her shoulder; before he started to read the article Paddy glanced up at his son, into the eyes so like Fee's, and he nodded. What had roused him to jealousy in Frank could never do so in Stuart; as if their love for Fee bound them tightly together instead of separating them.

Paddy read out loud, slowly, his tone growing sadder and sadder. The little headline said: BOXER RECEIVES LIFE SENTENCE.

> Francis Armstrong Cleary, aged 26, professional boxer, was convicted today in Goulburn District Court of the murder of Ronald Albert Cumming, aged 32, laborer, last July. The jury reached its verdict after only ten minutes' deliberation, recommending the most severe punishment the court could mete out. It was, said Mr. Justice FitzHugh-Cunneally, a simple open-and-closed case. Cumming and Cleary had quarreled violently in the public bar of the Harbor Hotel on July 23rd. Later the same night Sergeant Tom Beardsmore of the Goulburn police, accompanied by two constables, was called to the Harbor Hotel by its proprietor, Mr. James Ogilvie. In the lane behind the hotel the police discovered Cleary kicking at the head of the insensible Cumming. His fists were bloodstained and bore tufts of Cumming's hair. When arrested Cleary was drunk but lucid. He was charged with assault with intent to commit grievous bodily harm, but the charge was amended to murder after Cumming died of brain injuries in the Goulburn District Hospital next day.
>
> Mr. Arthur Whyte, K.C., entered a plea of not guilty by reason of insanity, but four medical witnesses for the Crown stated unequivocally that under the provisions of the M'Naghten rules Cleary could not be called insane. In addressing the jury,

Mr. Justice FitzHugh-Cunneally told them there was no question of guilt or innocence, the verdict was clearly guilty, but he requested them to take time considering their recommendation for either clemency or severity, as he would be guided by their opinion. When sentencing Cleary, Mr. Justice FitzHugh-Cunneally called his act "subhuman savagery," and regretted that the drunken unpremeditated nature of the crime precluded hanging, as he regarded Cleary's hands as a weapon quite as deadly as a gun or knife. Cleary was sentenced to life imprisonment at hard labor, the sentence to be served in Goulburn Gaol, this institution being one designed for violently disposed prisoners. Asked if he had anything so say, Cleary answered, "Just don't tell my mother."

Paddy looked at the top of the page to see the date: December 6, 1925. "It happened over three years ago," he said helplessly.

No one answered him or moved, for no one knew what to do; from the front of the house came the gleeful laughter of the twins, their high voices raised in chatter.

" 'Just—don't—tell my mother,' " said Fee numbly. "And no one did! Oh, God! My poor, poor Frank!"

Paddy wiped the tears from his face with the back of his free hand, then squatted down in front of her, patting her lap gently.

"Fee dear, pack your things. We'll go to him."

She half-rose before sinking back, her eyes in her small white face starred and glistening as if dead, pupils huge and gold-filmed.

"I can't go," she said without a hint of agony, yet making everyone feel that the agony was there. "It would kill him to see me. Oh, Paddy, it would kill him! I know him so well—his pride, his ambition, his determination to be someone important. Let him bear the shame alone, it's what he wants. You read it. 'Just don't tell my mother.' We've got to help him keep his secret. What good will it do him or us to see him?"

Paddy was still weeping, but not for Frank; for the life which had gone from Fee's face, for the dying in her eyes. A Jonah, that's what the lad had always been; the bitter bringer of blight, forever standing between Fee and himself, the cause of her withdrawal from his heart and the hearts of *his* children. Every time it looked as if there might be happiness in store for Fee, Frank took it away. But Paddy's love for her was as deep and impossible to eradicate as hers was for Frank; he could never use the lad as his whipping boy again, not after that night in the presbytery.

So he said, "Well, Fee, if you think it's better not to attempt to get in touch with him, we won't. Yet I'd like to know he was all right, that whatever can be done for him is being done. How about if I write to Father de Bricassart and ask him to look out for Frank?"

The eyes didn't liven, but a faint pink stole into her cheeks. "Yes, Paddy, do that. Only make sure he knows not to tell Frank we found out. Perhaps it would ease Frank to think for certain that we don't know."

Within a few days Fee regained most of her energy, and her interest in redecorating the big house kept her occupied. But her quietness became dour again, only less grim, encapsulated by an expressionless calm. It seemed she cared more for how the big house would eventually look than she did for her family's welfare. Perhaps she assumed they could look after themselves spiritually, and that Mrs. Smith and the maids were there to look after them physically.

Yet the discovery of Frank's plight had profoundly affected everyone. The older boys grieved deeply for their mother, spent sleepless nights remembering her face at that awful moment. They loved her, and her cheerfulness during the previous few weeks had given them a glimpse of her which was never to leave them, and was to inspire them with a passionate desire to bring it back again. If their father had been the pivot upon which their lives turned until then, from that moment on their mother was put alongside him. They began to treat her with a tender, absorbed care no amount of indifference on her part could banish. From Paddy to Stu the Cleary males conspired to make Fee's life whatever she wanted, and they demanded adherence to this end from everyone. No one must ever harm her or hurt her again. And when Paddy presented her with the pearls she took them with a brief, expressionless word of thanks, no pleasure or interest in her perusal; but everyone was thinking how different her reaction would have been were it not for Frank.

Had the move to the big house not occurred, poor Meggie would have suffered a great deal more than she did, for without admitting her into full, exclusively male membership of the protect-Mum society (perhaps sensing that her participation was more grudging than theirs), her father and older brothers expected that Meggie should shoulder all the tasks Fee obviously found repugnant. As it turned out, Mrs. Smith and the maids shared the burden with Meggie. Chiefly repugnant to Fee was the care of her two youngest sons, but Mrs. Smith assumed full charge of Jims and Patsy with such ardor Meggie couldn't feel sorry for her, instead in a way she felt glad that these two could at last belong entirely to the housekeeper. Meggie grieved for her mother, too, but by no means as wholeheartedly as the men, for her loyalties were sorely tried; the big vein of motherliness in her was deeply offended by Fee's mounting indifference to Jims and Patsy. When I have my children, she would think to herself, I'm *never* going to love one of them more than the rest.

Living in the big house was certainly very different. At first it was strange to have a bedroom to oneself, and for the women, not to have to worry about any sort of household duty, inside or outside. Minnie, Cat and

Mrs. Smith among them coped with everything from washing and ironing to cooking and cleaning, and were horrified by offers of help. In return for plenty of food and a small wage, an endless procession of swaggies were temporarily entered on the station books as rouse-abouts, to chop the wood for the homestead fires, feed the fowls and pigs, do the milking, help old Tom take care of the lovely gardens, do all the heavy cleaning.

Paddy had been communicating with Father Ralph.

"The income from Mary's estate comes to roughly four million pounds a year, thanks to the fact that Michar Limited is a privately owned company with most of its assets sunk in steel, ships and mining," wrote Father Ralph. "So what I've assigned to you is a mere drop in the Carson bucket, and doesn't even amount to one-tenth of Drogheda station profits in a year. Don't worry about bad years, either. The Drogheda station account is so heavily in the black I can pay you out of its interest forever, if necessary. So what money comes to you is no more than you deserve, and doesn't dent Michar Limited. It's station money you're getting, not company money. I require no more of you than to keep the station books up to date and honestly entered for the auditors."

It was after he had this particular letter that Paddy held a conference in the beautiful drawing room on a night when everyone was at home. He sat with his steel-rimmed reading half-glasses perched on his Roman nose, in a big cream chair, his feet comfortably disposed on a matching ottoman, his pipe in a Waterford ashtray.

"How nice this is." He smiled, looking around with pleasure. "I think we ought to give Mum a vote of thanks for it, don't you, boys?"

There were murmurs of assent from the "boys"; Fee inclined her head from where she sat in what had been Mary Carson's wing chair, re-covered now in cream watered silk. Meggie curled her feet around the ottoman she had chosen instead of a chair, and kept her eyes doggedly on the sock she was mending.

"Well, Father de Bricassart has sorted everything out and has been very generous," Paddy continued. "He's put seven thousand pounds in the bank in my name, and opened a savings account for everyone with two thousand pounds in each. I am to be paid four thousand pounds a year as the station manager, and Bob will be paid three thousand a year as the assistant manager. All the working boys—Jack, Hughie and Stu—will be paid two thousand a year, and the little boys are to get one thousand a year each until they're old enough to decide what they want to do.

"When the little boys are grown up, the estate will guarantee each of them a yearly income equal to a full working member of Drogheda, even if they don't want to work on Drogheda. When Jims and Patsy turn twelve, they'll be sent to Riverview College in Sydney to board and be educated at the expense of the estate.

"Mum is to have two thousand pounds a year for herself, and so is Meggie. The household account will be kept at five thousand pounds, though why Father thinks we need so much to run a house, I don't know. He says in case we want to make major alterations. I have his instructions as to how much Mrs. Smith, Minnie, Cat and Tom are to be paid, and I must say he's generous. Other wages I decide on myself. But my first decision as manager is to put on at least six more stockmen, so Drogheda can be run as it should be. It's too much for a handful." That was the most he ever said about his sister's management.

No one had ever heard of having so much money; they sat silent, trying to assimilate their good fortune.

"We'll never spend the half of it, Paddy," said Fee. "He hasn't left us anything to spend it on."

Paddy looked at her gently. "I know, Mum. But isn't it nice to think we'll never have to worry about money again?" He cleared his throat. "Now it seems to me that Mum and Meggie in particular are going to be at a bit of a loose end," he went on. "I was never much good at figures, but Mum can add and subtract and divide and multiply like an arithmetic teacher. So Mum is going to be the Drogheda bookkeeper, instead of Harry Gough's office. I never realized it, but Harry has employed one chap just to deal with Drogheda's accounts, and at the moment he's a man short, so he doesn't mind passing it back to us at all. In fact, he was the one who suggested Mum might make a good bookkeeper. He's going to send someone out from Gilly to teach you properly, Mum. It's quite complicated, apparently. You've got to balance the ledgers, the cash books, the journals, record everything in the log book, and so on. Enough to keep you pretty busy, only it won't take the starch out of you the way cooking and washing did, will it?"

It was on the tip of Meggie's tongue to shout: What about *me?* I did just as much washing and cooking as Mum!

Fee was actually smiling, for the first time since the news about Frank. "I'll enjoy the job, Paddy, really I will. It will make me feel like a part of Drogheda."

"Bob is going to teach you how to drive the new Rolls, because you're going to have to be the one to go into Gilly to the bank and see Harry. Besides, it will do you good to know you can drive anywhere you want without depending on one of us being around. We're too isolated out here. I've always meant to teach you girls how to drive, but there's never been the time before. All right, Fee?"

"All right, Paddy," she said happily.

"Now, Meggie, we've got to deal with you."

Meggie laid her sock and needle down, looked up at her father in a mixture of inquiry and resentment, sure she knew what he was going to say: her mother would be busy with the books, so it would be her job to supervise the house and its environs.

"I'd hate to see you turn into an idle, snobby miss like some of the graziers' daughters we know," Paddy said with a smile which robbed his words of any contempt. "So I'm going to put you to work at a full-time job, too, wee Meggie. You're going to look after the inside paddocks for us—Borehead, Creek, Carson, Winnemurra and North Tank. You're also going to look after the Home Paddock. You'll be responsible for the stock horses, which ones are working and which ones are being spelled. During musters and lambing we'll all pitch in together, of course, but otherwise you'll manage on your own, I reckon. Jack can teach you to work the dogs and use a stock whip. You're a terrible tomboy still, so I thought you might like to work in the paddocks more than lie around the house," he finished, smiling more broadly than ever.

Resentment and discontent had flown out the window while he talked; he was once more Daddy, who loved her and thought of her. What had been the matter with her, to doubt him so? She was so ashamed of herself she felt like jabbing the big darning needle into her leg, but she was too happy to contemplate self-infliction of pain for very long, and anyway, it was just an extravagant way of expressing her remorse.

Her face shone. "Oh, Daddy, I'll love it!"

"What about me, Daddy?" asked Stuart.

"The girls don't need you around the house anymore, so you'll be out in the paddocks again, Stu."

"All right, Daddy." He looked at Fee longingly, but said nothing.

Fee and Meggie learned to drive the new Rolls-Royce Mary Carson had taken delivery of a week before she died, and Meggie learned to work the dogs while Fee learned to keep the books.

If it hadn't been for Father Ralph's continued absence, Meggie for one would have been absolutely happy. This was what she had always longed to do: be out there in the paddocks astride a horse, doing stockman's work. Yet the ache for Father Ralph was always there, too, the memory of his kiss something to be dreamed about, treasured, felt again a thousand times. However, memory wasn't a patch on reality; try as she would, the actual sensation couldn't be conjured up, only a shadow of it, like a thin sad cloud.

When he wrote to tell them about Frank, her hopes that he would use this as a pretext to visit them were abruptly shatttered. His description of the trip to see Frank in Goulburn Gaol was carefully worded, stripped of the pain it had engendered, giving no hint of Frank's steadily worsening psychosis. He had tried vainly to have Frank committed to Morisset asylum for the criminally insane, but no one had listened. So he simply passed on an idealistic image of a Frank resigned to paying for his sins to society, and in a passage heavily underlined told Paddy Frank had no idea they knew what had happened. It had come to his ears, he assured Frank, through Sydney newspapers, and he would make sure the family never knew. After being told this, Frank settled better, he said, and left it at that.

Paddy talked of selling Father Ralph's chestnut mare. Meggie used the rangy black gelding she had ridden for pleasure as a stock horse, for it was lighter-mouthed and nicer in nature than the moody mares or mean geldings in the yards. Stock horses were intelligent, and rarely placid. Even a total absence of stallions didn't make them very amiable animals.

"Oh, please, Daddy, I can ride the chestnut, too!" Meggie pleaded. "Think how awful it would be if after all his kindnesses to us, Father should come back to visit and discover we had sold his horse!"

Paddy stared at her thoughtfully. "Meggie, I don't think Father will come back."

"But he might! You never know!"

The eyes so like Fee's were too much for him; he couldn't bring himself to hurt her more than she was already hurt, poor little thing. "All right then, Meggie, we'll keep the mare, but make sure you use both the mare and the gelding regularly, for I won't have a fat horse on Drogheda, do you hear?"

Until then she hadn't liked to use Father Ralph's own mount, but after that she alternated to give both the animals in the stables a chance to work off their oats.

It was just as well Mrs. Smith, Minnie and Cat doted on the twins, for with Meggie out in the paddocks and Fee sitting for hours at her escritoire in the drawing room, the two little fellows had a wonderful time. They were into everything, but with such glee and constant good humor that no one could be angry with them for very long. At night in her little house Mrs. Smith, long converted to Catholicism, knelt to her prayers with such deep thankfulness in her heart she could scarcely contain it. Children of her own had never come to gladden her when Rob had been alive, and for years the big house had been childless, its occupants forbidden to mix with the inhabitants of the stockmen's houses down by the creek. But when the Clearys came they were Mary Carson's kin, and there were children at last. Especially now, with Jims and Patsy permanent residents of the big house.

It had been a dry winter, and the summer rains didn't come. Knee-high and lush, the tawny grass dried out in the stark sun until even the inner core of each blade was crisp. To look across the paddocks required slitted eyes and a hat brim drawn far down on the forehead; the grass was mirror-silver, and little spiral whirlwinds sped busily among shimmering blue mirages, transferring dead leaves and fractured grass blades from one restless heap to another.

Oh, but it was dry! Even the trees were dry, the bark falling from them in stiff, crunchy ribbons. No danger yet of the sheep starving—the grass would last another year at least, maybe more—but no one liked to see everything so dry. There was always a good chance the rain would not come next year, or the year after. In a good year they got ten to fifteen inches, in a bad year less than five, perhaps close to none at all.

In spite of the heat and the flies, Meggie loved life out in the paddocks, walking the chestnut mare behind a bleating mob of sheep while the dogs lay flat on the ground, tongues lolling, deceptively inattentive. Let one sheep bolt out of the tightly packed cluster and the nearest dog would be away, a streak of vengeance, sharp teeth hungering to nip into a hapless heel.

Meggie rode ahead of her mob, a welcome relief after breathing their dust for several miles, and opened the paddock gate. She waited patiently while the dogs, reveling in this chance to show her what they could do, bit and goaded the sheep through. It was harder mustering and droving cattle, for they kicked or charged, often killing an unwary dog; that was when the human herdsman had to be ready to do his bit, use his whip, but the dogs loved the spice of danger working cattle. However, to drove cattle was not required of her; Paddy attended to that himself.

But the dogs never ceased to fascinate her; their intelligence was phenomenal. Most of the Drogheda dogs were kelpies, coated in rich brownish tan with creamy paws, chests and eyebrows, but there were Queensland blues too, larger, with blue-grey coats dappled in black, and all varieties of crossbreds between kelpie and blue. The bitches came in heat, were scientifically mated, increased and whelped; after weaning and growing, their pups were tried out in the paddocks, and if good were kept or sold, if no good shot.

Whistling her dogs to heel, Meggie shut the gate on the mob and turned the chestnut mare toward home. Nearby was a big stand of trees, stringybark and ironbark and black box, an occasional wilga on its outskirts. She rode into its shade thankfully, and having now the leisure to look around, let her eyes roam in delight. The gums were full of budgies, skawking and whistling their parodies of songbirds; finches wheeled from branch to branch; two sulphur-crested cockatoos sat with their heads to one side watching her progress with twinkling eyes; willy-wagtails fossicked in the dirt for ants, their absurd rumps bobbing; crows carked eternally and mournfully. Theirs was the most obnoxious noise in the whole bush song repertoire, so devoid of joy, desolate and somehow soul-chilling, speaking of rotting flesh, of carrion and blowflies. To think of a crow singing like a bellbird was impossible; cry and function fitted perfectly.

Of course there were flies everywhere; Meggie wore a veil over her hat, but her bare arms were constantly plagued, and the chestnut mare's tail never stopped swishing, its flesh never stopped shivering and creeping for a second. It amazed Meggie that even through the thickness of hide and hair, a horse could feel something as delicate and airy as a fly. They drank sweat, which was why they tormented horses and humans so, but humans never let them do what sheep did, so they used the sheep for a more intimate purpose, laying their eggs around the rump wool, or wherever the wool was damp and dirty.

The air was full of the noise of bees, and alive with brilliant quick dragonflies seeking out the bore drains, alive with exquisitely colored butterflies and day moths. Her horse turned over a piece of rotting log with a hoof; Meggie stared at its underside, her skin crawling. There were witchetty grubs, fat and white and loathsome, wood lice and slugs, huge centipedes and spiders. From burrows rabbits hopped and skittled, flashed back inside with white powder puffs up in the air, then turned to peer out, noses twitching. Farther on an echidna broke off its quest after ants, panicked at her approach. Burrowing so fast that its strong clawed feet were hidden in seconds, it began to disappear under a huge log. Its antics as it dug were amusing, the cruel spines lying flat all over its body to streamline its entry into the ground, earth flying in heaps.

She came out of the timber on the main track to the homestead. A sheet of dappled grey occupied its dust, galahs picking for insects or grubs, but as they heard her coming they took to the air en masse. It was like being inundated by a magenta-pink wave; breasts and underwings soared above her head, the grey turned magically to rich pink. If I had to leave Drogheda tomorrow, she thought, never again to come back, in my dreams I'd live Drogheda in a wash of pink galah undersides. . . . It must be getting very dry farther out; the kangas are coming in, more and more of them. . . .

A great mob of kangaroos, maybe two thousand strong, was startled out of its placid grazing by the galahs and took off into the distance in long, graceful leaps which swallowed the leagues faster than any other animal save the emu. Horses couldn't keep up with them.

In between these delightful bouts of nature-studying she thought of Ralph, as always. Privately Meggie had never catalogued what she felt for him as a schoolgirl crush, simply called it love, as they did in books. Her symptoms and feelings were no different from those of an Ethel M. Dell heroine. Nor did it seem fair that a barrier as artificial as his priesthood could stand between her and what she wanted of him, which was to have him as her husband. To live with him as Daddy did with Mum, in such harmony he would adore her the way Daddy did Mum. It had never seemed to Meggie that her mother did very much to earn her father's adoration, yet worship her he did. So Ralph would soon see that to live with her was far better than living on his own; for it had not dawned upon her that Ralph's priesthood was something he could not abandon under any circumstances. Yes, she knew it was forbidden to have a priest as husband or lover, but she had got into the habit of getting around it by stripping

Ralph of his religious office. Her formal education in Catholicism had never advanced to discussions of the nature of priestly vows, and she was not herself in need of religion, so didn't pursue it voluntarily. Obtaining no satisfaction from praying, Meggie obeyed the laws of the Church simply because not to do so meant burning in Hell throughout eternity.

In her present daydream she rambled through the bliss of living with him and sleeping with him, as Daddy did with Mum. Then the thought of his nearness excited her, made her shift in the saddle restlessly; she translated it into a deluge of kisses, having no other criterion. Riding the paddocks hadn't advanced her sexual education at all, for the mere sniff of a dog in the far distance drove all desire to mate out of any animal's mind, and as on all stations, indiscriminate mating was not allowed. When the rams were sent among the ewes of a particular paddock, Meggie was dispatched elsewhere, and the sight of one dog humping another was simply the signal to flick the pair with her whip, stop their "playing."

Perhaps no human being is equipped to judge which is worse: inchoate longing with its attendant restlessness and irritability, or specific desire with its willful drive to achieve the desire. Poor Meggie longed, quite what for she didn't know, but the basic pull was there, and it dragged her inexorably in the direction of Ralph de Bricassart. So she dreamed of him, yearned for him, wanted him; and mourned, that in spite of his declared love for her she meant so little to him that he never came to see her.

Into the middle of her thoughts rode Paddy, heading for the homestead on the same course as she was; smiling, she reined in the chestnut mare and waited for him to catch up.

"What a nice surprise," said Paddy, walking his old roan beside his daughter's middle-aged mare.

"Yes, it is," she said. "Is it dry farther out?"

"A bit worse than this, I think. Lord, I've never seen so many kangas! It must be bone dry out Milparinka way. Martin King was talking of a big shoot, but I don't see how an army of machine guns could reduce the number of kangas by enough to see the difference."

He was so nice, so thoughtful and forgiving and loving; and it was rarely that she ever had the chance to be with him without at least one of the boys in attendance. Before she could change her mind, Meggie asked the doubting question, the one which gnawed and preyed in spite of all her internal reassurances.

"Daddy, why doesn't Father de Bricassart ever come to see us?"

"He's busy, Meggie," Paddy answered, but his voice had become wary.

"But even priests have holidays, don't they? He used to love Drogheda so, I'm sure he'd want to spend his holidays here."

"In one way priests have holidays, Meggie, but in another way they're never off duty. For instance, every day of their lives they have to say Mass, even if quite alone. I think Father de Bricassart is a very wise man, and knows that it's never possible to go back to a way of life that's gone. For him, wee Meggie, Drogheda's a bit of the past. If he came back, it wouldn't give him the same sort of pleasure it used to."

"You mean he's forgotten us," she said dully.

"No, not really. If he had, he wouldn't write so often, or demand news about each of us." He turned in his saddle, his blue eyes pitying. "I think it's best that he doesn't ever come back, so I don't encourage him to think of it by inviting him."

"Daddy!"

Paddy plunged into muddy waters doggedly. "Look, Meggie, it's wrong for you to dream about a priest, and it's time you understood that. You've kept your secret pretty well, I don't think anyone else knows how you feel about him, but it's to me your questions come, isn't it? Not many, but enough. Now take it from me, you've got to stop, hear it? Father de Bricassart took holy vows I know he has absolutely no intention of breaking, and you've mistaken his fondness for you. He was a grown man when he met you, and you were a little girl. Well, that's how he thinks of you, Meggie, to this very day."

She didn't answer, nor did her face change. Yes, he thought, she's Fee's daughter, all right.

After a while she said tautly, "But he could stop being a priest. It's just that I haven't had a chance to talk to him about it."

The shock on Paddy's face was too genuine not to believe it, so Meggie found it more convincing than his words, vehement though they were.

"Meggie! Oh, good God, that's the worst of this bush existence! You ought to be in school, my girl, and if Auntie Mary had died sooner I would have packed you off to Sydney in time to get at least a couple of years under your belt. But you're too old, aren't you? I wouldn't have them laugh at you at your age, poor wee Meggie." He continued more gently, spacing his words to give them a sharp, lucid cruelty, though it was not his intention to be cruel, only to dispel illusions once and for all. "Father de Bricassart is a *priest,* Meggie. He can never, never stop being a priest, understand that. The vows he took are sacred, too solemn to break. Once a man is a priest there can be no turning away, and his supervisors in the seminary make absolutely sure that he knows what he's swearing before he does. A man who takes those vows knows beyond any doubt that once taken they can't be broken, ever. Father de Bricassart took them, and he'll never break them." He sighed. "Now you know, Meggie, don't you? From this moment you have no excuse to daydream about Father de Bricassart."

They had come in from the front of the homestead,

so the stables were closer than the stockyards; without a word, Meggie turned the chestnut mare toward the stables, and left her father to continue alone. For a while he kept turning around to look after her, but when she had disappeared inside the fence around the stables he dug his roan in the ribs and finished his ride at a canter, hating himself and the necessity of saying what he had. Damn the man-woman thing! It seemed to have a set of rules at variance with all others.

Father Ralph de Bricassart's voice was very cold, yet it was warmer than his eyes, which never veered from the young priest's pallid face as he spoke his stiff, measured words.

"You have not conducted yourself as Our Lord Jesus Christ demands His priests conduct themselves. I think you know it better than we who censure you could ever know it, but I must still censure you on behalf of your Archbishop, who stands to you not only as a fellow priest but as your superior. You owe him perfect obedience, and it is not your place to argue with his sentiments or his decisions.

"Do you really understand the disgrace you've brought on yourself, on your parish, and especially on the Church you purport to love more than any human being? Your vow of chastity was as solemn and binding as your other vows, and to break it is to sin grievously. You will never see the woman again, of course, but it behooves us to assist you in your struggles to overcome temptation. Therefore we have arranged that you leave immediately for duty in the parish of Darwin, in the Northern Territory. You will proceed to Brisbane tonight on the express train, and from there you will proceed, again by train, to Longreach. In Longreach you will board a QANTAS plane for Darwin. Your belongings are being packed at this moment and will be on the express before it departs, so there is no need for you to return to your present parish.

"Now go to the chapel with Father John and pray. You will remain in the chapel until it is time to join the train. For your comfort and consolation, Father John will travel with you to Darwin. You are dismissed."

They were wise and aware, the priests in administration; they would permit the sinner no opportunity to have further contact with the young girl he had taken as his mistress. It had become the scandal of his present parish, and very embarrassing. As for the girl—let her wait, and watch, and wonder. From now until he arrived in Darwin he would be watched by the excellent Father John, who had his orders, then after that every letter he sent from Darwin would be opened, and he would not be allowed to make any long-distance phone calls. She would never know where he had gone, and he would never be able to tell her. Nor would he be given any chance to take up with another girl. Darwin was a frontier town; women were almost nonexistent. His vows were absolute, he could never be released from them; if he was too weak to police himself, the Church must do it for him.

After he had watched the young priest and his appointed watchdog go from the room, Father Ralph got up from his desk and walked through to an inner chamber. Archbishop Cluny Dark was sitting in his customary chair, and at right angles to him another man in purple sash and skullcap sat quietly. The Archbishop was a big man, with a shock of beautiful white hair and intensely blue eyes; he was a vital sort of fellow, with a keen sense of humor and a great love of the table. His visitor was quite the antithesis; small and thin, a few sparse strands of black hair around his skullcap and beneath them an angular, ascetic face, a sallow skin with a heavy beard shadow, and large dark eyes. In age he might have been anywhere between thirty and fifty, but in actual fact he was thirty-nine, three years older than Father Ralph de Bricassart.

"Sit down, Father, have a cup of tea," said the Archbishop heartily. "I was beginning to think we'd have to send for a fresh pot. Did you dismiss the young man with a suitable admonition to mend his conduct?"

"Yes, Your Grace," said Father Ralph briefly, and seated himself in the third chair around the tea table, loaded with wafer-thin cucumber sandwiches, pink and white iced fairy cakes, hot buttered scones with crystal dishes of jam and whipped cream, a silver tea service and Aynsley china cups washed with a delicate coating of gold leaf.

"Such incidents are regrettable, my dear Archbishop, but even we who are ordained the priests of Our Dear Lord are weak, all-too-human creatures. I find it in my heart to pity him deeply, and I shall pray tonight that he finds more strength in the future," the visitor said.

His accent was distinctly foreign, his voice soft, with a hint of sibilance in its *s*'s. By nationality he was Italian, by title he was His Grace the Archbishop Papal Legate to the Australian Catholic Church, and by name he was Vittorio Scarbanza di Contini-Verchese. His was the delicate role of providing a link between the Australian hierarchy and the Vatican nerve center; which meant he was the most important priest in this section of the world.

Before being given this appointment he had of course hoped for the United States of America, but on thinking about it he decided Australia would do very nicely. If in population though not in area it was a much smaller country, it was also far more Catholic. Unlike the rest of the English-speaking world, it was no social comedown in Australia to be Catholic, no handicap to an aspiring politician or businessman or judge. And it was a rich country, it supported the Church well. No need to fear he would be forgotten by Rome while he was in Australia.

The Archbishop Papal Legate was also a very subtle man, and his eyes over the gold rim of his teacup were fixed not on Archbishop Cluny Dark but on Father

Ralph de Bricassart, soon to become his own secretary. That Archbishop Dark liked the priest enormously was a well-known fact, but the Archbishop Papal Legate was wondering how well *he* was going to like such a man. They were all so big, these Irish-Australian priests, they towered far above him; he was so weary of forever having to tilt his head up to see their faces. Father de Bricassart's manner to his present master was perfect: light, easy, respectful but man-to-man, full of humor. How would he adjust to working for a far different master? It was customary to appoint the Legatal secretary from the ranks of the Italian Church, but Father Ralph de Bricassart held great interest for the Vatican. Not only did he have the curious distinction of being personally rich (contrary to popular opinion, his superiors were not empowered to take his money from him, and he had not volunteered to hand it over), but he had single-handedly brought a great fortune into the Church. So the Vatican had decided that the Archbishop Papal Legate was to take Father de Bricassart as his secretary, to study the young man and find out exactly what he was like.

One day the Holy Father would have to reward the Australian Church with a cardinal's biretta, but it would not be yet. Therefore it was up to him to study priests in Father de Bricassart's age group, and of these Father de Bricassart was clearly the leading candidate. So be it. Let Father de Bricassart try his mettle against an Italian for a while. It might be interesting. But why couldn't the man have been just a little smaller?

As he sipped his tea gratefully Father Ralph was unusually quiet. The Archbishop Papal Legate noticed that he ate a small sandwich triangle and eschewed the other delicacies, but drank four cups of tea thirstily, adding neither sugar nor milk. Well, that was what his report said; in his personal living habits the priest was remarkably abstemious, his only weakness being a good (and very fast) car.

"Your name is French, Father," said the Archbishop Papal Legate softly, "but I understand you are an Irishman. How comes this phenomenon? Was your family French, then?"

Father Ralph shook his head, smiling. "It's a Norman name, Your Grace, very old and honorable. I am a direct descendant of one Ranulf de Bricassart, who was a baron in the court of William the Conqueror. In 1066 he came to invade England with William, and one of his sons took English land. The family prospered under the Norman kings of England, and later on some of them crossed the Irish Sea during the time of Henry the Fourth, and settled within the Pale. When Henry the Eighth removed the English Church from Rome's authority we kept the faith of William, which meant we felt we owed our first allegiance to Rome, not to London. But when Cromwell set up the Commonwealth we lost our lands and titles, and they were never restored to us. Charles had English favorites to reward with Irish land. It is not causeless, you know, the Irish hatred of the English.

"However, we descended to relative obscurity, still loyal to the Church, and to Rome. My older brother has a successful stud farm in County Meath, and hopes to breed a Derby or a Grand National winner. I am the second son, and it has always been a family tradition that the second son embrace the Church if he feels the wish for it. I'm very proud of my name and my lineage, you know. For fifteen hundred years there have been de Bricassarts."

Ah, that was good! An old, aristocratic name and a perfect record of keeping the faith through emigrations and persecutions.

"And the Ralph?"

"A constriction of Ranulf, Your Grace."

"I see."

"I'm going to miss you greatly, Father," said Archbishop Cluny Dark, piling jam and whipped cream on half a scone and popping it whole into his mouth.

Father Ralph laughed at him. "You place me in a dilemma, Your Grace! Here I am seated between my old master and my new, and if I answer to please one, I must displease the other. But may I say I shall miss Your Grace, while looking forward to serving Your Grace?"

It was well said, a diplomat's answer. Archbishop di Contini-Verchese began to think he might do well with such a secretary. But too good-looking by far, with those fine features, the striking coloring, the magnificent body.

Father Ralph lapsed back into silence, staring at the tea table without seeing it. He was seeing the young priest he had just disciplined, the look in those already tormented eyes as he realized they were not even going to let him say goodbye to his girl. Dear God, what if it had been him, and the girl Meggie? One could get away with it for a while if one was discreet; forever if one limited women to the yearly vacation away from the parish. But let a serious devotion to one woman enter the picture and they would inevitably find out.

There were times when only kneeling on the marble floor of the palace chapel until he was stiff with physical pain prevented him from catching the next train back to Gilly and Drogheda. He had told himself that he was simply the victim of loneliness, that he missed the human affection he had known on Drogheda. He told himself nothing had changed when he yielded to a passing weakness and kissed Meggie back; that his love for her was still located in realms of fancy and delight, that it had not passed into a different world which had a distracting, disturbing wholeness to it the earlier dreams had not. For he couldn't admit anything had changed, and he kept Meggie in his mind as a little girl, shutting out any visions which might contradict this.

He had been wrong. The pain didn't fade. It seemed to grow worse, and in a colder, uglier way. Before, his loneliness had been an impersonal thing, he had never been able to say to himself that the presence in his life of any one being could remedy it. But now loneliness had a name: Meggie. Meggie, Meggie, Meggie . . .

He came out of his reverie to find Archbishop di Contini-Verchese staring at him unwinkingly, and those large dark eyes were far more dangerously omniscient than the round vivid orbs of his present master. Far too intelligent to pretend there was nothing causing his brown study, Father Ralph gave his master-to-be as penetrating a look as he was receiving, then smiled faintly and shrugged his shoulders, as if to say: Every man has sadness in him, and it is no sin to remember a grief.

"Tell me, Father, has the sudden slump in economic affairs affected your charge?" the Italian prelate asked smoothly.

"So far we have nothing to worry about, Your Grace. Michar Limited isn't easily affected by fluctuations in the market. I should imagine those whose fortunes are less carefully invested than Mrs. Carson's are the ones who stand to lose the most. Of course the station Drogheda won't do as well; the price of wool is falling. However, Mrs. Carson was too clever to sink her money into rural pursuits; she preferred the solidity of metal. Though to my mind this is an excellent time to buy land, not only stations in the country but houses and buildings in the major cities. Prices are ridiculously low, but they can't remain low forever. I don't see how we can lose on real estate in years to come if we buy now. The Depression will be over one day."

"Quite," said the Archbishop Papal Legate. So not only was Father de Bricassart something of a diplomat, he was also something of a businessman as well! Truly Rome had better keep her eye upon him.

9

But it was 1930, and Drogheda knew all about the Depression. Men were out of work all over Australia. Those who could stopped paying rent and tying themselves down to the futility of looking for work when there was none. Left to fend alone, wives and children lived in humpies on municipal land and queued for the dole; fathers and husbands had gone tramping. A man stowed his few essentials inside his blanket, tied it with thongs and slung it across his back before setting out on the track, hoping at least for handouts of food from the stations he crossed, if not employment. Humping a bluey through the Outback beat sleeping in the Sydney Domain.

The price of food was low, and Paddy stocked the Drogheda pantries and storehouses to overflowing. A man could always be sure of having his tuckerbag filled when he arrived on Drogheda. The strange thing was that the parade of drifters constantly changed; once full of a good hot meal and loaded with provisions for the track, they made no attempt to remain, but wandered on in search of only they knew what. Not every place was as hospitable or generous as Drogheda by any means, which only added to the puzzle of why men on the track seemed not to want to stay. Perhaps the weariness and the purposelessness of having no home, no place to go, made them continue to drift. Most managed to live, some died and if found were buried before the crows and pigs picked their bones clean. The Outback was a huge place, and lonely.

But Stuart was permanently in residence again, and the shotgun was never far from the cookhouse door. Good stockmen were easy to come by, and Paddy had nine single men on his books in the old jackaroo barracks, so Stuart could be spared from the paddocks. Fee stopped keeping cash lying about, and had Stuart make a camouflaged cupboard for the safe behind the chapel altar. Few of the swaggies were bad men. Bad men preferred to stay in the cities and the big country towns, for life on the track was too pure, too lonely and scant of pickings for bad men. Yet no one blamed Paddy for not wanting to take chances with his women; Drogheda was a very famous name, and might conceivably attract what few undesirables there were on the track.

That winter brought bad storms, some dry, some wet, and the following spring and summer brought rain so heavy that Drogheda grass grew lusher and longer than ever.

Jims and Patsy were plowing through their correspondence lessons at Mrs. Smith's kitchen table, and chattered now of what it would be like when it was time to go to Riverview, their boarding school. But Mrs. Smith would grow so sharp and sour at such talk that they learned not to speak of leaving Drogheda when she was within hearing distance.

The dry weather came back; the thigh-high grass dried out completely and baked to a silver crisp in a rainless summer. Inured by ten years of the black-soil plains to the hey-ho, up we go, hey-ho, down we go oscillations of drought and flood, the men shrugged and went about each day as if it were the only one that could ever matter. This was true; the main business was essentially to survive between one good year and the next, whenever it might be. No one could predict the rain. There was a man in Brisbane called Inigo Jones who wasn't bad at long-range weather predictions, using a novel concept of sun spot activity, but out on the black-soil plains no one put much credence in what he had to say. Let Sydney and Melbourne brides petition him for forecasts; the black-soil plainsmen would stick with that old sensation in their bones.

In the winter of 1932 the dry storms came back, along with bitter cold, but the lush grass kept dust to a minimum and the flies weren't as numerous as usual. No consolation to the freshly shorn sheep, which shivered miserably. Mrs. Dominic O'Rourke, who lived in a wooden house of no particular distinction, adored to entertain visitors from Sydney; one of the highlights of her tour program was paying a call at Drogheda homestead, to show her visitors that even out on the black-soil plains some people lived graciously. And the subject would always turn to those skinny, drowned-rat-looking sheep, left to face the winter minus the five- and six-inch-long fleeces they would have grown by the time summer heat arrived. But, as Paddy said gravely to one such visitor, it made for better wool. The wool was the thing, not the sheep. Not long after he made that statement a letter appeared in the *Sydney Morning Herald,* demanding prompt parliamentary legislation to end what it called "grazier cruelty." Poor Mrs. O'Rourke was horrified, but Paddy laughed until his sides ached.

"Just as well the silly bloke never saw a shearer rip up a sheep's belly and sew it with a baling needle," he comforted the embarrassed Mrs. O'Rourke. "It's not worth getting upset about, Mrs. Dominic. Down in the city they don't know how the other half lives, and they can afford the luxury of doting on their animals as if they were children. Out here it's different. You'll never see man, woman or child in need of help go ignored out here, yet in the city those same people who dote on their pets will completely ignore a cry of help from a human being."

Fee looked up. "He's right, Mrs. Dominic," she said. "We all have contempt for whatever there's too many of. Out here it's sheep, but in the city it's people."

Only Paddy was far afield that day in August when the big storm broke. He got down from his horse, tied the animal securely to a tree and sat beneath a wilga to wait it out. Shivering in fear, his five dogs huddled together near him, while the sheep he had been intending to transfer to another paddock scattered into jumpy little groups trotting aimlessly in all directions. And it was a terrible storm, reserving the worst of its fury until the center of the maelstrom was directly overhead. Paddy stuffed his fingers in his ears, shut his eyes and prayed.

Not far from where he sat with the down-dropping wilga leaves clashing restlessly in the rising wind was a small collection of dead stumps and logs surrounded by tall grass. In the middle of the white, skeletal heap was one massive dead gum, its bare body soaring forty feet toward the night-black clouds, spindling at its top into a sharp, jagged point.

A blossoming blue fire so bright it seared his eyes through their closed lids made Paddy jump to his feet, only to be thrown down like a toy in the heave of a huge explosion. He lifted his face from the earth to see the final glory of the lightning bolt playing shimmering halos of glaring blue and purple all up and down the dead spear of gum tree; then, so quickly he hardly had time to understand what was happening, everything caught fire. The last drop of moisture had long since evaporated from the tissues of that decayed cluster, and the grass everywhere was long and dry as paper. Like some defiant answer of the earth to the sky, the giant tree shot a pillar of flame far beyond its tip, the logs and stumps around it went up at the same moment, and in a circle from around the center great sheets of fire swept in the swirling wind, round and round and round. Paddy had not even time to reach his horse.

The parched wilga caught and the gum resin at its tender heart exploded outward. There were solid walls of fire in every direction Paddy looked; the trees were burning fiercely and the grass beneath his feet was roaring into flames. He could hear his horse screaming and his heart went out to it; he could not leave the poor beast to die tied up and helpless. A dog howled, its howl changing to a shriek of agony almost human. For a moment it flared and danced, a living torch, then subsided into the blazing grass. More howls as the other dogs, fleeing, were enveloped by the racing fire, faster in the gale than anything on foot or wing. A streaming meteor scorched his hair as he stood for a millisecond debating which way was the best to get to his horse; he looked down to see a great cockatoo roasting at his feet.

Suddenly Paddy knew this was the end. There was no way out of the inferno for himself or his horse. Even as he thought it, a desiccated stringybark behind him shot flames in every direction, the gum in it exploding. The skin on Paddy's arm shriveled and blackened, the hair of his head dimmed at last by something brighter. To die so is indescribable; for fire works its way from outside to in. The last things that go, finally cooked to the point of nonfunction, are brain and heart. His clothes on fire, Paddy capered screaming and screaming through the holocaust. And every awful cry was his wife's name.

All the other men made it back to Drogheda homestead ahead of the storm, turned their mounts into the stockyard and headed for either the big house or the jackaroo barracks. In Fee's brightly lit drawing room with a log fire roaring in the cream-and-pink marble fireplace the Cleary boys sat listening to the storm, not tempted these days to go outside and watch it. The beautiful pungent smell of burning eucalyptus wood in the grate and the heaped cakes and sandwiches on the afternoon tea trolley were too alluring. No one expected Paddy to make it in.

About four o'clock the clouds rolled away to the east, and everyone unconsciously breathed easier; somehow it was impossible to relax during a dry storm, even though every building on Drogheda was equipped with a lightning conductor. Jack and Bob got up and went outside to get a little fresh air, they said, but in reality to release pent breath.

"Look!" said Bob, pointing westward.

Above the trees that ringed the Home Paddock round, a great bronze pall of smoke was growing, its margins torn to tattered streamers in the high wind.

"God Jesus!" Jack cried, running inside to the telephone.

"Fire, fire!" he shouted into the receiver, while those still inside the room turned to gape at him, then ran outside to see. "Fire on Drogheda, and a big one!" Then he hung up; it was all he needed to say to the Gilly switch and to those along the line who habitually picked up when the first tinkle came. Though there had not been a big fire in the Gilly district since the Clearys had come to Drogheda, everyone knew the routine.

The boys scattered to get horses, and the stockmen were piling out of the jackaroo barracks, while Mrs. Smith unlocked one of the storehouses and doled out hessian bags by the dozen. The smoke was in the west and the wind was blowing from that direction, which meant the fire would be heading for the homestead. Fee took off her long skirt and put on a pair of Paddy's pants, then ran with Meggie for the stables; every pair of hands capable of holding a bag would be needed.

In the cookhouse Mrs. Smith stoked up the range firebox and the maids began bringing down huge pots from their ceiling hooks.

"Just as well we killed a steer yesterday," said the housekeeper. "Minnie, here's the key to the liquor storehouse. You and Cat fetch all the beer and rum we've got, then start making damper bread while I carry on with the stew. And hurry, *hurry!*"

The horses, unsettled by the storm, had smelled smoke and were hard to saddle; Fee and Meggie backed the two trampling, restive thoroughbreds outside the stable into the yard to tackle them better. As Meggie wrestled with the chestnut mare two swaggies came pounding down the track from the Gilly road.

"Fire, Missus, fire! Got a couple of spare horses? Give us a few bags."

"Down that way to the stockyards. Dear God, I hope none of you are caught out there!" said Meggie, who didn't know where her father was.

The two men grabbed hessian bags and water bags from Mrs. Smith; Bob and the men had been gone five minutes. The two swaggies followed, and last to leave, Fee and Meggie rode at a gallop down to the creek, across it and away toward the smoke.

Behind them Tom, the garden rouseabout, finished filling the big water truck from the bore-drain pump, then started the engine. Not that any amount of water short of a downpour from the sky would help put out a fire this big, but he would be needed to keep the bags damp, and the people wielding them. As he shoved the truck down into bottom gear to grind up the far creek bank he looked back for a moment at the empty head stockman's house, the two vacant houses beyond it; there was the homestead's soft underbelly, the only place where flammable things came close enough to the trees on the far side of the creek to catch. Old Tom looked westward, shook his head in sudden decision, and managed to get the truck back across the creek and up the near bank in reverse. They'd never stop that fire out in the paddocks; they'd return. On top of the gully and just beside the head stockman's house, in which he had been camping, he attached the hose to the tank and began saturating the building, then passed beyond it to the two smaller dwellings, hosed them down. This was where he could help the most; keep those three homes so wet they'd never catch.

As Meggie rode beside Fee the ominous cloud in

the west grew, and stronger and stronger on the wind came the smell of burning. It was growing dark; creatures fleeing from the west came thicker and thicker across the paddock, kangaroos and wild pigs, frightened sheep and cattle, emus and goannas, rabbits by the thousands. Bob was leaving the gates open, she noticed as she rode from Borehead into Billa-Billa; every paddock on Drogheda had a name. But sheep were so stupid they would blunder into a fence and stop three feet from an open gate, never see it.

The fire had gone ten miles when they reached it, and it was spreading laterally as well, along a front expanding with every second. As the long dry grass and the high wind took it leaping from timber stand to timber stand they sat their frightened, jobbing horses and looked into the west helplessly. No use trying to stop it here; an army couldn't stop it here. They would have to go back to the homestead and defend that if they could. Already the front was five miles wide; if they didn't push their weary mounts they too would be caught, and passed. Too bad for the sheep, too bad. But it couldn't be helped.

Old Tom was still hosing the houses by the creek when they clattered through the thin blanket of water on the ford.

"Good bloke, Tom!" Bob shouted. "Keep it up until it gets too hot to stay, then get out in plenty of time, hear me? No rash heroism; you're more important than some bits of wood and glass."

The homestead grounds were full of cars, and more headlights were bouncing and glaring down the road from Gilly; a large group of men stood waiting for them as Bob turned into the horse yards.

"How big is it, Bob?" Martin King asked.

"Too big to fight, I think," said Bob despairingly. "I reckon it's about five miles wide and in this wind it's traveling almost as fast as a horse can gallop. I don't know if we can save the homestead, but I think Horry ought to get ready to defend his place. He's going to get it next, because I don't see how we can ever stop it."

"Well, we're overdue for a big fire. The last big one was in 1919. I'll organize a party to go to Beel-Beel, but there are plenty of us and more coming. Gilly can put out close to five hundred men to fight a fire. Some of us will stay here to help. Thank God I'm west of Drogheda is all I can say."

Bob grinned. "You're a bloody comfort, Martin."

Martin looked around. "Where's your father, Bob?"

"West of the fire, like Bugela. He was out in Wilga mustering some ewes for the lambing, and Wilga's at least five miles west of where the fire started, I reckon."

"No other men you're worried about?"

"Not today, thank heavens."

In a way it was like being in a war, Meggie thought as she entered the house: a controlled speed, a concern for food and drink, the keeping up of one's strength and courage. And the threat of imminent disaster. As more men arrived they went to join those already in the Home Paddock, cutting down the few trees that had sprung up close to the creek bank, and clearing away any overlong grass on the perimeter. Meggie remembered thinking when she first arrived on Drogheda how much prettier the Home Paddock might have been, for compared to the wealth of timber all around it, it was bare and bleak. Now she understood why. The Home Paddock was nothing less than a gigantic circular firebreak.

Everyone talked of the fires Gilly had seen in its seventy-odd years of existence. Curiously enough, fires were never a major threat during prolonged drought, because there wasn't sufficient grass then to keep a fire going far. It was times like this, a year or two after heavy rain had made the grass grow so long and tinder-lush, that Gilly saw its big fires, the ones which sometimes burned out of control for hundreds of miles.

Martin King had taken charge of the three hundred men remaining to defend Drogheda. He was the senior grazier of the district, and had fought fires for fifty years.

"I've got 150,000 acres on Bugela," he said, "and in 1905 I lost every sheep and every tree on the place. It took me fifteen years to recover, and I thought for a while I wouldn't, because wool wasn't fetching much in those days, nor was beef."

The wind was still howling, the smell of burning was everywhere. Night had fallen, but the western sky was lit to unholy brilliance and lowering smoke was beginning to make them cough. Not long afterward they saw the first flames, vast tongues leaping and writhing a hundred feet into the smoke, and a roaring came to their ears like a huge crowd overexcited at a football game. The trees on the western side of the timber ringing the Home Paddock caught and went up in a solid sheet of fire; as Meggie watched petrified from the homestead veranda she could see little pygmy silhouettes of men outlined against them, jumping and cavorting like anguished souls in Hell.

"Meggie, will you get in here and stack those plates on the sideboard, girl! We're not at a picnic, you know!" came her mother's voice. She turned away reluctantly.

Two hours later the first relay of exhausted men staggered in to snatch food and drink, gather up their waning strength to go back and fight on. For this had the station women toiled, to make sure there was stew and damper bread, tea and rum and beer aplenty, even for three hundred men. In a fire, everyone did what he or she was best equipped to do, and that meant the women cooked to keep up the superior physical strength of the men. Case after case of liquor emptied and was replaced by new cases; black from soot and reeling with fatigue, the men stood to drink copiously and stuff huge chunks of damper into their mouths, gobble down a plateful of stew when it had cooled, gulp a last tumbler of rum, then out again to the fire.

In between trips to the cookhouse Meggie watched the fire, awed and terrified. In its way it had a beauty beyond the beauty of anything earthly, for it was a thing of the skies, of suns so far away their light came coldly, of God and the Devil. The front had galloped on eastward, they were completely surrounded now, and Meggie could pick out details the undefined holocaust of the front did not permit. Now there were black and orange and red and white and yellow; a tall tree in black silhouette rimmed with an orange crust that simmered and glowered; red embers floating and pirouetting like frolicsome phantoms in the air above; yellow pulsations from the exhausted hearts of burned-out trees; a shower of spinning crimson sparks as a gum exploded; sudden licks of orange-and-white flames from something that had resisted until now, and finally yielded its being to the fire. Oh, yes, it was beautiful in the night; she would carry the memory of it all her life.

A sudden increase in the wind velocity sent all the women up the wistaria boughs onto the silver iron roof muffled in bags, for all the men were out in the Home Paddock. Armed with wet bags, their hands and knees scorched even through the bags they wore, they beat out embers on the frying roof, terrified the iron might give way under the coals, drop flaming pieces down into the wooden struts below. But the worst of the fire was ten miles eastward on Beel-Beel.

Drogheda homestead was only three miles from the eastern boundary of the property, it being closest to Gilly. Beel-Beel adjoined it, and beyond that farther east lay Narrengang. When the wind picked up from forty to sixty miles an hour the whole district knew nothing but rain could prevent the fire burning on for weeks, and laying waste to hundreds of square miles of prime land.

Through the worst of the blaze the houses by the creek had endured, with Tom like a man possessed filling his tank truck, hosing, filling again, hosing again. But the moment the wind increased the houses went up, and Tom retreated in the truck, weeping.

"You'd better get down on your knees and thank God the wind didn't pick up while the front was to the west of us," said Martin King. "If it had, not only would the homestead have gone, but us as well. God Jesus, I hope they're all right on Beel-Beel!"

Fee handed him a big glass of neat rum; he was not a young man, but he had fought as long as it was needed, and directed operations with a master's touch.

"It's silly," she said to him, "but when it looked as if it all might go I kept thinking of the most peculiar things. I didn't think of dying, or of the children, or of this beautiful house in ruins. All I could think of were my sewing basket, my half-done knitting, the box of odd buttons I'd been saving for years, my heart-shaped cake pans Frank made me years ago. How could I survive without them? All the little things, you know, the things which can't be replaced, or bought in a shop."

"That's how most women think, as a matter of fact. Funny, isn't it, how the mind reacts? I remember in 1905 my wife running back into the house while I yelled after her like a madman, just to get a tambour with a bit of fancywork on it." He grinned. "But we got out in time, though we lost the house. When I built the new place, the first thing she did was finish the fancywork. It was one of those old-fashioned samplers, you know the sort I mean. And it said 'Home Sweet Home.' " He put down the empty glass, shaking his head over the strangeness of women. "I must go. Gareth Davies is going to need us on Narrengang, and unless I miss my guess so will Angus on Rudna Hunish."

Fee whitened. "Oh, Martin! So far away?"

"The word's out, Fee. Booroo and Bourke are rallying."

For three days more the fire rampaged eastward on

a front that kept widening and widening, then came a sudden heavy fall of rain that lasted for nearly four days, and quenched every last coal. But it had gone over a hundred miles and laid a charred, blackened path twenty miles wide from midway out across Drogheda to the boundary of the last property in the Gillanbone district eastward, Rudna Hunish.

Until it began to rain no one expected to hear from Paddy, for they thought him safely on the far side of the burned zone, cut off from them by heat in the ground and the still-flaring trees. Had the fire not brought the telephone line down, Bob thought they would have got a call from Martin King, for it was logical that Paddy would strike westward for shelter at Bugela homestead. But when the rain had been falling for six hours and there was still no sign of him, they began to worry. For almost four days they had been assuring themselves continually that there was no reason to be anxious, that of course he was just cut off, and had decided to wait until he could head for his own home rather than go to Bugela.

"He ought to be in by now," said Bob, pacing up and down the drawing room while the others watched; the irony of it was that the rain had brought a dank chill into the air, and once more a bright fire burned in the marble hearth.

"What do you think, Bob?" Jack asked.

"I think it's high time we went looking for him. He might be hurt, or he might be on foot and facing a long walk home. His horse might have panicked and thrown him, he might be lying somewhere unable to walk. He had food for overnight, but nothing like enough for four days, though he won't have passed out from starvation yet. Best not to create a fuss just now, so I won't recall the men from Narrengang. But if we don't find him by nightfall I'll ride to Dominic's and we'll get the whole district out tomorrow. Lord, I wish those PMG blokes would get a move on with those phone lines!"

Fee was trembling, her eyes feverish, almost savage.

"I'll put on a pair of trousers," she said. "I can't bear to sit here waiting."

"Mum, stay home!" Bob pleaded.

"If he's hurt it might be anywhere, Bob, and he might be in any sort of condition. You sent the stockmen to Narrengang, and that leaves us mighty short for a search party. If I go paired with Meggie the two of us will be strong enough together to cope with whatever we find, but if Meggie goes on her own she'll have to search with one of you, and that's wasting her, not to mention me."

Bob gave in. "All right, then. You can have Meggie's gelding; you rode it to the fire. Everyone take a rifle, and plenty of shells."

They rode off across the creek and into the heart of that blasted landscape. Not a green or a brown thing was left anywhere, just a vast expanse of soggy black coals, incredibly still steaming after hours of rain. Every leaf of every tree was frizzled to a curling limp string, and where the grass had been they could see little black bundles here and there, sheep caught in the fire, or an occasional bigger mound which had been a steer or a pig. Their tears mingled with the rain on their faces.

Bob and Meggie headed the little procession, Jack and Hughie in the middle, Fee and Stuart bringing up the rear. For Fee and Stuart it was a peaceful progress; they drew comfort from being close together, not talking, each content in the company of the other. Sometimes the horses drew close or shied apart at the sight of some new horror, but it seemed not to affect the last pair of riders. The mud made the going slow and hard, but the charred, matted grass lay like a coir-rope rug on the soil to give the horses a foothold. And every few yards they expected to see Paddy appear over the far flat horizon, but time went on and he never did.

With sinking hearts they realized the fire had begun farther out than first imagined, in Wilga paddock. The storm clouds must have disguised the smoke until the fire had gone quite a long way. The borderland was astonishing. One side of a clearly drawn line was just black, glistening tar, while the other side was the land as they had always known it, fawn and blue and drear in the rain, but alive. Bob stopped and drew back to talk to everyone.

"Well, here's where we start. I'm going due west from here; it's the most likely direction and I'm the strongest. Has everyone got plenty of ammunition? Good. If you find anything, three shots in the air, and those who hear must answer with one shot each. Then wait. Whoever fired the three shots will fire three more five minutes later, and keep on firing three shots every five minutes. Those who hear, one shot in answer.

"Jack, you go south along the fire line. Hughie, you go southwest. I'm going west. Mum and Meggie, you go northwest. Stu, follow the fire line due north. And go slowly, everyone, please. The rain doesn't make it any easier to see far, and there's a lot of timber out here in places. Call often; he might not see you where he would hear you. But remember, no shots unless you find something, because he didn't have a gun with him and if he should hear a shot and be out of voice range to answer, it would be dreadful for him.

"Good luck, and God bless."

Like pilgrims at the final crossroads they straggled apart in the steady grey rain, getting farther and farther away from each other, smaller and smaller, until each disappeared along the appointed path.

Stuart had gone a bare half mile when he noticed that a stand of burned timber drew very close to the fire's demarcation line. There was a little wilga as black and crinkled as a pickaninny's mop, and the remains of a great stump standing close to the charred boundary. What he saw was Paddy's horse, sprawled and fused into the trunk of a big gum, and two of Paddy's dogs, little black stiff things with all four limbs poking up like sticks. He got down from his horse, boots sinking ankle deep in mud, and took his rifle from its saddle scabbard. His lips moved, praying, as he picked his slippery way across the sticky coals. Had it not been for the horse and the dogs he might have hoped for a swaggie or some down-and-out wayfarer caught, trapped. But Paddy was horsed and had five dogs with him; no one on the track rode a horse or had more than one dog. This was too far inside Drogheda land to think of drovers, or stockmen from Bugela to the west. Farther away were three more incinerated dogs; five altogether, five dogs. He knew he would not find a sixth, nor did he.

And not far from the horse, hidden as he approached by a log, was what had been a man. There could be no mistake. Glistening and shiny in the rain, the black thing lay on its back, and its back was arched like a great bow so that it bent upward in the middle and did not touch the ground except at the buttocks and shoulders. The arms were flung apart and curved at the elbows as if beseeching heaven, the fingers with the flesh dropping off them to reveal charred bones were clawing and grasping at nothing. The legs were splayed apart also but flexed at the knees, and the blob of a head looked up sightless, eyeless at the sky.

For a moment Stuart's clear, all-seeing gaze rested on his father, and saw not the ruined shell but the man, as he had been in life. He pointed his rifle at the sky, fired a shot, reloaded, fired a second shot, reloaded, let off the third. Faintly in the distance he heard one answering report, then, farther off and very faintly, a second answer. It was then he remembered the closer shot would have come from his mother and sister. They were north-west, he was north. Without waiting the stipulated five minutes, he put another shell in the rifle breech, pointed the gun due south, and fired. A pause to reload, the second shot, reload, the third shot. He put the weapon back on the ground and stood looking south, his head cocked, listening. This time the first answer was from the west, Bob's shot, the second from Jack or Hughie, and the third from his mother. He sighed in relief; he didn't want the women reaching him first.

Thus he didn't see the great wild pig emerge from the trees to the north; he smelled it. As big as a cow, its massive bulk rolled and quivered on short, powerful legs as it drove its head down, raking at the burned wet ground. The shots had disturbed it, and it was in pain. The sparse black hair on one side of its body was singed off and the skin was redly raw; what Stuart smelled as he stared into the south was the delectable odor of bubbled pork skin, just as it is on a roasted joint fresh from the oven and crisp all over the slashed outer husk. Surprised out of the curiously peaceful sorrow he always seemed to have known, his head turned, even as he thought to himself that he must have been here before, that this sodden black place had been etched into some part of his brain on the day of his birth.

Stooping, he groped for the rifle, remembering it wasn't loaded. The boar stood perfectly still, its little reddened eyes mad with pain, the great yellow tusks sharp and curving upward in a half circle. Stuart's horse neighed, smelling the beast; the pig's massive head swung to watch it, then lowered for the charge. While its attention was on the horse Stuart saw his only chance, bent quickly for the rifle and snapped the breech open, his other hand in his jacket pocket for a shell. All around the rain was dropping down, muffling other sounds in its own unchanging patter. But the pig heard the bolt slide back, and at the last moment changed the direction of its charge from the horse to Stuart. It was almost upon him when he got one shot off straight into the beast's chest, without slowing it down. The tusks slewed up and sideways, and caught him in the groin. He fell, blood appearing like a faucet turned all the way on and saturating his clothes, spurting over the ground.

Turning awkwardly as it began to feel the bullet, the pig came back to gore him again, faltered, swayed, and tottered. The whole of that fifteen-hundred-pound bulk came down across him, and crushed his face into the tarry mud. For a moment his hands clawed at the ground on either side in a frantic, futile struggle to be free; this then was what he had always known, why he had never hoped or dreamed or planned, only sat and drunk of the living world so deeply there had not been time to grieve for his waiting fate. He thought: Mum, Mum! I can't stay with you, Mum!, even as his heart burst within him.

"I wonder why Stu hasn't fired again?" Meggie asked her mother as they trotted toward the sound of those two first triple volleys, not able to go any faster in the mud, and desperately anxious.

"I suppose he decided we'd heard," Fee said. But in the back of her mind she was remembering Stuart's face as they parted in different directions on the search, the way his hand had gone out to clasp hers, the way he had smiled at her. "We can't be far away now," she said, and pushed her mount into a clumsy, sliding canter.

But Jack had got there first, so had Bob, and they headed the women off as they came across the last of the living land toward the place where the bushfire had begun.

"Don't go in, Mum," said Bob as she dismounted.

Jack had gone to Meggie, and held her arms.

The two pairs of grey eyes turned, not so much in bewilderment or dread as in knowledge, as if they did not need to be told anything.

"Paddy?" asked Fee in a voice not like her own.

"Yes. And Stu."

Neither of her sons could look at her.

"Stu? *Stu! What do you mean, Stu?* Oh, God, what is it, what's happened? Not both of them—no!"

"Daddy got caught in the fire; he's dead. Stu must have disturbed a boar, and it charged him. He shot it, but it fell on him as it was dying and smothered him. He's dead too, Mum."

Meggie screamed and struggled, trying to break free of Jack's hands, but Fee stood between Bob's grimy, bloody ones as if turned to stone, her eyes as glassy as a gazing-ball.

"It is too much," she said at last, and looked up at Bob with the rain running down her face and her hair in straggling wisps around her neck like golden runnels. "Let me go to them, Bob. I am the wife of one and the mother of one. You can't keep me away—you have no right to keep me away. Let me go to them."

Meggie had quietened, and stood within Jack's arms with her head on his shoulder. As Fee began to walk across the ruins with Bob's arm around her waist, Meggie looked after them, but she made no move to follow. Hughie appeared out of the dimming rain; Jack nodded toward his mother and Bob.

"Go after them, Hughie, stay with them. Meggie and I are going back to Drogheda, to bring the dray." He let Meggie go, and helped her onto the chestnut mare. "Come on, Meggie; it's nearly dark. We can't leave them out all night in this, and they won't go until we get back."

It was impossible to put the dray or anything else wheeled upon the mud; in the end Jack and old Tom chained a sheet of corrugated iron behind two draft horses, Tom leading the team on a stock horse while Jack rode ahead with the biggest lamp Drogheda possessed.

Meggie stayed at the homestead and sat in front of the drawing room fire while Mrs. Smith tried to persuade her to eat, tears running down her face to see the girl's still, silent shock, the way she did not weep. At the sound of the front door knocker she turned and went to answer it, wondering who on earth had managed to get through the mud, and as always astonished at the speed with which news traveled the lonely miles between the far-flung homesteads.

Father Ralph was standing on the veranda, wet and muddy, in riding clothes and oilskins.

"May I come in, Mrs. Smith?"

"Oh, Father, Father!" she cried, and threw herself into his astounded arms. "How did you know?"

"Mrs. Cleary telegrammed me, a manager-to-owner courtesy I appreciated very much. I got leave to come from Archbishop di Contini-Verchese. What a mouthful! Would you believe I have to say it a hundred times a day? I flew up. The plane bogged as it landed and pitched on its nose, so I knew what the ground was like before I so much as stepped on it. Dear, beautiful Gilly! I left my suitcase with Father Watty at the presbytery and cadged a horse from the Imperial publican, who thought I was crazy and bet me a bottle of Johnnie Walker Black Label I'd never get through the mud. Oh, Mrs. Smith, don't cry so! My dear, the world hasn't come to an end because of a fire, no matter how big and nasty it was!" he said, smiling and patting her heaving shoulders. "Here am I doing my best to make light of it, and you're just not doing your best to respond. Don't cry so, please."

"Then you don't know," she sobbed.

"What? Know what? What is it—what's happened?"

"Mr. Cleary and Stuart are dead."

His face drained of color; his hands pushed the housekeeper away. "Where's Meggie?" he barked.

"In the drawing room. Mrs. Cleary's still out in the paddock with the bodies. Jack and Tom have gone to bring them in. Oh, Father, sometimes in spite of my faith I can't help thinking God is too cruel! Why did He have to take both of them?"

But all Father Ralph had stayed to hear was where Meggie was; he had gone into the drawing room shedding his oilskins as he went, trailing muddy water behind him.

"Meggie!" he said, coming to her and kneeling at one side of her chair, taking her cold hands in his wet ones firmly.

She slipped from the chair and crawled into his arms, pillowed her head on his dripping shirt and closed her eyes, so happy in spite of her pain and grief that she never wanted the moment to end. He had come, it was a vindication of her power over him, she hadn't failed.

"I'm wet, darling Meggie; you'll get soaked," he whispered, his cheek on her hair.

"It doesn't matter. You've come."

"Yes, I've come. I wanted to be sure you were safe, I had a feeling I was needed, I had to see for myself. Oh, Meggie, your father and Stu! How did it happen?"

"Daddy was caught in the fire, and Stu found him. He was killed by a boar; it fell on him after he shot it. Jack and Tom have gone out to bring them in."

He said no more, but held her and rocked her as if she were a baby until the heat of the fire partially dried his shirt and hair and he felt some of the stiffness drain from her. Then he put his hand beneath her chin, tilted her head until she looked up at him, and without thinking kissed her. It was a confused impulse not rooted in desire, just something he instinctively offered when he saw what lay in the grey eyes. Something apart, a different kind of sacrament. Her arms slid up under his to meet across his back; he could not stop himself flinching, suppress the exclamation of pain.

She drew back a little. "What's the matter?"

"I must have bruised my ribs when the plane came in. We bogged to the fuselage in good old Gilly mud, so it was a pretty rough landing. I wound up balanced on the back of the seat in front of me."

"Here, let me see."

Fingers steady, she unbuttoned the damp shirt and peeled it off his arms, pulled it free of his breeches. Under the surface of the smooth brown skin a purpling ugly patch extended from one side clear across to the other below the rib cage; her breath caught.

"Oh, Ralph! You rode all the way from Gilly with this? How it must have hurt! Do you feel all right? No faintness? You might have ruptured something inside!"

"No, I'm fine, and I didn't feel it, honestly. I was so anxious to get here, make sure you were all right, that

I suppose I simply eliminated it from my mind. If I was bleeding internally I'd have known about it long before now, I expect. God, Meggie, *don't!*"

Her head had gone down, she was delicately touching her lips to the bruise, her palms sliding up his chest to his shoulders with a deliberate sensuousness that staggered him. Fascinated, terrified, meaning to free himself at any cost, he pulled her head away; but somehow all he succeeded in doing was having her back in his arms, a snake coiled tightly about his will, strangling it. Pain was forgotten, Church was forgotten, God was forgotten. He found her mouth, forced it open hungrily, wanting more and more of her, not able to hold her close enough to assuage the ghastly drive growing in him. She gave him her neck, bared her shoulders where the skin was cool, smoother and glossier than satin; it was like drowning, sinking deeper and deeper, gasping and helpless. Mortality pressed down on him, a great weight crushing his soul, liberating the bitter dark wine of his senses in a sudden flood. He wanted to weep; the last of his desire trickled away under the burden of his mortality, and he wrenched her arms from about his wretched body, sat back on his heels with his head sunken forward, seeming to become utterly absorbed in watching his hands tremble on his knees. Meggie, what have you done to me, what might you do to me if I let you?

"Meggie, I love you, I always will. But I'm a priest, I can't. . . . I just can't!"

She got to her feet quickly, straightened her blouse, stood looking down at him and smiling a twisted smile which only threw the failed pain in her eyes into greater emphasis.

"It's all right, Ralph. I'll go and see if Mrs. Smith can get you something to eat, then I'll bring you the horse liniment. It's marvelous for bringing out a bruise; stops the soreness much better than kisses ever could, I daresay."

"Is the phone working?" he managed to say.

"Yes. They strung a temporary line on the trees and reconnected us a couple of hours ago."

But it was some minutes after she left him before he could compose himself sufficiently to seat himself at Fee's escritoire.

"Give me trunks, please, switch. This is Father de Bricassart at Drogheda— Oh, hello, Doreen; still on the switch, I see. Nice to hear your voice, too. One never knows who switch is in Sydney; she's just a bored voice. I want to put an urgent call through to His Grace the Archbishop Papal Legate in Sydney. His number is XX-2324. And while I'm waiting for Sydney, put me through to Bugela, Doreen."

There was barely time to tell Martin King what had happened before Sydney was on the line, but one word to Bugela was enough. Gilly would know from him and the eavesdroppers on the party line, and those who wished to brave a ride through Gilly mud would be at the funerals.

"Your Grace? This is Father de Bricassart. . . . Yes, thank you, I arrived safely, but the plane's bogged to its fuselage in mud and I'll have to come back by train. . . . Mud, Your Grace, *m-u-d mud!* No, Your Grace, everything up here becomes impassable when it rains. I had to ride from Gillanbone to Drogheda on horseback; that's the only way one can even try in rain. . . . That's why I'm phoning, Your Grace. It was as well I came. I suppose I must have had some sort of premonition. . . . Yes, things are bad, very bad. Padraic Cleary and his son Stuart are dead, one burned to death in the fire, one smothered by a boar. . . . A *b-o-a-r boar,* Your Grace, a wild pig. . . . Yes, you're right, one does speak a slightly bizarre English up here."

All down the faint line he could hear gasps from the listeners, and grinned in spite of himself. One couldn't yell into the phone that everybody must get off the line—it was the sole entertainment of a mass nature Gilly had to offer its contact-hungry citizens—but if they would only get off the line His Grace might stand a better chance of hearing. "With your permission, Your Grace, I'll remain to conduct the funerals and make sure the widow and her surviving children are all right. . . . Yes, your Grace, thank you. I'll return to Sydney as soon as I can."

Switch was listening, too; he clicked the lever and spoke again immediately. "Doreen, put me back to Bugela, please." He talked to Martin King for a few minutes, and decided since it was August and winter-cold to delay the funerals until the day after this coming day. Many people would want to attend in spite of the mud and be prepared to ride to get there, but it was slow and arduous work.

Meggie came back with the horse liniment, but made no offer to rub it on, just handed him the bottle silently. She informed him abruptly that Mrs. Smith was laying him a hot supper in the small dining room in an hour, so he would have time to bathe. He was uncomfortably aware that in some way Meggie thought he had failed her, but he didn't know why she should think so, or on what basis she had judged him. She *knew* what he was; why was she angry?

In grey dawnlight the little cavalcade escorting the bodies reached the creek, and stopped. Though the water was still contained within its banks, the Gillan had become a river in full spate, running fast and thirty feet deep. Father Ralph swam his chestnut mare across to meet them, stole around his neck and the instruments of his calling in a saddlebag. While Fee, Bob, Jack, Hughie and Tom stood around, he stripped the canvas off the bodies and prepared to anoint them. After Mary Carson nothing could sicken him; yet he found nothing repugnant about Paddy and Stu. They were both black after their fashion, Paddy from the fire and Stu from suffocation, but the priest kissed them with love and respect.

For fifteen miles the rough sheet of iron had jarred

and bounced over the ground behind the team of draft horses, scarring the mud with deep gouges which would still be visible years later, even in the grass of other seasons. But it seemed they could go no farther; the swirling creek would keep them on its far side, with Drogheda only a mile away. They stood staring at the tops of the ghost gums, clearly visible even in the rain.

"I have an idea," said Bob, turning to Father Ralph. "Father, you're the only one on a fresh horse; it will have to be you. Ours will only swim the creek once—they've got no more in them after the mud and the cold. Go back and find some empty forty-four-gallon drums, and seal their lids shut so they can't possibly leak or slip off. Solder them if necessary. We'll need twelve of them, ten if you can't find more. Tie them together and bring them back across the creek. We'll lash them under the iron and float it across like a barge."

Father Ralph did as he was told without question; it was a better idea than any he had to offer. Dominic O'Rourke of Dibban-Dibban had ridden in with two of his sons; he was a neighbor and not far away as distances went. When Father Ralph explained what had to be done they set about it quickly, scouring the sheds for empty drums, tipping chaff and oats out of drums empty of petrol but in use for storage, searching for lids, soldering the lids to the drums if they were rust-free and looked likely to withstand the battering they would get in the water. The rain was still falling, falling. It wouldn't stop for another two days.

"Dominic, I hate to ask it of you, but when these people come in they're going to be half dead. We'll have to hold the funerals tomorrow, and even if the Gilly undertaker could make the coffins in time, we'd never get them out through the mud. Can any of you have a go at making a couple of coffins? I only need one man to swim the creek with me."

The O'Rourke sons nodded; they didn't want to see what the fire had done to Paddy or the boar to Stuart.

"We'll do it, Dad," said Liam.

Dragging the drums behind their horses, Father Ralph and Dominic O'Rourke rode down to the creek and swam it.

"There's one thing, Father!" shouted Dominic. "We don't have to dig graves in this bloody mud! I used to think old Mary was putting on the dog a bit too much when she put a marble vault in her backyard for Michael, but right at this minute if she was here, I'd kiss her!"

"Too right!" yelled Father Ralph.

They lashed the drums under the sheet of iron, six on either side, tied the canvas shroud down firmly, and swam the exhausted draft horses across on the rope which would finally tow the raft. Dominic and Tom sat astride the great beasts, and at the top of the Drogheda-side bank paused, looking back, while those still marooned hooked up the makeshift barge, pushed it to the bank and shoved it in. The draft horses began walking, Tom and Dominic cooeeing shrilly as the raft began to float. It bobbed and wallowed badly, but it stayed afloat long enough to be hauled out safely; rather than waste time dismantling the pontoons, the two impromptu postilions urged their mounts up the track toward the big house, the sheet of iron sliding along on its drums better than it had without them.

There was a ramp up to great doors at the baling end of the shearing shed, so they put the raft and its burden in the huge empty building amid the reeks of tar, sweat, lanolin and dung. Muffled in oilskins, Minnie and Cat had come down from the big house to take first vigil, and knelt one on either side of the iron bier, rosary beads clicking, voices rising and falling in cadences too well known to need the effort of memory.

The house was filling up. Duncan Gordon had arrived from Each-Uisge, Gareth Davies from Narrengang, Horry Hopeton from Beel-Beel, Eden Carmichael from Barcoola. Old Angus MacQueen had flagged down one of the ambling local goods trains and ridden with the engine driver to Gilly, where he borrowed a horse from Harry Gough and rode out with him. He had covered over two hundred miles of mud, one way or another.

"I'm wiped out, Father," Horry said to the priest later as the seven of them sat in the small dining room eating steak-and-kidney pie. "The fire went through me from one end to the other and left hardly a sheep alive or a tree green. Lucky the last few years have been good is all I can say. I can afford to restock, and if this rain keeps up the grass will come back real quick. But heaven help us from another disaster during the next ten years, Father, because I won't have anything put aside to meet it."

"Well, you're smaller than me, Horry," Gareth Davies said, cutting into Mrs. Smith's meltingly light flaky pastry with evident enjoyment. Nothing in the line of disasters could depress a black-soil plainsman's appetite for long; he needed his food to meet them. "I reckon I lost about half of my acreage, and maybe two-thirds of my sheep, worse luck. Father, we need your prayers."

"Aye," said old Angus. "I wasna sae hard hit as wee Horry and Garry, Father, but bad enough for a' that. I lost sixty thoosand of ma acres, and half ma wee sheep. 'Tis times like this, Father, make me wish I hadna left Skye as a young laddie."

Father Ralph smiled. "It's a passing wish, Angus, you know that. You left Skye for the same reason I left Clunamara. It was too small for you."

"Aye, nae doot. The heather doesna make sic a bonnie blaze as the gums, eh, Father?"

It would be a strange funeral, thought Father Ralph as he looked around; the only women would be Drogheda women, for all the visiting mourners were men. He had taken a huge dose of laudanum to Fee after Mrs. Smith had stripped her, dried her and put her into the big bed she had shared with Paddy, and when she refused to drink it, weeping hysterically, he had held her nose and tipped it ruthlessly down her throat. Funny, he hadn't thought of Fee breaking down. It had worked quickly, for she hadn't eaten in twenty-four hours. Knowing she was sound asleep, he rested easier. Meggie he kept tabs on; she was out in the cookhouse at the moment helping Mrs. Smith prepare food. The boys were all in bed, so exhausted they could hardly manage to peel off their wet things before collapsing. When Minnie and Cat concluded their stint of the vigil custom demanded because the bodies lay in a deserted, unblessed place, Gareth Davies and his son Enoch were taking over; the others allotted hour-long spans among themselves as they talked and ate.

None of the young men had joined their elders in the dining room. They were all in the cookhouse ostensibly helping Mrs. Smith, but in reality so they could look at Meggie. When he realized this fact Father Ralph was both annoyed and relieved. Well, it was out of their ranks she must choose her husband, as she inevitably would. Enoch Davies was twenty-nine, a "black Welshman," which meant he was black-haired and very dark-eyed, a handsome man; Liam O'Rourke was twenty-six, sandy-haired and blue-eyed, like his twenty-five-year-old brother Rory; Connor Carmichael was the spit of his sister, older at thirty-two, and very good-looking indeed, if a little arrogant; the pick of the bunch in Father Ralph's estimation was old Angus's grandson Alastair, the closest to Meggie in age at twenty-four and a sweet young man, with his grandfather's beautiful blue Scots eyes and hair already gray, a family trait. Let her fall in love with one of them, marry him, have the children she wanted so badly. Oh, God, my God, if You will do that for me, I'll gladly bear the pain of loving her, gladly. . . .

No flowers smothered these coffins, and the vases all

around the chapel were empty. What blossoms had survived the terrible heat of the fiery air two nights ago had succumbed to the rain, and laid themselves down against the mud like ruined butterflies. Not even a stalk of bottle brush, or an early rose. And everyone was tired, so tired. Those who had ridden the long miles in the mud to show their liking for Paddy were tired, those who had brought the bodies in were tired, those who had slaved to cook and clean were tired, Father Ralph was so tired he felt as if he moved in a dream, eyes sliding away from Fee's pinched, hopeless face, Meggie's expression of mingled sorrow and anger, the collective grief of that collective cluster Bob, Jack and Hughie. . . .

He gave no eulogy; Martin King spoke briefly and movingly on behalf of those assembled, and the priest went on into the Requiem immediately. He had as a matter of course brought his chalice, his sacraments and a stole, for no priest stirred without them when he went offering comfort or aid, but he had no vestments with him, and the house possessed none. But old Angus had called in at the presbytery in Gilly on his way, and carried the black mourning garb of a Requiem Mass wrapped in an oilskin across his saddle. So he stood properly attired with the rain hissing against the windows, drumming on the iron roof two stories up.

Then out into it, the grieving rain, across the lawn all browned and scorched by heat, to the little white-railinged cemetery. This time there were pallbearers willing to shoulder the plain rectangular boxes, slipping and sliding in the mud, trying to see where they were going through the rain beating in their eyes. And the little bells on the Chinese cook's grave tinkled drably: Hee Sing, Hee Sing, Hee Sing.

It got itself over and done with. The mourners departed on their horses, backs hunched inside their oilskins, some of them staring miserably at the prospect of ruin, others thanking God they had escaped death and the fire. And Father Ralph got his few things together, knowing he must go before he couldn't go.

He went to see Fee, where she sat at the escritoire staring mutely down at her hands.

"Fee, will you be all right?" he asked, sitting where he could see her.

She turned toward him, so still and quenched within her soul that he was afraid, and closed his eyes.

"Yes, Father, I'll be all right. I have the books to keep, and five sons left—six if you count Frank, only I don't suppose we can count Frank, can we? Thank you for that, more than I can ever say. It's such a comfort to me knowing your people are watching out for him, making his life a little easier. Oh, if I could see him, just once!"

She was like a lighthouse, he thought; flashes of grief every time her mind came round to that pitch of emotion which was too great to be contained. A huge flare, and then a long period of nothing.

"Fee, I want you to think about something."

"Yes, what?" She was dark again.

"Are you listening to me?" he asked sharply, worried and suddenly more frightened than before.

For a long moment he thought she had retreated so far into herself even the harshness of his voice hadn't penetrated, but up blazed the beacon again, and her lips parted. "My poor Paddy! My poor Stuart! My poor Frank!" she mourned, then got herself under that iron control once more, as if she was determined to elongate her periods of darkness until the light shone no more in her lifetime.

Her eyes roamed the room without seeming to recognize it. "Yes, Father, I'm listening," she said.

"Fee, what about your daughter? Do you ever remember that you have a daughter?"

The grey eyes lifted to his face, dwelled on it almost pityingly. "Does any woman? What's a daughter? Just a reminder of the pain, a younger version of oneself who will do all the things one has done, cry the same tears. No, Father. I try to forget I have a daughter—if I do think of her, it is as one of my sons. It's her sons a mother remembers."

"Do you cry tears, Fee? I've only seen them once."

"You'll never see them again, for I've finished with tears forever." Her whole body quivered. "Do you know something, Father? Two days ago I discovered how much I love Paddy, but it was like all of my life —too late. Too late for him, too late for me. If you knew how I wanted the chance to take him in my arms, tell him I loved him! Oh, God, I hope no other human being ever has to feel my pain!"

He turned away from that suddenly ravaged face, to give it time to don its calm, and himself time to cope with understanding the enigma who was Fee.

He said, "No one else can ever feel *your* pain."

One corner of her mouth lifted in a stern smile. "Yes. That's a comfort, isn't it? It may not be enviable, but my pain is *mine.*"

"Will you promise me something, Fee?"

"If you like."

"Look after Meggie, don't forget her. Make her go to the local dances, let her meet a few young men, encourage her to think of marriage and a home of her own. I saw all the young men eyeing her today. Give her the opportunity to meet them again under happier circumstances than these."

"Whatever you say, Father."

Sighing, he left her to the contemplation of her thin white hands.

Meggie walked with him to the stables, where the Imperial publican's bay gelding had been stuffing itself on hay and bran and dwelling in some sort of equine heaven for two days. He flung the publican's battered saddle on its back and bent to strap the surcingle and girth while Meggie leaned against a bale of straw and watched him.

"Father, look what I found," she said as he finished and straightened. She held out her hand, in it one pale, pinkish-gray rose. "It's the only one. I found it on a bush under the tank stands, at the back. I suppose it didn't get the same heat in the fire, and it was sheltered from the rain. So I picked it for you. It's something to remember me by."

He took the half-open bloom from her, his hand not quite steady, and stood looking down at it. "Meggie, I need no reminder of you, not now, not ever. I carry you within me, you know that. There's no way I could hide it from you, is there?"

"But sometimes there's a reality about a keepsake," she insisted. "You can take it out and look at it, and remember when you see it all the things you might forget otherwise. Please take it, Father."

"My name is Ralph," he said. He opened his little sacrament case and took out the big missal which was his own property, bound in costly mother-of-pearl. His dead father had given it to him at his ordination, thirteen long years ago. The pages fell open at a great thick white ribbon; he turned over several more, laid the rose down, and shut the book upon it. "Do you want a keepsake from me, Meggie, is that it?"

"Yes."

"I won't give you one. I want you to forget me, I want you to look around your world and find some good kind man, marry him, have the babies you want so much. You're a born mother. You mustn't cling to me, it isn't right. I can never leave the Church, and I'm going to be completely honest with you, for your own sake. I don't want to leave the Church, because I don't love you the way a husband will, do you understand? Forget me, Meggie!"

"Won't you kiss me goodbye?"

For answer he pulled himself up on the publican's bay and walked it to the door before putting on the publican's old felt hat. His blue eyes flashed a moment, then the horse moved out into the rain and slithered reluctantly up the track toward Gilly. She did not attempt to follow him, but stayed in the gloom of the damp stable, breathing in the smells of horse dung and hay; it reminded her of the barn in New Zealand, and of Frank.

Thirty hours later Father Ralph walked into the Archbishop Papal Legate's chamber, crossed the room to kiss his master's ring, and flung himself wearily into a chair. It was only as he felt those lovely, omniscient eyes on him that he realized how peculiar he must look, why so many people had stared at him since he got off the train at Central. Without remembering the suitcase Father Watty Thomas was keeping for him at the presbytery, he had boarded the night mail with two minutes to spare and come six hundred miles in a cold train clad in shirt, breeches and boots, soaking wet, never noticing the chill. So he looked down at himself with a rueful smile, then across at the Archbishop.

"I'm sorry, Your Grace. So much has happened I didn't think how odd I must look."

"Don't apologize, Ralph." Unlike his predecessor, he preferred to call his secretary by his Christian name. "I think you look very romantic and dashing. Only a trifle too secular, don't you agree?"

"Very definitely on the secular bit, anyway. As to the romantic and dashing, Your Grace, it's just that you're not used to seeing what is customary garb in Gillanbone."

"My dear Ralph, if you took it into your head to don sackcloth and ashes, you'd manage to make yourself seem romantic and dashing! The riding habit suits you, though, it really does. Almost as well as a soutane, and don't waste your breath telling me you aren't very well aware it becomes you more than a priest's black suit. You have a peculiar and a most attractive way of moving, and you have kept your fine figure; I think perhaps you always will. I also think that when I am recalled to Rome I shall take you with me. It will afford me great amusement to watch your effect on our short, fat Italian prelates. The beautiful sleek cat among the plump startled pigeons."

Rome! Father Ralph sat up in his chair.

"Was it very bad, my Ralph?" the Archbishop went on, smoothing his beringed milky hand rhythmically across the silky back of his purring Abyssinian cat.

"Terrible, Your Grace."

"These people, you have a great fondness for them."

"Yes."

"And do you love all of them equally, or do you love some of them more than others?"

But Father Ralph was at least as wily as his master, and he had been with him now long enough to know how his mind worked. So he parried the smooth question with deceptive honesty, a trick he had discovered lulled His Grace's suspicions at once. It never occurred to that subtle, devious mind that an outward display of frankness might be more mendacious than any evasion.

"I do love all of them, but as you say, some more than others. It's the girl Meggie I love the most. I've always felt her my special responsibility, because the family is so son-oriented they forget she exists."

"How old is this Meggie?"

"I'm not sure exactly. Oh, somewhere around twenty, I imagine. But I made her mother promise to lift her head out of her ledgers long enough to make sure the girl got to a few dances, met a few young men. She's going to waste her life away stuck on Drogheda, which is a shame."

He spoke nothing but the truth; the Archbishop's ineffably sensitive nose sniffed it out at once. Though he was only three years his secretary's senior, his career within the Church hadn't suffered the checks Ralph's had, and in many ways he felt immeasurably older than

Ralph would ever be; the Vatican sapped one of some vital essence if one was exposed to it very early, and Ralph possessed that vital essence in abundance.

Relaxing his vigilance somewhat, he continued to watch his secretary and resumed his interesting game of working out precisely what made Father Ralph de Bricassart tick. At first he had been sure there would be a fleshly weakness, if not in one direction, in another. Those stunning good looks and the accompanying body must have made him the target of many desires, too much so to preserve innocence or unawareness. And as time went on he had found himself half right; the awareness was undoubtedly there, but with it he began to be convinced was a genuine innocence. So whatever Father Ralph burned for, it was not the flesh. He had thrown the priest together with skilled and quite irresistible homosexuals if one was a homosexual; no result. He had watched him with the most beautiful women in the land; no result. Not a flicker of interest or desire, even when he was not in the slightest aware he was under observation. For the Archbishop did not always do his own watching, and when he employed minions it was not through secretarial channels.

He had begun to think Father Ralph's weaknesses were pride in being a priest, and ambition; both were facets of personality he understood, for he possessed them himself. The Church had places for ambitious men, as did all great and self-perpetuating institutions. Rumor had it that Father Ralph had cheated these Clearys he purported to love so much out of their rightful inheritance. If indeed he had, he was well worth hanging on to. And how those wonderful blue eyes had blazed when he mentioned Rome! Perhaps it was time he tried another gambit. He poked forward a conversational pawn lazily, but his eyes under hooded lids were very keen.

"I had news from the Vatican while you were away,

Ralph," he said, shifting the cat slightly. "My Sheba, you are selfish; you make my legs numb."

"Oh?" Father Ralph was sinking down in his chair, and his eyes were having a hard time staying open.

"Yes, you may go to bed, but not before you have heard my news. A little while ago I sent a personal and private communication to the Holy Father, and an answer came back today from my friend Cardinal Monteverdi—I wonder if he is a descendant of the Renaissance musician? Why do I never remember to ask him when I see him? Oh, Sheba, must you insist upon digging in your claws when you are happy?"

"I'm listening, Your Grace, I haven't fallen asleep yet," said Father Ralph, smiling. "No wonder you like cats so much. You're one yourself, playing with your prey for your own amusement." He snapped his fingers. "Here, Sheba, leave him and come to me! He is unkind."

The cat jumped down off the purple lap immediately, crossed the carpet and leaped delicately onto the priest's knees, stood waving its tail and sniffing the strange smells of horses and mud, entranced. Father Ralph's blue eyes smiled into the Archbishop's brown ones, both half closed, both absolutely alert.

"How do you do that?" demanded the Archbishop. "A cat will never go to anyone, but Sheba goes to you as if you gave her caviar and valerian. Ingrate animal."

"I'm waiting, Your Grace."

"And you punish me for it, taking my cat from me. All right, you have won, I yield. Do you ever lose? An interesting question. You are to be congratulated, my dear Ralph. In future you will wear the miter and the cope, and be addressed as My Lord, Bishop de Bricassart."

That brought the eyes wide open! he noted with glee. For once Father Ralph didn't attempt to dissimulate, or conceal his true feelings. He just beamed.

FOUR

1933-1938 Luke

10

It was amazing how quickly the land mended; within a week little green shoots of grass were poking out of the gluey morass, and within two months the roasted trees were coming into leaf. If the people were tough and resilient, it was because the land gave them no opportunity to be otherwise; those who were faint in heart or lacking a fanatical streak of endurance did not stay long in the Great Northwest. But it would be years before the scars faded. Many coats of bark would have to grow and fall to eucalyptoid tatters before the tree trunks became white or red or grey again, and a certain percentage of the timber would not regenerate at all, but remain dead and dark. And for years disintegrating skeletons would dew the plains, subsiding into the matting of time, gradually covered by dust and marching little hoofs. And straggling out across Drogheda to the west the sharp deep channels cut by the corners of a makeshift bier in the mud remained, were pointed out by wanderers who knew the story to more wanderers who did not, until the tale became a part of black-soil plains lore.

Drogheda lost perhaps a fifth of its acreage in the fire, and 25,000 sheep, a mere bagatelle to a station whose sheep tally in the recent good years lay in the neighborhood of 125,000. There was absolutely no point in railing at the malignity of fate, or the wrath of

God, however those concerned might choose to regard a natural disaster. The only thing to do was cut the losses and begin again. In no case was it the first time, and in no case did anyone assume it would be the last.

But to see Drogheda's homestead gardens bare and brown in spring hurt badly. Against drought they could survive thanks to Michael Carson's water tanks, but in a fire nothing survived. Even the wistaria failed to bloom; when the flames came its tender clusters of buds were just forming, and shriveled. Roses were crisped, pansies were dead, stocks turned to sepia straw, fuchsias in shady spots withered past rejuvenation, babies'-breath smothered, sweet pea vines were sere and scentless. What had been bled from the water tanks during the fire was replaced by the heavy rain that followed hard on it, so everyone on Drogheda sacrificed a nebulous spare time to helping old Tom bring the gardens back.

Bob decided to keep on with Paddy's policy of more hands to run Drogheda, and put on three more stockmen; Mary Carson's policy had been to keep no permanent non-Cleary men on her books, preferring to hire extra hands at mustering, lambing and shearing time, but Paddy felt the men worked better knowing they had permanent jobs, and it didn't make much difference in the long run. Most stockmen were chronically afflicted with itchy feet, and never stayed very long anywhere.

The new houses sitting farther back from the creek were inhabited by married men; old Tom had a neat new three-room cottage under a pepper tree behind the horse yards, and cackled with proprietary glee every time he entered it. Meggie continued to look after some of the inner paddocks, and her mother the books.

Fee had taken over Paddy's task of communicating with Bishop Ralph, and being Fee failed to pass on any information save those items concerned with the running of the station. Meggie longed to snatch his letters, read them greedily, but Fee gave her no chance to do so, locking them in a steel box the moment she had digested their contents. With Paddy and Stu gone there was just no reaching Fee. As for Meggie, the minute Bishop Ralph had gone Fee forgot all about her promise. Meggie answered dance and party invitations with polite negatives; aware of it, Fee never remonstrated with her or told her she ought to go. Liam O'Rourke seized any opportunity to drive over; Enoch Davies phoned constantly, so did Connor Carmichael and Alastair MacQueen. But with each of them Meggie was preoccupied, curt, to the point where they despaired of interesting her.

The summer was very wet, but not in spates protracted enough to cause flooding, only keeping the ground perpetually muddy and the thousand-mile Barwon-Darling flowing deep, wide and strong. When winter came sporadic rain continued; the flying brown sheets were made up of water, not dust. Thus the Depression march of foot-loose men along the track tapered off, for it was hell tramping through the black-soil plains in a wet season, and with cold added to damp, pneumonia raged among those not able to sleep under warm shelter.

Bob was worried, and began to talk of foot rot among the sheep if it kept up; merinos couldn't take much moisture in the ground without developing diseased hoofs. The shearing had been almost impossible, for shearers would not touch soaked wool, and unless the mud dried before lambing many offspring would die in the sodden earth and the cold.

The phone jangled its two longs, one short for Drogheda; Fee answered and turned.

"Bob, the AML&F for you."

"Hullo, Jimmy, Bob here. . . . Yeah, righto. . . . Oh, good! References all in order? . . . Righto, send him out to see me. . . . Righto, if he's that good you can tell him he's probably got the job, but I still want to see him for myself; don't like pigs in pokes and don't trust references. . . . Righto, thanks. Hooroo."

Bob sat down again. "New stockman coming, a good bloke according to Jimmy. Been working out on the West Queensland plains around Longreach and Charleville. Was a drover, too. Good references and all aboveboard. Can sit anything with four legs and a tail, used to break horses. Was a shearer before that, gun shearer too, Jimmy says, over two fifty a day. That's what makes me a bit suspicious. Why would a gun shearer want to work for stockman's wages? Not too often a gun shearer will give up the boggi for a saddle. Be handy paddock-crutching, though, eh?"

With the passing of the years Bob's accent grew more drawling and Australian but his sentences shorter in compensation. He was creeping up toward thirty, and much to Meggie's disappointment showed no sign of being smitten with any of the eligible girls he met at the few festivities decency forced them to attend. For one thing he was painfully shy, and for another he seemed utterly wrapped in the land, apparently preferring to love it without distraction. Jack and Hughie grew more and more like him; indeed, they could have passed for triplets as they sat together on one of the hard marble benches, the closest to comfortable housebound relaxation they could get. They seemed actually to prefer camping out in the paddocks, and when sleeping at home stretched out on the floors of their bedrooms, frightened that beds might soften them. The sun, the wind and the dryness had weathered their fair, freckled skins to a sort of mottled mahogany, in which their blue eyes shone pale and tranquil, with the deep creases beside them speaking of gazing into far distances and silver-beige grass. It was almost impossible to tell what age they were, or which was the oldest and which the youngest. Each had Paddy's Roman nose and kind homely face, but better bodies than Paddy's, which had been stooped and arm-elongated from so many years shearing. They had developed the spare, easy beauty of horsemen instead. Yet for women and comfort and pleasure they did not pine.

"Is the new man married?" asked Fee, drawing neat lines with a ruler and a red-inked pen.

"Dunno, didn't ask. Know tomorrow when he comes."

"How is he getting here?"

"Jimmy's driving him out; got to see about those old wethers in Tankstand."

"Well, let's hope he stays awhile. If he's not married he'll be off again in a few weeks, I suppose. Wretched people, stockmen," said Fee.

Jims and Patsy were boarding at Riverview, vowing they wouldn't stay at school a minute longer than the fourteen years of age which was legal. They burned for the day when they would be out in the paddocks with Bob, Jack and Hughie, when Drogheda could run on family again and the outsiders would be welcome to come and go as frequently as they pleased. Sharing the family passion for reading didn't endear Riverview to them at all; a book could be carried in a saddlebag or a jacket pocket and read with far more pleasure in the noonday shade of a wilga than in a Jesuit classroom. It had been a hard transition for them, boarding school. The big-windowed classrooms, the spacious green playing fields, the wealth of gardens and facilities meant nothing to them, nor did Sydney with its museums, concert halls and art galleries. They chummed up with the sons of other graziers and spent their leisure hours longing for home, or boasting about the size and splendor of Drogheda to awed but believing ears; anyone west of Burren Junction had heard of mighty Drogheda.

Several weeks passed before Meggie saw the new stockman. His name had been duly entered in the books, Luke O'Neill, and he was already talked about in the big house far more than stockmen usually were. For one thing, he had refused to bunk in the jackaroos' barracks but had taken up residence in the last empty house upon the creek. For another, he had introduced himself to Mrs. Smith, and was in that lady's good books, though she didn't usually care for stockmen. Meggie was quite curious about him long before she met him.

Since she kept the chestnut mare and the black gelding in the stables rather than the stockyards and was mostly obliged to start out later of a morning than the men, she would often go long periods of time without running into any of the hired people. But she finally met Luke O'Neill late one afternoon as the summer sun was flaring redly over the trees and the long shadows crept toward the gentle oblivion of night. She was coming back from Borehead to the ford across the creek, he was coming in from southeast and farther out, also on a course for the ford.

The sun was in his eyes, so she saw him before he saw her, and he was riding a big mean bay with a black mane and tail and black points; she knew the animal well because it was her job to rotate the work horses, and she had wondered why this particular beast was not so much in evidence these days. None of the men cared for it, never rode it if they could help. Apparently the new stockman didn't mind it at all, which certainly indicated he could ride, for it was a notorious early-morning bucker and had a habit of snapping at its rider's head the moment he dismounted.

It was hard to tell a man's height when he was on horseback, for Australian stockmen used small English saddles minus the high cantle and horn of the American saddle, and rode with their knees bent, sitting very upright. The new man seemed tall, but sometimes height was all in the trunk, the legs disproportionately short, so Meggie reserved judgment. However, unlike most stockmen he preferred a white shirt and white moleskins to grey flannel and grey twill; somewhat of a dandy, she decided, amused. Good luck to him, if he didn't mind the bother of so much washing and ironing.

"G'day, Missus!" he called as they converged, doffing his battered old grey felt hat and replacing it rakishly on the back of his head.

Laughing blue eyes looked at Meggie in undisguised admiration as she drew alongside.

"Well, you're certainly not the Missus, so you've got to be the daughter," he said. "I'm Luke O'Neill."

Meggie muttered something but wouldn't look at him again, so confused and angry she couldn't think of any appropriately light conversation. Oh, it wasn't fair! How dare someone else have eyes and face like Father Ralph! Not the way he looked at her: the mirth was something of his own and he had no love burning for her there; from the first moment of seeing Father Ralph kneeling in the dust of the Gilly station yard Meggie had seen love in his eyes. To look into *his* eyes and not see *him!* It was a cruel joke, a punishment.

Unaware of the thoughts his companion harbored, Luke O'Neill kept his wicked bay beside Meggie's demure mare as they splashed through the creek, still running strong from so much rain. She was a beauty, all right! That hair! What was simply carrots on the male Clearys was something else again on this little sprig. If only she would look up, give him a better chance to see that face! Just then she did, with such a look on it that his brows came together, puzzled; not as if she hated him, exactly, but as if she was trying to see something and couldn't, or had seen something and wished she hadn't. Or whatever. It seemed to upset her, anyway. Luke was not used to being weighed in a feminine balance and found wanting. Caught naturally in a delicious trap of sunset-gold hair and soft eyes, his interest only fed on her displeasure and disappointment. Still she was watching him, pink mouth fallen slightly open, a silky dew of sweat on her upper lip and forehead because it was so hot, her reddish-gold brows arched in seeking wonderment.

He grinned to reveal Father Ralph's big white teeth;

yet it was not Father Ralph's smile. "Do you know you look exactly like a baby, all oh! and ah!?"

She looked away. "I'm sorry, I didn't mean to stare. You reminded me of someone, that's all."

"Stare all you like. It's better than looking at the top of your head, pretty though that might be. Who do I remind you of?"

"No one important. It's just strange, seeing someone familiar and yet terribly unfamiliar."

"What's your name, little Miss Cleary?"

"Meggie."

"Meggie . . . It hasn't got enough dignity, it doesn't suit you a bit. I'd rather you were called something like Belinda or Madeline, but if Meggie's the best you've got to offer, I'll go for it. What's the Meggie stand for —Margaret?"

"No, Meghann."

"Ah, now that's more like! I'll call you Meghann."

"No, you won't!" she snapped. "I detest it!"

But he only laughed. "You've had too much of your own way, little Miss Meghann. If I want to call you Eustacia Sophronia Augusta, I will, you know."

They had reached the stockyards; he slipped off his bay, aiming a punch at its snapping head which rocked it into submission, and stood, obviously waiting for her to offer him her hands so he could help her down. But she touched the chestnut mare with her heels and walked on up the track.

"Don't you put the dainty lady with the common old stockmen?" he called after her.

"Certainly not!" she answered without turning.

Oh, it wasn't fair! Even on his own two feet he was like Father Ralph; as tall, as broad in the shoulders and narrow in the hips, and with something of the same grace, though differently employed. Father Ralph moved like a dancer, Luke O'Neill like an athlete. His hair was as thick and black and curling, his eyes as blue, his nose as fine and straight, his mouth as well cut.

And yet he was no more like Father Ralph than—than—than a ghost gum, so tall and pale and splendid, was like a blue gum, also tall and pale and splendid.

After that chance meeting Meggie kept her ears open for opinions and gossip about Luke O'Neill. Bob and the boys were pleased with his work and seemed to get along well with him; apparently he hadn't a lazy bone in his body, according to Bob. Even Fee brought his name up in conversation one evening by remarking that he was a very handsome man.

"Does he remind you of anyone?" Meggie asked idly, flat on her stomach on the carpet reading a book.

Fee considered the question for a moment. "Well, I suppose he's a bit like Father de Bricassart. The same build, the same coloring. But it isn't a striking likeness; they're too different as men.

"Meggie, I wish you'd sit in a chair like a lady to read! Just because you're in jodhpurs you don't have to forget modesty entirely."

"Pooh!" said Meggie. "As if anyone notices!"

And so it went. There was a likeness, but the men behind the faces were so unalike only Meggie was plagued by it, for she was in love with one of them and resented finding the other attractive. In the kitchen she found he was a prime favorite, and also discovered how he could afford the luxury of wearing white shirts and white breeches into the paddocks; Mrs. Smith washed and ironed them for him, succumbing to his ready, beguiling charm.

"Och, what a fine Irishman he is and all!" Minnie sighed ecstatically.

"He's an Australian," said Meggie provocatively.

"Born here, maybe, Miss Meggie darlin', but wit' a name like O'Neill now, he's as Irish as Paddy's pigs, not meanin' any disrespect to yer sainted father, Miss Meggie, may he rest in peace and sing wit' the angels. Mr. Luke not Irish, and him wit' that black hair, thim blue eyes? In the old days the O'Neills was the kings of Ireland."

"I thought the O'Connors were," said Meggie slyly.

Minnie's round little eyes twinkled. "Ah, well now, Miss Meggie, 'twas a big country and all."

"Go on! It's about the size of Drogheda! And anyway, O'Neill is an Orange name; you can't fool me."

"It is that. But it's a great Irish name and it existed before there were Orangemen ever thought of. It is a name from Ulster parts, so it's logical there'd have to be a few of thim Orange, isn't it now? But there was the O'Neill of Clandeboy and the O'Neill Mor back when, Miss Meggie darlin'."

Meggie gave up the battle; Minnie had long since lost any militant Fenian tendencies she might once have possessed, and could pronounce the word "Orange" without having a stroke.

About a week later she ran into Luke O'Neill again, down by the creek. She suspected he had lain in wait for her, but she didn't know what to do about it if he had.

"Good afternoon, Meghann."

"Good afternoon," said she, looking straight between the chestnut mare's ears.

"There's a woolshed ball at Braich y Pwll next Saturday night. Will you come with me?"

"Thank you for asking me, but I can't dance. There wouldn't be any point."

"I'll teach you how to dance in two flicks of a dead lamb's tail, so that's no obstacle. Since I'll be taking the squatter's sister, do you think Bob might let me borrow the old Rolls, if not the new one?"

"I said I wouldn't go!" she said, teeth clenched.

"*You* said you couldn't dance, *I* said I'd teach you. You never said you wouldn't go with me if you could dance, so I assumed it was the dancing you objected to, not me. Are you going to back out?"

Exasperated, she glared at him fiercely, but he only laughed at her.

"You're spoiled rotten, young Meghann; it's time you didn't get all your own way."

"I'm not spoiled!"

"Go on, tell me another! The only girl, all those brothers to run round after you, all this land and money, a posh house, servants? I know the Catholic Church owns it, but the Clearys aren't short of a penny either."

That was the big difference between them! she thought triumphantly; it had been eluding her since she met him. Father Ralph would never have fallen for outward trappings, but this man lacked his sensitivity; he had no in-built antennae to tell him what lay beneath the surface. He rode through life without an idea in his head about its complexity or its pain.

Flabbergasted, Bob handed over the keys to the new Rolls without a murmur; he had stared at Luke for a moment without speaking, then grinned.

"I never thought of Meggie going to a dance, but take her, Luke, and welcome! I daresay she'd like it, the poor little beggar. She never gets out much. We ought to think of taking her, but somehow we never do."

'Why don't you and Jack and Hughie come, too?" Luke asked, apparently not averse to company.

Bob shook his head, horrified. "No, thanks. We're not too keen on dances."

Meggie wore her ashes-of-roses dress, not having anything else to wear; it hadn't occurred to her to use some of the stockpiling pounds Father Ralph put in the bank in her name to have dresses made for parties and balls. Until now she had managed to refuse invitations, for men like Enoch Davies and Alastair MacQueen were easy to discourage with a firm no. They didn't have Luke O'Neill's gall.

But as she stared at herself in the mirror she thought she just might go into Gilly next week when Mum made her usual trip, visit old Gert and have her make up a few new frocks.

For she hated wearing this dress; if she had owned one other even remotely suitable, it would have been off in a second. Other times, a different black-haired man; it was so tied up with love and dreams, tears and loneliness, that to wear it for such a one as Luke O'Neill seemed a desecration. She had grown used to hiding what she felt, to appearing always calm and outwardly happy. Self-control was growing around her thicker than bark on a tree, and sometimes in the night she would think of her mother, and shiver.

Would she end up like Mum, cut off from all feeling? Was this how it begàn for Mum back in the days when there was Frank's father? And what on earth would Mum do, what would she say if she knew Meggie had learned the truth about Frank? Oh, that scene in the presbytery! It seemed like yesterday, Daddy and Frank facing each other, and Ralph holding her so hard he hurt. Shouting those awful things. Everything had fallen into place. Meggie thought she must always have known, once she did. She had grown up enough to realize there was more to getting babies than she used to think; some sort of physical contact absolutely forbidden between any but a married couple. What disgrace and humiliation poor Mum must have gone through over Frank. No wonder she was the way she was. If it happened to her, Meggie thought, she would want to die. In books only the lowest, cheapest girls had babies outside of marriage; yet Mum wasn't cheap, could never have been cheap. With all her heart Meggie wished Mum could talk to her about it, or that she herself had the courage to bring up the subject. Perhaps in some small way she might have been able to help. But Mum wasn't the sort of person one could approach, nor would Mum do the approaching. Meggie sighed at herself in the mirror, and hoped nothing like that ever happened to her.

Yet she was young; at times like this, staring at herself in the ashes-of-roses dress, she wanted to feel, wanted emotion to blow over her like a strong hot wind. She didn't want to plod like a little automaton for the rest of her life, she wanted change and vitality and love. Love, and a husband, and babies. What was the use of hungering after a man she could never have? He didn't want her, he never would want her. He said he loved her, but not as a husband would love her. Because he was married to the Church. Did all men do that, love some inanimate thing more than they could love a woman? No, surely not all men. The difficult ones, perhaps, the complex ones with their seas of doubts and objections, rationalities. But there had to be simpler men, men who could surely love a woman before all else. Men like Luke O'Neill, for instance.

"I think you're the most beautiful girl I've ever seen," said Luke as he started the Rolls.

Compliments were quite out of Meggie's ken; she gave him a startled sidelong glance and said nothing.

"Isn't this nice?" Luke asked, apparently not upset at her lack of enthusiasm. "Just turn a key and press a button on the dashboard and the car starts. No cranking a handle, no hoping the darned donk catches before a man's exhausted. This is the life, Meghann, no doubt about it."

"You won't leave me alone, will you?" she asked.

"Good Lord, no! You've come with me, haven't you? That means you're mine all night long, and I don't intend giving anyone else a chance."

"How old are you, Luke?"

"Thirty. How old are you?"

"Almost twenty-three."

"As much as that, eh? You look like a baby."

"I'm not a baby."

"Oho! Have you ever been in love, then?"

"Once."

"Is that all? At twenty-three? Good Lord! I'd been in and out of love a dozen times by your age."

"I daresay I might have been, too, but I meet very

few people to fall in love with on Drogheda. You're the first stockman I remember who said more than a shy hello."

"Well, if you won't go to dances because you can't dance, you're on the outside looking in right there, aren't you? Never mind, we'll fix that up in no time. By the end of the evening you'll be dancing, and in a few weeks we'll have you a champion." He glanced at her quickly. "But you can't tell me some of the squatters off other stations haven't tried to get you to come to the odd dance with them. Stockmen I can understand, you're a cut above the usual stockman's inclinations, but some of the sheep cockies must have given you the glad eye."

"If I'm a cut above stockmen, why did you ask me?" she parried.

"Oh, I've got all the cheek in the world." He grinned. "Come on now, don't change the subject. There must be a few blokes around Gilly who've asked."

"A few," she admitted. "But I've really never wanted to go. You pushed me into it."

"Then the rest of them are sillier than pet snakes," he said. "I know a good thing when I see it."

She wasn't too sure that she cared for the way he talked, but the trouble with Luke was that he was a hard man to put down.

Everyone came to a woolshed dance, from squatters' sons and daughters to stockmen and their wives if any, maidservants, governesses, town dwellers of all ages and sexes. For instance, these were occasions when female schoolteachers got the opportunity to fraternize with the stock-and-station-agent apprentices, the bank johnnies and the real bushies off the stations.

The grand manners reserved for more formal affairs were not in evidence at all. Old Mickey O'Brien came out from Gilly to play the fiddle, and there was always someone on hand to man the piano accordion or the button accordion, taking turns to spell each other as

Mickey's accompanists while the old violinist sat on a barrel or a wool bale for hours playing without a rest, his pendulous lower lip drooling because he had no patience with swallowing; it interfered with his tempo,

But it was not the sort of dancing Meggie had seen at Mary Carson's birthday party. This was energetic round-dancing: barn dances, jigs, polkas, quadrilles, reels, mazurkas, Sir Roger de Coverleys, with no more than a passing touching of the partner's hands, or a wild swirling in rough arms. There was no sense of intimacy, no dreaminess. Everyone seemed to view the proceedings as a simple dissipation of frustrations; romantic intrigues were furthered better outside, well away from the noise and bustle.

Meggie soon discovered she was much envied her big handsome escort. He was the target of almost as many seductive or languishing looks as Father Ralph used to be, and more blatantly so. As Father Ralph used to be. Used to be. How terrible to have to think of him in the very remotest of all past tenses.

True to his word, Luke left her alone only so long as it took him to visit the Men's. Enoch Davies and Liam O'Rourke were there, and eager to fill his place alongside her. He gave them no opportunity whatsoever, and Meggie herself seemed too dazed to understand that she was quite within her rights to accept invitations to dance from men other than her escort. Though she didn't hear the comments, Luke did, secretly laughing. What a damned cheek the fellow had, an ordinary stockman, stealing her from under their noses! Disapproval meant nothing to Luke. They had had their chances; if they hadn't made the most of them, hard luck.

The last dance was a waltz. Luke took Meggie's hand and put his arm about her waist, drew her against him. He was an excellent dancer. To her surprise she found she didn't need to do anything more than follow where he propelled her. And it was a most extraordinary sensation to be held so against a man, to feel the muscles of his chest and thighs, to absorb his body warmth. Her brief contacts with Father Ralph had been so intense she had not had time to perceive discrete things, and she had honestly thought that what she felt in his arms she would never feel in anyone else's. Yet though this was quite different, it was exciting; her pulse rate had gone up, and she knew he sensed it by the way he turned her suddenly, gripped her more closely, put his cheek on her hair.

As the Rolls purred home, making light of the bumpy track and sometimes no track at all, they didn't speak very much. Braich y Pwll was seventy miles from Drogheda, across paddocks with never a house to be seen all the way, no lights of someone's home, no intrusion of humanity. The ridge which cut across Drogheda was not more than a hundred feet higher than the rest of the land, but out on the black-soil plains to reach the crest of it was like being on top of an Alp to a Swiss. Luke stopped the car, got out and came round to open Meggie's door. She stepped down beside him, trembling a little; was he going to spoil everything by trying to kiss her? It was so quiet, so far from anyone!

There was a decaying dogleg wooden fence wandering off to one side, and holding her elbow lightly to make sure she didn't stumble in her frivolous shoes, Luke helped Meggie across the uneven ground, the rabbit holes. Gripping the fence tightly and looking out over the plains, she was speechless; first from terror, then, her panic dying as he made no move to touch her, from wonder.

Almost as clearly as the sun could, the moon's still pale light picked out vast sweeping stretches of distance, the grass shimmering and rippling like a restless sigh, silver and white and grey. Leaves on trees sparkled suddenly like points of fire when the wind turned their glossy tops upward, and great yawning gulfs of shadows spread under timber stands as mysteriously as mouths of the underworld. Lifting her head, she tried to count the stars and could not; as delicate as drops of dew on a wheeling spider's web the pinpoints flared, went out, flared, went out, in a rhythm as timeless as God. They seemed to hang over her like a net, so beautiful, so very silent, so watchful and searching of the soul, like jewel eyes of insects turned brilliant in a spotlight, blind as to expression and infinite as to seeing power. The only sounds were the wind hot in the grass, hissing trees, an occasional clank from the cooling Rolls, and a sleepy bird somewhere close complaining because they had broken its rest; the sole smell the fragrant, indefinable scent of the bush.

Luke turned his back on the night, pulled out his tobacco pouch and booklet of rice papers, and began to roll himself a cigarette.

"Were you born out here, Meghann?" he asked, rubbing the strands of leaf back and forth in his palm, lazily.

"No, I was born in New Zealand. We came to Drogheda thirteen years ago."

He slipped the shaped tendrils into their paper sheath, twiddled it expertly between thumb and forefinger, then licked it shut, poked a few wisps back inside the tube with a match end, struck the match and lit up.

"You enjoyed yourself tonight, didn't you?"

"Oh, yes!"

"I'd like to take you to all the dances."

"Thank you."

He fell silent again, smoking quietly and looking back across the roof of the Rolls at the stand of timber where the irate bird still twittered querulously. When only a small remnant of the tube sputtered between his stained fingers he dropped it on the ground and screwed his boot heel viciously down upon it until he was sure it was out. No one kills a cigarette as dead as an Australian bushman.

Sighing, Meggie turned from the moon vista, and he helped her to the car. He was far too wise to kiss her at this early stage, because he intended to marry her if he could; let her want to be kissed, first.

But there were other dances, as the summer wore on and wore itself down in bloody, dusty spendor; gradually the homestead got used to the fact that Meggie had found herself a very good-looking boyfriend. Her brothers forbore to tease, for they loved her and liked him well enough. Luke O'Neill was the hardest worker they had ever employed; no better recommendation than that existed. At heart more working class than squatter class, it never occurred to the Cleary men to judge him by his lack of possessions. Fee, who might have weighed him in a more selective balance, didn't care sufficiently to do so. Anyway, Luke's calm assumption that he was different from your average stockman bore fruit; because of it, he was treated more like one of themselves.

It became his custom to call up the track at the big house when he was in at night and not out in the paddocks; after a while Bob declared it was silly for him to eat alone when there was plenty on the Cleary table, so he ate with them. After that it seemed rather senseless to send him a mile down the track to sleep when he was nice enough to want to stay talking to Meggie until late, so he was bidden to move into one of the small guesthouses out behind the big house.

By this time Meggie thought about him a great deal, and not as disparagingly as she had at first, always comparing him to Father Ralph. The old sore was healing. After a while she forgot that Father Ralph had smiled *so* with the same mouth, while Luke smiled *thus,* that Father Ralph's vivid blue eyes had had a distant stillness to them while Luke's glittered with restless passion. She was young and she had never quite got to savor love, if for a moment or two she had tasted it. She wanted to roll it round on her tongue, get the bouquet of it into her lungs, spin it dizzying to her brain. Father Ralph was Bishop Ralph; he would never, never come back to her. He had sold her for thirteen million pieces of silver, and it rankled. If he hadn't used the phrase that night by the borehead she would not have wondered, but he had used it, and countless were the nights since when she had lain puzzling as to what he could possibly have meant.

And her hands itched with the feel of Luke's back when he held her close in a dance; she was stirred by him, his touch, his crisp vitality. Oh, she never felt that dark liquid fire in her bones for him, she never thought that if she didn't see him again she would wither and dry up, she never twitched and trembled because he looked at her. But she had grown to know men like Enoch Davies, Liam O'Rourke, Alastair MacQueen better as Luke squired her to more and more of the district affairs, and none of them moved her the way Luke O'Neill did. If they were tall enough to oblige her to look up, they would turn out not to have Luke's eyes, or if they had the same sort of eyes, they wouldn't have his hair. Something was always lacking which wasn't lacking in Luke, though just what it was Luke possessed she didn't know. Aside from the fact that he reminded her of Father Ralph, that is, and she refused to admit her attraction had no better basis than that.

They talked a lot, but always about general things; shearing, the land, the sheep, or what he wanted out of life, or perhaps about the places he had seen, or some political happening. He read an occasional book but he wasn't an inveterate reader like Meggie, and try as she would, she couldn't seem to persuade him to read this or that book simply because she had found it interesting. Nor did he lead the conversation into intellectual depths; most interesting and irritating of all, he never evinced any interest in her life, or asked her what she wanted from it. Sometimes she longed to talk about matters far closer to her heart than sheep or rain, but if she made a leading statement he was expert at deflecting her into more impersonal channels.

Luke O'Neill was clever, conceited, extremely hard-working and hungry to enrich himself. He had been born in a wattle-and-daub shanty exactly on the Tropic of Capricorn, outside the town of Longreach in Western Queensland. His father was the black sheep of a prosperous but unforgiving Irish family, his mother was the daughter of the German butcher in Winton; when she insisted on marrying Luke senior, she also was disowned. There were ten children in that humpy, none of whom possessed a pair of shoes—not that shoes mattered much in torrid Longreach. Luke senior, who shore for a living when he felt like it (but mostly all he felt like doing was drinking OP rum), died in a fire at the Blackall pub when young Luke was twelve years old. So as soon as he could Luke took himself off on the shearing circuit as a tar boy, slapping molten tar on jagged wounds if a shearer slipped and cut flesh as well as wool.

One thing Luke was never afraid of, and that was hard work; he thrived on it the way some men thrived on its opposite, whether because his father had been a barfly and a town joke or because he had inherited his German mother's love of industry no one had ever bothered to find out.

As he grew older he graduated from tar boy to shed hand, running down the board catching the great heavy fleeces as they flew off the boggis in one piece billowing up like kites, and carrying them to the wool-rolling table to be skirted. From that he learned to skirt, picking the dirt-encrusted edges off the fleeces and transferring them to bins ready for the attention of the classer, who was shed aristocrat: the man who like a wine-taster or a perfume-tester cannot be trained unless he also has instinct for the job. And Luke didn't have a classer's instinct; either he turned to pressing or to shearing if he wanted to earn more money, which he certainly did. He had the strength to man the press, tamp down the graded fleeces into massive bales, but a gun shearer could make more money.

By now he was well known in Western Queensland as a good worker, so he had no trouble getting himself a learner's pen. With grace, coordination, strength and endurance, all necessary and luckily present in Luke, a man could become a gun shearer. Soon Luke was shearing his two hundred-plus a day six days a week, a quid a hundred; and this with the narrow handpiece resembling a boggi lizard, hence its name. The big New Zealand handpieces with their wide, coarse combs and cutters were illegal in Australia, though they doubled a shearer's tally.

It was grueling work; bending from his height with a sheep clamped between his knees, sweeping his boggi in blows the length of the sheep's body to free the wool in one piece and leave as few second cuts as possible, close enough to the loose kinky skin to please the shed boss, who would be down in a second on any shearer not conforming to his rigorous standards. He didn't mind the heat and the sweat and the thirst which forced him to drink upward of three gallons of water a day, he didn't even mind the tormenting hordes of flies, for he was born in fly country. Nor did he mind the sheep, which were mostly a shearer's nightmare; cobblers, wets, overgrowns, snobs, dags, fly-strikes, they came in all varieties, and they were all merinos, which meant wool all the way down to their hoofs and noses, and a cobbled fragile skin which moved like slippery paper.

No, it wasn't the work itself Luke minded, for the harder he worked the better he felt; what irked him were the noise, the being shut inside, the stench. No place on earth was quite the hell a shearing shed was. Se he decided he wanted to be the boss cocky, the man who strolled up and down the lines of stooping shearers to watch the fleeces he owned being stripped away by that smooth, flawless motion.

> At the end of the floor in his cane-bottomed chair
> Sits the boss of the board with his eyes every-
> where.

That was what the old shearing song said, and that was who Luke O'Neill decided to be. The boss cocky, the head peanut, the grazier, the squatter. Not for him the perpetual stoop, the elongated arms of a lifelong shearer; he wanted the pleasure of working out in the open air while he watched the money roll in. Only the prospect of becoming a dreadnought shearer might have kept Luke inside a shed, one of the rare handful of men who managed to shear over three hundred merino sheep a day, all to standard, and using narrow boggis. They made fortunes on the side by betting. But unfortunately he was just a little too tall, those extra seconds bending and ducking mounted up to the difference between gun and dreadnought.

His mind turned within its limitations to another method of acquiring what he hungered for; at about this stage in his life he discovered how attractive he was to women. His first try had been in the guise of a stockman on Gnarlunga, as that station had an heir who was female, fairly young and fairly pretty. It had been sheer bad luck that in the end she preferred the Pommy jackaroo whose more bizarre exploits were becoming bush legend. From Gnarlunga he went to Bingelly and got a job breaking horses, his eye on the homestead where the aging and unattractive heiress lived with her widowed father. Poor Dot, he had so nearly won her; but in the end she had fallen in with her father's wishes and married the spry sexagenarian who owned the neighboring property.

These two essays cost him over three years of his life, and he decided twenty months per heiress was far too long and boring. It would suit him better for a while to journey far and wide, continually on the move, until within this much larger sweep he found another likely prospect. Enjoying himself enormously, he began to drove the Western Queensland stock routes, down the Cooper and the Diamantina, the Barcoo and the Bulloo Overflow dwindling through the top corner of western New South Wales. He was thirty, and it was more than time he found the goose who would lay at least part of his golden egg.

Everyone had heard of Drogheda, but Luke's ears pricked up when he discovered there was an only daughter. No hope she'd inherit, but perhaps they'd want to dower her with a modest 100,000 acres out around Kynuna or Winton. This was nice country around Gilly, but too cramped and forested for him. Luke yearned for the enormity of far western Queensland, where the grass stretched into infinity and trees were mostly something a man remembered as being vaguely eastward. Just the grass, on and on and on with no beginning and no end, where a man was lucky to graze one sheep for every ten acres he owned. Because sometimes there was no grass, just a flat desert of cracked, panting black soil. The grass, the sun, the heat and the flies; to each man his own kind of heaven, and this was Luke O'Neill's.

He had prised the rest of the Drogheda story out of Jimmy Strong, the AML&F stock-and-station agent who drove him out that first day, and it had been a bitter blow to discover the Catholic Church owned Drogheda. However, he had learned how few and far between female heirs to properties were; when Jimmy Strong went on to say that the only daughter had a nice little cash sum of her own and many doting brothers, he decided to carry on as planned.

But though Luke had long decided his life's objective lay in 100,000 acres out around Kynuna or Winton, and worked toward it with single-minded zeal, the truth was that at heart he loved hard cash far more than what it might eventually buy him; not the possession of land, nor its inherent power, but the prospect of stockpiling rows of neat figures in his bankbook, *in his name*. It hadn't been Gnarlunga or Bingelly he had wanted so desperately, but their value in hard cash. A man who genuinely wanted to be the boss cocky would never have settled for landless Meggie Cleary. Nor would he have loved the physical act of working hard as did Luke O'Neill.

The dance at the Holy Cross hall in Gilly was the thirteenth dance Luke had taken Meggie to in as many weeks. How he discovered where they were and how he wangled some of the invitations Meggie was too naïve to guess, but regularly on a Saturday he would ask Bob for the keys to the Rolls, and take her somewhere within 150 miles.

Tonight it was cold as she stood by a fence looking across a moonless landscape, and under her feet she could feel the crunch of frost. Winter was coming. Luke's arm came around her and drew her in to his side.

"You're cold," he said. "I'd better get you home."

"No, it's all right now, I'm getting warm," she answered breathlessly.

She felt a change in him, a change in the arm held loosely and impersonally across her back. But it was nice to lean against him, to feel the warmth radiating from his body, the different construction of his frame. Even through her cardigan she was conscious of his hand, moving now in small, caressing circles, a tentative and questioning massage. If at this stage she announced she was cold he would stop; if she said nothing, he would take it as tacit permission to proceed. She was young, she wanted so badly to savor love properly. This was the only man outside of Ralph who interested her, so why not see what his kisses were like? Only let them be different! Let them not be like Ralph's kisses!

Taking her silence as acquiescence, Luke put his other hand on her shoulder, turned her to face him, and bent his head. Was that how a mouth really felt? Why, it was no more than a sort of pressure! What was she supposed to do to indicate liking? She moved her lips under his and at once wished she had not. The pushing down increased; he opened his mouth wide, forced her lips apart with his teeth and tongue, and ran the tongue around the inside of her mouth. Revolting. Why had it seemed so different when Ralph kissed her? She hadn't been aware then of how wet and faintly nauseating it was; she hadn't seemed to think at all, only open to him like a casket when the well-known hand touches a secret spring. What on earth was he *doing?* Why did her body jump so, cling to him when her mind wanted badly to pull away?

Luke had found the sensitive spot on her side, and kept his fingers on it to make her writhe; so far she wasn't exactly enthusiastic. Breaking the kiss, he put his mouth hard against the side of her neck. She seemed to like that better, her hands came up around him and she gasped, but when he slid his lips down her throat at the same time as his hand attempted to push her dress off her shoulder, she gave him a sharp shove and stepped quickly away.

"That's enough, Luke!"

The episode had disappointed her, half-repelled her. Luke was very aware of it as he helped her into the car and rolled a much-needed cigarette. He rather fancied himself as a lover, none of the girls so far had ever complained—but then they hadn't been ladies like Meggie. Even Dot MacPherson, the Bingelly heiress, richer by far than Meggie, was as rough as bags, no posh Sydney boarding school and all that crap. In spite of his looks Luke was about on a par with the average rural workingman when it came to sexual experience; he knew little of the mechanics beyond what he liked himself, and he knew nothing of the theory. The numerous girls he had made love to were nothing loath to assure him they liked it, but that meant he had to rely on a certain amount of personal information, not always honest, either. A girl went into any affair hoping for marriage when the man was as attractive and hard-working as Luke, so a girl was as likely as not to lie her head off to please him. And nothing pleased a man more than being told he was the best ever. Luke never dreamed how many men aside from himself had been fooled with that one.

Still thinking about old Dot, who had given in and done as her father wanted after he locked her in the shearers' barracks for a week with a fly-blown carcass, Luke mentally shrugged his shoulders. Meggie was going to be a tough nut to crack and he couldn't afford to frighten or disgust her. Fun and games would have to wait, that was all. He'd woo her the way she obviously wanted, flowers and attention and not too much slap-and-tickle.

For a while an uncomfortable silence reigned, then Meggie sighed and slumped back in her seat.

"I'm sorry, Luke."

"I'm sorry, too. I didn't mean to offend you."

"Oh, no, you didn't offend me, truly! I suppose I'm not very used to it. . . . I was frightened, not offended."

"Oh, Meghann!" He took one hand off the wheel and put it over her clasped ones. "Look, don't worry about it. You're a bit of a girl and I went too fast. Let's forget it."

"Yes, let's," she said.

"Didn't *he* kiss you?" Luke asked curiously.

"Who?'

Was there fear in her voice? But why should there be fear in her voice? "You said you'd been in love once, so I thought you knew the ropes. I'm sorry, Meghann. I should have realized that stuck all the way out here in a family like yours, what you meant was you had a schoolgirl crush on some bloke who never noticed you."

Yes, yes, yes! Let him think that! "You're quite right, Luke; it was just a schoolgirl crush."

Outside the house he drew her to him again and gave her a gentle, lingering kiss without any open-mouth tongue business. She didn't respond exactly, but clearly she liked it; he went off to his guesthouse more satisfied that he hadn't ruined his chances.

Meggie dragged herself to bed and lay looking up at the soft round halo the lamp cast on the ceiling. Well, one thing had been established: there was nothing in Luke's kisses to remind her of Ralph's. And once or twice toward the end she had felt a flicker of dismayed excitement, when he had dug his fingers into her side and when he had kissed her neck. No use equating Luke with Ralph, and she wasn't sure anymore that she wanted to try. Better forget Ralph; he couldn't be her husband. Luke could.

The second time Luke kissed her Meggie behaved quite differently. They had been to a wonderful party on Rudna Hunish, the limit of the territorial boundary Bob had drawn around their jaunts, and the evening had gone well from its beginning. Luke was in his best form, joking so much on the way out he kept her helpless with laughter, then warmly loving and attentive toward her all through the party. And Miss Carmichael had been so determined to take him away from her! Stepping in where Alastair MacQueen and Enoch Davies feared to go, she attached herself to them and flirted with Luke blatantly, forced him for the sake of good manners to ask her to dance. It was a formal affair, the dancing ballroom style, and the dance Luke gave Miss Carmichael was a slow waltz. But he had come back to Meggie immediately it was over and said nothing, only cast his eyes toward the ceiling in a way which left her in no doubt that to him Miss Carmichael was a bore. And she loved him for it; ever since the day the lady had interfered with her pleasure at the Gilly Show, Meggie had disliked her. She had never forgotten the way Father Ralph had ignored the lady to lift a small girl over a puddle; now tonight Luke showed himself in those same colors. Oh, bravo! Luke, you're splendid!

It was a very long way home, and very cold. Luke had cajoled a packet of sandwiches and a bottle of champagne out of old Angus MacQueen, and when they were nearly two-thirds of the way home he stopped the car. Heaters in cars were extremely rare in Australia then as now, but the Rolls was equipped with a heater; that night it was very welcome, for the frost lay two inches thick on the ground.

"Oh, isn't it nice to sit without a coat on a night like this?" Meggie smiled, taking the little silver collapsible cup of champagne Luke gave her, and biting into a ham sandwich.

"Yes, it is. You look so pretty tonight, Meghann."

What was it about the color of her eyes? Grey wasn't normally a color he cared for, too anemic, but looking at her grey eyes he could have sworn they held every color in the blue end of the spectrum, violet and indigo and the sky on a rich clear day, deep mossy green, a hint of tawny yellow. And they glowed like soft, half-opaque jewels, framed by those long curling lashes which glittered as if they had been dipped in gold. He reached out and delicately brushed his finger along the lashes of one eye, then solemnly looked down at its tip.

"Why, Luke! What's the matter?"

"I couldn't resist seeing for myself that you don't have a pot of gold powder on your dressing table. Do you know you're the only girl I've ever met with real gold on her eyelashes?"

"Oh!" She touched them herself, looked at her finger, laughed. "So I have! It doesn't come off at all." The champagne was tickling her nose and fizzing in her stomach; she felt wonderful.

"And real gold eyebrows that have the same shape as a church roof, and the most beautiful real gold hair

. . . I always expect it to be hard like metal, yet it's soft and fine like a baby's. . . . And skin you must use gold powder on, it shines so . . . And the most beautiful mouth, just made for kissing . . ."

She sat staring at him with that tender pink mouth slightly open, the way it had been on their first meeting; he reached out and took the empty cup from her.

"I think you need a little more champagne," he said, filling it.

"I must admit this is nice, to stop and give ourselves a little break from the track. And thank you for thinking of asking Mr. MacQueen for the sandwiches and wine."

The big Rolls engine ticked gently in the silence, warm air pouring almost soundlessly through the vents; two separate kinds of lulling noise. Luke unknotted his tie and pulled it off, opened his shirt collar. Their jackets were on the back seat, too warm for the car.

"Oh, that feels good! I don't know who invented ties and then insisted a man was only properly dressed when he wore one, but if ever I meet him, I'll strangle him with his own invention."

He turned abruptly, lowered his face to hers, and seemed to catch the rounded curve of her lips exactly into his, like two pieces of a jigsaw puzzle; though he didn't hold her or touch her elsewhere she felt locked to him and let her head follow as he leaned back, drawing her forward onto his chest. His hands came up to clasp her head, the better to work at that dizzying, amazingly responsive mouth, drain it. Sighing, he abandoned himself to feeling nothing else, at home at last with those silky baby's lips finally fitting his own. Her arm slid around his neck, quivering fingers sank into his hair, the palm of her other hand coming to rest on the smooth brown skin at the base of his throat. This time he didn't hurry, though he had risen and hardened before giving her the second cup of champagne, just from looking at her. Not releasing her head, he kissed her cheeks, her closed eyes, the curving bones of the orbits beneath her brows, came back to her cheeks because they were so satiny, came back to her mouth because its infantile shape drove him mad, had driven him mad since the day he first saw her.

And there was her throat, the little hollow at its base, the skin of her shoulder so delicate and cool and dry. . . . Powerless to call a halt, almost beside himself with fear lest she should call a halt, he removed one hand from her head and plucked at the long row of buttons down the back of her dress, slid it off her obedient arms, then the straps of her loose satin slip. Face buried between her neck and shoulder, he passed the tips of his fingers down her bare back, feeling her startled little shivers, the sudden hard points to her breasts. He pushed his face lower in a blind, compulsive touch-search of one cold, cushioned surface, lips parted, pressing down, until they closed over taut ruched flesh. His tongue lingered for a dazed minute, then his hands clutched in agonized pleasure on her back and he sucked, nipped, kissed, sucked. . . . The old eternal impulse, his particular preference, and it never failed. It was so good, good, good, *goooooood!* He did not cry out, only shuddered for a wrenching, drenching moment, and swallowed in the depths of his throat.

Like a satiated nursling, he let the nipple pop out of his mouth, formed a kiss of boundless love and gratitude against the side of her breast, and lay utterly still except for the heaves of his breathing. He could feel her mouth in his hair, her hand down inside his shirt, and suddenly he seemed to recollect himself, opened his eyes. Briskly he sat up, pulled her slip straps up her arms, then her dress, and fastened all the buttons deftly.

"You'd better marry me, Meghann," he said, eyes soft and laughing. "I don't think your brothers would approve one little bit of what we just did."

"Yes, I think I'd better too," she agreed, lids lowered, a delicate flush in her cheeks.

"Let's tell them tomorrow morning."

"Why not? The sooner the better."

"Next Saturday I'll drive you into Gilly. We'll see Father Thomas—I suppose you'd like a church wedding—arrange for the banns, and buy an engagement ring."

"Thank you, Luke."

Well, that was that. She had committed herself, there could be no turning back. In a few weeks or however long it took to call banns, she would marry Luke O'Neill. She would be . . . Mrs. Luke O'Neill! How strange! Why did she say yes? Because *he* told me I must, *he* said I was to do it. But why? To remove *him* from danger? To protect himself, or me? Ralph de Bricassart, sometimes I think I hate you. . . .

The incident in the car had been startling and disturbing. Not a bit like that first time. So many beautiful, terrifying sensations. Oh, the touch of his hands! That electrifying tugging at her breast sending vast widening rings clear through her! And he did it right at the moment her conscience had reared its head, told the mindless thing she seemed to have become that he was taking off her clothes, that she must scream, slap him, run away. No longer lulled and half senseless from champagne, from warmth, from the discovery that it was delicious to be kissed when it was done right, his first great gulping taking-in of her breast had transfixed her, stilled common sense, conscience and all thought of flight. Her shoulders came up off his chest, her hips seemed to subside against him, her thighs and that unnamed region at their top rammed by his squeezing hands against a ridge of his body hard as a rock, and she had just wanted to stay like that for the rest of her days, shaken to her soul and yawning empty, wanting. . . . Wanting what? She didn't know. In the moment at which he had put her away from him she hadn't wanted to go, could even have flown at him like a savage. But it had set the seal on her hardening resolve to marry

Luke O'Neill. Not to mention that she was convinced he had done to her the thing which made babies start.

No one was very surprised at the news, and no one dreamed of objecting. The only thing which did startle them was Meggie's adamant refusal to write and tell Bishop Ralph, her almost hysterical rejection of Bob's idea that they invite Bishop Ralph to Drogheda and have a big house wedding. No, no, no! She had screamed it at them; Meggie who never raised her voice. Apparently she was miffed that he had never come back to see them, maintaining that her marriage was her own business, that if he didn't have the common decency to come to Drogheda for no reason, she was not going to furnish him with an obligation he could not refuse.

So Fee promised not to say a word in her letters; she seemed not to care one way or the other, nor did she seem interested in Meggie's choice of a husband. Keeping the books of a station as large as Drogheda was a full-time job. Fee's records would have served a historian with a perfect description of life on a sheep station, for they didn't simply consist of figures and ledgers. Every movement of every mob of sheep was rigidly described, the changes of the seasons, the weather each day, even what Mrs. Smith served for dinner. The entry in the log book for Sunday, July 22, 1934, said: *Sky clear, no cloud, temperature at dawn 34 degrees. No Mass today. Bob in, Jack out at Murrimbah with 2 stockmen, Hughie out at West Dam with 1 stockman, Beerbarrel droving 3-year wethers from Budgin to Winnemurra. Temperature high at 3 o'clock, 85 degrees. Barometer steady, 30.6 inches. Wind due west. Dinner menu corned beef, boiled potatoes, carrots and cabbage, then plum duff. Meghann Cleary is to marry Mr. Luke O'Neill, stockman, on Saturday August 25 at the Holy Cross Church, Gillanbone. Entered 9 o'clock evening, temperature 45 degrees, moon last quarter.*

11

Luke bought Meggie a diamond engagement ring, modest but quite pretty, its twin quarter-carat stones set in a pair of platinum hearts. The banns were called for noon on Saturday, August 25th, in the Holy Cross Church. This would be followed by a family dinner at the Hotel Imperial, to which Mrs. Smith, Minnie and Cat were naturally invited, though Jims and Patsy had been left in Sydney after Meggie said firmly that she couldn't see the point in bringing them six hundred miles to witness a ceremony they didn't really understand. She had received their letters of congratulations; Jims's long, rambling and childlike, Patsy's consisting of three words, "Lots of luck." They knew Luke, of course, having ridden the Drogheda paddocks with him during their vacations.

Mrs. Smith was grieved at Meggie's insistence on as small an affair as possible; she had hoped to see the only girl married on Drogheda with flags flying and cymbals clashing, days of celebration. But Meggie was so against a fuss she even refused to wear bridal regalia; she would be married in a day dress and an ordinary hat, which could double afterwards as her traveling outfit.

"Darling, I've decided where to take you for our honeymoon," Luke said, slipping into a chair opposite hers the Sunday after they had made their wedding plans.

"Where?"

"North Queensland. While you were at the dressmaker I got talking to some chaps in the Imperial bar, and they were telling me there's money to be made up in cane country, if a man's strong and not afraid of hard work."

"But Luke, you already have a good job here!"

"A man doesn't feel right, battening on his in-laws. I want to get us the money to buy a place out in Western Queensland, and I want it before I'm too old to work it. A man with no education finds it hard to get high-paying work in this Depression, but there's a shortage of men in North Queensland, and the money's at least ten times what I earn as a stockman on Drogheda."

"Doing what?"

"Cutting sugar cane."

"Cutting sugar cane? That's coolie labor"

"No, you're wrong. Coolies aren't big enough to do it as well as the white cutters, and besides, you know as well as I do that Australian law forbids the importation of black or yellow men to do slave labor or work for wages lower than a white man's, take the bread out of a white Australian's mouth. There's a shortage of cutters and the money's terrific. Not too many blokes are big enough or strong enough to cut cane. But *I* am. It won't beat me!"

"Does this mean you're thinking of making our home in North Queensland, Luke?"

"Yes."

She stared past his shoulder through the great bank of windows at Drogheda: the ghost gums, the Home Paddock, the stretch of trees beyond. Not to live on Drogheda! To be somewhere Bishop Ralph could never find her, to live without ever seeing him again, to cleave to this stranger sitting facing her so irrevocably there could be no going back. . . . The grey eyes rested on Luke's vivid, impatient face and grew more beautiful, but unmistakably sadder. He sensed it only; she had no tears there, her lids didn't droop, or the corners of her mouth. But he wasn't concerned with whatever sorrows Meggie owned, for he had no intention of letting her become so important to him she caused him worry on her behalf. Admittedly she was something of a bonus to a man who had tried to marry Dot MacPherson of Bingelly, but her physical desirability and tractable nature only increased Luke's guard over his own heart. No woman, even one as sweet and beautiful as Meggie Cleary, was ever going to gain sufficient power over him to tell him what to do.

So, remaining true to himself, he plunged straight into the main thing on his mind. There were times when guile was necessary, but in this matter it wouldn't serve him as well as bluntness.

"Meghann, I'm an old-fashioned man," he said.

She stared at him, puzzled. "Are you?" she asked, her tone implying: Does it matter?

"Yes," he said. "I believe that when a man and woman marry, all the woman's property should become the man's. The way a dowry did in the old days. I know you've got a bit of money, and I'm telling you now that when we marry you're to sign it over to me. It's only fair you know what's in my mind while you're still single, and able to decide whether you want to do it."

It had never occurred to Meggie that she would retain her money; she had simply assumed when she married it would become Luke's, not hers. All save the most educated and sophisticated Australian women were reared to think themselves more or less the chattels of their men, and this was especially true of Meggie. Daddy had always ruled Fee and his children, and since his death Fee had deferred to Bob as his successor. The man owned the money, the house, his wife and his children. Meggie had never questioned his right to do so.

"Oh!" she exclaimed. "I didn't know signing anything was necessary, Luke. I thought that what was mine automatically became yours when we married."

"It used to be like that, but those stupid drongos in Canberra stopped it when they gave women the vote. I want everything to be fair and square between us, Meghann, so I'm telling you now how things are going to be."

She laughed, "It's all right, Luke, I don't mind."

She took it like a good old-fashioned wife; Dot wouldn't have given in so readily. "How much have you got?" he asked.

"At the moment, fourteen thousand pounds. Every year I get two thousand more."

He whistled. "Fourteen thousand pounds! Phew! That's a lot of money, Meghann. Better to have me look after it for you. We can see the bank manager next week, and remind me to make sure everything coming in in the future gets put in my name, too. I'm not going to touch a penny of it, you know that. It's to buy our station later on. For the next few years we're both going to work hard, and save every penny we earn. All right?"

She nodded. "Yes, Luke."

A simple oversight on Luke's part nearly scotched the wedding in midplan. He was not a Catholic. When Father Watty found out he threw up his hands in horror.

"Dear Lord, Luke, why didn't you tell me earlier? Indeed and to goodness, it will take all of our energies to have you converted and baptized before the wedding!"

Luke stared at Father Watty, astonished. "Who said anything about converting, Father? I'm quite happy as I am being nothing, but if it worries you, write me down as a Calathumpian or a Holy Roller or whatever you like. But write me down a Catholic you will not."

In vain they pleaded; Luke refused to entertain the

idea of conversion for a moment. "I've got nothing against Catholicism or Eire, and I think the Catholics in Ulster are hard done by. But I'm Orange, and I'm not a turncoat. If I was a Catholic and you wanted me to convert to Methodism, I'd react the same. It's being a turncoat I object to, not being a Catholic. So you'll have to do without me in the flock, Father, and that's that."

"Then you can't get married!"

"Why on earth not? If you don't want to marry us, I can't see why the Reverend up at the Church of England will object, or Harry Gough the J.P."

Fee smiled sourly, remembering her contretemps with Paddy and a priest; she had won that encounter.

"But, Luke, I *have* to be married in church!" Meggie protested fearfully. "If I'm not, I'll be living in sin!"

"Well, as far as I'm concerned, living in sin is a lot better than turning my coat inside out," said Luke, who was sometimes a curious contradiction; much as he wanted Meggie's money, a blind streak of stubbornness in him wouldn't let him back down.

"Oh, stop all this silliness!" said Fee, not to Luke but to the priest. "Do what Paddy and I did and have an end to argument! Father Thomas can marry you in the presbytery if he doesn't want to soil his church!"

Everyone stared at her, amazed, but it did the trick; Father Watkin gave in and agreed to marry them in the presbytery, though he refused to bless the ring.

Partial Church sanction left Meggie feeling she was sinning, but not badly enough to go to Hell, and ancient Annie the presbytery housekeeper did her best to make Father Watty's study as churchlike as possible, with great vases of flowers and many brass candlesticks. But it was an uncomfortable ceremony, the very displeased priest making everyone feel he only went through with it to save himself the embarrassment of a secular wedding elsewhere. No Nuptial Mass, no blessings.

However, it was done. Meggie was Mrs. Luke

O'Neill, on her way to North Queensland and a honeymoon somewhat delayed by the time it would take getting there. Luke refused to spend that Saturday night at the Imperial, for the branch-line train to Goondiwindi left only once a week, on Saturday night, to connect with the Goondiwindi–Brisbane mail train on Sunday. This would bring them to Bris on Monday in time to catch the Cairns express.

The Goondiwindi train was crowded. They had no privacy and sat up all night because it carried no sleeping cars. Hour after hour it trundled its erratic, grumpy way northeast, stopping interminably every time the engine driver felt like brewing a billy of tea for himself, or to let a mob of sheep wander along the rails, or to have a yarn with a drover.

"I wonder why they pronounce *Goon*diwindi *Gun*diwindi if they don't want to spell it that way?" Meggie asked idly as they waited in the only place open in Goondiwindi on a Sunday, the awful institutional-green station waiting room with its hard black wooden benches. Poor Meggie, she was nervous and ill at ease.

"How do I know?" sighed Luke, who didn't feel like talking and was starving into the bargain. Since it was Sunday they couldn't even get a cup of tea; not until the Monday-morning breakfast stop on the Brisbane mail did they get an opportunity to fill their empty stomachs and slake their thirst. Then Brisbane, into South Bris station, the trek across the city to Roma Street Station and the Cairns train. Here Meggie discovered Luke had booked them two second-class upright seats.

"Luke, we're not short of money!" she said, tired and exasperated. "If you forgot to go to the bank, I've got a hundred pounds Bob gave me here in my purse. Why didn't you get us a first-class sleeping compartment?"

He stared down at her, astounded. "But it's only three nights and three days to Dungloe! Why spend money on a sleeper when we're both young, healthy and strong? Sitting up on a train for a while won't kill you, Meghann! It's about time you realized you've married a plain old workingman, not a bloody squatter!"

So Meggie slumped in the window seat Luke seized for her and rested her trembling chin on her hand to look out the window so Luke wouldn't notice her tears. He had spoken to her as one speaks to an irresponsible child, and she was beginning to wonder if indeed this was how he regarded her. Rebellion began to stir, but it was very small and her fierce pride forbade the indignity of quarreling. Instead she told herself she was this man's wife, but it was such a new thing he wasn't used to it. Give him time. They would live together, she would cook his meals, mend his clothes, look after him, have his babies, be a good wife to him. Look how much Daddy had appreciated Mum, how much he had adored her. Give Luke time.

They were going to a town called Dungloe, only fifty miles short of Cairns, which was the far northern terminus of the line which ran all the way along the Queensland coast. Over a thousand miles of narrow three-foot-six-gauge rail, rocking and pitching back and forth, every seat in the compartment occupied, no chance to lie down or stretch out. Though it was far more densely settled countryside than Gilly, and far more colorful, she couldn't summon up interest in it.

Her head ached, she could keep no food down and the heat was much, much worse than anything Gilly had ever cooked up. The lovely pink silk wedding dress was filthy from soot blowing in the windows, her skin was clammy with a sweat which wouldn't evaporate, and what was more galling than any of her physical discomforts, she was close to hating Luke. Apparently not in the least tired or out of sorts because of the journey, he sat at his ease yarning with two men going to Cardwell. The only times he glanced in her direction he also got up, leaned across her so carelessly she shrank, and flung a rolled-up newspaper out the window to some event-hungry gang of tattered men beside the line with steel hammers in their hands, calling:

"Paip! Paip!"

"Fettlers looking after the rails," he explained as he sat down again the first time it happened.

And he seemed to assume she was quite as happy and comfortable as he was, that the coastal plain flying by was fascinating her. While she sat staring at it and not seeing it, hating it before she had so much as set foot on it.

At Cardwell the two men got off, and Luke went to the fish-and-chip shop across the road from the station to bring back a newspaper-wrapped bundle.

"They say Cardwell fish has to be tasted to be believed, Meghann love. The best fish in the world. Here, try some. It's your first bit of genuine Bananaland food. I tell you, there's no place like Queensland."

Meggie glanced at the greasy pieces of batter-dipped fish, put her handkerchief to her mouth and bolted for the toilet. He was waiting in the corridor when she came out some time later, white and shaking.

"What's the matter? Aren't you feeling well?"

"I haven't felt well since we left Goondiwindi."

"Good Lord! Why didn't you tell me?"

"Why didn't you notice?"

"You looked all right to me."

"How far is it now?" she asked, giving up.

"Three to six hours, give or take a bit. They don't run to timetable up here too much. There's plenty of room now those blokes are gone; lie down and put your tootsies in my lap."

"Oh, don't baby-talk me!" she snapped tartly. "It would have been a lot better if they'd got off two days ago in Bundaberg!"

"Come on now, Meghann, be a good sport! Nearly there. Only Tully and Innisfail, then Dungloe."

It was late afternoon when they stepped off the train,

Meggie clinging desperately to Luke's arm, too proud to admit she wasn't able to walk properly. He asked the stationmaster for the name of a workingmen's hotel, picked up their cases and walked out onto the street, Meggie behind him weaving drunkenly.

"Only to the end of the block on the other side of the street," he comforted. "The white two-storied joint."

Though their room was small and filled to overflowing with great pieces of Victorian furniture, it looked like heaven to Meggie, collapsing on the edge of the double bed.

"Lie down for a while before dinner, love. I'm going out to find my landmarks," he said, sauntering from the room looking as fresh and rested as he had on their wedding morning. That had been Saturday, and this was late Thursday afternoon; five days sitting up in crowded trains, choked by cigarette smoke and soot.

The bed was rocking monotonously in time to the clickety-click of steel wheels passing over rail joins, but Meggie turned her head into the pillow gratefully, and slept, and slept.

Someone had taken off her shoes and stockings, and covered her with a sheet; Meggie stirred, opened her eyes and looked around. Luke was sitting on the window ledge with one knee drawn up, smoking. Her movement made him turn to look at her, and he smiled.

"A nice bride you are! Here I am looking forward to my honeymoon and my wife conks out for nearly two days! I was a bit worried when I couldn't wake you up, but the publican says it hits women like that, the trip up in the train and the humidity. He said just let you sleep it off. How do you feel now?"

She sat up stiffly, stretched her arms and yawned, "I feel much better, thank you. Oh, Luke! I know I'm young and strong, but I'm a woman! I can't take the sort of physical punishment you can."

He came to sit on the edge of the bed, rubbing her

arm in a rather charming gesture of contrition. "I'm sorry, Meghann, I really am. I didn't think of your being a woman. Not used to having a wife with me, that's all. Are you hungry, darling?"

"Starved. Do you realize it's almost a week since I've eaten?"

"Then why don't you have a bath, put on a clean dress and come outside to look at Dungloe?"

There was a Chinese café next door to the hotel, where Luke led Meggie for her first-ever taste of Oriental food. She was so hungry anything would have tasted good, but this was superb. Nor did she care if it was made of rats' tails and sharks' fins and fowls' bowels, as rumor had it in Gillanbone, which only possessed a café run by Greeks who served steak and chips. Luke had brown-bagged two quart bottles of beer from the hotel and insisted she drink a glass in spite of her dislike for beer.

"Go easy on the water at first," he advised. "Beer won't give you the trots."

Then he took her arm and walked her around Dungloe proudly, as if he owned it. But then, Luke was born a Queenslander. What a place Dungloe was! It had a look and a character far removed from western towns. In size it was probably the same as Gilly, but instead of rambling forever down one main street. Dungloe was built in ordered square blocks, and all its shops and houses were painted white, not brown. Windows were vertical wooden transoms, presumably to catch the breeze, and wherever possible roofs had been dispensed with, like the movie theater, which had a screen, transomed walls and rows of ship's canvas desk chairs, but no roof at all.

All around the edge of the town encroached a genuine jungle. Vines and creepers sprawled everywhere—up posts, across roofs, along walls. Trees sprouted casually in the middle of the road, or had houses built around them, or perhaps had grown up through the houses. It was impossible to tell which had come first, trees or human habitations, for the overwhelming impression was one of uncontrolled, hectic growth of vegetation. Coconut palms taller and straighter than the Drogheda ghost gums waved fronds against a deep, swimming blue sky; everywhere Meggie looked was a blaze of color. No brown-and-grey land, this. Every kind of tree seemed to be in flower—purple, orange, scarlet, pink, blue, white.

There were many Chinese in black silk trousers, tiny black-and-white shoes with white socks, white Mandarin-collared shirts, pigtails down their backs. Males and females looked so alike Meggie found it difficult to tell which were which. Almost the entire commerce of the town seemed to be in the hands of Chinese; a large department store, far more opulent than anything Gilly possessed, bore a Chinese name: AH WONG'S, said the sign.

All the houses were built on top of very high piles, like the old head stockman's residence on Drogheda. This was to achieve maximum air circulation, Luke explained, and keep the termites from causing them to fall down a year after they were built. At the top of each pile was a tin plate with turned-down edges; termites couldn't bend their bodies in the middle and thus couldn't crawl over the tin parapet into the wood of the house itself. Of course they feasted on the piles, but when a pile rotted it was removed and replaced by a new one. Much easier and less expensive than putting up a new house. Most of the gardens seemed to be jungle, bamboo and palms, as if the inhabitants had given up trying to keep floral order.

The men and women shocked her. To go for dinner and a walk with Luke she had dressed as custom demanded in heeled shoes, silk stockings, satin slip, floating silk frock with belt and elbow sleeves. On her head was a big straw hat, on her hands were gloves. And what irritated her the most was an uncomfortable feeling from the way people stared that *she* was the one improperly dressed!

The men were bare-footed, bare-legged and mostly bare-chested, wearing nothing but drab khaki shorts; the few who covered their chests did so with athletic singlets, not shirts. The women were worse. A few wore skimpy cotton dresses clearly minus anything in the way of underwear, no stockings, sloppy sandals. But the majority wore short shorts, went bare-footed and shielded their breasts with indecent little sleeveless vests. Dungloe was a civilized town, not a beach. But here were its native white inhabitants strolling around in brazen undress; the Chinese were better clad.

There were bicycles everywhere, hundreds of them; a few cars, no horses at all. Yes, very different from Gilly. And it was hot, hot, hot. They passed a thermometer which incredibly said a mere ninety degrees; in Gilly at 115 degrees it seemed cooler than this. Meggie felt as if she moved through solid air which her body had to cut like wet, steamy butter, as if when she breathed her lungs filled with water.

"Luke, I can't bear it! Please, can we go back?" she gasped after less than a mile.

"If you want. You're feeling the humidity. It rarely gets below ninety percent, winter or summer, and the temperature rarely gets below eighty-five or above ninety-five. There's not much of a seasonal variation, but in summer the monsoons send the humidity up to a hundred percent all the flaming time."

"Summer rain, not winter?"

"All year round. The monsoons always come, and when they're not blowing, the southeast trades are. They carry a lot of rain, too. Dungloe has an annual rainfall of between one and three hundred inches."

Three hundred inches of rain a year! Poor Gilly ecstatic if it got a princely fifteen, while here as much as three hundred fell, two thousand miles from Gilly.

"Doesn't it cool off at night?" Meggie asked as they

reached the hotel; hot nights in Gilly were bearable compared to this steam bath.

"Not very much. You'll get used to it." He opened the door to their room and stood back for her to enter. "I'm going down to the bar for a beer, but I'll be back in half an hour. That ought to give you enough time."

Her eyes flew to his face, startled. "Yes, Luke."

Dungloe was seventeen degrees south of the equator, so night fell like a thunderclap; one minute it seemed the sun was scarcely setting, and the next minute pitch-black darkness spread itself thick and warm like treacle. When Luke came back Meggie had switched off the light and was lying in the bed with the sheet pulled up to her chin. Laughing, he reached out and tugged it off her, threw it on the floor.

"It's hot enough, love! We won't need a sheet."

She could hear him walking about, see his faint shadow shedding its clothes. "I put your pajamas on the dressing table," she whispered.

"Pajamas? In weather like this? I know in Gilly they'd have a stroke at the thought of a man not wearing pajamas, but this is Dungloe! Are you really wearing a nightie?"

"Yes."

"Then take it off. The bloody thing will only be a nuisance anyway."

Fumbling, Meggie managed to wriggle out of the lawn nightgown Mrs. Smith had embroidered so lovingly for her wedding night, thankful that it was too dark for him to see her. He was right; it was much cooler lying bare and letting the breeze from the wide-open transoms play over her thinly. But the thought of another hot body in the bed with her was depressing.

The springs creaked; Meggie felt damp skin touch her arm and jumped. He turned on his side, pulled her into his arms and kissed her. At first she lay passively, trying not to think of that wide-open mouth and its probing, indecent tongue, but then she began to struggle to be free, not wanting to be close in the heat, not wanting to be kissed, not wanting Luke. It wasn't a bit like that night in the Rolls coming back from Rudna Hunish. She couldn't seem to feel anything in him which thought of her, and some part of him was pushing insistently at her thighs while one hand, its nails squarely sharp, dug into her buttocks. Her fear blossomed into terror, she was overwhelmed in more than a physical way by his strength and determination, his lack of awareness of her. Suddenly he let her go, sat up and seemed to fumble with himself, snapping and pulling at something.

"Better be safe," he gasped. "Lie on your back, it's time. No, not like that! Open your legs, for God's sake! Don't you know anything?"

No, no, Luke, I don't! she wanted to cry. This is horrible, obscene; whatever it is you're doing to me can't possibly be permitted by the laws of Church or men! He actually lay down on top of her, lifted his hips and poked at her with one hand, the other so firmly in her hair she didn't dare move. Twitching and jumping at the alien thing between her legs, she tried to do as he wanted, spread her legs wider, but he was much broader than she was, and her groin muscles went into crampy spasm from the weight of him and the unaccustomed posture. Even through the darkening mists of fright and exhaustion she could sense the gathering of some mighty power; as he entered her a long high scream left her lips.

"Shut *up!*" he groaned, took his hand out of her hair and clamped it defensively over her mouth. "What do you want to do, make everyone in this bloody pub think I'm murdering you? Lie still and it won't hurt any more than it has to! Lie still, *lie still!*"

She fought like one possessed to be rid of that ghastly, painful thing, but his weight pinned her down and his hand deadened her cries, the agony went on and on. Utterly dry because he hadn't roused her, the even drier condom scraped and rasped her tissues as he worked himself in and out, faster and faster, the breath beginning to hiss between his teeth; then some change stilled him, made him shudder, swallow hard. The pain dulled to raw soreness and he mercifully rolled off her to lie on his back, gasping.

"It'll be better for you the next time," he managed to say. "The first time always hurts the woman."

Then why didn't you have the decency to tell me that beforehand? she wanted to snarl, but she hadn't the energy to utter the words, she was too busy wanting to die. Not only because of the pain, but also from the discovery that she had possessed no identity for him, only been an instrument.

The second time hurt just as much, and the third; exasperated, expecting her discomfort (for so he deemed it) to disappear magically after the first time and thus not understanding why she continued to fight and cry out, Luke grew angry, turned his back on her and went to sleep. The tears slipped sideways from Meggie's eyes into her hair; she lay on her back wishing for death, or else for her old life on Drogheda.

Was that what Father Ralph had meant years ago, when he had told her of the hidden passageway to do with having children? A nice way to find out what he meant. No wonder he had preferred not to explain it more clearly himself. Yet Luke had liked the activity well enough to do it three times in quick succession. Obviously it didn't hurt him. And for that she found herself hating him, hating it.

Exhausted, so sore moving was agony, Meggie inched herself over onto her side with her back to Luke, and wept into the pillow. Sleep eluded her, though Luke slept so soundly her small timid movements never caused so much as a change in the pattern of his breathing. He was an economical sleeper and a quiet one, he neither snored nor flopped about, and she thought while waiting for the late dawn that if it had just been a matter of lying down together, she might have found him nice to be with. And the dawn came as quickly and joylessly as darkness had; it seemed strange not to hear roosters crowing, the other sounds of a rousing Drogheda with its sheep and horses and pigs and dogs.

Luke woke, and rolled over, she felt him kiss her on the shoulder and was so tired, so homesick that she forgot modesty, didn't care about covering herself.

"Come on, Meghann, let's have a look at you," he commanded, his hand on her hip. "Turn over, like a good little girl."

Nothing mattered this morning; Meggie turned over, wincing, and lay looking up at him dully. "I don't like Meghann," she said, the only form of protest she could manage. "I do wish you'd call me Meggie."

"I don't like Meggie. But if you really dislike Meghann so much, I'll call you Meg." His gaze roved her body dreamily. "What a nice shape you've got." He touched one breast, pink nipple flat and unaroused. "Especially these." Bunching the pillows into a heap, he lay back on them and smiled. "Come on, Meg, kiss me. It's your turn to make love to me, and maybe you'll like that better, eh?"

I never want to kiss you again as long as I live, she thought, looking at the long, heavily muscled body, the mat of dark hair on the chest diving down the belly in a thin line and then flaring into a bush, out of which grew the deceptively small and innocent shoot which could cause so much pain. How hairy his legs were! Meggie had grown up with men who never removed a layer of their clothes in the presence of women, but open-necked shirts showed hairy chests in hot weather. They were all fair men, and not offensive to her; this dark man was alien, repulsive. Ralph had a head of hair just as dark, but well she remembered that smooth, hairless brown chest.

"Do as you're told, Meg! Kiss me."

Leaning over, she kissed him; he cupped her breasts

in his palms and made her go on kissing him, took one of her hands and pushed it down to his groin. Startled, she took her unwilling mouth away from his to look at what lay under her hand, changing and growing.

"Oh, please, Luke, not again!" she cried. "Please, not again! Please, please!"

The blue eyes scanned her speculatively. "Hurts that much? All right, we'll do something different, but for God's sake try to be enthusiastic!"

Pulling her on top of him, he pushed her legs apart, lifted her shoulders and attached himself to her breast, as he had done in the car the night she committed herself to marrying him. There only in body, Meggie endured it; at least he didn't put himself inside her, so it didn't hurt any more than simply moving did. What strange creatures men were, to go at this as if it was the most pleasurable thing in the world. It was disgusting, a mockery of love. Had it not been for her hope that it would culminate in a baby, Meggie would have refused flatly to have anything more to do with it.

"I've got you a job," Luke said over breakfast in the hotel dining room.

"What? Before I've had a chance to make our home nice, Luke? Before we've even *got* a home?"

"There's no point in our renting a house, Meg. I'm going to cut cane; it's all arranged. The best gang of cutters in Queensland is a gang of Swedes, Poles and Irish led by a bloke called Arne Swenson, and while you were sleeping off the journey I went to see him. He's a man short and he's willing to give me a trial. That means I'll be living in barracks with them. We cut six days a week, sunrise to sunset. Not only that, but we move around up and down the coast, wherever the next job takes us. How much I earn depends on how much sugar I cut, and if I'm good enough to cut with Arne's gang I'll be pulling in more than twenty quid a week. Twenty quid a week! Can you imagine that?"

"Are you trying to tell me we won't be living togther, Luke?"

"We can't, Meg! The men won't have a woman in the barracks, and what's the use of your living alone in a house? You may as well work, too; it's all money toward our station."

"But where will I live? What sort of work can I do? There's no stock to drove up here."

"No, more's the pity. That's why I've got you a live-in job, Meg. You'll get free board, I won't have the expense of keeping you. You're going to work as a housemaid on Himmelhoch, Ludwig Mueller's place. He's the biggest cane cocky in the district and his wife's an invalid, can't manage the house on her own. I'll take you there tomorrow morning."

"But when will I see you, Luke?"

"On Sundays. Luddie understands you're married; he doesn't mind if you disappear on Sundays."

"Well! You've certainly arranged things to your satisfaction, haven't you?"

"I reckon. Oh, Meg, we're going to be rich! We'll work hard and save every penny, and it won't be long before we can buy ourselves the best station in Western Queensland. There's the fourteen thousand I've got in the Gilly bank, the two thousand a year more coming in there, and the thirteen hundred or more a year we can earn between us. It won't be long, love, I promise. Grin and bear it for me, eh? Why be content with a rented house when the harder we work now means the sooner you'll be looking around your own kitchen?"

"If it's what you want." She looked down at her purse. "Luke, did you take my hundred pounds?"

"I put it in the bank. You can't carry money like that around, Meg."

"But you took every bit of it! I don't have a penny! What about spending money?"

"Why on earth do you want spending money? You'll be out at Himmelhoch in the morning, and you can't spend anything there. I'll take care of the hotel bill. It's time you realized you've married a workingman, Meg, that you're not the pampered squatter's daughter with money to burn. Mueller will pay your wages straight into my bank account, where they'll stay along with mine. I'm not spending the money on myself, Meg, you know that. Neither of us is going to touch it, because it's for our future, our station."

"Yes, I understand. You're very sensible, Luke. But what if I should have a baby?"

For a moment he was tempted to tell her the truth, that there would be no baby until the station was a reality, but something in her face made him decide not to.

"Well, let's cross that bridge when we come to it, eh? I'd rather we didn't have one until we've got our station, so let's just hope we don't."

No home, no money, no babies. No husband, for that matter. Meggie started to laugh. Luke joined her, his teacup lifted in a toast.

"Here's to French letters," he said.

In the morning they went out to Himmelhoch on the local bus, an old Ford with no glass in its windows and room for twelve people. Meggie was feeling better, for Luke had left her alone when she offered him a breast, and seemed to like it quite as well as that other awful thing. Much and all as she wanted babies, her courage had failed her. The first Sunday that she wasn't sore at all, she told herself, she would be willing to try again. Perhaps there was a baby already on the way, and she needn't bother with it ever again unless she wanted more. Eyes brighter, she looked around her with interest as the bus chugged out along the red dirt road.

It was breath-taking country, so different from Gilly; she had to admit there was a grandeur and beauty here Gilly quite lacked. Easy to see there was never a shortage of water. The soil was the color of freshly spilled blood, brilliant scarlet, and the cane in the fields not fallow was a perfect contrast to the soil: long bright-green blades waving fifteen or twenty feet above claret-colored stalks as thick as Luke's arm. Nowhere in the world, raved Luke, did cane grow as tall or as rich in sugar; its yield was the highest known. That bright-red soil was over a hundred feet deep, and so stuffed with exactly the right nutrients the cane couldn't help but be perfect, especially considering the rainfall. And nowhere else in the world was it cut by white men, at the white man's driving, money-hungry pace.

"You look good on a soapbox, Luke," said Meggie ironically.

He glanced sideways at her, suspiciously, but refrained from comment because the bus had stopped on the side of the road to let them off.

Himmelhoch was a large white house on top of a hill, surrounded by coconut palms, banana palms and beautiful smaller palms whose leaves splayed outward in great fans like the tails of peacocks. A grove of bamboo forty feet high cut the house off from the worst of the northwest monsoonal winds; even with its hill elevation it was still mounted on top of fifteen-foot piles.

Luke carried her case; Meggie toiled up the red road beside him, gasping, still in correct shoes and stockings, her hat wilting around her face. The cane baron himself wasn't in, but his wife came onto the veranda as they mounted the steps, balancing herself between two sticks. She was smiling; looking at her dear kind face, Meggie felt better at once.

"Come in, come in!" she said in a strong Australian accent.

Expecting a German voice, Meggie was immeasurably cheered. Luke put her case down, shook hands when the lady took her right one off its stick, then pounded away down the steps in a hurry to catch the bus on its return journey. Arne Swenson was picking him up outside the pub at ten o'clock.

"What's your first name, Mrs. O'Neill?"

"Meggie."

"Oh, that's nice. Mine is Anne, and I'd rather you called me Anne. It's been so lonely up here since my girl left me a month ago, but it's not easy to get good house help, so I've been battling on my own. There's only Luddie and me to look after; we have no children. I hope you're going to like living with us, Meggie."

"I'm sure I will, Mrs. Mueller—Anne."

"Let me show you to your room. Can you manage the case? I'm not much good at carrying things, I'm afraid."

The room was austerely furnished, like the rest of the house, but it looked out on the only side of the house where the view was unimpeded by some sort of windbreak, and shared the same stretch of veranda as the living room, which seemed very bare to Meggie with its cane furniture and lack of fabric.

"It's just too hot up here for velvet or chintz," Anne explained. "We live with wicker, and as little on ourselves as decency allows. I'll have to educate you, or you'll die. You're hopelessly overclothed."

She herself was in a sleeveless, low-necked vest and a pair of short shorts, out of which her poor twisted legs poked doddering. In no time at all Meggie found herself similarly clad, loaned from Anne until Luke could be persuaded to buy her new clothes. It was humiliating to have to explain that she was allowed no money, but at least having to endure this attenuated her embarrassment over wearing so little.

"Well, you certainly decorate my shorts better than I do," said Anne. She went on with her breezy lecture. "Luddie will bring you firewood; you're not to cut your own or drag it up the steps. I wish we had electricity like the places closer in to Dunny, but the government is slower than a wet week. Maybe next year the line will reach as far as Himmelhoch, but until then it's the awful old fuel stove, I'm afraid. But you wait, Meggie!

The minute they give us power we'll have an electric stove, electric lights and a refrigerator."

"I'm used to doing without them."

"Yes, but where you come from the heat is dry. This is far, far worse. I'm just frightened that your health will suffer. It often does in women who weren't born and brought up here; something to do with the blood. We're on the same latitude south as Bombay and Rangoon are north, you know; not fit country for man or beast unless born to it." She smiled. "Oh, it's nice having you already! You and I are going to have a wonderful time! Do you like reading? Luddie and I have a passion for it."

Meggie's face lit up. "Oh, yes!"

"Splendid! You'll be too content to miss that big handsome husband of yours."

Meggie didn't answer. Miss Luke? Was he handsome? She thought that if she never saw him again she would be perfectly happy. Except that he *was* her husband, that the law said she had to make her life with him. She had gone into it with her eyes open; she had no one to blame save herself. And perhaps as the money came in and the station in Western Queensland became a reality, there would be time for Luke and her to live together, settle down, know each other, get along.

He wasn't a bad man, or unlikable; it was just that he had been alone so long he didn't know how to share himself with someone else. And he was a simple man, ruthlessly single of purpose, untormented. What he desired was a concrete thing, even if a dream; it was a positive reward which would surely come as the result of unremitting work, grinding sacrifice. For that one had to respect him. Not for a moment did she think he would use the money to give himself luxuries; he had meant what he said. It would stay in the bank.

The trouble was he didn't have the time or the inclination to understand a woman, he didn't seem to know a woman was different, needed things he didn't need, as he needed things she didn't. Well, it could be worse. He might have put her to work for someone far colder and less considerate than Anne Mueller. On top of this hill she wouldn't come to any harm. But oh, it was so far from Drogheda!

That last thought came again after they finished touring the house, and stood together on the living room veranda looking out across Himmelhoch. The great fields of cane (one couldn't call them paddocks, since they were small enough to encompass with the eyes) plumed lushly in the wind, a restlessly sparkling and polished-by-rain green, falling away in a long slope to the jungle-clad banks of a great river, wider by far than the Barwon. Beyond the river the cane lands rose again, squares of poisonous green interspersed with bloody fallow fields, until at the foot of a vast mountain the cultivation stopped, and the jungle took over. Behind the cone of mountain, farther away, other peaks reared and died purple into the distance. The sky was a richer, denser blue than Gilly skies, puffed with white billows of thick cloud, and the color of the whole was vivid, intense.

"That's Mount Bartle Frere," said Anne, pointing to the isolated peak. "Six thousand feet straight up out of a sea-level plain. They say it's solid tin, but there's no hope of mining it for the jungle."

On the heavy, idle wind came a strong, sickening stench Meggie hadn't stopped trying to get out of her nostrils since stepping off the train. Like decay, only not like decay; unbearably sweet, all-pervasive, a tangible presence which never seemed to diminish no matter how hard the breeze blew.

"What you can smell is molasses," said Anne as she noticed Meggie's flaring nose; she lit a tailor-made Ardath cigarette.

"It's disgusting."

"I know. That's why I smoke. But to a certain extent you get used to it, though unlike most smells it never quite disappears. Day in and day out, the molasses is always there."

"What are the buildings on the river with the black chimney?"

"That's the mill. It processes the cane into raw sugar. What's left over, the dry remnants of the cane minus its sugar content, is called bagasse. Both raw sugar and bagasse are sent south to Sydney for further refining. Out of raw sugar they get molasses, treacle, golden syrup, brown sugar, white sugar and liquid glucose. The bagasse is made into fibrous building board like Masonite. Nothing is wasted, absolutely nothing. That's why even in this Depression growing cane is still a very profitable business."

Arne Swenson was six feet two inches tall, exactly Luke's height, and just as handsome. His bare body was coated a dark golden brown by perpetual exposure to the sun, his thatch of bright yellow hair curled all over his head; the fine Swedish features were so like Luke's in type that it was easy to see how much Norse blood had percolated into the veins of the Scots and Irish.

Luke had abandoned his moleskins and white shirt in favor of shorts. With Arne he climbed into an ancient, wheezing model-T utility truck and headed for where the gang was cutting out by Goondi. The secondhand bicycle he had bought lay in the utility's tray along with his case, and he was dying to begin work.

The other men had been cutting since dawn and didn't lift their heads when Arne appeared from the direction of the barracks, Luke in tow. The cutting uniform consisted of shorts, boots with thick woolen socks, and canvas hats. Eyes narrowing, Luke stared at the toiling men, who were a peculiar sight. Coal-black dirt covered them from head to foot, with sweat making bright pink streaks down chests, arms, backs.

"Soot and muck from the cane," Arne explained. "We have to burn it before we can cut it."

He bent down to pick up two instruments, gave one to Luke and kept one. "This is a cane knife," he said, hefting his. "With this you cut the cane. Very easy if you know how." He grinned, proceeding to demonstrate and making it look far easier than it probably was.

Luke looked at the deadly thing he gripped, which was not at all like a West Indian machete. It widened into a large triangle instead of tapering to a point, and had a wicked hook like a rooster's spur at one of the two blade ends.

"A machete is too small for North Queensland cane," Arne said, finished his demonstration. "This is the right toy, you'll find. Keep it sharp, and good luck."

Off he went to his own section, leaving Luke standing undecided for a moment. Then, shrugging, he started work. Within minutes he understood why they left it to slaves and to races not sophisticated enough to know there were easier ways to make a living; like shearing, he thought with wry humor. Bend, hack, straighten, clutch the unwieldy topheavy bunch securely, slide its length through the hands, whack off the leaves, drop it in a tidy heap, go to the next cluster of stems, bend, hack, straighten, hack, add it to the heap. . . .

The cane was alive with vermin: rats, bandicoots, cockroaches, toads, spiders, snakes, wasps, flies and bees. Everything that could bite viciously or sting unbearably was well represented. For that reason the cutters burned the cane first, preferring the filth of working charred crops to the depredations of green, living cane. Even so they were stung, bitten and cut. If it hadn't been for the boots Luke's feet would have been worse off than his hands, but no cutter ever wore gloves. They slowed a man down, and time was money in this game. Besides, gloves were sissy.

At sundown Arne called a halt, and came to see how Luke had fared.

"Hey, mate not bad!" he shouted, thumping Luke on the back. "Five tons; not bad for a first day!"

It was not a long walk back to the barracks, but tropical night fell so suddenly it was dark as they arrived. Before going inside they collected naked in a communal shower, then, towels around their waists, they trooped into the barracks, where whichever cutter on cook duty that week had mountains of whatever was his specialty ready on the table. Today it was steak and potatoes, damper bread and jam roly-poly; the men fell on it and wolfed every last particle down, ravenous.

Two rows of iron pallets faced each other down either side of a long room made of corrugated iron; sighing and cursing the cane with an originality a bullocky might have envied, the men flopped naked on top of unbleached sheets, drew their mosquito nets down from the rings and within moments were asleep, vague shapes under gauzy tents.

Arne detained Luke. "Let me see your hands." He inspected the bleeding cuts, the blisters, the stings. "Bluebag them first, then use this ointment. And if you take my advice you'll rub coconut oil into them every night of your life. You've got big hands, so if your back can take it you'll make a good cutter. In a week you'll harden, you won't be so sore."

Every muscle in Luke's splendid body had its own separate ache; he was conscious of nothing but a vast, crucifying pain. Hands wrapped and anointed, he stretched himself on his allotted bed, pulled down his mosquito net and closed his eyes on a world of little suffocating holes. Had he dreamed what he was in for he would never have wasted his essence on Meggie; she had become a withered, unwanted and unwelcome idea in the back of his mind, shelved. He knew he would never have anything for her while he cut the cane.

It took him the predicted week to harden, and attain the eight-ton-a-day minimum Arne demanded of his gang members. Then he settled down to becoming better than Arne. He wanted the biggest share of the money, maybe a partnership. But most of all he wanted to see that same look that came into every face for Arne directed at himself; Arne was something of a god, for he was the best cutter in Queensland, and that probably meant he was the best cutter in the world. When they went into a town on Saturday night the local men couldn't buy Arne enough rums and beers, and the local women whirred about him like hummingbirds. There were many similarities between Arne and Luke. They were both vain and enjoyed evoking intense female admiration, but admiration was as far as it went. They had nothing to give to women; they gave it all to the cane.

For Luke the work had a beauty and a pain he seemed to have been waiting all his life to feel. To bend and straighten and bend in that ritual rhythm was to participate in some mystery beyond the scope of ordinary men. For, as watching Arne taught him, to do this superbly was to be a top member of the most elite band of workingmen in the world; he could bear himself with pride no matter where he was, knowing that almost every man he met would never last a day in a cane field. The King of England was no better than he, and the King of England would admire him if he knew him. He could look with pity and contempt on doctors, lawyers, pen-pushers, cockies. To cut sugar the money-hungry white man's way—that was the greatest achievement.

He would sit on the edge of his cot feeling the ribbed, corded muscles of his arm swell, look at the horny, scarred palms of his hands, the tanned length of his beautifully structured legs, and smile. A man who could do this and not only survive but like it was a *man*. He wondered if the King of England could say as much.

It was four weeks before Meggie saw Luke. Each Sunday she powdered her sticky nose, put on a pretty silk dress—though she gave up the purgatory of slips and stockings—and waited for her husband, who never came. Anne and Luddie Mueller said nothing, just watched her animation fade as each Sunday darkened dramatically, like a curtain falling on a brilliantly lit, empty stage. It wasn't that she wanted him, precisely; it was just that he was hers, or she was his, or however best it might be described. To imagine that he didn't even think of her while she passed her days and weeks waiting with him in her thoughts all the time, to imagine that was to be filled with rage, frustration, bitterness, humiliation, sorrow. Much as she had loathed those two nights at the Dunny pub, at least then she had come first with him; now she found herself actually wishing she had bitten off her tongue sooner than cried out in pain. That was it, of course. Her suffering had made him tire of her, ruined his own pleasure. From anger at him, at his indifference to her pain, she passed to remorse, and ended in blaming it all on herself.

The fourth Sunday she didn't bother dressing up, just padded around the kitchen bare-footed in shorts and vest, getting a hot breakfast for Luddie and Anne, who enjoyed this incongruity once a week. At the sound of footsteps on the back stairs she turned from bacon sizzling in the pan; for a moment she simply stared at the big, hairy fellow in the doorway. Luke? Was this Luke? He seemed made of rock, inhuman. But the effigy crossed the kitchen, gave her a smacking kiss and sat down at the table. She broke eggs into the pan and put on more bacon.

Anne Mueller came in, smiled civilly and inwardly fumed at him. Wretched man, what was he about, to leave his new wife neglected for so long?

"I'm glad to see you've remembered you have a wife," she said. "Come out onto the veranda, sit with Luddie and me and we'll all have breakfast. Luke, help Meggie carry the bacon and eggs. I can manage the toast rack in my teeth."

Ludwig Mueller was Australian-born, but his German heritage was clearly on him: the beefy red complexion not able to cope with beer and sun combined, the square grey head, the pale-blue Baltic eyes. He and his wife liked Meggie very much, and counted themselves fortunate to have acquired her services. Especially was Luddie grateful, seeing how much happier Anne was since that goldy head had been glowing around the house.

"How's the cutting, Luke?" he asked, shoveling eggs and bacon onto his plate.

"If I said I liked it, would you believe me?" Luke laughed, heaping his own plate.

Luddie's shrewd eyes rested on the handsome face, and he nodded. "Oh, yes. You've got the right sort of temperament and the right sort of body, I think. It makes you feel better than other men, superior to them." Caught in his heritage of cane fields, far from academia and with no chance of exchanging one for the other, Luddie was an ardent student of human nature; he read great fat tomes bound in Morocco leather with names on their spines like Freud and Jung, Huxley and Russell.

"I was beginning to think you were never going to come and see Meggie," Anne said, spreading ghee on her toast with a brush; it was the only way they could have butter up here, but it was better than none.

"Well, Arne and I decided to work on Sundays for a while. Tomorrow we're off to Ingham."

"Which means poor Meggie won't see you too often."

"Meg understands. It won't be for more than a couple of years, and we do have the summer layoff. Arne says he can get me work at the CSR in Sydney then, and I might take Meg with me."

"Why do you have to work so hard, Luke?" asked Anne.

"Got to get the money together for my property out west, around Kynuna. Didn't Meg mention it?"

"I'm afraid our Meggie's not much good at personal talk. You tell us, Luke."

The three listeners sat watching the play of expression on the tanned, strong face, the glitter of those very blue eyes; since he had come before breakfast Meggie hadn't uttered a word to anyone. On and on he talked about the marvelous country Back of Beyond; the grass, the big grey brolga birds mincing delicately in the dust of Kynuna's only road, the thousands upon thousands of flying kangaroos, the hot dry sun.

"And one day soon a big chunk of all that is going to be mine. Meg's put a bit of money toward it, and at the pace we're working it won't take more than four or five years. Sooner, if I was content to have a poorer place, but knowing what I can earn cutting sugar, I'm tempted to cut a bit longer and get a really decent bit of land." He leaned forward, big scarred hands around his teacup. "Do you know I nearly passed Arne's tally the other day? Eleven tons I cut *in one day!*"

Luddie's whistle was genuinely admiring, and they embarked upon a discussion of tallies. Meggie sipped her strong dark milkless tea. Oh, Luke! First it had been a couple of years, now it was four or five, and who knew how long it would be the next time he mentioned a period of years? Luke loved it, no one could mistake that. So would he give it up when the time came? Would he? For that matter, did she want to wait around to find out? The Muellers were very kind and she was far from overworked, but if she had to live without a husband, Drogheda was the best place. In the month of her stay at Himmelhoch she hadn't felt really well for one single day; she didn't want to eat, she suffered bouts of painful diarrhea, she seemed dogged by lethargy and couldn't shake it off. Not used to feeling anything but tiptop well, the vague malaise frightened her.

After breakfast Luke helped her wash the dishes, then took her for a walk down to the nearest cane field, talking all the time about the sugar and what it was like to cut it, what a beaut life it was out in the open air, what a beaut lot of blokes they were in Arne's gang, how different it was from shearing, and how much better.

They turned and walked up the hill again; Luke led her into the exquisitely cool cavern under the house, between the piles. Anne had made a conservatory out of it, stood pieces of terra-cotta pipe of differing lengths and girths upright, then filled them with soil and planted trailing, dangling things in them; orchids of every kind and color, ferns, exotic creepers and bushes. The ground was soft and redolent of wood chips; great wire baskets hung from the joists overhead, full of ferns or orchids or tuberoses; staghorns in bark nests grew on the piles; magnificent begonias in dozens of brilliant colors had been planted around the bases of the pipes. It was Meggie's favorite retreat, the one thing of Himmelhoch's she preferred to anything of Drogheda's. For Drogheda could never hope to grow so much on one small spot; there just wasn't enough moisture in the air.

"Isn't this lovely, Luke? Do you think perhaps after a couple of years up here we might be able to rent a house for me to live in? I'm dying to try something like this for myself."

"What on earth do you want to live alone in a house for? This isn't Gilly, Meg; it's the sort of place where a woman on her own isn't safe. You're much better off here, believe me. Aren't you happy here?"

"I'm as happy as one can be in someone else's home."

"Look, Meg, you've just got to be content with what you have now until we move out west. We can't spend money renting houses and having you live a life of leisure and still save. Do you hear me?"

"Yes, Luke."

He was so upset he didn't do what he had intended to do when he led her under the house, namely kiss her. Instead he gave her a casual smack on the bottom which hurt a little too much to be casual, and set off down the road to the spot where he had left his bike propped against a tree. He had pedaled twenty miles to see her rather than spend money on a rail motor and a bus, which meant he had to pedal twenty miles back.

"The poor little soul!" said Anne to Luddie. "I could kill him!"

January came and went, the slackest month of the year for cane cutters, but there was no sign of Luke. He had murmured about taking Meggie to Sydney, but instead he went to Sydney with Arne and without her. Arne was a bachelor and had an aunt with a house in Rozelle, within walking distance (no tram fares; save money) of the CSR, the Colonial Sugar Refineries. Within those gargantuan concrete walls like a fortress on a hill, a cutter with connections could get work. Luke and Arne kept in trim stacking sugar bags, and swimming or surfing in their spare time.

Left in Dungloe with the Muellers, Meggie sweated her way through The Wet, as the monsoon season was called. The Dry lasted from March to November and in this part of the continent wasn't exactly dry, but compared to The Wet it was heavenly. During The Wet the skies just opened and vomited water, not all day but in fits and starts; in between deluges the land steamed, great clouds of white vapor rising from the cane, the soil, the jungle, the mountains.

And as time went on Meggie longed for home more and more. North Queensland, she knew now, could never become home to her. For one thing, the climate didn't suit her, perhaps because she had spent most of her life in dryness. And she hated the loneliness, the unfriendliness, the feeling of remorseless lethargy. She hated the prolific insect and reptile life which made each night an ordeal of giant toads, tarantulas, cockroaches, rats; nothing seemed to keep them out of the house, and she was terrified of them. They were so huge, so aggressive, so *hungry*. Most of all she hated the dunny, which was not only the local patois for toilet but the diminutive for Dungloe, much to the delight of the local populace, who punned on it perpetually. But a Dunny dunny left one's stomach churning in revolt, for in this seething climate holes in the ground were out of the question because of typhoid and other enteric fevers. Instead of being a hole in the ground, a Dunny dunny was a tarred tin can which stank, and as it filled came alive with noisome maggots and worms. Once a week the can was removed and replaced with an empty one, but once a week wasn't soon enough.

Meggie's whole spirit rebelled against the casual local acceptance of such things as normal; a lifetime in North Queensland couldn't reconcile her to them. Yet dismally she reflected that it probably would be a whole lifetime, or at least until Luke was too old to cut the sugar. Much as she longed for and dreamed of Drogheda, she was far too proud to admit to her family that her husband neglected her; sooner than admit that, she'd take the lifetime sentence, she told herself fiercely.

Months went by, then a year, and time crept toward the second year's end. Only the constant kindness of the Muellers kept Meggie in residence at Himmelhoch, trying to resolve her dilemma. Had she written to ask Bob for the fare home he would have sent it by return telegram, but poor Meggie couldn't face telling her family that Luke kept her without a penny in her purse. The day she did tell them was the day she would leave Luke, never to go back to him, and she hadn't made up her mind yet to take such a step. Everything in her upbringing conspired to prevent her leaving Luke: the sacredness of her marriage vows, the hope she might have a baby one day, the position Luke occupied as husband and master of her destiny. Then there were the things which sprang from her own nature: that stubborn, stiff-necked pride, and the niggling conviction that the situation was as much her fault as Luke's. If there wasn't something wrong with her, Luke might have behaved far differently.

She had seen him six times in the eighteen months of her exile, and often thought, quite unaware such a thing as homosexuality existed, that by rights Luke should have married Arne, because he certainly lived with Arne and much preferred his company. They had gone into full partnership and drifted up and down the thousand-mile coast following the sugar harvest, living, it seemed, only to work. When Luke did come to see her he didn't attempt any kind of intimacy, just sat around for an hour or two yarning to Luddie and Anne, took his wife for a walk, gave her a friendly kiss, and was off again.

The three of them, Luddie, Anne and Meggie, spent all their spare time reading. Himmelhoch had a library far larger than Drogheda's few shelves, more erudite and more salacious by far, and Meggie learned a great deal while she read.

One Sunday in June of 1936 Luke and Arne turned up together, very pleased with themselves. They had come, they said, to give Meggie a real treat, for they were taking her to a ceilidh.

Unlike the general tendency of ethnic groups in Australia to scatter and become purely Australian, the various nationalities in the North Queensland peninsula tended to preserve their traditions fiercely: the Chinese, the Italians, the Germans and the Scots-Irish, these four groups making up the bulk of the population. And when the Scots threw a ceilidh every Scot for miles attended.

To Meggie's astonishment, Luke and Arne were wearing kilts, looking, she thought when she got her breath back, absolutely magnificent. Nothing is more masculine on a masculine man than a kilt, for it swings with a long clean stride in a flurry of pleats behind and stays perfectly still in front, the sporran like a loin guard, and below the mid-knee hem strong fine legs in diamond checkered hose, buckled shoes. It was far too hot to wear the plaid and the jacket; they had contented themselves with white shirts open halfway down their chests, sleeves rolled up above their elbows.

"What's a ceilidh anyway?" she asked as they set off.

"It's Gaelic for a gathering, a shindig."

"Why on earth are you wearing kilts?"

"We won't be let in unless we are, and we're well known at all the ceilidhs between Bris and Cairns."

"Are you now? I imagine you must indeed go to quite a few, otherwise I can't see Luke outlaying money for a kilt. Isn't that so, Arne?"

"A man's got to have some relaxation," said Luke, a little defensively.

The ceilidh was being held in a barnlike shack falling to rack and ruin down in the midst of the mangrove swamps festering about the mouth of the Dungloe River. Oh, what a country this was for smells! Meggie thought in despair, her nose twitching to yet another indescribably disgusting aroma. Molasses, mildew, dunnies, and now mangroves. All the rotting effluvia of the seashore rolled into one smell.

Sure enough, every man arriving at the shed wore a kilt; as they went in and she looked around, Meggie understood how drab a peahen must feel when dazzled by the vivid gorgeousness of her mate. The women were overshadowed into near nonexistence, an impression which the later stages of the evening only sharpened.

Two pipers in the complex, light-blue-based Anderson tartan were standing on a rickety dais at one end of the hall, piping a cheerful reel in perfect synchrony, sandy hair on end, sweat running down ruddy faces.

A few couples were dancing, but most of the noisy activity seemed to be centered around a group of men who were passing out glasses of what was surely Scotch whiskey. Meggie found herself thrust into a corner with several other women, and was content to stay there watching, fascinated. Not one woman wore a clan tartan, for indeed no Scotswoman wears the kilt, only the plaid, and it was too hot to drape a great heavy piece of material around the shoulders. So the women wore their dowdy North Queensland cotton dresses, which stuttered into limp silence beside the men's kilts. There was the blazing red and white of Clan Menzies, the cheery black and yellow of Clan MacLeod of Lewis, the windowpane blue and red checks of Clan Skene, the vivid complexity of Clan Ogilvy, the lovely red, grey and black of Clan MacPherson. Luke in Clan MacNeil, Arne in the Sassenach's Jacobean tartan. Beautiful!

Luke and Arne were obviously well known and well liked. How often did they come without her, then? And what had possessed them to bring her tonight? She sighed, leaned against the wall. The other women were eyeing her curiously, especially the rings on her wedding finger; Luke and Arne were the objects of much feminine admiration, herself the object of much feminine envy. I wonder what they'd say if I told them the big dark one, who is my husband, has seen me precisely twice in the last eight months, and never sees me with the idea of getting into a bed? Look at the pair of them, the conceited Highland fops! And neither of them Scottish at all, just playacting because they know they look sensational in kilts and they like to be the center of attention. You magnificent pair of frauds! You're too much in love with yourselves to want or need love from anyone else.

At midnight the women were relegated to standing around the walls; the pipers skirled into "Caber Feidh" and the serious dancing began. For the rest of her life, whenever she heard the sound of a piper Meggie was back in that shed. Even the swirl of a kilt could do it; there was that dreamlike merging of sound and sight, of life and brilliant vitality, which means a memory so piercing, so spellbinding, that it will never be lost.

Down went the crossed swords on the floor; two men

in Clan MacDonald of Sleat kilts raised their arms above their heads, hands flicked over like ballet dancers, and very gravely, as if at the end the swords would be plunged into their breasts, began to pick their delicate way through, between, among the blades.

A high shrill scream ripped above the airy wavering of the pipes, the tune became "All the Blue Bonnets over the Border," the sabers were scooped up, and every man in the room swung into the dance, arms linking and dissolving, kilts flaring. Reels, strathspeys, flings; they danced them all, feet on the board floor sending echoes among the rafters, buckles on shoes flashing, and every time the pattern changed someone would throw back his head, emit that shrill, ululating whoop, set off trains of cries from other exuberant throats. While the women watched, forgotten.

It was close to four in the morning when the ceilidh broke up; outside was not the astringent crispness of Blair Atholl or Skye but the torpor of a tropical night, a great heavy moon dragging itself along the spangled wastes of the heavens, and over it all the stinking miasma of mangroves. Yet as Arne drove them off in the wheezing old Ford, the last thing Meggie heard was the drifting dwindling lament "Flowers o' the Forest," bidding the revelers home. Home. Where was home?

"Well, did you enjoy that?" asked Luke.

"I would have enjoyed it more had I danced more," she answered.

"What, at a ceilidh? Break it down, Meg! Only the men are supposed to dance, so we're actually pretty good to you women, letting you dance at all."

"It seems to me only men do a lot of things, and especially if they're good things, enjoyable things."

"Well, excuse me!" said Luke stiffly. "Here was I thinking you might like a bit of a change, which was why I brought you. I didn't have to, you know! And if you're not grateful I won't bring you again."

"You probably don't have any intention of doing so,

anyway," said Meggie. "It isn't good to admit me into your life. I learned a lot these past few hours, but I don't think it's what you intended to teach me. It's getting harder to fool me, Luke. In fact, I'm fed up with you, with the life I'm leading, with everything!"

"Ssssh!" he hissed, scandalized. "We're not alone!"

"Then *come* alone!" she snapped. "When do I ever get the chance to see you alone for more than a few minutes?"

Arne pulled up at the bottom of the Himmelhoch hill, grinning at Luke sympathetically. "Go on, mate," he said. "Walk her up; I'll wait here for you. No hurry."

"I mean it, Luke!" Meggie said as soon as they were out of Arne's hearing. "The worm's turning, do you hear me? I know I promised to obey you, but you promised to love and cherish me, so we're both liars! I want to go home to Drogheda!"

He thought of her two thousand pounds a year and of its ceasing to be put in his name.

"Oh, Meg!" he said helplessly. "Look, sweetheart, it won't be forever, I promise! And this summer I'm going to take you to Sydney with me, word of an O'Neill! Arne's aunt has a flat coming vacant in her house, and we can live there for three months, have a wonderful time! Bear with me another year or so in the cane, then we'll buy our property and settle down, eh?"

The moon lit up his face; he looked sincere, upset, anxious, contrite. And very like Ralph de Bricassart.

Meggie relented, because she still wanted his babies. "All right," she said. "Another year. But I'm holding you to that promise of Sydney, Luke, so remember!"

12

Once a month Meggie wrote a dutiful letter to Fee, Bob and the boys, full of descriptions of North Queensland, carefully humorous, never hinting of any differences between her and Luke. That pride again. As far as Drogheda knew, the Muellers were friends of Luke's with whom she boarded because Luke traveled so much. Her genuine affection for the couple came through in every word she wrote about them, so no one on Drogheda worried. Except that it grieved them she never came home. Yet how could she tell them that she didn't have the money to visit without also telling them how miserable her marriage to Luke O'Neill had become?

Occasionally she would nerve herself to insert a casual question about Bishop Ralph, and even less often Bob would remember to pass on the little he learned from Fee about the Bishop. Then came a letter full of him.

"He arrived out of the blue one day, Meggie," Bob's letter said, "looking a bit upset and down in the mouth. I must say he was floored not to find you here. He was spitting mad because we hadn't told him about you and Luke, but when Mum said you'd got a bee in your bonnet about it and didn't want us to tell him, he shut up and never said another word. But I thought he missed you more than he would any of the rest of us, and I suppose that's quite natural because you spent more time with him than the rest of us, and I think he always thought of you as his little sister. He wandered around as if he couldn't believe you wouldn't pop up all of a sudden, poor chap. We didn't have any pictures to show him either, and I never thought until he asked to see them that it was funny you never had any wedding pictures taken. He asked if you had any kids, and I said I didn't think so. You don't, do you, Meggie? How long is it now since you were married? Getting on for two years? Must be, because this is July. Time flies, eh? I hope you have some kids soon, because I think the Bishop would be pleased to hear of it. I offered to give him your address, but he said no. Said it wouldn't be any use because he's going to Athens, Greece, for a while with the archbishop he works for. Some Dago name four yards long, I never can remember it. Can you imagine, Meggie, they're flying? 'Struth! Anyway, once he found out you weren't on Drogheda to go round with him he didn't stay long, just took a ride or two, said Mass for us every day, and went six days after he got here."

Meggie laid the letter down. He knew, he knew! At last he knew. What had he thought, how much had it grieved him? And why had he pushed her to do this? It hadn't made things any better. She didn't love Luke, she never would love Luke. He was nothing more than a substitute, a man who would give her children similar in type to those she might have had with Ralph de Bricassart. Oh, God, what a mess!

Archbishop di Contini-Verchese preferred to stay in a secular hotel than avail himself of the offered quarters in an Athens Orthodox palace. His mission was a very delicate one, of some moment; there were matters long overdue for discussion with the chief prelates of the

Greek Orthodox Church, the Vatican having a fondness for Greek and Russian Orthodoxy that it couldn't have for Protestantism. After all, the Orthodoxies were schisms, not heresies; their bishops, like Rome's, extended back to Saint Peter in an unbroken line.

The Archbishop knew his appointment for this mission was a diplomatic testing, a stepping stone to greater things in Rome. Again his gift for languages had been a boon, for it was his fluent Greek which had tipped the balance in his favor. They had sent for him all the way to Australia, flown him out.

And it was unthinkable that he go without Bishop de Bricassart, for he had grown to rely upon that amazing man more and more with the passing of the years. A Mazarin, truly a Mazarin; His Grace admired Cardinal Mazarin far more than he did Cardinal Richelieu, so the comparison was high praise. Ralph was everything the Church liked in her high officials. His theology was conservative, so were his ethics; his brain was quick and subtle, his face gave away nothing of what went on behind it; and he had an exquisite knack of knowing just how to please those he was with, whether he liked them or loathed them, agreed with them or differed from them. A sycophant he was not, a diplomat he was. If he was repeatedly brought to the attention of those in the Vatican hierarchy, his rise to prominence would be certain. And that would please His Grace di Contini-Verchese, for he didn't want to lose contact with His Lordship de Bricassart.

It was very hot, but Bishop Ralph didn't mind the dry Athens air after Sydney's humidity. Walking rapidly, as usual in boots, breeches and soutane, he strode up the rocky ramp to the Acropolis, through the frowning Propylon, past the Erechtheum, on up the incline with its slippery rough stones to the Parthenon, and down to the wall beyond.

There, with the wind ruffling his dark curls, a little grey about the ears now, he stood and looked across the white city to the bright hills and the clear, astonishing aquamarine of the Aegean Sea. Right below him was the Plaka with its rooftop cafés, its colonies of Bohemians, and to one side a great theater lapped up the rock. In the distance were Roman columns, Crusader forts and Venetian castles, but never a sign of the Turks. What amazing people, these Greeks. To hate the race who had ruled them for seven hundred years so much that once freed they hadn't left a mosque or a minaret standing. And so ancient, so full of rich heritage. His Normans had been fur-clad barbarians when Pericles clothed the top of the rock in marble, and Rome had been a rude village.

Only now, eleven thousand miles away, was he able to think of Meggie without wanting to weep. Even so, the distant hills blurred for a moment before he brought his emotions under control. How could he possibly blame her, when he had told her to do it? He understood at once why she had been determined not to tell him; she didn't want him to meet her new husband, or be a part of her new life. Of course in his mind he had assumed she would bring whomever she married to Gillanbone if not to Drogheda itself, that she would continue to live where he knew her to be safe, free from care and danger. But once he thought about it, he could see this was the last thing she would want. No, she had been bound to go away, and so long as she and this Luke O'Neill were together, she wouldn't come back. Bob said they were saving to buy a property in Western Queensland, and that news had been the death knell. Meggie meant never to come back. As far as he was concerned, she intended to be dead.

But are you happy, Meggie? Is he good to you? Do you love him, this Luke O'Neill? What kind of man is he, that you turned from me to him? What was it about him, an ordinary stockman, that you liked better than Enoch Davies or Liam O'Rourke or Alastair MacQueen? Was it that *I* didn't know him, that *I* could make no comparisons? Did you do it to torture me, Meggie, to pay me back? But why are there no children? What's the matter with the man, that he roams up and down the state like a vagabond and puts you to live with friends? No wonder you have no child; he's not with you long enough. Meggie, why? Why did you marry this Luke O'Neill?

Turning, he made his way down from the Acropolis, and walked the busy streets of Athens. In the open-air markets around Evripidou Street he lingered, fascinated by the people, the huge baskets of kalamari and fish reeking in the sun, the vegetables and tinsel slippers hung side by side; the women amused him, their unashamed and open cooing over him, a legacy of a culture basically very different from his puritanical own. Had their unabashed admiration been lustful (he could not think of a better word) it would have embarrassed him acutely, but he accepted it in the spirit intended, as an accolade for extraordinary physical beauty.

The hotel was on Omonia Square, very luxurious and expensive. Archbishop di Contini-Verchese was sitting in a chair by his balcony windows, quietly thinking; as Bishop Ralph came in he turned his head, smiling.

"In good time, Ralph. I would like to pray."

"I thought everything was settled? Are there sudden complications, Your Grace?"

"Not of that kind. I had a letter from Cardinal Monteverdi today, expressing the wishes of the Holy Father."

Bishop Ralph felt his shoulders tighten, a curious prickling of the skin around his ears. "Tell me."

"As soon as the talks are over—and they are over—I am to proceed to Rome. There I am to be blessed with the biretta of a cardinal, and continue my work in Rome under the direct supervision of His Holiness."

"Whereas I?"

"You will become Archbishop de Bricassart, and go back to Australia to fill my shoes as Papal Legate."

The prickling skin around his ears flushed red hot; his head whirled, rocked. He, a non-Italian, to be honored with the Papal Legation! It was unheard of! Oh, depend on it, he would be Cardinal de Bricassart yet!

"Of course you will receive training and instruction in Rome first. That will take about six months, during which I will be with you to introduce you to those who are my friends. I want them to know you, because the time will come when I shall send for you, Ralph, to help me with my work in the Vatican."

"Your Grace, I can't thank you enough! It's due to you, this great chance."

"God grant I am sufficiently intelligent to see when a man is too able to leave in obscurity, Ralph! Now let us kneel and pray. God is very good."

His rosary beads and missal were sitting on a table nearby; hand trembling, Bishop Ralph reached for the beads and knocked the missal to the floor. It fell open at the middle. The Archbishop, who was closer to it, picked it up and looked curiously at the brown, tissue-thin shape which had once been a rose.

"How extraordinary! Why do you keep this? Is it a memory of your home, or perhaps of your mother?" The eyes which saw through guile and dissimulation were looking straight at him, and there was no time to disguise his emotion, or his apprehension.

"No." He grimaced. "I want no memories of my mother."

"But it must have great meaning for you, that you store it so lovingly within the pages of the book most dear to you. Of what does it speak?"

"Of a love as pure as that I bear my God, Vittorio. It does the book nothing but honor."

"That I deduced, because I know you. But the love, does it endanger your love for the Church?"

"No. It was for the Church I forsook her, that I always will forsake her. I've gone so far beyond her, and I can never go back again."

"So at last I understand the sadness! Dear Ralph, it is not as bad as you think, truly it is not. You will live to do great good for many people, you will be loved by many people. And she, having the love which is contained in such an old, fragrant memory as this, will never want. Because you kept the love alongside the rose."

"I don't think she understands at all."

"Oh, yes. If you have loved her thus, then she is woman enough to understand. Otherwise you would have forgotten her, and abandoned this relic long since."

"There have been times when only hours on my knees have stopped me from leaving my post, going to her."

The Archbishop eased himself out of his chair and came to kneel beside his friend, this beautiful man whom he loved as he had loved few things other than his God and his Church, which to him were indivisible.

"You will not leave, Ralph, and you know it well. You belong to the Church, you always have and you always will. The vocation for you is a true one. We shall pray now, and I shall add the Rose to my prayers for the rest of my life. Our Dear Lord sends us many griefs and much pain during our progress to eternal life. We must learn to bear it, I as much as you."

At the end of August Meggie got a letter from Luke to say he was in Townsville Hospital with Weil's disease, but that he was in no danger and would be out soon.

"So it looks like we don't have to wait until the end of the year for our holiday, Meg. I can't go back to the cane until I'm one hundred percent fit, and the best way to make sure I am is to have a decent holiday. So I'll be along in a week or so to pick you up. We're going to Lake Eacham on the Atherton Tableland for a couple of weeks, until I'm well enough to go back to work."

Meggie could hardly believe it, and didn't know if

she wanted to be with him or not, now that the opportunity presented itself. Though the pain of her mind had taken a lot longer to heal than the pain of her body, the memory of her honeymoon ordeal in the Dunny pub had been pushed from thought so long it had lost the power to terrify her, and from her reading she understood better now that much of it had been due to ignorance, her own and Luke's. Oh, dear Lord, pray this holiday would mean a child! If she could only have a baby to love it would be so much easier. Anne wouldn't mind a baby around, she'd love it. So would Luddie. They had told her so a hundred times, hoping Luke would come once for long enough to rectify his wife's barren loveless existence.

When she told them what the letter said they were delighted, but privately skeptical.

"Sure as eggs is eggs that wretch will find some excuse to be off without her," said Anne to Luddie.

Luke had borrowed a car from somewhere, and picked Meggie up early in the morning. He looked thin, wrinkled and yellow, as if he had been pickled. Shocked, Meggie gave him her case and climbed in beside him.

"What is Weil's disease, Luke? You said you weren't in any danger, but it looks to me as if you've been very sick indeed."

"Oh, it's just some sort of jaundice most cutters get sooner or later. The cane rats carry it, we pick it up through a cut or sore. I'm in good health, so I wasn't too sick compared to some who get it. The quacks say I'll be fit as a fiddle in no time."

Climbing up through a great gorge filled with jungle, the road led inland, a river in full spate roaring and tumbling below, and at one spot a magnificent waterfall spilling to join it from somewhere up above, right athwart the road. They drove between the cliff and the angling water in a wet, glittering archway of fantastic light and shadow. And as they climbed the air grew cool, exquisitely fresh; Meggie had forgotten how good cool air made her feel. The jungle leaned across them, so impenetrable no one ever dared to enter it. The bulk of it was quite invisible under the weight of leafy vines lying sagging from treetop to treetop, continuous and endless, like a vast sheet of green velvet flung across the forest. Under the eaves Meggie caught glimpses of wonderful flowers and butterflies, cartwheeling webs with great elegant speckled spiders motionless at their hubs, fabulous fungi chewing at mossy trunks, birds with long trailing red or blond tails.

Lake Eacham lay on top of the tableland, idyllic in its unspoiled setting. Before night fell they strolled out onto the veranda of their boardinghouse to look across the still water. Meggie wanted to watch the enormous fruit bats called flying foxes wheel like precursors of doom in thousands down toward the places where they found their food. They were monstrous and repulsive, but singularly timid, entirely benign. To see them come across a molten sky in dark, pulsating sheets was awesome; Meggie never missed watching for them from the Himmelhoch veranda.

And it was heaven to sink into a soft cool bed, not have to lie still until one spot was sweat-saturated and then move carefully to a new spot, knowing the old one wouldn't dry out anyway. Luke took a flat brown packet out of his case, picked a handful of small round objects out of it and laid them in a row on the bedside table.

Meggie reached out to take one, inspect it. "What on earth is it?" she asked curiously.

"A French letter." He had forgotten his decision of two years ago, not to tell her he practiced contraception. "I put it on myself before I go inside you. Otherwise I might start a baby, and we can't afford to do that until we get our place." He was sitting naked on the side of the bed, and he was thin, ribs and hips protruding. But his blue eyes shone, he reached out to clasp her hand as it held the French letter. "Nearly there,

Meg, nearly there! I reckon another five thousand pounds will buy us the best property to be had west of Charters Towers."

"Then you've got it," she said, her voice quite calm. "I can write to Bishop de Bricassart and ask him for a loan of the money. He won't charge us interest."

"You most certainly won't!" he snapped. "Damn it, Meg, where's your pride? We'll work for what we have, not borrow! I've never owed anyone a penny in all my life, and I'm not going to start now."

She scarcely heard him, glaring at him through a haze of brilliant red. In all her life she had never been so angry! Cheat, liar, egotist! How dared he do it to her, trick her out of a baby, try to make her believe he ever had any intention of becoming a grazier! He'd found his niche, with Arne Swenson and the sugar.

Concealing her rage so well it surprised her, she turned her attention back to the little rubber wheel in her hand. "Tell me about these French letter things. How do they stop me having a baby?"

He came to stand behind her, and contact of their bodies made her shiver; from excitement he thought, from disgust she knew.

"Don't you know anything, Meg?"

"No," she lied. Which was true about French letters, at any rate; she could not remember ever seeing a mention of them.

His hands played with her breasts, tickling. "Look, when I come I make this—I don't know—stuff, and if I'm up inside you with nothing on, it stays there. When it stays there long enough or often enough, it makes a baby."

So that was it! He *wore* the thing, like a skin on a sausage! Cheat!

Turning off the light, he drew her down onto the bed, and it wasn't long before he was groping for his anti-baby device; she heard him making the same sounds he had made in the Dunny pub bedroom, knowing now they meant he was pulling on the French letter. The cheat! But how to get around it?

Trying not to let him see how much he hurt her, she endured him. Why did it have to hurt so, if this was a natural thing?

"It's no good, is it, Meg?" he asked afterward. "You must be awfully small for it to keep on hurting so much after the first time. Well, I won't do it again. You don't mind if I do it on your breast, do you?"

"Oh, what does it matter?" she asked wearily. "If you mean you're not going to hurt me, all right!"

"You might be a bit more enthusiastic, Meg!"

"What for?"

But he was rising again; it was two years since he had had time or energy for this. Oh, it was nice to be with a woman, exciting and forbidden. He didn't feel at all married to Meg; it wasn't any different from getting a bit in the paddock behind the Kynuna pub, or having high-and-mighty Miss Carmichael against the shearing shed wall. Meggie had nice breasts, firm from all that riding, just the way he liked them, and he honestly preferred to get his pleasure at her breast, liking the sensation of unsheathed penis sandwiched between their bellies. French letters cut a man's sensitivity a lot, but not to don one when he put himself inside her was asking for trouble.

Groping, he pulled at her buttocks and made her lie on top of him, then seized one nipple between his teeth, feeling the hidden point swell and harden on his tongue. A great contempt for him had taken possession of Meggie; what ridiculous creatures men were, grunting and sucking and straining for what they got out of it. He was becoming more excited, kneading her back and bottom, gulping away for all the world like a great overgrown kitten sneaked back to its mother. His hips began to move in a rhythmic, jerky fashion, and sprawled across him awkwardly because she was hating it too much to try helping him, she felt the tip of his unprotected penis slide between her legs.

Since she was not a participant in the act, her thoughts were her own. And it was then the idea came. As slowly and unobtrusively as she could, she maneuvered him until he was right at the most painful part of her; with a great indrawn breath to keep her courage up, she forced the penis in, teeth clenched. But though it did hurt, it didn't hurt nearly as much. Minus its rubber sheath, his member was more slippery, easier to introduce and far easier to tolerate.

Luke's eyes opened. He tried to push her away, but oh, God! It was unbelievable without the French letter; he had never been inside a woman bare, had never realized what a difference it made. He was so close, so excited he couldn't bring himself to push her away hard enough, and in the end he put his arms round her, unable to keep up his breast activity. Though it wasn't manly to cry out, he couldn't prevent the noise leaving him, and afterward kissed her softly.

"Luke?"

"What?"

"Why can't we do that every time? Then you wouldn't have to put on a French letter."

"We shouldn't have done it that time, Meg, let alone again. I was right in you when I came."

She leaned over him, stroking his chest. "But don't you see? I'm sitting up! It doesn't stay there at all, it runs right out again! Oh, Luke, please! It's so much nicer, it doesn't hurt nearly as much. I'm sure it's all right, because I can feel it running out. Please!"

What human being ever lived who could resist the repetition of perfect pleasure when offered so plausibly? Adam-like, Luke nodded, for at this stage he was far less informed than Meggie.

"I suppose there's truth in what you say, and it's much nicer for me when you're not fighting it. All right, Meg, we'll do it that way from now on."

And in the darkness she smiled, content. For it had *not* all run out. The moment she felt him shrink out of her she had drawn up all the internal muscles into a knot, slid off him onto her back, stuck her crossed knees in the air casually and hung on to what she had with every ounce of determination in her. Oho, my fine gentleman, I'll fix you yet! You wait and see, Luke O'Neill! I'll get my baby if it kills me!

Away from the heat and humidity of the coastal plain Luke mended rapidly. Eating well, he began to put the weight he needed back again, and his skin faded from the sickly yellow to its usual brown. With the lure of an eager, responsive Meggie in his bed it wasn't too difficult to persuade him to prolong the original two weeks into three, and then into four. But at the end of a month he rebelled.

"There's no excuse, Meg. I'm as well as I've ever been. We're sitting up here on top of the world like a king and queen, spending money. Arne needs me."

"Won't you reconsider, Luke? If you really wanted to, you could buy your station now."

"Let's hang on a bit longer the way we are, Meg."

He wouldn't admit it, of course, but the lure of the sugar was in his bones, the strange fascination some men have for utterly demanding labor. As long as his young man's strength held up, Luke would remain faithful to the sugar. The only thing Meggie could hope for was to force him into changing his mind by giving him a child, an heir to the property out around Kynuna.

So she went back to Himmelhoch to wait and hope. Please, please, let there be a baby! A baby would solve everything, so please let there be a baby. And there was. When she told Anne and Luddie, they were overjoyed. Luddie especially turned out to be a treasure. He did the most exquisite smocking and embroidery, two crafts Meggie had never had time to master, so while he pushed a tiny needle through delicate fabric with his horny, magical hands, Meggie helped Anne get the nursery together.

The only trouble was the baby wasn't sitting well, whether because of the heat or her unhappiness Meggie didn't know. The morning sickness was all day, and persisted long after it should have stopped; in spite of her very slight weight gain she began to suffer badly from too much fluid in the tissues of her body, and her blood pressure went up to a point at which Doc Smith became apprehensive. At first he talked of hospital in Cairns for the remainder of her pregnancy, but after a long think about her husbandless, friendless situation he decided she would be better off with Luddie and Anne, who did care for her. For the last three weeks of her term, however, she must definitely go to Cairns.

"And try to get her husband to come and see her!" he roared to Luddie.

Meggie had written right away to tell Luke she was pregnant, full of the usual feminine conviction that once the not-wanted was an irrefutable fact, Luke would become wildly enthusiastic. His answering letter scotched any such delusions. He was furious. As far as he was concerned, becoming a father simply meant he would have two nonworking mouths to feed, instead of none. It was a bitter pill for Meggie to swallow, but swallow it she did; she had no choice. Now the coming child bound her to him as tightly as her pride.

But she felt ill, helpless, utterly unloved; even the baby didn't love her, didn't want to be conceived or born. She could feel it inside her, the weakly tiny creature's feeble protests against growing into being. Had she been able to tolerate the two-thousand-mile rail journey home, she would have gone, but Doc Smith shook his head firmly. Get on a train for a week or more, even in broken stages, and that would be the end of the baby. Disappointed and unhappy though she was, Meggie wouldn't consciously do anything to harm the baby. Yet as time went on her enthusiasm and her longing to have someone of her own to love withered in her; the incubus child hung heavier, more resentful.

Doc Smith talked of an earlier transfer to Cairns; he wasn't sure Meggie could survive a birth in Dungloe, which had only a cottage infirmary. Her blood pressure was recalcitrant, the fluid kept mounting; he talked of toxemia and eclampsia, other long medical words which frightened Anne and Luddie into agreeing, much as they longed to see the baby born at Himmelhoch.

By the end of May there were only four weeks left to go, four weeks until Meggie could rid herself of this intolerable burden, this ungrateful child. She was learning to hate it, the very being she had wanted so much before discovering what trouble it would cause. *Why* had she assumed Luke would look forward to the baby once its existence was a reality? Nothing in his attitude or conduct since their marriage indicated he would.

Time she admitted it was a disaster, abandoned her silly pride and tried to salvage what she could from the ruins. They had married for all the wrong reasons: he for her money, she as an escape from Ralph de Bricassart while trying to retain Ralph de Bricassart. There had never been any pretense at love, and only love might have helped her and Luke to overcome the enormous difficulties their differing aims and desires created.

Oddly enough, she never seemed able to hate Luke, where she found herself hating Ralph de Bricassart more and more frequently. Yet when all was said and done, Ralph had been far kinder and fairer to her than Luke. Not once had he encouraged her to dream of him in any roles save priest and friend, for even on the two occasions when he had kissed her, she had begun the move herself.

Why be so angry with him, then? Why hate Ralph and not Luke? Blame her own fears and inadequacies, the huge, outraged resentment she felt because he had consistently rejected her when she loved and wanted him so much. And blame that stupid impulse which had led her to marry Luke O'Neill. A betrayal of her own self and Ralph. No matter if she could never have married him, slept with him, had his child. No matter if he didn't want her, and he *didn't* want her. The fact remained that he was who she wanted, and she ought never to have settled for less.

But knowing the wrongs couldn't alter them. It was still Luke O'Neill she had married, Luke O'Neill's child she was carrying. How could she be happy at the thought of Luke O'Neill's child, when even he didn't want it? Poor little thing. At least when it was born it would be its own piece of humanity, and could be loved as that. Only . . . What wouldn't she give, for Ralph de Bricassart's child? The impossible, the never-to-be. He served an institution which insisted on having all of him, even that part of him she had no use for, his manhood. That Mother Church required from him as a sacrifice to her power as an institution, and thus wasted him, stamped his being out of being, made sure that when he stopped he would be stopped forever. Only one day she would have to pay for her greed. One day there wouldn't be any more Ralph de Bricassarts, because they'd value their manhood enough to see that her demanding it of them was a useless sacrifice, having no meaning whatsoever. . . .

Suddenly she stood up and waddled through to the living room, where Anne was sitting reading an underground copy of Norman Lindsay's banned novel, *Redheap,* very obviously enjoying every forbidden word.

"Anne, I think you're going to get your wish."

Anne looked up absently. "What, dear?"

"Phone Doc Smith. I'm going to have this wretched baby here and now."

"Oh, my God! Get into the bedroom and lie down—not your bedroom, ours!"

Cursing the whims of fate and the determination of babies, Doc Smith hurried out from Dungloe in his battered car with the local midwife in the back and as much equipment as he could carry from his little cottage hospital. No use taking her there; he could do as much for her at Himmelhoch. But Cairns was where she ought to be.

"Have you let the husband know?" he asked as he pounded up the front steps, his midwife behind him.

"I sent a telegram. She's in my room; I thought it would give you more space."

Hobbling in their wake, Anne went into her bedroom. Meggie was lying on the bed, wide-eyed and giving no indication of pain except for an occasional spasm of her hands, a drawing-in of her body. She turned her head to smile at Anne, and Anne saw that the eyes were very frightened.

"I'm glad I never got to Cairns" she said. "My mother never went to hospital to have hers, and Daddy said once she had a terrible time with Hal. But she survived, and so will I. We're hard to kill, we Cleary women."

It was hours later when the doctor joined Anne on the veranda.

"It's a long, hard business for the little woman. First babies are rarely easy, but this one's not lying well and she just drags on without getting anywhere. If she was in Cairns she could have a Caesarean, but that's out of the question here. She'll just have to push it out all by herself."

"Is she conscious?"

"Oh, yes. Gallant little soul, doesn't scream or complain. The best ones usually have the worst time of it in my opinion. Keeps asking me if Ralph's here yet, and I have to tell her some lie about the Johnstone in flood. I thought her husband's name was Luke?"

"It is."

"Hmmm! Well, maybe that's why she's asking for this Ralph, whoever he is. Luke's no comfort, is he?"

"Luke's a bastard."

Anne leaned forward, hands on the veranda railing. A taxi was coming from the Dunny road, and had turned off up the incline to Himmelhoch. Her excellent eyesight just discerned a black-haired man in the back, and she crowed with relief and joy.

"I don't believe what I see, but I think Luke's finally remembered he's got a wife!"

"I'd best go back to her and leave you to cope with him, Anne. I won't mention it to her, in case it isn't him. If it is him, give him a cup of tea and save the hard stuff for later. He's going to need it."

The taxi drew up; to Anne's surprise the driver got out and went to the back door to open it for his passenger. Joe Castiglione, who ran Dunny's sole taxi, wasn't usually given to such courtesies.

"Himmelhoch, Your Grace," he said, bowing deeply.

A man in a long, flowing black soutane got out, a purple grosgrain sash about his waist. As he turned, Anne thought for a dazed moment that Luke O'Neill was playing some elaborate trick on her. Then she saw that this was a far different man, a good ten years older than Luke. My God! she thought as the graceful figure mounted her steps two at a time. He's the handsomest chap I've ever seen! An archbishop, no less! What does a Catholic archbishop want with a pair of old Lutherans like Luddie and me?

"Mrs. Mueller?" he asked, smiling down at her with kind, aloof blue eyes. As if he had seen much he would give anything not to have seen, and had managed to stop feeling long ago.

"Yes, I'm Anne Mueller."

"I'm Archbishop Ralph de Bricassart, His Holiness's Legate in Australia. I understand you have a Mrs. Luke O'Neill staying with you?"

"Yes, sir." Ralph? *Ralph?* Was *this* Ralph?

"I'm a very old friend of hers. I wonder if I might see her, please?"

"Well, I'm sure she'd be delighted, Archbishop"—

no, that wasn't right, one didn't say Archbishop, one said Your Grace, like Joe Castiglione—"under more normal circumstances, but at the moment Meggie's in labor, and having a very hard time."

Then she saw that he hadn't succeeded in stopping feeling at all, only disciplined it to a doglike abjection at the back of his thinking mind. His eyes were so blue she felt she drowned in them, and what she saw in them now made her wonder what Meggie was to him, and what he was to Meggie.

"I *knew* something was wrong! I've felt that something was wrong for a long time, but of late my worry's become an obsession. I had to come and see for myself. Please, let me see her! If you wish for a reason, I am a priest."

Anne had never intended to deny him. "Come along, Your Grace, through here, please." And as she shuffled slowly between her two sticks she kept thinking: Is the house clean and tidy? Have I dusted? Did we remember to throw out that smelly old leg of lamb, or is it all through the place? What a time for a man as important as this one to come calling! Luddie, will you never get your fat arse off that tractor and come in? The boy should have found you hours ago!

He went past Doc Smith and the midwife as if they didn't exist to drop on his knees beside the bed, his hand reaching for hers.

"Meggie!"

She dragged herself out of the ghastly dream into which she had sunk, past caring, and saw the beloved face close to hers, the strong black hair with two white wings in its darkness now, the fine aristocratic features a little more lined, more patient if possible, and the blue eyes looking into hers with love and longing. How had she ever confused Luke with him? There was no one like him, there never would be for her, and she had betrayed what she felt for him. Luke was the dark side of the mirror; Ralph was as splendid as the sun, and as remote. Oh, how beautiful to see him!

"Ralph, help me," she said.

He kissed her hand passionately, then held it to his cheek. "Always, my Meggie, you know that."

"Pray for me, and the baby. If anyone can save us, you can. You're much closer to God than we are. No one wants us, no one has ever wanted us, even you."

"Where's Luke?"

"I don't know, and I don't care." She closed her eyes and rolled her head upon the plllow, but the fingers in his gripped strongly, wouldn't let him go.

Then Doc Smith touched him on the shoulder. "Your Grace, I think you ought to step outside now."

"If her life is in danger, you'll call me?"

"In a second."

Luddie had finally come in from the cane, frantic because there was no one to be seen and he didn't dare enter the bedroom.

"Anne, is she all right?" he asked as his wife came out with the Archbishop.

"So far. Doc won't commit himself, but I think he's got hope. Luddie, we have a visitor. This is Archbishop Ralph de Bricassart, an old friend of Meggie's."

Better versed than his wife, Luddie dropped on one knee and kissed the ring on the hand held out to him. "Sit down, Your Grace, talk to Anne. I'll go and put a kettle on for some tea."

"So you're Ralph," Anne said, propping her sticks against a bamboo table while the priest sat opposite her with the folds of his soutane falling about him, his glossy black riding boots clearly visible, for he had crossed his knees. It was an effeminate thing for a man to do, but he was a priest so it didn't matter; yet there was something intensely masculine about him, crossed legs or no. He was probably not as old as she had first thought; in his very early forties, perhaps. What a waste of a magnificent man!

"Yes, I'm Ralph."

"Ever since Meggie's labor started she's been asking for someone called Ralph. I must admit I was puzzled. I don't ever remember her mentioning a Ralph before."

"She wouldn't."

"How do you know Meggie, Your Grace? For how long?"

The priest smiled wryly and clasped his thin, very beautiful hands together so they made a pointed church roof. "I've known Meggie since she was ten years old, only days off the boat from New Zealand. You might in all truth say that I've known Meggie through flood and fire and emotional famine, and through death, and life. All that we have to bear. Meggie is the mirror in which I'm forced to view my mortality."

"You love her!" Anne's tone was surprised.

"Always."

"It's a tragedy for both of you."

"I had hoped only for me. Tell me about her, what's happened to her since she married. It's many years since I've seen her, but I haven't been happy about her."

"I'll tell you, but only after you've told me about Meggie. Oh, I don't mean personal things, only about what sort of life she led before she came to Dunny. We know absolutely nothing of her, Luddie and I, except that she used to live somewhere near Gillanbone. We'd like to know more, because we're very fond of her. But she would never tell us a thing—pride, I think."

Luddie carried in a tray loaded with tea and food, and sat down while the priest gave them an outline of Meggie's life before she married Luke.

"I would never have guessed it in a million years! To think Luke O'Neill had the temerity to take her from all that and put her to work as a housemaid! And had the hide to stipulate that her wages be put in *his* bankbook! Do you know the poor little thing has never had a penny in her purse to spend on herself since she's been here? I had Luddie give her a cash bonus last

Christmas, but by then she needed so many things it was all spent in a day, and she'd never take more from us."

"Don't feel sorry for Meggie," said Archbishop Ralph a little harshly. "I don't think she feels sorry for herself, certainly not over lack of money. It's brought little joy to her after all, has it? She knows where to go if she can't do without it. I'd say Luke's apparent indifference has hurt her far more than the lack of money. My poor Meggie!"

Between them Anne and Luddie filled in the outline of Meggie's life, while Archbishop de Bricassart sat, his hands still steepled, his gaze on the lovely sweeping fan of a traveler's palm outside. Not once did a muscle in his face move, or a change come into those detachedly beautiful eyes. He had learned much since being in the service of Vittorio Scarbanza, Cardinal di Contini-Verchese.

When the tale was done he sighed, and shifted his gaze to their anxious faces. "Well, it seems we must help her, since Luke will not. If Luke truly doesn't want her, she'd be better off back on Drogheda. I know you don't want to lose her, but for her sake try to persuade her to go home. I shall send you a check from Sydney for her, so she won't have the embarrassment of asking her brother for money. Then when she gets home she can tell them what she likes." He glanced toward the bedroom door and moved restlessly. "Dear God, let the child be born!"

But the child wasn't born until nearly twenty-four hours later, and Meggie almost dead from exhaustion and pain. Doc Smith had given her copious doses of laudanum, that still being the best thing, in his old-fashioned opinion; she seemed to drift whirling through spiraling nightmares in which things from without and within ripped and tore, clawed and spat, howled and whined and roared. Sometimes Ralph's face would come into focus for a small moment, then go again on a heaving tide of pain; but the memory of him persisted, and while he kept watch she knew neither she nor the baby would die.

Pausing, while the midwife coped alone, to snatch food and a stiff tot of rum and check that none of his other patients were inconsiderate enough to think of dying, Doc Smith listened to as much of the story as Anne and Luddie thought wise to tell him.

"You're right, Anne," he said. "All that riding is probably one of the reasons for her trouble now. When the sidesaddle went out it was a bad thing for women who must ride a lot. Astride develops the wrong muscles."

"I'd heard that was an old wives' tale," said the Archbishop mildly.

Doc Smith looked at him maliciously. He wasn't fond of Catholic priests, deemed them a sanctimonious lot of driveling fools.

"Think what you like," he said. "But tell me, Your Grace, if it came down to a choice between Meggie's life and the baby's, what would your conscience advise?"

"The Church is adamant on that point, Doctor. No choice must ever be made. The child cannot be done to death to save the mother, nor the mother done to death to save the child." He smiled back at Doc Smith just as maliciously. "But if it should come to that, Doctor, I won't hesitiate to tell you to save Meggie, and the hell with the baby."

Doc Smith gasped, laughed, and clapped him on the back. "Good for you! Rest easy, I won't broadcast what you said. But so far the child's alive, and I can't see what good killing it is going to do."

But Anne was thinking to herself: I wonder what your answer would have been if the child was yours, Archbishop?

About three hours later, as the afternoon sun was sliding sadly down the sky toward Mount Bartle Frere's misty bulk, Doc Smith came out of the bedroom.

"Well, it's over," he said with some satisfaction. "Meggie's got a long road ahead of her, but she'll be all right, God willing. And the baby is a skinny, cranky, five-pound girl with a whopping great head and a temper to match the most poisonous red hair I've ever seen on a newborn baby. You couldn't kill that little mite with an axe, and I know, because I nearly tried."

Jubilant, Luddie broke out the bottle of champagne he had been saving, and the five of them stood with their glasses brimming; priest, doctor, midwife, farmer and cripple toasted the health and well-being of the mother and her screaming, crotchety baby. It was the first of June, the first day of the Australian winter.

A nurse had arrived to take over from the midwife, and would stay until Meggie was pronounced out of all danger. The doctor and the midwife left, while Anne, Luddie and the Archbishop went to see Meggie.

She looked so tiny and wasted in the double bed that Archbishop Ralph was obliged to store away another, separate pain in the back of his mind, to be taken out later, inspected and endured. Meggie, my torn and beaten Meggie . . . I shall love you always, but I cannot give you what Luke O'Neill did, however grudgingly.

The grizzling scrap of humanity responsible for all this lay in a wicker bassinet by the far wall, not a bit appreciative of their attention as they stood around her and peered down. She yelled her resentment, and kept on yelling. In the end the nurse lifted her, bassinet and all, and put her in the room designated as her nursery.

"There's certainly nothing wrong with her lungs." Archbishop Ralph smiled, sitting on the edge of the bed and taking Meggie's pale hand.

"I don't think she likes life much," Meggie said with an answering smile. How much older he looked! As fit and supple as ever, but immeasurably older. She turned her head to Anne and Luddie, and held out her other hand. "My dear good friends! Whatever would I have done without you? Have we heard from Luke?"

"I got a telegram saying he was too busy to come, but wishing you good luck."

"Big of him," said Meggie.

Anne bent quickly to kiss her check. "We'll leave you to talk with the Archbishop, dear. I'm sure you've got a lot of catching up to do." Leaning on Luddie, she crooked her finger at the nurse, who was gaping at the priest as if she couldn't believe her eyes. "Come on, Nettie, have a cup of tea with us. His Grace will let you know if Meggie needs you."

"What are you going to call your noisy daughter?" he asked as the door closed and they were alone.

"Justine."

"It's a very good name, but why did you choose it?"

"I read it somewhere, and I liked it."

"Don't you want her, Meggie?"

Her face had shrunk, and seemed all eyes; they were soft and filled with a misty light, no hate but no love either. "I suppose I want her. Yes, I do want her. I schemed enough to get her. But while I was carrying her I couldn't feel anything for her, except that *she* didn't want me. I don't think Justine will ever be mine, or Luke's, or anyone's. I think she's always going to belong to herself."

"I must go, Meggie," he said gently.

Now the eyes grew harder, brighter: her mouth twisted into an unpleasant shape. "I expected *that!* Funny how the men in my life all scuttle off into the woodwork, isn't it?"

He winced. "Don't be bitter, Meggie. I can't bear to leave thinking of you like this. No matter what's happened to you in the past, you've always retained your sweetness and it's the thing about you I find most endearing. Don't change, don't become hard because of this. I know it must be terrible to think that Luke didn't care enough to come, but don't change. You wouldn't be my Meggie anymore."

But still she looked at him half as if she hated him. "Oh, come off it, Ralph! I'm not your Meggie, I never was! You didn't want me, you sent me to him, to Luke. What do you think I am, some sort of saint, or a nun? Well, I'm not! I'm an ordinary human being, and you've spoiled my life! All the years I've loved you, and wanted to forget you, but then I married a man I thought looked a little bit like you, and he doesn't want me or need me either. Is it so much to ask of a man, to be needed and wanted by him?"

She began to sob, mastered it; there were fine lines of pain on her face that he had never seen before, and he knew they weren't the kind that rest and returning health would smooth away.

"Luke's not a bad man, or even an unlikable one," she went on. "Just a man. You're all the same, great big hairy moths bashing yourselves to pieces after a silly flame behind a glass so clear your eyes don't see it. And if you do manage to blunder your way inside the glass to fly into the flame, you fall down burned and dead. While all the time out there in the cool night there's food, and love, and baby moths to get. But do you see it, do you want it? No! It's back after the flame again, beating yourselves senseless until you burn yourselves dead!"

He didn't know what to say to her, for this was a side of her he had never seen. Had it always been there, or had she grown it out of her terrible trouble and abandonment? Meggie, saying things like this? He hardly heard what she said, he was so upset that she should say it, and so didn't understand that it came from her loneliness, and her guilt.

"Do you remember the rose you gave me the night I left Drogheda?" he asked tenderly.

"Yes, I remember." The life had gone out of her voice, the hard light out of her eyes. They stared at him now like a soul without hope, as expressionless and glassy as her mother's.

"I have it still, in my missal. And every time I see a rose that color, I think of you. Meggie, I love you. You're my rose, the most beautiful human image and thought in my life."

Down went the corners of her mouth again, up shone that tense, glittering fierceness with the tang of hate in it. "An image, a thought! A *human* image and thought! Yes, that's right, that's all I am to you! You're nothing but a romantic, dreaming fool, Ralph de Bricassart! You have no more idea of what life is all about than the moth I called you! No wonder you became a priest! You couldn't live with the ordinariness of life if you were an ordinary man any more than ordinary man Luke does!

"You say you love me, but you have no idea what love is; you're just mouthing words you've memorized because you think they sound good! What floors me is why you men haven't managed to dispense with us women altogether, which is what you'd like to do, isn't it? You should work out a way of marrying each other; you'd be divinely happy!"

"Meggie, don't! Please don't!"

"Oh, go away! I don't want to look at you! And you've forgotten one thing about your precious roses, Ralph—they've got nasty, hooky thorns!"

He left the room without looking back.

Luke never bothered to answer the telegram informing him he was the proud father of a five-pound girl named Justine. Slowly Meggie got better, and the baby began to thrive. Perhaps if Meggie could have managed to feed her she might have developed more rapport with the scrawny, bad-tempered little thing, but she had absolutely no milk in the plenteous breasts Luke had so loved to suck. That's an ironic justice, she thought. She dutifully changed and bottle-fed the red-faced, redheaded morsel just as custom dictated she should, waiting for the commencement of some wonderful, surging emotion. But it never came; she felt no desire to smother the tiny face with kisses, or bite the wee fingers, or do any of the thousand silly things mothers loved to do with babies. It didn't feel like her baby, and it didn't want or need her any more than she did it. It, it! Her, her! She couldn't even remember to call it her.

Luddie and Anne never dreamed Meggie did not adore Justine, that she felt less for Justine than she had for any of her mother's younger babies. Whenever Justine cried Meggie was right there to pick her up, croon to her, rock her, and never was a baby drier or more comfortable. The strange thing was that Justine didn't seem to want to be picked up or crooned over; she quieted much faster if she was left alone.

As time went on she improved in looks. Her infant skin lost its redness, acquired that thin blue-veined transparency which goes so often with red hair, and her little arms and legs filled out to pleasing plumpness. The hair began to curl and thicken and to assume forever the same violent shade her grandfather Paddy had owned. Everyone waited anxiously to see what color her eyes would turn out to be, Luddie betting on her father's blue, Anne on her mother's grey, Meggie without an opinion. But Justine's eyes were very definitely her own, and unnerving to say the least. At six weeks they began to change, and by the ninth week had gained their final color and form. No one had even seen anything like them. Around the outer rim of the iris was a very dark grey ring, but the iris itself was so pale it couldn't be called either blue or grey; the closest description of the color was a sort of dark white. They were riveting, uncomfortable, inhuman eyes, rather blind-looking; but as time went on it was obvious Justine saw through them very well.

Though he didn't mention it, Doc Smith had been worried by the size of her head when she was born, and kept a close watch on it for the first six months of her life; he had wondered, especially after seeing those strange eyes, if she didn't perhaps have what he still called water on the brain, though the textbooks these days were calling it hydrocephalus. But it appeared Justine wasn't suffering from any kind of cerebral dysfunction or malformation; she just had a very big head, and as she grew the rest of her more or less caught up to it.

Luke stayed away. Meggie had written to him repeatedly, but he neither answered nor came to see his child. In a way she was glad; she wouldn't have known what to say to him, and she didn't think he would be at all entranced with the odd little creature who was his daughter. Had Justine been a strapping big son he might have relented, but Meggie was fiercely glad she wasn't. She was living proof the great Luke O'Neill wasn't perfect, for if he was he would surely have sired nothing but sons.

The baby thrived better than Meggie did, recovered faster from the birth ordeal. By the time she was four months old she ceased to cry so much and began to amuse herself as she lay in her bassinet, fiddling and pinching at the rows of brightly colored beads strung within her reach. But she never smiled at anyone, even in the guise of gas pains.

The Wet came early, in October, and it was a very wet Wet. The humidity climbed to 100 percent and stayed there; every day for hours the rain roared and whipped about Himmelhoch, melting the scarlet soil, drenching the cane, filling the wide, deep Dungloe River but not overflowing it, for its course was so short the water got away into the sea quickly enough. While Justine lay in her bassinet contemplating her world through those strange eyes, Meggie sat dully watching Bartle Frere disappear behind a wall of dense rain, then reappear.

The sun would come out, writhing veils of steam issue from the ground, the wet cane shimmer and sparkle diamond prisms, and the river seem like a great gold snake. Then hanging right across the vault of the sky a double rainbow would materialize, perfect throughout its length on both bows, so rich in its coloring against the sullen dark-blue clouds that all save a North Queensland landscape would have been paled and diminished. Being North Queensland, nothing was washed out by its ethereal glow, and Meggie thought she knew why the Gillanbone countryside was so brown and grey; North Queensland had usurped its share of the palette as well.

One day at the beginning of December, Anne came out onto the veranda and sat down beside her, watching her. Oh, she was so thin, so lifeless! Even the lovely goldy hair had dulled.

"Meggie, I don't know whether I've done the wrong thing, but I've done it anyway, and I want you at least to listen to me before you say no."

Meggie turned from the rainbows, smiling. "You sound so solemn, Anne! What is it I must listen to?"

"Luddie and I are worried about you. You haven't picked up properly since Justine was born, and now The Wet's here you're looking even worse. You're not eating and you're losing weight. I've never thought the climate here agreed with you, but as long as nothing happened to drag you down you managed to cope with it. Now we think you're sick, and unless something's done you're going to get really ill."

She drew a breath. "So a couple of weeks ago I wrote to a friend of mine in the tourist bureau, and booked you a holiday. And don't start protesting about the expense; it won't dent Luke's resources or ours. The Archbishop sent us a very big check for you, and your brother sent us another one for you and the baby—I think he was hinting go home for a while—from everyone on Drogheda. And after we talked it over, Luddie and I decided the best thing we could do was spend some of it on a holiday for you. I don't think going home to Drogheda is the right sort of holiday, though. What Luddie and I feel you need most is a thinking time. No Justine, no us, no Luke, no Drogheda. Have you ever been on your own, Meggie? It's time you were. So we've booked you a cottage on Matlock Island for two months, from the beginning of January to the beginning of March. Luddie and I will look after Justine. You know she won't come to any harm, but if we're the slightest bit worried about her, you have our word we'll notify you right away, and the island's on the phone so it wouldn't take long to fetch you back."

The rainbows had gone, so had the sun; it was getting ready to rain again.

"Anne, if it hadn't been for you and Luddie these past three years, I would have gone mad. You know that. Sometimes in the night I wake up wondering what would have happened to me had Luke put me with people less kind. You've cared for me more than Luke has."

"Twaddle! If Luke had put you with unsympathetic people you would have gone back to Drogheda, and who knows? Maybe that might have been the best course."

"No. It hasn't been pleasant, this thing with Luke, but it was far better for me to stay and work it out."

The rain was beginning to inch its way across the dimming cane blotting out everything behind its edge, like a grey cleaver.

"You're right, I'm not well," Meggie said. "I haven't been well since Justine was conceived. I've tried to pull myself up, but I suppose one reaches a point where there isn't the energy to do it. Oh, Anne, I'm so tired and discouraged! I'm not even a good mother to Justine, and I owe her that. I'm the one caused her to be; she didn't ask for it. But mostly I'm discouraged because Luke won't even give me a chance to make him happy. He won't live with me or let me make a home for him; he doesn't want our children. I don't love him —I never did love him the way a woman ought to love the man she marries, and maybe he sensed it from the word go. Maybe if I had loved him, he would have acted differently. So how can I blame him? I've only myself to blame, I think."

"It's the Archbishop you love, isn't it?"

"Oh, ever since I was a little girl! I was hard on him when he came. Poor Ralph! I had no right to say what I did to him, because he never encouraged me, you know. I hope he's had time to understand that I was in pain, worn out, and terribly unhappy. All I could think was it ought by rights to be his child and it never would be, never could be. It isn't fair! Protestant clergy can marry, why can't Catholic? And don't try to tell me ministers don't care for their flocks the way priests do, because I won't believe you. I've met heartless priests and wonderful ministers. But because of the celibacy of priests I've had to go away from Ralph, make my home and my life with someone else, have someone else's baby. And do you know something, Anne? That's as disgusting a sin as Ralph breaking his vows, or more so. I resent the Church's implication that my loving Ralph or his loving me is wrong!"

"Go away for a while, Meggie. Rest and eat and sleep and stop fretting. Then maybe when you come back you can somehow persuade Luke to buy that station instead of talking about it. I know you don't love him, but I think if he gave you half a chance you might be happy with him."

The grey eyes were the same color as the rain falling in sheets all around the house; their voices had risen to shouting pitch to be audible above the incredible din on the iron roof.

"But that's just it, Anne! When Luke and I went up to Atherton I realized at last that he'll never leave the sugar while he's got the strength to cut it. He loves the life, he really does. He loves being with men as strong and independent as he is himself; he loves roaming from one place to the other. He's always been a wanderer, now I come to think of it. As for needing a woman for pleasure if nothing else, he's too exhausted by the cane. And how can I put it? Luke is the kind of man who quite genuinely doesn't care if he eats his food off a packing crate and sleeps on the floor. Don't you see? One can't appeal to him as to one who likes nice things, because he doesn't. Sometimes I think he despises nice things, pretty things. They're soft, they might make him soft. I have absolutely no enticements powerful enough to sway him from his present way of life."

She glanced up impatiently at the veranda roof, as if tired of shouting. "I don't know if I'm strong enough to take the loneliness of having no home for the next ten or fifteen years, Anne, or however long it's going to take Luke to wear himself out. It's lovely here with you; I don't want you to think I'm ungrateful. But I want a *home!* I want Justine to have brothers and sisters, I want to dust my own furniture, I want to make curtains for my own windows, cook on my own stove for my own man. Oh, Anne! I'm just an ordinary sort of a woman; I'm not ambitious or intelligent or well educated, you know that. All I want is a husband, children, my own home. And a bit of love from *someone!*"

Anne got out her handkerchief, wiped her eyes and tried to laugh. "What a soppy pair we are! But I do understand, Meggie, really I do. I've been married to Luddie for ten years, the only truly happy ones of my life. I had infantile paralysis when I was five years old, and it left me like this. I was convinced no one would ever look at me. Nor did they, God knows. When I met Luddie I was thirty years old, teaching for a living. He was ten years younger than me, so I couldn't take him seriously when he said he loved me and wanted to marry me. How terrible, Meggie, to ruin a very young man's life! For five years I treated him to the worst display of downright nastiness you could imagine, but he always came back for more. So I married him, and I've been happy. Luddie says he is, but I'm not sure. He's had to give up a lot, including children, and he looks older than I do these days, poor chap."

"It's the life, Anne, and the climate."

The rain stopped as suddenly as it had begun; the sun came out, the rainbows waxed to full glory in the steamy sky, Mount Bartle Frere loomed lilac out of the scudding clouds.

Meggie spoke again. "I'll go. I'm very grateful to you for thinking of it; it's probably what I need. But are you sure Justine won't be too much trouble?"

"Lord, no! Luddie's got it all worked out. Anna Maria, who used to work for me before you came, has a younger sister, Annunziata, who wants to go nursing in Townsville. But she won't be sixteen until March, and she finishes school in a few days. So while you're away she's going to come here. She's an expert foster mother, too. There are hordes of babies in the Tesoriero clan."

"Matlock Island. Where is it?"

"Just near Whitsunday Passage on the Great Barrier Reef. It's very quiet and private, mostly a honeymoon resort, I suppose. You know the sort of thing—cottages instead of a central hotel. You won't have to go to dinner in a crowded dining room, or be civil to a whole heap of people you'd rather not talk to at all. And at this time of year it's just about deserted, because of the danger of summer cyclones. The Wet isn't a problem, but no one ever seems to want to go to the Reef in summer. Probably because most of the people who go to the Reef come from Sydney or Melbourne, and summer down there is lovely without going away. In June and July and August the southerners have it booked out for three years ahead."

13

On the last day of 1937 Meggie caught the train to Townsville. Though her holiday had scarcely begun, she already felt much better, for she had left the molasses reek of Dunny behind her. The biggest settlement in North Queensland, Townsville was a thriving town of several thousands living in white wooden houses atop stilts. A tight connection between train and boat left her with no time to explore, but in a way Meggie wasn't sorry she had to rush to the wharf without a chance to think; after that ghastly voyage across the Tasman sixteen years ago she wasn't looking forward to thirty-six hours in a ship much smaller than the *Wahine*.

But it was quite different, a whispering slide in glassy waters, and she was twenty-six, not ten. The air was between cyclones, the sea was exhausted; though it was only midday Meggie put her head down and slept dreamlessly until the steward woke her at six the next morning with a cup of tea and a plate of plain sweet biscuits.

Up on deck was a new Australia, different again. In a high clear sky, delicately colorless, a pink and pearly glow suffused slowly upward from the eastern rim of the ocean until the sun stood above the horizon and the light lost its neonatal redness, became day. The ship was slithering soundlessly through water which had no taint, so translucent over the side that one could look fathoms down to grottoes of purple and see the forms of vivid fish flashing by. In distant vistas the sea was a greenish-hued aquamarine, splotched with wine-dark stains where weed or coral covered the floor, and on all sides it seemed islands with palmy shores of brilliant white sand just grew out of it spontaneously like crystals in silica—jungle-clad and mountainous islands or flat, bushy islands not much higher than the water.

"The flat ones are the true coral islands," explained a crewman. "If they're ring-shaped and enclose a lagoon they're called atolls, but if they're just a lump of reef risen above the sea they're called cays. The hilly islands are the tops of mountains, but they're still surrounded by coral reefs, and they have lagoons."

"Where's Matlock Island?" Meggie asked.

He looked at her curiously; a lone woman going on holiday to a honeymoon island like Matlock was a contradiction in terms. "We're sailing down Whitsunday Passage now, then we head out to the Pacific edge of the reef. Matlock's ocean side is pounded by the big breakers that come in for a hundred miles off the deep Pacific like express trains, roaring so you can't hear yourself think. Can you imagine riding the same wave for a hundred miles?" He sighed wistfully. "We'll be at Matlock before sundown, madam."

And an hour before sundown the little ship heaved its way through the backwash of the surf whose spume rose like a towering misty wall into the eastern sky. A jetty on spindling piles doddered literally half a mile out across the reef exposed by low tide, behind it a high, craggy coastline which didn't fit in with Meggie's expectations of tropical splendor. An elderly man stood waiting, helped her from ship to jetty, and took her cases from a crewman.

"How d'you do, Mrs. O'Neill," he greeted her. "I'm Rob Walter. Hope your husband gets the chance to come after all. Not too much company on Matlock this time of year; it's really a winter resort."

They walked together down the uneasy planking, the exposed coral molten in the dying sun and the fearsome sea a reflected, tumultuous glory of crimson foam.

"Tide's out, or you'd have had a rougher trip. See the mist in the east? That's the edge of the Great Barrier Reef itself. Here on Matlock we hang onto it by the skin of our teeth; you'll feel the island shaking all the time from the pounding out there." He helped her into a car. "This is the windward side of Matlock—a bit wild and unwelcome looking, eh? But you wait until you see the leeward side, ah! Something like, it is."

They hurtled with the careless speed natural to the only car on Matlock down a narrow road of crunchy coral bones, through palms and thick undergrowth with a tall hill rearing to one side, perhaps four miles across the island's spine.

"Oh, how beautiful!" said Meggie.

They had emerged on another road which ran all around the looping sandy shores of the lagoon side, crescent-shaped and hollow. Far out was more white spray where the ocean broke in dazzling lace on the edges of the lagoon reef, but within the coral's embrace the water was still and calm, a polished silver mirror tinged with bronze.

"Island's four miles wide and eight long," her guide explained. They drove past a straggling white building with a deep veranda and shoplike windows. "The general store," he said with a proprietary flourish. "I live there with the Missus, and she's not too happy about a lone woman coming here, I can tell you. Thinks I'll be seduced was how she put it. Just as well the bureau said you wanted complete peace and quiet, because it soothed the Missus a bit when I put you in the farthest-out place we have. There's not a soul in your direction; the only other couple here are on the other side. You can lark around without a stitch on—no one will see you. The Missus isn't going to let me out of her sight while you're here. When you need something, just pick up your phone and I'll bring it out. No sense walking all the way in. And Missus or no, I'll call in on you once a day at sunset, just to make sure you're all right. Best that you're in the house then—and wear a proper dress, in case the Missus comes along for the ride."

A one-story structure with three rooms, the cottage had its own private curve of white beach between two prongs of the hill diving into the sea, and here the road ended. Inside it was very plain, but comfortable. The island generated its own power, so there was a little refrigerator, electric light, the promised phone, and even a wireless set. The toilet flushed, the bath had fresh water; more modern amenities than either Drogheda or Himmelhoch, Meggie thought in amusement. Easy to see most of the patrons were from Sydney or Melbourne, and so inured to civilization they couldn't do without it.

Left alone while Rob sped back to his suspicious Missus, Meggie unpacked and surveyed her domain. The big double bed was a great deal more comfortable than her own nuptial couch had been. But then, this was a genuine honeymoon paradise and the one thing its clients would demand was a decent bed; the clients of the Dunny pub were usually too drunk to object to herniating springs. Both the refrigerator and the overhead cupboards were well stocked with food, and on the counter stood a great basket of bananas, passionfruit, pineapples and mangoes. No reason why she shouldn't sleep well, and eat well.

For the first week Meggie seemed to do nothing but eat and sleep; she hadn't realized how tired she was, nor that Dungloe's climate was what had killed her appetite. In the beautiful bed she slept the moment she lay down, ten and twelve hours at a stretch, and food had an appeal it hadn't possessed since Drogheda. She seemed to eat every minute she was awake, even carrying mangoes into the water with her. Truth to tell, that was the most logical place to eat mangoes other than a bathtub; they just ran juice. Since her tiny beach lay within the lagoon, the sea was mirror calm and quite free of currents, very shallow. All of which she loved, because she couldn't swim a stroke. But in water so salty it seemed almost to hold her up, she began to experiment; when she could float for ten seconds at a time she was delighted. The sensation of being freed from the pull of the earth made her long to be able to move as easily as a fish.

So if she mourned her lack of company, it was only because she would have liked to have someone to teach her to swim. Other than that, being on her own was wonderful. How right Anne had been! All her life there had been people in the house. To have no one was such a relief, so utterly peaceful. She wasn't lonely at all; she didn't miss Anne or Luddie or Justine or Luke, and for the first time in three years she didn't yearn for Drogheda. Old Rob never disturbed her solitude, just chugged far enough down the road each sunset to make sure her friendly wave from the veranda wasn't a signal of distress, turned the car and puttered off again, his surprisingly pretty Missus grimly riding shotgun. Once he phoned her to say he was taking the other couple in residence out in his glass-bottomed boat, and would she like to come along?

It was like having a ticket of admission to a whole new planet, peering through the glass down into that teeming, exquisitely fragile world, where delicate forms were buoyed and bolstered by the loving intimacy of water. Live coral, she discovered, wasn't garishly hued from dyes the way it was in the souvenir counter of the store. It was soft pink or beige or blue-grey, and around every knob and branch wavered a marvelous rainbow of color, like a visible aura. Great anemones twelve inches wide fluttered fringes of blue or red or orange or purple tentacles; white fluted clams as big as rocks beckoned unwary explorers to take a look inside with tantalizing glimpses of colorful, restless things through feathery lips; red lace fans swayed in water winds;

bright-green ribbons of weed danced loose and drifting. Not one of the four in the boat would have been in the least surprised to see a mermaid: a gleam of polished breast, a twisting glitter of tail, lazily spinning clouds of hair, an alluring smile taunting the siren's spell to sailors. But the fish! Like living jewels they darted in thousands upon thousands, round like Chinese lanterns, slender like bullets, raimented in colors which glowed with life and the light-splitting quality water imparts, some on fire with scales of gold and scarlet, some cool and silvery blue, some swimming rag bags gaudier than parrots. There were needle-nosed garfish, pug-nosed toadfish, fanged barracuda, a cavernous-mawed grouper lurking half seen in a grotto, and once a sleek grey nurse shark which seemed to take forever to pass silently beneath them.

"But don't worry," said Rob. "We're too far south here for sea wasps, so if anything on the Reef is going to kill you, it's most likely to be a stonefish. Never go walking on the coral without your shoes."

Yes, Meggie was glad she went. But she didn't yearn to go again, or make friends with the couple Rob brought along. She immersed herself in the sea, and walked, and lay in the sun. Curiously enough, she didn't even miss having books to read, for there always seemed to be something interesting to watch.

She had taken Rob's advice and stopped wearing clothes. At first she had tended to behave like a rabbit catching whiffs of dingo on the breeze, bolting for cover if a twig cracked or a coconut fell like a cannonball from a palm. But after several days of patent solitude she really began to feel no one would come near her, that indeed it was as Rob said, a completely private domain. Shyness was wasted. And walking the tracks, lying in the sand, paddling in that warm salty water, she began to feel like an animal born and brought up in a cage, suddenly let loose in a gentle, sunny, spacious and welcoming world.

Away from Fee, her brothers, Luke, the unsparing, unthinking domination of her whole life, Meggie discovered pure leisure; a whole kaleidoscope of thought patterns wove and unwove novel designs in her mind. For the first time in her life she wasn't keeping her conscious self absorbed in work thoughts of one description or another. Surprised, she realized that keeping physically busy is the most effective blockade against totally mental activity human beings can erect.

Years ago Father Ralph had asked her what she thought about, and she had answered: Daddy and Mum, Bob, Jack, Hughie, Stu, the little boys, Frank, Drogheda, the house, work, the rainfall. She hadn't said him, but he was at the top of the list, always. Now add to those Justine, Luke, Luddie and Anne, the cane, homesickness, the rainfall. And always, of course, the lifesaving release she found in books. But it had all come and gone in such tangled, unrelated clumps and chains; no opportunity, no *training* to enable her to sit down quietly and think out who exactly was Meggie Cleary, Meggie O'Neill? What did she want? What did she think she was put on this earth for? She mourned the lack of training, for that was an omission no amount of time on her own could ever rectify. However, here was the time, the peace, the laziness of idle physical well-being; she could lie on the sand and try.

Well, there was Ralph. A wry, despairing laugh. Not a good place to start, but in a sense Ralph was like God; everything began and ended with him. Since the day he had knelt in the sunset dust of the Gilly station yard to take her between his hands, there had been Ralph, and though she never saw him again as long as she lived, it seemed likely that her last thought this side of the grave would be of him. How frightening, that one person could mean so much, so many things.

What had she said to Anne? That her wants and needs were quite ordinary—a husband, children, a home of her own. Someone to love. It didn't seem much to ask; after all, most women had the lot. But how many of the women who had them were truly content? Meggie thought she would be, because for her they were so hard to come by.

Accept it, Meggie Cleary. Meggie *O'Neill*. The someone you want is Ralph de Bricassart, and you just can't have him. Yet as a man he seems to have ruined you for anyone else. All right, then. Assume that a man and the someone to love can't occur. It will have to be children to love, and the love you receive will have to come from those children. Which in turn means Luke, and Luke's children.

Oh, dear God, dear God! No, not *dear* God! What's God ever done for me, except deprive me of Ralph? We're not too fond of each other, God and I. And do You know something, God? You don't frighten me the way You used to. How much I feared You, Your punishment! All my life I've trodden the straight and narrow, from fear of You. And what's it got me? Not one scrap more than if I'd broken every rule in Your book. You're a fraud, God, a demon of fear. You treat us like children, dangling punishment. But You don't frighten me anymore. Because it isn't Ralph I ought to be hating, it's You. It's all Your fault, not poor Ralph's. He's just living in fear of You, the way I always have. That he could love You is something I can't understand. I don't see what there is about You to love.

Yet how can I stop loving a man who loves God? No matter how hard I try, I can't seem to do it. He's the moon, and I'm crying for it. Well, you've just got to stop crying for it, Meggie O'Neill, that's all there is to it. You're going to have to content yourself with Luke, and Luke's children. By hook or by crook you're going to wean Luke from the wretched sugar, and live with him out where there aren't even any trees. You're going to tell the Gilly bank manager that your future income stays in your own name, and you're going to use it to have the comforts and conveniences in your treeless home that Luke won't think to provide for you. You're going to use it to educate Luke's children properly, and make sure they never want.

And that's all there is to be said about it, Meggie O'Neill. I'm Meggie O'Neill, not Meggie de Bricassart. It even sounds silly, Meggie de Bricassart. I'd have to be Meghann de Bricassart, and I've always hated Meghann. Oh, will I ever stop regretting that they're not Ralph's children? That's the question, isn't it? Say it to yourself, over and over again: Your life is your own, Meggie O'Neill, and you're *not* going to waste it dreaming of a man and children you can never have.

There! That's telling yourself! No use thinking of what's past, what *must* be buried. The future's the thing, and the future belongs to Luke, to Luke's children. It doesn't belong to Ralph de Bricassart. He is the past.

Meggie rolled over in the sand and wept as she hadn't wept since she was three years old: noisy wails, with only the crabs and the birds to hear her desolation.

Anne Mueller had chosen Matlock Island deliberately, planning to send Luke there as soon as she could. The moment Meggie was on her way she sent Luke a telegram saying Meggie needed him desperately, please to come. By nature she wasn't given to interfering in other people's lives, but she loved and pitied Meggie, and adored the difficult, capricious scrap Meggie had borne and Luke fathered. Justine must have a home, and both her parents. It would hurt to see her go away, but better that than the present situation.

Luke arrived two days later. He was on his way to the CSR in Sydney, so it didn't cost him much time to go out of his way. Time he saw the baby; if it had been a boy he would have come when it was born, but news of a girl had disappointed him badly. If Meggie insisted on having children, let them at least be capable of carrying on the Kynuna station one day. Girls were no flaming use at all; they just ate a man out of house and home and when they were grown up they went and worked for someone else instead of staying put like boys to help their old father in his last years.

"How's Meg?" he asked as he came up onto the front veranda. "Not sick, I hope?"

"You hope. No, she's not sick. I'll tell you in a minute. But first come and see your beautiful daughter."

He stared down at the baby, amused and interested but not emotionally moved, Anne thought.

"She's got the queerest eyes I've ever seen," he said. "I wonder whose they are?"

"Meggie says as far as she knows no one in her family."

"Nor mine. She's a throwback, the funny little thing. Doesn't look too happy, does she?"

"How could she look happy?" Anne snapped, hanging on to her temper grimly. "She's never seen her father, she has no real home and not much likelihood of one before she's grown up if you go on the way you are!"

"I'm saving, Anne!" he protested.

"Rubbish! I know how much money you've got. Friends of mine in Charters Towers send me the local paper from time to time, so I've seen the ads for western properties a lot closer in than Kynuna, and a lot more fertile. There's a Depression on, Luke! You could pick up a beauty of a place for a lot less by far than the amount you have in the bank, and you know it."

"Now that's just it! There's a Depression on, and west of the ranges a bloody terrible drought from Junee to the Isa. It's in its second year and there's no rain at all, not a drop. Right now I'll bet Drogheda's hurting, so what do you think it's like out around Winton and Blackall? No, I reckon I ought to wait."

"Wait until the price of land goes up in a good wet season? Come off it, Luke! Now's the time to buy! With Meggie's assured two thousand a year, you can wait out a ten-year drought! Just don't stock the place. Live on Meggie's two thousand a year until the rains come, then put your stock on."

"I'm not ready to leave the sugar yet," he said, stubbornly, still staring at his daughter's strange light eyes.

"And that's the truth at last, isn't it? Why don't you admit it, Luke? You don't want to be married, you'd rather live the way you are at the moment, hard, among men, working your innards out, just like one out of every two Australian men I've ever known! What is it about this frigging country, that its men prefer being with other men to having a home life with their wives and children? If the bachelor's life is what they truly want, why on earth do they try marriage at all? Do you know how many deserted wives there are in Dunny alone, scraping an existence and trying to rear their children without fathers? Oh, he's just off in the sugar, he'll be back, you know, it's only for a little while. Hah! And every mail they're there hanging over the front gate waiting for the postie, hoping the bastard's sent them a little money. And mostly he hasn't, sometimes he has—not enough, but something to keep things going!"

She was trembling with rage, her gentle brown eyes sparking. "You know, I read in the *Brisbane Mail* that Australia has the highest percentage of deserted wives in the civilized world? It's the only thing we beat every other country at—isn't that a record to be proud of!"

"Go easy, Anne! I haven't deserted Meg; she's safe and she's not starving. What's the matter with you?"

"I'm sick of the way you treat your wife, that's what! For the love of God, Luke, grow up, shoulder your responsibilities for a while! You've got a wife and baby! You should be making a home for them—be a husband and a father, not a bloody stranger!"

"I will, I will! But I can't yet; I've got to carry on in the sugar for a couple more years just to make sure. I don't want to say I'm living off Meg, which is what I'd be doing until things got better."

Anne lifted her lip contemptuously. "Oh, bullshit! You married her for her money, didn't you?"

A dark-red flush stained his brown face. He wouldn't look at her. "I admit the money helped, but I married her because I liked her better than anyone else."

"You *liked* her! What about loving her?"

"Love! What's love? Nothing but a figment of women's imagination, that's all." He turned away from the crib and those unsettling eyes, not sure someone with eyes like that couldn't understand what was being said. "And if you've quite finished telling me off, where's Meg?"

"She wasn't well. I sent her away for a while. Oh, don't panic! Not on your money. I was hoping I could persuade you to join her, but I see that's impossible."

"Out of the question. Arne and I are on our way to Sydney tonight."

"What shall I tell Meggie when she comes back?"

He shrugged, dying to get away. "I don't care. Oh, tell her to hang on a while longer. Now that she's gone ahead with the family business, I wouldn't mind a son."

Leaning against the wall for support, Anne bent over the wicker basket and lifted the baby up, then managed to shuffle to the bed and sit down. Luke made no move to help her, or take the baby; he looked rather frightened of his daughter.

"Go away, Luke! You don't deserve what you've got. I'm sick of the sight of you. Go back to bloody Arne, and the flaming sugar, and the backbreak!"

At the door he paused. "What did she call it? I've forgotten its name."

"Justine, Justine, *Justine!*"

"Bloody stupid name," he said, and went out.

Anne put Justine on the bed and burst into tears. God damn all men but Luddie, God damn them! Was it the soft, sentimental, almost womanish streak in Luddie made him capable of loving? Was Luke right? Was it just a figment of women's imaginations? Or was it something only women were able to feel, or men with a little woman in them? No woman could ever hold Luke, no woman ever had. What he wanted no woman could ever give him.

But by the next day she had calmed down, no longer feeling she had tried for nothing. A postcard from Meggie had come that morning, waxing enthusiastic about Matlock Island and how well she was. Something good had come out of it. Meggie was feeling better. She would come back as the monsoons diminished and be able to face her life. But Anne resolved not to tell her about Luke.

So Nancy, short for Annunziata, carried Justine out onto the front veranda, while Anne hobbled out with the baby's wants in a little basket between her teeth; clean diaper, tin of powder and toys. She settled in a cane chair, took the baby from Nancy and began to feed her from the bottle of Lactogen Nancy had warmed. It was very pleasant, life was very pleasant; she had done her best to make Luke see sense, and if she had failed, at least it meant Meggie and Justine would remain at Himmelhoch a while longer. She had no doubt that eventually Meggie would realize there was no hope of salvaging her relationship with Luke, and would then return to Drogheda. But Anne dreaded the day.

A red English sports car roared off the Dunny road and up the long, hilly drive; it was new and expensive, its bonnet strapped down with leather, its silver exhausts and scarlet paintwork glittering. For a while she didn't recognize the man who vaulted over the low door, for he wore the North Queensland uniform of a pair of shorts and nothing else. My word, what a beautiful bloke! she thought, watching him appreciatively and with a twinge of memory as he took the steps two at a time. I wish Luddie wouldn't eat so much; he could do with a bit of this chap's condition. Now, he's no chicken—look at those marvelous silver temples—but I've never seen a cane cutter in better nick.

When the calm, aloof eyes looked into hers, she realized who he was.

"My God!" she said, and dropped the baby's bottle.

He retrieved it, handed it to her and leaned against the veranda railing, facing her: "It's all right. The teat didn't strike the ground; you can feed her with it."

The baby was just beginning a deprived quiver. Anne stuck the rubber in her mouth and got enough breath back to speak. "Well, Your Grace, this *is* a surprise!" Her eyes slid over him, amused. "I must say you don't exactly look like an archbishop. Not that you ever did, even in the proper togs. I always imagine archbishops of any religious denomination to be fat and self-satisfied."

"At the moment I'm not an archbishop, only a priest on a well-earned holiday, so you can call me Ralph. Is this the little thing caused Meggie so much trouble when I was here last? May I have her? I think I can manage to hold the bottle at the appropriate angle."

He settled into a chair alongside Anne, took baby and bottle and continued to feed her, his legs crossed casually.

"Did Meggie name her Justine?"

"Yes."

"I like it. Good Lord, look at the color of her hair! Her grandfather all over."

"That's what Meggie says. I hope the poor little mite doesn't come out in a million freckles later on, but I think she will."

"Well, Meggie's sort of a redhead and she isn't a bit freckled. Though Meggie's skin is a different color and texture, more opaque." He put the empty bottle down, sat the baby bolt upright on his knee, facing him, bent her forward in a salaam and began rhythmically rubbing her back hard. "Among my other duties I have to visit Catholic orphanages, so I'm quite deedy with babies. Mother Gonzaga at my favorite infants' home always says this is the only way to burp a baby. Holding it over one's shoulder doesn't flex the body forward enough, the wind can't escape so easily, and when it does come up there's usually lots of milk as well. This way the baby's bent in the middle, which corks the milk in while it lets the gas escape." As if to prove his point, Justine gave several huge eructations but held her gorge. He laughed, rubbed again, and when nothing further happened settled her in the crook of his arm comfortably. "What fabulously exotic eyes! Magnificent, aren't they? Trust Meggie to have an unusual baby."

"Not to change the subject, but what a father you'd have made, Father."

"I like babies and children, I always have. It's much easier for me to enjoy them, since I don't have any of the unpleasant duties fathers do."

"No, it's because you're like Luddie. You've got a bit of woman in you."

Apparently Justine, normally so isolationist, returned his liking; she had gone to sleep. Ralph settled her more snugly and pulled a packet of Capstans from his shorts pocket.

"Here, give them to me. I'll light one for you."

"Where's Meggie?" he asked, taking a lit cigarette from her. "Thank you. I'm sorry, please take one for yourself."

"She's not here. She never really got over the bad time she had when Justine was born, and The Wet seemed to be the last straw. So Luddie and I sent her away for two months. She'll be back around the first of March; another seven weeks to go."

The moment Anne spoke she was aware of the change in him; as if the whole of his purpose had suddenly evaporated, and the promise of some very special pleasure.

He drew a long breath. "This is the second time I've come to say goodbye and not found her. . . . Athens, and now again. I was away for a year then and it might have been a lot longer; I didn't know at the time. I had never visited Drogheda since Paddy and Stu died, yet when it came I found I couldn't leave Australia without seeing Meggie. And she'd married, gone away. I wanted to come after her, but I knew it wouldn't have been fair to her or to Luke. This time I came because I knew I couldn't harm what isn't there."

"Where are you going?"

"To Rome, to the Vatican. Cardinal di Contini-Verchese has taken over the duties of Cardinal Monteverdi, who died not long ago. And he's asked for me, as I knew he would. It's a great compliment, but more than that. I cannot refuse to go."

"How long will you be away?"

"Oh, a very long time, I think. There are war rumbles in Europe, though it seems so far away up here. The Church in Rome needs every diplomat she has, and thanks to Cardinal di Contini-Verchese I'm classified as a diplomat. Mussolini is closely allied to Hitler, birds of a feather, and somehow the Vatican has to reconcile two opposing ideologies, Catholicism and Fascism. It won't be easy. I speak German very well, learned Greek when I was in Athens and Italian when I was in Rome. I also speak French and Spanish fluently." He sighed. "I've always had a talent for languages, and I cultivated it deliberately. It was inevitable that I would be transferred."

"Well, Your Grace, unless you're sailing tomorrow you can still see Meggie."

The words popped out before Anne let herself stop to think; why shouldn't Meggie see him once before he went away, especially if, as he seemed to think, he was going to be away a very long time?

His head turned toward her. Those beautiful, distant blue eyes were very intelligent and very hard to fool. Oh, yes, he was a born diplomat! He knew exactly what she was saying, and every reason at the back of her mind. Anne found herself hanging breathlessly on his answer, but for a long time he said nothing, just sat staring out over the emerald cane toward the brimming river, with the baby forgotten in the crook of his arm. Fascinated, she stared at his profile—the curve of eyelid, the straight nose, the secretive mouth, the determined chin. What forces was he marshaling while he contemplated the view? What complicated balances of love, desire, duty, expediency, will power, longing, did he weigh in his mind, and which against which? His hand lifted the cigarette to his lips; Anne saw the fingers tremble and soundlessly let go her breath. He was not indifferent, then.

For perhaps ten minutes he said nothing; Anne lit him another Capstan, handed it to him in place of the burned-out stub. It, too, he smoked down steadiliy, not once lifting his gaze from the far mountains and the monsoon clouds lowering the sky.

"Where is she?" he asked then in a perfectly normal voice, throwing the second stub over the veranda railing after the first.

And on what she answered depended his decision; it was her turn to think. Was one right to push other human beings on a course which led one knew not where, or to what? Her loyalty was all to Meggie; she didn't honestly care an iota what happened to this man. In his way he was no better than Luke. Off after some male thing with never the time or the inclination to put a woman ahead of it, running and clutching at some dream which probably only existed in has addled head. No more substance than the smoke from the mill dissipating itself in the heavy, molasses-laden air. But it was what he wanted, and he would spend himself and his life in chasing it.

He hadn't lost his good sense, no matter what Meggie meant to him. Not even for her—and Anne was beginning to believe he loved Meggie more than anything except that strange ideal—would he jeopardize the chance of grasping what he wanted in his hands one day. No, not even for her. So if she answered that Meggie was in some crowded resort hotel where he might be recognized, he wouldn't go. No one knew better than he that he wasn't the sort who could become anonymous in a crowd. She licked her lips, found her voice.

"Meggie's in a cottage on Matlock Island."

"On where?"

"Matlock Island. It's a resort just off Whitsunday Passage, and it's specially designed for privacy. Besides, at this time of the year there's hardly a soul on it." She couldn't resist adding, "Don't worry, no one will see you!"

"How reassuring." Very gently he eased the sleeping baby out of his arms, handed her to Anne. "Thank you," he said, going to the steps. Then he turned back, in his eyes a rather pathetic appeal. "You're quite wrong," he said. "I just want to see her, no more than that. I shall never involve Meggie in anything which might endanger her immortal soul."

"Or your own, eh? Then you'd better go as Luke O'Neill; he's expected. That way you'll be sure to create no scandal, for Meggie or for yourself."

"And what if Luke turns up?"

"There's no chance of that. He's gone to Sydney and he won't be back until March. The only way he could have known Meggie was on Matlock is through me, and I didn't tell him, Your Grace."

"Does Meggie expect Luke?"

Anne smiled wryly. "Oh, dear me, no."

"I shan't harm her," he insisted. "I just want to see her for a little while, that's all."

"I'm well aware of it, Your Grace. But the fact remains that you'd harm her a great deal less if you wanted more," said Anne.

When old Rob's car came sputtering along the road Meggie was at her station on the cottage veranda, hand raised in the signal that everything was fine and she needed nothing. He stopped in the usual spot to reverse, but before he did so a man in shorts, shirt and sandals sprang out of the car, suitcase in hand.

"Hooroo, Mr. O'Neill!" Rob yelled as he went.

But never again would Meggie mistake them, Luke O'Neill and Ralph de Bricassart. That wasn't Luke; even at the distance and in the fast-fading light she wasn't deceived. She stood dumbly and waited while he walked down the road toward her, Ralph de Bricassart. He had decided he wanted her after all. There could be no other reason for his joining her in a place like this, calling himself Luke O'Neill.

Nothing in her seemed to be functioning, not legs or mind or heart. This was Ralph come to claim her, why couldn't she feel? Why wasn't she running down the road to his arms, so utterly glad to see him nothing else mattered? This was Ralph, and he was all she had ever wanted out of living; hadn't she just spent more than a week trying to get that fact out of her mind? God damn him, God damn him! Why the *hell* did he have to come when she was finally beginning to get him out of her thoughts, if not out of her heart? Oh, it was all going to start again! Stunned, sweating, angry, she stood woodenly waiting, watching that graceful form grow larger.

"Hello, Ralph," she said through clenched teeth, not looking at him.

"Hello, Meggie."

"Bring your case inside. Would you like a hot cup of tea?" As she spoke she led the way into the living room, still not looking at him.

"That would be nice," he said, as stilted as she.

He followed her into the kitchen and watched while she plugged in an electric jug, filled the teapot from a little hot-water geyser over the sink, and busied herself getting cups and saucers down from a cupboard. When she handed him the big five-pound tin of Arnotts biscuits he took a couple of handfuls of cookies out of it and put them on a plate. The jug boiled, she emptied the hot water out of the teapot, spooned loose tea into it and filled it with bubbling water. While she carried the cookie plate and the teapot, he followed with the cups and saucers, back into the living room.

The three rooms had been built alongside each other, the bedroom opening off one side of the living room and the kitchen off the other, with the bathroom beyond it. This meant the house had two verandas, one facing the road and the other the beach. Which in turn meant they each had somewhere excusable to look without having to look at each other. Full darkness had fallen with tropical suddenness, but the air through the wide-open sliding doors was filled with the lapping of water, the distant surf on the reef, the coming and going of the warm soft wind.

They drank the tea in silence, though neither could eat a biscuit, and the silence stretched on after the tea was finished, he shifting his gaze to her and she keeping hers steadfastly on the breezy antics of a baby palm outside the road-veranda doors.

"What's the matter, Meggie?" he asked, so gently and tenderly her heart knocked frantically, and seemed to die from the pain of it, the old query of the grown man to the little girl. He hadn't come to Matlock to see the woman at all. He had come to see the child. It was the child he loved, not the woman. The woman he had hated from the moment she came into being.

Round and up came her eyes to his, amazed, outraged, furious; even now, even now! Time suspended, she stared at him so, and he was forced to see, breath caught astounded, the grown woman in those glass-clear eyes. Meggie's eyes. Oh, God, Meggie's eyes!

He had meant what he said to Anne Mueller; he just wanted to see her, nothing more. Though he loved her, he hadn't come to be her lover. Only to see her, talk to her, be her friend, sleep on the living room couch while he tried once more to unearth the taproot of that eternal fascination she possessed for him, thinking that if only he could see it fully exposed, he might gain the spiritual means to eradicate it.

It had been hard to adjust to a Meggie with breasts, a waist, hips; but he had done it because when he looked into her eyes, there like the pool of light in a sanctuary lamp shone his Meggie. A mind and a spirit whose pulls he had never been free from since first meeting her, still unchanged inside that distressingly changed body; but while he could see proof of their continued existence in her eyes, he could accept the altered body, discipline his attraction to it.

And, visiting his own wishes and dreams upon her, he had never doubted she wanted to do the same until she had turned on him like a goaded cat, at Justine's birth. Even then, after the anger and hurt died in him, he had attributed her behavior to the pain she had gone through, spiritual more than physical. Now, seeing her at last as she was, he could pinpoint to a second the moment when she had shed the lenses of childhood, donned the lenses of a woman: that interlude in the Drogheda cemetery after Mary Carson's birthday party. When he had explained to her why he couldn't show her any special attention, because people might deem him interested in her as a man. She had looked at him with something in her eyes he had not understood, then looked away, and when she turned back the expression was gone. From that time, he saw now, she had thought of him in a different light; she hadn't kissed him in a passing weakness when she had kissed him, then gone back to thinking of him in the old way, as he had her. He had perpetuated his illusions, nurtured them, tucked them into his unchanging way of life as best he could, worn them like a hair shirt. While all the time she had furnished her love for him with woman's objects.

Admit it, he had physically wanted her from the time of their first kiss, but the want had never plagued him the way his love for her had; seeing them as separate and distinct, not facets of the same thing. She, poor misunderstood creature, had never succumbed to this particular folly.

At that moment, had there been any way he could have got off Matlock Island, he would have fled from her like Orestes from the Eumenides. But he couldn't quit the island, and he did have the courage to remain in her presence rather than senselessly walk the night. What can I do, how can I possibly make reparation? I *do* love her! And if I love her, it has to be because of the way she is now, not because of a juvenile way station along her road. It's womanly things I've always loved in her; the bearing of the burden. So, Ralph de Bricassart, take off your blinkers, see her as she really is, not as she was long ago. Sixteen years ago, sixteen long incredible years . . . I am forty-four and she is twenty-six; neither of us is a child, but I am by far the more immature.

You took it for granted the minute I stepped out of Rob's car, isn't that so, Meggie? You assumed I had given in at last. And before you even had time to get your breath back I had to show you how wrong you were. I ripped the fabric of your delusion apart as if it had been a dirty old rag. Oh, Meggie! What have I done to you? How could I have been so blind, so utterly self-centered? I've accomplished nothing in coming to see you, unless it is to cut you into little pieces. All these years we've been loving at cross-purposes.

Still she was looking into his eyes, her own filling with shame, humiliation, but as the expressions flew across his face to the final one of despairing pity she seemed to realize the magnitude of her mistake, the horror of it. And more than that: the fact that he knew her mistake.

Go, run! Run, Meggie, get out of here with the scrap of pride he's left you! The instant she thought it she acted on it, she was up out of her chair and fleeing.

Before she could reach the veranda he caught her, the impetus of her flight spinning her round against him so hard he staggered. It didn't matter, any of it, the grueling battle to retain his soul's integrity, the long pressing down of will upon desire; in moments he had gone lifetimes. All that power held dormant, sleeping, only needing the detonation of a touch to trigger a chaos in which mind was subservient to passion, mind's will extinguished in body's will.

Up slid her arms around his neck, his across her back, spasmed; he bent his head, groped with his mouth for hers, found it. Her mouth, no longer an unwanted, unwelcome memory but real; her arms about him as if she couldn't bear to let him go; the way she seemed to lose even the feel of her bones; how dark she was like the night, tangled memory and desire, unwanted memory and unwelcome desire. The years he must have longed for this, longed for her and denied her power, kept himself even from the thought of her as a woman!

Did he carry her to the bed, or did they walk? He thought he must have carried her, but he could not be sure; only that she was there upon it, he was there upon it, her skin under his hands, his skin under hers. Oh, God! My Meggie, my Meggie! How could they rear me from infancy to think you profanation?

Time ceased to tick and began to flow, washed over him until it had no meaning, only a depth of dimension more real than real time. He could feel her yet he did not feel her, not as a separate entity; wanting to make her finally and forever a part of himself, a graft which was himself, not a symbiosis which acknowledged her as distinct. Never again would he not know the upthrusts of breasts and belly and buttocks; the folds and crevices in between. Truly she was made for him, for he had made her; for sixteen years he had shaped and molded her without knowing that he did, let alone why he did. And he forgot that he had ever given her away, that another man had shown her the end of what he had begun for himself, had always intended for himself, for she was his downfall, his rose; his creation. It was a dream from which he would never again awaken, not as long as he was a man, with a man's body. *Oh, dear God! I know, I know!* I know why I kept her as an idea and a child within me for so long after she had grown beyond both, but why does it have to be learned like this?

Because at last he understood that what he had aimed to be was *not* a man. Not a man, never a man; something far greater, something beyond the fate of a mere man. Yet after all his fate was here under his hands, struck quivering and alight with him, her man. *A man, forever a man.* Dear Lord, couldst Thou not have kept this from me? I am a man, I can never be God; it was a delusion, that life in search of godhead. Are we all the same, we priests, yearning to be God? We abjure the one act which irrefutably proves us men.

He wrapped his arms about her and looked down with eyes full of tears at the still, faintly lit face, watched its rosebud mouth drop open, gasp, become a helpless O of astonished pleasure. Her arms and legs were round him, living ropes which bound him to her, silkily, sleekly tormented him; he put his chin into her shoulder and his cheek against the softness of hers, gave himself over to the maddening, exasperating drive of a man grappling with fate. His mind reeled, slipped, became utterly dark and blindingly bright; for one moment he was within the sun, then the brilliance faded, grew grey, and went out. This was being a man. He could be no more. But that was not the source of the pain. The pain was in the final moment, the finite moment, the empty, desolate realization: ecstasy is fleeting. He couldn't bear to let her go, not now that he had her; he had made her for himself. So he clung to her like a drowning man to a spar in a lonely sea, and soon, buoyant, rising again on a tide grown quickly familiar, he succumbed to the inscrutable fate which is a man's.

What was sleep? Meggie wondered. A blessing, a respite from life, an echo of death, a demanding nuisance? Whatever it was, he had yielded himself to it, and lay with his arm over her and his head beside her shoulder, possessive even in it. She was tired, too, but she would not let herself sleep. Somehow she felt if she relaxed her grasp on consciousness he might not be there when she picked it up again. Later she could sleep, after he was awake and the secretive, beautiful mouth uttered its first words. What would he say to her? Would he regret it? Had she been a pleasure to him worth what he had abandoned? So many years he had fought it, made her fight it with him; she could hardly make herself believe he had lain down his arms at last, but there had been things he had said in the night and in the midst of his pain which blotted out his long denial of her.

She was supremely happy, happier than she could remember ever being. From the moment he had pulled her back from the door it had been a body poem, a thing of arms and hands and skin and utter pleasure. I was made for him, and only for him. . . . That's why I felt so little with Luke! Borne out beyond the limits of endurance on her body's tide, all she could think was that to give him everything she could was more necessary to her than life itself. He must never regret it, never. Oh, his pain! There had been moments when she seemed actually to feel it as if it had been her own. Which only contributed to her happiness; there was some justice in his pain.

He was awake. She looked down into his eyes and saw the same love in their blueness which had warmed her, given her purpose since childhood; and with it a great, shadowed fatigue. Not a weariness of the body, but a weariness of the soul.

He was thinking that in all his life he had never woken in the same bed as another person; it was in a way more intimate than the sexual act preceding it, a deliberate indication of emotional ties, a cleaving to her. Light and empty as the air so alluringly full of marine tang and sun-soaked vegetation, he drifted for a while on the wings of a different kind of freedom: the relief of relinquishing his mandate to fight her, the peace of losing a long, incredibly bloody war and finding the surrender far sweeter than the battles. Ah, but I gave you a good fight, my Meggie! Yet in the end it isn't your fragments I must glue together, but the dismembered chunks of myself.

You were put in my life to show me how false, how presumptuous is the pride of a priest of my kind; like Lucifer I aspired to that which is God's alone, and like Lucifer, I fell. I had the chastity, the obedience, even the poverty before Mary Carson. But until this morning

I have never known humility. Dear Lord, if she meant nothing to me it would be easier to bear, but sometimes I think I love her far more than I do Thee, and that, too, is a part of Thy punishment. Her I do not doubt; Thou? A trick, a phantom, a jest. *How* can I love a jest? And yet, I do.

"If I could get the energy together, I'd go for a swim and then make breakfast," he said, desperate for something to say, and felt her smile against his chest.

"Go for the swim part, I'll make the breakfast. And there's no need to put anything on here. No one comes."

"Truly paradise!" He swung his legs off the bed, sat up and stretched. "It's a beautiful morning. I wonder if that's an omen."

Already the pain of parting; just because he had left the bed; she lay watching him as he walked to the sliding doors giving onto the beach, stepped outside and paused. He turned, held out his hand.

"Come with me? We can get breakfast together."

The tide was in, the reef covered, the early sun hot but the restless summer wind cool; coarse grass sent feelers down onto the crumbling, unsandlike sand, where crabs and insects scuttled after pickings.

"I feel as if I've never seen the world before," he said, staring.

Meggie clutched at his hand; she felt visited, and found this sunny aftermath more incomprehensible than the night's dreamy reality. Her eyes rested on him, aching. It was time out of mind, a different world.

So she said, "Not this world. How could you? This is our world, for as long as it lasts."

"What's Luke like?" he asked, over breakfast.

She put her head on one side, considering. "Not as much like you physically as I used to think, because in those days I missed you more, I hadn't got used to doing without you. I believe I married him because he reminded me of you. At any rate, I had made up my mind to marry someone, and he stood head and shoulders above the rest. I don't mean in worthiness, or niceness, or any of the things women are supposed to find desirable in a husband. Just in some way I can't put a finger on. Except perhaps that he *is* like you. He doesn't need women, either."

His face twisted. "Is that how you see me, Meggie?"

"Truthfully? I think so. I'll never understand why, but I think so. There's something in Luke and in you which believes that needing a woman is a weakness. I don't mean to sleep with; I mean to need, really need."

"And accepting that, you can still want us?"

She shrugged, smiled with a trace of pity. "Oh, Ralph! I don't say it isn't important, and it's certainly caused me a lot of unhappiness, but it is the way things are. I'd be a fool to waste myself trying to eradicate it, when it can't be eradicated. The best I can do is exploit the weakness, not ignore its existence. Because I want and need, too. And apparently I want and need people like you and Luke, or I wouldn't have spent myself over the pair of you the way I have. I'd have married a good, kind, simple man like my father, someone who did want and need me. But there's a streak of Samson in every man, I think. It's just that in men like you and Luke, it's more pronounced."

He didn't seem at all insulted; he was smiling. "My wise Meggie!"

"That's not wisdom, Ralph. Just common sense. I'm not a very wise person at all, you know that. But look at my brothers. I doubt the older ones at any rate will ever get married, or have girlfriends even. They're terribly shy, they're frightened of the power a woman might have over them, and they're quite wrapped up in Mum."

Day followed day, and night followed night. Even the heavy summer rains were beautiful, to be walked in naked and listened to on the iron roof, as warm and full of caresses as the sun. And when the sun was out they walked too, lazed on the beach, swam; for he was teaching her to swim.

Sometimes when he didn't know he was being watched Meggie would look at him and try desperately to imprint his face upon her brain's core, remembering how in spite of the love she had borne Frank, with the passing of the years his image had dimmed, the *look* of him. There were the eyes, the nose, the mouth, the stunning silver wings in that black hair, the long hard body which had kept the slenderness and tautness of youth, yet had set a little, lost elasticity. And he would turn to find her watching him, a look in his eyes of haunted grief, a doomed look. She understood the implicit message, or thought she did; he must go, back to the Church and his duties. Never again with the same spirit, perhaps, but more able to serve. For only those who have slipped and fallen know the vicissitudes of the way.

One day, when the sun had gone down far enough to bloody the sea and stain the coral sand a hazy yellow, he turned to her as they lay on the beach.

"Meggie, I've never been so happy, or so unhappy."

"I know, Ralph."

"I believe you do. Is it why I love you? You're not much out of the ordinary way, Meggie, and yet you aren't ordinary at all. Did I sense it, all those years ago? I must have, I suppose. My passion for titian hair! Little did I know where it would lead me. I love you, Meggie."

"Are you leaving?"

"Tomorrow. I must. My ship sails for Genoa in less than a week."

"Genoa?"

"Rome, actually. For a long time, perhaps the rest of my life. I don't know."

"Don't worry, Ralph, I'll let you go without any fuss. My time is almost up, too. I'm leaving Luke, I'm going home to Drogheda."

"Oh, my dear! Not because of this, because of me?"

"No, of course not," she lied. "I'd made up my mind before you arrived. Luke doesn't want me or need me, he won't miss me in the slightest. But I need a home, somewhere of my own, and I think now that Drogheda is always going to be that place. It isn't right that poor Justine should grow up in a house where I'm the servant, though I know Anne and Luddie don't think of me like a servant. But it's how I think of myself, and how Justine will think of me when she's old enough to understand she hasn't a normal sort of home. In a way she never will enjoy that, but I must do as much for her as I can. So I'm going back to Drogheda."

"I'll write to you, Meggie."

"No, don't. Do you think I need letters, after this? I don't want anything between us which might endanger you, fall into the hands of unscrupulous people. So no letters. If you're ever in Australia it would be natural and normal of you to visit Drogheda, though I'm warning you, Ralph, to think before you do. There are only two places in the world where you belong to me ahead of God—here on Matlock, and on Drogheda."

He pulled her into his arms and held her, stroking her bright hair. "Meggie, I wish with all my heart I could marry you, never be apart from you again. I don't want to leave you. . . . And in a way I'll never be free of you again. I wish I hadn't come to Matlock. But we can't change what we are, and perhaps it's just as well. I know things about myself I would never have known or faced if I hadn't come. It's better to contend with the known than the unknown. I love you. I always have, and I always will. Remember it."

The next day Rob appeared for the first time since he had dropped Ralph, and waited patiently while they said their farewells. Obviously not a couple of newlyweds, for he'd come later than she and was leaving first. Not illicit lovers, either. They were married; it was written all over them. But they were fond of each other, very fond indeed. Like him and his Missus; a big difference in age, and that made for a good marriage.

"Goodbye, Meggie."

"Goodbye, Ralph. Take care of yourself."

"I will. And you."

He bent to kiss her; in spite of her resolution she clung to him, but when he plucked her hands from around his neck she put them stiffly behind her and kept them there.

He got into the car and sat while Rob reversed, then stared ahead through the windscreen without once looking back at her. It was a rare man who could do that, Rob reflected, without ever having heard of Orpheus. They drove in silence through the rain forest and came at last to the sea side of Matlock, and the long jetty. As they shook hands Rob looked into his face, wondering. He had never seen eyes so human, or so sad. The aloofness has passed from Archbishop Ralph's gaze forever.

When Meggie came back to Himmelhoch Anne knew at once she would lose her. Yes, it was the same Meggie—but so much more, somehow. Whatever Archbishop Ralph might have told himself before he went to Matlock, on Matlock things had gone Meggie's way at last, not his. About time, too.

She took Justine into her arms as if she only now understood what having Justine meant, and stood rocking the little thing while she looked around the room, smiling. Her eyes met Anne's, so alive, so shining with emotion that Anne felt her own eyes fill with reciprocal tears of that same joy.

"I can't thank you enough, Anne."

"Pish, for what?"

"For sending Ralph. You must have known it would mean I'd leave Luke, so I thank you just that much more, dear. Oh, you have no idea what it did for me! I had made up my mind I was going to stay with Luke, you know. Now I'm going back to Drogheda, and I'm never going to leave it again."

"I hate to see you go and especially I hate to see Justine go, but I'm glad for both of you, Meggie. Luke will never give you anything but unhappiness."

"Do you know here he is?"

"Back from the CSR. He's cutting near Ingham."

"I'll have to go and see him, tell him. And, much as I loathe the idea, sleep with him."

"What?"

The eyes shone. "I'm two weeks overdue, and I'm never a day overdue. The only other time I was, Justine was starting. I'm pregnant, Anne, I *know* I am!"

"My God!" Anne gasped at Meggie as if she had never seen her before; and perhaps she had not. She licked her lips and stammered, "It could be a false alarm."

But Meggie shook her head positively. "Oh, no. I'm pregnant. There are some things one just knows."

"A nice pickle if you are," Anne muttered.

"Oh, Anne, don't be blind! Don't you see what this means? I can never have Ralph, I've always known I could never have Ralph. But I have, I have!" She laughed, gripping Justine so hard Anne was frightened the baby would scream, but strangely she did not. "I've got the part of Ralph the Church can never have, the part of him which carries on from generation to generation. Through me he'll continue to live, because I know it's going to be a son! And that son will have sons, and they'll have sons—I'll beat God yet. I've loved Ralph since I was ten years old, and I suppose I'll still be loving him if I live to be a hundred. But he isn't mine, where his child will be. Mine, Anne, *mine!"*

"Oh, Meggie!" Anne said helplessly.

The passion died, the exhilaration; she became once more familiar Meggie, quiet and sweet but with the faint thread of iron, the capacity to bear much. Only now Anne trod carefully, wondering just what she had done in sending Ralph de Bricassart to Matlock Island. Was it possible for anyone to change this much? Anne didn't think so. It must have been there all the time, so well hidden its presence was rarely suspected. There was far more than a faint thread of iron in Meggie; she was solid steel.

"Meggie, if you love me at all, please remember something for me?"

The grey eyes crinkled at the corners. "I'll try!"

"I've picked up most of Luddie's tomes over the years, when I've run out of my own books. Especially the ones with the ancient Greek stories, because they fascinate me. They say the Greeks have a word for everything, and that there's no human situation the Greeks didn't describe."

"I know. I've read some of Luddie's books, too."

"Then don't you remember? The Greeks say it's a sin against the gods to love something beyond all reason. And do you remember that they say when someone *is* loved so, the Gods become jealous, and strike the object down in the very fullness of its flower? There's a lesson in it, Meggie. It's profane to love too much."

"Profane, Anne, that's the key word! I shan't love Ralph's baby profanely, but with the purity of the Blessed Mother herself."

Anne's brown eyes were very sad. "Ah, but did she love purely? The object of her love was struck down in the very fullness of His flower, wasn't He?"

Meggie put Justine in her cot. "What must be, must be. Ralph I can't have, his baby I can. I feel . . . oh, as if there's a purpose to my life after all! That's been the worst thing about these three and a half years, Anne. I was beginning to think there was no purpose to my life." She smiled briskly, decisively. "I'm going to protect this child in every way I can, no matter what the cost to myself. And the first thing is that no one, including Luke, shall ever imply it has no right to the only name I'm at liberty to give it. The very thought of sleeping with Luke makes me ill, but I'll do it. I'd sleep with the Devil himself if it could help this baby's future. Then I'm going home to Drogheda, and I hope I never see Luke again." She turned from the cot. "Will you and Luddie come to see us? Drogheda always has room for friends."

"Once a year, for as many years as you'll have us. Luddie and I want to see Justine grow up."

* * *

Only the thought of Ralph's baby kept Meggie's sagging courage up as the little rail motor rocked and jolted the long miles to Ingham. Had it not been for the new life she was sure was growing in her, getting into a bed with Luke ever again would have been the ultimate sin against herself; but for Ralph's baby she would indeed have entered into a contract with the Devil.

From a practical viewpoint it wasn't going to be easy either, she knew that. But she had laid her plans with what foresight she could, and with Luddie's aid, oddly enough. It hadn't been possible to conceal much from him; he was too shrewd, and too deeply in Anne's confidence. He had looked at Meggie sadly, shaken his head, and then proceeded to give her some excellent advice. The actual aim of her mission hadn't been mentioned, of course, but Luddie was as adept at adding two and two as most people who read massive tomes.

"You won't want to have to tell Luke you're leaving him when he's worn out after the cane," said Luddie delicately. "Much better if you catch him in a good mood, isn't it? Best thing is, see him on a Saturday night or a Sunday after it's been his week cooking. The grapevine says Luke's the best cook on the cutting circuit—learned to cook when he was low man on the shearing totem pole, and shearers are much fussier eaters than cutters. Means cooking doesn't upset him, you know. Probably finds it as easy as falling off a log. That's the speed, then, Meggie. You slap the news on him when he's feeling real good after a week in the barracks kitchen."

It seemed to Meggie lately that she had gone a long way from blushing days; she looked at Luddie steadily without going the least bit pink.

"Could you find out which week Luke cooks, Luddie? Or is there any way I could find out, if you can't?"

"Oh, she's apples," he said cheerfully. "I've got my branches on the old grapevine. I'll find out."

It was mid Saturday afternoon when Meggie checked into the Ingham pub that looked the most respectable. All North Queensland towns were famous for one thing: they had pubs on all four corners of every block. She put her small case in her room, then made her way back to the unlovely foyer to find a telephone. There was a Rugby League football team in town for a preseason training match, and the corridors were full of half-naked, wholly drunk players who greeted her appearance with cheers and affectionate pats on the back and behind. By the time she got the use of the phone she was shaking with fright; everything about this venture seemed to be an ordeal. But through the din and the looming drunken faces she managed to call Braun's, the farm where Luke's gang was cutting, and ask that a message be relayed to him that his wife was in Ingham, wanting to see him. Seeing her fear, the publican walked back to her room with her, and waited until he heard her turn the key.

Meggie leaned against the door, limp with relief; if it meant she didn't eat again until she was back in Dunny, she wasn't venturing to the dining room. Luckily the publican had put her right next to the women's bathroom, so she ought to be able to make that journey when necessary. The moment she thought her legs would hold her up she wobbled to the bed and sat on it, her head bowed, looking at her quivering hands.

All the way down she had thought about the best way of going about it, and everything in her cried, Quickly, quickly! Until coming to live at Himmelhoch she had never read a description of a seduction, and even now, armed with several such recountings, she wasn't confident of her ability to go about one herself. But that was what she had to do, for she knew once she started to talk to Luke it would be all over. Her tongue itched to tell him what she really thought of him. But more than that, the desire to be back on Drogheda with Ralph's baby made safe consumed her.

Shivering in the sultry sugary air she took off her

clothes and lay down on the bed, eyes closed, willing herself not to think beyond the expediency of making Ralph's baby safe.

The footballers didn't worry Luke at all when he entered the pub alone at nine o'clock; by then most of them were insensible, and the few still on their feet were too far gone to notice anything farther away than their beer glasses.

Luddie had been exactly right; at the end of his week's stint as cook Luke was rested, eager for a change and oozing goodwill. When Braun's young son had brought Meggie's message down to the barracks he was just washing the last of the supper dishes and planning to cycle into Ingham, join Arne and the blokes on their customary Saturday-night binge. The prospect of Meggie was a very agreeable alternative; ever since that holiday on the Atherton he had found himself wanting her occasionally in spite of his physical exhaustion. Only his horror of starting her off on the let's-settle-down-in-our-own-home cry had kept him away from Himmelhoch whenever he was near Dunny. But now she had come to him, and he was not at all averse to a night in bed. So he finished the dishes in a hurry, and was lucky enough to be picked up by a truck after he had pedaled a scant half mile. But as he walked his bike the three blocks from where his ride had dropped him to the pub where Meggie was staying, some of his anticipation flattened. All the chemist shops were closed, and he didn't have any French letters. He stopped, stared in a window full of moth-eaten, heat-stippled chocolates and dead blowflies, then shrugged. Well, he'd just have to take his chances. It would only be tonight, and if there was a baby, with any luck it would be a boy this time.

Meggie jumped nervously when she heard his knock, got off the bed and padded over to the door.

"Who is it?" she called.

"Luke," came his voice.

She turned the key, opened the door a tiny way, and stepped behind it as Luke pushed it wider. The moment he was inside she slammed it shut, and stood looking at him. He looked at her; at the breasts which were bigger, rounder, more enticing than ever, the nipples no longer pale pink but a rich dark red from the baby. If he had been in need of stimuli they were more than adequate; he reached out to pick her up, and carried her to the bed.

By daylight she still hadn't spoken a word, though her touch had welcomed him to a pitch of fevered want he had never before experienced. Now she lay moved away from him, and curiously divorced from him.

He stretched luxuriously, yawned, cleared his throat. "What brings you down to Ingham, Meg?" he asked.

Her head turned; she regarded him with wide, contemptuous eyes.

"Well, what brings you here?" he repeated, nettled.

No reply, only the same steady, stinging gaze, as if she couldn't be bothered answering. Which was ridiculous, after the night.

Her lips opened; she smiled. "I came to tell you I'm going home to Drogheda," she said.

For a moment he didn't believe her, then he looked at her face more closely and saw she meant it, all right. "Why?" he asked.

"I told you what would happen if you didn't take me to Sydney," she said.

His astonishment was absolutely genuine. "But, Meg! That's flaming eighteen months ago! And I *gave* you a holiday! Four bloody expensive weeks on the Atherton! I couldn't afford to take you to Sydney on top of that!"

"You've been to Sydney twice since then, both times without me," she said stubbornly. "I can understand the first time, since I was expecting Justine, but heaven knows I could have done with a holiday away from The Wet this last January."

"Oh, Christ!"

"What a skinflint you are, Luke," she went on gently. "Twenty thousand pounds you've had from me, money that's rightfully mine, and yet you begrudge the few measly pounds it would have cost you to take me to Sydney. You and your money! You make me sick."

"I haven't touched it," he said feebly. "It's there, every penny of it, and more besides."

"Yes, that's right. Sitting in the bank, where it always will. You haven't any intention of spending it, have you? You want to adore it, like a golden calf. Admit it, Luke, you're a miser. And what an unforgivable idiot you are into the bargain! To treat your wife and daughter the way you wouldn't dream of treating a pair of dogs, to ignore their existences, let alone their needs! You complacent, conceited, self-centered *bastard!*"

White-faced, trembling, he searched for speech; to have Meg turn on him, especially after the night, was like being bitten to death by a butterfly. The injustice of her accusations appalled him, but there didn't seem to be any way he could make her understand the purity of his motives. Womanlike, she saw only the obvious; she just couldn't appreciate the grand design at back of it all.

So he said, "Oh, Meg!" in tones of bewilderment, despair, resignation. "I've never ill-treated you," he added. "No, I definitely haven't! There's no one could say I was cruel to you. No one! You've had enough to eat, a roof over your head, you've been warm—"

"Oh, yes," she interrupted. "That's one thing I'll grant you. I've never been warmer in my life." She shook her head, laughed. "What's the use? It's like talking to a brick wall."

"I might say the same!"

"By all means do," said Meggie icily, getting off the bed and slipping on her panties. "I'm not going to divorce you," she said. "I don't want to marry again. If you want a divorce, you know where to find me. Technically speaking, I'm the one at fault, aren't I? I'm deserting you—or at least that's the way the courts in this country will see it. You and the judge can cry on each other's shoulders about the perfidies and ingratitude of women."

"I never deserted you," he maintained.

"You can keep my twenty thousand pounds, Luke. But not another penny do you ever get from me. My future income I'm going to use to support Justine, and perhaps another child if I'm lucky."

"So that's it!" he said. "All you were after was another bloody baby, wasn't it? That's why you came down here—a swan song, a little present from me for you to take back to Drogheda with you! Another bloody baby, not *me!* It never was me, was it? To you I'm just a breeder! Christ, what a have!"

"That's all most men are to most women," she said maliciously. "You bring out the worst in me, Luke, in more ways than you'll ever understand. Be of good cheer! I've earned you more money in the last three and a half years than the sugar has. If there is another child, it's none of your concern. As of this minute I never want to see you again, not as long as I live."

She was into her clothes. As she picked up her handbag and the little case by the door she turned back, her hand on the knob.

"Let me give you a little word of advice, Luke. In case you ever get yourself another woman, when you're too old and too tired to give yourself to the cane any more. You can't kiss for toffee. You open your mouth too wide, you swallow a woman whole like a python. Saliva's fine, but not a deluge of it." She wiped her hand viciously across her mouth. "You make me want to be sick! Luke O'Neill, the great I-am! You're a nothing!"

After she had gone he sat on the edge of the bed staring at the closed door for a long while. Then he shrugged and started to dress. Not a long procedure, in North Queensland. Just a pair of shorts. If he hurried he could get a ride back to the barracks with Arne and the blokes. Good old Arne. Dear old mate. A man was a fool. Sex was one thing, but a man's mates were quite another.

FIVE

1938-1953 Fee

14

Not wanting anyone to know of her return, Meggie rode out to Drogheda on the mail truck with old Bluey Williams, Justine in a basket on the seat beside her. Bluey was delighted to see her and eager to know what she had been doing for the last four years, but as they neared the homestead he fell silent, divining her wish to come home in peace.

Back to brown and silver, back to dust, back to that wonderful purity and spareness North Queensland so lacked. No profligate growth here, no hastening of decay to make room for more; only a slow, wheeling inevitability like the constellations. Kangaroos, more than ever. Lovely little symmetrical wilgas, round and matronly, almost coy. Galahs, soaring in pink waves of undersides above the truck. Emus at full run. Rabbits, hopping out of the road with white powder puffs flashing cheekily. Bleached skeletons of dead trees in the grass. Mirages of timber stands on the far curving horizon as they came across the Dibban-Dibban plain, only the unsteady blue lines across their bases to indicate that the trees weren't real. The sound she had so missed but never thought to miss, crows carking desolately. Misty brown veils of dust whipped along by the dry autumn wind like dirty rain. And the grass, the silver-beige grass of the Great Northwest, stretching to the sky like a benediction.

Drogheda, Drogheda! Ghost gums and sleepy giant pepper trees a-hum with bees. Stockyards and buttery yellow sandstone buildings, alien green lawn around the big house, autumn flowers in the garden, wallflowers and zinnias, asters and dahlias, marigolds and calendulas, chrysanthemums, roses, roses. The gravel of the backyard, Mrs. Smith standing gaping, then laughing, crying, Minnie and Cat running, old stringy arms like chains around her heart. For Drogheda was home, and here was her heart, for always.

Fee came out to see what all the fuss was about.

"Hello, Mum. I've come home."

The grey eyes didn't change, but in the new growth of her soul Meggie understood. Mum *was* glad; she just didn't know how to show it.

"Have you left Luke?" Fee asked, taking it for granted that Mrs. Smith and the maids were as entitled to know as she was herself.

"Yes. I shall never go back to him. He didn't want a home, or his children, or me."

"Children?"

"Yes. I'm going to have another baby."

Oohs and aahs from the servants, and Fee speaking her judgment in that measured voice, gladness underneath.

"If he doesn't want you, then you were right to come home. We can look after you here."

Her old room, looking out across the Home Paddock, the gardens. And a room next door for Justine, the new baby when it came. Oh, it was so good to be home!

Bob was glad to see her, too. More and more like Paddy, he was becoming a little bent and sinewy as the sun baked his skin and his bones to dryness. He had the same gentle strength of character, but perhaps because he had never been the progenitor of a large family, he lacked Paddy's fatherly mien. And he was like Fee, also. Quiet, self-contained, not one to air his feelings or opinions. He had to be into his middle thirties, Meggie thought in sudden surprise, and still he wasn't married. Then Jack and Hughie came in, two duplicate Bobs without his authority, their shy smiles welcoming her home. That must be it, she reflected; they are so shy, it is the land, for the land doesn't need articulateness or social graces. It needs only what they bring to it, voiceless love and wholehearted fealty.

The Cleary men were all home that night, to unload a truck of corn Jims and Patsy had picked up from the AML&F in Gilly.

"I've never seen it so dry, Meggie," Bob said. "No rain in two years, not a drop. And the bunnies are a bigger curse than the kangas; they're eating more grass than sheep and kangas combined. We're going to try to hand-feed, but you know what sheep are."

Only too well did Meggie know what sheep were. Idiots, incapable of understanding even the rudiments of survival. What little brain the original animal had ever possessed was entirely bred out of these woolly aristocrats. Sheep wouldn't eat anything but grass, or scrub cut from their natural environment. But there just weren't enough hands to cut scrub to satisfy over a hundred thousand sheep.

"I take it you can use me?" she asked.

"Can we! You'll free up a man's hands for scrub-cutting, Meggie, if you'll ride the inside paddocks the way you used to."

True as their word, the twins were home for good. At fourteen they quit Riverview forever, couldn't head back to the black-oil plains quickly enough. Already they looked like juvenile Bobs, Jacks and Hughies, in what was gradually replacing the old-fashioned grey twill and flannel as the uniform of the Great Northwest grazier: white moleskin breeches, white shirt, a flat-crowned grey felt hat with a broad brim, and ankle-high elastic-sided riding boots with flat heels. Only the handful of half-caste aborigines who lived in Gilly's shanty section aped the cowboys of the American West, in high-heeled fancy boots and ten-gallon Stetsons. To a black-soil plainsman such gear was a useless affectation, a part of a different culture. A man couldn't walk through the scrub in high-heeled boots, and a man often had to walk through the scrub. And a ten-gallon Stetson was far too hot and heavy.

The chestnut mare and the black gelding were both dead; the stables were empty. Meggie insisted she was happy with a stock horse, but Bob went over to Martin King's to buy her two of his part-thoroughbred hacks —a creamy mare with a black mane and tail, and a leggy chestnut gelding. For some reason the loss of the old chestnut mare hit Meggie harder than her actual parting from Ralph, a delayed reaction; as if in this the fact of his going was more clearly stated. But it was so good to be out in the paddocks again, to ride with the dogs, eat the dust of a bleating mob of sheep, watch the birds, the sky, the land.

It was terribly dry. Drogheda's grass had always managed to outlast the droughts Meggie remembered, but this was different. The grass was patchy now; in between its tussocks the dark ground showed, cracked into a fine network of fissures gaping like parched mouths. For which mostly thank the rabbits. In the four years of her absence they had suddenly multiplied out of all reason, though she supposed they had been bad for many years before that. It was just that almost overnight their numbers had reached far beyond saturation point. They were everywhere, and they, too, ate the precious grass.

She learned to set rabbit traps, hating in a way to see the sweet little things mangled in steel teeth, but too much of a land person herself to flinch from doing what had to be done. To kill in the name of survival wasn't cruelty.

"God rot the homesick Pommy who shipped the first rabbits out from England," said Bob bitterly.

They were not native to Australia, and their sentimental importation had completely upset the ecological balance of the continent where sheep and cattle had not, these being scientifically grazed from the moment of their introduction. There was no natural Australian predator to control the rabbit numbers, and imported foxes didn't thrive. Man must be an unnatural predator, but there were too few men, too many rabbits.

After Meggie grew too big to sit a horse, she spent her days in the homestead with Mrs. Smith, Minnie and Cat, sewing or knitting for the little thing squirming inside her. He (she always thought of it as he) was a part of her as Justine never had been; she suffered no sickness or depression, and looked forward eagerly to bearing him. Perhaps Justine was inadvertently responsible for some of this; now that the little pale-eyed thing was changing from a mindless baby to an extremely intelligent girl child, Meggie found herself fascinated with the process and the child. It was a long time since she had been indifferent to Justine, and she yearned to lavish love upon her daughter, hug her, kiss her, laugh with her. To be politely rebuffed was a shock, but that was what Justine did at every affectionate overture.

When Jims and Patsy left Riverview, Mrs. Smith had thought to get them back under her wing again, then came the disappointment of discovering they were away in the paddocks most of the time. So Mrs. Smith turned to little Justine, and found herself as firmly shut out as Meggie was. It seemed that Justine didn't want to be hugged, kissed or made to laugh.

She walked and talked early, at nine months. Once upon her feet and in command of a very articulate tongue, she proceeded to go her own way and do precisely whatever she wanted. Not that she was either noisy or defiant; simply that she was made of very hard metal indeed. Meggie knew nothing about genes, but if she had she might have pondered upon the result of an intermingling of Cleary, Armstrong and O'Neill. It couldn't fail to be powerful human soup.

But the most dismaying thing was Justine's dogged

refusal to smile or laugh. Every soul on Drogheda turned inside out performing antics to make her germinate a grin, without success. When it came to innate solemnity she outdid her grandmother.

On the first of October, when Justine was exactly sixteen months old, Meggie's son was born on Drogheda. He was almost four weeks early and not expected; there were two or three sharp contractions, the water broke, and he was delivered by Mrs. Smith and Fee a few minutes after they rang for the doctor. Meggie had scarcely had time to dilate. The pain was minimal, the ordeal so quickly over it might hardly have been; in spite of the stitches she had to have because his entry into the world had been so precipitate, Meggie felt wonderful. Totally dry for Justine, her breasts were full to overflowing. No need for bottles or tins of Lactogen this time.

And he was so beautiful! Long and slender, with a quiff of flaxen hair atop his perfect little skull, and vivid blue eyes which gave no hint of changing later to some other color. How could they change? They were Ralph's eyes, as he had Ralph's hands, Ralph's nose and mouth, even Ralph's feet. Meggie was unprincipled enough to be very thankful Luke had been much the same build and coloring as Ralph, much the same in features. But the hands, the way the brows grew in, the downy widow's peak, the shape of the fingers and toes; they were so much Ralph, so little Luke. Better hope no one remembered which man owned what.

"Have you decided on his name?" asked Fee; he seemed to fascinate her.

Meggie watched her as she stood holding him, and was grateful. Mum was going to love again; oh, maybe not the way she had loved Frank, but at least she would feel something.

"I'm going to call him Dane."

"What a queer name! Why? Is it an O'Neill family name? I thought you were finished with the O'Neills?"

"It's got nothing to do with Luke. This is *his* name, no one else's. I hate family names; it's like wishing a piece of someone different onto a new person. I called Justine Justine simply because I liked the name, and I'm calling Dane Dane for the same reason.

"Well, it does have a nice ring to it," Fee admitted.

Meggie winced; her breasts were too full. "Better give him to me, Mum. Oh, I hope he's hungry! And I hope old Blue remembers to bring that breast pump. Otherwise you're going to have to drive into Gilly for it."

He was hungry; he tugged at her so hard his gummy little mouth hurt. Looking down on him, the closed eyes with their dark, gold-tipped lashes, the feathery brows, the tiny working cheeks, Meggie loved him so much the love hurt her more than his sucking ever could.

He is enough; he has to be enough, I'll not get any more. But by God, Ralph de Bricassart, by that God you love more than me, you'll never know what I stole from you—and from Him. I'm never going to tell you about Dane. Oh, my baby! Shifting on the pillows to settle him more comfortably into the crook of her arm, to see more easily that perfect little face. My baby! You're mine, and I'm never going to give you up to anyone else. Least of all to your father, who is a priest and can't acknowledge you. Isn't that wonderful?

The boat docked in Genoa at the beginning of April. Archbishop Ralph landed in an Italy bursting into full, Mediterranean spring, and caught a train to Rome. Had he requested it he could have been met, chauffeured in a Vatican car to Rome, but he dreaded to feel the Church close around him again; he wanted to put the moment off as long as he could. The Eternal City. It was truly that, he thought, staring out of the taxi windows at the campaniles and domes, and pigeon-strewn plazas, the ambitious fountains, the Roman columns with their bases buried deep in the centuries. Well, to him they were all superfluities. What mattered to him was the part of Rome called the Vatican, its sumptuous public rooms, its anything but sumptuous private rooms.

A black-and-cream-robed Dominican monk led him through high marble corridors, amid bronze and stone figures worthy of a museum, past great paintings in the styles of Giotto, Raphael, Botticelli, Fra Angelico. He was in the public rooms of a great cardinal, and no doubt the wealthy Contini-Verchese family had given much to enhance their august scion's surroundings.

In a room of ivory and gold, rich with color from tapestries and pictures, French carpeted and furnished, everywhere touches of crimson, sat Vittorio Scarbanza, Cardinal di Contini-Verchese. The small smooth hand, its ruby ring glowing, was extended to him in welcome; glad to fix his eyes downward, Archbishop Ralph crossed the room, knelt, took the hand to kiss the ring. And laid his cheek against the hand, knowing he couldn't lie, though he had meant to right up until the moment his lips touched that symbol of spiritual power, temporal authority.

Cardinal Vittorio put his other hand on the bent shoulder, nodding a dismissal to the monk, then as the door closed softly his hand went from shoulder to hair, rested in its dark thickness, smoothed it back tenderly from the half-averted forehead. It had changed; soon it would be no longer black, but the color of iron. The bent spine stiffened, the shoulders went back, and Archbishop Ralph looked directly up into his master's face.

Ah, there had been a change! The mouth had drawn in, knew pain and was more vulnerable; the eyes, so beautiful in color and shape and setting, were yet completely different from the eyes he still remembered as if bodily they had never left him. Cardinal Vittorio had always had a fancy that the eyes of Jesus were blue, and like Ralph's: calm, removed from what He saw and therefore able to encompass all, understand all. But perhaps it had been a mistaken fancy. How could one feel for humanity and suffer oneself without its showing in the eyes?

"Come, Ralph, sit down."

"Your Eminence, I wish to confess."

"Later, later! First we will talk, and in English. There are ears everywhere these days, but, thank our dear Jesus, not English-speaking ears. Sit down, Ralph, please. Oh, it is so good to see you! I have missed your wise counsel, your rationality, your perfect brand of companionship. They have not given me anyone I like half so well as you."

He could feel his brain clicking into the formality already, feel the very thoughts in his mind take on more stilted phrasing; more than most people, Ralph de Bricassart knew how everything about one changed with one's company, even one's speech. Not for these ears the easy fluency of colloquial English. So he sat down not far away, and directly opposite the slight figure in its scarlet moiré, the color changing yet not changing, of a quality which made its edges fuse with the surroundings rather than stand out from them.

The desperate weariness he had known for weeks seemed to be easing a little from his shoulders; he wondered why he had dreaded this meeting so, when he had surely known in his heart he would be understood, forgiven. But that wasn't it, not it at all. It was his own guilt at having failed, at being less than he had aspired to be, at disappointing a man who had been interested, tremendously kind, a true friend. His guilt at walking into this pure presence no longer pure himself.

"Ralph, we are priests, but we are something else before that; something we were before we became priests, and which we cannot escape in spite of our exclusiveness. We are men, with the weaknesses and failings of men. There is nothing you can tell me which could alter the impressions I formed of you during our years together, nothing you could tell me which will make me think less of you, or like you less. For many years I have known that you had escaped this realization of our intrinsic weakness, of our humanity, but I knew you must come to it, for we all do. Even the Holy Father, who is the most humble and human of us all."

"I broke my vows, Your Eminence. That isn't easily forgiven. It's sacrilege."

"Poverty you broke years ago, when you accepted the bequest of Mrs. Mary Carson. Which leaves chastity and obedience, does it not?"

"Then all three were broken, Your Eminence."

"I wish you would call me Vittorio, as you used to! I am not shocked, Ralph, nor disappointed. It is as Our Lord Jesus Christ wills, and I think perhaps you had a great lesson to learn which could not be learned in any way less destructive. God is mysterious, His reasons beyond our poor comprehension. But I think what you did was not done lightly, your vows thrown away as having no value. I know you very well. I know you to be proud, very much in love with the idea of being a priest, very conscious of your exclusiveness. It is possible that you needed this particular lesson to reduce that pride, make you understand that you are first a man, and therefore not as exclusive as you think. Is it not so?"

"Yes. I lacked humility, and I believe in a way I aspired to be God Himself. I've sinned most grievously and inexcusably. I can't forgive myself, so how can I hope for divine forgiveness?"

"The pride, Ralph, *the pride!* It is not your place to forgive, do you not understand that yet? Only God can forgive. Only God! And He will forgive if the sincere repentance is there. He has forgiven greater sins from far greater saints, you know, as well as from far greater villains. Do you think Prince Lucifer is not forgiven? He was forgiven in the very moment of his rebellion. His fate as ruler of Hell is his own, not God's doing. Did he not say it? 'Better to rule in Hell than serve in Heaven!' For he could not overcome his pride, he could not bear to subjugate his will to the Will of Someone else, even though that Someone was God Himself. I do not want to see you make the same mistake, my dearest friend. Humility was the one quality you lacked, and it is the very quality which makes a great saint—or a great man. Until you can leave the matter of forgiveness to God, you will not have acquired true humility."

The strong face twisted. "Yes, I know you're right. I *must* accept what I am without question, only strive to be better without having pride in what I am. I repent, therefore I shall confess and await forgiveness. I *do* repent, bitterly." He sighed; his eyes betrayed the conflict his measured words couldn't, not in this room.

"And yet, Vittorio, in a way there was nothing else I could do. Either I ruined her, or I took the ruin upon myself. At the time there didn't seem to be a choice, because I do love her. It wasn't her fault that I've never wanted the love to extend to a physical plane. Her fate became more important than my own, you see. Until that moment I had always considered myself first, as more important than she, because I was a priest, and she was a lesser being. But I saw that I was responsible for what she is. . . . I should have let her go when she was a child, but I didn't. I kept her in my heart and she knew it. If I had truly plucked her out she would have known that, too, and she would have become someone I couldn't influence." He smiled. "You see that I have much to repent. I tried a little creating of my own."

"It was the Rose?"

The head went back; Archbishop Ralph looked at the elaborate ceiling with its gilded moldings and baroque Murano chandelier. "Could it have been anyone else? She's my only attempt at creation."

"And will she be all right, the Rose? Did you do her more harm by this than in denying her?"

"I don't know, Vittorio. I wish I did! At the time it just seemed the only thing to do. I'm not gifted with Promethean foresight, and emotional involvement makes one a poor judge. Besides, it simply . . . happened! But I think perhaps she needed most what I gave her, the recognition of her identity as a woman. I don't mean that *she* didn't know she was a woman. I mean *I* didn't know. If I had first met her as a woman it might have been different, but I knew her as a child for many years."

"You sound rather priggish, Ralph, and not yet ready for forgiveness. It hurts, does it not? That you could have been human enough to yield to human weakness. Was it really done in such a spirit of noble self-sacrifice?"

Startled, he looked into the liquid dark eyes, saw himself reflected in them as two tiny manikins of insignificant proportion. "No," he said. "I'm a man, and as a man I found a pleasure in her I didn't dream existed. I didn't know a woman felt like that, or could be the source of such profound joy. I wanted never to leave her, not only because of her body, but because I just loved to be with her—talk to her, not talk to her, eat the meals she cooked, smile at her, share her thoughts. I shall miss her as long as I live."

There was something in the sallow ascetic visage which unaccountably reminded him of Meggie's face in that moment of parting; the sight of a spiritual burden being taken up, the resoluteness of a character well able to go forward in spite of its loads, its griefs, its pain. What had he known, the red silk cardinal whose only human addiction seemed to be his languid Abyssinian cat?

"I can't repent of what I had with her in that way," Ralph went on when His Eminence didn't speak. "I repent the breaking of vows as solemn and binding as my life. I can never again approach my priestly duties in the same light, with the same zeal. I repent that bitterly. But Meggie?" The look on his face when he uttered her name made Cardinal Vittorio turn away to do battle with his own thoughts.

"To repent of Meggie would be to murder her." He passed his hand tiredly across his eyes. "I don't know if that's very clear, or even if it gets close to saying what I mean. I can't for the life of me ever seem to express what I feel for Meggie adequately." He leaned forward in his chair as the Cardinal turned back, and watched his twin images grow a little larger. Vittorio's eyes were like mirrors; they threw back what they saw and didn't permit one a glimpse of what went on behind them. Meggie's eyes were exactly the opposite; they went down and down and down, all the way to her soul. "Meggie is a benediction," he said. "She's a holy thing to me, a different kind of sacrament."

"Yes, I understand," sighed the Cardinal. "It is well you feel so. In Our Lord's eyes I think it will mitigate the great sin. For your own sake you had better confess to Father Giorgio, not to Father Guillermo. Father Giorgio will not misinterpret your feelings and your reasoning. He will see the truth. Father Guillermo is less perceptive, and might deem your true repentance debatable." A faint smile crossed his thin mouth like a wispy shadow. "They, too, are men, my Ralph, those who hear the confessions of the great. Never forget it as long as you live. Only in their priesthood do they act as vessels containing God. In all else they are men. And the forgiveness they mete out comes from God, but the ears which listen and judge belong to men."

There was a discreet knock on the door; Cardinal Vittorio sat silently and watched the tea tray being carried to a buhl table.

"You see, Ralph? Since my days in Australia I have become addicted to the afternoon tea habit. They make it quite well in my kitchen, though they used not to at first." He held up his hand as Archbishop Ralph started to move toward the teapot. "Ah, no! I shall pour it myself. It amuses me to be 'mother.' "

"I saw a great many black shirts in the streets of Genoa and Rome," said Archbishop Ralph, watching Cardinal Vittorio pour.

"The special cohorts of Il Duce. We have a very difficult time ahead of us, my Ralph. The Holy Father is adamant that there be no fracture between the Church and the secular government of Italy, and he is right in this as in all things. No matter what happens, we must remain free to minister to all our children, even should a war mean our children will be divided, fighting each other in the name of a Catholic God. Wherever our hearts and our emotions might lie, we must endeavor always to keep the Church removed from political ideologies and international squabbles. I wanted you to come to me because I can trust your face not to give away what your brain is thinking no matter what your eyes might be seeing, and because you have the best diplomatic turn of mind I have ever encountered."

Archbishop Ralph smiled ruefully. "You'll further my career in spite of me, won't you! I wonder what would have happened to me if I hadn't met you?"

"Oh, you would have become Archbishop of Sydney, a nice post and an important one," said His Eminence with a golden smile. "But the ways of our lives lie not in our hands. We met because it was meant to be, just as it is meant that we work together now for the Holy Father."

"I can't see success at the end of the road," said Archbishop Ralph. "I think the result will be what the result of impartiality always is. No one will like us, and everyone will condemn us."

"I know that, so does His Holiness. But we can do nothing else. And there is nothing to prevent our praying in private for the speedy downfall of Il Duce and Der Führer, is there?"

"Do you really think there will be war?"

"I cannot see any possibility of avoiding it."

His Eminence's cat stalked out of the sunny corner where it had been sleeping, and jumped upon the scarlet shimmering lap a little awkwardly, for it was old.

"Ah, Sheba! Say hello to your old friend Ralph, whom you used to prefer to me."

The satanic yellow eyes regarded Archbishop Ralph haughtily, and closed. Both men laughed.

15

Drogheda had a wireless set. Progress had finally come to Gillanbone in the shape of an Australian Broadcasting Commission radio station, and at long last there was something to rival the party line for mass entertainment. The wireless itself was a rather ugly object in a walnut case which sat on a small exquisite cabinet in the drawing room, its car-battery power source hidden in the cupboard underneath.

Every morning Mrs. Smith, Fee and Meggie turned it on to listen to the Gillanbone district news and weather, and every evening Fee and Meggie turned it on to listen to the ABC national news. How strange it was to be instantaneously connected with Outside; to hear of floods, fires, rainfall in every part of the nation, an uneasy Europe, Australian politics, without benefit of Bluey Williams and his aged newspapers.

When the national news on Friday, September 1st, announced that Hitler had invaded Poland, only Fee and Meggie were home to hear it, and neither of them paid any attention. There had been speculation for months; besides, Europe was half a world away. Nothing to do with Drogheda, which was the center of the universe. But on Sunday, September 3rd all the men were in from the paddocks to hear Father Watty

Thomas say Mass, and the men were interested in Europe. Neither Fee nor Meggie thought to tell them of Friday's news, and Father Watty, who might have, left in a hurry for Narrengang.

As usual, the wireless set was switched on that evening for the national news. But instead of the crisp, absolutely Oxford tones of the announcer, there came the genteel, unmistakably Australian voice of the Prime Minister, Robert Gordon Menzies.

"Fellow Australians. It is my melancholy duty to inform you officially that in consequence of the persistence by Germany in her invasion of Poland, Great Britain has declared war upon her, and that, as a result, Australia is also at war. . . .

"It may be taken that Hitler's ambition is not to unite all the German people under one rule, but to bring under that rule as many countries as can be subdued by force. If this is to go on, there can be no security in Europe and no peace in the world. . . . There can be no doubt that where Great Britain stands, there stand the people of the entire British world. . . .

"Our staying power, and that of the Mother Country, will be best assisted by keeping our production going, continuing our avocations and business, maintaining employment, and with it, our strength. I know that in spite of the emotions we are feeling, Australia is ready to see it through.

"May God, in His mercy and compassion, grant that the world may soon be delivered from this agony."

There was a long silence in the drawing room, broken by the megaphonal tones of a short-wave Neville Chamberlain speaking to the British people; Fee and Meggie looked at their men.

"If we count Frank, there are six of us," said Bob into the silence. "All of us except Frank are on the land, which means they won't want to let us serve. Of our present stockmen, I reckon six will want to go and two will want to stay."

"I want to go!" said Jack, eyes shining.

"And me," said Hughie eagerly.

"And us," said Jims on behalf of himself and the inarticulate Patsy.

But they all looked at Bob, who was the boss.

"We've got to be sensible," he said. "Wool is a staple of war, and not only for clothes. It's used as packing in ammunition and explosives, for all sorts of funny things we don't hear of, I'm sure. Plus we have beef cattle for food, and the old wethers and ewes go for hides, glue, tallow, lanolin—all war staples.

"So we can't go off and leave Drogheda to run itself, no matter what we might want to do. With a war on it's going to be mighty hard to replace the stockmen we're bound to lose. The drought's in its third year, we're scrub-cutting, and the bunnies are driving us silly. For the moment our job's here on Drogheda; not very exciting compared to getting into action, but just as necessary. We'll be doing our best bit here."

The male faces had fallen, the female ones lightened.

"What if it goes on longer than old Pig Iron Bob thinks it will?" asked Hughie, giving the Prime Minister his national nickname.

Bob thought hard, his weatherbeaten visage full of frowning lines. "If things get worse and it goes on for a long time, then I reckon as long as we've got two stockmen we can spare two Clearys, but only if Meggie's willing to get back into proper harness and work the inside paddocks. It would be awfully hard and in good times we wouldn't stand a chance, but in this drought I reckon five men and Meggie working seven days a week could run Drogheda. Yet that's asking a lot of Meggie, with two little babies."

"If it has to be done, Bob, it has to be done," said Meggie. "Mrs. Smith won't mind doing her bit by taking charge of Justine and Dane. When you give the word that I'm needed to keep Drogheda up to full production, I'll start riding the inside paddocks."

"Then that's us, the two who can be spared," said Jims, smiling.

"No, it's Hughie and I," said Jack quickly.

"By rights it ought to be Jims and Patsy," Bob said slowly. "You're the youngest and least experienced as stockmen, where as soldiers we'd all be equally inexperienced. But you're only sixteen now, chaps."

"By the time things get worse we'll be seventeen," offered Jims. "We'll look older than we are, so we won't have any trouble enlisting if we've got a letter from you witnessed by Harry Gough."

"Well, right at the moment no one is going. Let's see if we can't bring Drogheda up to higher production, even with the drought and the bunnies."

Meggie left the room quietly, went upstairs to the nursery. Dane and Justine were asleep, each in a white-painted cot. She passed her daughter by, and stood over her son, looking down at him for a long time.

"Thank God you're only a baby," she said.

It was almost a year before the war intruded upon the little Drogheda universe, a year during which one by one the stockmen left, the rabbits continued to multiply, and Bob battled valiantly to keep the station books looking worthy of a wartime effort. But at the beginning of June 1940 came the news that the British Expeditionary Force had been evacuated from the European mainland at Dunkirk; volunteers for the second Australian Imperial Force poured in thousands into the recruiting centers, Jims and Patsy among them.

Four years of riding the paddocks in all weathers had passed the twins' faces and bodies beyond youth, to that ageless calm of creases at the outer corners of the eyes, lines down the nose to the mouth. They presented their letters and were accepted without comment. Bushmen were popular. They could usually shoot well, knew the value of obeying an order, and they were tough.

Jims and Patsy had enlisted in Dubbo, but camp was

to be Ingleburn, outside Sydney, so everyone saw them off on the night mail. Cormac Carmichael, Eden's youngest son, was on the same train for the same reason, going to the same camp as it turned out. So the two families packed their boys comfortably into a first-class compartment and stood around awkwardly, aching to weep and kiss and have something warming to remember, but stifled by their peculiar British mistrust of demonstrativeness. The big C-36 steam locomotive howled mournfully, the stationmaster began blowing his whistle.

Meggie leaned over to peck her brothers on their cheeks self-consciously, then did the same to Cormac, who looked just like his oldest brother, Connor; Bob, Jack and Hughie wrung three different young hands; Mrs. Smith, weeping, was the only one who did the kissing and cuddling everyone was dying to do. Eden Carmichael, his wife and aging but still handsome daughter with him, went through the same formalities. Then everyone was outside on the Gilly platform, the train was jerking against its buffers and creeping forward.

"Goodbye, goodbye!" everyone called, and waved big white handkerchiefs until the train was a smoky streak in the shimmering sunset distance.

Together as they had requested, Jims and Patsy were gazetted to the raw, half-trained Ninth Australian Division and shipped to Egypt at the beginning of 1941, just in time to become a part of the rout at Benghazi. The newly arrived General Erwin Rommel had put his formidable weight on the Axis end of the seesaw and begun the first reversal of direction in the great cycling rushes back and forth across North Africa. And, while the rest of the British forces retreated ignominiously ahead of the new Afrika Korps back to Egypt, the Ninth Australian Division was detailed to occupy and hold Tobruk, an outpost in Axis-held territory. The only thing which made the plan feasible was that it was still accessible by sea and could be supplied as long as British ships could move in the Mediterranean. The Rats of Tobruk holed up for eight months, and saw action after action as Rommel threw everything he had at them from time to time, without managing to dislodge them.

"Do youse know why youse is here?" asked Private Col Stuart, licking the paper on his cigarette and rolling it shut lazily.

Sergeant Bob Malloy shifted his Digger hat far enough upward to see his questioner from under its brim. "Shit, no," he said, grinning; it was an oft-asked query.

"Well, it's better than whiting gaiters in the bloody glasshouse," said Private Jims Cleary, pulling his twin brother's shorts down a little so he could rest his head comfortably on soft warm belly.

"Yair, but in the glasshouse youse don't keep getting shot at," objected Col, flicking his dead match at a sunbathing lizard.

"I know this much, mate," said Bob, rearranging his hat to shade his eyes. "I'd rather get shot at than die of fuckin' boredom."

They were comfortably disposed in a dry, gravelly dugout just opposite the mines and barbed wire which cut off the southwest corner of the perimeter; on the other side Rommel hung doggedly on to his single piece of the Tobruk territory. A big .50-caliber Browning machine gun shared the hole with them, cases of ammunition neatly beside it, but no one seemed very energetic or interested in the possibility of attack. Their rifles were propped against one wall, bayonets glittering in the brilliant Tobruk sun. Flies buzzed everywhere, but all four were Australian bushmen, so Tobruk and North Africa held no surprises in the way of heat, dust or flies.

"Just as well youse is twins, Jims," said Col, throwing pebbles at the lizard, which didn't seem disposed to move. "Youse look like a pair of poofters, all tied up together."

"You're just jealous." Jims grinned, stroking Patsy's belly. "Patsy's the best pillow in Tobruk."

"Yair, all right for you, but what about poor Patsy? Go on, Harpo, say something!" Bob teased.

Patsy's white teeth appeared in a smile, but as usual he remained silent. Everyone had tried to get him to talk, but no one had ever succeeded beyond an essential yes or no; in consequence nearly everyone called him Harpo, after the voiceless Marx brother.

"Hear the news?" asked Col suddenly.

"What?"

"The Seventh's Matildas got plastered by the eighty-eights at Halfaya. Only gun in the desert big enough to wipe out a Matilda. Went through them big buggers of tanks like a dose of salts."

"Oh, yeah, tell me another!" said Bob skeptically. "I'm a sergeant and I never heard a whisper, you're a private and you know all about it. Well, mate, there's just nothing Jerry's got capable of wiping out a brigade of Matildas."

"I was in Morshead's tent on a message from the CO when I heard it come through on the wireless, and it is true," Col maintained.

For a while no one spoke; it was necessary to every inhabitant of a beleaguered outpost like Tobruk that he believe implicitly his own side had sufficient military thrust to get him out. Col's news wasn't very welcome, more so because not one soldier in Tobruk held Rommel lightly. They had resisted his efforts to blow them out because they genuinely believed the Australian fighting man had no peer save a Gurkha, and if faith is nine-tenths of power, they had certainly proved themselves formidable.

"Bloody Poms," said Jims. "What we need in North Africa is more Aussies."

The chorus of agreement was interrupted by an explosion on the rim of the dugout which blew the lizard into nothing and sent the four soldiers diving for the machine gun and their rifles.

"Fuckin' Dago grenade, all splinters and no punch," Bob said with a sigh of relief. "If that was a Hitler special we'd be playing our harps for sure, and wouldn't you like that, eh, Patsy?"

At the beginning of Operation Crusader the Ninth Australian Division was evacuated by sea to Cairo, after a weary, bloody siege which seemed to have accomplished nothing. However, while the Ninth had been holed up inside Tobruk, the steadily swelling ranks of British troops in North Africa had become the British Eighth Army, its new commander General Bernard Law Montgomery.

Fee wore a little silver brooch formed into the rising sun emblem of the AIF; suspended on two chains below it was a silver bar, on which she had two gold stars, one for each son under arms. It assured everyone she met that she, too, was Doing Her Bit for the Country. Because her husband was not a soldier, nor her son, Meggie wasn't entitled to wear a brooch. A letter had come from Luke informing her that he would keep on cutting the sugar; he thought she would like to know in case she had been worried he might join up. There was no indication that he remembered a word of what she had said that morning in the Ingham pub. Laughing wearily and shaking her head, she had dropped the letter in Fee's wastepaper basket, wondering as she did so if Fee worried about her sons under arms. What did she really think of the war? But Fee never said a word, though she wore her brooch every single day, all day.

Sometimes a letter would come from Egypt, falling into tatters when it was spread open because the censor's scissors had filled it with neat rectangular holes, once the names of places or regiments. Reading these letters was largely a matter of piecing together much out of virtually nothing, but they served one purpose which cast all others into the shade: while ever they came, the boys were still alive.

There had been no rain. It was as if even the divine elements conspired to blight hope, for 1941 was the fifth year of a disastrous drought. Meggie, Bob, Jack, Hughie and Fee were desperate. The Drogheda bank account was rich enough to buy all the feed necessary to keep the sheep alive, but most of the sheep wouldn't eat. Each mob had a natural leader, the Judas; only if they could persuade the Judas to eat did they stand a hope with the rest, but sometimes even the sight of a chewing Judas couldn't impress the rest of the mob into emulating it.

So Drogheda, too, was seeing its share of bloodletting, and hating it. The grass was all gone, the ground a dark cracked waste lightened only by grey and dun-brown timber stands. They armed themselves with knives as well as rifles; when they saw an animal down someone would cut its throat to spare it a lingering death, eyeless from the crows. Bob put on more cattle and hand-fed them to keep up Drogheda's war effort. There was no profit to be had in it with the price of feed, for the agrarian regions closer in were just as hard hit by lack of rain as the pastoral regions farther out. Crop returns were abysmally low. However, word had come from Rome that they were to do what they could regardless of the cost.

What Meggie hated most of all was the time she had to put in working the paddocks. Drogheda had managed to retain only one of its stockmen, and so far there were no replacements; Australia's greatest shortage had always been manpower. So unless Bob noticed her irritability and fatigue, and gave her Sunday off, Meggie worked the paddocks seven days a week. However, if Bob gave her time off it meant he himself worked harder, so she tried not to let her distress show. It never occurred to her that she could simply refuse to ride as a stockman, plead her babies as an excuse. They were well cared for, and Bob needed her so much more than they did. She didn't have the insight to understand her babies needed her, too; thinking of her longing to be with them as selfishness when they were so well cared for by loving and familiar hands. It *was* selfish, she told herself. Nor did she have the kind of confidence that might have told her that in her children's eyes she was just as special as they were to her. So she rode the paddocks, and for weeks on end got to see her children only after they were in bed for the night.

Whenever Meggie looked at Dane her heart turned over. He was a beautiful child; even strangers on the streets of Gilly remarked on it when Fee took him into town. His habitual expression was a smiling one, his nature a curious combination of quietness and deep, sure happiness; he seemed to have grown into his identity and acquired his self-knowledge with none of the pain children usually experience, for he rarely made mistakes about people or things, and nothing ever exasperated or bewildered him. To his mother his likeness to Ralph was sometimes very frightening, but apparently no one else ever noticed. Ralph had been gone from Gilly for a long time, and though Dane had the same features, the same build, he had one great difference, which tended to cloud the issue. His hair wasn't black like Ralph's, it was a pale gold; not the color of wheat or sunset but the color of Drogheda grass, gold with silver and beige in it.

From the moment she set eyes on him, Justine adored her baby brother. Nothing was too good for Dane, nothing too much trouble to fetch or present in his honor. Once he began to walk she never left his side, for which Meggie was very grateful, worrying that Mrs. Smith and the maids were getting too old to keep a satisfactorily sharp eye on a small boy. On one of her rare Sundays off Meggie took her daughter onto her lap and spoke to her seriously about looking after Dane.

"I can't be here at the homestead to look after him myself," she said, "so it all depends on you, Justine. He's your baby brother and you must always watch out for him, make sure he doesn't get into danger or trouble."

The light eyes were very intelligent, with none of the rather wandering attention span typical of a four-year-old. Justine nodded confidently. "Don't worry, Mum," she said briskly. "I'll always look after him for you."

"I wish I could myself," Meggie sighed.

"I don't," said her daughter smugly. "I like having Dane all to myself. So don't worry. I won't let anything happen to him."

Meggie didn't find the reassurance a comfort, though it was reassuring. This precocious little scrap was going to steal her son from her, and there was no way she could avert it. Back to the paddocks, while Justine staunchly guarded Dane. Ousted by her own daughter, who was a monster. Who on earth did she take after? Not Luke, not herself, not Fee.

At least these days she was smiling and laughing. She was four years old before she saw anything funny in anything, and that she ever did was probably due to Dane, who had laughed from babyhood. Because he laughed, so did she. Meggie's children learned from each other all the time. But it was galling, knowing they could get on without their mother very well. By the time this wretched conflict is over, Meggie thought, he'll be too old to feel what he should for me. He's always going to be closer to Justine. Why is it that every time I think I've got my life under control, something happens? I didn't ask for this war or this drought, but I've got them.

Perhaps it was as well Drogheda was having such a hard time of it. If things had been easier, Jack and Hughie would have been off to enlist in a second. As it was, they had no choice but to buckle down and salvage what they could out of the drought which would come to be called the Great Drought. Over a million square miles of crop- and stock-bearing land was affected, from southern Victoria to the waist-high Mitchell grasslands of the Northern Territory.

But the war rivaled the drought for attention. With the twins in North Africa, the homestead people followed that campaign with painful eagerness as it pushed and pulled back and forth across Libya. Their heritage was working class, so they were ardent Labor supporters and loathed the present government, Liberal by name but conservative by nature. When in August of 1941 Robert Gordon Menzies stepped down, admitting he couldn't govern, they were jubilant, and when on October 3rd the Labor leader John Curtin was asked to form a government, it was the best news Drogheda had heard in years.

All through 1940 and 1941 unease about Japan had been growing, especially after Roosevelt and Churchill cut off her petroleum supplies. Europe was a long way away and Hitler would have to march his armies twelve thousand miles in order to invade Australia, but Japan was Asia, part of the Yellow Peril poised like a descending pendulum above Australia's rich, empty, underpopulated pit. So no one in Australia was at all surprised when the Japanese attacked Pearl Harbor; they had simply been waiting for it to come, somewhere. Suddenly the war was very close, and might even become their own backyard. There were no great oceans separating Australia from Japan, only big islands and little seas.

On Christmas Day 1941, Hong Kong fell; but the Japs would never succeed in taking Singapore, everyone said, relieved. Then news came of Japanese landings in Malay and in the Philippines; the great naval base at the toe of the Malayan peninsula kept its huge, flat-trajectoried guns trained on the sea, its fleet at the ready. But on February 8th, 1942, the Japanese crossed the narrow

Strait of Johore, landed on the north side of Singapore Island and came across to the city behind its impotent guns. Singapore fell without even a struggle.

And then great news! All the Australian troops in North Africa were to come home. Prime Minister Curtin rode the swells of Churchillian wrath undismayed, insisting that Australia had first call on Australian men. The Sixth and Seventh Australian Divisions embarked in Alexandria quickly; the Ninth, still recovering in Cairo from its battering at Tobruk, was to follow as soon as more ships could be provided. Fee smiled, Meggie was delirious with joy. Jims and Patsy were coming home.

Only they didn't. While the North waited for its troopships the seesaw tipped again; the Eighth Army was in full retreat back from Benghazi. Prime Minister Churchill struck a bargain with Prime Minister Curtin. The Ninth Australian Division would remain in North Africa, in exchange for the shipment of an American division to defend Australia. Poor soldiers, shuttled around by decisions made in offices not even belonging to their own countries. Give a little here, take a little there.

But it was a hard jolt for Australia, to discover that the Mother Country was booting all her Far Eastern chicks out of the nest, even a poult as fat and promising as Australia.

On the night of October 23rd, 1942, it was very quiet in the desert. Patsy shifted slightly, found his brother in the darkness, and leaned like a small child right into the curve of his shoulder. Jims's arm went around him and they sat together in companionable silence. Sergeant Bob Malloy nudged Private Col Stuart, grinned.

"Pair of poofs," he said.

"Fuck you, too," said Jims.

"Come on, Harpo, say something," Col murmured.

Patsy gave him an angelic smile only half seen in the

darkness, opened his mouth and hooted an excellent imitation of Harpo Marx's horn. Everyone for several yards hissed at Patsy to shut up; there was an all-quiet alert on.

"Christ, this waiting's killing me," Bob sighed.

Patsy spoke in a shout: "It's the silence that's killing me!"

"You fuckin' side-show fraud, I'll do the killing!" Col croaked hoarsely, reaching for his bayonet.

"For Crissake pipe down!" came the captain's whisper. "Who's the bloody idiot yelling?"

"Patsy," chorused half a dozen voices.

The roar of laughter floated reassuringly across the minefields, died down in a stream of low-toned profanity from the captain. Sergeant Malloy glanced at his watch; the second hand was just sweeping up to 9:40 pip-emma.

Eight hundred and eighty-two British guns and howitzers spoke together. The heavens reeled, the ground lifted, expanded, could not settle, for the barrage went on and on without a second's diminution in the mind-shattering volume of noise. It was no use plugging fingers in ears; the gargantuan booming came up through the earth and traveled inward to the brain via the bones. What the effect must have been on Rommel's front the troops of the Ninth in their trenches could only imagine. Usually it was possible to pick out this type and size of artillery from that, but tonight their iron throats chorused in perfect harmony, and thundered on as the minutes passed.

The desert lit not with the light of day but with the fire of the sun itself; a vast billowing cloud of dust rose like coiling smoke thousands of feet, glowing with the flashes of exploding shells and mines, the leaping flames of massive concentrations of detonating casings, igniting payloads. Everything Montgomery had was aimed at the minefields—guns, howitzers, mortars. And everything Montgomery had was thrown as fast as the sweating artillery crews could throw it, slaves feeding the maws of their weapons like small frantic birds a huge cuckoo; gun casings grew hot, the time between recoil and reload shorter and shorter as the artillerymen got carried away on their own impetus. Madmen, maddened, they danced a stereotyped pattern of attendance on their fieldpieces.

It was beautiful, wonderful—the high point of an artilleryman's life, which he lived and relived in his dreams, waking and sleeping, for the rest of his anticlimactic days. And yearned to have back again, those fifteen minutes with Montgomery's guns.

Silence. Stilled, absolute silence, breaking like waves on distended eardrums; unbearable silence. Five minutes before ten, exactly. The Ninth got up and moved forward out of its trenches into no man's land, fixing bayonets, feeling for ammunition clips, releasing safety catches, checking water bottles, iron rations, watches, tin hats, whether bootlaces were well tied, the location of those carrying the machine guns. It was easy to see, in the unholy glow of fires and red-hot sand melted into glass; but the dust pall hung between the Enemy and them, they were safe. For the moment. On the very edge of the minefields they halted, waited.

Ten pip-emma, on the dot. Sergeant Malloy put his whistle to his lips and blew a shrill blast up and down the company lines; the captain shouted his forward command. On a two-mile front the Ninth stepped off into the minefields and the guns began again behind them, bellowing. They could see where they were going as if it had been day, the howitzers trained on shortest range bursting shells not yards in front of them. Every three minutes the range lifted another hundred yards; advance those hundred yards praying it was only through antitank mines, or that the S-mines, the man mines, had been shelled out of existence by Montgomery's guns. There were still Germans and Italians in the field, outposts of machine guns, 50-mm small artillery, mortars. Sometimes a man would step on an unexploded S-mine, have time to see it leap upward out of the sand before it blew him in half.

No time to think, no time to do anything save crab-scuttle in time to the guns, a hundred yards forward every three minutes, praying. Noise, light, dust, smoke, gut-watering terror. Minefields which had no end, two or three miles of them to the other side, and no going back. Sometimes in the tiny pauses between barrages came the distant, eerie skirl of a bagpipe on the roasting gritty air; on the left of the Ninth Australian, the Fifty-first Highlanders were trekking through the minefields with a piper to lead every company commander. To a Scot the sound of his piper drawing him into battle was the sweetest lure in the world, and to an Australian very friendly, comforting. But to a German or an Italian it was hackle-raising.

The battle went on for twelve days, and twelve days is a very long battle. The Ninth was lucky at first; its casualties were relatively light through the minefields and through those first days of continued advance into Rommel's territory.

"You know, I'd rather be me and get shot at than be a sapper," said Col Stuart, leaning on his shovel.

"I dunno, mate; I think they've got the best of it," growled his sergeant. "Waiting behind the fuckin' lines until we've done all the work, then out they toddle with their bloody minesweepers to clear nice little paths for the fuckin' tanks."

"It isn't the tanks at fault, Bob; it's the brass who deploy them," Jims said, patting the earth down around the top of his section of their new trench with the flat of his spade. "Christ, though, I wish they'd decide to keep us in one place for a while! I've dug more dirt in the last five days than a bloody anteater."

"Keep digging, mate," said Bob unsympathetically.

"Hey, look!" cried Col, pointing skyward.

Eighteen RAF light bombers came down the valley

in perfect flying-school formation, dropping their sticks of bombs among the Germans and Italians with deadly accuracy.

"Bloody beautiful," said Sergeant Bob Malloy, his long neck tilting his head at the sky.

Three days later he was dead; a huge piece of shrapnel took off his arm and half his side in a fresh advance, but no one had time to stop except to pluck his whistle from what was left of his mouth. Men were going down now like flies, too tired to maintain the initial pitch of vigilance and swiftness; but what miserable barren ground they took they held on to, in the face of a bitter defense by the cream of a magnificent army. It had become to them all no more than a dumb, stubborn refusal to be defeated.

The Ninth held off Graf von Sponeck and Lungerhausen while the tanks broke out to the south, and finally Rommel was beaten. By November 8 he was trying to rally beyond the Egyptian border, and Montgomery was left in command of the entire field. A very important tactical victory, Second Alamein; Rommel had been forced to leave behind many of his tanks, guns and equipment. Operation Torch could commence its push eastward from Morocco and Algeria with more security. There was still plenty of fight in the Desert Fox, but a large part of his brush was on the ground at El Alamein. The biggest and most decisive battle of the North African theater had been fought, and Field Marshal Viscount Montgomery of Alamein was its victor.

Second Alamein was the swan song of the Ninth Australian Division in North Africa. They were finally going home to contend with the Japanese, on the mainland of New Guinea. Since March of 1941 they had been more or less permanently in the front line, arriving poorly trained and equipped, but going home now with a reputation exceeded only by the Fourth Indian

Division. And with the Ninth went Jims and Patsy, safe and whole.

Of course they were granted leave to go home to Drogheda. Bob drove into Gilly to collect them from the Goondiwindi train, for the Ninth was based in Brisbane and would depart after jungle training for New Guinea. When the Rolls swept round the drive all the women were out on the lawn waiting, Jack and Hughie hanging back a little but just as eager to see their young brothers. Every sheep left alive on Drogheda could drop dead if it so desired, but this was a holiday.

Even after the car stopped and they got out, no one moved. They looked so different. Two years in the desert had ruined their original uniforms; they were dressed in a new issue of jungle green, and looked like strangers. For one thing, they seemed to have grown inches, which indeed they had; the last two years of their development had occurred far from Drogheda, and had pushed them way above their older brothers. Not boys any more but men, though not men in the Bob-Jack-Hughie mold; hardship, battle euphoria and violent death had made something out of them Drogheda never could. The North African sun had dried and darkened them to rosy mahogany, peeled away every layer of childhood. Yes, it was possible to believe these two men in their simple uniforms, slouch hats pinned above their left ears with the badge of the AIF rising sun, had killed fellow men. It was in their eyes, blue as Paddy's but sadder, without his gentleness.

"My boys, my boys!" cried Mrs. Smith, running to them, tears streaming down her face. No, it didn't matter what they had done, how much they had changed; they were still her little babies she had washed, diapered, fed, whose tears she had dried, whose wounds she had kissed better. Only the wounds they harbored now were beyond her power to heal.

Then everyone was around them, British reserve

broken down, laughing, crying, even poor Fee patting them on their backs, trying to smile. After Mrs. Smith there was Meggie to kiss, Minnie to kiss, Cat to kiss, Mum to hug bashfully, Jack and Hughie to wring by the hand speechlessly. The Drogheda people would never know what it was like to be home, they could never know how much this moment had been longed for, feared for.

And how the twins ate! Army tucker was never like this, they said, laughing. Pink and white fairy cakes, chocolate-soaked lamingtons rolled in coconut, steamed spotted dog pudding, pavlova dripping passionfruit and cream from Drogheda cows. Remembering their stomachs from earlier days, Mrs. Smith was convinced they'd be ill for a week, but as long as there was unlimited tea to wash it down, they didn't seem to have any trouble with their digestions.

"A bit different from Wog bread, eh, Patsy?"

"Yair."

"What's Wog mean?" asked Mrs. Smith.

"A Wog's an Arab, but a Wop's an Italian, right, Patsy?"

"Yair."

It was peculiar. They would talk, or at least Jims would talk, for hours about North Africa: the towns, the people, the food, the museum in Cairo, life on board a troopship, in rest camp. But no amount of questioning could elicit anything but vague, change-the-subject answers as to what the actual fighting had been like, what Gazala, Benghazi, Tobruk, El Alamein had been like. Later on after the war was over the women were to find this constantly; the men who had actually been in the thick of battle never opened their mouths about it, refused to join the ex-soldiers' clubs and leagues, wanted nothing to do with institutions perpetuating the memory of war.

Drogheda held a party for them. Alastair MacQueen was in the Ninth as well and was home, so of course

Rudna Hunish held a party. Dominic O'Rourke's two youngest sons were in the Sixth in New Guinea, so even though they couldn't be present, Dibban-Dibban held a party. Every property in the district with a son in uniform wanted to celebrate the safe return of the three Ninth boys. Women and girls flocked around them, but the Cleary returned heroes tried to escape at every opportunity, more scared than they had been on any field of war.

In fact, Jims and Patsy didn't seem to want to have anything to do with women; it was to Bob, Jack and Hughie they clung. Late into the night after the women had gone to bed they sat talking to the brothers who had been forced to remain behind, opening their sore, scarred hearts. And they rode the paddocks of parched Drogheda, in its seventh year of the drought, glad to be in civvies.

Even so racked and tortured, to Jims and Patsy the land was ineffably lovely, the sheep comforting, the late roses in the garden a perfume of some heaven. And somehow they had to drink of it all so deeply they'd never again forget, for that first going away had been a careless one; they had had no idea what it would be like. When they left this time it would be with every moment hoarded to remember and treasure, and with Drogheda roses pressed into their wallets along with a few blades of scarce Drogheda grass. To Fee they were kind and pitying, but to Meggie, Mrs. Smith, Minnie and Cat they were loving, very tender. They had been the real mothers.

What delighted Meggie most was the way they loved Dane, played with him for hours, took him with them for rides, laughed with him, rolled him over and over on the lawn. Justine seemed to frighten them; but then, they were awkward with anyone female whom they didn't know as well as they knew the older women. Besides which, poor Justine was furiously jealous of the way they monopolized Dane's company, for it meant she had no one to play with.

"He's a bonzer little bloke, Meggie," said Jims to Meggie when she came out onto the veranda one day; he was sitting in a cane chair watching Patsy and Dane playing on the lawn.

"Yes, he is a little beauty, isn't he?" She smiled, sitting where she could see her youngest brother. Her eyes were soft with pity; they had been her babies, too. "What's the matter, Jims? Can't you tell me?"

His eyes lifted to hers, wretched with some deep pain, but he shook his head as if not even tempted. "No, Meggie. It isn't anything I could ever tell a woman."

"What about when all this is over and you marry? Won't you want to tell your wife?"

"Us marry? I don't think so. War takes all that out of a man. We were itching to go, but we're wiser now. If we married we'd have sons, and for what? See them grow up, get pushed off to do what we've done, see what we've seen?"

"Don't, Jims, don't!"

His gaze followed hers, to Dane chuckling in glee because Patsy was holding him upside down.

"Don't ever let him leave Drogheda, Meggie. On Drogheda he can't come to any harm," said Jims.

Archbishop de Bricassart ran down the beautiful high corridor, heedless of the surprised faces turning to watch him; he burst into the Cardinal's room and stopped short. His Eminence was entertaining Monsieur Papée, the Polish government-in-exile's ambassador to the Holy See.

"Why, Ralph! What is it?"

"It's happened, Vittorio. Mussolini has been overthrown."

"Dear Jesus! The Holy Father, does he know?"

"I telephoned Castel Gandolfo myself, though the

radio should have it any minute. A friend at German headquarters phoned me."

"I do hope the Holy Father has his bags packed," said Monsieur Papée with a faint, a very faint relish.

"If we disguised him as a Franciscan mendicant he might get out, not otherwise," Archbishop Ralph snapped. "Kesselring has the city sealed tighter than a drum."

"He wouldn't go anyway," said Cardinal Vittorio.

Monsieur Papée got up. "I must leave you, Your Eminence. I am the representative of a government which is Germany's enemy. If His Holiness is not safe, nor am I. There are papers in my rooms I must attend to."

Prim and precise, diplomat to his fingertips, he left the two priests alone.

"He was here to intercede for his persecuted people?"

"Yes. Poor man, he cares so much for them."

"And don't we?"

"Of course we do, Ralph! But the situation is more difficult than he knows."

"The truth of the matter is he's not believed."

"Ralph!"

"Well, isn't it the truth? The Holy Father spent his early years in Munich, he fell in love with the Germans and he still loves them, in spite of everything. If proof in the form of those poor wasted bodies was laid out in front of his eyes, he'd say it must be the Russians did it. Not his so-dear Germans, never a people as cultured and civilized as they are!"

"Ralph, you are not a member of the Society of Jesus, but you are here only because you have taken a personal oath of allegiance to the Holy Father. You have the hot blood of your Irish and Norman forebears, but I beg of you, be sensible! Since last September we have been only waiting for the axe to fall, praying Il Duce would remain to shelter us from German reprisal.

Adolf Hitler has a curious streak of contradiction in his personality, for there are two things he knows to be his enemies yet wishes if at all possible to preserve: the British Empire and the Holy Catholic Church of Rome. But when pushed to it, he has done his level best to crush the British Empire. Do you think he would not crush us, too, if we push him to it? One word of denunciation from us as to what is happening in Poland and he will certainly crush us. And what earthly good do you think our denouncing that would achieve, my friend? We have no armies, no soldiers. Reprisal would be immediate, and the Holy Father would be sent to Berlin, which is what he fears. Do you not remember the puppet pope in Avignon all those centuries ago? Do you want *our* Pope a puppet in Berlin?"

"I'm sorry, Vittorio, I can't see it that way. I say we *must* denounce Hitler, shout his barbarity from the rooftops! If he has us shot we'll die martyrs, and that would be more effective still."

"You are not usually obtuse, Ralph! He would not have us shot at all. He understands the impact of martyrdom just as well as we do. The Holy Father would be shipped to Berlin, and we would be shipped quietly to Poland. Poland, Ralph, *Poland!* Do you want to die in Poland of less use than you are now?"

Archbishop Ralph sat down, clenched his hands between his knees, stared rebelliously out the window at the doves soaring, golden in the setting sun, toward their cote. At forty-nine he was thinner than of yore, and was aging as splendidly as he did most things.

"Ralph, we are what we are. Men, but only as a secondary consideration. First we are priests."

"That wasn't how you listed our priorities when I came back from Australia, Vittorio."

"I meant a different thing then, and you know it. You are being difficult. I mean now that we cannot think as men. We must think as priests, because that is the most important aspect of our lives. Whatever we may think or want to do as men, our allegiance is to the Church, and to *no* temporal power! Our loyalty lies *only* with the Holy Father! You vowed obedience, Ralph. Do you wish to break it again? The Holy Father is infallible in all matters affecting the welfare of God's Church."

"He's wrong! His judgment's biased. All of his energies are directed toward fighting Communism. He sees Germany as its greatest enemy, the only real factor preventing the westward spread of Communism. He wants Hitler to remain firmly in the German saddle, just as he was content to see Mussolini rule Italy."

"Believe me, Ralph, there are things you do not know. He is the Pope, he *is* infallible! If you deny that, you deny your very faith."

The door opened discreetly, but hastily.

"Your Eminence, Herr General Kesselring."

Both prelates rose, their late differences smoothed from their faces, smiling.

"This is a great pleasure, Your Excellency. Won't you sit down? Would you like tea?"

The conversation was conducted in German, since many of the senior members of the Vatican spoke it. The Holy Father was fond of speaking and listening to German.

"Thank you, Your Eminence, I would. Nowhere else in Rome does one get such superbly *English* tea."

Cardinal Vittorio smiled guilelessly. "It is a habit I acquired while I was the Papal Legate in Australia, and which, for all my innate Italianness, I have not been able to break."

"And you, Your Grace?"

"I'm an Irishman, Herr General. The Irish, too, are brought up on tea."

General Albert Kesselring always responded to Archbishop de Bricassart as one man to another; after these slight, oily Italian prelates he was so refreshing, a man without subtlety or cunning, straightforward.

"As always, Your Grace, I am amazed at the purity of your German accent," he complimented.

"I have an ear for languages, Herr General, which means it's like all talents—not worth praising."

"What may we do for Your Excellency?" asked the Cardinal sweetly.

"I presume you will have heard of the fate of Il Duce by now?"

"Yes, Your Excellency, we have."

"Then you will know in part why I came. To assure you that all is well, and to ask you if perhaps you would convey the message to those summering at Castel Gandolfo? I'm so busy at the moment it's impossible for me to visit Castel Gandolfo myself."

"The message will be conveyed. You are so busy?"

"Naturally. You must surely realize this is now an enemy country for us Germans?"

"This, Herr General? This is not Italian soil, and no man is an enemy here except those who are evil."

"I beg your pardon, Your Eminence. Naturally I was referring to Italy, not to the Vatican. But in the matter of Italy I must act as my Führer commands. Italy will be occupied, and my troops, present until now as allies, will become policemen."

Archbishop Ralph, sitting comfortably and looking as if he had never had an ideological struggle in his life, watched the visitor closely. Did he know what his Führer was doing in Poland? How could he *not* know?

Cardinal Vittorio arranged his face into an anxious look. "Dear General, not Rome herself, surely? Ah, no! Rome, with her history, her priceless artifacts? If you bring troops within her seven hills there will be strife, destruction. I beg of you, not that!"

General Kesselring looked uncomfortable. "I hope it won't come to that, Your Eminence. But I took an oath also, I too am under orders. I must do as my Führer wishes."

"You'll try for us, Herr General? Please, you must!

I was in Athens some years ago," said Archbishop Ralph quickly, leaning forward, his eyes charmingly wide, a lock of white-sprinkled hair falling across his brow; he was well aware of his effect on the general, and used it without compunction. "Have you been in Athens, sir?"

"Yes, I have," said the general dryly.

"Then I'm sure you know the story. How it took men of relatively modern times to destroy the buildings atop the Acropolis? Herr General, Rome stands as she always was, a monument to two thousand years of care, attention, love. Please, I beg of you! Don't endanger Rome."

The general stared at him in startled admiration; his uniform became him very well, but no better than the soutane with its touch of imperial purple became Archbishop Ralph. He, too, had the look of a soldier, a soldier's sparely beautiful body, and the face of an angel. So must the Archangel Michael look; not a smooth young Renaissance boy but an aging perfect man, who had loved Lucifer, fought him, banished Adam and Eve, slain the serpent, stood at God's right hand. Did he know how he looked? He was indeed a man to remember.

"I shall do my best, Your Grace, I promise you. To a certain extent the decision is mine, I admit it. I am, as you know, a civilized man. But you're asking a lot. If I declare Rome an open city, it means I cannot blow up her bridges or convert her buildings into fortresses, and that might well be to Germany's eventual disadvantage. What assurances do I have that Rome won't repay me with treachery if I'm kind to her?"

Cardinal Vittorio pursed his lips and made kissing noises at his cat, an elegant Siamese nowadays; he smiled gently, and looked at the Archbishop. "Rome would never repay kindness with treachery, Herr General. I am sure when you do find the time to visit those summering at Castel Gandolfo that you will receive the same assurances. Here, Kheng-see, my sweetheart! Ah, what a lovely girl you are!" His hands pressed it down on his scarlet lap, caressed it.

"An unusual animal, Your Eminence."

"An aristocrat, Herr General. Both the Archbishop and myself bear old and venerable names, but beside her lineage, ours are as nothing. Do you like her name? It is Chinese for silken flower. Apt, is it not?"

The tea had arrived, was being arranged; they were all quiet until the lay sister left the room.

"You won't regret a decision to declare Rome an open city, Your Excellency," said Archbishop Ralph to the new master of Italy with a melting smile. He turned to the Cardinal, charm falling away like a dropped cloak, not needed with this beloved man. "Your Eminence, do you intend to be 'mother,' or shall I do the honors?"

" 'Mother'?" asked General Kesselring blankly.

Cardinal di Contini-Verchese laughed. "It is our little joke, we celibate men. Whoever pours the tea is called 'mother.' An *English* saying, Herr General."

That night Archbishop Ralph was tired, restless, on edge. He seemed to be doing nothing to help end this war, only dicker about the preservation of antiquities, and he had grown to loathe Vatican inertia passionately. Though he was conservative by nature, sometimes the snaillike caution of those occupying the highest Church positions irked him intolerably. Aside from the humble nuns and priests who acted as servants, it was weeks since he had spoken to an ordinary man, someone without a political, spiritual or military axe to grind. Even prayer seemed to come less easily to him these days, and God seemed light-years away, as if He had withdrawn to allow His human creatures full rein in destroying the world He had made for them. What he needed, he thought, was a stiff dose of Meggie and Fee, or a stiff dose of someone who wasn't interested in the fate of the Vatican or of Rome.

His Grace walked down the private stairs into the great basilica of Saint Peter's, whence his aimless progress had led him. Its doors were locked these days the moment darkness fell, a sign of the uneasy peace which lay over Rome more telling than the companies of grey-clad Germans moving through Roman streets. A faint, ghostly glow illuminated the yawning empty apse; his footsteps echoed hollowly on the stone floor as he walked, stopped and merged with the silence as he genuflected in front of the High Altar, began again. Then, between one foot's noise of impact and the next, he heard a gasp. The flashlight in his hand sprang into life; he leveled his beam in the direction of the sound, not frightened so much as curious. This was his world; he could defend it secure from fear.

The beam played upon what had become in his eyes the most beautiful piece of sculpture in all creation: the Pietà of Michelangelo. Below the stilled stunned figures was another face, made not of marble but of flesh, all shadowed hollows and deathlike.

"Ciao," said His Grace, smiling.

There was no answer, but he saw that the clothes were those of a German infantryman of lowest rank; his ordinary man! That he was a German didn't matter.

"Wie geht's?" he asked, still smiling.

A movement caused sweat on a wide, intellectual brow to flash suddenly out of the dimness.

"Du bist krank?" he asked then, wondering if the lad, for he was no more, was ill.

Came the voice, at last: *"Nein."*

Archbishop Ralph laid his flashlight down on the floor and went forward, put his hand under the soldier's chin and lifted it to look into the dark eyes, darker in the darkness.

"What's the matter?" he asked in German, and laughed. "There!" he continued, still in German. "You don't know it, but that's been my main function in life—to ask people what's the matter. And, let me tell you, it's a question which has got me into a lot of trouble in my time."

"I came to pray," said the lad in a voice too deep for his age, with a heavy Bavarian accent.

"What happened, did you get locked in?"

"Yes, but that isn't what the matter is."

His grace picked up the flashlight. "Well, you can't stay here all night, and I haven't got a key to the doors. Come with me." He began walking back toward the private stairs leading up to the papal palace, talking in a slow, soft voice. "I came to pray myself, as a matter of fact. Thanks to your High Command, it's been a rather nasty day. That's it, up here. . . . We'll have to hope that the Holy Father's staff don't assume I've been arrested, but can see I'm doing the escorting, not you."

After that they walked for ten more minutes in silence, through corridors, out into open courts and gardens, inside hallways, up steps; the young German did not seem anxious to leave his protector's side, for he kept close. At last His Grace opened a door and led his waif into a small sitting room, sparsely and humbly furnished, switched on a lamp and closed the door.

They stood staring at each other, able to see. The German soldier saw a very tall man with a fine face and blue, discerning eyes; Archbishop Ralph saw a child tricked out in the garb which all of Europe found fearsome and awe-inspiring. A child; no more than sixteen years old, certainly. Of average height and youthfully thin, he had a frame promising later bulk and strength, and very long arms. His face had rather an Italianate cast, dark and patrician, extremely attractive; wide, dark brown eyes with long black lashes, a magnificent head of wavy black hair. There was nothing usual or ordinary about him after all, even if his role was an ordinary one; in spite of the fact that he had longed to talk to an average, ordinary man, His Grace was interested.

"Sit down," he said to the boy, crossing to a chest

and unearthing a bottle of Marsala wine. He poured some into two glasses, gave the boy one and took his own to a chair from which he could watch the fascinating countenance comfortably. "Are they reduced to drafting children to do their fighting?" he asked, crossing his legs.

"I don't know," said the boy. "I was in a children's home, so I'd be taken early anyway."

"What's your name, lad?"

"Rainer Moerling Hartheim," said the boy, rolling it out with great pride.

"A magnificent name," said the priest gravely.

"It is, isn't it? I chose it myself. They called me Rainer Schmidt at the home, but when I went into the army I changed it to the name I've always wanted."

"You were an orphan?"

"The Sisters called me a love child."

Archbishop Ralph tried not to smile; the boy had such dignity and self-possession, now he had lost his fear. Only what had frightened him? Not being found, or being locked in the basilica.

"Why were you so frightened, Rainer?"

The boy sipped his wine gingerly, looked up with a pleased expression. "Good, it's sweet." He made himself more comfortable. "I wanted to see Saint Peter's because the Sisters always used to talk about it and show us pictures. So when they posted us to Rome I was glad. We got here this morning. The minute I could, I came." He frowned. "But it wasn't as I had expected. I thought I'd feel closer to Our Lord, being in His own Church. Instead it was only enormous and cold. I couldn't feel Him."

Archbishop Ralph smiled. "I know what you mean. But Saint Peter's isn't really a church, you know. Not in the sense most churches are. Saint Peter's is *the* Church. It took me a long time to get used to it, I remember."

"I wanted to pray for two things," the boy said, nodding his head to indicate he had heard but that it wasn't what he wished to hear.

"For the things which frighten you?"

"Yes. I thought being in Saint Peter's might help."

"What are the things which frighten you, Rainer?"

"That they'll decide I'm a Jew, and that my regiment will be sent to Russia after all."

"I see. No wonder you're frightened. Is there indeed a possibility they'll decide you're a Jew?"

"Well, look at me!" said the boy simply. "When they were writing down my particulars they said they'd have to check. I don't know if they can or not, but I suppose the Sisters might know more than they ever told me."

"If they do, they'll not pass it on," said His Grace comfortingly. "They'll know why they're being asked."

"Do you really think so? Oh, I hope so!"

"Does the thought of having Jewish blood disturb you?"

"What my blood is doesn't matter," said Rainer. "I was born a German, that's the only important thing."

"Only they don't look at it like that, do they?"

"No."

"And Russia? There's no need to worry about Russia now, surely. You're in Rome, the opposite direction."

"This morning I heard our commander saying we might be sent to Russia after all. It isn't going well there."

"You're a child," said Archbishop Ralph abruptly. "You ought to be in school."

"I wouldn't be now anyway." The boy smiled. "I'm sixteen, so I'd be working." He sighed. "I would have liked to keep going to school. Learning is important."

Archbishop Ralph started to laugh, then got up and refilled the glasses. "Don't take any notice of me, Rainer. I'm not making any sense. Just thoughts, one after the other. It's my hour for them, thoughts. I'm not a very good host, am I?"

"You're all right," said the boy.

"So," said His Grace, sitting down again. "Define yourself, Rainer Moerling Hartheim."

A curious pride settled on the young face. "I'm a German, and a Catholic. I want to make Germany a place where race and religion won't mean persecution, and I'm going to devote my life to that end, if I live."

"I shall pray for you—that you live, and succeed."

"Would you?" asked the boy shyly. "Would you really pray for me personally, by name?"

"Of course. In fact, you've taught me something. That in my business there is only one weapon at my disposal—prayer. I have no other function."

"Who are you?" asked Rainer, the wine beginning to make him blink drowsily.

"I'm Archbishop Ralph de Bricassart."

"Oh! I thought you were an ordinary priest!"

"I *am* an ordinary priest. Nothing more."

"I'll strike a bargain with you!" said the boy, his eyes sparkling. "You pray for me, Father, and if I live long enough to get what I want, I'll come back to Rome to let you see what your prayers have done."

The blue eyes smiled tenderly. "All right, it's a bargain. And when you come, I'll tell you what *I* think happened to my prayers." He got up. "Stay there, little politician. I'll find you something to eat."

They talked until dawn glowed round the domes and campaniles, and the wings of pigeons whirred outside the window. Then the Archbishop conducted his guest through the public rooms of the palace, watching his awe with delight, and let him out into the cool, fresh air. Though he didn't know it, the boy with the splendid name was indeed to go to Russia, carrying with him a memory oddly sweet and reassuring: that in Rome, in Our Lord's own Church, a man was praying for him every day, by name.

By the time the Ninth was ready to be shipped to New Guinea, it was all over bar the mopping up. Disgruntled, the most elite division in Australian military history could only hope there might be further glory to amass somewhere else, chasing the Japanese back up through Indonesia. Guadalcanal had defeated all Japanese hopes in the drive for Australia. And yet, like the Germans, they yielded bitterly, grudgingly. Though their resources were pitifully stretched, their armies foundering from lack of supplies and reinforcements, they made the Americans and the Australians pay for every inch they gained back. In retreat, the Japanese abandoned Buna, Gona, Salamaua, and slipped back up the north coast, to Lae and Finschafen.

On the fifth of September 1943 the Ninth Division was landed from the sea just east of Lae. It was hot, the humidity was 100 percent, and it rained every afternoon though The Wet wasn't due for another two full months. The threat of malaria meant everyone was taking Atabrine, and the little yellow tablets made everyone feel as sick as if they had the actual malaria. Already the constant moisture meant permanently damp boots and socks; feet were becoming spongy, the flesh between the toes raw and bloody. Mocka and mosquito bites turned angry, ulcerated.

In Port Moresby they had seen the wretched state of the New Guinea natives, and if they couldn't stand the climate without developing yaws, beriberi, malaria, pneumonia, chronic skin diseases, enlarged livers and spleens, there wasn't much hope for the white man. There were survivors of Kokoda in Port Moresby as well, victims not so much of the Japanese but of New Guinea, emaciated, masses of sores, delirious with fever. Ten times as many had died from pneumonia nine thousand feet up in freezing cold wearing thin tropical kit as died from the Japanese. Greasy dank mud, unearthly forests which glowed with cold pale spectral light after dark from phosphorescent fungi, precipitous climbs over a gnarled tangle of exposed roots which meant a man couldn't look up for a second and was a sitting duck for a sniper. It was about as different from North Africa as any place could get, and the Ninth wasn't a bit sorry it had stayed to fight the two Alameins instead of Kokoda Trail.

Lae was a coastal town amid heavily forested grasslands, far from the eleven-thousand-foot elevations of the deep interior, and far more salubrious as a battleground than Kokoda. Just a few European houses, a petrol pump, and a collection of native huts. The Japanese were as ever game, but few in number and impoverished, as worn out from New Guinea as the Australians they had been fighting, as disease ridden. After the massive ordnance and extreme mechanization of North Africa it was strange never to see a mortar or a fieldpiece; just Owen guns and rifles, with bayonets in place all the time. Jims and Patsy liked hand-to-hand fighting, they liked to go in close together, guard each other. It was a terrible comedown after the Afrika Korps, though, there was no doubt about it. Pint-size yellow men who all seemed to wear glasses and have buck teeth. They had absolutely no martial panache.

Two weeks after the Ninth landed at Lae, there were no more Japanese. It was, for spring in New Guinea, a very beautiful day. The humidity had dropped twenty points, the sun shone out of a sky suddenly blue instead of steamily white, the watershed reared green, purple and lilac beyond the town. Discipline had relaxed, everyone seemed to be taking the day off to play cricket, walk around, tease the natives to make them laugh and display their blood-red, toothless gums, the result of chewing betel nut. Jims and Patsy were strolling through the tall grass beyond the town, for it reminded them of Drogheda; it was the same bleached, tawny color, and long the way Drogheda grass was after a season of heavy rain.

"Won't be long now until we're back, Patsy," said Jims. "We've got the Nips on the run, and Jerry, too. Home, Patsy, home to Drogheda! I can hardly wait."

"Yair," said Patsy.

They walked shoulder to shoulder, much closer than was permissible between ordinary men; they would touch each other sometimes, not consciously but as a man touches his own body, to relieve a mild itch or absently assure himself it is still all there. How nice it was to feel genuinely sunny sun on their faces instead of a molten ball in a Turkish bath! Every so often they would lift their muzzles to the sky, flare their nostrils to take in the scent of hot light on Drogheda-like grass, dream a little that they were back there, walking toward a wilga in the daze of noon to lie down through the worst of it, read a book, drowse. Roll over, feel the friendly, beautiful earth through their skins, sense a mighty heart beating away down under somewhere, like a mother's heart to a sleepy baby.

"Jims! Look! A dinkum Drogheda budgie!" said Patsy, shocked into speaking.

Perhaps budgerigars were natives of the Lae country, too, but the mood of the day and this quite unexpected reminder of home suddenly triggered a wild elation in Patsy. Laughing, feeling the grass tickling his bare legs, he took off after it, snatching his battered slouch hat from his head and holding it out as if he truly believed he could snare the vanishing bird. Smiling, Jims stood watching him.

He was perhaps twenty yards away when the machine gun ripped the grass to flying shreds around him; Jims saw his arms go up, his body spin round so that the arms seemed stretched out in supplication. From waist to knees he was brilliant blood, life's blood.

"Patsy, Patsy!" Jims screamed; in every cell of his own body he felt the bullets, felt himself ebbing, dying.

His legs opened in a huge stride, he gained momentum to run, then his military caution asserted itself and he dived headlong into the grass just as the machine gun opened up again.

"Patsy, Patsy, are you all right?" he cried stupidly, having seen that blood.

Yet incredibly, "Yair," came a faint answer.

Inch by inch Jims dragged himself forward through the fragrant grass, listening to the wind, the rustlings of his own progress.

When he reached his brother he put his head against the naked shoulder, and wept.

"Break it down," said Patsy. "I'm not dead yet."

"How bad is it?" Jims asked, pulling down the blood-soaked shorts to see blood-soaked flesh, shivering.

"Doesn't feel as if I'm going to die, anyway."

Men had appeared all around them, the cricketers still wearing their leg pads and gloves; someone went back for a stretcher while the rest proceeded to silence the gun at the far side of the clearing. The deed was done with more than usual ruthlessness, for everyone was fond of Harpo. If anything happened to him, Jims would never be the same.

A beautiful day; the budgerigar had long gone, but other birds trilled and twittered fearlessly, silenced only during the actual battle.

"Patsy's bloody lucky," said the medic to Jims some time later. "There must be a dozen bullets in him, but most of them hit the thighs. The two or three higher up seem to have embedded themselves in pelvic bone or muscle. As far as I can judge, his gut's in one piece, so is his bladder. The only thing is . . ."

"Well, what?" Jims prompted impatiently; he was still shaking, and blue around the mouth.

"Difficult to say anything for certain at this stage, of course, and I'm not a genius surgeon like some of the blokes in Moresby. They'll be able to tell you a lot more. But the urethra has been damaged, so have many of the tiny little nerves in the perineum. I'm pretty sure he can be patched up as good as new, except maybe for the nerves. Nerves don't patch up too well, unfortunately." He cleared his throat. "What I'm trying to say is that he might never have much sensation in the genital region."

Jims dropped his head, looked at the ground through a crystal wall of tears. "At least he's alive," he said.

He was granted leave to fly to Port Moresby with his brother, and to stay until Patsy was pronounced out of danger. The injuries were little short of miraculous. Bullets had scattered all around the lower abdomen without penetrating it. But the Ninth medic had been right; lower pelvic sensation was badly impaired. How much he might regain later on no one was prepared to say.

"It doesn't much matter," said Patsy from the stretcher on which he was to be flown to Sydney. "I was never too keen on marrying, anyway. Now, you look after yourself, Jims, do you hear? I hate leaving you."

"I'll look after myself, Patsy. Christ!" Jims grinned, holding hard onto his brother's hand. "Fancy having to spend the rest of the war without my best mate. I'll write and tell you what it's like. Say hello to Mrs. Smith and Meggie and Mum and the brothers for me, eh? Half your luck, going home to Drogheda."

Fee and Mrs. Smith flew down to Sydney to meet the American plane which brought Patsy from Townsville; Fee remained only a few days, but Mrs. Smith stayed on in a Randwick hotel close to the Prince of Wales military hospital. Patsy remained there for three months. His part in the war was over. Many tears had Mrs. Smith shed; but there was much to be thankful for, too. In one way he would never be able to lead a full life, but he could do everything else: ride, walk, run. Mating didn't seem to be in the Cleary line, anyway. When he was discharged from hospital Meggie drove down from Gilly in the Rolls, and the two women tucked him up on the back seat amid blankets and magazines, praying for one more boon: that Jims would come home, too.

16

Not until the Emperor Hirohito's delegate signed Japan's official surrender did Gillanbone believe the war was finally over. The news came on Sunday, September 2, 1945, which was exactly six years after the start. Six agonizing years. So many places empty, never to be filled again: Dominic O'Rourke's son Rory, Horry Hopeton's son John, Eden Carmichael's son Cormac. Ross MacQueen's youngest son, Angus, would never walk again, Anthony King's son David would walk but never see where he was going, Paddy Cleary's son Patsy would never have children. And there were those whose wounds weren't visible, but whose scars went just as deep; who had gone off gaily, eager and laughing, but came home quietly, said little, and laughed only rarely. Who could have dreamed when it began that it would go on so long, or take such a toll?

Gillanbone was not a particularly superstitious community, but even the most cynical resident shivered that Sunday, September 2nd. For on the same day that the war ended, so did the longest drought in the history of Australia. For nearly ten years no useful rain had fallen, but that day the clouds filled the sky thousands of feet deep, blackly, cracked themselves open and poured twelve inches of rain on the thirsty earth. An inch of rain may not mean the breaking of a drought, it might not be followed by anything more, but twelve inches of rain means *grass.*

Meggie, Fee, Bob, Jack, Hughie and Patsy stood on the veranda watching it through the darkness, sniffing the unbearably sweet perfume of rain on parched and crumbling soil. Horses, sheep, cattle and pigs spraddled their legs against the shifting of the melting ground and let the water pour over their twitching bodies; most of them had been born since rain like this had last passed across their world. In the cemetery the rain washed the dust away, whitened everything, washed the dust off the outstretched wings of the bland Botticelli angel. The creek produced a tidal wave, its roaring flood mingling with the drumming of the soaking rain. Rain, rain! Rain. Like a benediction from some vast inscrutable hand, long withheld, finally given. The blessed, wonderful rain. For rain meant grass, and grass was life.

A pale-green fuzz appeared, poked its little blades skyward, ramified, burgeoned, grew a darker green as it lengthened, then faded and waxed fat, became the silver-beige, knee-high grass of Drogheda. The Home Paddock looked like a field of wheat, rippling with every mischievous puff of wind, and the homestead gardens exploded into color, great buds unfurling, the ghost gums suddenly white and lime-green again after nine years of griming dust. For though Michael Carson's insane proliferation of water tanks still held enough to keep the homestead gardens alive, dust had long settled on every leaf and petal, dimmed and drabbed. And an old legend had been proven fact: Drogheda did indeed have sufficient water to survive ten years of drought, but only for the homestead.

Bob, Jack, Hughie and Patsy went back to the paddocks, began seeing how best to restock; Fee opened a brand-new bottle of black ink and savagely screwed the lid down on her bottle of red ink; Meggie saw an end coming to her life in the saddle, for it would not be long before Jims was home and men turned up looking for jobs.

After nine years there were very few sheep or cattle left, only the prize breeders which were always penned and hand-fed in any time, the nucleus of champion stock, rams and bulls. Bob went east to the top of the Western slopes to buy ewes of good blood line from properties not so hard hit by the drought. Jims came home. Eight stockmen were added to the Drogheda payroll. Meggie hung up her saddle.

It was not long after this that Meggie got a letter from Luke, the second since she had left him.

"Not long now, I reckon," he said. "A few more years in the sugar should see me through. The old back's a bit sore these days, but I can still cut with the best of them, eight or nine tons a day. Arne and I have twelve other gangs cutting for us, all good blokes. Money's getting very loose, Europe wants sugar as fast as we can produce it. I'm making over five thousand quid a year, saving almost all of it. Won't be long now, Meg, before I'm out around Kynuna. Maybe when I get things together you might want to come back to me. Did I give you the kid you wanted? Funny, how women get their hearts set on kids. I reckon that's what really broke us up, eh? Let me know how you're getting on, and how Drogheda weathered the drought. Yours, Luke."

Fee came out onto the veranda, where Meggie sat with the letter in her hand, staring absently out across the brilliant green of the homestead lawns.

"How's Luke?"

"The same as ever, Mum. Not a bit changed. Still on about a little while longer in the damned sugar, the place he's going to have one day out around Kynuna."

"Do you think he'll ever actually do it?"

"I suppose so, one day."

"Would you go to join him, Meggie?"

"Not in a million years."

Fee sat down in a cane chair beside her daughter, pulling it round so she could see Meggie properly. In the distance men were shouting, hammers pounded; at long last the verandas and the upper-story windows of the homestead were being enclosed by fine wire mesh to screen out the flies. For years Fee had held out, obdurate. No matter how many flies there were, the lines of the house would never be spoiled by ugly netting. But the longer the drought dragged on the worse the flies became, until two weeks before it ended Fee had given in and hired a contractor to enclose every building on the station, not only the homestead itself but all the staff houses and barracks as well.

But electrify she would not, though since 1915 there had been a "donk," as the shearers called it, to supply power to the shearing shed. Drogheda without the gentle diffusion of lamps? It wasn't to be thought of. However, there was one of the new gas stoves which burned off cylindered gas on order, and a dozen of the new kerosene refrigerators; Australian industry wasn't yet on a peacetime footing, but eventually the new appliances would come.

"Meggie, why don't you divorce Luke, marry again?" Fee asked suddenly. "Enoch Davies would have you in a second; he's never looked at anyone else."

Meggie's lovely eyes surveyed her mother in wonder. "Good Lord, Mum, I do believe you're actually talking to me as one woman to another!"

Fee didn't smile; Fee still rarely smiled. "Well, if you aren't a woman by now, you'll never be one. I'd say you qualified. I must be getting old; I feel garrulous."

Meggie laughed, delighted at her mother's overture, and anxious not to destroy this new mood. "It's the rain, Mum. It must be. Oh, isn't it wonderful to see grass on Drogheda again, and green lawns around the homestead?"

"Yes, it is. But you're side-stepping my question. Why not divorce Luke, marry again?"

"It's against the laws of the Church."

"Piffle!" exclaimed Fee, but gently. "Half of you is me, and I'm not a Catholic. Don't give me that, Meggie. If you really wanted to marry, you'd divorce Luke."

"Yes, I suppose I would. But I don't want to marry again. I'm quite happy with my children and Drogheda."

A chuckle very like her own echoed from the interior of the bottle-brush shrubbery nearby, its drooping scarlet cylinders hiding the author of the chuckle.

"Listen! There he is, that's Dane! Do you know at his age he can sit a horse as well as I can?" She leaned forward. "Dane! What are you up to? Come out of there this instant!"

He crawled out from under the closest bottle brush, his hands full of black earth, suspicious black smears all around his mouth.

"Mum! Did you know soil tastes good? It really does, Mum, honestly!"

He came to stand in front of her; at seven he was tall, slender, gracefully strong, and had a face of delicate porcelain beauty.

Justine appeared, came to stand beside him. She too was tall, but skinny rather than slender, and atrociously freckled. It was hard to see what her features were like beneath the brown spots, but those unnerving eyes were as pale as they had been in infancy, and the sandy brows and lashes were too fair to emerge from the freckles. Paddy's fiercely red tresses rioted in a mass of curls around her rather pixyish face. No one could have called her a pretty child, but no one ever forgot her, not merely on account of the eyes but also because she had remarkable strength of character. Astringent, forthright and uncompromisingly intelligent, Justine at eight cared as little what anyone thought of her as she had when a baby. Only one person was very close to her: Dane. She still adored him, and still regarded him as her own property.

Which had led to many a tussle of wills between her

and her mother. It had been a rude shock to Justine when Meggie hung up her saddle and got back to being a mother. For one thing, Justine didn't seem to need a mother, since she was convinced she was right about everything. Nor was she the sort of little girl who required a confidante, or warm approval. As far as she was concerned, Meggie was mostly someone who interfered with her pleasure in Dane. She got on a lot better with her grandmother, who was just the sort of person Justine heartily approved of; she kept her distance and assumed one had a little sense.

"I *told* him not to eat dirt," Justine said.

"Well, it won't kill him, Justine, but it isn't good for him, either." Meggie turned to her son. "Dane, why?"

He considered the question gravely. "It was there, so I ate it. If it was bad for me, wouldn't it taste bad, too? It tastes good."

"Not necessarily," Justine interrupted loftily. "I give up on you, Dane, I really do. Some of the best-tasting things are the most poisonous."

"Name one!" he challenged.

"Treacle!" she said triumphantly.

Dane had been very ill after finding a tin of treacle in Mrs. Smith's pantry and eating the lot. He admitted the thrust, but countered. "I'm still here, so it can't be all that poisonous."

"That's only because you vomited. If you hadn't vomited, you'd be dead."

This was inarguable. He and his sister were much of a height, so he tucked his arm companionably through hers and they sauntered away across the lawn toward their cubbyhouse, which their uncles had erected as instructed amid the down-drooping branches of a pepper tree. Danger from bees had led to much adult opposition to this site, but the children were proven right. The bees dwelled with them amicably. For, said the children, pepper trees were the nicest of all trees, very private. They had such a dry, fragrant smell, and the grapelike clusters of tiny pink globules they bore crumbled into crisp, pungent pink flakes when crushed in the hand.

"They're so different from each other, Dane and Justine, yet they get along so well together," said Meggie. "It never ceases to amaze me. I don't think I've ever seen them quarrel, though how Dane avoids quarreling with some one as determined and stubborn as Justine, I don't understand."

But Fee had something else on her mind. "Lord, he's the living image of his father," she said, watching Dane duck under the lowest fronds of the pepper tree and disappear from sight.

Meggie felt herself go cold, a reflex response which years of hearing people say this had not scotched. It was just her own guilt, of course. People always meant Luke. Why not? There were basic similarities between Luke O'Neill and Ralph de Bricassart. But try as she would, she could never be quite natural when Dane's likeness to his father was commented upon.

She drew a carefully casual breath. "Do you think so, Mum?" she asked, nonchalantly swinging her foot. "I can never see it myself. Dane is nothing like Luke in nature or attitude to life."

Fee laughed. It came out as a snort, but it was a genuine laugh. Grown pallid with age and encroaching cataracts, her eyes rested on Meggie's startled face, grim and ironic. "Do you take me for a fool, Meggie? I don't mean Luke O'Neill. I mean Dane is the living image of Ralph de Bricassart."

Lead. Her foot was made of lead. It dropped to the Spanish tiles, her leaden body sagged, the lead heart within her breast struggled against its vast weight to beat. Beat, damn you, beat! You've got to go on beating for my son!

"Why, Mum!" Her voice was leaden, too. "Why, Mum, what an extraordinary thing to say! *Father Ralph de Bricassart?"*

"How many people of that name do you know? Luke O'Neill never bred that boy; he's Ralph de Bricassart's son. I knew it the minute I took him out of you at his birth."

"Then—why haven't you said something? Why wait until he's seven years old to make such an insane and unfounded accusation?"

Fee stretched her legs out, crossed them daintily at the ankles. "I'm getting old at last, Meggie. And things don't hurt as much anymore. What a blessing old age can be! It's so good to see Drogheda coming back, I feel better within myself because of it. For the first time in years I feel like talking."

"Well, I must say when you decide to talk you really know how to pick your subject! Mum, you have absolutely no right to say such a thing. It isn't true!" said Meggie desperately, not sure if her mother was bent on torture or commiseration.

Suddenly Fee's hand came out, rested on Meggie's knee, and she was smiling—not bitterly or contemptuously, but with a curious sympathy. "Don't lie to *me,* Meggie. Lie to anyone else under the sun, but don't lie to *me*. Nothing will ever convince me Luke O'Neill fathered that boy. I'm not a fool, I have eyes. There's no Luke in him, there never was because there couldn't be. He's the image of the priest. Look at his hands, the way his hair grows in a widow's peak, the shape of his face, the eyebrows, the mouth. Even how he moves. Ralph de Bricassart, Meggie, Ralph de Bricassart."

Meggie gave in, the enormity of her relief showing in the way she sat, loosely now, relaxed. "The distance in his eyes. That's what I notice myself most of all. Is it so obvious? Does everyone know, Mum?"

"Of course not," said Fee positively. "People don't look any further than the color of the eyes, the shape of the nose, the general build. Like enough to Luke's. I knew because I'd been watching you and Ralph de Bricassart for years. All he had to do was crook his little finger and you'd have gone running, so a fig for your 'it's against the laws of the Church' when it comes to divorce. You were panting to break a far more serious law of the Church than the one about divorce. Shameless, Meggie, that's what you were. Shameless!" A hint of hardness crept into her voice. "But he was a stubborn man. His heart was set on being a perfect priest; you came a very bad second. Oh, idiocy! It didn't do him any good, did it? It was only a matter of time before something happened."

Around the corner of the veranda someone dropped a hammer, and let fly with a string of curses; Fee winced, shuddered. "Dear heaven, I'll be glad when they're done with the screening!" She got back to the subject. "Did you think you fooled me when you wouldn't have Ralph de Bricassart to marry you to Luke? *I* knew. You wanted him as the bridegroom, not as the officiating cleric. Then when he came to Drogheda before he left for Athens and you weren't here, I knew sooner or later he'd have to go and find you. He wandered around the place as lost as a little boy at the Sydney Royal Easter Show. Marrying Luke was the smartest move you made, Meggie. As long as he knew you were pining for him Ralph didn't want you, but the minute you became somebody else's he exhibited all the classical signs of the dog in the manger. Of course he'd convinced himself that his attachment to you was as pure as the driven snow, but the fact remained that he needed you. You were necessary to him in a way no other woman ever had been, or I suspect ever will be. Strange," said Fee with real puzzlement. "I always wondered what on earth he saw in you, but I suppose mothers are always a little blind about their daughters until they're too old to be jealous of youth. You are about Justine, the same as I was about you."

She leaned back in her chair, rocking slightly, her eyes half closed, but she watched Meggie like a scientist his specimen.

"Whatever it was he saw in you," she went on, "he saw it the first time he met you, and it never left off enchanting him. The hardest thing he had to face was your growing up, but he faced it that time he came to find you gone, married. Poor Ralph! He had no choice but to look for you. And he did find you, didn't he? I knew it when you came home, before Dane was born. Once you had Ralph de Bricassart it wasn't necessary to stay any longer with Luke."

"Yes," sighed Meggie, "Ralph found me. But it didn't solve anything for us, did it? I knew he would never be willing to give up his God. It was for that reason I was determined to have the only part of him I ever could. His child. Dane."

"It's like listening to an echo," Fee said, laughing her rusty laugh. "You might be me, saying that."

"Frank?"

The chair scraped; Fee got up, paced the tiles, came back and stared hard at her daughter. "Well, well! Tit for tat, eh, Meggie? How long have *you* known?"

"Since I was a little girl. Since the time Frank ran away."

"His father was married already. He was a lot older than me, an important politician. If I told you his name, you'd recognize it. There are streets named for him all over New Zealand, a town or two probably. But for the purpose, I'll call him Pakeha. It's Maori for 'white man,' but it'll do. He's dead now, of course. I have a trace of Maori blood in me, but Frank's father was half Maori. It showed in Frank because he got it from both of us. Oh, but I loved that man! Perhaps it was the call of our blood, I don't know. He was handsome. A big man with a mop of black hair and the most brilliant, laughing black eyes. He was everything Paddy wasn't—cultured, sophisticated, very charming. I loved him to the point of madness. And I thought I'd never love anyone else; I wallowed in that delusion so long I left it too late, too late!" Her voice broke. She turned to look at the garden. "I have a lot to answer for, Meggie, believe me."

"So that's why you loved Frank more than the rest of us," Meggie said.

"I thought I did, because he was Pakeha's son and the rest belonged to Paddy," She sat down, made a queer, mournful noise. "So history does repeat itself. I had a quiet laugh when I saw Dane, I tell you."

"Mum, you're an extraordinary woman!"

"Am I?" The chair creaked; she leaned forward. "Let me whisper you a little secret, Meggie. Extraordinary or merely ordinary, I'm a very unhappy woman. For one reason or another I've been unhappy since the day I met Pakeha. Mostly my own fault. I loved him, but what he did to me shouldn't happen to any woman. And there was Frank. . . . I kept hanging on to Frank, and ignoring the rest of you. Ignoring Paddy, who was the best thing ever happened to me. Only I didn't see it. I was too busy comparing him with Pakeha. Oh, I was grateful to him, and I couldn't help but see what a fine man he was. . . ." She shrugged. "Well, all that's past. What I wanted to say was that it's wrong, Meggie. You know that, don't you?"

"No, I don't. The way I see it, the Church is wrong, expecting to take that from her priests as well."

"Funny, how we always infer the Church is feminine. You stole a woman's man, Meggie, just as I did."

"Ralph had absolutely no allegiance to any woman, except to me. The Church isn't a woman, Mum. It's a thing, an institution."

"Don't bother trying to justify yourself to me. I know all the answers. I thought as you do myself, at the time. Divorce was out of the question for him. He was one of the first people of his race to attain political greatness; he had to choose between me and his people. What man could resist a chance like that to be noble? Just as your Ralph chose the Church, didn't he? So I thought,

I don't care. I'll take what I can get of him, I'll have his child to love at least."

But suddenly Meggie was too busy hating her mother to be able to pity her, too busy resenting the inference that she herself had made just as big a mess of things. So she said, "Except that I far outdid you in subtlety, Mum. *My* son has a name no one can take from him, even including Luke."

Fee's breath hissed between her teeth. "Nasty! Oh, you're deceptive, Meggie! Butter wouldn't melt in your mouth, would it? Well, my father *bought* my husband to give Frank a name and get rid of me: I'll bet you never knew that! How did you know?"

"That's my business."

"You're going to pay, Meggie. Believe me, you're going to pay. You won't get away with it any more than I did. I lost Frank in the worst way a mother could; I can't even see him and I long to. . . . You wait! You'll lose Dane, too."

"Not if I can help it. You lost Frank because he couldn't pull in tandem with Daddy. I made sure Dane had no daddy to harness him. *I'll* harness him instead, to Drogheda. Why do you think I'm making a stockman out of him already? He'll be safe on Drogheda."

"Was Daddy? Was Stuart? Nowhere is safe. And you won't keep Dane here if he wants to go. Daddy didn't harness Frank. That was it. Frank couldn't be harnessed. And if you think you, a woman, can harness Ralph de Bricassart's son, you've got another think coming. It stands to reason, doesn't it? If neither of us could hold the father, how can we hope to hold the son?"

"The only way I can lose Dane is if you open your mouth, Mum. And I'm warning you, I'd kill you first."

"Don't bother, I'm not worth swinging for. Your secret's safe with me; I'm just an interested onlooker. Yes indeed, that's all I am. An onlooker."

"Oh, Mum! What could possibly have made you like this? Why like this, so unwilling to give?"

Fee sighed. "Events which took place years before you were even born," she said pathetically.

But Meggie shook her fist vehemently. "Oh, no, you don't! After what you've just told me? You're not going to get away with flogging that dead horse to me ever again! Rubbish, rubbish, rubbish! Do you hear me, Mum? You've wallowed in it for most of your life, like a fly in syrup!"

Fee smiled broadly, genuinely pleased. "I used to think having a daughter wasn't nearly as important as having sons, but I was wrong. I enjoy you, Meggie, in a way I can never enjoy my sons. A daughter's an equal. Sons aren't, you know. They're just defenseless dolls we set up to knock down at our leisure."

Meggie stared. "You're remorseless. Tell me, then, where *do* we go wrong?"

"In being born," said Fee.

Men were returning home in thousands upon thousands, shedding their khaki uniforms and slouch hats for civvies. And the Labor government, still in office, took a long, hard look at the great properties of the western plains, some of the bigger stations closer in. It wasn't right that so much land should belong to one family, when men who had done their bit for Australia needed room for their belongings and the country needed more intensive working of its land. Six million people to fill an area as big as the United States of America, but a mere handful of those six million holding vast tracts in a handful of names. The biggest properties would have to be subdivided, yield up some of their acreages to the war veterans.

Bugela went from 150,000 acres to 70,000; two returned soldiers got 40,000 acres each off Martin King. Rudna Hunish had 120,000 acres, therefore Ross MacQueen lost 60,000 acres and two more returned soldiers were endowed. So it went. Of course the government compensated the graziers, though at lower figures than the open market would have given. And it hurt. Oh, it hurt. No amount of argument prevailed with Canberra; properties as large as Bugela and Rudna Hunish would be partitioned. It was self-evident no man needed so much, since the Gilly district had many thriving stations of less than 50,000 acres.

What hurt the most was the knowledge that this time it seemed the returned soldiers would persevere. After the First World War most of the big stations had gone through the same partial resumption, but it had been poorly done, the fledgling graziers without training or experience; gradually the squatters bought their filched acres back at rock-bottom prices from discouraged veterans. This time the government was prepared to train and educate the new settlers at its own expense.

Almost all the squatters were avid members of the Country Party, and on principle loathed a Labor government, identifying it with blue-collar workers in industrial cities, trade unions and feckless Marxist intellectuals. The unkindest cut of all was to find that the Clearys, who were known Labor voters, were not to see a single acre pared from the formidable bulk of Drogheda. Since the Catholic Church owned it, naturally it was subdivision-exempt. The howl was heard in Canberra, but ignored. It came very hard to the squatters, who always thought of themselves as the most powerful lobby group in the nation, to find that he who wields the Canberra whip does pretty much as he likes. Australia was heavily federal, its state governments virtually powerless.

Thus, like a giant in a Lilliputian world, Drogheda carried on, all quarter of a million acres of it.

The rain came and went, sometimes adequate, sometimes too much, sometimes too little, but not, thank God, ever another drought like the great one. Gradually the number of sheep built up and the quality of the wool improved over pre-drought times, no mean feat.

Breeding was the "in" thing. People talked of Haddon Rig near Warren, started actively competing with its owner, Max Falkiner, for the top ram and ewe prizes at the Royal Easter Show in Sydney. And the price of wool began to creep up, then skyrocketed. Europe, the United States and Japan were hungry for every bit of fine wool Australia could produce. Other countries yielded coarser wools for heavy fabrics, carpets, felts; but only the long, silky fibers from Australian merinos could make a woolen textile so fine it slipped through the fingers like softest lawn. And that sort of wool reached its peak out on the black-soil plains of northwest New South Wales and southwest Queensland.

It was as if after all the years of tribulation, a just reward had arrived. Drogheda's profits soared out of all imagination. Millions of pounds every year. Fee sat at her desk radiating contentment, Bob put another two stockmen on the books. If it hadn't been for the rabbits, pastoral conditions would have been ideal, but the rabbits were as much of a blight as ever.

On the homestead life was suddenly very pleasant. The wire screening had excluded flies from all Drogheda interiors; now that it was up and everyone had grown used to its appearance, they wondered how they had ever survived without it. For there were multiple compensations for the look of it, like being able to eat al fresco on the veranda when it was very hot, under the tapping leaves of the wistaria vine.

The frogs loved the screening, too. Little fellows they were, green with a delicate overlay of glossy gold. On suckered feet they crept up the outside of the mesh to stare motionless at the diners, very solemn and dignified. Suddenly one would leap, grab at a moth almost bigger than itself, and settle back into inertia with two-thirds of the moth flapping madly out of its overladen mouth. It amused Dane and Justine to time how long it took a frog to swallow a big moth completely, staring gravely through the wire and every ten minutes getting a little more moth down. The insect lasted a long time, and would often still be kicking when the final piece of wingtip was engulfed.

"Erckle! What a fate!" chuckled Dane. "Fancy half of you still being alive while the other half of you is busy being digested."

Avid reading—that Drogheda passion—had given the two O'Neill children excellent vocabularies at an early age. They were intelligent, alert and interested in everything. Life was particularly pleasant for them. They had their thoroughbred ponies, increasing in size as they did; they endured their correspondence lessons at Mrs. Smith's green kitchen table; they played in the pepper tree cubbyhouse; they had pet cats, pet dogs, even a pet goanna, which walked beautifully on a leash and answered to its name. Their favorite pet was a miniature pink pig, as intelligent as any dog, called Iggle-Piggle.

So far from urban congestion, they caught few diseases and never had colds or influenza. Meggie was terrified of infantile paralysis, diphtheria, anything which might swoop out of nowhere to carry them off, so whatever vaccines became available they received. It was an ideal existence, full of physical activity and mental stimulation.

When Dane was ten and Justine eleven they were sent to boarding school in Sydney, Dane to Riverview as tradition demanded, and Justine to Kincoppal. When she put them on the plane the first time, Meggie watched as their white, valiantly composed little faces stared out of a window, handkerchiefs waving; they had never been away from home before. She had wanted badly to go with them, see them settled in for herself, but opinion was so strongly against her she yielded. From Fee down to Jims and Patsy, everyone felt they would do a great deal better on their own.

"Don't mollycoddle them," said Fee sternly.

But indeed she felt like two different people as the

DC-3 took off in a cloud of dust and staggered into the shimmering air. Her heart was breaking at losing Dane, and light at the thought of losing Justine. There was no ambivalence in her feelings about Dane; his gay, even-tempered nature gave and accepted love as naturally as breathing. But Justine was a lovable, horrible monster. One had to love her, because there was much to love: her strength, her integrity, her self-reliance—lots of things. The trouble was that she didn't permit love the way Dane did, nor did she ever give Meggie the wonderful feeling of being needed. She wasn't matey or full of pranks, and she had a disastrous habit of putting people down, chiefly, it seemed, her mother. Meggie found much in her that had been exasperating in Luke, but at least Justine wasn't a miser. For that much be thankful.

A thriving airline meant that all the children's vacations, even the shortest ones, could be spent on Drogheda. However, after an initial period of adjustment both children enjoyed their schooling. Dane was always homesick after a visit to Drogheda, but Justine took to Sydney as if she had always lived there, and spent her Drogheda time longing to be back in the city. The Riverview Jesuits were delighted; Dane was a marvelous student, in the classroom and on the playing field. The Kincoppal nuns, on the other hand, were definitely not delighted; no one with eyes and a tongue as sharp as Justine's could hope to be popular. A class ahead of Dane, she was perhaps the better student of the two, but only in the classroom.

The *Sydney Morning Herald* of August 4th, 1952, was very interesting. Its big front page rarely bore more than one photograph, usually middle and high up, the interest story of the day. And that day the picture was a handsome portrait of Ralph de Bricassart.

His Grace Archbishop Ralph de Bricassart, at

the present time aide to the Secretary of State of the Holy See of Rome, was today created Cardinal de Bricassart by His Holiness Pope Pius XII.

Ralph Raoul, Cardinal de Bricassart has had a long and illustrious association with the Roman Catholic Church in Australia, extending from his arrival as a newly ordained priest in July 1919 to his departure for the Vatican in March 1938.

Born on September 23, 1893, in the Republic of Ireland, Cardinal de Bricassart was the second son of a family which can trace its descent from Baron Ranulf de Bricassart, who came to England in the train of William the Conqueror. By tradition, Cardinal de Bricassart espoused the Church. He entered the seminary at the age of seventeen, and upon his ordination was sent to Australia. His first months were spent in the service of the late Bishop Michael Clabby, in the Diocese of Winnemurra.

In June 1920 he was transferred to serve as pastor of Gillanbone, in northwestern New South Wales. He was made Monsignor, and continued at Gillanbone until December 1928. From there he became private secretary to His Grace Archbishop Cluny Dark, and finally private secretary to the then Archbishop Papal Legate, His Eminence Cardinal di Contini-Verchese. During this time he was created Bishop. When Cardinal di Contini-Verchese was transferred to Rome to commence his remarkable career at the Vatican, Bishop de Bricassart was created Archbishop, and returned to Australia from Athens as the Papal Legate himself. He held this important Vatican appointment until his transfer to Rome in 1938; since that time his rise within the central hierarchy of the Roman Catholic Church has been spectacular. Now 58 years of age, he is rumored to be one of the few men actively concerned in the determination of papal policy.

A *Sydney Morning Herald* representative talked to some of Cardinal de Bricassart's ex-parishioners in the Gillanbone area yesterday. He is well remembered, and with much affection. This rich sheep district is predominantly Roman Catholic in its religious adherence.

"Father de Bricassart founded the Holy Cross Bush Bibliophilic Society," said Mr. Harry Gough, Mayor of Gillanbone. "It was—for the time especially—a remarkable service, splendidly endowed first by the late Mrs. Mary Carson, and after her death by the Cardinal himself, who has never forgotten us or our needs."

"Father de Bricassart was the finest-looking man I've ever seen," said Mrs. Fiona Cleary, present doyenne of Drogheda, one of the largest and most prosperous stations in New South Wales. "During his time in Gilly he was a great spiritual support to his parishioners, and particularly to those of us on Drogheda, which as you know now belongs to the Catholic Church. During floods he helped us move our stock, during fires he came to our aid, even if it was only to bury our dead. He was, in fact, an extraordinary man in every way, and he had more charm than any man I've ever met. One could see he was meant for great things. Indeed we remember him, though it's over twenty years since he left us. Yes, I think it's quite truthful to say that there are some around Gilly who still miss him very much."

During the war the then Archbishop de Bricassart served His Holiness loyally and unswervingly, and is credited with having influenced Field Marshal Albert Kesselring in deciding to maintain Rome as an open city after Italy became a German enemy. Florence, which had asked in vain for the same privilege, lost many of its treasures, only restored later because Germany lost the war. In the immediate postwar period, Cardinal de Bricassart helped thousands of displaced persons seek asylum in new countries, and was especially vigorous in aiding the Australian immigration program.

Though by birth he is an Irishman, and though it seems he will not exert his influence as Cardinal de Bricassart in Australia, we still feel that to a large extent Australia may rightly claim this remarkable man as her own.

Meggie handed the paper back to Fee, and smiled at her mother ruefully.

"One must congratulate him, as I said to the *Herald* reporter. They didn't print that, did they? Though they printed your little eulogy almost verbatim, I see. What a barbed tongue you've got! At least I know where Justine gets it from. I wonder how many people will be smart enough to read between the lines of what you said?"

"He will, anyway, if he ever sees it."

"I wonder does he remember us?" Meggie sighed.

"Undoubtedly. After all, he still finds time to administer Drogheda himself. Of course he remembers us, Meggie. How could he forget?"

"True, I had forgotten Drogheda. We're right up there on top of the earnings, aren't we? He must be very pleased. With our wool at a pound per pound in the auctions, the Drogheda wool check this year must have made even the gold mines look sick. Talk about Golden Fleece. Over four million pounds, just from shaving our baa-lambs."

"Don't be cynical, Meggie, it doesn't suit you," said Fee; her manner toward Meggie these days, though often mildly withering, was tempered with respect and affection. "We've done well enough, haven't we? Don't forget we get our money every year, good or bad. Didn't he pay Bob a hundred thousand as a bonus, the rest of us fifty thousand each? If he threw us off Drogheda tomorrow we could afford to buy Bugela, even at today's inflated land prices. And how much has he given your children? Thousands upon thousands. Be fair to him."

"But my children don't know it, and they're not going to find out. Dane and Justine will grow up to think they must make their own ways in the world, without benefit of dear Ralph Raoul, Cardinal de Bricassart. Fancy his second name being Raoul! Very Norman, isn't it?"

Fee got up, walked over to the fire and threw the front page of the *Herald* onto the flames. Ralph Raoul, Cardinal de Bricassart shuddered, winked at her, and then shriveled up.

"What will you do if he comes back, Meggie?"

Meggie sniffed. "Fat chance!"

"He might," said Fee enigmatically.

He did, in December. Very quietly, without anyone knowing, driving an Aston Martin sports car all the way from Sydney himself. Not a word about his presence in Australia had reached the press, so no one on Drogheda had the remotest suspicion he was coming. When the car pulled in to the gravelly area at one side of the house there was no one about, and apparently no one had heard him arrive, for no one came out onto the veranda.

He had felt the miles from Gilly in every cell of his body, inhaled the odors of the bush, the sheep, the dry grass sparkling restlessly in the sun. Kangaroos and emus, galahs and goannas, millions of insects buzzing and flipping, ants marching across the road in treacly columns, fat pudgy sheep everywhere. He loved it so, for in one curious aspect it conformed to what he loved in all things; the passing years scarcely seemed to brush it.

Only the fly screening was different, but he noted with amusement that Fee hadn't permitted the big house veranda facing the Gilly road to be enclosed like the rest, only the windows opening onto it. She was right, of course; a great expanse of mesh would have ruined the lines of that lovely Georgian façade. How long did ghost gums live? These must have been transplanted from the Dead Heart interior eighty years ago. The bougainvillaea in their high branches was one sliding mass of copper and purple.

It was already summer, two weeks left before Christmas, and the Drogheda roses were at their height. There were roses everywhere, pink and white and yellow, crimson like heart's blood, scarlet like a cardinal's soutane. In among the wistaria, green now, rambling roses drowsed pink and white, fell off the veranda roof, down the wire mesh, clung lovingly to the black shutters of the second story, stretched tendrils past them to the sky. The tank stands were quite smothered from sight now, so were the tanks themselves. And one color was everywhere among the roses, a pale pinkish-grey. Ashes of roses? Yes, that was the name of the color. Meggie must have planted them, it had to be Meggie.

He heard Meggie's laugh, and stood motionless, quite terrified, then made his feet go in the direction of the sound, gone down to delicious giggling trills. Just the way she used to laugh when she was a little girl. There it was! Over there, behind a great clump of pinkish-grey roses near a pepper tree. He pushed the clusters of blossoms aside with his hand, his mind reeling from their perfume, and that laugh.

But Meggie wasn't there, only a boy squatting in the lush lawn, teasing a little pink pig which ran in idiotic rushes up to him, galloped off, sidled back. Unconscious of his audience, the boy threw his gleaming head back and laughed. Meggie's laugh, from that unfamiliar throat. Without meaning to, Cardinal Ralph let the roses fall into place and stepped through them, heedless of the thorns. The boy, about twelve or fourteen years of age, just prepubescent, looked up, startled; the pig squealed, curled up its tail tightly and ran off.

Clad in an old pair of khaki shorts and nothing else,

bare-footed, he was golden brown and silky-skinned, his slender, boyish body already hinting at later power in the breadth of the young square shoulders, the well-developed calf and thigh muscles, the flat belly and narrow hips. His hair was a little long and loosely curly, just the bleached color of Drogheda grass, his eyes through absurdly thick black lashes intensely blue. He looked like a very youthful escaped angel.

"Hello," said the boy, smiling.

"Hello," said Cardinal Ralph, finding it impossible to resist the charm of that smile. "Who are you?"

"I'm Dane O'Neill," answered the boy. "Who are you?"

"My name is Ralph de Bricassart."

Dane O'Neill. He was Meggie's boy, then. She had not left Luke O'Neill after all, she had gone back to him, borne this beautiful lad who might have been his, had he not married the Church first. How old had he been when he married the Church? Not much older than this, not very much more mature. Had he waited, the boy might well have been his. What nonsense, Cardinal de Bricassart! If you hadn't married the Church you would have remained in Ireland to breed horses and never known your fate at all, never known Drogheda or Meggie Cleary.

"May I help you?" asked the boy politely, getting to his feet with a supple grace Cardinal Ralph recognized, and thought of as Meggie's.

"Is your father here, Dane?"

"My *father?*" The dark, finely etched brows knitted. "No, he's not here. He's never been here."

"Oh, I see. Is your mother here, then?"

"She's in Gilly, but she'll be back soon. My Nanna is in the house, though. Would you like to see her? I can take you." Eyes as blue as cornflowers stared at him, widened, narrowed. "Ralph de Bricassart. I've heard of you. Oh! *Cardinal* de Bricassart! Your Eminence, I'm sorry! I didn't mean to be rude."

Though he had abandoned his clerical regalia in favor of boots, breeches and a white shirt, the ruby ring was still on his finger, must never be withdrawn as long as he lived. Dane O'Neill knelt, took Cardinal Ralph's slender hand in his own slender ones, and kissed the ring reverently.

"It's all right, Dane. I'm not here as Cardinal de Bricassart. I'm here as a friend of your mother's and your grandmother's."

"I'm sorry, Your Eminence, I ought to have recognized your name the minute I heard it. We say it often enough round here. Only you pronounce it a bit differently, and your Christian name threw me off. My mother will be very glad to see you, I know."

"Dane, Dane, where are you?" called an impatient voice, very deep and entrancingly husky.

The hanging fronds of the pepper tree parted and a girl of about fifteen ducked out, straightened. He knew who she was immediately, from those astonishing eyes. Meggie's daughter. Covered in freckles, sharp-faced, small-featured, disappointingly unlike Meggie.

"Oh, hello. I'm sorry, I didn't realize we had a visitor. I'm Justine O'Neill."

"Jussy, this is Cardinal de Bricassart!" Dane said in a loud whisper. "Kiss his ring, quickly!"

The blind-looking eyes flashed scorn. "You're a real prawn about religion, Dane," she said without bothering to lower her voice. "Kissing a ring is unhygienic; I won't do it. Besides, how do we know this is Cardinal de Bricassart? He looks like an old-fashioned grazier to me. You know, like Mr. Gordon."

"He is, he is!" insisted Dane. "Please, Jussy, be good! Be good for *me!*"

"I'll be good, but only for you. But I won't kiss his ring, even for you. Disgusting. How do I know who kissed it last? They might have had a cold."

"You don't have to kiss my ring, Justine. I'm here on a holiday; I'm not being a cardinal at the moment."

"That's good, because I'll tell you frankly, I'm an atheist," said Meggie Cleary's daughter calmly. "After four years at Kincoppal I think it's all a load of utter codswallop."

"That's your privilege," said Cardinal Ralph, trying desperately to look as dignified and serious as she did. "May I find your grandmother?"

"Of course. Do you need us?" Justine asked.

"No, thank you. I know my way."

"Good." She turned to her brother, still gaping up at the visitor. "Come on, Dane, help me. Come on!"

But though Justine tugged painfully at his arm, Dane stayed to watch Cardinal Ralph's tall, straight figure disappear behind the roses.

"You really are a prawn, Dane. What's so special about him?"

"He's a cardinal!" said Dane. "Imagine that! A real live cardinal on Drogheda!"

"Cardinals," said Justine, "are Princes of the Church. I suppose you're right, it *is* rather extraordinary. But I don't like him."

Where else would Fee be, except at her desk? He stepped through the windows into the drawing room, but these days that necessitated opening a screen. She must have heard him, but kept on working, back bent, the lovely golden hair gone to silver. With difficulty he remembered she must be all of seventy-two years old.

"Hello, Fee," he said.

When she raised her head he saw a change in her, of what precise nature he couldn't be sure; the indifference was there, but so were several other things. As if she had mellowed and hardened simultaneously, become more human, yet human in a Mary Carson mold. God, these Drogheda matriarchs! Would it happen to Meggie, too, when her turn came?

"Hello, Ralph," she said, as if he stepped through the windows every day. "How nice to see you."

"Nice to see you, too."

"I didn't know you were in Australia."

"No one does. I have a few weeks' holiday."

"You're staying with us, I hope?"

"Where else?" His eyes roamed round the magnificent walls, rested on Mary Carson's portrait. "You know, Fee, your taste is impeccable, unerring. This room rivals anything in the Vatican. Those black egg shapes with the roses are a stroke of genius."

"Why, thank you! We try our humble best. Personally I prefer the dining room; I've done it again since you were here last. Pink and white and green. Sounds awful, but wait until you see it. Though why I try, I don't know. It's your house, isn't it?"

"Not while there's a Cleary alive, Fee," he said quietly.

"How comforting. Well, you've certainly come up in the world since your Gilly days, haven't you? Did you see the *Herald* article about your promotion?"

He winced. "I did. Your tongue's sharpened, Fee."

"Yes, and what's more, I'm enjoying it. All those years I shut up and never said a thing! I didn't know what I was missing." She smiled. "Meggie's in Gilly, but she'll be back soon."

Dane and Justine came through the windows.

"Nanna, may we ride down to the borehead?"

"You know the rules. No riding unless your mother gives her permission personally. I'm sorry, but they're your mother's orders. Where are your manners? Come and be introduced to our visitor."

"I've already met them."

"Oh."

"I'd have thought you'd be away at boarding school," he said to Dane, smiling.

"Not in December, Your Eminence. We're off for two months—the summer holidays."

Too many years away; he had forgotten that southern hemisphere children would enjoy their long vacation during December and January.

"Are you going to be staying here long, Your Eminence?" Dane queried, still fascinated.

"His Eminence will be with us for as long as he can manage, Dane," said his grandmother, "but I think he's going to find it a little wearing to be addressed as Your Eminence all the time. What shall it be? Uncle Ralph?"

"Uncle!" exclaimed Justine. "You know 'uncle' is against the family rules, Nanna! Our uncles are just Bob, Jack, Hughie, Jims and Patsy. So that means he's Ralph."

"Don't be so rude, Justine! What on earth's the matter with your manners?" demanded Fee.

"No, Fee, it's all right. I'd prefer that everyone call me plain Ralph, really," the Cardinal said quickly. Why did she dislike him so, the odd mite?

"I couldn't!" gasped Dane. "I couldn't call you just *Ralph!"*

Cardinal Ralph crossed the room, took the bare shoulders between his hands and smiled down, his blue eyes very kind, and vivid in the room's shadows. "Of course you can, Dane. It isn't a sin."

"Come on, Dane, let's get back to the cubbyhouse," Justine ordered.

Cardinal Ralph and his son turned toward Fee, looked at her together.

"Heaven help us!" said Fee. "Go on, Dane, go outside and play, will you?" She clapped her hands. "Buzz!"

The boy ran for his life, and Fee edged toward her books. Cardinal Ralph took pity on her and announced that he would go to the cookhouse. How little the place had changed! Still lamplit, obviously. Still redolent of beeswax and great vases of roses.

He stayed talking to Mrs. Smith and the maids for a long time. They had grown much older in the years since he had left, but somehow age suited them more than it did Fee. Happy. That's what they were. Genuinely almost perfectly happy. Poor Fee, who wasn't happy. It made him hungry to see Meggie, see if she was happy.

But when he left the cookhouse Meggie wasn't back, so to fill in time he strolled through the grounds toward the creek. How peaceful the cemetery was; there were six bronze plaques on the mausoleum wall, just as there had been last time. He must see that he himself was buried here; he must remember to instruct them, when he returned to Rome. Near the mausoleum he noticed two new graves, old Tom, the garden rouseabout, and the wife of one of the stockmen, who had been on the payroll since 1946. Must be some sort of record. Mrs. Smith thought he was still with them because his wife lay here. The Chinese cook's ancestral umbrella was quite faded from all the years of fierce sun, had dwindled from its original imperial red through the various shades he remembered to its present whitish-pink, almost ashes of roses. Meggie, Meggie. You went back to him after me, you bore him a son.

It was very hot; a little wind came, stirred the weeping willows along the creek, made the bells on the Chinese cook's umbrella chime their mournful tinny tune: Hee Sing, Hee Sing, Hee Sing. TANKSTAND CHARLIE HE WAS A GOOD BLOKE. That had faded, too, was practically indecipherable. Well, it was fitting. Graveyards ought to sink back into the bosom of Mother Earth, lose their human cargo under a wash of time, until it all was gone and only the air remembered, sighing. He didn't want to be buried in a Vatican crypt, among men like himself. Here, among people who had really lived.

Turning, his eyes caught the glaucous glance of the marble angel. He raised his hand, saluted it, looked across the grass toward the big house. And she was coming, Meggie. Slim, golden, in a pair of breeches and a white man's shirt exactly like his own, a man's grey felt hat on the back of her head, tan boots on her feet. Like a boy, like her son, who should have been his son.

He was a man, but when he too lay here there would be nothing left living to mark the fact.

She came on, stepped over the white fence, came so close all he could see were her eyes, those grey, light-filled eyes which hadn't lost their beauty or their hold over his heart. Her arms were around his neck, his fate again within his touch, it was as if he had never been away from her, that mouth alive under his, not a dream; so long wanted, so long. A different kind of sacrament, dark like the earth, having nothing to do with the sky.

"Meggie, Meggie," he said, his face in her hair, her hat on the grass, his arms around her.

"It doesn't seem to matter, does it? Nothing ever changes," she said, eyes closed.

"No, nothing changes," he said, believing it.

"This is Drogheda, Ralph. I warned you, on Drogheda you're mine, not God's."

"I know. I admit it. But I came." He drew her down onto the grass. "Why, Meggie?"

"Why what?" Her hand was stroking his hair, whiter than Fee's now, still thick, still beautiful.

"Why did you go back to Luke? Have his son?" he asked jealously.

Her soul looked out from behind its lucent grey windows and veiled its thoughts from him. "He forced me to," she said blandly. "It was only once. But I had Dane, so I'm not sorry. Dane was worth everything I went through to get him."

"I'm sorry, I had no right to ask. I gave you to Luke in the first place, didn't I?"

"That's true, you did."

"He's a wonderful boy. Does he look like Luke?"

She smiled secretly, plucked at the grass, laid her hand inside his shirt, against his chest. "Not really. Neither of my children looks very much like Luke, or me."

"I love them because they're yours."

"You're as sentimental as ever. Age suits you, Ralph.

I knew it would, I hoped I'd have the chance to see it. Thirty years I've known you! It seems like thirty days."

"Thirty years? As many as that?"

"I'm forty-one, my dear, so it must be." She got to her feet. "I was officially sent to summon you inside. Mrs. Smith is laying on a splendid tea in your honor, and later on when it's a bit cooler there's to be roast leg of pork, with lots of crackling."

He began to walk with her, slowly. "Your son laughs just like you, Meggie. His laugh was the first human noise I heard on Drogheda. I thought he was you; I went to find you and I discovered him instead."

"So he was the first person you saw on Drogheda."

"Why, yes, I suppose he was."

"What did you think of him, Ralph?" she asked eagerly.

"I liked him. How could I not, when he's your son? But I was attracted to him very strongly, far more so than to your daughter. She doesn't like me, either."

"Justine might be my child, but she's a prize bitch. I've learned to swear in my old age, mostly thanks to Justine. And you, a little. And Luke, a little. And the war, a little. Funny how they all mount up."

"You've changed a lot, Meggie."

"Have I?" The soft, full mouth curved into a smile. "I don't think so, really. It's just the Great Northwest, wearing me down, stripping off the layers like Salome's seven veils. Or like an onion, which is how Justine would rather put it. No poetry, that child. I'm the same old Meggie, Ralph, only more naked."

"Perhaps so."

"Ah, but *you've* changed, Ralph."

"In what way, my Meggie?"

"As if the pedestal rocks with every passing breeze, and as if the view from up there is a disappointment."

"It is." He laughed soundlessly. "And to think I once had the temerity to say you weren't anything out of the ordinary! I take it back. You're the one woman, Meggie. *The one!*"

"What happened?"

"I don't know. Did I discover even Church idols have feet of clay? Did I sell myself for a mess of pottage? Am I grasping at nothing?" His brows drew togther, as if in pain. "And that's it, perhaps, in a nutshell. I'm a mass of clichés. It's an old, sour, petrified world, the Vatican world."

"I was more real, but you could never see it."

"There was nothing else I could do, truly! I knew where I should have gone, but I couldn't. With you I might have been a better man, if less august. But I just couldn't, Meggie. Oh, I wish I could make you see that!"

Her hand stole along his bare arm, tenderly. "Dear Ralph, I do see it. I know, I know. . . . Each of us has something within us which won't be denied, even if it makes us scream aloud to die. We are what we are, that's all. Like the old Celtic legend of the bird with the thorn in its breast, singing its heart out and dying. Because it has to, it's driven to. We can know what we do wrong even before we do it, but self-knowledge can't affect or change the outcome, can it? Everyone singing his own little song, convinced it's the most wonderful song the world has ever heard. Don't you see? We create our own thorns, and never stop to count the cost. All we can do is suffer the pain, and tell ourselves it was well worth it."

"That's what I don't understand. The pain." He glanced down at her hand, so gently on his arm, hurting him so unbearably. "Why the pain, Meggie?"

"Ask God, Ralph," said Meggie. "He's the authority on pain, isn't He? He made us what we are, He made the whole world. Therefore He made the pain, too."

Bob, Jack, Hughie, Jims and Patsy were in for dinner, since it was Saturday night. Tomorrow Father

Watty was due out to say Mass, but Bob called him and sa d no one would be there. A white lie, to preserve Cardinal Ralph's anonymity. The five Cleary boys were more like Paddy than ever, older, slower in speech, as steadfast and enduring as the land. And how they loved Dane! Their eyes never seemed to leave him, even followed him from the room when he went to bed. It wasn't hard to see they lived for the day when he would be old enough to join them in running Drogheda.

Cardinal Ralph had also discovered the reason for Justine's enmity. Dane had taken a fancy to him, hung on his words, lingered near him; she was plain jealous.

After the children had gone upstairs, he looked at those who were left: the brothers, Meggie, Fee.

"Fee, leave your desk for a moment," he said. "Come and sit here with us. I want to talk to all of you."

She still carried herself well and hadn't lost her figure, only slackened in the breasts, thickened very slightly in the waist; more a shaping due to old age than to an actual weight gain. Silently she seated herself in one of the big cream chairs opposite the Cardinal, with Meggie to one side, and the brothers on stone benches close by.

"It's about Frank," he said.

The name hung between them, resounding distantly.

"What about Frank?" asked Fee composedly.

Meggie laid her knitting down, looked at her mother, then at Cardinal Ralph. "Tell us, Ralph," she said quickly, unable to bear her mother's composure a moment longer.

"Frank has served almost thirty years in jail, do you realize that?" asked the Cardinal. "I know my people kept you informed as we arranged, but I had asked them not to distress you unduly. I honestly couldn't see what good it could do Frank or yourselves to hear the harrowing details of his loneliness and despair, because there was nothing any of us might have done. I think Frank would have been released some years ago had he not gained a reputation for violence and instability during his early years in Goulburn Gaol. Even as late as the war, when some other prisoners were released into armed service, poor Frank was refused."

Fee glanced up from her hands. "It's his temper," she said without emotion.

The Cardinal seemed to be having some difficulty in finding the right words; while he sought for them, the family watched him in mingled dread and hope, though it wasn't Frank's welfare they cared about.

"It must be puzzling you greatly why I came back to Australia after all these years," Cardinal Ralph said finally, not looking at Meggie. "I haven't always been mindful of your lives, and I know it. From the day I met you, I've thought of myself first, put myself first. And when the Holy Father rewarded my labors on behalf of the Church with a cardinal's mantle, I asked myself if there was any service I could do the Cleary family which in some way would tell them how deeply I care." He drew a breath, focused his gaze on Fee, not on Meggie. "I came back to Australia to see what I could do about Frank. Do you remember, Fee, that time I spoke to you after Paddy and Stu died? Twenty years ago, and I've never been able to forget the look in your eyes. So much energy and vitality, crushed."

"Yes," said Bob abruptly, his eyes riveted on his mother. "Yes, that's it."

"Frank is being paroled," said the Cardinal. "It was the only thing I could do to show you that I *do* care."

If he had expected a sudden, dazzling blaze of light from out of Fee's long darkness, he would have been very disappointed; at first it was no more than a small flicker, and perhaps the toll of age would never really permit it to shine at full brightness. But in the eyes of Fee's sons he saw its true magnitude, and knew a sense of his own purpose he hadn't felt since that time during the war when he had talked to the young German soldier with the imposing name.

"Thank you," said Fee.

"Will you welcome him back to Drogheda?" he asked the Cleary men.

"This is his home, it's where he ought to be," Bob answered elliptically.

Everyone nodded agreement save Fee, who seemed intent on some private vision.

"He isn't the same Frank," Cardinal Ralph went on gently. "I visited him in Goulburn Gaol to tell him the news before I came here, and I had to let him know everyone on Drogheda had always been aware what had happened to him. If I tell you that he didn't take it hard, it might give you some idea of the change in him. He was simply . . . grateful. And so looking forward to seeing his family again, especially you, Fee."

"When's he being released?" Bob asked, clearing his throat, pleasure for his mother clearly warring with fear of what would happen when Frank returned.

"In a week or two. He'll come up on the night mail. I wanted him to fly, but he said he preferred the train."

"Patsy and I will meet him," Jims offered eagerly, then his face fell. "Oh! We don't know what he looks like!"

"No," said Fee. "I'll meet him myself. On my own. I'm not in my dotage yet; I can still drive to Gilly."

"Mum's right," said Meggie firmly, forestalling a chorus of protests from her brothers. "Let Mum meet him on her own. She's the one ought to see him first."

"Well, I have work to do," said Fee gruffly, getting up and moving toward her desk.

The five brothers rose as one man. "And I reckon it's our bedtime," said Bob, yawning elaborately. He smiled shyly at Cardinal Ralph. "It will be like old times, to have you saying Mass for us in the morning."

Meggie folded her knitting, put it away, got up. "I'll say good night, too, Ralph."

"Good night, Meggie." His eyes followed her as she

went out of the room, then turned to Fee's hunched back. "Good night, Fee."

"I beg your pardon? Did you say something?"

"I said good night."

"Oh! Good night, Ralph."

He didn't want to go upstairs so soon after Meggie. "I'm going for a walk before I turn in, I think. Do you know something, Fee?"

"No." Her voice was absent.

"You don't fool me for a minute."

She snorted with laughter, an eerie sound. "Don't I? I wonder about that."

Late, and the stars. The southern stars, wheeling across the heavens. He had lost his hold upon them forever, though they were still there, too distant to warm, too remote to comfort. Closer to God, Who was a wisp between them. For a long time he stood looking up, listening to the wind in the trees, smiling.

Reluctant to be near Fee, he used the flight of stairs at the far end of the house; the lamp over her desk still burned and he could see her bent silhouette there, working. Poor Fee. How much she must dread going to bed, though perhaps when Frank came home it would be easier. Perhaps.

At the top of the stairs silence met him thickly; a crystal lamp on a narrow hall table shed a dim pool of light for the comfort of nocturnal wanderers, flickering as the night breeze billowed the curtains inward around the window next to it. He passed it by, his feet on the heavy carpeting making no sound.

Meggie's door was wide open, more light welling through it; blocking the rays for a moment, he shut her door behind him and locked it. She had donned a loose wrapper and was sitting in a chair by the window looking out across the invisible Home Paddock, but her head turned to watch him walk to the bed, sit on its edge. Slowly she got up and came to him.

"Here, I'll help you get your boots off. That's the reason I never wear knee ones myself. I can't get them off without a jack, and a jack ruins good boots."

"Did you wear that color deliberately, Meggie?"

"Ashes of roses?" She smiled. "It's always been my favorite color. It doesn't clash with my hair."

He put one foot on her backside while she pulled a boot off, then changed it for the bare foot.

"Were you so sure I'd come to you, Meggie?"

"I told you. On Drogheda you're mine. Had you not come to me, I'd have gone to you, make no mistake." She drew his shirt over his head, and for a moment her hand rested with luxurious sensitivity on his bare back, then she went across to the lamp and turned it out, while he draped his clothes over a chair back. He could hear her moving about, shedding her wrapper. And tomorrow morning I'll say Mass. But that's tomorrow morning, and the magic has long gone. There is still the night, and Meggie. I have wanted her. She, too, is a sacrament.

Dane was disappointed. "I thought you'd wear a red soutane!" he said.

"Sometimes I do, Dane, but only within the walls of the palace. Outside it, I wear a black soutane with a red sash, like this."

"Do you really have a palace?"

"Yes."

"Is it full of chandeliers?"

"Yes, but so is Drogheda."

"Oh, Drogheda!" said Dane in disgust. "I'll bet ours are little ones compared to yours. I'd love to see your palace, and you in a red soutane."

Cardinal Ralph smiled. "Who knows, Dane? Perhaps one day you will."

The boy had a curious expression always at the back of his eyes; a distant look. When he turned during the Mass, Cardinal Ralph saw it reinforced, but he didn't recognize it, only felt its familiarity. No man sees himself in a mirror as he really is, nor any woman.

Luddie and Anne Mueller were due in for Christmas, as indeed they were every year. The big house was full of light-hearted people, looking forward to the best Christmas in years; Minnie and Cat sang tunelessly as they worked, Mrs. Smith's plump face was wreathed in smiles, Meggie relinquished Dane to Cardinal Ralph without comment, and Fee seemed much happier, less glued to her desk. The men seized upon any excuse to make it back in each night, for after a late dinner the drawing room buzzed with conversation, and Mrs. Smith had taken to preparing a bedtime supper snack of melted cheese on toast, hot buttered crumpets and raisin scones. Cardinal Ralph protested that so much good food would make him fat, but after three days of Drogheda air, Drogheda people and Drogheda food, he seemed to be shedding the rather gaunt, haggard look he had worn when he arrived.

The fourth day came in very hot. Cardinal Ralph had gone with Dane to bring in a mob of sheep, Justine sulked alone in the pepper tree, and Meggie lounged on a cushioned cane settee on the veranda. Her bones felt limp, glutted, and she was very happy. A woman can live without it quite well for years at a stretch, but it was nice, when it was the one man. When she was with Ralph every part of her came alive except that part which belonged to Dane; the trouble was, when she was with Dane every part of her came alive except that which belonged to Ralph. Only when both of them were present in her world simultaneously, as now, did she feel utterly complete. Well, it stood to reason. Dane was her son, but Ralph was her man.

Yet one thing marred her happiness; Ralph hadn't seen. So her mouth remained closed upon her secret. If he couldn't see it for himself, why should she tell him? What had he ever done, to earn the telling? That he could think for a moment she had gone back to Luke willingly was the last straw. He didn't deserve to be told, if he could think that of her. Sometimes she felt Fee's pale, ironic eyes upon her, and she would stare back, unperturbed. Fee understood, she really did. Understood the half-hate, the resentment, the desire to pay back the lonely years. Off chasing rainbows, that was Ralph de Bricassart; and why should she gift him with the most exquisite rainbow of all, his son? Let him be deprived. Let him suffer, never knowing he suffered.

The phone rang its Drogheda code; Meggie listened idly, then realizing her mother must be elsewhere, she got up reluctantly and went to answer it.

"Mrs. Fiona Cleary, please," said a man's voice.

When Meggie called her name, Fee returned to take the receiver.

"Fiona Cleary speaking," she said, and as she stood listening the color faded gradually from her face, making it look as it had looked in the days after Paddy and Stu died; tiny and vulnerable. "Thank you," she said, and hung up.

"What is it, Mum?"

"Frank's been released. He's coming up on the night mail this afternoon." She looked at her watch. "I must leave soon; it's after two."

"Let me come with you," Meggie offered, so filled with her own happiness she couldn't bear to see her mother disappointed; she sensed that this meeting couldn't be pure joy for Fee.

"No, Meggie, I'll be all right. You take care of things here, and hold dinner until I get back."

"Isn't it wonderful, Mum? Frank's coming home in time for Christmas!"

"Yes," said Fee, "it is wonderful."

No one traveled on the night mail these days if they could fly, so by the time it had huffed the six hundred miles from Sydney, dropping its mostly second-class passengers at this small town or that, few people were left to be disgorged in Gilly.

The stationmaster had a nodding acquaintance with Mrs. Cleary but would never have dreamed of engaging her in conversation, so he just watched her descend the wooden steps from the overhead footbridge, and left her alone to stand stiffly on the high platform. She was a stylish old girl, he thought; up-to-date dress and hat, high-heeled shoes, too. Good figure, not many lines on her face really for an old girl; just went to show what the easy life of a grazier could do for a woman.

So that on the surface Frank recognized his mother more quickly than she did him, though her heart knew him at once. He was fifty-two years old, and the years of his absence were those which had carried him from youth to middle age. The man who stood in the Gilly sunset was too thin, gaunt almost, very pale; his hair was cropped halfway up his head, he wore shapeless clothes which hung on a frame still hinting at power for all its small size, and his well-shaped hands were clamped on the brim of a grey felt hat. He wasn't stooped or ill-looking, but he stood helplessly twisting that hat between his hands and seemed not to expect anyone to meet him, nor to know what next he ought to do.

Fee, controlled, walked briskly down the platform.

"Hello, Frank," she said.

He lifted the eyes which used to flash and sparkle so, set now in the face of an aging man. Not Frank's eyes at all. Exhausted, patient, intensely weary. But as they absorbed the sight of Fee an extraordinary expression came into them, wounded, utterly defenseless, filled with the appeal of a dying man.

"Oh, Frank!" she said, and took him in her arms, rocking his head on her shoulder. "It's all right, it's all right," she crooned, and softer still, "It's all right!"

He sat slumped and silent in the car at first, but as

the Rolls picked up speed and headed out of town he began to take an interest in his surroundings, and glanced out of the window.

"It looks exactly the same," he whispered.

"I imagine it does. Time moves slowly out here."

They crossed the rumbling wooden-planked bridge over the thin, muddy river lined with weeping willows, most of its bed exposed in a tangle of roots and gravel, pools lying in still brown patches, gum trees growing everywhere in the stony wastes.

"The Barwon," he said. "I never thought I'd see it again."

Behind them rose an enormous cloud of dust, in front of them the road sped straight as a perspective exercise across a great grassy plain devoid of trees.

"The road's new, Mum?" He seemed desperate to find conversation, make the situation appear normal.

"Yes, they put it through from Gilly to Milparinka just after the war ended."

"They might have sealed it with a bit of tar instead of leaving it the same old dirt."

"What for? We're used to eating dust out here, and think of the expense of making a bed strong enough to resist the mud. The new road is straight, they keep it well graded and it cut out thirteen of our twenty-seven gates. Only fourteen left between Gilly and the homestead, and just you wait and see what we've done to them, Frank. No more opening and closing gates."

The Rolls ran up a ramp toward a steel gate which lifted lazily; the moment the car passed under it and got a few yards down the track, the gate lowered itself closed.

"Wonders never cease!" said Frank.

"We were the first station around here to install the automatic ramp gates—only between the Milparinka road and the homestead, of course. The paddock gates still have to be opened and closed by hand."

"Well, I reckon the bloke that invented these gates

must have opened and closed a lot in his time, eh?" Frank grinned; it was the first sign of amusement he had shown.

But then he fell silent, so his mother concentrated on her driving, unwilling to push him too quickly. When they passed under the last gate and entered the Home Paddock, he gasped.

"I'd forgotten how lovely it is," he said.

"It's home," said Fee. "We've looked after it."

She drove the Rolls down to the garages and then walked with him back to the big house, only this time he carried his case himself.

"Would you rather have a room in the big house, Frank, or a guesthouse all to yourself?" his mother asked.

"I'll take a guesthouse, thanks." The exhausted eyes rested on her face. "It will be nice to be able to get away from people," he explained. That was the only reference he ever made to conditions in jail.

"I think it will be better for you," she said, leading the way into her drawing room. "The big house is pretty full at the moment, what with the Cardinal here, Dane and Justine home, and Luddie and Anne Mueller arriving the day after tomorrow for Christmas." She pulled the bell cord for tea and went quickly round the room lighting the kerosene lamps.

"Luddie and Anne Mueller?" he asked.

She stopped in the act of turning up a wick, looked at him. "It's been a long time, Frank. The Muellers are friends of Meggie's." The lamp trimmed to her satisfaction, she sat down in her wing chair. "We'll have dinner in an hour, but first we'll have a cup of tea. I have to wash the dust of the road out of my mouth."

Frank seated himself awkwardly on the edge of one of the cream silk ottomans, gazing at the room in awe. "It looks so different from the days of Auntie Mary."

Fee smiled. "Well, I think so," she said.

Then Meggie came in, and it was harder to assimilate the fact of Meggie grown into a mature woman than to see his mother old. As his sister hugged and kissed him he turned his face away, shrank inside his baggy coat and searched beyond her to his mother, who sat looking at him as if to say: It doesn't matter, it will all seem normal soon, just give it time. A minute later, while he was still searching for something to say to this stranger, Meggie's daughter came in; a tall, skinny young girl who sat down stiffly, her big hands pleating folds in her dress, her light eyes fixed first on one face, then on another. Meggie's son entered with the Cardinal and went to sit on the floor beside his sister, a beautiful, calmly aloof boy.

"Frank, this is marvelous," said Cardinal Ralph, shaking him by the hand, then turning to Fee with his left brow raised. "A cup of tea? Very good idea."

The Cleary men came into the room together, and that was very hard, for they hadn't forgiven him at all. Frank knew why; it was the way he had hurt their mother. But he didn't know of anything to say which would make them understand any of it, nor could he tell them of the pain, the loneliness, or beg forgiveness. The only one who really mattered was his mother, and she had never thought there was anything to forgive.

It was the Cardinal who tried to hold the evening together, who led the conversation round the dinner table and then afterward back in the drawing room, chatting with diplomatic ease and making a special point of including Frank in the gathering.

"Bob, I've meant to ask you ever since I arrived—where are the rabbits?" the Cardinal asked. "I've seen millions of burrows, but nary a rabbit."

"The rabbits are all dead," Bob answered.

"Dead?"

"That's right, from something called myxomatosis. Between the rabbits and the drought years, Australia was just about finished as a primary producing nation by nineteen forty-seven. We were desperate," said Bob, warming to his theme and grateful to have something to discuss which would exclude Frank.

At which point Frank unwittingly antagonized his next brother by saying, "I knew it was bad, but not as bad as all that." He sat back, hoping he had pleased the Cardinal by contributing his mite to the discussion.

"Well, I'm not exaggerating, believe me!" said Bob tartly; how would Frank know?

"What happened?" the Cardinal asked quickly.

"The year before last the Commonwealth Scientific and Industrial Research Organization started an experimental program in Victoria, infecting rabbits with this virus thing they'd bred. I'm not sure what a virus is, except I think it's a sort of germ. Anyway, they called theirs the myxomatosis virus. At first it didn't seem to spread too well, though what bunnies caught it all died. But about a year after the experimental infection it began to spread like wildfire, they think mosquito-borne, but something to do with saffron thistle as well. And the bunnies have died in millions and millions ever since, it's just wiped them out. You'll sometimes see a few sickies around with huge lumps all over their faces, very ugly-looking things. But it's a marvelous piece of work, Ralph, it really is. Nothing else can catch myxomatosis, even close relatives. So thanks to the blokes at the CSIRO, the rabbit plague is no more."

Cardinal Ralph stared at Frank. "Do you realize what it is, Frank? Do you?"

Poor Frank shook his head, wishing everyone would let him retreat into anonymity.

"Mass-scale biological warfare. I wonder does the rest of the world know that right here in Australia between 1949 and 1952 a virus war was waged against a population of trillions upon trillions, and succeeded in obliterating it? Well! It's feasible, isn't it? Not simply yellow journalism at all, but scientific fact. They may as well bury their atom bombs and hydrogen bombs. I know it had to be done, it was absolutely necessary, and it's probably the world's most unsung major scientific achievement. But it's terrifying, too."

Dane had been following the conversation closely. "Biological warfare? I've never heard of it. What is it exactly, Ralph?"

"The words are new, Dane, but I'm a papal diplomat and the pity of it is that I must keep abreast of words like 'biological warfare.' In a nutshell, the term means myxomatosis. Breeding a germ capable of specifically killing and maiming only one kind of living being."

Quite unself-consciously Dane made the Sign of the Cross, and leaned back against Ralph de Bricassart's knees. "We had better pray, hadn't we?"

The Cardinal looked down on his fair head, smiling.

That eventually Frank managed to fit into Drogheda life at all was thanks to Fee, who in the face of stiff male Cleary opposition continued to act as if her oldest son had been gone but a short while, and had never brought disgrace on his family or bitterly hurt his mother. Quietly and inconspicuously she slipped him into the niche he seemed to want to occupy, removed from her other sons; nor did she encourage him to regain some of the vitality of other days. For it had all gone; she had known it the moment he looked at her on the Gilly station platform. Swallowed up by an existence the nature of which he refused to discuss with her. The most she could do for him was to make him as happy as possible, and surely the way to do that was to accept the now Frank as the always Frank.

There was no question of his working the paddocks, for his brothers didn't want him, nor did he want a kind of life he had always hated. The sight of growing things pleased him, so Fee put him to potter in the homestead gardens, left him in peace. And gradually the Cleary men grew used to having Frank back in the family bosom, began to understand that the threat Frank used to represent to their own welfare was quite empty.

Nothing would ever change what their mother felt for him, it didn't matter whether he was in jail or on Drogheda, she would still feel it. The important thing was that to have him on Drogheda made her happy. He didn't intrude upon their lives, he was no more or no less than always.

Yet for Fee it wasn't a joy to have Frank home again; how could it be? Seeing him every day was simply a different kind of sorrow from not being able to see him at all. The terrible grief of having to witness a ruined life, a ruined man. Who was her most beloved son, and must have endured agonies beyond her imagination.

One day after Frank had been home about six months, Meggie came into the drawing room to find her mother sitting looking through the big windows to where Frank was clipping the great bank of roses alongside the drive. She turned away, and something in her calmly arranged face sent Meggie's hands up to her heart.

"Oh, Mum!" she said helplessly.

Fee looked at her, shook her head and smiled. "It doesn't matter, Meggie," she said.

"If only there was something I could do!"

"There is. Just carry on the way you have been. I'm very grateful. You've become an ally."

SIX

1954-1965 *Dane*

[illegible] moments did he seem [illegible] realize there was an e[illegible]
[illegible] most men tread [illegible] choice, [illegible] as long as they
[illegible]bly could.
He told her backstage at the C[illegible]den, after a performance. It had been settled with Rome that d[illegible]; he

17

"Well," said Justine to her mother, "I've decided what I'm going to do."

"I thought it was already decided. Arts at Sydney University, isn't that right?"

"Oh, that was just a red herring to lull you into a false sense of security while I made my plans. But now it's all set, so I can tell you."

Meggie's head came up from her task, cutting fir-tree shapes in cookie dough; Mrs. Smith was ill and they were helping out in the cookhouse. She regarded her daughter wearily, impatiently, helplessly. What could one do with someone like Justine? If she announced she was going off to train as a whore in a Sydney bordello, Meggie very much doubted whether she could be turned aside. Dear, horrible Justine, queen among juggernauts.

"Go on, I'm all agog," she said, and went back to producing cookies.

"I'm going to be an actress."

"A *what?"*

"An actress."

"Good Lord!" The fir trees were abandoned again. "Look, Justine, I hate to be a spoilsport and truly I don't mean to hurt your feelings, but do you think you're—well, quite physically equipped to be an actress?"

"Oh, Mum!" said Justine, disgusted. "Not a film star; an actress! I don't want to wiggle my hips and stick out my breasts and pout my wet lips! I want to act." She was pushing chunks of defatted beef into the corning barrel. "I have enough money to support myself during whatever sort of training I choose, isn't that right?"

"Yes, thanks to Cardinal de Bricassart."

"Then it's all settled. I'm going to study acting with Albert Jones at the Culloden Theater, and I've written to the Royal Academy of Dramatic Art in London, asking that I be put on their waiting list."

"Are you quite sure, Jussy?"

"Quite sure. I've known for a long time." The last piece of bloody beef was tucked down under the surface of the corning solution; Justine put the lid on the barrel with a thump. "There! I hope I never see another bit of corned beef as long as I live."

Meggie handed her a completed tray of cookies. "Put these in the oven, would you? Four hundred degrees. I must say this comes as something of a surprise. I thought little girls who wanted to be actresses role-played constantly, but the only person I've ever seen you play has been yourself."

"Oh, Mum! There you go again, confusing film stars with actresses. Honestly, you're hopeless."

"Well, aren't film stars actresses?"

"Of a very inferior sort. Unless they've been on the stage first, that is. I mean, even Laurence Olivier does an occasional film."

There was an autographed picture of Laurence Olivier on Justine's dressing table; Meggie had simply deemed it juvenile crush stuff, though at the time she remembered thinking at least Justine had taste. The friends she sometimes brought home with her to stay a few days usually treasured pictures of Tab Hunter and Rory Calhoun.

"I still don't understand," said Meggie, shaking her head. "An actress!"

Justine shrugged. "Well, where else can I scream and yell and howl but on a stage? I'm not allowed to do any of those here, or at school, or *anywhere!* I like screaming and yelling and howling, dammit!"

"But you're so good at art, Jussy! Why not be an artist?" Meggie persevered.

Justine turned from the huge gas stove, flicked her finger against a cylinder gauge. "I must tell the kitchen rouseabout to change bottles; we're low. It'll do for today, though." The light eyes surveyed Meggie with pity. "You're so impractical, Mum, really. I thought it was supposed to be the children who didn't stop to consider a career's practical aspects. Let me tell you, I don't want to starve to death in a garret and be famous after I'm dead. I want to enjoy a bit of fame while I'm still alive, and be very comfortable financially. So I'll paint as a hobby and act for a living. How's that?"

"You've got an income from Drogheda, Jussy," Meggie said desperately, breaking her vow to remain silent no matter what. "It would never come to starving in a garret. If you'd rather paint, it's all right. You can."

Justine looked alert, interested. "How much have I got, Mum?"

"Enough that if you preferred, you need never work at anything."

"What a bore! I'd end up talking on the telephone and playing bridge; at least that's what the mothers of most of my school friends do. Because I'd be living in Sydney, not on Drogheda. I like Sydney *much* better than Drogheda." A gleam of hope entered her eye. "Do I have enough to pay to have my freckles removed with this new electrical treatment?"

"I should think so. But why?"

"Because then someone might see my face, that's why."

"I thought looks didn't matter to an actress?"

"Enough's enough, Mum. My freckles are a pain."

"Are you sure you wouldn't rather be an artist?"

"Quite sure, thank you." She did a little dance. "I'm going to tread the boards, Mrs. Worthington!"

"How did you get yourself into the Culloden?"

"I auditioned."

"And they *took* you?"

"Your faith in your daughter is touching, Mum. Of course they took me! I'm superb, you know. One day I shall be very famous."

Meggie beat green food coloring into a bowl of runny icing and began to drizzle it over already baked fir trees. "Is it important to you, Justine? Fame?"

"I should say so." She tipped sugar in on top of butter so soft it had molded itself to the inner contours of the bowl; in spite of the gas stove instead of the wood stove, the cookhouse was very hot. "I'm absolutely iron-bound determined to be famous."

"Don't you want to get married?"

Justine looked scornful. "Not bloody likely! Spend *my* life wiping snotty noses and cacky bums? Salaaming to some man not half my equal even though he thinks he's better? Ho ho ho, not me!"

"Honestly, you're the dizzy limit! Where do you pick up your language?"

Justine began cracking eggs rapidly and deftly into a basin, using one hand. "At my exclusive ladies' college, of course." She drubbed the eggs unmercifully with a French whisk. "We were quite a decent bunch of girls, actually. Very cultured. It isn't every gaggle of silly adolescent females can appreciate the delicacy of a Latin limerick:

> There was a Roman from Vinidium
> Whose shirt was made of iridium;

When asked why the vest,
He replied, *"Id est*
Bonum sanguinem praesidium."

Meggie's lips twitched. "I'm going to hate myself for asking, but what did the Roman say?"

" 'It's a bloody good protection.' "

"Is that all? I thought it was going to be a lot worse. You surprise me. But getting back to what we were saying, dear girl, in spite of your neat effort to change the subject, what's wrong with marriage?"

Justine imitated her grandmother's rare snort of ironic laughter. "Mum! Really! You're a fine one to ask that, I must say."

Meggie felt the blood well up under her skin, and looked down at the tray of bright-green trees. "Don't be impertinent, even if you are a ripe old seventeen."

"Isn't it odd?" Justine asked the mixing bowl. "The minute one ventures onto strictly parental territory, one becomes impertinent. I just said: You're a fine one to ask. Perfectly true, dammit! I'm not necessarily implying you're a failure, or a sinner, or worse. Actually I think you've shown remarkable good sense, dispensing with your husband. What have you needed one for? There's been tons of male influence for your children with the Unks around, you've got enough money to live on. I agree with you! Marriage is for the birds."

"You're just like your father!"

"Another evasion. Whenever I displease you, I become just like my father. Well, I'll have to take your word for that, since I've never laid eyes on the gentleman."

"When are you leaving?" Meggie asked desperately.

Justine grinned. "Can't wait to get rid of me, eh? It's all right, Mum, I don't blame you in the least. But I can't help it, I just love shocking people, especially you. How about taking me into the 'drome tomorrow?"

"Make it the day after. Tomorrow I'll take you to

the bank. You'd better know how much you've got. And, Justine . . ."

Justine was adding flour and folding expertly, but she looked up at the change in her mother's voice. "Yes?"

"If ever you're in trouble, come home, please. We've always got room for you on Drogheda, I want you to remember that. Nothing you could ever do would be so bad you couldn't come home."

Justine's gaze softened. "Thanks, Mum. You're not a bad old stick underneath, are you?"

"Old?" gasped Meggie. "I am not old! I'm only forty-three!"

"Good Lord, as much as that?"

Meggie hurled a cookie and hit Justine on the nose. "Oh, you wretch!" she laughed. "What a monster you are! Now I feel like a hundred."

Her daughter grinned.

At which moment Fee walked in to see how things in the cookhouse were going; Meggie hailed her arrival with relief.

"Mum, do you know what Justine just told me?"

Fee's eyes were no longer up to anything beyond the uttermost effort of keeping the books, but the mind at back of those smudged pupils was as acute as ever.

"How could I possibly know what Justine just told you?" she inquired mildly, regarding the green cookies with a slight shudder.

"Because sometimes it strikes me that you and Jussy have little secrets from me, and now, the moment my daughter finishes telling me her news, in you walk when you never do."

"Mmmmmm, at least they taste better than they look," commented Fee, nibbling. "I assure you, Meggie, I don't encourage your daughter to conspire with me behind your back. What have you done to upset the applecart now, Justine?" she asked, turning to where Justine was pouring her sponge mixture into greased and floured tins.

"I told Mum I was going to be an actress, Nanna, that's all."

"That's all, eh? Is it true, or only one of your dubious jokes?"

"Oh, it's true. I'm starting at the Culloden."

"Well, well, well!" said Fee, leaning against the table and surveying her own daughter ironically. "Isn't it amazing how chidren have minds of their own, Meggie?"

Meggie didn't answer.

"Do you disapprove, Nanna?" Justine growled, ready to do battle.

"I? Disapprove? It's none of my business what you do with your life, Justine. Besides, I think you'll make a good actress."

"You *do?"* gasped Meggie.

"Of course she will," said Fee. "Justine's not the sort to choose unwisely, are you, my girl?"

"No." Justine grinned, pushing a damp curl out of her eye. Meggie watched her regarding her grandmother with an affection she never seemed to extend to her mother.

"You're a good girl, Justine," Fee pronounced, and finished the cookie she had started so unenthusiastically. "Not bad at all, but I wish you'd iced them in white."

"You can't ice trees in white," Meggie contradicted.

"Of course you can when they're firs; it might be snow," her mother said.

"Too late now, they're vomit green," laughed Justine.

"Jus*tine!"*

"Ooops! Sorry, Mum, didn't mean to offend you. I always forget you've got a weak stomach."

"I haven't got a weak stomach," said Meggie, exasperated.

"I came to see if there was any chance of a cuppa,"

Fee broke in, pulling out a chair and sitting down. "Put on the kettle, Justine, like a good girl."

Meggie sat down, too. "Do you really think this will work out for Justine, Mum?" she asked anxiously.

"Why shouldn't it?" Fee answered, watching her granddaughter attending to the tea ritual.

"It might be a passing phase."

"Is it a passing phase, Justine?" Fee asked.

"No," Justine said tersely, putting cups and saucers on the old green kitchen table.

"Use a plate for the biscuits, Justine, don't put them out in their barrel," said Meggie automatically, "and for pity's sake don't dump the whole milk can on the table, put some in a proper afternoon tea jug."

"Yes, Mum, sorry, Mum," Justine responded, equally mechanically. "Can't see the point of frills in the kitchen. All I've got to do is put whatever isn't eaten back where it came from, and wash up a couple of extra dishes."

"Just do as you're told; it's so much nicer."

"Getting back to the subject," Fee pursued, "I don't think there's anything to discuss. It's my opinion that Justine ought to be allowed to try, and will probably do very well."

"I wish I could be so sure," said Meggie glumly.

"Have you been on about fame and glory, Justine?" her grandmother demanded.

"They enter the picture," said Justine, putting the old brown kitchen teapot on the table defiantly and sitting down in a hurry. "Now don't complain, Mum; I'm not making tea in a silver pot for the kitchen and that's final."

"The teapot is perfectly appropriate." Meggie smiled.

"Oh, that's good! There's nothing like a nice cup of tea," sighed Fee, sipping. "Justine, why do you persist in putting things to your mother so badly? You know it isn't a question of fame and fortune. It's a question of self, isn't it?"

"Self, Nanna?"

"Of course. Self. Acting is what you feel you were meant to do, isn't that right?"

"Yes."

"Then why couldn't you have explained it so to your mother? Why upset her with a lot of flippant nonsense?"

Justine shrugged, drank her tea down and pushed the empty cup toward her mother for more. "Dunno," she said.

"I-dont-know," Fee corrected. "You'll articulate properly on the stage, I trust. But self is why you want to be an actress, isn't it?"

"I suppose so," answered Justine reluctantly.

"Oh, that stubborn, pigheaded Cleary pride! It will be your downfall, too, Justine, unless you learn to rule it. That stupid fear of being laughed at, or held up to some sort of ridicule. Though why you think your mother would be so cruel I don't know." She tapped Justine on the back of her hand. "Give a little, Justine; cooperate."

But Justine shook her head and said, "I can't."

Fee sighed. "Well, for what earthly good it will do you, child, you have my blessing on your enterprise."

"Ta, Nanna, I appreciate it."

"Then kindly show your appreciation in a concrete fashion by finding your uncle Frank and telling him there's tea in the kitchen, please."

Justine went off, and Meggie stared at Fee.

"Mum, you're amazing, you really are."

Fee smiled. "Well, you have to admit I never tried to tell any of my children what to do."

"No, you never did," said Meggie tenderly. "We did appreciate it, too."

The first thing Justine did when she arrived back in Sydney was begin to have her freckles removed. Not a quick process, unfortunately; she had so many it would take about twelve months, and then she would have to stay out of the sun for the rest of her life, or they would come back. The second thing she did was to find herself an apartment, no mean feat in Sydney at that time, when people built private homes and regarded living en masse in buildings as anathema. But eventually she found a two-room flat in Neutral Bay, in one of the huge old waterside Victorian mansions which had fallen on hard times and been made over into dingy semi-apartments. The rent was five pounds ten shillings a week, outrageous considering that the bathroom and kitchen were communal, shared by all the tenants. However, Justine was quite satisfied. Though she had been well trained domestically, she had few homemaker instincts.

Living in Bothwell Gardens was more fascinating than her acting apprenticeship at the Culloden, where life seemed to consist in skulking behind scenery and watching other people rehearse, getting an occasional walk-on, memorizing masses of Shakespeare, Shaw and Sheridan.

Including Justine's, Bothwell Gardens had six flats, plus Mrs. Devine the landlady. Mrs. Devine was a sixty-five-year-old Londoner with a doleful sniff, protruding eyes and a great contempt for Australia and Australians, though she wasn't above robbing them. Her chief concern in life seemed to be how much gas and electricity cost, and her chief weakness was Justine's next-door neighbor, a young Englishman who exploited his nationality cheerfully.

"I don't mind giving the old duck an occasional tickle while we reminisce," he told Justine. "Keeps her off my back, you know. You girls aren't allowed to run electric radiators even in winter, but *I* was given one and *I'm* allowed to run it all summer as well if I feel like it."

"Pig," said Justine dispassionately.

His name was Peter Wilkins, and he was a traveling

salesman. "Come in and I'll make you a nice cuppa sometime," he called after her, rather taken with those pale, intriguing eyes.

Justine did, careful not to choose a time when Mrs. Devine was lurking jealously about, and got quite used to fighting Peter off. The years of riding and working on Drogheda had endowed her with considerable strength, and she was untroubled by shibboleths like hitting below the belt.

"God damn you, Justine!" gasped Peter, wiping the tears of pain from his eyes. "Give in, girl! You've got to lose it sometime, you know! This isn't Victorian England, you aren't expected to save it for marriage."

"I have no intention of saving it for marriage," she answered, adjusting her dress. "I'm just not sure who's going to get the honor, that's all."

"You're nothing to write home about!" he snapped nastily; she had really hurt.

"No, that I'm not. Sticks and stones, Pete. You can't hurt me with words. And there are plenty of men who will shag anything if it's a virgin."

"Plenty of women, too! Watch the front flat."

"Oh, I do, I do," said Justine.

The two girls in the front flat were lesbians, and had hailed Justine's advent gleefully until they realized she not only wasn't interested, she wasn't even intrigued. At first she wasn't quite sure what they were hinting at, but after they spelled it out baldly she shrugged her shoulders, unimpressed. Thus after a period of adjustment she became their sounding board, their neutral confidante, their port in all storms; she bailed Billie out of jail, took Bobbie to the Mater hospital to have her stomach pumped out after a particularly bad quarrel with Billie, refused to take sides with either of them when Pat, Al, Georgie and Ronnie hove in turns on the horizon. It did seem a very insecure kind of emotional life, she thought. Men were bad enough, but at least they had the spice of intrinsic difference.

So between the Culloden and Bothwell Gardens and girls she had known from Kincoppal days, Justine had quite a lot of friends, and was a good friend herself. She never told them all her troubles as they did her; she had Dane for that, though what few troubles she admitted to having didn't appear to prey upon her. The thing which fascinated her friends the most about her was her extraordinary self-discipline; as if she had trained herself from infancy not to let circumstances affect her well-being.

Of chief interest to everyone called a friend was how, when and with whom Justine would finally decide to become a fulfilled woman, but she took her time.

Arthur Lestrange was Albert Jones's most durable juvenile lead, though he had wistfully waved goodbye to his fortieth birthday the year before Justine arrived at the Culloden. He had a good body, was a steady, reliable actor and his clean-cut, manly face with its surround of yellow curls was always sure to evoke audience applause. For the first year he didn't notice Justine, who was very quiet and did exactly as she was told. But at the end of the year her freckle treatments were finished, and she began to stand out against the scenery instead of blending into it.

Minus the freckles and plus makeup to darken her brows and lashes, she was a good-looking girl in an elfin, understated way. She had none of Luke O'Neill's arresting beauty, or her mother's exquisiteness. Her figure was passable though not spectacular, a trifle on the thin side. Only the vivid red hair ever stood out. But on a stage she was quite different; she could make people think she was as beautiful as Helen of Troy or as ugly as a witch.

Arthur first noticed her during a teaching period, when she was required to recite a passage from Conrad's *Lord Jim* using various accents. She was extraordinary, really; he could feel the excitement in Albert Jones, and finally understood why Al devoted so much time to her. A born mimic, but far more than that; she gave character to every word she said. And there was the voice, a wonderful natural endowment for any actress, deep, husky, penetrating.

So when he saw her with a cup of tea in her hand, sitting with a book open on her knees, he came to sit beside her.

"What are you reading?"

She looked up, smiled. "Proust."

"Don't you find him a little dull?"

"Proust dull? Not unless one doesn't care for gossip, surely. That's what he is, you know. A terrible old gossip."

He had an uncomfortable conviction that she was intellectually patronizing him, but he forgave her. No more than extreme youth.

"I heard you doing the Conrad. Splendid."

"Thank you."

"Perhaps we could have coffee together sometime and discuss your plans"

"If you like," she said, returning to Proust.

He was glad he had stipulated coffee, rather than dinner; his wife kept him on short commons, and dinner demanded a degree of gratitude he couldn't be sure Justine was ready to manifest. However, he followed his casual invitation up, and bore her off to a dark little place in lower Elizabeth Street, where he was reasonably sure his wife wouldn't think of looking for him.

In self-defense Justine had learned to smoke, tired of always appearing goody-goody in refusing offered cigarettes. After they were seated she took her own cigarettes out of her bag, a new pack, and peeled the top cellophane from the flip-top box carefully, making sure the larger piece of cellophane still sheathed the bulk of the packet. Arthur watched her deliberateness, amused and interested.

"Why on earth go to so much trouble? Just rip it all off, Justine."

"How untidy!"

He picked up the box and stroked its intact shroud reflectively. "Now, if I was a disciple of the eminent Sigmund Freud . . ."

"If you were Freud, what?" She glanced up, saw the waitress standing beside her. "Cappuccino, please."

It annoyed him that she gave her own order, but he let it pass, more intent on pursuing the thought in his mind. "Vienna, please. Now, getting back to what I was saying about Freud. I wonder what he'd think of this? He might say . . ."

She took the packet off him, opened it, removed a cigarette and lit it herself without giving him time to find his matches. "Well?"

"He'd think you liked to keep membranous substances intact, wouldn't he?"

Her laughter gurgled through the smoky air, caused several male heads to turn curiously. "Would he now? Is that a roundabout way of asking me if I'm still a virgin, Arthur?"

He clicked his tonque, exasperated. "Justine! I can see that among other things I'll have to teach you the fine art of prevarication."

"Among what other things, Arthur?" She leaned her elbows on the table, eyes gleaming in the dimness. "Well, what do you need to learn?"

"I'm pretty well educated, actually."

"In everything?"

"Heavens, you do know how to emphasize words, don't you? Very good, I must remember how you said that."

"There are things which can only be learned from firsthand experience," he said softly, reaching out a hand to tuck a curl behind her ear.

"Really? I've always found observation adequate."

"Ah, but what about when it comes to love?" He

put a delicate deepness into the word. "How can you play Juliet without knowing what love is?"

"A good point. I agree with you."

"Have you ever been in love?"

"No."

"Do you know anything about love?" This time he put the vocal force on "anything," rather than "love."

"Nothing at all."

"Ah! Then Freud would have been right, eh?"

She picked up her cigarettes and looked at their sheathed box, smiling. "In some things, perhaps."

Quickly he grasped the bottom of the cellophane, pulled it off and held it in his hand, dramatically crushed it and dropped it in the ashtray, where it squeaked and writhed, expanded. "I'd like to teach you what being a woman is, if I may."

For a moment she said nothing, intent on the antics of the cellophane in the ashtray, then she struck a match and carefully set fire to it. "Why not?" she asked the brief flare. "Yes, why not?"

"Shall it be a divine thing of moonlight and roses, passionate wooing, or shall it be short and sharp, like an arrow?" he declaimed, hand on heart.

She laughed. "Really, Arthur! I hope it's *long* and sharp, myself. But no moonlight and roses, please. My stomach's not built for passionate wooing."

He stared at her a little sadly, shook his head. "Oh, Justine! Everyone's stomach is built for passionate wooing—even yours, you cold-blooded young vestal. One day, you wait and see. You'll long for it."

"Pooh!" She got up. "Come on, Arthur, let's get the deed over and done with before I change my mind."

"Now? Tonight?"

"Why on earth not? I've got plenty of money for a hotel room, if you're short."

The Hotel Metropole wasn't far away; they walked through the drowsing streets with her arm tucked cozily in his, laughing. It was too late for diners and too early for the theaters to be out, so there were few people around, just knots of American sailors off a visiting task force, and groups of young girls window-shopping with an eye to sailors. No one took any notice of them, which suited Arthur fine. He popped into a chemist shop while Justine waited outside, emerged beaming happily.

"Now we're all set, my love."

"What did you buy? French letters?"

He grimaced. "I should hope not. A French letter is like coming wrapped in a page of the *Reader's Digest*—condensed tackiness. No, I got you some jelly. How do you know about French letters, anyway?"

"After seven years in a Catholic boarding school? What do you think we did? Prayed?" She grinned. "I admit we didn't *do* much, but we talked about everything."

Mr. and Mrs. Smith surveyed their kingdom, which wasn't bad for a Sydney hotel room of that era. The days of the Hilton were still to come. It was very large, and had superb views of the Sydney Harbor Bridge. There was no bathroom, of course, but there was a basin and ewer on a marble-topped stand, a fitting accompaniment to the enormous Victorian relics of furniture.

"Well, what do I do now?" she asked, pulling the curtains back. "It's a beautiful view, isn't it?"

"Yes. As to what you do now, you take your pants off, of course."

"Anything else?" she asked mischievously.

He sighed. "Take it all off, Justine! If you don't feel skin with skin it isn't nearly so good."

Neatly and briskly she got out of her clothes, not a scrap coyly, clambered up on the bed and spread her legs apart. "Is this right, Arthur?"

"Good Lord!" he said, folding his trousers carefully; his wife always looked to see if they were crushed.

"What? What's the matter?"

"You really are a redhead, aren't you?"

"What did you expect, purple feathers?"

"Facetiousness doesn't set the right mood, darling, so stop it this instant." He sucked in his belly, turned, strutted to the bed and climbed onto it, began dropping expert little kisses down the side of her face, her neck, over her left breast. "Mmmmmm, you're nice." His arms went around her. "There! Isn't this nice?"

"I suppose so. Yes, it *is* quite nice."

Silence fell, broken only by the sound of kisses, occasional murmurs. There was a huge old dressing table at the far end of the bed, its mirror still tilted to reflect love's arena by some erotically minded previous tenant.

"Put out the light, Arthur."

"Darling, no! Lesson number one. There's no aspect of love which won't bear the light."

Having done the preparatory work with his fingers and deposited the jelly where it was supposed to be, Arthur managed to get himself between Justine's legs. A bit sore but quite comfortable, if not lifted into ecstasy at least feeling rather motherly, Justine looked over Arthur's shoulder and straight down the bed into the mirror.

Foreshortened, their legs looked weird with his darkly matted ones sandwiched between her smooth de-freckled ones; however, the bulk of the image in the mirror consisted of Arthur's buttocks, and as he maneuvered they spread and contracted, hopped up and down, with two quiffs of yellow hair like Dagwood's just poking above the twin globes and waving at her cheerfully.

Justine looked; looked again. She stuffed her fist against her mouth wildly, gurgling and moaning.

"There, there, my darling, it's all right! I've broken you already, so it can't hurt too much," he whispered.

Her chest began to heave; he wrapped his arms closer about her and murmured inarticulate endearments.

Suddenly her head went back, her mouth opened in a long, agonized wail, and became peal after peal of uproarious laughter. And the more limply furious he got, the harder she laughed, pointing her finger helplessly toward the foot of the bed, tears streaming down her face. Her whole body was convulsed, but not quite in the manner poor Arthur had envisioned.

In many ways Justine was a lot closer to Dane than their mother was, and what they felt for Mum belonged to Mum. It didn't impinge upon or clash with what they felt for each other. That had been forged very early, and had grown rather than diminished. By the time Mum was freed from her Drogheda bondage they were old enough to be at Mrs. Smith's kitchen table, doing their correspondence lessons; the habit of finding solace in each other had been established for all time.

Though they were very dissimilar in character, they also shared many tastes and appetites, and those they didn't share they tolerated in each other with instinctive respect, as a necessary spice of difference. They knew each other very well indeed. Her natural tendency was to deplore human failings in others and ignore them in herself; his natural tendency was to understand and forgive human failings in others, and be merciless upon them in himself. She felt herself invincibly strong; he knew himself perilously weak.

And somehow it all came together as a nearly perfect friendship, in the name of which nothing was impossible. However, since Justine was by far the more talkative, Dane always got to hear a lot more about her and what she was feeling than the other way around. In some respects she was a little bit of a moral imbecile, in that nothing was sacred, and he understood that his function was to provide her with the scruples she lacked within herself. Thus he accepted his role of passive listener with a tenderness and compassion which would have irked Justine enormously had she suspected them.

Not that she ever did; she had been bending his ear about absolutely anything and everything since he was old enough to pay attention.

"Guess what I did last night?" she asked, carefully adjusting her big straw hat so her face and neck were well shaded.

"Acted in your first starring role," Dane said.

"Prawn! As if I wouldn't tell you so you could be there to see me. Guess again."

"Finally copped a punch Bobbie meant for Billie."

"Cold as a stepmother's breast."

He shrugged his shoulders, bored. "Haven't a clue."

They were sitting in the Domain on the grass, just below the Gothic bulk of Saint Mary's Cathedral. Dane had phoned to let Justine know he was coming in for a special ceremony in the cathedral, and could she meet him for a while first in the Dom? Of course she could; she was dying to tell him the latest episode.

Almost finished his last year at Riverview, Dane was captain of the school, captain of the cricket team, the Rugby, handball and tennis teams. And dux of his class into the bargain. At seventeen he was two inches over six feet, his voice had settled into its final baritone, and he had miraculously escaped such afflictions as pimples, clumsiness and a bobbing Adam's apple. Because he was so fair he wasn't really shaving yet, but in every other way he looked more like a young man than a schoolboy. Only the Riverview uniform categorized him.

It was a warm, sunny day. Dane removed his straw boater school hat and stretched out on the grass, Justine sitting hunched beside him, her arms about her knees to make sure all exposed skin was shaded. He opened one lazy blue eye in her direction.

"What did you do last night, Jus?"

"I lost my virginity. At least I *think* I did."

Both his eyes opened. "You're a prawn."

"Pooh! High time, I say. How can I hope to be a

good actress if I don't have a clue what goes on between men and women?"

"You ought to save yourself for the man you marry."

Her face twisted in exasperation. "Honestly, Dane, sometimes you're so archaic I'm embarrassed! Suppose I don't meet the man I marry until I'm forty? What do you expect me to do? Sit on it all those years? Is that what you're going to do, save it for marriage?"

"I don't think I'm going to get married."

"Well, nor am I. In which case, why tie a blue ribbon around it and stick it in my nonexistent hope chest? I don't want to die wondering."

He grinned. "You can't, now." Rolling over onto his stomach, he propped his chin on his hand and looked at her steadily, his face soft, concerned. "Was it all right? I mean, was it awful? Did you hate it?"

Her lips twitched, remembering. "I didn't hate it, at any rate. It wasn't awful, either. On the other hand, I'm afraid I don't see what everyone raves about. Pleasant is as far as I'm prepared to go. And it isn't as if I chose just anyone; I selected someone very attractive and old enough to know what he was doing."

He sighed. "You *are* a prawn, Justine. I'd have been a lot happier to hear you say, 'He's not much to look at, but we met and I couldn't help myself.' I can accept that you don't want to wait until you're married, but it's still something you've got to want because of the person. Never because of the act, Jus. I'm not surprised you weren't ecstatic."

All the gleeful triumph faded from her face. "Oh, damn you, now you've made me feel awful! If I didn't know you better, I'd say you were trying to put me down—or my motives, at any rate."

"But you do know me better, don't you? I'd never put you down, but sometimes your motives are plain thoughtlessly silly." He adopted a tolling, monotonous voice. "I am the voice of your conscience, Justine O'Neill."

"You are, too, you prawn." Shade forgotten, she flopped back on the grass beside him so he couldn't see her face. "Look, you know why. Don't you?"

"Oh, Jussy," he said sadly, but whatever he was going to add was lost, for she spoke again, a little savagely.

"I'm never, never, *never* going to love anyone! If you love people, they kill you. If you need people, they kill you. They do, I tell you!"

It always hurt him, that she felt left out of love, and hurt more that he knew himself the cause. If there was one overriding reason why she was so important to him, it was because she loved him enough to bear no grudges, had never made him feel a moment's lessening of her love through jealousy or resentment. To him, it was a cruel fact that she moved on an outer circle while he was the very hub. He had prayed and prayed things would change, but they never did. Which hadn't lessened his faith, only pointed out to him with fresh emphasis that somewhere, sometime, he would have to pay for the emotion squandered on him at her expense. She put a good face on it, had managed to convince even herself that she did very well on that outer orbit, but he felt her pain. He *knew*. There was so much worth loving in her, so little worth loving in himself. Without a hope of understanding differently, he assumed he had the lion's share of love because of his beauty, his more tractable nature, his ability to communicate with his mother and the other Drogheda people. And because he was male. Very little escaped him beyond what he simply couldn't know, and he had had Justine's confidence and companionship in ways no one else ever had. Mum mattered to Justine far more than she would admit.

But I will atone, he thought. I've had everything. Somehow I've got to pay it back, make it up to her.

Suddenly he chanced to see his watch, came to his feet bonelessly; huge though he admitted his debt to his sister was, to Someone else he owed even more.

"I've got to go, Jus."

"You and your bloody Church! When are you going to grow out of it?"

"Never, I hope."

"When will I see you?"

"Well, since today's Friday, tomorrow of course, eleven o'clock, here."

"Okay. Be a good boy."

He was already several yards away, Riverview boater back on his head, but he turned to smile at her. "Am I ever anything else?"

She grinned. "Bless you, no. You're too good to be true; I'm the one always in trouble. See you tomorrow."

There were huge padded red leather doors inside the vestibule of Saint Mary's; Dane poked one open and slipped inside. He had left Justine a little earlier than was strictly necessary, but he always liked to get into a church before it filled, became a shifting focus of sighs, coughs, rustles, whispers. When he was alone it was so much better. There was a sacristan kindling branches of candles on the high altar; a deacon, he judged unerringly. Head bowed, he genuflected and made the Sign of the Cross as he passed in front of the tabernacle, then quietly slid into a pew.

On his knees, he put his head on his folded hands and let his mind float freely. He didn't consciously pray, but rather became an intrinsic part of the atmosphere, which he felt as dense yet ethereal, unspeakably holy, brooding. It was as if he had turned into a flame in one of the little red glass sanctuary lamps, always just fluttering on the brink of extinction, sustained by a small puddle of some vital essence, radiating a minute but enduring glow out into the far darknesses. Stillness, formlessness, forgetfulness of his human identity; these were what Dane got from being in a church. Nowhere else did he feel so right, so much at peace with himself, so removed from pain. His lashes lowered, his eyes closed.

From the organ gallery came the shuffling of feet, a preparatory wheeze, a breathy expulsion of air from pipes. The Saint Mary's Cathedral Boys' School choir was coming in early to sandwich a little practice between now and the coming ritual. It was only a Friday midday Benediction, but one of Dane's friends and teachers from Riverview was celebrating it, and he had wanted to come.

The organ gave off a few chords, quietened into a rippling accompaniment, and into the dim stone-lace arches one unearthly boy's voice soared, thin and high and sweet, so filled with innocent purity the few people in the great empty church closed their eyes, mourned for that which could never come to them again.

Panis angelicus
Fit panis hominum,
Dat panis coelicus
Figuris terminum,
O res mirabilis,
Manducat Dominus,
Pauper, pauper,
Servus et humilis. . . .

Bread of angels, heavenly bread, O thing of wonder. Out of the depths have I cried unto Thee, O Lord; Lord, hear my voice! Let Thine ear be attuned to the sounds of my supplication. Turn not away, O Lord, turn not away. For Thou art my Sovereign, my Master, my God, and I am Thy humble servant. In Thine eyes only one thing counts, goodness. Thou carest not if Thy servants be beautiful or ugly. To Thee only the heart matters; in Thee all is healed, in Thee I know peace.

Lord, it is lonely. I pray it be over soon, the pain of life. They do not understand that I, so gifted, find so much pain in living. But Thou dost, and Thy comfort is all which sustains me. No matter what Thou requirest of me, O Lord, shall be given, for I love

Thee. And if I might presume to ask anything of Thee, it is that in Thee all else shall be forever forgotten. . . .

"You're very quiet, Mum," said Dane. "Thinking of what? Of Drogheda?"

"No," said Meggie drowsily. "I'm thinking that I'm getting old. I found half a dozen grey hairs this morning, and my bones ache."

"You'll never be old, Mum," he said comfortably.

"I wish that were true, love, but unfortunately it isn't. I'm beginning to need the borehead, which is a sure sign of old age."

They were lying in the warm winter sun on towels spread over the Drogheda grass, by the borehead. At the far end of the great pool boiling water thundered and splashed, the reek of sulphur drifted and floated into nothing. It was one of the great winter pleasures, to swim in the borehead. All the aches and pains of encroaching age were soothed away, Meggie thought, and turned to lie on her back, her head in the shade of the log on which she and Father Ralph had sat so long ago. A very long time ago; she was unable to conjure up even a faint echo of what she must have felt when Ralph had kissed her.

Then she heard Dane get up, and opened her eyes. He had always been her baby, her lovely little boy; though she had watched him change and grow with proprietary pride, she had done so with an image of the laughing baby superimposed on his maturing face. It had not yet occurred to her that actually he was no longer in any way a child.

However, the moment of realization came to Meggie at that instant, watching him stand outlined against the crisp sky in his brief cotton swimsuit.

My God, it's all over! The babyhood, the boyhood. *He's a man.* Pride, resentment, a female melting at the quick, a terrific consciousness of some impending tragedy, anger, adoration, sadness; all these and more Meggie felt, looking up at her son. It is a terrible thing to create a man, and more terrible to create a man like this. So amazingly male, so amazingly beautiful.

Ralph de Bricassart, plus a little of herself. How could she not be moved at seeing in its extreme youth the body of the man who had joined in love with her? She closed her eyes, embarrassed, hating having to think of her son as a man. Did he look at her and see a woman these days, or was she still that wonderful cipher, Mum? God damn him, God damn him! How dared he grow up?

"Do you know anything about women, Dane?" she asked suddenly, opening her eyes again.

He smiled. "The birds and the bees, you mean?"

"That you know, with Justine for a sister. When she discovered what lay between the covers of physiology textbooks she blurted it all out to everyone. No, I mean have you ever put any of Justine's clinical treatises into practice?"

His head moved in a quick negative shake, he slid down onto the grass beside her and looked into her face. "Funny you should ask that, Mum. I've been wanting to talk to you about it for a long time, but I didn't know how to start."

"You're only eighteen, love. Isn't it a bit soon to be thinking of putting theory into practice?" Only eighteen. Only. He was a man, wasn't he?

"That's it, what I wanted to talk to you about. Not putting it into practice at all."

How cold the wind was, blowing down from the Great Divide. Peculiar, she hadn't noticed until now. Where was her robe? "Not putting it into practice at all," she said dully, and it was not a question.

"That's right. I don't want to, ever. Not that I haven't thought about it, or wanted a wife and children. I have. But I can't. Because there isn't enough room to love them and God as well, not the way I want to love God. I've known that for a long time. I don't seem to remember a time when I didn't, and the older I become the greater my love for God grows. It's a great mystery, loving God."

Meggie lay looking into those calm, distant blue eyes. Ralph's eyes, as they used to be. But ablaze with something quite alien to Ralph's. Had he had it, at eighteen? Had he? Was it perhaps something one could only experience at eighteen? By the time she entered Ralph's life, he was ten years beyond that. Yet her son was a mystic, she had always known it. And she didn't think that at any stage of his life Ralph had been mystically inclined. She swallowed, wrapped the robe closer about her lonely bones.

"So I asked myself," Dane went on, "what I could do to show Him how much I loved Him. I fought the answer for a long time, I didn't want to see it. Because I wanted a life as a man, too, very much. Yet I knew what the offering had to be, I knew. . . . There's only one thing I can offer Him, to show Him nothing else will ever exist in my heart before Him. I must offer up His only rival; that's the sacrifice He demands of me. I am His servant, and He will have no rivals. I have had to choose. All things He'll let me have and enjoy, save that." He sighed, plucked at a blade of Drogheda grass. "I must show Him that I understand why He gave me so much at my birth. I must show Him that I realize how unimportant my life as a man is."

"You can't do it, I won't let you!" Meggie cried, her hand reaching for his arm, clutching it. How smooth it felt, the hint of great power under the skin, just like Ralph's. *Just like Ralph's!* Not to have some glossy girl put her hand there, as a right?

"I'm going to be a priest," said Dane. "I'm going to enter His service completely, offer everything I have and am to Him, as His priest. Poverty, chastity and obedience. He demands no less than all from His chosen servants. It won't be easy, but I'm going to do it."

The look in her eyes! As if he had killed her, ground her into the dust beneath his foot. That he should have to suffer this he hadn't known, dreaming only of her pride in him, her pleasure at giving her son to God. They *said* she'd be thrilled, uplifted, completely in accord. Instead she was staring at him as if the prospect of his priesthood was her death sentence.

"It's all I've ever wanted to be," he said in despair, meeting those dying eyes. "Oh, Mum, can't you understand? I've never, never wanted to be anything but a priest! I *can't* be anything but a priest!"

Her hand fell from his arm; he glanced down and saw the white marks of her fingers, the little arcs in his skin where her nails had bitten deeply. Her head went up, she laughed on and on and on, huge hysterical peals of bitter, derisive laughter.

"Oh, it's too good to be true!" she gasped when she could speak again, wiping the tears from the corners of her eyes with a trembling hand. "The incredible irony! Ashes of roses, he said that night riding to the borehead. And I didn't understand what he meant. Ashes thou wert, unto ashes return. To the Church thou belongest, to the Church thou shalt be given. Oh, it's beautiful, beautiful! God rot God, I say! God the sod! The utmost Enemy of women, that's what God is! Everything we seek to do, He seeks to undo!"

"Oh, don't! Oh, don't! Mum, don't!" He wept for her, for her pain, not understanding her pain or the words she was saying. His tears fell, twisted in his heart; already the sacrifice had begun, and in a way he hadn't dreamed. But though he wept for her, not even for her could he put it aside, the sacrifice. The offering must be made, and the harder it was to make, the more valuable it must be in His eyes.

She had made him weep, and never in all his life until now had she made him weep. Her own rage and grief were put away resolutely. No, it wasn't fair to visit herself upon him. What he was his genes had made him. Or his God. Or Ralph's God. He was the light of her life, her son. He should not be made to suffer because of her, ever.

"Dane, don't cry," she whispered, stroking the angry marks on his arm. "I'm sorry, I didn't mean it. You gave me a shock, that's all. Of course I'm glad for you, truly I am! How could I not be? I was shocked; I just didn't expect it, that's all." She chuckled, a little shakily. "You did rather drop it on me like a rock."

His eyes cleared, regarded her doubtfully. Why had he imagined he killed her? Those were Mum's eyes as he had always known them; full of love, very much alive. The strong young arms gathered her close, hugged her. "You're *sure* you don't mind?"

"Mind? A good Catholic mother mind her son becoming a priest? Impossible!" She jumped to her feet. "Brr! How cold it's got! Let's be getting back."

They hadn't taken the horses, but a jeeplike Land-Rover; Dane climbed behind the wheel, his mother sat beside him.

"Do you know where you're going?" asked Meggie, drawing in a sobbing breath, pushing the tumbled hair out of her eyes.

"Saint Patrick's College, I suppose. At least until I find my feet. Perhaps then I'll espouse an order. I'd rather like to be a Jesuit, but I'm not quite sure enough of that to go straight into the Society of Jesus."

Meggie stared at the tawny grass bouncing up and down through the insect-spattered windscreen. "I have a much better idea, Dane."

"Oh?" He had to concentrate on driving; the track dwindled a bit and there were always new logs across it.

"I shall send you to Rome, to Cardinal de Bricassart. You remember him, don't you?"

"Do I remember him? What a question, Mum! I don't think I could forget him in a million years. He's my example of the perfect priest. If I could be the priest he is, I'd be very happy."

"Perfection is as perfection does!" said Meggie tartly. "But I shall give you into his charge, because I know he'll look after you for my sake. You can enter a seminary in Rome."

"Do you really mean it, Mum? Really?" Anxiety pushed the joy out of his face. "Is there enough money? It would be much cheaper if I stayed in Australia."

"Thanks to the selfsame Cardinal de Bricassart, my dear, you'll never lack money."

At the cookhouse door she pushed him inside. "Go and tell the girls and Mrs. Smith," she said. "They'll be absolutely thrilled."

One after the other she put her feet down, made them plod up the ramp to the big house, to the drawing room where Fee sat, miraculously not working but talking to Anne Mueller instead, over an afternoon tea tray. As Meggie came in they looked up, saw from her face that something serious had happened.

For eighteen years the Muellers had been visiting Drogheda, expecting that was how it always would be. But Luddie Mueller had died suddenly the preceding autumn, and Meggie had written immediately to Anne to ask her if she would like to live permanently on Drogheda. There was plenty of room, a guest cottage for privacy; she could pay board if she was too proud not to, though heaven knew there was enough money to keep a thousand permanent houseguests. Meggie saw it as a chance to reciprocate for those lonely Queensland years, and Anne saw it as salvation. Himmelhoch without Luddie was horribly lonely. Though she had put on a manager, not sold the place; when she died it would go to Justine.

"What is it, Meggie?" Anne asked.

Meggie sat down. "I think I've been struck by a retributory bolt of lightning."

"What?"

"You were right, both of you. You said I'd lose him. I didn't believe you, I actually thought I could beat God. But there was never a woman born who could beat God. He's a Man."

Fee poured Meggie a cup of tea. "Here, drink this," she said, as if tea had the restorative powers of brandy. "How have you lost him?"

"He's going to become a priest." She began to laugh, weeping at the same time.

Anne picked up her sticks, hobbled to Meggie's chair and sat awkwardly on its arm, stroking the lovely red-gold hair. "Oh, my dear! But it isn't as bad as all that."

"Do you know about Dane?" Fee asked Anne.

"I've always known," said Anne.

Meggie sobered. "It isn't as bad as all that? It's the beginning of the end, don't you see? Retribution. I stole Ralph from God, and I'm paying with my son. You told me it was stealing, Mum, don't you remember? I didn't want to believe you, but you were right, as always."

"Is he going to Saint Pat's?" Fee asked practically.

Meggie laughed more normally. "That's no sort of reparation, Mum. I'm going to send him to Ralph, of course. Half of him is Ralph; let Ralph finally enjoy him." She shrugged. "He's more important than Ralph, and I knew he'd want to go to Rome."

"Did you ever tell Ralph about Dane?" asked Anne; it wasn't a subject ever discussed.

"No, and I never will. Never!"

"They're so alike he might guess."

"Who, Ralph? He'll never guess! That much I'm going to keep. I'm sending him *my* son, but no more than that. I'm not sending him *his* son."

"Beware of the jealousy of the gods, Meggie," said Anne softly. "They might not have done with you yet."

"What more can they do to me?" mourned Meggie.

When Justine heard the news she was furious, though

for the last three or four years she had had a sneaking suspicion it was coming. On Meggie it burst like a clap of thunder, but on Justine it descended like an expected shower of icy water.

First of all, because Justine had been at school in Sydney with him, and as his confidante had listened to him talk of the things he didn't mention to his mother. Justine knew how vitally important his religion was to Dane; not only God, but the mystical significance of Catholic rituals. Had he been born and brought up a Protestant, she thought, he was the type to have eventually turned to Catholicism to satisfy something in his soul. Not for Dane an austere, calvinistic God. His God was limned in stained glass, wreathed in incense, wrapped in lace and gold embroidery, hymned in musical complexity, and worshipped in lovely Latin cadences.

Too, it was a kind of ironic perversity that someone so wonderfully endowed with beauty should deem it a crippling handicap, and deplore its existence. For Dane did. He shrank from any reference to his looks; Justine fancied he would far rather have been born ugly, totally unprepossessing. She understood in part why he felt so, and perhaps because her own career lay in a notoriously narcissistic profession, she rather approved of his attitude toward his appearance. What she couldn't begin to understand was why he positively loathed his looks, instead of simply ignoring them.

Nor was he highly sexed, for what reason she wasn't sure: whether he had taught himself to sublimate his passions almost perfectly, or whether in spite of his bodily endowments some necessary cerebral essence was in short supply. Probably the former, since he played some sort of vigorous sport every day of his life to make sure he went to bed exhausted. She knew very well that his inclinations were "normal," that is, heterosexual, and she knew what type of girl appealed to him —tall, dark and voluptuous. But he just wasn't sensually aware; he didn't notice the feel of things when he held them, or the odors in the air around him, or understand the special satisfaction of shape and color. Before he experienced a sexual pull the provocative object's impact had to be irresistible, and only at such rare moments did he seem to realize there was an earthly plane most men trod, of choice, for as long as they possibly could.

He told her backstage at the Culloden, after a performance. It had been settled with Rome that day; he was dying to tell her and yet he knew she wasn't going to like it. His religious ambitions were something he had never discussed with her as much as he wanted to, for she became angry. But when he came backstage that night it was too difficult to contain his joy any longer.

"You're a prawn," she said in disgust.

"It's what I want."

"Idiot."

"Calling me names won't change a thing, Jus."

"Do you think I don't know that? It affords me a little much-needed emotional release, that's all."

"I should think you'd get enough on the stage, playing Electra. You're really good, Jus."

"After this news I'll be better," she said grimly. "Are you going to Saint Pat's?"

"No. I'm going to Rome, to Cardinal de Bricassart. Mum arranged it."

"Dane, no! It's so far away!"

"Well, why don't you come, too, at least to England? With your background and ability you ought to be able to get a place somewhere without too much trouble."

She was sitting at a mirror wiping off Electra's paint, still in Electra's robes; ringed with heavy black arabesques, her strange eyes seemed even stranger. She nodded slowly. "Yes, I could, couldn't I?" she asked thoughtfully. "It's more than time I did. . . . Australia's getting a bit too small. . . . Right, mate! You're on! England it is!"

"Super! Just think! I get holidays, you know, one always does in the seminary, as if it was a university. We can plan to take them together, trip around Europe a bit, come home to Drogheda. Oh, Jus, I've thought it all out! Having you not far away makes it perfect."

She beamed. "It does, doesn't it? Life wouldn't be the same if I couldn't talk to you."

"That's what I was afraid you were going to say." He grinned. "But seriously, Jus, you worry me. I'd rather have you where I can see you from time to time. Otherwise who's going to be the voice of your conscience?"

He slid down between a hoplite's helmet and an awesome mask of the Pythoness to a position on the floor where he could see her, coiling himself into an economical ball, out of the way of all the feet. There were only two stars' dressing rooms at the Culloden and Justine didn't rate either of them yet. She was in the general dressing room, among the ceaseless traffic.

"Bloody old Cardinal de Bricassart!" she spat. "I hated him the moment I laid eyes on him!"

Dane chuckled. "You didn't, you know."

"I did! I did!"

"No, you didn't. Aunt Anne told me one Christmas hol, and I'll bet you don't know."

"What don't I know?" she asked warily.

"That when you were a baby he fed you a bottle and burped you, rocked you to sleep. Aunt Anne said you were a horrible cranky baby and hated being held, but when he held you, you really liked it."

"It's a flaming lie!"

"No, it's not." He grinned. "Anyway, why do you hate him so much now?"

"I just do. He's like a skinny old vulture, and he gives me the dry heaves."

"I like him. I always did. The perfect priest, that's what Father Watty calls him. I think he is, too."

"Well, fuck him, *I* say!"

"Jus*tine!*"

"Shocked you that time, didn't I? I'll bet you never even thought I knew that word."

His eyes danced. *"Do* you know what it means? Tell me, Jussy, go on, I dare you!"

She could never resist him when he teased; her own eyes began to twinkle. "You might be going to be a Father Rhubarb, you prawn, but if you don't already know what it means, you'd better not investigate."

He grew serious. "Don't worry, I won't."

A very shapely pair of female legs stopped beside Dane, pivoted. He looked up, went red, looked away, and said, "Oh, hello, Martha," in a casual voice.

"Hello yourself."

She was an extremely beautiful girl, a little short on acting ability but so decorative she was an asset to any production; she also happened to be exactly Dane's cup of tea, and Justine had listened to his admiring comments about her more than once. Tall, what the movie magazines always called sexsational, very dark of hair and eye, fair of skin, with magnificent breasts.

Perching herself on the corner of Justine's table, she swung one leg provocatively under Dane's nose and watched him with an undisguised appreciation he clearly found disconcerting. Lord, he was really something! How had plain old cart-horse Jus collected herself a brother who looked like this? He might be only eighteen and it might be cradle-snatching, but who cared?

"How about coming over to my place for coffee and whatever?" she asked, looking down at Dane. "The two of you?" she added reluctantly.

Justine shook her head positively, her eyes lighting up at a sudden thought. "No, thanks, I can't. You'll have to be content with Dane."

He shook his head just as positively, but rather regretfully, as if he was truly tempted. "Thanks anyway, Martha, but I can't." He glanced at his watch as at a savior. "Lord, I've only got a minute left on my meter! How much longer are you going to be, Jus?"

"About ten minutes."

"I'll wait for you outside, all right?"

"Chicken!" she mocked.

Martha's dusky eyes followed him. "He is absolutely gorgeous. Why won't he look at me?"

Justine grinned sourly, scrubbed her face clean at last. The freckles were coming back. Maybe London would help; no sun. "Oh, don't worry, he looks. He'd like, too. But will he? Not Dane."

"Why? What's the matter with him? Never tell me he's a poof! Shit, why is it every gorgeous man I meet is a poof? I never thought Dane was, though; he doesn't strike me that way at all."

"Watch your language, you dumb wart! He most certainly isn't a poof. In fact, the day he looks at Sweet William, our screaming juvenile, I'll cut his throat and Sweet William's, too."

"Well, if he isn't a pansy and he likes, why doesn't he take? Doesn't he get my message? Does he think I'm too old for him?"

"Sweetie, at a hundred you won't be too old for the average man, don't worry about it. No, Dane's sworn off sex for life, the fool. He's going to be a priest."

Martha's lush mouth dropped open, she swung back her mane of inky hair. "Go on!"

"True, true."

"You mean to say all that's going to be *wasted?"*

"Afraid so. He's offering it to God."

"Then God's a bigger poofter than Sweet Willie."

"You might be right," said Justine. "He certainly isn't too fond of women, anyway. Second-class, that's us, way back in the Upper Circle. Front Stalls and the Mezzanine, strictly male."

"Oh."

Justine wriggled out of Electra's robe, flung a thin cotton dress over her head, remembered it was chilly outside, added a cardigan, and patted Martha kindly on the head. "Don't worry about it, sweetie. God was very good to you; he didn't give you any brains. Believe me, it's far more comfortable that way. You'll never offer the Lords of Creation any competition."

"I don't know, I wouldn't mind competing with God for your brother."

"Forget it. You're fighting the Establishment, and it just can't be done. You'd seduce Sweet Willie far quicker, take my word for it."

A Vatican car met Dane at the airport, whisked him through sunny faded streets full of handsome, smiling people; he glued his nose to the window and drank it all in, unbearably excited at seeing for himself the things he had seen only in pictures—the Roman columns, the rococo palaces, the Renaissance glory of Saint Peter's.

And waiting for him, clad this time in scarlet from head to foot, was Ralph Raoul, Cardinal de Bricassart. The hand was outstretched, its ring glowing; Dane sank on both knees to kiss it.

"Stand up, Dane, let me look at you."

He stood, smiling at the tall man who was almost exactly his own height; they could look each other in the eye. To Dane the Cardinal had an immense aura of spiritual power which made him think of a pope rather than a saint, yet those intensely sad eyes were not the eyes of a pope. How much he must have suffered to appear so, but how nobly he must have risen above his suffering to become this most perfect of priests.

And Cardinal Ralph gazed at the son he did not know was his son, loving him, he thought, because he was dear Meggie's boy. Just so would he have wanted to see a son of his own body; as tall, as strikingly good-looking, as graceful. In all his life he had never seen a man move so well. But far more satisfying than any physical beauty was the simple beauty of his soul. He had the strength of the angels, and something of their unearthliness. Had he been so himself, at eighteen? He tried to remember, span the crowded events of three-fifths of a lifetime; no, he had never been so. Was it because this one came truly of his own choice? For he himself had not, though he *had* had the vocation, of that much he still was sure.

"Sit down, Dane. Did you do as I asked, start to learn Italian?"

"At this stage I speak it fluently but without idiom, and I read it very well. Probably the fact that it's my fourth language makes it easier. I seem to have a talent for languages. A couple of weeks here and I ought to pick up the vernacular."

"Yes, you will. I, too, have a talent for languages."

"Well, they're handy," said Dane lamely. The awesome scarlet figure was a little daunting; it was suddenly hard to remember the man on the chestnut gelding at Drogheda.

Cardinal Ralph leaned forward, watching him.

"I pass the responsibility for him to you, Ralph," Meggie's letter had said. "I charge you with his well-being, his happiness. What I stole, I give back. It is demanded of me. Only promise me two things, and I'll rest in the knowledge you've acted in his best interests. First, promise me you'll make sure before you accept him that this is what he truly, absolutely wants. Secondly, that if this is what he wants, you'll keep your eye on him, make sure it remains what he wants. If he should lose heart for it, I want him back. For he belonged to me first. It is I who gives him to you."

"Dane, are you sure?" asked the Cardinal.

"Absolutely."

"Why?"

His eyes were curiously aloof, uncomfortably familiar, but familiar in a way which was of the past.

"Because of the love I bear Our Lord. I want to serve Him as His priest all of my days."

"Do you understand what His service entails, Dane?"

"Yes."

"That no other love must ever come between you and Him? That you are His exclusively, forsaking all others?"

"Yes."

"That His Will be done in all things, that in His service you must bury your personality, your individuality, your concept of yourself as uniquely important?"

"Yes."

"That if necessary you must face death, imprisonment, starvation in His Name? That you must own nothing, value nothing which might tend to lessen your love for Him?"

"Yes."

"Are you strong, Dane?"

"I am a man, Your Eminence. I am first a man. It will be hard, I know. But I pray that with His help I shall find the strength."

"Must it be this, Dane? Will nothing less than this content you?"

"Nothing."

"And if later on you should change your mind, what would you do?"

"Why, I should ask to leave," said Dane, surprised. "If I changed my mind it would be because I had genuinely mistaken my vocation, for no other reason. Therefore I should ask to leave. I wouldn't be loving Him any less, but I'd know this isn't the way He means me to serve Him."

"But once your final vows are taken and you are ordained, you realize there can be no going back, no dispensation, absolutely no release?"

"I understand that," said Dane patiently. "But if

there is a decision to be made, I will have come to it before then."

Cardinal Ralph leaned back in his chair, sighed. Had he ever been that sure? Had he ever been that strong? "Why to me, Dane? Why did you want to come to Rome? Why not have remained in Australia?"

"Mum suggested Rome, but it had been in my mind as a dream for a long time. I never thought there was enough money."

"Your mother is very wise. Didn't she tell you?"

"Tell me what, Your Eminence?"

"That you have an income of five thousand pounds a year and many thousands of pounds already in the bank in your own name?"

Dane stiffened. "No. She never told me."

"Very wise. But it's there, and Rome is yours if you want. Do you want Rome?"

"Yes."

"Why do you want *me,* Dane?"

"Because you're my conception of the perfect priest, Your Eminence."

Cardinal Ralph's face twisted. "No, Dane, you can't look up to me as that. I'm far from a perfect priest. I have broken all my vows, do you understand? I had to learn what you already seem to know in the most painful way a priest can, through the breaking of my vows. For I refused to admit that I was first a mortal man, and only after that a priest."

"Your Eminence, it doesn't matter," said Dane softly. "What you say doesn't make you any less my conception of the perfect priest. I think you don't understand what I mean, that's all. I don't mean an inhuman automaton, above the weaknesses of the flesh. I mean that you've suffered, and grown. Do I sound presumptuous? I don't intend to, truly. If I've offended you, I beg your pardon. It's just that it's so hard to express my thoughts! What I mean is that becoming a perfect priest must take years, terrible pain, and all the time keeping before you an ideal, and Our Lord."

The telephone rang; Cardinal Ralph picked it up in a slightly unsteady hand, spoke in Italian.

"Yes, thank you, we'll come at once." He got to his feet. "It's time for afternoon tea, and we're to have it with an old, old friend of mine. Next to the Holy Father he's probably the most important priest in the Church. I told him you were coming, and he expressed a wish to meet you."

"Thank you, Your Eminence."

They walked through corridors, then through pleasant gardens quite unlike Drogheda's, with tall cypresses and poplars, neat rectangles of grass surrounded by pillared walkways, mossy flagstones; past Gothic arches, under Renaissance bridges. Dane drank it in, loving it. Such a different world from Australia, so old, perpetual.

It took them fifteen minutes at a brisk pace to reach the palace; they entered, and passed up a great marble staircase hung with priceless tapestries.

Vittorio Scarbanza, Cardinal di Contini-Verchese was sixty-six now, his body partially crippled by a rheumatic complaint, but his mind as intelligent and alert as it had always been. His present cat, a Russian blue named Natasha, was curled purring in his lap. Since he couldn't rise to greet his visitors he contented himself with a wide smile, and beckoned them. His eyes passed from Ralph's beloved face to Dane O'Neill and widened, narrowed, fixed on him stilly. Within his chest he felt his heart falter, put the welcoming hand to it in an instinctive gesture of protection, and sat staring stupidly up at the younger edition of Ralph de Bricassart.

"Vittorio, are you all right?" Cardinal Ralph asked anxiously, taking the frail wrist between his fingers, feeling for a pulse.

"Of course. A little passing pain, no more. Sit down, sit down!"

"First, I'd like you to meet Dane O'Neill, who is as I told you the son of a very dear friend of mine. Dane, this is His Eminence Cardinal di Contini-Verchese."

Dane knelt, pressed his lips to the ring; over his bent tawny head Cardinal Vittorio's gaze sought Ralph's face, scanned it more closely than in many years. Very slightly he relaxed; she had never told him, then. And he wouldn't suspect, of course, what everyone who saw them together would instantly surmise. Not father-son, of course, but a close relationship of the blood. Poor Ralph! He had never seen himself walk, never watched the expressions on his own face, never caught the upward flight of his own left eyebrow. Truly God was good, to make men so blind.

"Sit down. The tea is coming. So, young man! You wish to be a priest, and have sought the assistance of Cardinal de Bricassart?"

"Yes, Your Eminence."

"You have chosen wisely. Under his care you will come to no harm. But you look a little nervous, my son. Is it the strangeness?"

Dane smiled Ralph's smile, perhaps minus conscious charm, but so much Ralph's smile it caught at an old, tired heart like a passing flick from barbed wire. "I'm overwhelmed, Your Eminence. I hadn't realized quite how important cardinals are. I never dreamed I'd be met at the airport, or be having tea with *you.*"

"Yes, it is unusual. . . . Perhaps a source of trouble, I see that. Ah, here is our tea!" Pleased, he watched it laid out, lifted an admonishing finger. "Ah, no! I shall be 'mother.' How do you take your tea, Dane?"

"The same as Ralph," he answered, blushed deeply. "I'm sorry, Your Eminence, I didn't mean to say that!"

"It's all right, Dane, Cardinal di Contini-Verchese understands. We met first as Dane and Ralph, and we knew each other far better that way, didn't we? Formality is new to our relationship. I'd prefer it remain Dane and Ralph in private. His Eminence won't mind, will you, Vittorio?"

"No. I am fond of Christian names. But returning to what I was saying about having friends in high places, my son. It could be a trifle uncomfortable for you when you enter whichever seminary is decided upon, this long friendship with our Ralph. To have to keep going into involved explanations every time the connection between you is remarked upon would be very tedious. Sometimes Our Lord permits of a little white lie"—he smiled, the gold in his teeth flashing—"and for everyone's comfort I would prefer that we resort to one such tiny fib. For it is difficult to explain satisfactorily the tenuous connections of friendship, but very easy to explain the crimson cord of blood. So we will say to all and sundry that Cardinal de Bricassart is your uncle, my Dane, and leave it at that," ended Cardinal Vittorio suavely.

Dane looked shocked, Cardinal Ralph resigned.

"Do not be disappointed in the great, my son," said Cardinal Vittorio gently. "They, too, have feet of clay, and resort to comfort via little white lies. It is a very useful lesson you have just learned, but looking at you, I doubt you will take advantage of it. However, you must understand that we scarlet gentlemen are diplomats to our fingertips. Truly I think only of you, my son. Jealousy and resentment are not strangers to seminaries any more than they are to secular institutions. You will suffer a little because they think Ralph is your uncle, your mother's brother, but you would suffer far more if they thought no blood bond linked you together. We are first men, and it is with men you will deal in this world as in others."

Dane bowed his head, then leaned forward to stroke the cat, pausing with his hand extended. "May I? I love cats, Your Eminence."

No quicker pathway to that old but constant heart could he have found. "You may. I confess she grows too heavy for me. She is a glutton, are you not, Natasha? Go to Dane; he is the new generation."

There was no possibility of Justine transferring herself and her belongings from the southern to the northern hemisphere as quickly as Dane had; by the time she worked out the season at the Culloden and bade a not unregretful farewell to Bothwell Gardens, her brother had been in Rome two months.

"How on earth did I manage to accumulate so much junk?" she asked, surrounded by clothes, papers, boxes.

Meggie looked up from where she was crouched, a box of steel wool soap pads in her hand.

"What were these doing under your bed?"

A look of profound relief swept across her daughter's flushed face. "Oh, thank God! Is that where they were? I thought Mrs. D's precious poodle ate them; he's been off color for a week and I wasn't game to mention my missing soap pads. But I *knew* the wretched animal ate them; he'll eat anything that doesn't eat him first. Not," continued Justine thoughtfully, "that I wouldn't be glad to see the last of him."

Meggie sat back on her heels, laughing. "Oh, Jus! Do you know how funny you are?" She threw the box onto the bed among a mountain of things already there. "You're no credit to Drogheda, are you? After all the care we took pushing neatness and tidiness into your head, too."

"I could have told you it was a lost cause. Do you want to take the soap pads back to Drogheda? I know I'm sailing and my luggage is unlimited, but I daresay there are tons of soap pads in London."

Meggie transferred the box into a large carton marked MRS. D. "I think we'd better donate them to Mrs. Devine; she has to render this flat habitable for the next tenant." An unsteady tower of unwashed dishes stood on the end of the table, sprouting gruesome whiskers of mold. "Do you ever wash your dishes?"

Justine chuckled unrepentantly. "Dane says I don't wash them at all, I shave them instead."

"You'd have to give this lot a haircut first. Why don't you wash them as you use them?"

"Because it would mean trekking down to the kitchen again, and since I usually eat after midnight, no one appreciates the patter of my little feet."

"Give me one of the empty boxes. I'll take them down and dispose of them now," said her mother, resigned; she had known before volunteering to come what was bound to be in store for her, and had been rather looking forward to it. It wasn't very often anyone had the chance to help Justine do anything; whenever Meggie had tried to help her she had ended feeling an utter fool. But in domestic matters the situation was reversed for once; she could help to her heart's content without feeling a fool.

Somehow it got done, and Justine and Meggie set out in the station wagon Meggie had driven down from Gilly, bound for the Hotel Australia, where Meggie had a suite.

"I wish you Drogheda people would buy a house at Palm Beach or Avalon," Justine said, depositing her case in the suite's second bedroom. "This is terrible, right above Martin Place. Just imagine being a hop, skip and jump from the surf! Wouldn't that induce you to hustle yourselves on a plane from Gilly more often?"

"Why should I come to Sydney? I've been down twice in the last seven years—to see Dane off, and now to see you off. If we had a house it would never be used."

"Codswallop."

"Why?"

"Why? Because there's more to the world than bloody Drogheda, dammit! That place, it drives me batty!"

Meggie sighed. "Believe me, Justine, there'll come a time when you'll yearn to come home to Drogheda."

"Does that go for Dane, too?"

Silence. Without looking at her daughter, Meggie took her bag from the table. "We'll be late. Madame Rocher said two o'clock. If you want your dresses before you sail, we'd better hurry."

"I am put in my place," Justine said, and grinned.

"Why is it, Justine, that you didn't introduce me to any of your friends? I didn't see a sign of anyone at Bothwell Gardens except Mrs. Devine," Meggie said as they sat in Germaine Rocher's salon watching the languid mannequins preen and simper.

"Oh, they're a bit shy. . . . I like that orange thing, don't you?"

"Not with your hair. Settle for the grey."

"Pooh! I think orange goes perfectly with my hair. In grey I look like something the cat dragged in, sort of muddy and half rotten. Move with the times, Mum. Redheads don't have to be seen in white, grey, black, emerald green or that horrible color you're so addicted to—what is it, ashes of roses? Victorian!"

"You have the name of the color right," Meggie said. She turned to look at her daughter. "You're a monster," she said wryly, but with affection.

Justine didn't pay any attention; it was not the first time she had heard it. "I'll take the orange, the scarlet, the purple print, the moss green, the burgundy suit. . . ."

Meggie sat torn between laughter and rage. What could one do with a daughter like Justine?

The *Himalaya* sailed from Darling Harbor three days later. She was a lovely old ship, flat-hulled and very seaworthy, built in the days when no one was in a tearing hurry and everyone accepted the fact England was four weeks away via Suez or five weeks away via the Cape of Good Hope. Nowadays even the ocean liners were streamlined, hulls shaped like destroyers to get there faster. But what they did to a sensitive stomach made seasoned sailors quail.

"What fun!" Justine laughed. "We've got a whole

lovely footie team in first class, so it won't be as dull as I thought. Some of them are gorgeous."

"Now aren't you glad I insisted on first class?"

"I suppose so."

"Justine, you bring out the worst in me, you always have," Meggie snapped, losing her temper at what she took for ingratitude. Just this once couldn't the little wretch at least pretend she was sorry to be going? "Stubborn, pig-headed, self-willed! You exasperate me."

For a moment Justine didn't answer, but turned her head away as if she was more interested in the fact that the all-ashore gong was ringing than in what her mother was saying. She bit the tremor from her lips, put a bright smile on them. "I know I exasperate you," she said cheerfully as she faced her mother. "Never mind, we are what we are. As you always say, I take after my dad."

They embraced self-consciously before Meggie slipped thankfully into the crowds converging on gangways and was lost to sight. Justine made her way up to the sun deck and stood by the rail with rolls of colored streamers in her hands. Far below on the wharf she saw the figure in the pinkish-grey dress and hat walk to the appointed spot, stand shading her eyes. Funny, at this distance one could see Mum was getting up toward fifty. Some way to go yet, but it was there in her stance. They waved in the same moment, then Justine threw the first of her streamers and Meggie caught its end deftly. A red, a blue, a yellow, a pink, a green, an orange; spiraling round and round, tugging in the breeze.

A pipe band had come to bid the football team farewell and stood with pennons flying, plaids billowing, skirling a quaint version of "Now Is the Hour." The ship's rails were thick with people hanging over, holding desperately to their ends of the thin paper streamers; on the wharf hundreds of people craned their necks upward, lingering hungrily on the faces going so far away, young faces mostly, off to see what the hub of civilization on the other side of the world was really like. They would live there, work there, perhaps come back in two years, perhaps not come back at all. And everyone knew it, wondered.

The blue sky was plumped with silver-white clouds and there was a tearing Sydney wind. Sun warmed the upturned heads and the shoulder blades of those leaning down; a great multicolored swath of vibrating ribbons joined ship and shore. Then suddenly a gap appeared between the old boat's side and the wooden struts of the wharf; the air filled with cries and sobs; and one by one in their thousands the streamers broke, fluttered wildly, sagged limply and crisscrossed the surface of the water like a mangled loom, joined the orange peels and the jellyfish to float away.

Justine kept doggedly to her place at the rail until the wharf was a few hard lines and little pink pinheads in the distance; the *Himalaya*'s tugs turned her, towed her helplessly under the booming decks of the Sydney Harbor Bridge, out into the mainstream of that exquisite stretch of sunny water.

It wasn't like going to Manly on the ferry at all, though they followed the same path past Neutral Bay and Rose Bay and Cremorne and Vaucluse; no. For this time it was out through the Heads, beyond the cruel cliffs and the high lace fans of foam, into the ocean. Twelve thousand miles of it, to the other side of the world. And whether they came home again or not, they would belong neither here nor there, for they would have lived on two continents and sampled two different ways of life.

Money, Justine discovered, made London a most alluring place. Not for her a penniless existence clinging to the fringes of Earl's Court—"Kangaroo Valley" they called it because so many Australians made it their headquarters. Not for her the typical fate of Australians in England, youth-hosteling on a shoestring, working for a pittance in some office or school or hospital, shivering thin-blooded over a tiny radiator in a cold, damp room. Instead, for Justine a mews flat in Kensington close to Knightsbridge, centrally heated; and a place in the company of Clyde Daltinham-Roberts, The Elizabethan Group.

When the summer came she caught a train to Rome. In afteryears she would smile, remembering how little she saw of that long journey across France, down Italy; her whole mind was occupied with the things she had to tell Dane, memorizing those she simply mustn't forget. There were so many she was bound to leave some out.

Was that Dane? The tall, fair man on the platform, was that Dane? He didn't look any different, and yet he was a stranger. Not of her world anymore. The cry she was going to give to attract his attention died unuttered; she drew back a little in her seat to watch him, for the train had halted only a few feet beyond where he stood, blue eyes scanning the windows without anxiety. It was going to be a pretty one-sided conversation when she told him about life since he had gone away, for she knew now there was no thirst in him to share what he experienced with her. Damn him! He wasn't her baby brother anymore; the life he was living had as little to do with her as it did with Drogheda. Oh, Dane! What's it like to live something twenty-four hours of every day?

"Hah! Thought I'd dragged you down here on a wild-goose chase, didn't you?" she said, creeping up behind him unseen.

He turned, squeezed her hands and stared down at her, smiling. "Prawn," he said lovingly, taking her bigger suitcase and tucking her free arm in his. "It's good to see you," he added as he handed her into the red Lagonda he drove everywhere; Dane had always been a sports car fanatic, and had owned one since he was old enough to hold a license.

"Good to see you, too. I hope you found me a nice pub, because I meant what I wrote. I refuse to be stuck in a Vatican cell among a heap of celibates." She laughed.

"They wouldn't have you, not with the Devil's hair. I've booked you into a little pension not far from me, but they speak English so you needn't worry if I'm not with you. And in Rome it's no problem getting around on English; there's usually someone who can speak it."

"Times like this I wish I had your gift for foreign languages. But I'll manage; I'm very good at mimes and charades."

"I have two months, Jussy, isn't it super? So we can take a look at France and Spain and still have a month on Drogheda. I miss the old place."

"Do you?" She turned to look at him, at the beautiful hands guiding the car expertly through the crazy Roman traffic. "I don't miss it at all; London's too interesting."

"You don't fool me," he said. "I know what Drogheda and Mum mean to you."

Justine clenched her hands in her lap but didn't answer him.

"Do you mind having tea with some friends of mine this afternoon?" he asked when they had arrived. "I rather anticipated things by accepting for you already. They're so anxious to meet you, and as I'm not a free man until tomorrow, I didn't like to say no."

"Prawn! Why should I mind? If this was London I'd be inundating you with my friends, so why shouldn't you? I'm glad you're giving me a look-see at the blokes in the seminary, though it's a bit unfair to me, isn't it? Hands off the lot of them."

She walked to the window, looked down at a shabby little square with two tired plane trees in its paved quadrangle, three tables strewn beneath them, and to one side a church of no particular architectural grace or beauty, covered in peeling stucco.

"Dane. . . ."

"Yes?"

"I do understand, really I do."

"Yes, I know." His face lost its smile. "I wish Mum did, Jus."

"Mum's different. She feels you deserted her; she doesn't realize you haven't. Never mind about her. She'll come round in time."

"I hope so." He laughed. "By the way, it isn't the blokes from the seminary you're going to meet today. I wouldn't subject them or you to such temptation. It's Cardinal de Bricassart. I know you don't like him, but promise you'll be good."

Her eyes lit with peculiar witchery. "I promise! I'll even kiss every ring that's offered to me."

"Oh, you remember! I was so mad at you that day, shaming me in front of him."

"Well, since then I've kissed a lot of things less hygienic than a ring. There's one horrible pimply youth in acting class with halitosis and decayed tonsils and a rotten stomach I had to kiss a total of twenty-nine times, and I can assure you, mate, that after him nothing's impossible." She patted her hair, turned from the mirror. "Have I got time to change?"

"Oh, don't worry about that. You look fine."

"Who else is going to be there?"

The sun was too low to warm the ancient square, and the leprous patches on the plane tree trunks looked worn, sick. Justine shivered.

"Cardinal di Contini-Verchese will be there."

She had heard that name, and opened her eyes wider. "Phew! You move in pretty exalted circles, don't you?"

"Yes. I try to deserve it."

"Does it mean some people make it hard on you in other areas of your life here, Dane?" she asked, shrewdly.

"No, not really. Who one knows isn't important. I never think of it, so nor does anyone else."

The room, the red men! Never in all her life had Justine been so conscious of the redundancy of women in the lives of some men as at that moment, walking into a world where women simply had no place except as humble nun servants. She was still in the olive-green linen suit she had put on outside Turin, rather crumpled from the train, and she advanced across the soft crimson carpet cursing Dane's eagerness to be there, wishing she had insisted on donning something less travel-marked.

Cardinal de Bricassart was on his feet, smiling; what a handsome old man he was.

"My dear Justine," he said, extending his ring with a wicked look which indicated he well remembered the last time, and searching her face for something she didn't understand. "You don't look at all like your mother."

Down on one knee, kiss the ring, smile humbly, get up, smile less humbly. "No, I don't, do I? I could have done with her beauty in my chosen profession, but on a stage I manage. Because it has nothing to do with what the face actually is, you know. It's what you and your art can convince people the face is."

A dry chuckle came from a chair; once more she trod to salute a ring on an aging wormy hand, but this time she looked up into dark eyes, and strangely in them saw love. Love for her, for someone he had never seen, could scarcely have heard mentioned. But it was there. She didn't like Cardinal de Bricassart any more now than she had at fifteen, but she warmed to this old man.

"Sit down, my dear," said Cardinal Vittorio, his hand indicating the chair next to him.

"Hello, pusskins," said Justine, tickling the blue-grey cat in his scarlet lap. "She's nice, isn't she?"

"Indeed she is."

"What's her name?"

"Natasha."

The door opened, but not to admit the tea trolley. A man, mercifully clad as a layman; one more red soutane, thought Justine, and I'll bellow like a bull.

But he was no ordinary man, even if he was a layman. They probably had a little house rule in the Vatican, continued Justine's unruly mind, which specifically barred ordinary men. Not exactly short, he was so powerfully built he seemed more stocky than he was, with massive shoulders and a huge chest, a big leonine head, long arms like a shearer. Ape-mannish, except that he exuded intelligence and moved with the gait of someone who would grasp whatever he wanted too quickly for the mind to follow. Grasp it and maybe crush it, but never aimlessly, thoughtlessly; with exquisite deliberation. He was dark, but his thick mane of hair was exactly the color of steel wool and of much the same consistency, could steel wool have been crimped into tiny, regular waves.

"Rainer, you come in good time," said Cardinal Vittorio, indicating the chair on his other side, still speaking in English. "My dear," he said, turning to Justine as the man finished kissing his ring and rose, "I would like you to meet a very good friend. Herr Rainer Moerling Hartheim. Rainer, this is Dane's sister, Justine."

He bowed, clicking his heels punctiliously, gave her a brief smile without warmth and sat down, just too far off to one side to see. Justine breathed a sigh of relief, especially when she saw that Dane had draped himself with the ease of habit on the floor beside Cardinal Ralph's chair, right in her central vision. While she could see someone she knew and loved well, she would be all right. But the room and the red men and now this dark man were beginning to irritate her more than Dane's presence calmed; she resented the way they shut her out. So she leaned to one side and tickled the cat again, aware that Cardinal Vittorio sensed and was amused by her reactions.

"Is she spayed?" asked Justine.

"Of course."

"Of course! Though why you needed to bother I don't know. Just being a permanent inhabitant of this place would be enough to neuter anyone's ovaries."

"On the contrary, my dear," said Cardinal Vittorio, enjoying her hugely. "It is we men who have psychologically neutered ourselves."

"I beg to differ, Your Eminence."

"So our little world antagonizes you?"

"Well, let's just say I feel a bit superfluous, Your Eminence. A nice place to visit, but I wouldn't want to live here."

"I cannot blame you. I also doubt that you like to visit. But you will get used to us, for you must visit us often, please."

Justine grinned. "I hate being on my best behavior," she confided. "It brings out the absolute worst in me—I can feel Dane's horrors from here without even looking at him."

"I was wondering how long it was going to last," said Dane, not at all put out. "Scratch Justine's surface and you find a rebel. That's why she's such a nice sister for me to have. I'm not a rebel, but I do admire them."

Herr Hartheim shifted his chair so that he could continue to keep her in his line of vision even when she straightened, stopped playing with the cat. At that moment the beautiful animal grew tired of the hand with an alien female scent, and without getting to its feet crawled delicately from red lap to grey, curling itself under Herr Hartheim's strong square stroking hands, purring so loudly that everyone laughed.

"Excuse me for living," said Justine, not proof against a good joke even when she was its victim.

"Her motor is as good as ever," said Herr Hartheim, the amusement working fascinating changes in his face.

His English was so good he hardly had an accent, but it had an American inflection; he rolled his *r*'s.

The tea came before everyone settled down again, and oddly enough it was Herr Hartheim who poured, handing Justine her cup with a much friendlier look than he had given her at introduction.

"In a British community," he said to her, "afternoon tea is the most important refreshment of the day. Things happen over teacups, don't they? I suppose because by its very nature it can be demanded and taken at almost any time between two and five-thirty, and talking is thirsty work."

The next half hour seemed to prove his point, though Justine took no part in the congress. Talk veered from the Holy Father's precarious health to the cold war and then the economic recession, all four men speaking and listening with an alertness Justine found absorbing, beginning to grope for the qualities they shared, even Dane, who was so strange, so much an unknown. He contributed actively, and it wasn't lost upon her that the three older men listened to him with a curious humility, almost as if he awed them. His comments were neither uninformed nor naïve, but they were different, original, *holy*. Was it for his holiness they paid such serious attention to him? That he possessed it, and they didn't? Was it truly a virtue they admired, yearned for themselves? Was it so rare? Three men so vastly different one from the other, yet far closer bound together than any of them were to Dane. How difficult it was to take Dane as seriously as they did! Not that in many ways he hadn't acted as an older brother rather than a younger; not that she wasn't aware of his wisdom, his intellect or his holiness. But until now he had been a part of her world. She had to get used to the fact that he wasn't anymore.

"If you wish to go straight to your devotions, Dane, I'll see your sister back to her hotel," commanded Herr

Rainer Moerling Hartheim without consulting anyone's wishes on the subject.

And so she found herself walking tongue-tied down the marble stairs in the company of that squat, powerful man. Outside in the yellow sheen of a Roman sunset he took her elbow and guided her into a black Mercedes limousine, its chauffeur standing to attention.

"Come, you don't want to spend your first evening in Rome alone, and Dane is otherwise occupied," he said, following her into the car. "You're tired and bewildered, so it's better you have company."

"You don't seem to be leaving me any choice, Herr Hartheim."

"I would rather you called me Rainer."

"You must be important, having a posh car and your own chauffeur."

"I'll be more important still when I'm chancellor of West Germany."

Justine snorted. "I'm surprised you're not already."

"Impudent! I'm too young."

"Are you?" She turned sideways to look at him more closely, discovering that his dark skin was unlined, youthful, that the deeply set eyes weren't embedded in the fleshy surrounds of age.

"I'm heavy and I'm grey, but I've been grey since I was sixteen and heavy since I've had enough to eat. At the present moment I'm a mere thirty-one."

"I'll take your word for it," she said, kicking her shoes off. "That's still old to me—I'm sweet *twenty-one*."

"You're a monster," he said, smiling.

"I suppose I must be. My mother says the same thing. Only I'm not sure what either of you means by monster, so you can give me your version, please."

"Have you already got your mother's version?"

"I'd embarrass the hell out of her if I asked."

"Don't you think you embarrass me?"

"I strongly suspect, Herr Hartheim, that you're a monster, too, so I doubt if anything embarrasses you."

"A monster," he said again under his breath. "All right then, Miss O'Neill, I'll try to define the term for you. Someone who terrifies others; rolls over the top of people; feels so strong only God can defeat; has no scruples and few morals."

She chuckled. "It sounds like you, to me. And I have so too got morals and scruples. I'm Dane's sister."

"You don't look a bit like him."

"More's the pity."

"His face wouldn't suit your personality."

"You're undoubtedly right, but with his face I might have developed a different personality."

"Depending on which comes first, eh, the chicken or the egg? Put your shoes on; we're going to walk."

It was warm, and growing dark; but the lights were brilliant, there were crowds it seemed no matter where they walked, and the roads were jammed with shrieking motor scooters, tiny aggressive Fiats, Goggomobils looking like hordes of panicked frogs. Finally he halted in a small square, its cobbles worn to smoothness by the feet of many centuries, and guided Justine into a restaurant.

"Unless you'd prefer al fresco?" he asked.

"Provided you feed me, I don't much care whether it's inside, outside, or halfway between."

"May I order for you?"

The pale eyes blinked a little wearily perhaps, but there was still fight in Justine. "I don't know that I go for all that high-handed masterful-male business," she said. "After all, how do you know what I fancy?"

"Sister Anna carries her banner," he murmured. "Tell me what sort of food you like, then, and I'll guarantee to please you. Fish? Veal?"

"A compromise? All right, I'll meet you halfway, why not? I'll have pâté, some scampi and a huge plate of saltimbocca, and after that I'll have a cassata and a cappuccino coffee. Fiddle around with that if you can."

"I ought to slap you," he said, his good humor quite unruffled. He gave her order to the waiter exactly as she had stipulated it, but in rapid Italian.

"You said I don't look a bit like Dane. Aren't I like him in any way at all?" she asked a little pathetically over coffee, too hungry to have wasted time talking while there was food on the table.

He lit her cigarette, then his own, and leaned into the shadows to watch her quietly, thinking back to his first meeting with the boy months ago. Cardinal de Bricassart minus forty years of life; he had seen it immediately, and then had learned they were uncle and nephew, that the mother of the boy and the girl was Ralph de Bricassart's sister.

"There is a likeness, yes," he said. "Sometimes even of the face. Expressions far more than features. Around the eyes and the mouth, in the way you hold your eyes open and your mouths closed. Oddly enough, not likenesses you share with your uncle the Cardinal."

"Uncle the Cardinal?" she repeated blankly.

"Cardinal de Bricassart. Isn't he your uncle? Now, I'm sure I was told he was."

"That old vulture? He's no relation of ours, thank heavens. He used to be our parish priest years ago, a long time before I was born."

She was very intelligent; but she was also very tired. Poor little girl—for that was what she was, a little girl. The ten years between them yawned like a hundred. To suspect would bring her world to ruins, and she was so valiant in defense of it. Probably she would refuse to see it, even if she were told outright. How to make it seem unimportant? Not labor the point, definitely not, but not drop it immediately, either.

"That accounts for it, then," he said lightly.

"Accounts for what?"

"The fact that Dane's likeness to the Cardinal is in general things—height, coloring, build."

"Oh! My grandmother told me our father was rather like the Cardinal to look at," said Justine comfortably.

"Haven't you ever seen your father?"

"Not even a picture of him. He and Mum separated for good before Dane was born." She beckoned the waiter. "I'd like another cappuccino, please."

"Justine, you're a savage! Let me order for you!"

"No, dammit, I won't! I'm perfectly capable of thinking for myself, and I don't need some bloody man always to tell me what I want and when I want it, do you hear?"

"Scratch the surface and one finds a rebel; that was what Dane said."

"He's right. Oh, if you knew how I hate being petted and cosseted and fussed over! I like to act for myself, and I *won't* be told what to do! I don't ask for quarter, but I don't give any, either."

"I can see that," he said dryly. "What made you so, *Herzchen?* Does it run in the family?"

"Does it? I honestly don't know. There aren't enough women to tell, I suppose. Only one per generation. Nanna, and Mum, and me. Heaps of men, though."

"Except in your generation there are not heaps of men. Only Dane."

"Due to the fact Mum left my father, I expect. She never seemed to get interested in anyone else. Pity, I think. Mum's a real homebody; she would have liked a husband to fuss over."

"Is she like you?"

"I don't think so."

"More importantly, do you like each other?"

"Mum and I?" She smiled without rancor, much as her mother would have done had someone asked her whether she liked her daughter. "I'm not sure if we *like* each other, but there is something there. Maybe it's a simple biological bond; I don't know." Her eyes kindled. "I've always wanted her to talk to me the way she does to Dane, and wanted to get along with her the way Dane does. But either there's something lacking in her, or something lacking in me. Me, I'd reckon. She's a much finer person than I am."

"I haven't met her, so I can't agree or disagree with your judgment. If it's of any conceivable comfort to you, *Herzchen,* I like you exactly the way you are. No, I wouldn't change a thing about you, even your ridiculous pugnacity."

"Isn't that nice of you? And after I insulted you, too. I'm not really like Dane, am I?"

"Dane isn't like anyone else in the world."

"You mean because he's so not of this world?"

"I suppose so." He leaned forward, out of the shadows into the weak light of the little candle in its Chianti bottle. "I am a Catholic, and my religion has been the one thing in my life which has never failed me, though I have failed it many times. I dislike speaking of Dane, because my heart tells me some things are better left undiscussed. Certainly you aren't like him in your attitude to life, or God. Let's leave it, all right?"

She looked at him curiously. "All right, Rainer, if you want. I'll make a pact with you—no matter what we discuss, it won't be the nature of Dane, or religion."

Much had happened to Rainer Moerling Hartheim since that meeting with Ralph de Bricassart in July 1943. A week afterward his regiment had been dispatched to the Eastern Front, where he spent the remainder of the war. Torn and rudderless, too young to have been indoctrinated into the Hitler Youth in its leisurely prewar days, he had faced the consequences of Hitler in feet of snow, without ammunition, the front line stretched so thin there was only one soldier for every hundred yards of it. And out of the war he carried two memories: that bitter campaign in bitter cold, and the face of Ralph de Bricassart. Horror and beauty, the Devil and God. Half crazed, half frozen, waiting defenseless for Khrushchev's guerrillas to drop from low-flying planes parachuteless into the snowdrifts, he beat his breast and muttered prayers. But he didn't know what he prayed for: bullets for his gun, escape from the Russians, his immortal soul, the man in the basilica, Germany, a lessening of grief.

In the spring of 1945 he had retreated back across Poland before the Russians, like his fellow soldiers with only one objective—to make it into British- or American-occupied Germany. For if the Russians caught him, he would be shot. He tore his papers into shreds and burned them, buried his two Iron Crosses, stole some clothes and presented himself to the British authorities on the Danish border. They shipped him to a camp for displaced persons in Belgium. There for a year he lived on the bread and gruel which was all the exhausted British could afford to feed the thousands upon thousands of people in their charge, waiting until the British realized their only course was release.

Twice officials of the camp had summoned him to present him with an ultimatum. There was a boat waiting in Ostend harbor loading immigrants for Australia. He would be given new papers and shipped to his new land free of charge, in return for which he would work for the Australian government for two years in whatever capacity they chose, after which his life would become entirely his own. Not slave labor; he would be paid the standard wage, of course. But on both occasions he managed to talk himself out of summary emigration. He had hated Hitler, not Germany, and he was not ashamed of being a German. Home meant Germany; it had occupied his dreams for over three years. The very thought of yet again being stranded in a country where no one spoke his language nor he theirs was anathema. So at the beginning of 1947 he found himself penniless on the streets of Aachen, ready to pick up the pieces of an existence he knew he wanted very badly.

He and his soul had survived, but not to go back to poverty and obscurity. For Rainer was more than a very ambitious man; he was also something of a genius. He went to work for Grundig, and studied the field which had fascinated him since he first got acquainted with radar: electronics. Ideas teemed in his brain, but he refused to sell them to Grundig for a millionth part of their value. Instead he gauged the market carefully, then married the widow of a man who had managed to keep a couple of small radio factories, and went into business for himself. That he was barely into his twenties didn't matter. His mind was characteristic of a far older man, and the chaos of postwar Germany created opportunities for young men.

Since his wedding had been a civil one, the Church permitted him to divorce his wife; in 1951 he paid Annelise Hartheim exactly twice the current value of her first husband's two factories, and did just that, divorced her. However, he didn't remarry.

What had happened to the boy in the frozen terror of Russia did not produce a soulless caricature of a man; rather it arrested the growth of softness and sweetness in him, and threw into high relief other qualities he possessed—intelligence, ruthlessness, determination. A man who has nothing to lose has everything to gain, and a man without feelings cannot be hurt. Or so he told himself. In actual fact, he was curiously similar to the man he had met in Rome in 1943; like Ralph de Bricassart he understood he did wrong even as he did it. Not that his awareness of the evil in him stopped him for a second; only that he paid for his material advancement in pain and self-torment. To many people it might not have seemed worth the price he paid, but to him it was worth twice the suffering. One day he was going to run Germany and make it what he had dreamed, he was going to scotch the

Aryan Lutheran ethic, shape a broader one. Because he couldn't promise to cease sinning he had been refused absolution in the confessional several times, but somehow he and his religion muddled through in one piece, until accumulated money and power removed him so many layers beyond guilt he could present himself repentant, and be shriven.

In 1955, one of the richest and most powerful men in the new West Germany and a fresh face in its Bonn parliament, he went back to Rome. To seek out Cardinal de Bricassart, and show him the end result of his prayers. What he had imagined that meeting might be he could not afterward remember, for from beginning to end of it he was conscious of only one thing: that Ralph de Bricassart was disappointed in him. He had known why, he hadn't needed to ask. But he hadn't expected the Cardinal's parting remark:

"I had prayed you would do better than I, for you were so young. No end is worth any means. But I suppose the seeds of our ruin are sown before our births."

Back in his hotel room he had wept, but calmed after a while and thought: What's past is done with; for the future I will be as he hoped. And sometimes he succeeded, sometimes he failed. But he tried. His friendship with the men in the Vatican became the most precious earthly thing in his life, and Rome became the place to which he fled when only their comfort seemed to stand between himself and despair. Comfort. Theirs was a strange kind. Not the laying on of hands, or soft words. Rather a balm from the soul, as if they understood his pain.

And he thought, as he walked the warm Roman night after depositing Justine in her pension, that he would never cease to be grateful to her. For as he had watched her cope with the ordeal of that afternoon interview, he had felt a stirring of tenderness. Bloody but unbowed, the little monster. She could match them every inch of the way; did they realize it? He felt, he decided, what he might have felt on behalf of a daughter he was proud of, only he had no daughter. So he had stolen her from Dane, carried her off to watch her aftermath reaction to that overpowering ecclesiasticism, and to the Dane she had never seen before; the Dane who was not and could not ever be a full-hearted part of her life.

The nicest thing about his personal God, he went on, was that He could forgive anything; He could forgive Justine her innate godlessness and himself the shutting down of his emotional powerhouse until such time as it was convenient to reopen it. Only for a while he had panicked, thinking he had lost the key forever. He smiled, threw away her cigarette. The key. . . . Well, sometimes keys had strange shapes. Perhaps it needed every kink in every curl of that red head to trip the tumblers; perhaps in a room of scarlet his God had handed him a scarlet key.

A fleeting day, over in a second. But on looking at his watch he saw it was still early, and knew the man who had so much power now that His Holiness lay near death would still be wakeful, sharing the nocturnal habits of his cat. Those dreadful hiccups filling the small room at Castel Gandolfo, twisting the thin, pale, ascetic face which had watched beneath the white crown for so many years; he was dying, and he was a great Pope. No matter what they said, he was a great Pope. If he had loved his Germans, if he still liked to hear German spoken around him, did it alter anything? Not for Rainer to judge that.

But for what Rainer needed to know at the moment, Castel Gandolfo was not the source. Up the marble stairs to the scarlet-and-crimson room, to talk to Vittorio Scarbanza, Cardinal di Contini-Verchese. Who might be the next Pope, or might not. For almost three years now he had watched those wise, loving dark eyes rest where they most liked to rest; yes, better to seek the answers from him than from Cardinal de Bricassart.

* * *

"I never thought I'd hear myself say it, but thank God we're leaving for Drogheda," said Justine, refusing to throw a coin in the Trevi Fountain. "We were supposed to take a look at France and Spain; instead we're still in Rome and I'm as unnecessary as a navel. Brothers!"

"Hmmm, so you deem navels unnecessary? Socrates was of the same opinion, I remember," said Rainer.

"Socrates was? I don't recollect that! Funny, I thought I'd read most of Plato, too." She twisted to stare at him, thinking the casual clothes of a holidaymaker in Rome suited him far better than the sober attire he wore for Vatican audiences.

"He was absolutely convinced navels were unnecessary, as a matter of fact. So much so that to prove his point he unscrewed his own navel and threw it away."

Her lips twitched. "And what happened?"

"His toga fell off."

"Hook! Hook!" She giggled. "Anyway, they didn't wear togas in Athens then. But I have a horrible feeling there's a moral in your story." Her face sobered. "Why do you bother with me, Rain?"

"Stubborn! I've told you before, my name is pronounced Ryner, not Rayner."

"Ah, but you don't understand," she said, looking thoughtfully at the twinkling streams of water, the dirty pool loaded with dirty coins. "Have you ever been to Australia?"

His shoulders shook, but he made no sound. "Twice I almost went, *Herzchen,* but I managed to avoid it."

"Well, if you had gone you'd understand. You have a magical name to an Australian, when it's pronounced my way. Rainer. Rain. Life in the desert."

Startled, he dropped his cigarette. "Justine, you aren't falling in love with me, are you?"

"What egotists men are! I hate to disappoint you, but no." Then, as if to soften any unkindness in her words, she slipped her hand into his, squeezed. "It's something much nicer."

"What could be nicer than falling in love?"

"Almost anything, I think. I don't want to need anyone like that, ever."

"Perhaps you're right. It's certainly a crippling handicap, taken on too early. So what is much nicer?"

"Finding a friend." Her hand rubbed his. "You are my friend, aren't you?"

"Yes." Smiling, he threw a coin in the fountain. "There! I must have given it a thousand D-marks over the years, just for reassurance that I would continue to feel the warmth of the south. Sometimes in my nightmares I'm cold again."

"You ought to feel the warmth of the real south," said Justine. "A hundred and fifteen in the shade, if you can find any."

"No wonder you don't feel the heat." He laughed the soundless laugh, as always; a hangover from the old days, when to laugh aloud might have tempted fate. "And the heat would account for the fact that you're hard-boiled."

"Your English is colloquial, but American. I would have thought you'd have learned English in some posh British university."

"No. I began to learn it from Cockney or Scottish or Midlands tommies in a Belgian camp, and didn't understand a word of it except when I spoke to the man who had taught it to me. One said 'abaht,' one said 'aboot,' one said 'aboat,' but they all meant 'about.' So when I got back to Germany I saw every motion picture I could, and bought the only records available in English, records made by American comedians. But I played them over and over again at home, until I spoke enough English to learn more."

Her shoes were off, as usual; awed, he had watched her walk barefooted on pavements hot enough to fry an egg, and over stony places.

"Urchin! Put your shoes on."

"I'm an Aussie; our feet are too broad to be comfortable in shoes. Comes of no really cold weather; we go barefoot whenever we can. I can walk across a paddock of bindy-eye burns and pick them out of my feet without feeling them," she said proudly. "I could probably walk on hot coals." Then abruptly she changed the subject. "Did you love your wife, Rain?"

"No."

"Did she love you?"

"Yes. She had no other reason to marry me."

"Poor thing! You used her, and you dropped her."

"Does it disappoint you?"

"No, I don't think so. I rather admire you for it, actually. But I do feel very sorry for her, and it makes me more determined than ever not to land in the same soup she did."

"Admire me?" His tone was blank, astonished.

"Why not? I'm not looking for the things in you she undoubtedly did, now am I? I like you, you're my friend. She loved you, you were her husband."

"I think, *Herzchen,*" he said a little sadly, "that ambitious men are not very kind to their women."

"That's because they usually fall for utter doormats of women, the 'Yes, dear, no, dear, three bags full, dear, and where would you like it put?' sort. Hard cheese all round, I say. If I'd been your wife, I'd have told you to go pee up a rope, but I'll bet she never did, did she?"

His lips quivered. "No, poor Annelise. She was the martyr kind, so her weapons were not nearly so direct or so deliciously expressed. I wish they made Australian films, so I knew your vernacular. The 'Yes, dear' bit I got, but I have no idea what hard cheese is."

"Tough luck, sort of, but it's more unsympathetic." Her broad toes clung like strong fingers to the inside of the fountain wall, she teetered precariously backward and righted herself easily. "Well, you were kind to her in the end. You got rid of her. She's far better off without you, though she probably doesn't think so. Whereas I can keep you, because I'll never let you get under my skin."

"Hard-boiled. You really are, Justine. And how did you find out these things about me?"

"I asked Dane. Naturally, being Dane he just gave me the bare facts, but I deduced the rest."

"From your enormous store of past experience, no doubt. What a fraud you are! They say you're a very good actress, but I find that incredible. How do you manage to counterfeit emotions you can never have experienced? As a person you're more emotionally backward than most fifteen-year-olds."

She jumped down, sat on the wall and leaned to put her shoes on, wriggling her toes ruefully. "My feet are swollen, dammit." There was no indication by a reaction of rage or indignation that she had even heard the last part of what he said. As if when aspersions or criticisms were leveled at her she simply switched off an internal hearing aid. How many there must have been. The miracle was that she didn't hate Dane.

"That's a hard question to answer," she said. "I must be able to do it or I wouldn't be so good, isn't that right? But it's like . . . a waiting. My life off the stage, I mean. I conserve myself, I can't spend it offstage. We only have so much to give, don't we? And up there I'm not myself, or perhaps more correctly I'm a succession of selves. We must all be a profound mixture of selves, don't you think? To me, acting is first and foremost intellect, and only after that, emotion. The one liberates the other, and polishes it. There's so much more to it than simply crying or screaming or producing a convincing laugh. It's wonderful, you know. Thinking myself into another self, someone I might have been, had the circumstances been there. That's the secret. Not becoming someone else, but incorporating the role into me as if she was myself. And so she becomes me." As though her excitement was too great to bear in stillness, she jumped to her feet. "Imagine, Rain! In twenty years' time I'll be able to say to myself, I've committed murders, I've suicided, I've gone mad, I've saved men or ruined them. *Oh!* The possibilities are endless!"

"And they will all be you." He rose, took her hand again. "Yes, you're quite right, Justine. You can't spend it offstage. In anyone else, I'd say you would in spite of that, but being you, I'm not so sure."

18

If they applied themselves to it, the Drogheda people could imagine that Rome and London were no farther away than Sydney, and that the grown-up Dane and Justine were still children going to boarding school. Admittedly they couldn't come home for all the shorter vacations of other days, but once a year they turned up for a month at least. Usually in August or September, and looking much as always. Very young. Did it matter whether they were fifteen and sixteen or twenty-two and twenty-three? And if the Drogheda people lived for that month in early spring, they most definitely never went round saying things like, Well, only a few weeks to go! or, Dear heaven, it's not a month since they left! But around July everyone's step became brisker, and permanent smiles settled on every face. From the cookhouse to the paddocks to the drawing room, treats and gifts were planned.

In the meantime there were letters. Mostly these reflected the personalities of their authors, but sometimes they contradicted. One would have thought, for instance, that Dane would be a meticulously regular correspondent and Justine a scrappy one. That Fee would never write at all. That the Cleary men would write twice a year. That Meggie would enrich the postal service with letters every day, at least to Dane. That Mrs. Smith, Minnie and Cat would send birthday and Christmas cards. That Anne Mueller would write often to Justine, never to Dane.

Dane's intentions were good, and he did indeed write regularly. The only trouble was he forgot to post his efforts, with the result that two or three months would go by without a word, and then Drogheda would receive dozens on the same mail run. The loquacious Justine wrote lengthy missives which were pure stream-of-consciousness, rude enough to evoke blushes and clucks of alarm, and entirely fascinating. Meggie wrote once every two weeks only, to both her children. Though Justine never received letters from her grandmother, Dane did quite often. He also got word regularly from all his uncles, about the land and the sheep and the health of the Drogheda women, for they seemed to think it was their duty to assure him all was truly well at home. However, they didn't extend this to Justine, who would have been flabbergasted by it anyway. For the rest, Mrs. Smith, Minnie, Cat and Anne Mueller, correspondence went as might be expected.

It was lovely reading letters, and a burden writing them. That is, for all save Justine, who experienced twinges of exasperation because no one ever sent her the kind she desired—fat, wordy and frank. It was from Justine the Drogheda people got most of their information about Dane, for his letters never plunged his readers right into the middle of a scene. Whereas Justine's did.

> Rain flew into London today [she wrote once], and he was telling me he saw Dane in Rome last week. Well, he sees a lot more of Dane than of me, since Rome is at the top of his travel agenda and London is rock bottom. So I must confess Rain is one of the prime reasons why I meet Dane in Rome every year before we come home. Dane

likes coming to London, only I won't let him if Rain is in Rome. Selfish. But you've no idea how I enjoy Rain. He's one of the few people I know who gives me a run for my money, and I wish we met more often.

In one respect Rain's luckier than I am. He gets to meet Dane's fellow students where I don't. I think Dane thinks I'm going to rape them on the spot. Or maybe he thinks they'll rape me. Hah. Only happen if they saw me in my Charmian costume. It's a stunner, people, it really is. Sort of up-to-date Theda Bara. Two little round bronze shields for the old tits, lots and lots of chains and what I reckon is a chastity belt—you'd need a pair of tin-cutters to get inside it, anyway. In a long black wig, tan body paint and my few scraps of metal I look a smasher.

. . . Where was I??? Oh, yes, Rain in Rome last week meeting Dane and his pals. They all went out on the tiles. Rain insists on paying, saves Dane embarrassment. It was some night. No women, natch, but everything else. Can you imagine *Dane* down on his knees in some seedy Roman bar saying "Fair daffodils, we haste to see thee weep so soon away" to a vase of daffodils? He tried for ten minutes to get the words of the quotation in their right order and couldn't, then he gave up, put one of the daffodils between his teeth instead and did a dance. Can you ever imagine *Dane* doing that? Rain says it's harmless and necessary, all work and no play, etc. Women being out, the next best thing is a skinful of grog. Or so Rain insists. Don't get the idea it happens often, it doesn't, and I gather when it does Rain is the ringleader, so he's along to watch out for them, the naïve lot of raw prawns. But I did laugh to think of Dane's halo slipping during the course of a flamenco dance with a daffodil.

It took Dane eight years in Rome to attain his priesthood, and at their beginning no one thought they could ever end. Yet those eight years used themselves up faster than any of the Drogheda people had imagined. Just what they thought he was going to do after he was ordained they didn't know, except that they did assume he would return to Australia. Only Meggie and Justine suspected he would want to remain in Italy, and Meggie at any rate could lull her doubts with memories of his content when he came back each year to his home. He was an Australian, he *would* want to come home. With Justine it was different. No one dreamed she would come home for good. She was an actress; her career would founder in Australia. Where Dane's career could be pursued with equal zeal anywhere at all.

Thus in the eighth year there were no plans as to what the children would do when they came for their annual holiday; instead the Drogheda people were planning their trip to Rome, to see Dane ordained a priest.

"We fizzled out," said Meggie.

"I beg your pardon, dear?" asked Anne.

They were sitting in a warm corner of the veranda reading, but Meggie's book had fallen neglected into her lap, and she was absently watching the antics of two willy-wagtails on the lawn. It had been a wet year; there were worms everywhere and the fattest, happiest birds anyone ever remembered. Bird songs filled the air from dawn to the last of dusk.

"I said we fizzled out," repeated Meggie, crowlike. "A damp squib. All that promise! Whoever would have guessed it in 1921, when we arrived on Drogheda?"

"How do you mean?"

"A total of six sons, plus me. And a year later, two more sons. What would you think? Dozens of children, half a hundred grandchildren? So look at us now. Hal and Stu are dead, none of the ones left alive seem to have any intention of ever getting married, and I, the only one not entitled to pass on the name, have been the only one to give Drogheda its heirs. And even then the gods weren't happy, were they? A son and a daughter. Several grandchildren at least, you might think. But what happens? My son embraces the priesthood and my daughter's an old maid career woman. Another dead end for Drogheda."

"I don't see what's so strange about it," said Anne. "After all, what could you expect from the men? Stuck out here as shy as kangas, never meeting the girls they might have married. And with Jims and Patsy, the war to boot. Could you see Jims marrying when he knows Patsy can't? They're far too fond of each other for that. And besides, the land's demanding in a neutered way. It takes just about all they've got to give, because I don't think they have a great deal. In a physical sense, I mean. Hasn't it ever struck you, Meggie? Yours isn't a very highly sexed family, to put it bluntly. And that goes for Dane and Justine, too. I mean, there are some people who compulsively hunt it like tomcats, but not your lot. Though perhaps Justine will marry. There's this German chap Rainer; she seems terribly fond of him."

"You've hit the nail on the head," said Meggie, in no mood to be comforted. "She seems terribly *fond* of him. Just that. After all, she's known him for seven years. If she wanted to marry him, it would have happened ages ago."

"Would it? I know Justine pretty well," answered Anne truthfully, for she did; better than anyone else on Drogheda, including Meggie and Fee. "I think she's terrified of committing herself to the kind of love marriage would entail, and I must say I admire Rainer. He seems to understand her very well. Oh, I don't say he's in love with her for sure, but if he is, at least he's got the sense to wait until she's ready to take the plunge." She leaned forward, her book falling forgotten to the tiles. "Oh, will you listen to that bird? I'm sure even a nightingale couldn't match it." Then she said what she had been wanting to say for weeks. "Meggie, why won't you go to Rome to see Dane ordained? Isn't that peculiar? Dane—or*dain*."

"I'm *not* going to Rome!" said Meggie between clenched teeth. "I shall never leave Drogheda again."

"Meggie, don't! You can't disappoint him so! Go, please! If you don't, Drogheda won't have a single woman there, because you're the only woman young enough to take the flight. But I tell you, if I thought for one minute my body would survive I'd be right on that plane."

"Go to Rome and see Ralph de Bricassart smirking? I'd rather be dead!"

"Oh, Meggie, Meggie! Why must you take out your frustrations on him, and on your son? You said it once yourself—it's your own fault. So beggar your pride, and go to Rome. Please!"

"It isn't a question of pride." She shivered. "Oh, Anne, I'm frightened to go! Because I don't believe it, I just don't! My flesh creeps when I think about it."

"And what about the fact he mightn't come home after he's a priest? Did that ever occur to you? He won't be given huge chunks of leave the way he was in the seminary, so if he decides to remain in Rome you may well have to take yourself there if you ever want to see him at all. Go to Rome, Meggie!"

"I can't. If you knew how frightened I am! It's not pride, or Ralph scoring one over on me, or any of the things I say it is to stop people asking me questions. Lord knows, I miss both my men so much I'd crawl on my knees to see them if I thought for a minute they wanted me. Oh, Dane would be glad to see me, but Ralph? He's forgotten I ever existed. I'm frightened, I tell you. I know in my bones that if I go to Rome something will happen. So I'm not going."

"What could happen, for pity's sake?"

"I don't know. . . . If I did, I'd have something to battle. A feeling, how can I battle a feeling? Because that's all it is. A premonition. As if the gods are gathering."

Anne laughed. "You're becoming a real old woman, Meggie. Stop!"

"I can't, I can't! And I *am* an old woman."

"Nonsense, you're just in brisk middle age. Well and truly young enough to hop on that plane."

"Oh, leave me alone!" said Meggie savagely, and picked up her book.

Occasionally a crowd with a purpose converges upon Rome. Not tourism, the voyeuristic sampling of past glories in present relics; not the filling in of a little slice of time between A and B, with Rome a point on the line between those two places. This is a crowd with a single uniting emotion; it bursts with pride, for it is coming to see its son, nephew, cousin, friend ordained a priest in the great basilica which is the most venerated church in the world. Its members put up in humble pensiones, luxury hotels, the homes of friends or relatives. But they are totally united, at peace with each other and with the world. They do the rounds dutifully; the Vatican Museum with the Sistine Chapel at its end like a prize for endurance; the Forum, the Colosseum, the Appian Way, the Spanish Steps, the greedy Trevi Fountain, the *son et lumière*. Waiting for the day, filling in time. They will be accorded the special privilege of a private audience with the Holy Father, and for them Rome will find nothing too good.

This time it wasn't Dane waiting on the platform to meet Justine, as it had been every other time; he was in retreat. Instead, Rainer Moerling Hartheim prowled the dirty paving like some great animal. He didn't greet her with a kiss, he never did; he just put an arm about her shoulders and squeezed.

"Rather like a bear," said Justine.

"A bear?"

"I used to think when I first met you that you were some sort of missing link, but I've finally decided you're more of a bear than a gorilla. It was an unkind comparison, the gorilla."

"And bears are kind?"

"Well, perhaps they do one to death just as quickly, but they're more cuddly." She linked her arm through his and matched his stride, for she was almost as tall as he. "How's Dane? Did you see him before he went into retreat? I could kill Clyde, not letting me go sooner."

"Dane is as always."

"You haven't been leading him astray?"

"Me? Certainly not. You look very nice, *Herzchen."*

"I'm on my very best behavior, and I bought out every couturier in London. Do you like my new short skirt? They call it the mini."

"Walk ahead of me, and I'll tell you."

The hem of the full silk skirt was about midthigh; it swirled as she turned and came back to him. "What do you think, Rain? Is it scandalous? I noticed no one in Paris is wearing this length yet."

"It proves a point, *Herzchen*—that with legs as good as yours, to wear a skirt one millimeter longer is scandalous. I'm sure the Romans will agree with me."

"Which means my arse will be black and blue in an hour instead of a day. Damn them! Though do you know something, Rain?"

"What?"

"I've never been pinched by a priest. All these years I've been flipping in and out of the Vatican with nary a pinch to my credit. So I thought maybe if I wore a miniskirt, I might be the undoing of some poor prelate yet."

"You might be my undoing." He smiled.

"No, really? In orange? I thought you hated me in orange, when I've got orange hair."

"It inflames the senses, such a busy color."

"You're teasing me," she said, disgusted, climbing into his Mercedes limousine, which had a German pennant fluttering from its bonnet talisman. "When did you get the little flag?"

"When I got my new post in the government."

"No wonder I rated a mention in the *News of the World*! Did you see it?"

"You know I never read rags, Justine."

"Well, nor do I; someone showed it to me," she said, then pitched her voice higher and endowed it with a shabby-genteel, fraightfully naice accent. "What up-and-coming carrot-topped Australian actress is cementing very cordial relations with what member of the West German cabinet?"

"They can't be aware how long we've known each other," he said tranquilly, stretching out his legs and making himself comfortable.

Justine ran her eyes over his clothes with approval; very casual, very Italian. He was rather in the European fashion swim himself, daring to wear one of the fishing-net shirts which enabled Italian males to demonstrate the hairiness of their chests.

"You should never wear a suit and collar and tie," she said suddenly.

"No? Why not?"

"Machismo is definitely your style—you know, what you've got on now, the gold medallion and chain on the hairy chest. A suit makes you look as if your waistline is bulging, when it really isn't at all."

For a moment he gazed at her in surprise, then the expression in his eyes became alert, in what she called his "concentrated thinking look." "A first," he said.

"What's a first?"

"In the seven years I've known you, you've never before commented upon my appearance except perhaps to disparage it."

"Oh, dear, haven't I?" she asked, looking a little

ashamed. "Heavens, I've thought of it often enough, and never disparagingly." For some reason she added hastily, "I mean, about things like the way you look in a suit."

He didn't answer, but he was smiling, as at a very pleasant thought.

That ride with Rainer seemed to be the last quiet thing to happen for days. Shortly after they returned from visiting Cardinal de Bricassart and Cardinal di Contini-Verchese, the limousine Rainer had hired deposited the Drogheda contingent at their hotel. Out of the corner of her eye Justine watched Rain's reaction to her family, entirely uncles. Right until the moment her eyes didn't find her mother's face, Justine had been convinced she would change her mind, come to Rome. That she hadn't was a cruel blow; Justine didn't know whether she ached more on Dane's behalf or on her own. But in the meantime here were the Unks, and she was undoubtedly their hostess.

Oh, they were so shy! Which one of them was which? The older they got, the more alike they looked. And in Rome they stuck out like—well, like Australian graziers on holiday in Rome. Each one was clad in the city-going uniform of affluent squatters: tan elastic-sided riding boots, neutral trousers, tan sports jackets of very heavy, fuzzy wool with side vents and plenty of leather patches, white shirts, knitted wool ties, flat-crowned grey hats with broad brims. No novelty on the streets of Sydney during Royal Easter Show time, but in a late Roman summer, extraordinary.

And I can say with double sincerity, thank God for Rain! How good he is with them. I wouldn't have believed anyone could stimulate Patsy into speech, but he's doing it, bless him. They're talking away like old hens, and *where* did he get Australian beer for them? He likes them, and he's interested, I suppose. Everything is grist to the mill of a German industrialist-politician, isn't it? How can he stick to his faith, being what he is? An enigma, that's what you are, Rainer Moerling Hartheim. Friend of popes and cardinals, friend of Justine O'Neill. Oh, if you weren't so ugly I'd kiss you, I'm so terribly grateful. Lord, fancy being stuck in Rome with the Unks and no Rain! You are well named.

He was sitting back in his chair, listening while Bob told him about shearing, and having nothing better to do because he had so completely taken charge, Justine watched him curiously. Mostly she noticed everything physical about people immediately, but just occasionally that vigilance slipped and people stole up on her, carved a niche in her life without her having made that vital initial assessment. For if it wasn't made, sometimes years would go by before they intruded into her thoughts again as strangers. Like now, watching Rain. That first meeting had been responsible, of course; surrounded by churchmen, awed, frightened, brazening it out. She had noticed only the obvious things: his powerful build, his hair, how dark he was. Then when he had taken her off to dinner the chance to rectify things had been lost, for he had forced an awareness of himself on her far beyond his physical attributes; she had been too interested in what the mouth was saying to look at the mouth.

He wasn't really ugly at all, she decided now. He looked what he was, perhaps, a mixture of the best and the worst. Like a Roman emperor. No wonder he loved the city. It was his spiritual home. A broad face with high, wide cheekbones and a small yet aquiline nose. Thick black brows, straight instead of following the curve of the orbits. Very long, feminine black lashes and quite lovely dark eyes, mostly hooded to hide his thoughts. By far his most beautiful possession was his mouth, neither full nor thin-lipped, neither small nor large, but very well shaped, with a distinct cut to the boundaries of its lips and a peculiar firmness in the way he held it; as if perhaps were he to relax his hold upon it, it might give away secrets about what he was really like. Interesting, to take a face apart which was already so well known, yet not known at all.

She came out of her reverie to find him watching her watch him, which was like being stripped naked in front of a crowd armed with stones. For a moment his eyes held hers, wide open and alert, not exactly startled, rather arrested. Then he transferred his gaze calmly to Bob, and asked a pertinent question about boggis. Justine gave herself a mental shake, told herself not to go imagining things. But it was fascinating, suddenly to see a man who had been a friend for years as a possible lover. And not finding the thought at all repulsive.

There had been a number of successors to Arthur Lestrange, and she hadn't wanted to laugh. Oh, I've come a long way since that memorable night. But I wonder have I actually progressed at all? It's very nice to have a man, and the hell with what Dane said about it being the *one* man. I'm not going to make it one man, so I'm not going to sleep with Rain; oh, no. It would change too many things, and I'd lose my friend. I need my friend, I can't afford to be without my friend. I shall keep him as I keep Dane, a male human being without any physical significance for me.

The church could hold twenty thousand people, so it wasn't crowded. Nowhere in the world had so much time and thought and genius been put into the creation of a temple of God; it paled the pagan works of antiquity to insignificance. It did. So much love, so much sweat. Bramante's basilica, Michelangelo's dome, Bernini's colonnade. A monument not only to God, but to Man. Deep under the *confessio* in a little stone room Saint Peter himself was buried; here the Emperor Charlemagne had been crowned. The echoes of old voices seemed to whisper among the pouring slivers of light, dead fingers polished the bronze rays behind the high altar and caressed the twisted bronze columns of the *baldacchino*.

He was lying on the steps, face down, as though dead. What was he thinking? Was there a pain in him that had no right to be there, because his mother had not come? Cardinal Ralph looked through his tears, and knew there was no pain. Beforehand, yes; afterward, certainly. But now, no pain. Everything in him was projected into the moment, the miracle. No room in him for anything which was not God. It was his day of days, and nothing mattered save the task at hand, the vowing of his life and soul to God. He could probably do it, but how many others actually had? Not Cardinal Ralph, though he still remembered his own ordination as filled with holy wonder. With every part of him he had tried, yet something he had withheld.

Not so august as this, my ordination, but I live it again through him. And wonder what he truly is, that in spite of our fears for him he could have passed among us so many years and not made an unfriend, let alone a real enemy. He is loved by all, and he loves all. It never crosses his mind for an instant that this state of affairs is extraordinary. And yet, when he came to us first he was not so sure of himself; *we* have given him that, for which perhaps our existences are vindicated. There have been many priests made here, thousands upon thousands, yet for him there is something special. Oh, Meggie! Why wouldn't you come to see the gift you've given Our Lord—the gift I could not, having given Him myself? And I suppose that's it, how he can be here today free of pain. Because for today I've been empowered to take his pain to myself, free him from it. I weep his tears, I mourn in his place. And that is how it should be.

Later he turned his head, looked at the row of Drogheda people in alien dark suits. Bob, Jack, Hughie, Jims, Patsy. A vacant chair for Meggie, then Frank. Justine's fiery hair dimmed under a black lace veil, the only female Cleary present. Rainer next to her. And then a lot of people he didn't know, but who shared in today as fully as the Drogheda people did. Only today it was different, today it was special for him. Today he felt almost as if he, too, had had a son to give. He smiled, and sighed. How must Vittorio feel, bestowing Dane's priesthood upon him?

Perhaps because he missed his mother's presence so acutely, Justine was the first person Dane managed to take aside at the reception Cardinal Vittorio and Cardinal Ralph gave for him. In his black soutane with the high white collar he looked magnificent, she thought; only not like a priest at all. Like an actor playing a priest, until one looked into the eyes. And there it was, the inner light, that something which transformed him from a very good-looking man into one unique.

"Father O'Neill," she said.

"I haven't assimilated it yet, Jus."

"That isn't hard to understand. I've never felt quite the way I did in Saint Peter's, so what it must have been like for you I can't imagine."

"Oh, I think you can, somewhere inside. If you truly couldn't, you wouldn't be such a fine actress. But with you, Jus, it comes from the unconscious; it doesn't erupt into thought until you need to use it."

They were sitting on a small couch in a far corner of the room, and no one came to disturb them.

After a while he said, "I'm so pleased Frank came," looking to where Frank was talking with Rainer, more animation in his face than his niece and nephew had ever seen. "There's an old Rumanian refugee priest I know," Dane went on, "who has a way of saying, 'Oh, the poor one!' with such compassion in his voice. . . . I don't know, somehow that's what I always find myself saying about our Frank. And yet, Jus, why?"

But Justine ignored the gambit, went straight to the crux. "I could kill Mum!" she said through her teeth. "She had no right to do this to you!"

"Oh, Jus! I understand. You've got to try, too. If it

had been done in malice or to get back at me I might be hurt, but you know her as well as I do, you know it's neither of those. I'm going down to Drogheda soon. I'll talk to her then, find out what's the matter."

"I suppose daughters are never as patient with their mothers as sons are." She drew down the corners of her mouth ruefully, shrugged. "Maybe it's just as well I'm too much of a loner ever to inflict myself on anyone in the mother role."

The blue eyes were very kind, tender; Justine felt her hackles rising, thinking Dane pitied her.

"Why don't you marry Rainer?" he asked suddenly.

Her jaw dropped, she gasped. "He's never asked me," she said feebly.

"Only because he thinks you'd say no. But it might be arranged."

Without thinking, she grabbed him by the ear, as she used to do when they were children. "Don't you dare, you dog-collared prawn! Not one word, do you hear? *I don't love Rain!* He's just a friend, and I want to keep it that way. If you so much as light a candle for it, I swear I'll sit down, cross my eyes and put a curse on you, and you remember how that used to scare the living daylights out of you, don't you?"

He threw back his head and laughed. "It wouldn't work, Justine! My magic is stronger than yours these days. But there's no need to get so worked up about it, you twit. I was wrong, that's all. I assumed there was a case between you and Rain."

"No, there isn't. After *seven years?* Break it down, pigs might fly." Pausing, she seemed to seek for words, then looked at him almost shyly. "Dane, I'm so happy for you. I think if Mum was here she'd feel the same. That's all it needs, for her to see you now, like this. You wait, she'll come around."

Very gently he took her pointed face between his hands, smiling down at her with so much love that her own hands came up to clutch at his wrists, soak it in through every pore. As if all those childhood years were remembered, treasured.

Yet behind what she saw in his eyes on her behalf she sensed a shadowy doubt, only perhaps doubt was too strong a word; more like anxiety. Mostly he was sure Mum would understand eventually, but he *was* human, though all save he tended to forget the fact.

"Jus, will you do something for me?" he asked as he let her go.

"Anything," she said, meaning it.

"I've got a sort of respite, to think about what I'm going to do. Two months. And I'm going to do the heavy thinking on a Drogheda horse after I've talked to Mum—somehow I feel I can't sort anything out until after I've talked to her. But first, well . . . I've got to get up my courage to go home. So if you could manage it, come down to the Peloponnese with me for a couple of weeks, tick me off good and proper about being a coward until I get so sick of your voice I put myself on a plane to get away from it." He smiled at her. "Besides, Jussy, I don't want you to think I'm going to exclude you from my life absolutely, any more than I will Mum. You need your old conscience around occasionally."

"Oh, Dane, of course I'll go!"

"Good," he said, then grinned, eyed her mischievously. "I really do need you, Jus. Having you bitching in my ear will be just like old times."

"Uh-uh-uh! No obscenities, *Father* O'Neill!"

His arms went behind his head, he leaned back on the couch contentedly. "I am! Isn't it marvelous? And maybe after I've seen Mum, I can concentrate on Our Lord. I think that's where my inclinations lie, you know. Simply thinking about Our Lord."

"You ought to have espoused an order, Dane."

"I still can, and I probably will. I have a whole lifetime; there's no hurry."

Justine left the party with Rainer, and after she talked of going to Greece with Dane, he talked of going to his office in Bonn.

"About bloody time," she said. "For a cabinet minister you don't seem to do much work, do you? All the papers call you a playboy, fooling around with carrot-topped Australian actresses, you old dog, you."

He shook his big fist at her. "I pay for my few pleasures in more ways than you'll ever know."

"Do you mind if we walk, Rain?"

"Not if you keep your shoes on."

"I have to these days. Miniskirts have their disadvantages; the days of stockings one could peel off easily are over. They've invented a sheer version of theatrical tights, and one can't shed those in public without causing the biggest furor since Lady Godiva. So unless I want to ruin a five-guinea pair of tights, I'm imprisoned in my shoes."

"At least you improve my education in feminine garb, under as well as over," he said mildly.

"Go on! I'll bet you've got a dozen mistresses, and undress them all."

"Only one, and like all good mistresses she waits for me in her negligee."

"Do you know, I believe we've never discussed your sex life before? Fascinating! What's she like?"

"Fair, fat, forty and flatulent."

She stopped dead. "Oh, you're kidding me," she said slowly. "I can't see you with a woman like *that.*"

"Why not?"

"You've got too much taste."

"*Chacun à son goût,* my dear. I'm nothing much to look at, myself—why should you assume I could charm a young and beautiful woman into being my mistress?"

"Because you could!" she said indignantly. "Oh, of course you could!"

"My money, you mean?"

"Not, *not* your money! You're teasing me, you always do! Rainer Moerling Hartheim, you're very well aware how attractive you are, otherwise you wouldn't wear gold medallions and netting shirts. Looks aren't everything—if they were, I'd still be wondering."

"Your concern for me is touching, *Herzchen.*"

"Why is it that when I'm with you I feel as if I'm forever running to catch up with you, and I never do?" Her spurt of temper died; she stood looking at him uncertainly. "You're not serious, are you?"

"Do you think I am?"

"No! You're not conceited, but you do know how very attractive you are."

"Whether I do or not isn't important. The important thing is that you think I'm attractive."

She was going to say: Of course I do; I was mentally trying you on as a lover not long ago, but then I decided it wouldn't work, I'd rather keep on having you for my friend. Had he let her say it, he might have concluded his time hadn't come, and acted differently. As it was, before she could shape the words he had her in his arms, and was kissing her. For at least sixty seconds she stood, dying, split open, smashed, the power in her screaming in wild elation to find a matching power. His mouth—it was *beautiful!* And his hair, incredibly thick, vital, something to seize in her fingers fiercely. Then he took her face between his hands and looked at her, smiling.

"I love you," he said.

Her hands had gone up to his wrists, but not to enclose them gently, as with Dane; the nails bit in, scored down to meat savagely. She stepped back two paces and stood rubbing her arm across her mouth, eyes huge with fright, breasts heaving.

"It couldn't work," she panted. "It could never work, Rain!"

Off came the shoes; she bent to pick them up, then turned and ran, and within three seconds the soft quick pad of her feet had vanished.

Not that he had any intention of following her, though apparently she had thought he might. Both his wrists were bleeding, and they hurt. He pressed his handkerchief first to one and then to the other, shrugged, put the stained cloth away, and stood concentrating on the pain. After a while he unearthed his cigarette case, took out a cigarette, lit it, and began to walk slowly. No one passing by could have told from his face what he felt. Everything he wanted within his grasp, reached for, lost. Idiot girl. When *would* she grow up? To feel it, respond to it, and deny it.

But he was a gambler, of the win-a-few, lose-a-few kind. He had waited seven long years before trying his luck, feeling the change in her at this ordination time. Yet apparently he had moved too soon. Ah, well. There was always tomorrow—or knowing Justine, next year, the year after that. Certainly he wasn't about to give up. If he watched her carefully, one day he'd get lucky.

The soundless laugh quivered in him; fair, fat, forty and flatulent. What had brought it to his lips he didn't know, except that a long time ago his ex-wife had said it to him. The four F's, describing the typical victim of gallstones. She had been a martyr to them, poor Annelise, even though she was dark, skinny, fifty and as well corked as a genie in a bottle. What am I thinking of Annelise for, now? My patient campaign of years turned into a rout, and I can do no better than poor Annelise. So, *Fräulein* Justine O'Neill! We shall see.

There were lights in the palace windows; he would go up for a few minutes, talk to Cardinal Ralph, who was looking old. Not well. Perhaps he ought to be persuaded into a medical examination. Rainer ached, but not for Justine; she was young, there was time. For Cardinal Ralph, who had seen his own son ordained, and not known it.

It was still early, so the hotel foyer was crowded. Shoes on, Justine crossed quickly to the stairs and ran up them, head bent. Then for some time her trembling hands couldn't find the room key in her bag and she thought she would have to go down again, brave the throng about the desk. But it was there; she must have passed her fingers over it a dozen times.

Inside at last, she groped her way to the bed, sat down on its edge and let coherent thought gradually return. Telling herself she was revolted, horrified, disillusioned; all the while staring drearily at the wide rectangle of pale light which was the night sky through the window, wanting to curse, wanting to weep. It could never be the same again, and that was a tragedy. The loss of the dearest friend. Betrayal.

Empty words, untrue; suddenly she knew very well what had frightened her so, made her flee from Rain as if he had attempted murder, not a kiss. The *rightness* of it! The feeling of coming home, when she didn't want to come home any more than she wanted the liability of love. Home was frustration, so was love. Not only that, even if the admission was humiliating; she wasn't sure she could love. If she was capable of it, surely once or twice her guard would have slipped; surely once or twice she would have experienced a pang of something more than tolerant affection for her infrequent lovers. It didn't occur to her that she deliberately chose lovers who would never threaten her self-imposed detachment, so much a part of herself by now that she regarded it as completely natural. For the first time in her life she had no reference point to assist her. There was no time in the past she could take comfort from, no once-deep involvement, either for herself or for those shadowy lovers. Nor could the Drogheda people help, because she had always withheld herself from them, too.

She had had to run from Rain. To say yes, commit herself to him, and then have to watch him recoil when he found out the extent of her inadequacy? Unbearable! He would learn what she was really like, and the knowledge would kill his love for her. Unbearable to say yes, and end in being rebuffed for all time. Far better to do any rebuffing herself. That way at least pride would be satisfied, and Justine owned all her mother's pride. Rain must *never* discover what she was like beneath all that brick flippancy.

He had fallen in love with the Justine he saw; she had not allowed him any opportunity to suspect the sea of doubts beneath. Those only Dane suspected—no, knew.

She bent forward to put her forehead against the cool bedside table, tears running down her face. That was why she loved Dane so, of course. Knowing what the real Justine was like, and still loving her. Blood helped, so did a lifetime of shared memories, problems, pains, joys. Whereas Rain was a stranger, not committed to her the way Dane was, or even the other members of her family. Nothing obliged him to love her.

She sniffled, wiped her palm around her face, shrugged her shoulders and began the difficult business of pushing her trouble back into some corner of her mind where it could lie peacefully, unremembered. She knew she could do it; she had spent all her life perfecting the technique. Only it meant ceaseless activity, continuous absorption in things outside herself. She reached over and switched on the bedside lamp.

One of the Unks must have delivered the letter to her room, for it was lying on the bedside table, a pale-blue air letter with Queen Elizabeth in its upper corner.

"Darling Justine," wrote Clyde Daltinham-Roberts, "Come back to the fold, you're *needed!* At once! There's a part going begging in the new season's repertoire, and a tiny little dicky-bird told me you just *might* want it. Desdemona, darling? With Marc Simpson as your Othello? Rehearsals for the principals start next week, *if* you're interested."

If she was interested! Desdemona! Desdemona in London! And with Marc Simpson as Othello! The opportunity of a lifetime. Her mood skyrocketed to a point where the scene with Rain lost significance, or rather assumed a different significance. Perhaps if she was very, very careful she might be able to keep Rain's love; a highly acclaimed, successful actress was too busy to share much of her life with her lovers. It was worth a try. If he looked as if he were getting too close to the truth, she could always back off again. To keep Rain in her life, but especially this new Rain, she would be prepared to do anything save strip off the mask.

In the meantime, news like this deserved some sort of celebration. She didn't feel up to facing Rain yet, but there were other people on hand to share her triumph. So she put on her shoes, walked down the corridor to the Unks' communal sitting room, and when Patsy let her in she stood with arms spread wide, beaming.

"Break out the beer, I'm going to be Desdemona!" she announced in ringing tones.

For a moment no one answered, then Bob said warmly, "That's nice, Justine."

Her pleasure didn't evaporate; instead it built up to an uncontrollable elation. Laughing, she flopped into a chair and stared at her uncles. What truly lovely men they were! Of course her news meant nothing to them! They didn't have a clue who Desdemona was. If she had come to tell them she was getting married, Bob's answer would have been much the same.

Since the beginning of memory they had been a part of her life, and sadly she had dismissed them as contemptuously as she did everything about Drogheda. The Unks, a plurality having nothing to do with Justine O'Neill. Simply members of a conglomerate who drifted in and out of the homestead, smiled at her shyly, avoided her if it meant conversation. Not that they didn't like her, she realized now; only that they sensed how foreign she was, and it made them uncomfortable. But in this Roman world which was alien to them and familiar to her, she was beginning to understand them better.

Feeling a glow of something for them which might

have been called love, Justine stared from one creased, smiling face to the next. Bob, who was the life force of the unit, the Boss of Drogheda, but in such an unobtrusive way; Jack, who merely seemed to follow Bob around, or maybe it was just that they got along so well together; Hughie, who had a streak of mischief the other two did not, and yet so very like them; Jims and Patsy, the positive and negative sides of a self-sufficient whole; and poor quenched Frank, the only one who seemed plagued by fear and insecurity. All of them save Jims and Patsy were grizzled now, indeed Bob and Frank were white-haired, but they didn't really look very different from the way she remembered them as a little girl.

"I don't know whether I ought to give you a beer," Bob said doubtfully, standing with a cold bottle of Swan in his hand.

The remark would have annoyed her intensely even half a day ago, but at the moment she was too happy to take offense.

"Look, love, I know it's never occurred to you to offer me one through the course of our sessions with Rain, but honestly I'm a big girl now, and I can handle a beer. I promise it isn't a sin." She smiled.

"Where's Rainer?" Jims asked, taking a full glass from Bob and handing it to her.

"I had a fight with him."

"With *Rainer?*"

"Well, yes. But it was all my fault. I'm going to see him later and tell him I'm sorry."

None of the Unks smoked. Though she had never asked for a beer before, on earlier occasions she had sat smoking defiantly while they talked with Rain; now it took more courage than she could command to produce her cigarettes, so she contented herself with the minor victory of the beer, dying to gulp it down thirstily but mindful of their dubious regard. Ladylike sips, Justine, even if you are dryer than a secondhand sermon.

"Rain's a bonzer bloke," said Hughie, eyes twinkling.

Startled, Justine suddenly realized why she had grown so much in importance in their thoughts: she had caught herself a man they'd like to have in the family. "Yes, he is rather," she said shortly, and changed the subject. "It was a lovely day, wasn't it?"

All the heads bobbed in unison, even Frank's, but they didn't seem to want to discuss it. She could see how tired they were, yet she didn't regret her impulse to visit them. It took a little while for near-atrophied senses and feelings to learn what their proper functions were, and the Unks were a good practice target. That was the trouble with being an island; one forgot there was anything going on beyond its shores.

"What's Desdemona?" Frank asked from the shadows where he hid.

Justine launched into a vivid description, charmed by their horror when they learned she would be strangled once a night, and only remembered how tired they must be half an hour later when Patsy yawned.

"I must go," she said, putting down her empty glass. She had not been offered a second beer; one was apparently the limit for ladies. "Thanks for listening to me blather."

Much to Bob's surprise and confusion, she kissed him good night; Jack edged away but was easily caught, while Hughie accepted the farewell with alacrity. Jims turned bright red, endured it dumbly. For Patsy, a hug as well as a kiss, because he was a little bit of an island himself. And for Frank no kiss at all, he averted his head; yet when she put her arms around him she could sense a faint echo of some intensity quite missing in the others. Poor Frank. Why was he like that?

Outside their door, she leaned for a moment against the wall. Rain loved her. But when she tried to phone his room the operator informed her he had checked out, returned to Bonn.

No matter. It might be better to wait until London to

see him, anyway. A contrite apology via the mail, and an invitation to dinner next time he was in England. There were many things she didn't know about Rain, but of one characteristic she had no doubt at all; he would come, because he hadn't a grudging bone in his body. Since foreign affairs had become his forte, England was one of his most regular ports of call.

"You wait and see, my lad," she said, staring into her mirror and seeing his face instead of her own. "I'm going to make England your most important foreign affair, or my name isn't Justine O'Neill."

It had not occurred to her that perhaps as far as Rain was concerned, her name was indeed the crux of the matter. Her patterns of behavior were set, and marriage was no part of them. That Rain might want to make her over into Justine Hartheim never even crossed her mind. She was too busy remembering the quality of his kiss, and dreaming of more.

There remained only the task of telling Dane she couldn't go to Greece with him, but about this she was untroubled. Dane would understand, he always did. Only somehow she didn't think she'd tell him *all* the reasons why she wasn't able to go. Much as she loved her brother, she didn't feel like listening to what would be one of his sternest homilies ever. He wanted her to marry Rain, so if she told him what her plans for Rain were, he'd cart her off to Greece with him if it meant forcible abduction. What Dane's ears didn't hear, his heart couldn't grieve about.

"Dear Rain," the note said. "Sorry I ran like a hairy goat the other night, can't think what got into me. The hectic day and everything, I suppose. Please forgive me for behaving like an utter prawn. I'm ashamed of myself for making so much fuss about a trifle. And I daresay the day had got to you, too, words of love and all, I mean. So I tell you what—you forgive me, and I'll forgive you. Let's be friends, please. I can't bear to be at outs with you. Next time you're in London, come to dinner at my place and we'll formally draft out a peace treaty."

As usual it was signed plain "Justine." No words even of affection; she never used them. Frowning, he studied the artlessly casual phrases as if he could see through them to what was really in her mind as she wrote. It was certainly an overture of friendship, but what else? Sighing, he was forced to admit probably very little. He had frightened her badly; that she wanted to retain his friendship spoke of how much he meant to her, but he very much doubted whether she understood exactly what she felt for him. After all, now she knew he loved her; if she had sorted herself out sufficiently to realize she loved him too, she would have come straight out with it in her letter. Yet why had she returned to London instead of going to Greece with Dane? He knew he shouldn't hope it was because of him, but despite his misgivings, hope began to color his thoughts so cheerfully he buzzed his secretary. It was 10 A.M. Greenwich Mean Time, the best hour to find her at home.

"Get me Miss O'Neill's London flat," he instructed, and waited the intervening seconds with a frown pulling at the inner corners of his brows.

"Rain!" Justine said, apparently delighted. "Did you get my letter?"

"This minute."

After a delicate pause she said. "And will you come to dinner soon?"

"I'm going to be in England this coming Friday and Saturday. Is the notice too short?"

"Not if Saturday evening is all right with you. I'm in rehearsal for Desdemona, so Friday's out."

"Desdemona?"

"That's right, you don't know! Clyde wrote to me in Rome and offered me the part. Marc Simpson as

Othello, Clyde directing personally. Isn't it wonderful? I came back to London on the first plane."

He shielded his eyes with his hand, thankful his secretary was safely in her outer office, not sitting where she could see his face. "Justine, *Herzchen,* that's marvelous news!" he managed to say enthusiastically. "I was wondering what brought you back to London."

"Oh, Dane understood," she said lightly, "and in a way I think he was quite glad to be alone. He had concocted a story about needing me to bitch at him to go home, but I think it was all more for his second reason, that he doesn't want me to feel excluded from his life now he's a priest."

"Probably," he agreed politely.

"Saturday evening, then," she said. "Around six, then we can have a leisurely peace treaty session with the aid of a bottle or two, and I'll feed you after we've reached a satisfactory compromise. All right?"

"Yes, of course. Goodbye, *Herzchen."*

Contact was cut off abruptly by the sound of her receiver going down; he sat for a moment with his still in his hand, then shrugged and replaced it on its cradle. Damn Justine! She was beginning to come between him and his work.

She continued to come between him and his work during the succeeding days, though it was doubtful if anyone suspected. And on Saturday evening a little after six he presented himself at her apartment, empty-handed as usual because she was a difficult person to bring gifts. She was indifferent to flowers, never ate candy and would have thrown a more expensive offering carelessly in some corner, then forgotten it. The only gifts Justine seemed to prize were those Dane had given her.

"Champagne before dinner?" he asked, looking at her in surprise.

"Well, I think the occasion calls for it, don't you? It was our first-ever breaking of relations, and this is our first-ever reconciliation," she answered plausibly, indicating a comfortable chair for him and settling herself on the tawny kangaroo-fur rug, lips parted as if she had already rehearsed replies to anything he might say next.

But conversation was beyond him, at least until he was better able to assess her mood, so he watched her in silence. Until he had kissed her it had been easy to keep himself partially aloof, but now, seeing her again for the first time since, he admitted that it was going to be a great deal harder in the future.

Probably even when she was a very old woman she would still retain something not quite fully mature about face and bearing; as though essential womanliness would always pass her by. That cool, self-centered, logical brain seemed to dominate her completely, yet for him she owned a fascination so potent he doubted if he would ever be able to replace her with any other woman. Never once had he questioned whether she was worth the long struggle. Possibly from a philosophical standpoint she wasn't. Did it matter? She was a goal, an aspiration.

"You're looking very nice tonight, *Herzchen,*" he said at last, tipping his champagne glass to her in a gesture half toast, half acknowledgment of an adversary.

A coal fire simmered unshielded in the small Victorian grate, but Justine didn't seem to mind the heat, huddled close to it with her eyes fixed on him. Then she put her glass on the hearth with a ringing snap and sat forward, her arms linked about her knees, bare feet hidden by folds of densely black gown.

"I can't stand beating around the bush," she said. "Did you mean it, Rain?"

Suddenly relaxing deeply, he lay back in his chair. "Mean what?"

"What you said in Rome . . . That you loved me."

"Is that what this is all about, *Herzchen?*"

She looked away, shrugged, looked back at him and nodded. "Well, of course."

"But why bring it up again? You told me what you thought, and I had gathered tonight's invitation wasn't extended to bring up the past, only plan a future."

"Oh, Rain! You're acting as if I'm making a fuss! Even if I was, surely you can see why."

"No, I can't." He put his glass down and bent forward to watch her more closely. "You gave me to understand most emphatically that you wanted no part of my love, and I had hoped you'd at least have the decency to refrain from discussing it."

It had not occurred to her that this meeting, no matter what its outcome, would be so uncomfortable; after all, he had put himself in the position of a suppliant, and ought to be waiting humbly for her to reverse her decision. Instead he seemed to have turned the tables neatly. Here she was feeling like a naughty schoolgirl called upon to answer for some idiotic prank.

"Look, sport, you're the one who changed the status quo, not me! I didn't ask you to come tonight so I could beg forgiveness for having wounded the great Hartheim ego!"

"On the defensive, Justine?"

She wriggled impatiently. "Yes, dammit! How do you manage to do that to me, Rain? Oh, I wish just once you'd let me enjoy having the upper hand!"

"If I did, you'd throw me out like a smelly old rag," he said, smiling.

"I can do that yet, mate!"

"Nonsense! If you haven't done it by now you never will. You'll go on seeing me because I keep you on the hop—you never know what to expect from me."

"Is that why you said you loved me?" she asked painfully. "Was it only a ploy to keep me on the hop?"

"What do you think?"

"I think you're a prize bastard!" she said through her teeth, and marched across the rug on her knees until she was close enough to give him the full benefit of her anger. "Say you love me again, you big Kraut prawn, and watch me spit in your eye!"

He was angry, too. "No, I'm not going to say it again! That isn't why you asked me to come, is it? My feelings don't concern you one bit, Justine. You asked me to come so you could experiment with your own feelings, and it didn't enter your mind to consider whether that was being fair to me."

Before she could move away he leaned forward, gripped her arms near the shoulders and clamped her body between his legs, holding her firmly. Her rage vanished at once; she flattened her palms on his thighs and lifted her face. But he didn't kiss her. He let go of her arms and twisted to switch off the lamp behind him, then relaxed his hold on her and laid his head back against the chair, so that she wasn't sure if he had dimmed the room down to glowing coals as the first move in his love-making, or simply to conceal his expression. Uncertain, afraid of outright rejection, she waited to be told what to do. She should have realized earlier that one didn't tamper with people like Rain. They were as invincible as death. Why couldn't she put her head on his lap and say: Rain, love me, I need you so much and I'm so sorry? Oh, surely if she could get him to make love to her some emotional key would turn and it would all come tumbling out, released. . . .

Still withdrawn, remote, he let her take off his jacket and tie, but by the time she began to unbutton his shirt she knew it wasn't going to work. The kind of instinctive erotic skills which could make the most mundane operation exciting were not in her repertoire. This was so important, and she was making an absolute mess of it. Her fingers faltered, her mouth puckered. She burst into tears.

"Oh, no! *Herzchen, liebchen,* don't cry!" He pulled her onto his lap and turned her head into his shoulder, his arms around her. "I'm sorry, *Herzchen,* I didn't mean to make you cry."

"Now you know," she said between sobs. "I'm a miserable failure; I told you it wouldn't work! Rain, I wanted so badly to keep you, but I knew it wouldn't work if I let you see how awful I am!"

"No, of course it wouldn't work. How could it? I wasn't helping you, *Herzchen.*" He tugged at her hair to bring her face up to his, kissed her eyelids, her wet cheeks, the corners of her mouth. "It's my fault, *Herzchen,* not yours. I was paying you back; I wanted to see how far you could go without encouragement. But I think I have mistaken your motives, *nicht wahr?*" His voice had grown thicker, more German. "And I say, if this is what you want you shall have it, but it shall be together."

"Please, Rain, let's call it off! I haven't got what it takes. I'll only disappoint you!"

"Oh, you've got it, *Herzchen,* I've seen it on the stage. How can you doubt yourself when you're with me?"

Which was so right her tears dried.

"Kiss me the way you did in Rome," she whispered.

Only it wasn't like the kiss in Rome at all. That had been something raw, startled, explosive; this was very languorous and deep, an opportunity to taste and smell and feel, settle by layers into voluptuous ease. Her fingers returned to the buttons, his went to the zipper of her dress, then he covered her hand with his and thrust it inside his shirt, across skin matted with fine soft hair. The sudden hardening of his mouth against her throat brought a helpless response so acute she felt faint, thought she was falling and found she had, flat on the silky rug with Rain looming above her. His shirt had come off, perhaps more, she couldn't see, only the fire glancing off his shoulders spread over her, and the beautiful stern mouth. Determined to destroy its discipline for all time, she locked her fingers in his hair and made him kiss her again, harder, harder!

And the feel of him! Like coming home, recognizing every part of him with her lips and hands and body, yet fabulous and strange. While the world sank down to the minute width of the firelight lapping against darkness, she opened herself to what he wanted, and learned something he had kept entirely concealed for as long as she had known him; that he must have made love to her in imagination a thousand times. Her own experience and newborn intuition told her so. She was completely disarmed. With any other man the intimacy and astonishing sensuality would have appalled her, but he forced her to see that these were things only she had the right to command. And command them she did. Until finally she cried for him to finish it, her arms about him so strongly she could feel the contours of his very bones.

The minutes wore away, wrapped in a sated peace. They had fallen into an identical rhythm of breathing, slow and easy, his head against her shoulder, her leg thrown across him. Gradually her rigid clasp on his back relaxed, became a dreamy, circular caress. He sighed, turned over and reversed the way they were lying, quite unconsciously inviting her to slide still deeper into the pleasure of being with him. She put her palm on his flank to feel the texture of his skin, slid her hand across warm muscle and cupped it around the soft, heavy mass in his groin. To feel the curiously alive, independent movements within it was a sensation quite new to her; her past lovers had never interested her sufficiently to want to prolong her sexual curiosity to this languid and undemanding aftermath. Yet suddenly it wasn't languid and undemanding at all, but so enormously exciting she wanted him all over again.

Still she was taken unaware, knew a suffocated surprise when he slipped his arms across her back, took her head in his hands and held her close enough to see there was nothing controlled about his mouth, shaped now solely because of her, and for her. Tenderness and humility were literally born in her in that moment. It must have shown in her face, for he was gazing at her with eyes grown so bright she couldn't bear them, and bent over to take his upper lip between her own. Thoughts and senses merged at last, but her cry was smothered soundless, an unuttered wail of gladness which shook her so deeply she lost awareness of everything beyond impulse, the mindless guidance of each urgent minute. The world achieved its ultimate contraction, turned in upon itself, and totally disappeared.

Rainer must have kept the fire going, for when gentle London daylight soaked through the folds of the curtains the room was still warm. This time when he moved Justine became conscious of it, and clutched his arm fearfully.

"Don't go!"

"I'm not, *Herzchen.*" He twitched another pillow from the sofa, pushed it behind his head and shifted her closer in to his side, sighing softly. "All right?"

"Yes."

"Are you cold?"

"No, but if you are we could go to bed."

"After making love to you for hours on a fur rug? What a comedown! Even if your sheets are black silk."

"They're ordinary old white ones, cotton. This bit of Drogheda is all right, isn't it?"

"Bit of Drogheda?"

"The rug! It's made of Drogheda kangaroos," she explained.

"Not nearly exotic or erotic enough. I'll order you a tiger skin from India."

"Reminds me of a poem I heard once:

> Would you like to sin
> With Elinor Glyn
> On a tiger skin?
> Or would you prefer

To err with her
On some other fur?

"Well, *Herzchen,* I must say it's high time you bounced back! Between the demands of Eros and Morpheus, you haven't been flippant in half a day." He smiled.

"I don't feel the need at the moment," she said with an answering smile, settling his hand comfortably between her legs. "The tiger skin doggerel just popped out because it was too good to resist, but I haven't got a single skeleton left to hide from you, so there's not much point in flippancy, is there?" She sniffed, suddenly aware of a faint odor of stale fish drifting on the air. "Heavens, you didn't get any dinner and now it's time for breakfast! I can't expect you to live on love!"

"Not if you expect such strenuous demonstrations of it, anyway."

"Go on, you enjoyed every moment of it."

"Indeed I did." He sighed, stretched, yawned. "I wonder if you have any idea how happy I am."

"Oh, I think so," she said quietly.

He raised himself on one elbow to look at her. "Tell me, was Desdemona the only reason you came back to London?"

Grabbing his ear, she tweaked it painfully. "Now it's my turn to pay you back for all those headmasterish questions! What do *you* think?"

He prized her fingers away easily, grinning. "If you don't answer me, *Herzchen,* I'll strangle you far more permanently than Marc does."

"I came back to London to do Desdemona, but because of you. I haven't been able to call my life my own since you kissed me in Rome, and well you know it. You're a very intelligent man, Rainer Moerling Hartheim."

"Intelligent enough to have known I wanted you for my wife almost the first moment I saw you," he said.

She sat up quickly. *"Wife?"*

"Wife. If I'd wanted you for my mistress I'd have taken you years ago, and I could have. I know how your mind works; it would have been relatively easy. The only reason I didn't was because I wanted you for my wife and I knew you weren't ready to accept the idea of a husband."

"I don't know that I am now," she said, digesting it.

He got to his feet, pulling her up to stand against him. "Well, you can put in a little practice by getting me some breakfast. If this was my house I'd do the honors, but in your kitchen you're the cook."

"I don't mind getting your breakfast this morning, but theoretically to commit myself until the day I die?" She shook her head. "I don't think that's my cup of tea, Rain."

It was the same Roman emperor's face, and imperially unperturbed by threats of insurrection. "Justine, this is not something to play with, nor am I someone to play with. There's plenty of time. You have every reason to know I can be patient. But get it out of your head entirely that this can be settled in any way but marriage. I have no wish to be known as anyone less important to you than a husband."

"I'm *not* giving up acting!" she said aggressively.

"Verfluchte Kiste, did I ask you to? Grow up, Justine! Anyone would think I was condemning you to a life sentence over a sink and stove! We're not exactly on the breadline, you know. You can have as many servants as you want, nannies for the children, whatever else is necessary."

"Erk!" said Justine, who hadn't thought of children.

He threw back his head and laughed. "Oh, *Herzchen,* this is what's known as the morning after with a vengeance! I'm a fool to bring up realities so soon, I know, but all you have to do at this stage is think about them. Though I give you fair warning—while you're making your decision, remember that if I can't have you for my wife, I don't want you at all."

She threw her arms around him, clinging fiercely. "Oh, Rain, don't make it so hard!" she cried.

Alone, Dane drove his Lagonda up the Italian boot, past Perugia, Firenze, Bologna, Ferrara, Padova, better by-pass Venezia, spend the night in Trieste. It was one of his favorite cities, so he stayed on the Adriatic coast a further two days before heading up the mountain road to Ljubljana, another night in Zagreb. Down the great Sava River valley amid fields blue with chicory flowers to Beograd, thence to Nis, another night. Macedonia and Skopje, still in crumbling ruins from the earthquake two years before; and Tito-Veles the vacation city, quaintly Turkish with its mosques and minarets. All the way down Yugoslavia he had eaten frugally, too ashamed to sit with a great plate of meat in front of him when the people of the country contented themselves with bread.

The Greek border at Evzone, beyond it Thessalonika. The Italian papers had been full of the revolution brewing in Greece; standing in his hotel bedroom window watching the bobbing thousands of flaming torches moving restlessly in the darkness of a Thessalonika night, he was glad Justine had not come.

"Pap-an-dre-ou! Pap-an-dre-ou! Pap-an-dre-ou!" the crowds roared, chanting, milling among the torches until after midnight.

But revolution was a phenomenon of cities, of dense concentrations of people and poverty; the scarred countryside of Thessaly must still look as it had looked to Caesar's legions, marching across the stubble-burned fields to Pompey at Pharsala. Shepherds slept in the shade of skin tents, storks stood one-legged in nests atop little old white buildings, and everywhere was a terrifying aridity. It reminded him, with its high clear sky, its brown treeless wastes, of Australia. And he breathed of it deeply, began to smile at the thought of going home. Mum would understand, when he talked to her.

Above Larisa he came onto the sea, stopped the car and got out. Homer's wine-dark sea, a delicate clear aquamarine near the beaches, purple-stained like grapes as it stretched to the curving horizon. On a greensward far below him stood a tiny round pillared temple, very white in the sun, and on the rise of the hill behind him a frowning Crusader fortress endured. Greece, you are very beautiful, more beautiful than Italy, for all that I love Italy. But here is the cradle, forever.

Panting to be in Athens, he pushed on, gunned the red sports car up the switchbacks of the Domokos Pass and descended its other side into Boeotia, a stunning panorama of olive groves, rusty hillsides, mountains. Yet in spite of his haste he stopped to look at the oddly Hollywoodish monument to Leonidas and his Spartans at Thermopylae. The stone said: "Stranger, go tell the Spartans that here we lie, in obedience to their command." It struck a chord in him, almost seemed to be words he might have heard in a different context; he shivered and went on quickly.

In melted sun he paused for a while above Kamena Voura, swam in the clear water looking across the narrow strait to Euboea; there must the thousand ships have sailed from Aulis, on their way to Troy. It was a strong current, swirling seaward; they must not have had to ply their oars very hard. The ecstatic cooings and strokings of the ancient black-garbed crone in the bathhouse embarrassed him; he couldn't get away from her fast enough. People never referred to his beauty to his face anymore, so most of the time he was able to forget it. Delaying only to buy a couple of huge, custard-filled cakes in the shop, he went on down the Attic coast and finally came to Athens as the sun was setting, gilding the great rock and its precious crown of pillars.

But Athens was tense and vicious, and the open admiration of the women mortified him; Roman women were more sophisticated, subtle. There was a feeling in the crowds, pockets of rioting, grim determination on the part of the people to have Papandreou. No, Athens wasn't herself; better to be elsewhere. He put the Lagonda in a garage and took the ferry to Crete.

And there at last, amid the olive groves, the wild thyme and the mountains, he found his peace. After a long bus ride with trussed chickens screeching and the all-pervasive reek of garlic in his nostrils, he found a tiny white-painted inn with an arched colonnade and three umbrellaed tables outside on the flagstones, gay Greek bags hanging festooned like lanterns. Pepper trees and Australian gum trees, planted from the new South Land in soil too arid for European trees. The gut roar of cicadas. Dust, swirling in red clouds.

At night he slept in a tiny cell-like room with shutters wide open, in the hush of dawn he celebrated a solitary Mass, during the day he walked. No one bothered him, he bothered no one. But as he passed the dark eyes of the peasants would follow him in slow amazement, and every face would crease deeper in a smile. It was hot, and so quiet, and very sleepy. Perfect peace. Day followed day, like beads slipping through a leathery Cretan hand.

Voicelessly he prayed, a feeling, an extension of what lay all through him, thoughts like beads, days like beads. Lord, I am truly Thine. For Thy many blessings I thank Thee. For the great Cardinal, his help, his deep friendship, his unfailing love. For Rome and the chance to be at Thy heart, to have lain prostrate before Thee in Thine own basilica, to have felt the rock of Thy Church within me. Thou hast blessed me above my worth; what can I do for Thee, to show my appreciation? I have not suffered enough. My life has been one long, absolute joy since I began in Thy service. I must suffer, and Thou Who suffered will know that. It is only through suffering that I may rise above myself, understand Thee better. For that is what this life is: the passage toward understanding Thy mystery. Plunge Thy spear into my breast, bury it there so deeply I am never able to withdraw it! Make me suffer. . . . For Thee I forsake all others, even my mother and my sister and the Cardinal. Thou alone art my pain, my joy. Abase me and I shall sing Thy beloved Name. Destroy me, and I shall rejoice. I love Thee. Only Thee . . .

He had come to the little beach where he liked to swim, a yellow crescent between beetling cliffs, and stood for a moment looking across the Mediterranean to what must be Libya, far below the dark horizon. Then he leaped lightly down the steps to the sand, kicked off his sneakers, picked them up, and trod through the softly yielding contours to the spot where he usually dropped shoes, shirt, outer shorts. Two young Englishmen talking in drawling Oxford accents lay like broiling lobsters not far away, and beyond them two women drowsily speaking in German. Dane glanced at the women and self-consciously hitched his swimsuit, aware they had stopped conversing and had sat up to pat their hair, smile at him.

"How goes it?" he asked the Englishmen, though in his mind he called them what all Australians call the English, Pommies. They seemed to be fixtures, since they were on the beach every day.

"Splendidly, old boy. Watch the current—it's too strong for us. Storm out there somewhere."

"Thanks." Dane grinned, ran down to the innocently curling wavelets and dived cleanly into shallow water like the expert surfer he was.

Amazing, how deceptive calm water could be. The current was vicious, he could feel it tugging at his legs to draw him under, but he was too strong a swimmer to be worried by it. Head down, he slid smoothly through the water, reveling in the coolness, the freedom. When he paused and scanned the beach he saw the two German women pulling on their caps, running down laughing to the waves.

Cupping his hands around his mouth, he called to them in German to stay in shallow water because of the current. Laughing, they waved acknowledgment. He put his head down then, swam again, and thought he heard a cry. But he swam a little farther, then stopped to tread water in a spot where the undertow wasn't so bad. There *were* cries; as he turned he saw the women struggling, their twisted faces screaming, one with her hands up, sinking. On the beach the two Englishmen had risen to their feet and were reluctantly approaching the water.

He flipped over onto his belly and flashed through the water, closer and closer. Panicked arms reached for him, clung to him, dragged him under; he managed to grip one woman around the waist long enough to stun her with a swift clip on the chin, then grabbed the other by the strap of her swimsuit, shoved his knee hard into her spine and winded her. Coughing, for he had swallowed water when he went under, he turned on his back and began towing his helpless burdens in.

The two Pommies were standing shoulder-deep, too frightened to venture any farther, for which Dane didn't blame them in the least. His toes just touched the sand; he sighed in relief. Exhausted, he exerted a last superhuman effort and thrust the women to safety. Fast regaining their senses, they began screaming again, thrashing about wildly. Gasping, Dane managed a grin. He had done his bit; the Poms could take over now. While he rested, chest heaving, the current had sucked him out again, his feet no longer brushed the bottom even when he stretched them downward. It had been a close call. If he hadn't been present they would certainly have drowned; the Poms hadn't the strength or skill to save them. But, said a voice, they only wanted to swim so they could be near *you;* until they saw *you* they hadn't any intention of going in. It was your fault they were in danger, your fault.

And as he floated easily a terrible pain blossomed in his chest, surely as a spear would feel, one long and red-hot shaft of screaming agony. He cried out, threw his arms up above his head, stiffening, muscles convulsed; but the pain grew worse, forced his arms down again, thrust his fists into his armpits, brought up his knees. My heart! I'm having a heart attack, I'm dying! My heart! I don't want to die! Not yet, not before I've begun my work, not before I've had a chance to prove myself! Dear Lord, help me! I don't want to die, I don't want to die!

The spasmed body stilled, relaxed; Dane turned onto his back, let his arms float wide and limp in spite of the pain. Wet-lashed, he stared up at the soaring vault of the sky. This is it; this is Thy spear, that I in my pride begged for not an hour ago. Give me the chance to suffer, I said, make me suffer. Now when it comes I resist, not capable of perfect love. Dearest Lord, Thy pain! I must accept it, I must not fight it, I must not fight Thy will. Thy hand is mighty and this is Thy pain, as Thou must have felt it on the Cross. My God, my God, I am Thine! If this is Thy will, so be it. Like a child I put myself into Thy infinite hand. Thou art too good to me. What have I done to deserve so much from Thee, and from the people who love me better than they love anyone else? Why hast Thou given me so much, when I am not worthy? *The pain, the pain!* Thou art so good to me. Let it not be long, I asked, and it has not been long. My suffering will be short, quickly over. Soon I shall see Thy face, but now, still in this life, I thank Thee. The pain! My dearest Lord, Thou art too good to me. *I love Thee!*

A huge tremor passed through the still, waiting body. His lips moved, murmured a Name, tried to smile. Then the pupils dilated, drove all the blue from his eyes forever. Safe on the beach at last, the two Englishmen dumped their weeping charges on the sand and stood looking for him. But the placid deep blue sea was empty, vast; the wavelets ran up rushing and retreated. Dane was gone.

Someone thought of the United States Air Force station nearby, and ran for help. Not thirty minutes after Dane had disappeared a helicopter took off, beat the air frantically and swooped in ever-increasing circles outward from the beach, searching. No one expected to see anything. Drowned men sank to the bottom and didn't come up for days. An hour passed; then fifteen miles out to sea they sighted Dane floating peacefully on the bosom of the deep, arms outstretched, face turned up to the sky. For a moment they thought he was alive and cheered, but as the craft came low enough to throw the water into hissing foam, it was plain he was dead. The coordinates were given over the helicopter's radio, a launch sped out, and three hours later returned.

Word had spread. The Cretans had loved to see him pass, loved to exchange a few shy words. Loved him, though they didn't know him. They flocked down to the sea, women all in black like dowdy birds, men in old-fashioned baggy trousers, white shirts open at the collar and sleeves rolled up. And stood in silent groups, waiting.

When the launch came in a burly master sergeant sprang out onto the sand, turned back to receive a blanket-draped form into his arms. He marched a few feet up the beach beyond the water line, and with the help of another man laid his burden down. The blanket fell apart; there was a high, rustling whisper from the Cretans. They came crowding around, pressing crucifixes to weather-beaten lips, the women softly keening, a wordless ohhhhhhhh! that had almost a melody in it, mournful, patient, earthbound, female.

It was about five in the afternoon; the barred sun was sliding westward behind the frowning cliff, but was still high enough to light up the little dark cluster on the beach, the long, still form on the sand with its golden skin, its closed eyes whose lashes were spiky from drying salt, the faint smile on the blued lips. A stretcher was brought forward, then all together Cretans and American servicemen bore Dane away.

Athens was in turmoil, rioting crowds overturning all order, but the USAF colonel got through to his superiors on a special frequency band, Dane's blue Australian passport in his hand. It said, as such documents do, nothing about him. His profession was simply marked "Student," and in the back under next of kin Justine's name was listed, with her London address. Unconcerned by the legal meaning of the term, he had put her name because London was far closer to Rome than Drogheda. In his little room at the inn, the square black case which housed his priestly implements had not been opened; it waited with his suitcase for directions as to where it should be sent.

When the phone rang at nine in the morning Justine rolled over, opened a bleary eye and lay cursing it, vowing she would have the bloody thing disconnected. Because the rest of the world thought it only right and proper to commence whatever they did at nine in the morning, why did they assume the same of her?

But it rang, and rang, and rang. Maybe it was Rain; that thought tipped the balance toward consciousness, and Justine got up, slopped reeling out to the living room. The German parliament was in urgent session; she hadn't seen Rain in a week and hadn't been optimistic about her chances of seeing him for at least another week. But perhaps the crisis had resolved, and he was calling to tell her he was on his way over.

"Hello?"

"Miss Justine O'Neill?"

"Yes, speaking."

"This is Australia House, in the Aldwych, you

know?" The voice had an English inflection, gave a name she was too tired to hear because she was still assimilating the fact that the voice was not Rain's.

"Okay, Australia House." Yawning, she stood on one foot and scratched its top with the sole of the other.

"Do you have a brother, a Mr. Dane O'Neill?"

Justine's eyes opened. "Yes, I do."

"Is he at present in Greece, Miss O'Neill?"

Both feet settled into the rug, stood braced. "Yes, that's right," It did not occur to her to correct the voice, explain it was Father, not Mister.

"Miss O'Neill, I very much regret to say that it is my unfortunate duty to give you some bad news."

"Bad news? Bad news? What is it? What's the matter? What's happened?"

"I regret to have to inform you that your brother, Mr. Dane O'Neill, was drowned yesterday in Crete, I understand in heroic circumstances, performing a sea rescue. However, you realize there is a revolution in Greece, and what information we have is sketchy and possibly not accurate."

The phone stood on a table near the wall and Justine leaned against the solid support the wall offered. Her knees buckled, she began to slide very slowly downward, wound up in a curled heap on the floor. Not laughing and not crying, she made noises somewhere in between, audible gasps. Dane drowned. Gasp. Dane dead. Gasp. Crete, Dane, drowned. Gasp. Dead, dead.

"Miss O'Neill? Are you there, Miss O'Neill?" asked the voice insistently.

Dead. Drowned. My brother!

"Miss O'Neill, answer me!"

"Yes, yes, yes, yes, *yes!* Oh, God, I'm here!"

"I understand you are his next of kin, therefore we must have your instructions as to what to do with the body. Miss O'Neill, are you there?"

"Yes, yes!"

"What do you want done with the body, Miss O'Neill?"

Body! He was a body, and they couldn't even say *his* body, they had to say *the* body. Dane, my Dane. He is a body. "Next of kin?" she heard her voice asking, thin and faint, torn by those great gasps. "I'm not Dane's next of kin. My mother is, I suppose."

There was a pause. "This is very difficult, Miss O'Neill. If you're not the next of kin, we've wasted valuable time." The polite sympathy gave way to impatience. "You don't seem to understand there's a revolution going on in Greece and the accident happened in Crete, even more remote and hard to contact. Really! Communication with Athens is virtually impossible and we have been instructed to forward the next of kin's personal wishes and instructions regarding the body immediately. Is your mother there? May I speak to her, please?"

"My mother's not here. She's in Australia."

"Australia? Lord, this gets worse and worse! Now we'll have to send a cable to Australia; more delays. If you are not the next of kin, Miss O'Neill, why did your brother's passport say you were?"

"I don't know," she said, and found she had laughed.

"Give me your mother's address in Australia; we'll cable her at once. We *have* to know what to do with the body! By the time cables get back and forth, this will mean a twelve-hour delay, I hope you realize that. It's going to be difficult enough without this mix-up."

"Phone her, then. Don't waste time with cables."

"Our budget does not extend to international phone calls, Miss O'Neill," said that stiff voice. "Now, will you please give me your mother's name and address?"

"Mrs. Meggie O'Neill," Justine recited, "Drogheda, Gillanbone, New South Wales, Australia." She spelled out the unfamiliar names for him.

"Once again, Miss O'Neill, my deepest regrets."

The receiver clicked, began the interminable burr of

the dial tone. Justine sat on the floor and let it slip into her lap. There was a mistake, it would all sort itself out. Dane drowned, when he swam like a champion? No, it wasn't true. But it is, Justine, you know it is, you didn't go with him to protect him and he drowned. You were his protector from the time he was a baby and you should have been there. If you couldn't save him, you should have been there to drown with him. And the only reason you didn't go with him was because you wanted to be in London so you could get Rain to make love to you.

Thinking was so hard. Everything was so hard. Nothing seemed to work, not even her legs. She couldn't get up, she would never get up again. There was no room in her mind for anyone but Dane, and her thoughts went in ever-diminishing circles around Dane. Until she thought of her mother, the Drogheda people. Oh, God. The news would come there, come to her, come to them. Mum didn't even have the lovely last sight of his face in Rome. They'll send the cable to the Gilly police, I suppose, and old Sergeant Ern will climb into his car and drive out all the miles to Drogheda, to tell my mother that her only son is dead. Not the right man for the job, and an almost-stranger. Mrs. O'Neill, my deepest, most heartfelt regrets, your son is dead. Perfunctory, courteous, empty words. . . . No! I can't let them do that to her, not to her, *she is my mother, too!* Not that way, not the way I had to hear it.

She pulled the other part of the phone off the table onto her lap, put the receiver to her ear and dialed the operator.

"Switch? Trunks, please, international. Hello? I want to place an urgent call to Australia, Gillanbone one-two-one-two. And please, please hurry."

Meggie answered the phone herself. It was late, Fee had gone to bed. These days she never felt like seeking her own bed early, she preferred to sit listening to the crickets and frogs, doze over a book, remember.

"Hello?"

"London calling, Mrs. O'Neill," said Hazel in Gilly.

"Hello, Justine," Meggie said, not perturbed. Jussy called, infrequently, to see how everything was.

"Mum? Is that you, Mum?"

"Yes, it's Mum here," said Meggie gently, sensing Justine's distress.

"Oh, Mum! Oh, Mum!" There was what sounded like a gasp, or a sob. "Mum, Dane's dead. Dane's dead!"

A pit opened at her feet. Down and down and down it went, and had no bottom. Meggie slid into it, felt its lips close over her head, and understood that she would never come out again as long as she lived. What more could the gods do? She hadn't known when she asked it. How could she have asked it, how could she not have known? Don't tempt the gods, they love it. In not going to see him in this most beautiful moment of his life, share it with him, she had finally thought to make the payment. Dane would be free of it, and free of her. In not seeing the face which was dearer to her than all other faces, she would repay. The pit closed in, suffocating. Meggie stood there, and realized it was too late.

"Justine, my dearest, be calm," said Meggie strongly, not a falter in her voice. "Calm yourself and tell me. Are you sure?"

"Australia House called me—they thought I was his next of kin. Some dreadful man who only wanted to know what I wanted done with the body. 'The body,' he kept calling Dane. As if he wasn't entitled to it anymore, as if it was anyone's." Meggie heard her sob. "God! I suppose the poor man hated what he was doing. Oh, Mum, Dane's dead!"

"How, Justine? Where? In Rome? Why hasn't Ralph called me?"

"No, not in Rome. The Cardinal probably doesn't know anything about it. In Crete. The man said he was drowned, a sea rescue. He was on holiday, Mum, he asked me to go with him and I didn't, I wanted to play Desdemona, I wanted to be with Rain. If I'd only been with him! If I had, it mightn't have happened. Oh, God, what can I do?"

"Stop it, Justine," said Meggie sternly. "No thinking like that, do you hear me? Dane would hate it, you know he would. Things happen, why we don't know. The important thing now is that you're all right, I haven't lost both of you. You're all I've got left now. Oh, Jussy, Jussy, it's so far away! The world's big, too big. Come home to Drogheda! I hate to think of you all alone."

"No, I've got to work. Work is the only answer for me. If I don't work, I'll go mad. I don't want people, I don't want comfort. Oh, Mum!" She began to sob bitterly. "How are we going to live without him?"

How indeed? Was that living? God's thou wert, unto God return. Dust to dust. Living's for those of us who failed. Greedy God, gathering in the good ones, leaving the world to the rest of us, to rot.

"It isn't for any of us to say how long we'll live," said Meggie. "Jussy, thank you so much for telling me yourself, for phoning."

"I couldn't bear to think of a stranger breaking the news, Mum. Not like that, from a stranger. What will you do? What can you do?"

With all her will Meggie tried to pour warmth and comfort across the miles to her devastated girl in London. Her son was dead, her daughter still lived. She must be made whole. If it was possible. In all her life Justine seemed only to have loved Dane. No one else, even herself.

"Dear Justine, don't cry. Try not to grieve. He wouldn't have wanted that, now would he? Come home, and forget. We'll bring Dane home to Drogheda, too.

At law he's mine again, he doesn't belong to the Church and they can't stop me. I'll phone Australia House right away, and the embassy in Athens if I can get through. He *must* come home! I'd hate to think of him lying somewhere far from Drogheda. Here is where he belongs, he'll have to come home. Come with him, Justine."

But Justine sat in a heap, shaking her head as if her mother could see. Come home? She could never come home again. If she had gone with Dane he wouldn't be dead. Come home, and have to look at her mother's face every day for the rest of her life? No, it didn't bear thinking of.

"No, Mum," she said, the tears rolling down her skin, hot like molten metal. Who on earth ever said people most moved don't weep? They don't know anything about it. "I shall stay here and work. I'll come home with Dane, but then I'm going back. I can't live on Drogheda."

For three days they waited in a purposeless vacuum, Justine in London, Meggie and the family on Drogheda, stretching the official silence into tenuous hope. Oh, surely after so long it would turn out to be a mistake, surely if it was true they would have heard by now! Dane would come in Justine's front door smiling, and say it was all a silly mistake. Greece was in revolt, all sorts of silly mistakes must have been made. Dane woud come in the door and laugh the idea of his death to scorn, he'd stand there tall and strong and alive, and he'd laugh. Hope began to grow, and grew with every minute they waited. Treacherous, horrible hope. He wasn't dead, no! Not *drowned,* not Dane who was a good enough swimmer to brave any kind of sea and live. So they waited, not acknowledging what had happened in the hope it would prove to be a mistake. Time later to notify people, let Rome know.

On the fourth morning Justine got the message. Like

an old woman she picked up the receiver once more, and asked for Australia.

"Mum?"

"Justine?"

"Oh, Mum, they've buried him already; we can't bring him home! What are we going to do? All they can say is that Crete is a big place, the name of the village isn't known, by the time the cable arrived he'd already been spirited away somewhere and disposed of. He's lying in an unmarked grave somewhere! I can't get a visa for Greece, no one wants to help, it's chaos. What are we going to do, Mum?"

"Meet me in Rome, Justine," said Meggie.

Everyone save Anne Mueller was there around the phone, still in shock. The men seemed to have aged twenty years in three days, and Fee, shrunken birdlike, white and crabbed, drifted about the house saying over and over, "Why couldn't it have been me? Why did they have to take him? I'm so old, so old! I wouldn't have minded going, why did it have to be him? Why couldn't it have been me? I'm so old!" Anne had collapsed, and Mrs. Smith, Minnie and Cat walked, slept tears.

Meggie stared at them silently as she put the phone down. This was Drogheda, all that was left. A little cluster of old men and old women, sterile and broken.

"Dane's lost," she said. "No one can find him; he's been buried somewhere on Crete. It's so far away! How could he rest so far from Drogheda? I'm going to Rome, to Ralph de Bricassart. If anyone can help us, he can."

Cardinal de Bricassart's secretary entered his room.

"Your Eminence, I'm sorry to disturb you, but a lady wishes to see you. I explained that there is a congress, that you are very busy and cannot see anyone, but she says she will sit in the vestibule until you have time for her."

"Is she in trouble, Father?"

"Great trouble, Your Eminence, that much is easy to see. She said I was to tell you her name is Meggie O'Neill." He gave it a lilting foreign pronunciation, so that it came out sounding like Meghee Onill.

Cardinal Ralph came to his feet, the color draining from his face to leave it as white as his hair.

"Your Eminence! Are you ill?"

"No, Father, I'm perfectly all right, thank you. Cancel my appointments until I notify you otherwise, and bring Mrs. O'Neill to me at once. We are not to be disturbed unless it is the Holy Father."

The priest bowed, departed. O'Neill. Of course! It was young Dane's name, he should have remembered. Save that in the Cardinal's palace everyone just said Dane. Ah, he had made a grave mistake, keeping her waiting. If Dane was His Eminence's dearly loved nephew then Mrs. O'Neill was his dearly loved sister.

When Meggie came into the room Cardinal Ralph hardly knew her. It was thirteen years since he had last seen her; she was fifty-three and he was seventy-one. Both of them aged now, instead of only him. Her face hadn't changed so much as settled, and into a mold unlike the one he had given her in his imagination. Substitute a trenchant incisiveness for sweetness, a touch of iron for softness; she resembled a vigorous, aging, willful martyr rather than the resigned, contemplative saint of his dreams. Her beauty was as striking as ever, her eyes still that clear silvery grey, but both had hardened, and the once vivid hair had faded to a drab beige, like Dane's without the life. Most disconcerting of all, she wouldn't look at him for long enough to satisfy his eager and loving curiosity.

Unable to greet this Meggie naturally, he stiffly indicated a chair. "Please sit down."

"Thank you," she said, equally stilted.

It was only when she was seated and he could gaze down upon her whole person that he noticed how visibly swollen her feet and ankles were.

"Meggie! Have you flown all the way through from Australia without breaking your journey? What's the matter?"

"Yes, I did fly straight through," she said. "For the past twenty-nine hours I've been sitting in planes between Gilly and Rome, with nothing to do except stare out the window at the clouds, and think." Her voice was harsh, cold.

"What's the matter?" he repeated impatiently, anxious and fearful.

She lifted her gaze from her feet and looked at him steadily.

There was something *awful* in her eyes; something so dark and chilling that the skin on the back of his neck crawled and automatically he put his hand up to stroke it.

"Dane is dead," said Meggie.

His hand slipped, flopped like a rag doll's into his scarlet lap as he sank into a chair. "Dead?" he asked slowly. "*Dane* dead?"

"Yes. He was drowned six days ago in Crete, rescuing some women from the sea."

He leaned forward, put his hands over his face. "Dead?" she heard him say indistinctly. "*Dane* dead? My beautiful boy! He can't be dead! Dane—he was the perfect priest—all that I couldn't be. What I lacked he had." His voice broke. "He always had it—that was what we all recognized—all of us who aren't perfect priests. *Dead?* Oh, dear Lord!"

"Don't bother about your dear Lord, Ralph," said the stranger sitting opposite him. "You have more important things to do. I came to ask for your help—not to witness your grief. I've had all those hours in the air to go over the way I'd tell you this, all those hours just staring out the window at the clouds knowing Dane is dead. After that, your grief has no power to move me."

Yet when he lifted his face from his hands her dead cold heart bounded, twisted, leaped. It was Dane's face, with a suffering written upon it that Dane would never live to feel. Oh, thank God! Thank God he's dead, can never now go through what this man has, what I have. Better he's dead than to suffer something like this.

"How can I help, Meggie?" he asked quietly, suppressing his own emotions to don the soul-deep guise of her spiritual counselor.

"Greece is in chaos. They've buried Dane somewhere on Crete, and I can't find out where, when, why. Except I suppose that my instructions directing that he be flown home were endlessly delayed by the civil war, and Crete is hot like Australia. When no one claimed him, I suppose they thought he had no one, and buried him." She leaned forward in her chair tensely. "I want my boy back, Ralph, I want him found and brought home to sleep where he belongs, on Drogheda. I promised Jims I'd keep him on Drogheda and I will, if I have to crawl on my hands and knees through every graveyard on Crete. No fancy Roman priest's tomb for him, Ralph, not as long as I'm alive to put up a legal battle. He's to come home."

"No one is going to deny you that, Meggie," he said gently. "It's consecrated Catholic ground, which is all the Church asks. I too have requested that I be buried on Drogheda."

"I can't get through all the red tape," she went on, as if he hadn't spoken. "I can't speak Greek, and I have no power or influence. So I came to you, to use yours. Get me back my son, Ralph!"

"Don't worry, Meggie, we'll get him back, though it may not be very quickly. The Left are in charge now, and they're very anti-Catholic. However, I'm not without friends in Greece, so it will be done. Let me start the wheels in motion immediately, and don't worry. He is a priest of the Holy Catholic Church, we'll get him back."

His hand had gone to the bell cord, but Meggie's coldly fierce gaze stilled it.

"You don't understand, Ralph. I don't want wheels set in motion. I want my son back—not next week or next month, but now! You speak Greek, you can get visas for yourself and me, you'll get results. I want you to come to Greece with me *now,* and help me get my son back."

There was much in his eyes: tenderness, compassion, shock, grief. But they had become the priest's eyes too, sane, logical, reasonable. "Meggie, I love your son as if he were my own, but I can't leave Rome at the moment. I'm not a free agent—you above all others should know that. No matter how much I may feel for you, how much I may feel on my own account, I can't leave Rome in the midst of a vital congress. I am the Holy Father's aide."

She reared back, stunned and outraged, then shook her head, half-smiling as if at the antics of some inanimate object beyond her power to influence; then she trembled, licked her lips, seemed to come to a decision and sat up straight and stiff. "Do you really love my son as if he were your own, Ralph?" she asked. "What would you do for a son of yours? Could you sit back then and say to *his* mother, No, I'm very sorry, I can't possibly take the time off? *Could* you say that to the mother of your son?"

Dane's eyes, yet not Dane's eyes. Looking at her; bewildered, full of pain, helpless.

"I have no son," he said, "but among the many, many things I learned from yours was that no matter how hard it is, my first and only allegiance is to Almighty God."

"Dane was your son too," said Meggie.

He stared at her blankly. "What?"

"I said, Dane was your son too. When I left Matlock Island I was pregnant. Dane was yours, not Luke O'Neill's."

"It—isn't—true!"

"I never intended you to know, even now," she said. "Would I lie to you?"

"To get Dane back? Yes," he said faintly.

She got up, came to stand over him in the red brocade chair, took his thin, parchmentlike hand in hers, bent and kissed the ring, the breath of her voice misting its ruby to milky dullness. "By all that you hold holy, Ralph, I swear that Dane was your son. He was not and could not have been Luke's. By his death I swear it."

There was a wail, the sound of a soul passing between the portals of Hell. Ralph de Bricassart fell forward out of the chair and wept, huddled on the crimson carpet in a scarlet pool like new blood, his face hidden in his folded arms, his hands clutching at his hair.

"Yes, cry!" said Meggie. "Cry, now that you know! It's right that one of his parents be able to shed tears for him. Cry, Ralph! For twenty-six years I had your son and you didn't even know it, you couldn't even see it. Couldn't see that he was you all over again! When my mother took him from me at birth she knew, but you never did. Your hands, your feet, your face, your eyes, your body. Only the color of his hair was his own; all the rest was you. Do you understand now? When I sent him here to you, I said it in my letter. 'What I stole, I give back.' Remember? Only we both stole, Ralph. We stole what you had vowed to God, and we've both had to pay."

She sat in her chair, implacable and unpitying, and watched the scarlet form in its agony on the floor. "I loved you, Ralph, but you were never mine. What I had of you, I was driven to steal. Dane was my part, all I could get from you. I vowed you'd never know, I vowed you'd never have the chance to take him away from me. And then he gave himself to you, of his own free will. The image of the perfect priest, he called you. What a laugh I had over that one! But not for anything would I have given you a weapon like knowing he was yours. Except for this. *Except for this!* For nothing less would I have told you. Though I don't suppose it matters now. He doesn't belong to either of us anymore. He belongs to God."

Cardinal de Bricassart chartered a private plane in Athens; he, Meggie and Justine brought Dane home to Drogheda, the living sitting silently, the dead lying silently on a bier, requiring nothing of this earth anymore.

I have to say this Mass, this Requiem for my son. Bone of my bone, my son. Yes, Meggie, I believe you. Once I had my breath back I would even have believed you without that terrible oath you swore. Vittorio knew the minute he set eyes on the boy, and in my heart I, too, must have known. Your laugh behind the roses from the boy—but my eyes looking up at me, as they used to be in my innocence. Fee knew. Anne Mueller knew. But not we men. We weren't fit to be told. For so you women think, and hug your mysteries, getting your backs on us for the slight God did you in not creating you in His Image. Vittorio knew, but it was the woman in him stilled his tongue. A masterly revenge.

Say it, Ralph de Bricassart, open your mouth, move your hands in the blessing, begin to chant the Latin for the soul of the departed. Who was your son. Whom you loved more than you loved his mother. Yes, more! For he was yourself all over again, in a more perfect mold.

"In Nomine Patris, et Filii, et Spiritus Sancti . . ."

The chapel was packed; they were all there who could be there. The Kings, the O'Rourkes, the Davieses, the Pughs, the MacQueens, the Gordons, the Carmichaels, the Hopetons. And the Clearys, the Drogheda people. Hope blighted, light gone. At the front in a great lead-lined casket, Father Dane O'Neill, covered in roses. Why were the roses always out when he came back to Drogheda? It was October, high spring. Of course they were out. The time was right.

"Sanctus . . . Sanctus . . . Sanctus . . ."

Be warned that the Holy of Holies is upon you. My Dane, my beautiful son. It is better so. I wouldn't have wanted you to come to this, what I already am. Why I say this for you, I don't know. You don't need it, you never needed it. What I grope for, you knew by instinct. It isn't you who is unhappy, it's those of us here, left behind. Pity us, and when our times come, help us.

"Ite, Missa est . . . Requiescat in pace. . . ."

Out across the lawn, down past the ghost gums, the roses, the pepper trees, to the cemetery. Sleep on, Dane, because only the good die young. Why do we mourn? You're lucky, to have escaped this weary life so soon. Perhaps that's what Hell is, a long term in earth-bound bondage. Perhaps we suffer our hells in living. . . .

The day passed, the mourners departed, the Drogheda people crept about the house and avoided each other; Cardinal Ralph looked early at Meggie, and could not bear to look again. Justine left with Jean and Boy King to catch the afternoon plane for Sydney, the night plane for London. He never remembered hearing her husky bewitching voice, or seeing those odd pale eyes. From the time when she had met him and Meggie in Athens to the time when she went with Jean and Boy King she had been like a ghost, her camouflage pulled closely around her. Why hadn't she called Rainer Hartheim, asked him to be with her? Surely she knew how much he loved her, how much he would want to be with her now? But the thought never stayed long enough in Cardinal Ralph's tired mind to call Rainer himself, though he had wondered about it off and on since before leaving Rome. They were strange, the Drogheda people. They didn't like company in grief; they preferred to be alone with their pain.

Only Fee and Meggie sat with Cardinal Ralph in the drawing room after a dinner left uneaten. No one said a word; the ormolu clock on the marble mantel ticked thunderously, and Mary Carson's painted eyes stared a mute challenge across the room to Fee's grandmother. Fee and Meggie sat together on a cream sofa, shoulders lightly touching; Cardinal Ralph never remembered their being so close in the old days. But they said nothing, did not look at each other or at him.

He tried to see what it was he had done wrong. Too much wrong, that was the trouble. Pride, ambition, a certain unscrupulousness. And love for Meggie flowering among them. But the crowning glory of that love he had never known. What difference would it have made to know his son was his son? Was it possible to love the boy more than he had? Would he have pursued a different path if he had known about his son? Yes! cried his heart. No, sneered his brain.

He turned on himself bitterly. Fool! You ought to have known Meggie was incapable of going back to Luke. You ought to have known at once whose child Dane was. She was so *proud* of him! All she could get from you, that was what she said to you in Rome. Well, Meggie. . . . In him you got the best of it. Dear God, Ralph, how could you not have known he was yours? You ought to have realized it when he came to you a man grown, if not before. She was waiting for you to see it, dying for you to see it; if only you had, she would have gone on her knees to you. But you were blind. You didn't want to see. Ralph Raoul, Cardinal de Bricassart, that was what you wanted; more than her, more than your son. *More than your son!*

The room had become filled with tiny cries, rustles, whispers; the clock was ticking in time with his heart. And then it wasn't in time anymore. He had got out of step with it. Meggie and Fee were swimming to their feet, drifting with frightened faces in a watery insubstantial mist, saying things to him he couldn't seem to hear.

"Aaaaaaah!" he cried, understanding.

He was hardly conscious of the pain, intent only on Meggie's arms around him, the way his head sank against her. But he managed to turn until he could see her eyes, and looked at her. He tried to say, Forgive me, and saw she had forgiven him long ago. She knew she had got the best of it. Then he wanted to say something so perfect she would be eternally consoled, and realized that wasn't necessary, either. Whatever she was, she could bear anything. *Anything!* So he closed his eyes and let himself feel, that last time, forgetfulness in Meggie.

SEVEN

1965-1969 Justine

19

Sitting at his Bonn desk with an early-morning cup of coffee, Rainer learned of Cardinal de Bricassart's death from his newspaper. The political storm of the past few weeks was diminishing at last, so he had settled to enjoy his reading with the prospect of soon seeing Justine to color his mood, and unperturbed by her recent silence. That he deemed typical; she was far from ready yet to admit the extent of her commitment to him.

But the news of the Cardinal's death drove all thought of Justine away. Ten minutes later he was behind the wheel of a Mercedes 280 SL, heading for the autobahn. The poor old man Vittorio would be so alone, and his burden was heavy at the best of times. Quicker to drive; by the time he fiddled around waiting for a flight, got to and from airports, he could be at the Vatican. And it was something positive to do, something he could control himself, always an important consideration to a man like him.

From Cardinal Vittorio he learned the whole story, too shocked at first to wonder why Justine hadn't thought to contact him.

"He came to me and asked me, did I know Dane was his son?" the gentle voice said, while the gentle hands smoothed the blue-grey back of Natasha.

"And you said?"

"I said I had guessed. I could not tell him more. But oh, his face! His face! I wept."

"It killed him, of course. The last time I saw him I thought he wasn't well, but he laughed at my suggestion that he see a doctor."

"It is as God wills. I think Ralph de Bricassart was one of the most tormented men I have ever known. In death he will find the peace he could not find here in this life."

"The boy, Vittorio! A tragedy."

"Do you think so? I like rather to think of it as beautiful. I cannot believe Dane found death anything but welcome, and it is not surprising that Our Dear Lord could not wait a moment longer to gather Dane unto Himself. I mourn, yes, not for the boy. For his mother, who must suffer so much! And for his sister, his uncles, his grandmother. No, I do not mourn for him. Father O'Neill lived in almost total purity of mind and spirit. What could death be for him but the entrance into everlasting life? For the rest of us, the passage is not so easy."

From his hotel Rainer dispatched a cable to London which he couldn't allow to convey his anger, hurt or disappointment. It merely said: MUST RETURN BONN BUT WILL BE IN LONDON WEEKEND STOP WHY DIDN'T YOU TELL ME QUERY ALL MY LOVE RAIN

On his desk in the office at Bonn were an express delivery letter from Justine, and a registered packet which his secretary informed him had come from Cardinal de Bricassart's lawyers in Rome. He opened this first, to learn that under the terms of Ralph de Bricassart's will he was to add another company to his already formidable list of directorships. Michar Limited. And Drogheda. Exasperated yet curiously touched, he understood that this was the Cardinal's way of telling him that in the final weighing he had not been found wanting, that those prayers during the war years had borne fruit. Into Rainer's hands he had delivered the future welfare of Meggie O'Neill and her people. Or so Rainer interpreted it, for the wording of the Cardinal's will was quite impersonal. It could not dare be otherwise.

He threw the packet into the basket for general non-secret correspondence, immediate reply, and opened the letter from Justine. It began badly, without any kind of salutation.

> Thank you for the cable. You've no idea how glad I am that we haven't been in touch these last couple of weeks, because I would have hated to have you around. At the time all I could think when I thought of you was, thank God you didn't know. You may find this hard to understand, but I don't want you anywhere near me. There is nothing pretty about grief, Rain, nor any way your witnessing mine could alleviate it. Indeed, you might say this has proved to me how little I love you. If I did truly love you I'd turn to you instinctively, wouldn't I? But I find myself turning away.
>
> Therefore I would much rather that we call it quits for good and all, Rain. I have nothing to give you, and I want nothing from you. This has taught me how much people mean if they're around for twenty-six years. I couldn't bear ever to go through this again, and you said it yourself, remember? Marriage or nothing. Well, I elect nothing.
>
> My mother tells me the old Cardinal died a few hours after I left Drogheda. Funny. Mum was quite cut up about his dying. Not that she said anything, but I know her. Beats me why she and Dane and you liked him so much. I never could, I thought he was too smarmy for words. An opinion I'm not prepared to change just because he's dead.

And that's it. All there is. I do mean what I say, Rain. Nothing is what I elect to have from you. Look after yourself.

She had signed it with the usual bold, black "Justine," and it was written with the new felt-tipped pen she had hailed so gleefully when he gave it to her, as an instrument thick and dark and positive enough to satisfy her.

He didn't fold the note and put it in his wallet, or burn it; he did what he did with all mail not requiring an answer—ran it through the electric shredder fixed to his wastebasket the minute he had finished reading it. Thinking to himself that Dane's death had effectively put an end to Justine's emotional awakening, and bitterly unhappy. It wasn't fair. He had waited so long.

At the weekend he flew to London anyway but not to see her, though he did see her. On the stage, as the Moor's beloved wife, Desdemona. Formidable. There was nothing he could do for her the stage couldn't, not for a while. *That's my good girl!* Pour it all out on the stage.

Only she couldn't pour it all out on the stage, for she was too young to play Hecuba. The stage was simply the one place offering peace and forgetfulness. She could only tell herself: Time heals all wounds—while not believing it. Asking herself why it should go on hurting so. When Dane was alive she hadn't really thought very much about him except when she was with him, and after they were grown up their time together had been limited, their vocations almost opposed. But his going had created a gap so huge she despaired of ever filling it.

The shock of having to pull herself up in the midst of a spontaneous reaction—I must remember to tell Dane about this, he'll get such a kick out of it—that was what hurt the most. And because it kept on occurring so often, it prolonged the grief. Had the circumstances surrounding his death been less horrifying she might have recovered more quickly, but the nightmare events of those few days remained vivid. She missed him unbearably; her mind would return again and again to the incredible fact of Dane dead, Dane who would never come back.

Then there was the conviction that she hadn't helped him enough. Everyone save her seemed to think he was perfect, didn't experience the troubles other men did, but Justine knew he had been plagued by doubts, had tormented himself with his own unworthiness, had wondered what people could see in him beyond the face and the body. Poor Dane, who never seemed to understand that people loved his goodness. Terrible to remember it was too late to help him now.

She also grieved for her mother. If his dying could do this to her, what must it have done to Mum? The thought made her want to run screaming and crying from memory, consciousness. The picture of the Unks in Rome for his ordination, puffing out their proud chests like pouter pigeons. That was the worst of all, visualizing the empty desolation of her mother and the other Drogheda people.

Be honest, Justine. Was this honestly the worst? Wasn't there something far more disturbing? She couldn't push the thought of Rain away, or what she felt as her betrayal of Dane. To gratify her own desires she had sent Dane to Greece alone, when to have gone with him might have meant life for him. There was no other way to see it. Dane had died because of her selfish absorption in Rain. Too late now to bring her brother back, but if in never seeing Rain again she could somehow atone, the hunger and the loneliness would be well worth it.

So the weeks went by, and then the months. A year, two years. Desdemona, Ophelia, Portia, Cleopatra. From the very beginning she flattered herself she behaved outwardly as if nothing had happened to ruin her world; she took exquisite care in speaking, laughing, relating to people quite normally. If there was a change, it was in that she was kinder than of yore, for people's griefs tended to affect her as if they were her own. But, all told, she was the same outward Justine—flippant, exuberant, brash, detached, acerbic.

Twice she tried to go home to Drogheda on a visit, the second time even going so far as to pay for her plane ticket. Each time an enormously important last-minute reason why she couldn't go cropped up, but she knew the real reason to be a combination of guilt and cowardice. She just wasn't able to nerve herself to confront her mother; to do so meant the whole sorry tale would come out, probably in the midst of a noisy storm of grief she had so far managed to avoid. The Drogheda people, especially her mother, must continue to go about secure in their conviction that Justine at any rate was all right, that Justine had survived it relatively unscathed. So, better to stay away from Drogheda. Much better.

Meggie caught herself on a sigh, suppressed it. If her bones didn't ache so much she might have saddled a horse and ridden, but today the mere thought of it was painful. Some other time, when her arthritis didn't make its presence felt so cruelly.

She heard a car, the thump of the brass ram's head on the front door, heard voices murmuring, her mother's tones, footsteps. Not Justine, so what did it matter?

"Meggie," said Fee from the veranda entrance, "we have a visitor. Could you come inside, please?"

The visitor was a distinguished-looking fellow in early middle age, though he might have been younger than he appeared. Very different from any man she had ever seen, except that he possessed the same sort of power and self-confidence Ralph used to have. *Used to have.* That most final of tenses, now truly final.

"Meggie, this is Mr. Rainer Hartheim," said Fee, standing beside her chair.

"Oh!" exclaimed Meggie involuntarily, very surprised at the look of the Rain who had figured so largely in Justine's letters from the old days. Then, remembering her manners, "Do sit down, Mr. Hartheim."

He too was staring, startled. "You're not a bit like Justine!" he said rather blankly.

"No, I'm not." She sat down facing him.

"I'll leave you alone with Mr. Hartheim, Meggie, as he says he wants to see you privately. When you're ready for tea you might ring," Fee commanded, and departed.

"You're Justine's German friend, of course," said Meggie, at a loss.

He pulled out his cigarette case. "May I?"

"Please do."

"Would you care for one, Mrs. O'Neill?"

"Thank you, no. I don't smoke." She smoothed her dress. "You're a long way from home, Mr. Hartheim. Have you business in Australia?"

He smiled, wondering what she would say if she knew that he was, in effect, the master of Drogheda. But he had no intention of telling her, for he preferred all the Drogheda people to think their welfare lay in the completely impersonal hands of the gentleman he employed to act as his go-between.

"Please, Mrs. O'Neill, my name is Rainer," he said, giving it the same pronunciation Justine did, while thinking wryly that this woman wouldn't use it spontaneously for some time to come; she was not one to relax with strangers. "No, I don't have any official business in Australia, but I do have a good reason for coming. I wanted to see you."

"To see *me?*" she asked in surprise. As if to cover sudden confusion, she went immediately to a safer subject: "My brothers speak of you often. You were very kind to them while they were in Rome for Dane's ordination." She said Dane's name without distress, as if she used it frequently. "I hope you can stay a few days, and see them."

"I can, Mrs. O'Neill," he answered easily.

For Meggie the interview was proving unexpectedly awkward; he was a stranger, he had announced that he had come twelve thousand miles simply to see her, and apparently he was in no hurry to enlighten her as to why. She thought she would end in liking him, but she found him slightly intimidating. Perhaps his kind of man had never come within her ken before, and this was why he threw her off-balance. A very novel conception of Justine entered her mind at that moment: her daughter could actually relate easily to men like Rainer Moerling Hartheim! She thought of Justine as a fellow woman at last.

Though aging and white-haired she was still very beautiful, he was thinking while she sat gazing at him politely; he was still surprised that she looked not at all like Justine, as Dane had so strongly resembled the Cardinal. How terribly lonely she must be! Yet he couldn't feel sorry for her in the way he did for Justine; clearly, she had come to terms with herself.

"How is Justine?" she asked.

He shrugged. "I'm afraid I don't know. I haven't seen her since before Dane died."

She didn't display astonishment. "I haven't seen her myself since Dane's funeral," she said, and sighed. "I'd hoped she would come home, but it begins to look as if she never will."

He made a soothing noise which she didn't seem to hear, for she went on speaking, but in a different voice, more to herself than to him.

"Drogheda is like a home for the aged these days," she said. "We need young blood, and Justine's is the only young blood left."

Pity deserted him; he leaned forward quickly, eyes glittering. "You speak of her as if she is a chattel of

Drogheda," he said, his voice now harsh. "I serve you notice, Mrs. O'Neill, she is *not!*"

"What right have you to judge what Justine is or isn't?" she asked angrily. "After all, you said yourself that you haven't seen her since before Dane died, and that's two years ago!"

"Yes, you're right. It's all of two years ago." He spoke more gently, realizing afresh what her life must be like. "You bear it very well, Mrs. O'Neill."

"Do I?" she asked, tightly trying to smile, her eyes never leaving his.

Suddenly he began to understand what the Cardinal must have seen in her to have loved her so much. It wasn't in Justine, but then he himself was no Cardinal Ralph; he looked for different things.

"Yes, you bear it very well," he repeated.

She caught the undertone at once, and flinched. "How do you know about Dane and Ralph?" she asked unsteadily.

"I guessed. Don't worry, Mrs. O'Neill, nobody else did. I guessed because I knew the Cardinal long before I met Dane. In Rome everyone thought the Cardinal was your brother, Dane's uncle, but Justine disillusioned me about that the first time I ever met her."

"Justine? Not Justine!" Meggie cried.

He reached out to take her hand, beating frantically against her knee. "No, no, *no,* Mrs. O'Neill! Justine has absolutely no idea of it, and I pray she never will! Her slip was quite unintentional, believe me."

"You're sure?"

"Yes, I swear it."

"Then in God's Name why doesn't she come home? Why won't she come to see me? Why can't she bring herself to look at my face?"

Not only her words but the agony in her voice told him what had tormented Justine's mother about her absence these last two years. His own mission's importance dwindled; now he had a new one, to allay Meggie's fears.

"For that *I* am to blame," he said firmly.

"You?" asked Meggie, bewildered.

"Justine had planned to go to Greece with Dane, and she's convinced that had she, he'd still be alive."

"Nonsense!" said Meggie.

"Quite. But though we know it's nonsense, Justine doesn't. It's up to *you* to make her see it."

"Up to me? You don't understand, Mr. Hartheim. Justine has never listened to me in all her life, and at this stage any influence I might once have had is completely gone. She doesn't even want to see my face."

Her tone was defeated but not abject. "I fell into the same trap my mother did," she went on matter-of-factly. "Drogheda is my life . . . the house, the books. . . . Here I'm needed, there's still some purpose in living. Here are people who rely on me. My children never did, you know. Never did."

"That's not true, Mrs. O'Neill. If it was, Justine could come home to you without a qualm. You underestimate the quality of the love she bears you. When I say I am to blame for what Justine is going through, I mean that she remained in London because of me, to be with me. But it is for you she suffers, not for me."

Meggie stiffened. "She has no right to suffer for me! Let her suffer for herself if she must, but not for *me*. Never for *me!*"

"Then you believe me when I say she has no idea of Dane and the Cardinal?"

Her manner changed, as if he had reminded her there were other things at stake, and she was losing sight of them. "Yes," she said, "I believe you."

"I came to see you because Justine needs your help and cannot ask for it," he announced. "You must convince her she needs to take up the threads of her life again—not a Drogheda life, but her own life, which has nothing to do with Drogheda."

He leaned back in his chair, crossed his legs and lit another cigarette. "Justine has donned some kind of hair shirt, but for all the wrong reasons. If anyone can make her see it, you can. Yet I warn you that if you choose to do so she will never come home, whereas if she goes on the way she is, she may well end up returning here permanently.

"The stage isn't enough for someone like Justine," he went on, "and the day is coming when she's going to realize that. Then she's going to opt for people—either her family and Drogheda, or me." He smiled at her with deep understanding. "But people are not enough for Justine either, Mrs. O'Neill. If Justine chooses me, she can have the stage as well, and that bonus Drogheda cannot offer her." Now he was gazing at her sternly, as if at an adversary. "I came to ask you to make sure she chooses me. It may seem cruel to say this, but I need her more than you possibly could."

The starch was back in Meggie. "Drogheda isn't such a bad choice," she countered. "You speak as if it would be the end of her life, but it doesn't mean that at all, you know. She could have the stage. This is a true community. Even if she married Boy King, as his grandfather and I have hoped for years, her children would be as well cared for in her absences as they would be were she married to you. This is her *home!* She knows and understands this kind of life. If she chose it, she'd certainly be very well aware what was involved. Can you say the same for the sort of life you'd offer her?"

"No," he said stolidly. "But Justine thrives on surprises. On Drogheda she'd stagnate."

"What you mean is, she'd be unhappy here."

"No, not exactly. I have no doubt that if she elected to return here, married this Boy King—who *is* this Boy King, by the way?"

"The heir to a neighboring property, Bugela, and an old childhood friend who would like to be more than a friend. His grandfather wants the marriage for dynastic reasons; I want it because I think it's what Justine needs."

"I see. Well, if she returned here and married Boy King, she'd learn to be happy. But happiness is a relative state. I don't think she would ever know the kind of satisfaction she would find with me. Because, Mrs. O'Neill, Justine loves me, not Boy King."

"Then she's got a very strange way of showing it," said Meggie, pulling the bell rope for tea. "Besides, Mr. Hartheim, as I said earlier, I think you overestimate my influence with her. Justine has never taken a scrap of notice of anything I say, let alone want."

"You're nobody's fool," he answered. "You know you can do it if you want to. I can ask no more than that you think about what I've said. Take your time, there's no hurry. I'm a patient man."

Meggie smiled. "Then you're a rarity," she said.

He didn't broach the subject again, nor did she. During the week of his stay he behaved like any other guest, though Meggie had a feeling he was trying to show her what kind of man he was. How much her brothers liked him was clear; from the moment word reached the paddocks of his arrival, they all came in and stayed in until he left for Germany.

Fee liked him, too; her eyes had deteriorated to the point where she could no longer keep the books, but she was far from senile. Mrs. Smith had died in her sleep the previous winter, not before her due time, and rather than inflict a new housekeeper on Minnie and Cat, both old but still hale, Fee had passed the books completely to Meggie and more or less filled Mrs. Smith's place herself. It was Fee who first realized Rainer was a direct link with that part of Dane's life no one on Drogheda had ever had opportunity to share, so she asked him to speak of it. He obliged gladly, having quickly noticed that none of the Drogheda people were at all reluctant to talk of Dane, and derived great pleasure from listening to new tales about him.

Behind her mask of politeness Meggie couldn't get away from what Rain had told her, couldn't stop dwelling on the choice he had offered her. She had long since given up hope of Justine's return, only to have him almost guarantee it, admit too that Justine would be happy if she did return. Also, for one other thing she had to be intensely grateful to him: he had laid the ghost of her fear that somehow Justine had discovered the link between Dane and Ralph.

As for marriage to Rain, Meggie didn't see what she could do to push Justine where apparently she had no desire to go. Or was it that she didn't want to see? She had ended in liking Rain very much, but his happiness couldn't possibly matter as much to her as the welfare of her daughter, of the Drogheda people, and of Drogheda itself. The crucial question was, how vital to Justine's future happiness was Rain? In spite of his contention that Justine loved him, Meggie couldn't remember her daughter ever saying anything which might indicate that Rain held the same sort of importance for her as Ralph had done for Meggie.

"I presume you will see Justine sooner or later," Meggie said to Rain when she drove him to the airport. "When you do, I'd rather you didn't mention this visit to Drogheda."

"If you prefer," he said. "I would only ask you to think about what I've said, and take your time." But even as he made his request, he couldn't help feeling that Meggie had reaped far more benefit from his visit than he had.

When the mid-April came that was two and a half years after Dane's death, Justine experienced an overwhelming desire to see something that wasn't rows of houses, too many sullen people. Suddenly on this beautiful day of soft spring air and chilly sun, urban London was intolerable. So she took a District Line train to Kew Gardens, pleased that it was a Tuesday and she would have the place almost to herself. Nor was she working that night, so it didn't matter if she exhausted herself tramping the byways.

She knew the park well, of course. London was a joy to any Drogheda person, with its masses of formal flower beds, but Kew was in a class all its own. In the old days she used to haunt it from April to the end of October, for every month had a different floral display to offer.

Mid-April was her favorite time, the period of daffodils and azaleas and flowering trees. There was one spot she thought could lay some claim to being one of the world's loveliest sights on a small, intimate scale, so she sat down on the damp ground, an audience of one, to drink it in. As far as the eye could see stretched a sheet of daffodils; in mid-distance the nodding yellow horde of bells flowed around a great flowering almond, its branches so heavy with white blooms they dipped downward in arching falls as perfect and still as a Japanese painting. Peace. It was so hard to come by.

And then, her head far back to memorize the absolute beauty of the laden almond amid its rippling golden sea, something far less beautiful intruded. Rainer Moerling Hartheim, of all people, threading his careful way through clumps of daffodils, his bulk shielded from the chilly breeze by the inevitable German leather coat, the sun glittering in his silvery hair.

"You'll get a cold in your kidneys," he said, taking off his coat and spreading it lining side up on the ground so they could sit on it.

"How did you find me here?" she asked, wriggling onto a brown satin corner.

"Mrs. Kelly told me you had gone to Kew. The rest was easy. I just walked until I found you."

"I suppose you think I ought to be falling all over you in gladness, tra-la?"

"Are you?"

"Same old Rain, answering a question with a question. No, I'm not glad to see you. I thought I'd managed to make you crawl up a hollow log permanently."

"It's hard to keep a good man up a hollow log permanently. How are you?"

"I'm all right."

"Have you licked your wounds enough?"

"No."

"Well, that's to be expected, I suppose. But I began to realize that once you had dismissed me you'd never again humble your pride to make the first move toward reconciliation. Whereas I, *Herzchen,* am wise enough to know that pride makes a very lonely bedfellow."

"Don't go getting any ideas about kicking it out to make room for yourself, Rain, because I'm warning you, I am not taking you on in that capacity."

"I don't want you in that capacity anymore."

The promptness of his answer irritated her, but she adopted a relieved air and said, "Honestly?"

"If I did, do you think I could have borne to keep away from you so long? You were a passing fancy in that way, but I still think of you as a dear friend, and miss you as a dear friend."

"Oh, Rain, so do I!"

"That's good. Am I admitted as a friend, then?"

"Of course."

He lay back on the coat and put his arms behind his head, smiling at her lazily. "How old are you, thirty? In those disgraceful clothes you look more like a scrubby schoolgirl. If you don't need me in your life for any other reason, Justine, you certainly do as your personal arbiter of elegance."

She laughed. "I admit when I thought you might pop up out of the woodwork I did take more interest in my appearance. If I'm thirty, though, you're no spring chook yourself. You must be forty at least. Doesn't seem like such a huge difference anymore, does it? You've lost weight. Are you all right, Rain?"

"I was never fat, only big, so sitting at a desk all the time has shrunk me, not made me expand."

Sliding down and turning onto her stomach, she put her face close to his, smiling. "Oh, Rain, it's so good to see you! No one else gives me a run for my money."

"Poor Justine! And you have so much of it these days, don't you?"

"Money?" She nodded. "Odd, that the Cardinal should have left all of his to me. Well, half to me and half to Dane, but of course I was Dane's sole legatee." Her face twisted in spite of herself. She ducked her head away and pretended to look at one daffodil in a sea of them until she could control her voice enough to say, "You know, Rain, I'd give my eyeteeth to learn just what the Cardinal was to my family. A friend, only that? More than that, in some mysterious way. But just what, I don't know. I wish I did."

"No, you don't." He got to his feet and extended his hand. "Come, *Herzchen,* I'll buy you dinner anywhere you think there will be eyes to see that the breach between the carrot-topped Australian actress and the certain member of the German cabinet is healed. My reputation as a playboy has deteriorated since you threw me out."

"You'll have to watch it, my friend. They don't call me a carrot-topped *Australian* actress any more—these days I'm that lush, gorgeous, titian-haired *British* actress, thanks to my immortal interpretation of Cleopatra. Don't tell me you didn't know the critics are calling me the most exotic Cleo in years?" She cocked her arms and hands into the pose of an Egyptian hieroglyph.

His eyes twinkled. "Exotic?" he asked doubtfully.

"Yes, exotic," she said firmly.

Cardinal Vittorio was dead, so Rain didn't go to Rome very much anymore. He came to London instead. At first Justine was so delighted she didn't look any further than the friendship he offered, but as the months passed and he failed by word or look to mention their previous relationship, her mild indignation became something more disturbing. Not that she wanted a resumption of that other relationship, she told herself constantly; she had finished completely with that sort of thing, didn't need or desire it anymore. Nor did she permit her mind to dwell on an image of Rain so successfully buried she remembered it only in traitorous dreams.

Those first few months after Dane died had been dreadful, resisting the longing to go to Rain, feel him with her in body and spirit, knowing full well he would be if she let him. But she could not allow this with his face overshadowed by Dane's. It was right to dismiss him, right to battle to obliterate every last flicker of desire for him. And as time went on and it seemed he was going to stay out of her life permanently, her body settled into unaroused torpor, and her mind disciplined itself to forget.

But now Rain was back it was growing much harder. She itched to ask him whether he remembered that other relationship—how *could* he have forgotten it? Certainly for herself she had quite finished with such things, but it would have been gratifying to learn he hadn't; that is, provided of course such things for him spelled Justine, and only Justine.

Pipe dreams. Rain didn't have the mien of a man who was wasting away of unrequited love, mental or physical, and he never displayed the slightest wish to reopen that phase of their lives. He wanted her for a friend, enjoyed her as a friend. Excellent! It was what she wanted, too. Only . . . *could* he have forgotten? No, it wasn't possible—but God damn him if he had!

The night Justine's thought processes reached so far, her season's role of Lady Macbeth had an interesting savagery quite alien to her usual interpretation. She didn't sleep very well afterward, and the following morning brought a letter from her mother which filled her with vague unease.

Mum didn't write often anymore, a symptom of the long separation which affected them both, and what letters there were were stilted, anemic. This was different, it contained a distant mutter of old age, an underlying weariness which poked up a word or two above the surface inanities like an iceberg. Justine didn't like it. Old. *Mum,* old!

What was happening on Drogheda? Was Mum trying to conceal some serious trouble? Was Nanna ill? One of the Unks? God forbid, Mum herself? It was three years since she had seen any of them, and a lot could happen in three years, even if it wasn't happening to Justine O'Neill. Because her own life was stagnant and dull, she ought not to assume everyone else's was, too.

That night was Justine's "off" night, with only one more performance of *Macbeth* to go. The daylight hours had dragged unbearably, and even the thought of dinner with Rain didn't carry its usual anticipatory pleasure. Their friendship was useless, futile, static, she told herself as she scrambled into a dress exactly the orange he hated most. Conservative old fuddy-duddy! If Rain didn't like her the way she was, he could lump her. Then, fluffing up the low bodice's frills around her meager chest, she caught her own eyes in the mirror and laughed ruefully. Oh, what a tempest in a teacup! She was acting exactly like the kind of female she most despised. It was probably very simple. She was stale, she needed a rest. Thank God for the end of Lady M! *But what was the matter with Mum?*

Lately Rain was spending more and more time in London, and Justine marveled at the ease with which he commuted between Bonn and England. No doubt having a private plane helped, but it had to be exhausting.

"Why *do* you come to see me so often?" she asked out of the blue. "Every gossip columnist in Europe thinks it's great, but I confess I sometimes wonder if you don't simply use me as an excuse to visit London."

"It's true that I use you as a blind from time to time," he admitted calmly. "As a matter of fact, you've been dust in certain eyes quite a lot. But it's no hardship being with you, because I like being with you." His dark eyes dwelled on her face thoughtfully. "You're very quiet tonight, *Herzchen.* Is anything worrying you?"

"No, not really." She toyed with her dessert and pushed it aside uneaten. "At least, only a silly little thing. Mum and I don't write every week anymore—it's so long since we've seen each other there's nothing much to say—but today I had such a strange letter from her. Not typical at all."

His heart sank; Meggie had indeed taken her time thinking about it, but instinct told him this was the commencement of her move, and that it was not in his favor. She was beginning her play to get her daughter back for Drogheda, perpetuate the dynasty.

He reached across the table to take Justine's hand; she was looking, he thought, more beautiful with maturity, in spite of that ghastly dress. Tiny lines were beginning to give her ragamuffin face dignity, which it badly needed, and character, which the person behind had always owned in huge quantities. But how deep did her surface maturity go? That was the whole trouble with Justine; she didn't even want to look.

"Herzchen, your mother is lonely," he said, burning his boats. If this was what Meggie wanted, how could he continue to think himself right and her wrong? Justine was her daughter; she must know her far better than he.

"Yes, perhaps," said Justine with a frown, "but I can't help feeling there's something more at base of it. I mean, she must have been lonely for years, so why this sudden whatever it is? I can't put my finger on it, Rain, and maybe that's what worries me the most."

"She's growing older, which I think you tend to forget. It's very possible things are beginning to prey upon her which she found easier to contend with in the past." His eyes looked suddenly remote, as if the brain behind was concentrating very hard on something at variance with what he was saying. "Justine, three years ago she lost her only son. Do you think that pain grows less as time passes? I think it must grow worse. He is gone, and she must surely feel by now that you are gone, too. After all, you haven't even been home to visit her."

She shut her eyes. "I will, Rain, I will! I promise I will, and soon! You're right, of course, but then you always are. I never thought I'd come to miss Drogheda, but lately I seem to be developing quite an affection for it. As if I am a part of it after all."

He looked suddenly at his watch, smiled ruefully. "I'm very much afraid tonight is one of those occasions when I've used you, *Herzchen*. I hate to ask you to find your own way home, but in less than an hour I have to meet some very important gentlemen in a top-secret place, to which I must go in my own car, driven by the triple-A-security-clearanced Fritz."

"Cloak and dagger!" she said gaily, concealing her hurt. "Now I know why those sudden taxis! *I* am to be entrusted to a cabby, but not the future of the Common Market, eh? Well, just to show you how little I need a taxi or your security-clearanced Fritz, I'm going to catch the tube home. It's quite early." His fingers lay rather limply around hers; she lifted his hand and held it against her cheek, then kissed it. "Oh, Rain, I don't know what I'd do without you!"

He put the hand in his pocket, got to his feet, came round and pulled out her chair with his other hand. "I'm your friend," he said. "That's what friends are for, not to be done without."

But once she parted from him, Justine went home in a very thoughtful mood, which turned rapidly into a depressed one. Tonight was the closest he had come to any kind of personal discussion, and the gist of it had been that he felt her mother was terribly lonely, growing old, and that she ought to go home. Visit, he had said; but she couldn't help wondering if he had actually meant stay. Which rather indicated that whatever he felt for her in the past was well and truly of the past, and he had no wish to resurrect it.

It had never occurred to her before to wonder if he might regard her as a nuisance, a part of his past he would like to see buried in decent obscurity on some place like Drogheda; but maybe he did. In which case, why had he re-entered her life nine months ago? Because he felt sorry for her? Because he felt he owed her some kind of debt? Because he felt she needed some sort of push toward her mother, for Dane's sake? He had been very fond of Dane, and who knew what they had talked about during those long visits to Rome when she hadn't been present? Maybe Dane had asked him to keep an eye on her, and he was doing just that. Waited a decent interval to make sure she wouldn't show him the door, then marched back into her life to fulfill some promise made to Dane. Yes, that was very likely the answer. Certainly he was no longer in love with her. Whatever attraction she had once possessed for him must have died long since; after all, she had treated him abominably. She had only herself to blame.

Upon the heels of which thought she wept miserably, succeeded in getting enough hold upon herself to tell herself not to be so stupid, twisted about and thumped her pillow in a fruitless quest after sleep, then lay defeated trying to read a script. After a few pages the words began traitorously to blur and swim together, and try as she would to use her old trick of bulldozing despair into some back corner of her mind, it ended in overwhelming her. Finally as the slovenly light of a late London dawn seeped through the windows she sat down at her desk, feeling the cold, hearing the distant growl of traffic, smelling the damp, tasting the sourness. Suddenly the idea of Drogheda seemed wonderful. Sweet pure air, a naturally broken silence. Peace.

She picked up one of her black felt-tipped pens and began a letter to her mother, her tears drying as she wrote.

I just hope you understand why I haven't been home since Dane died [she said], but no matter what you think about that, I know you'll be pleased to hear that I'm going to rectify my omission permanently.

Yes, that's right. I'm coming home for good, Mum. You were right—the time has come when I long for Drogheda. I've had my flutter, and I've discovered it doesn't mean anything to me at all. What's in it for me, trailing around a stage for the rest of my life? And what else is there here for me aside from the stage? I want something safe, permanent, enduring, so I'm coming home to Drogheda, which is all those things. No more empty dreams. Who knows? Maybe I'll marry Boy King if he still wants me, finally do something worthwhile with my life, like having a tribe of little Northwest plainsmen. I'm tired, Mum, so tired I don't know what I'm saying, and I wish I had the power to write what I'm feeling.

Well, I'll struggle with it another time. Lady Macbeth is over and I hadn't decided what to do with the coming season yet, so I won't inconvenience anyone by deciding to bow out of acting. London is teeming with actresses. Clyde can replace me adequately in two seconds, but you can't, can you? I'm sorry it's taken me thirty-one years to realize that.

Had Rain not helped me it might have taken even longer, but he's a most perceptive bloke. He's never met you, yet he seems to understand you better than I do. Still, they say the onlooker sees the game best. That's certainly true of him. I'm fed up with him, always supervising my life from his Olympian heights. He seems to think he owes Dane some sort of debt or promise, and he's forever making a nuisance of himself popping over to see me; only I've finally realized that *I'm* the nuisance. If I'm safely on Drogheda the debt or promise or whatever it was is canceled, isn't it? He ought to be grateful for the plane trips I'll save him, anyway.

As soon as I've got myself organized I'll write again, tell you when to expect me. In the meantime, remember that in my strange way I do love you.

She signed her name without its usual flourish, more like the "Justine" which used to appear on the bottom of dutiful letters written from boarding school under the eagle eye of a censoring nun. Then she folded the sheets, put them in an airmail envelope and addressed it. On the way to the theater for the final performance of *Macbeth* she posted it.

She went straight ahead with her plans to quit England. Clyde was upset to the extent of a screaming temper tantrum which left her shaking, then overnight he turned completely about and gave in with huffy good grace. There was no difficulty at all in disposing of the lease to the mews flat for it was in a high-demand category; in fact, once the word leaked out people rang every five minutes until she took the phone off the hook. Mrs. Kelly, who had "done" for her since those far-off days when she had first come to London, plodded dolefully around amid a jungle of wood shavings and crates, bemoaning her fate and surreptitiously putting the phone back on its cradle in the hope someone would ring with the power to persuade Justine to change her mind.

In the midst of the turmoil, someone with that power did ring, only not to persuade her to change her mind; Rain didn't even know she was going. He merely asked her to act as his hostess for a dinner party he was giving at his house on Park Lane.

"What do you mean, house on Park Lane?" Justine squeaked, astonished.

"Well, with growing British participation in the European Economic Community, I'm spending so much time in England that it's become more practical for me to have some sort of local *pied-à-terre,* so I've leased a house on Park Lane," he explained.

"Ye gods, Rain, you flaming secretive bastard! How long have you had it?"

"About a month."

"And you let me go through that idiotic charade the other night and said nothing? God damn you!" She was so angry she couldn't speak properly.

"I was going to tell you, but I got such a kick out of your thinking I was flying over all the time that I couldn't resist pretending a bit longer," he said with a laugh in his voice.

"I could kill you!" she ground from between her teeth, blinking away tears.

"No, *Herzchen,* please! Don't be angry! Come and be my hostess, then you can inspect the premises to your heart's content."

"Suitably chaperoned by five million other guests, of course! What's the matter, Rain, don't you trust yourself alone with me? Or is it me you don't trust?"

"You won't be a guest," he said, answering the first part of her tirade. "You'll be my hostess, which is quite different. Will you do it?"

She wiped the tears away with the back of her hand and said gruffly, "Yes."

It turned out to be more enjoyable than she had dared hope, for Rain's house was truly beautiful and he himself in such a good mood Justine couldn't help but become infected by it. She arrived properly though a little too flamboyantly gowned for his taste, but after an involuntary grimace at first sight of her shocking-pink slipper satin, he tucked her arm through his and conducted her around the premises before the guests arrived. Then during the evening he behaved perfectly, treating her in front of the others with an offhand intimacy which made her feel both useful and wanted. His guests were so politically important her brain didn't want to think about the sort of decisions they must have to make. Such *ordinary* people, too. That made it worse.

"I wouldn't have minded so much if even one of them had displayed symptoms of the Chosen Few," she said to him after they had gone, glad of the chance to be alone with him and wondering how quickly he was going to send her home. "You know, like Napoleon or Churchill. There's a lot to be said for being convinced one is a man of destiny, if one is a statesman. Do you regard yourself as a man of destiny?"

He winced. "You might choose your questions better when you're quizzing a German, Justine. No, I don't, and it isn't good for politicians to deem themselves men of destiny. It might work for a very few, though I doubt it, but the vast bulk of such men cause themselves and their countries endless trouble."

She had no desire to argue the point. It had served its purpose in getting a certain line of conversation started; she could change the subject without looking too obvious. "The wives were a pretty mixed bunch, weren't they?" she asked artlessly. "Most of them were far less presentable than I was, even if you don't approve of hot pink. Mrs. Whatsit wasn't too bad, and Mrs. Hoojar simply disappeared into the matching wallpaper, but Mrs. Gumfoozler was abominable. How does her husband manage to put up with her? Oh, men are such fools about choosing their wives!"

"Jus*tine!* When will you learn to remember names? It's as well you turned me down, a fine politician's wife you would have made. I heard you er-umming when you couldn't remember who they were. Many men with abominable wives have succeeded very well, and just as many with quite perfect wives haven't succeeded at all. In the long run it doesn't matter, because it's the caliber of the man which is put to the test. There are few men who marry for reasons purely politic."

That old ability to put her in her place could still shock; she made him a mock salaam to hide her face, then sat down on the rug.

"Oh, do get up, Justine!"

Instead she defiantly curled her feet under her and leaned against the wall to one side of the fireplace, stroking Natasha. She had discovered on her arrival that after Cardinal Vittorio's death Rain had taken his cat; he seemed very fond of it, though it was old and rather crotchety.

"Did I tell you I was going home to Drogheda for good?" she asked suddenly.

He was taking a cigarette out of his case; the big hands didn't falter or tremble, but proceeded smoothly with their task. "You know very well you didn't tell me," he said.

"Then I'm telling you now."

"When did you come to this decision?"

"Five days ago. I'm leaving at the end of this week, I hope. It can't come soon enough."

"I see."

"Is that all you've got to say about it?"

"What else is there to say, except that I wish you happiness in whatever you do?" He spoke with such complete composure she winced.

"Why, thank you!" she said airily. "Aren't you glad I won't be in your hair much longer?"

"You're not in my hair, Justine," he answered.

She abandoned Natasha, picked up the poker and began rather savagely nudging the crumbling logs, which had burned away to hollow shells; they collapsed inward in a brief flurry of sparks, and the heat of the fire abruptly decreased. "It must be the demon of destructiveness in us, the impulse to poke the guts out of a fire. It only hastens the end. But what a beautiful end, isn't it, Rain?"

Apparently he wasn't interested in what happened to fires when they were poked, for he merely asked, "By the end of the week, eh? You're not wasting much time."

"What's the point in delaying?"

"And your career?"

"I'm sick of my career. Anyway, after Lady Macbeth what is there left to do?"

"Oh, grow up, Justine! I could shake you when you come out with such sophomoric rot! Why not simply say you're not sure the theater has any challenge for you anymore, and that you're homesick?"

"All right, all right, *all right!* Have it any way you bloody well want! I was being my usual flippant self. Sorry I offended!" She jumped to her feet. "Dammit, where are my shoes? What's happened to my coat?"

Fritz appeared with both articles of clothing, and drove her home. Rain excused himself from accompanying her, saying he had things to do, but as she left he was sitting by the freshly built up fire, Natasha on his lap, looking anything but busy.

"Well," said Meggie to her mother, "I hope we've done the right thing."

Fee peered at her, nodded. "Oh, yes, I'm sure of it. The trouble with Justine is that she isn't capable of making a decision like this, so we don't have any choice. We must make it for her."

"I'm not sure I like playing God. I *think* I know what she really wants to do, but even if I could tax her with it face to face, she'd prevaricate."

"The Cleary pride," said Fee, smiling faintly. "It does crop up in the most unexpected people."

"Go on, it's not all Cleary pride! I've always fancied there was a little dash of Armstrong in it as well."

But Fee shook her head. "No. Whyever I did what I did, pride hardly entered into it. That's the purpose of old age, Meggie. To give us a breathing space before we die, in which to see why we did what we did."

"Provided senility doesn't render us incapable first," said Meggie dryly. "Not that there's any danger of that in you. Nor in me, I suppose."

"Maybe senility's a mercy shown to those who couldn't face retrospection. Anyway, you're not old enough yet to say you've avoided senility. Give it another twenty years."

"Another *twenty years!*" Meggie echoed, dismayed. "Oh, it sounds so long!"

"Well, you could have made those twenty years less lonely, couldn't you?" Fee asked, knitting industriously.

"Yes, I could. But it wouldn't have been worth it, Mum. Would it?" She tapped Justine's letter with the knob of one ancient knitting needle, the slightest trace of doubt in her tone. "I've dithered long enough. Sitting here ever since Rainer came, hoping I wouldn't need to do anything at all, hoping the decision wouldn't rest with me. Yet he was right. In the end, it's been for me to do."

"Well, you might concede I did a bit too," Fee protested, injured. "That is, once you surrendered enough of your pride to tell me all about it."

"Yes, you helped," said Meggie gently.

The old clock ticked; both pairs of hands continued to flash about the tortoise-shell stems of their needles.

"Tell me something, Mum," said Meggie suddenly. "Why did you break over Dane when you didn't over Daddy or Frank or Stu?"

"Break?" Fee's hands paused, laid down the needles: she could still knit as well as in the days when she could see perfectly. "How do you mean, break?"

"As though it killed you."

"They all killed me, Meggie. But I was younger for the first three, so I had the energy to conceal it better. More reason, too. Just like you now. But Ralph knew how I felt when Daddy and Stu died. You were too young to have seen it." She smiled. "I adored Ralph, you know. He was . . . someone special. Awfully like Dane."

"Yes, he was. I never realized you'd seen that, Mum—I mean their natures. Funny. You're a Darkest Africa to me. There are so many things about you I don't know."

"I should hope so!" said Fee with a snort of laughter. Her hands remained quiet. "Getting back to the original subject—if you can do this now for Justine, Meggie, I'd say you've gained more from your troubles than I did from mine. I wasn't willing to do as Ralph asked and look out for you. I wanted my memories . . . nothing but my memories. Whereas you've no choice. Memories are all you've got."

"Well, they're a comfort, once the pain dies down. Don't you think so? I had twenty-six whole years of Dane, and I've learned to tell myself that what happened *must* be for the best, that he must have been spared some awful ordeal he might not have been strong enough to endure. Like Frank, perhaps, only not the same. There are worse things than dying, we both know that."

"Aren't you bitter at all?" asked Fee.

"Oh, at first I was, but for their sakes I've taught myself not to be."

Fee resumed her knitting. "So when we go, there will be no one," she said softly. "Drogheda will be no more. Oh, they'll give it a line in the history books, and some earnest young man will come to Gilly to interview anyone he can find who remembers, for the book he's going to write about Drogheda. Last of the mighty New South Wales stations. But none of his readers will ever know what it was really like, because they couldn't. They'd have to have been a part of it."

"Yes," said Meggie, who hadn't stopped knitting. "They'd have to have been a part of it."

Saying goodbye to Rain in a letter, devastated by grief and shock, had been easy; in fact enjoyable in a cruel way, for she had lashed back then—I'm in agony, so ought you to be. But this time Rain hadn't put himself in a position where a Dear John letter was possible. It had to be dinner at their favorite restaurant. He hadn't suggested his Park Lane house, which disappointed but didn't surprise her. No doubt he intended saying even his final goodbyes under the benign gaze of Fritz. Certainly he wasn't taking any chances.

For once in her life she took care that her appearance should please him; the imp which usually prodded her into orange frills seemed to have retired cursing. Since Rain liked unadorned styles, she put on a floor-length silk jersey dress of dull burgundy red, high to the neck, long tight sleeves. She added a big flat collar of tortuous gold studded with garnets and pearls, and matching bracelets on each wrist. What horrible, horrible hair. It was never disciplined enough to suit him. More makeup than normal, to conceal the evidence of her depression. There. She would do if he didn't look too closely.

He didn't seem to; at least he didn't comment upon weariness or possible illness, even made no reference to the exigencies of packing. Which wasn't a bit like him. And after a while she began to experience a sensation that the world must be ending, so different was he from his usual self.

He wouldn't help her make the dinner a success, the sort of affair they could refer to in letters with reminiscent pleasure and amusement. If she could only have persuaded herself that he was simply upset at her going, it might have been all right. But she couldn't. His mood just wasn't that sort. Rather, he was so distant she felt as if she were sitting with a paper effigy, one-dimensional and anxious to be off floating in the breeze, far from her ken. As if he had said goodbye to her already, and this meeting was a superfluity.

"Have you had a letter from your mother yet?" he asked politely.

"No, but I don't honestly expect one. She's probably bereft of words."

"Would you like Fritz to take you to the airport tomorrow?"

"Thanks, I can catch a cab," she answered ungraciously. "I wouldn't want you to be deprived of his services."

"I have meetings all day, so I assure you it won't inconvenience me in the slightest."

"I *said* I'd take a cab!"

He raised his eyebrows. "There's no need to shout, Justine. Whatever you want is all right with me."

He wasn't calling her *Herzchen* any more; of late she had noticed its frequency declining, and tonight he had not used the old endearment once. Oh, what a dismal, depressing dinner this was! Let it be over soon! She found she was looking at his hands and trying to remember what they felt like, but she couldn't. Why wasn't life neat and well organized, why did things like Dane have to happen? Perhaps because she thought of Dane, her mood suddenly plummeted to a point where she couldn't bear to sit still a moment longer, and put her hands on the arms of her chair.

"Do you mind if we go?" she asked. "I'm developing a splitting headache."

At the junction of the High Road and Justine's little mews Rain helped her from the car, told Fritz to drive around the block, and put his hand beneath her elbow courteously to guide her, his touch quite impersonal. In the freezing damp of a London drizzle they walked slowly across the cobbles, dripping echoes of their footsteps all around them. Mournful, lonely footsteps.

"So, Justine, we say goodbye," he said.

"Well, for the time being, at any rate," she answered brightly, "but it's not forever, you know. I'll be across from time to time, and I hope you'll find the time to come down to Drogheda."

He shook his head. "No. This is goodbye, Justine. I don't think we have any further use for each other."

"You mean you haven't any further use for me," she said, and managed a fairly creditable laugh. "It's all right, Rain! Don't spare me, I can take it!"

He took her hand, bent to kiss it, straightened, smiled into her eyes and walked away.

There was a letter from her mother on the mat. Justine stooped to pick it up, dropped her bag and wrap where it had lain, her shoes nearby, and went into the living room. She sat down heavily on a packing crate, chewing at her lip, her eyes resting for a moment in wondering, bewildered pity on a magnificent head-and-shoulders study of Dane taken to commemorate his ordination. Then she caught her bare toes in the act of caressing the rolled-up kangaroo-fur rug, grimaced in distaste and got up quickly.

A short walk to the kitchen, that was what she needed. So she took a short walk to the kitchen, where she opened the refrigerator, reached for the cream jug, opened the freezer door and withdrew a can of filter coffee. With one hand on the cold-water tap to run water for her coffee, she looked around wide-eyed, as if she had never seen the room before. Looked at the flaws in the wallpaper, at the smug philodendron in its basket hung from the ceiling, at the black pussy-cat clock wagging its tail and rolling its eyes at the spectacle of time being so frivolously frittered away. PACK HAIRBRUSH, said the blackboard in large capitals. On the table lay a pencil sketch of Rain she had done some weeks ago. And a packet of cigarettes. She took one and lit it, put the kettle on the stove and remembered her mother's letter, which was still screwed up in one hand. May as well read it while the water heated. She sat down at the kitchen table, flipped the drawing of Rain onto the floor and planted her feet on top of it. Up yours, too, Rainer Moerling Hartheim! See if I care, you great dogmatic leather-coated Kraut twit. Got no further use for me, eh? Well, nor have I for you!

My dear Justine [said Meggie]
No doubt you're proceeding with your usual impulsive speed, so I hope this reaches you in time. If anything I've said lately in my letters has caused this sudden decision of yours, please forgive me. I didn't mean to provoke such a drastic reaction. I suppose I was simply looking for a bit of sympathy, but I always forget that under that tough skin of yours, you're pretty soft.

Yes, I'm lonely, terribly so. Yet it isn't anything your coming home could possibly rectify. If you stop to think for a moment, you'll see how true that is. What do you hope to accomplish by coming home? It isn't within your power to restore to me what I've lost, and you can't make reparation either. Nor is it purely *my* loss. It's your loss too, and Nanna's, and all the rest. You seem to have an idea, and it's quite a mistaken idea, that in some way you were responsible. This present impulse looks to me suspiciously like an act of contrition. That's pride and presumption, Justine. Dane was a grown man, not a helpless baby. *I* let him go, didn't I? If I had let myself feel the way you do, I'd be sitting here blaming myself into a mental asylum because I had permitted him to live his own life. But I'm not sitting here blaming myself. We're none of us God, though I think I've had more chance to learn that than you.

In coming home, you're handing me your life like

a sacrifice. *I don't want it.* I never have wanted it. And I refuse it now. You don't belong on Drogheda, you never did. If you still haven't worked out where you do belong, I suggest you sit down right this minute and start some serious thinking. Sometimes you really are awfully dense. Rainer is a very nice man, but I've never yet met a man who could possibly be as altruistic as you seem to think he is. For Dane's sake indeed! Do grow up, Justine!

My dearest one, a light has gone out. For *all* of us, a light has gone out. And there's absolutely nothing you can do about it, don't you understand? I'm not insulting you by trying to pretend I'm perfectly happy. Such isn't the human condition. But if you think we here on Drogheda spend our days weeping and wailing, you're quite wrong. We enjoy our days, and one of the main reasons why is that our lights for you still burn. Dane's light is gone forever. Please, dear Justine, try to accept that.

Come home to Drogheda by all means, we'd love to see you. But not for good. You'd never be happy settled here permanently. It is not only a needless sacrifice for you to make, but a useless one. In your sort of career, even a year spent away from it would cost you dearly. So stay where you belong, be a good citizen of your world.

The pain. It was like those first few days after Dane died. The same sort of futile, wasted, unavoidable pain. The same anguished impotence. No, of course there was nothing she could do. No way of making up, no way.

Scream! The kettle was whistling already. Hush, kettle, hush! Hush for Mummy! How does it feel to be Mummy's only child, kettle? Ask Justine, *she* knows. Yes, Justine knows all about being the only child. But

I'm not the child she wants, that poor fading old woman back on the ranch. Oh, Mum! Oh, Mum . . . Do you think if I humanly could, I wouldn't? New lamps for old, my life for his! It isn't fair, that Dane was the one to die. . . . She's right. My going back to Drogheda can't alter the fact that *he* never can. Though he lies there forever, he never can. A light has gone out, and I can't rekindle it. But I see what she means. My light still burns in her. Only not on Drogheda.

Fritz answered the door, not clad in his smart navy chauffeur's uniform, clad in his smart butler's morning suit instead. But as he smiled, bowed stiffly and clicked his heels in good old-fashioned German manner, a thought occurred to Justine; did he do double duty in Bonn, too?

"Are you simply Herr Hartheim's humble servant, Fritz, or are you really his watchdog?" she asked, handing him her coat.

Fritz remained impassive. "Herr Hartheim is in his study, Miss O'Neill."

He was sitting looking at the fire, leaning a little forward, Natasha curled sleeping on the hearth. When the door opened he looked up, but didn't speak, didn't seem glad to see her.

So Justine crossed the room, knelt, and laid her forehead on his lap. "Rain, I'm so sorry for all the years, and I can't atone," she whispered.

He didn't rise to his feet, draw her up with him; he knelt beside her on the floor.

"A miracle," he said.

She smiled at him. "You never did stop loving me, did you?"

"No, *Herzchen,* never."

"I must have hurt you very much."

"Not in the way you think. I knew you loved me, and I could wait. I've always believed a patient man must win in the end."

"So you decided to let me work it out for myself. You weren't a bit worried when I announced I was going home to Drogheda, were you?"

"Oh, yes. Had it been another man I would not have been perturbed, but Drogheda? A formidable opponent. Yes, I worried."

"You knew I was going before I told you, didn't you?"

"Clyde let the cat out of the bag. He rang Bonn to ask me if there was any way I could stop you, so I told him to play along with you for a week or two at any rate, and I'd see what I could do. Not for his sake, *Herzchen*. For my own. I'm no altruist."

"That's what Mum said. But this house! Did you have it a month ago?"

"No, nor is it mine. However, since we will need a London house if you're to continue with your career, I'd better see what I can do to acquire it. That is, provided you like it. I'll even let you have the redecorating of it, if you promise faithfully not to deck it out in pink and orange."

"I've never realized quite how devious you are. Why didn't you just say you still loved me? I wanted you to!"

"No. The evidence was there for you to see it for yourself, and you had to see if for yourself."

"I'm afraid I'm chronically blind. I didn't really see for myself, I had to have some help. My mother finally forced me to open my eyes. I had a letter from her tonight, telling me not to come home."

"She's a marvelous person, your mother."

"I know you've met her, Rain—when?"

"I went to see her about a year ago. Drogheda is magnificent, but it isn't you, *Herzchen*. At the time I went to try to make your mother see that. You've no idea how glad I am she has, though I don't think anything I said was very enlightening."

She put her fingers up to touch his mouth. "I doubted myself, Rain. I always have. Maybe I always will."

"Oh, *Herzchen,* I hope not! For me there can never be anyone else. Only you. The whole world has known it for years. But words of love mean nothing. I could have screamed them at you a thousand times a day without affecting your doubts in the slightest. So I haven't spoken my love, Justine, I've lived it. How could you doubt the feelings of your most faithful gallant?" He sighed. "Well, at least it hasn't come from me. Perhaps you'll continue to find your mother's word good enough."

"Please don't say it like that! Poor Rain, I think I've worn even your patience to a thread. Don't be hurt that it came from Mum. It doesn't *matter!* I've knelt in abasement at your feet!"

"Thank God the abasement will only last for tonight," he said more cheerfully. "You'll bounce back tomorrow."

The tension began to leave her; the worst of it was over. "What I like—no, *love*—about you the most is that you give me such a good run for my money I never do quite catch up."

His shoulders shook. "Then look at the future this way, *Herzchen.* Living in the same house with me might afford you the opportunity to see how it can be done." He kissed her brows, her cheeks, her eyelids. "I would have you no other way than the way you are, Justine. Not a freckle of your face or a cell of your brain."

She slid her arms around his neck, sank her fingers into that satisfying hair. "Oh, if you knew how I've longed to do this!" she said. "I've never been able to forget."

The cable said: HAVE JUST BECOME MRS RAINER MOERLING HARTHEIM STOP PRIVATE CEREMONY THE VATICAN STOP PAPAL BLESSINGS ALL OVER THE PLACE STOP THAT IS DEFINITELY BEING MARRIED EXCLAMATION WE WILL BE DOWN ON A DELAYED HONEYMOON AS SOON AS POSSIBLE BUT EUROPE IS GOING TO BE

HOME STOP LOVE TO ALL AND FROM RAIN TOO STOP JUSTINE

Meggie put the form down on the table and stared wide-eyed through the window at the wealth of autumn roses in the garden. Perfume of roses, bees of roses. And the hibiscus, the bottlebrush, the ghost gums, the bougainvillaea up above the world so high, the pepper trees. How beautiful the garden was, how alive. To see its small things grow big, change, and wither; and new little things come again in the same endless, unceasing cycle.

Time for Drogheda to stop. Yes, more than time. Let the cycle renew itself with unknown people. I did it all to myself, I have no one else to blame. And I cannot regret one single moment of it.

The bird with the thorn in its breast, it follows an immutable law; it is driven by it knows not what to impale itself, and die singing. At the very instant the thorn enters there is no awareness in it of the dying to come; it simply sings and sings until there is not the life left to utter another note. But we, when we put the thorns in our breasts, we know. We understand. And still we do it. Still we do it.